BLACKWATER

Jeannette Arroyo

and

Ren Graham

Henry Holt and Company

New York

Please note, this book was illustrated by both creators, who alternate drawing chapters in their own styles, which makes for a unique and dynamic illustration package.

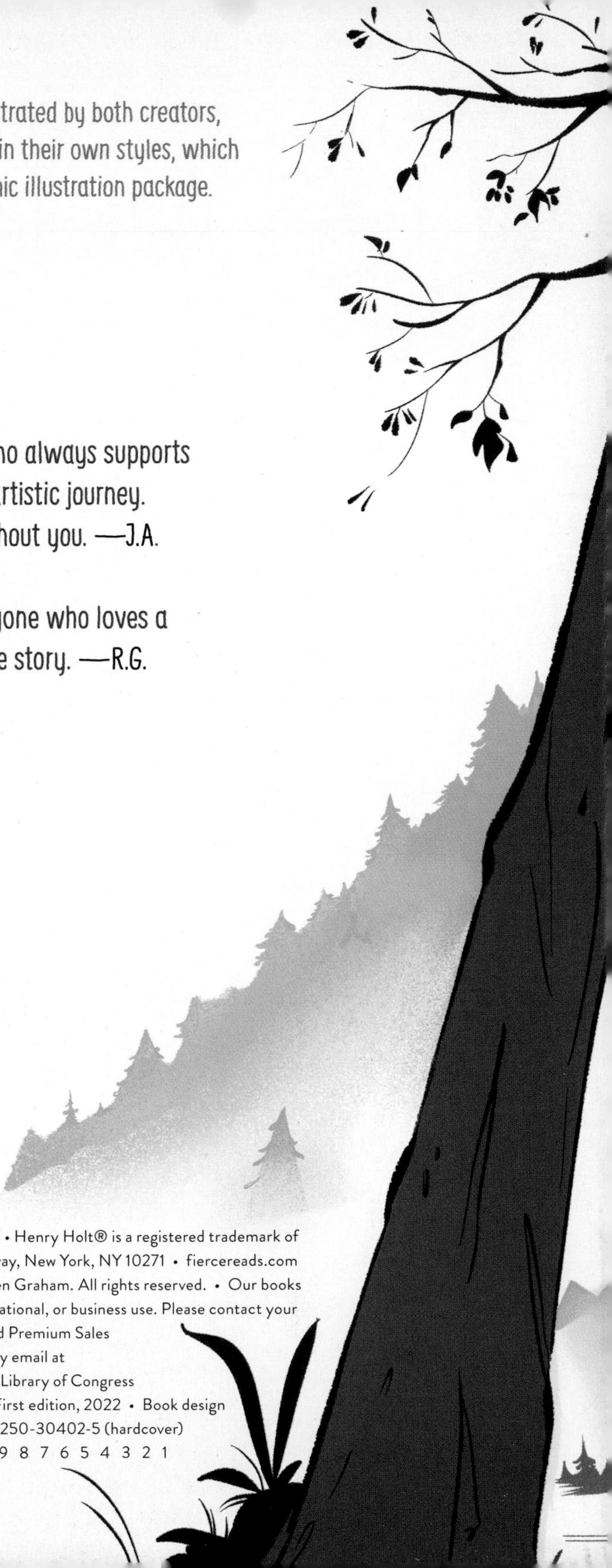

To my amazing family, who always supports
and encourages my artistic journey.
I wouldn't be here without you. —J.A.

To my family and everyone who loves a
supernatural romance story. —R.G.

Henry Holt and Company, *Publishers since 1866* • Henry Holt® is a registered trademark of Macmillan Publishing Group, LLC • 120 Broadway, New York, NY 10271 • fiercereads.com

• Our books may be purchased in bulk for promotional, educational, or business use. Please contact your local bookseller or the Macmillan Corporate and Premium Sales Department at (800) 221-7945 ext. 5442 or by email at MacmillanSpecialMarkets@macmillan.com. • Library of Congress Cataloging-in-Publication Data is available. • First edition, 2022 • Book design by Lisa Vega • Printed in China. • ISBN 978-1-250-30402-5 (hardcover) ISBN 978-1-250-77705-8 (paperback) • 10 9 8 7 6 5 4 3 2 1

CHAPTER ONE
BEGINNING

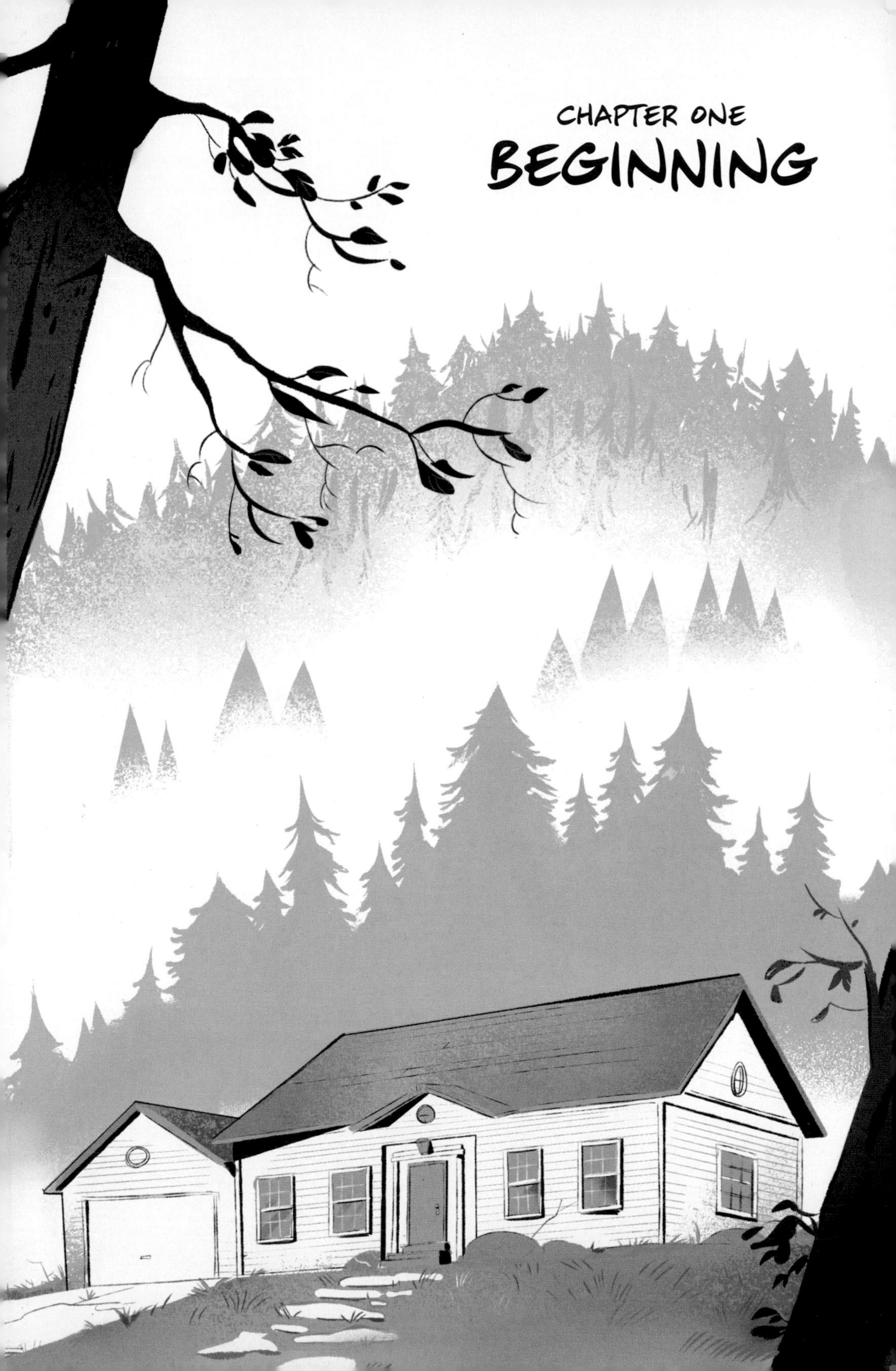

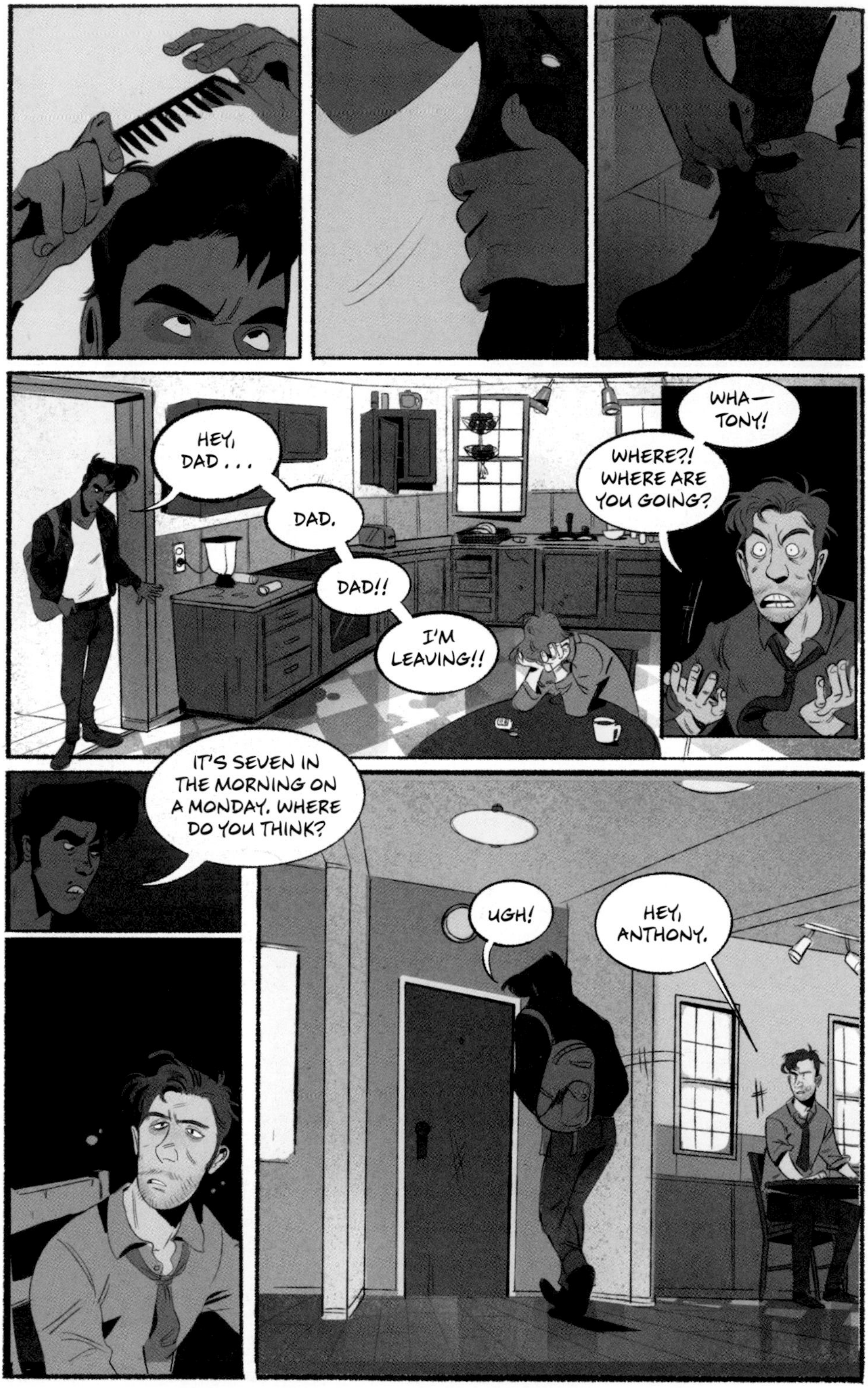
HEY, DAD . . .
DAD.
DAD!!
I'M LEAVING!!
WHA— TONY!
WHERE?! WHERE ARE YOU GOING?
IT'S SEVEN IN THE MORNING ON A MONDAY. WHERE DO YOU THINK?
UGH!
HEY, ANTHONY.

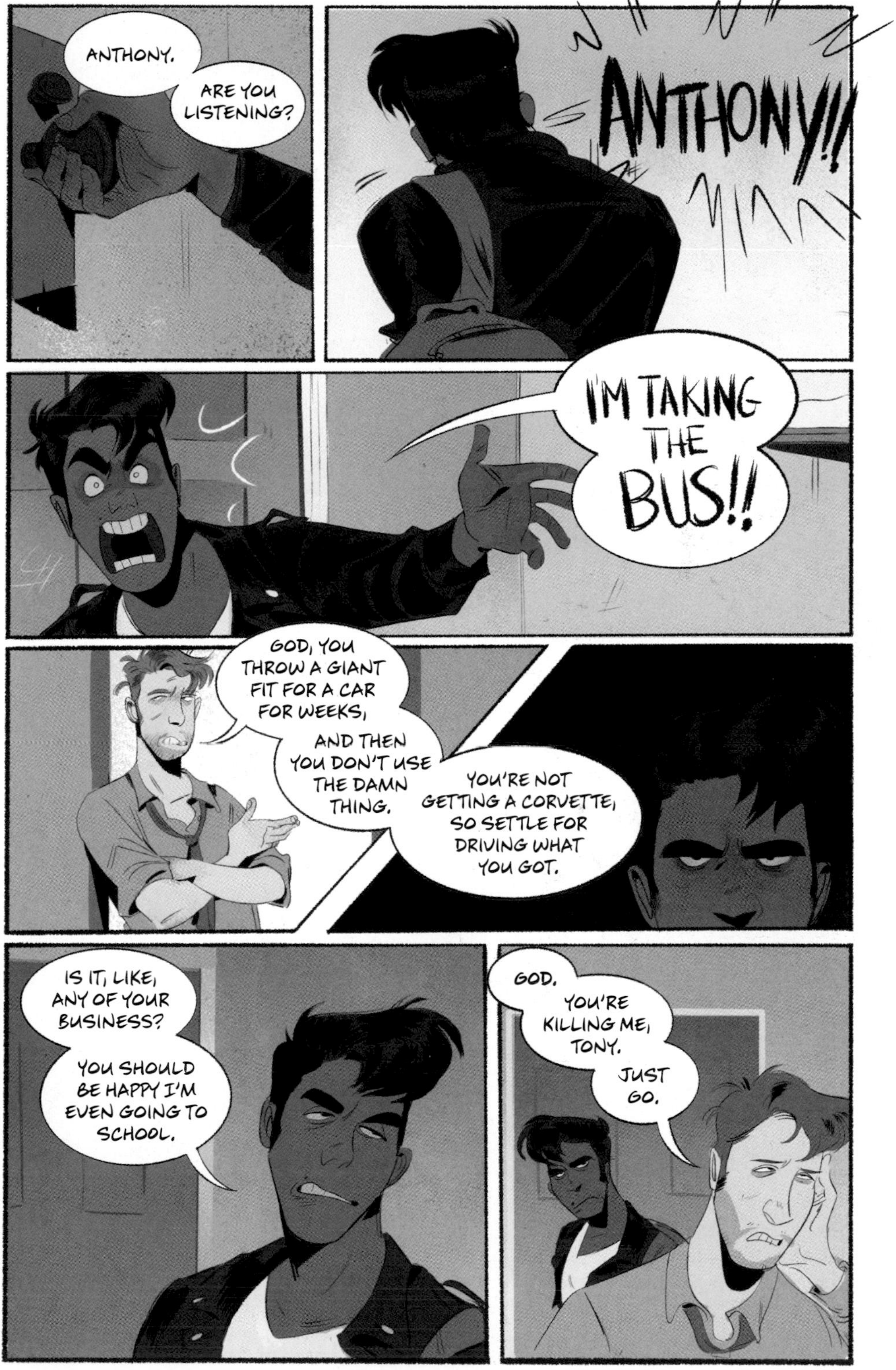
ANTHONY.
ARE YOU LISTENING?
ANTHONY!!
I'M TAKING THE BUS!!
GOD, YOU THROW A GIANT FIT FOR A CAR FOR WEEKS,
AND THEN YOU DON'T USE THE DAMN THING.
YOU'RE NOT GETTING A CORVETTE, SO SETTLE FOR DRIVING WHAT YOU GOT.
IS IT, LIKE, ANY OF YOUR BUSINESS?
YOU SHOULD BE HAPPY I'M EVEN GOING TO SCHOOL.
GOD.
YOU'RE KILLING ME, TONY.
JUST GO.

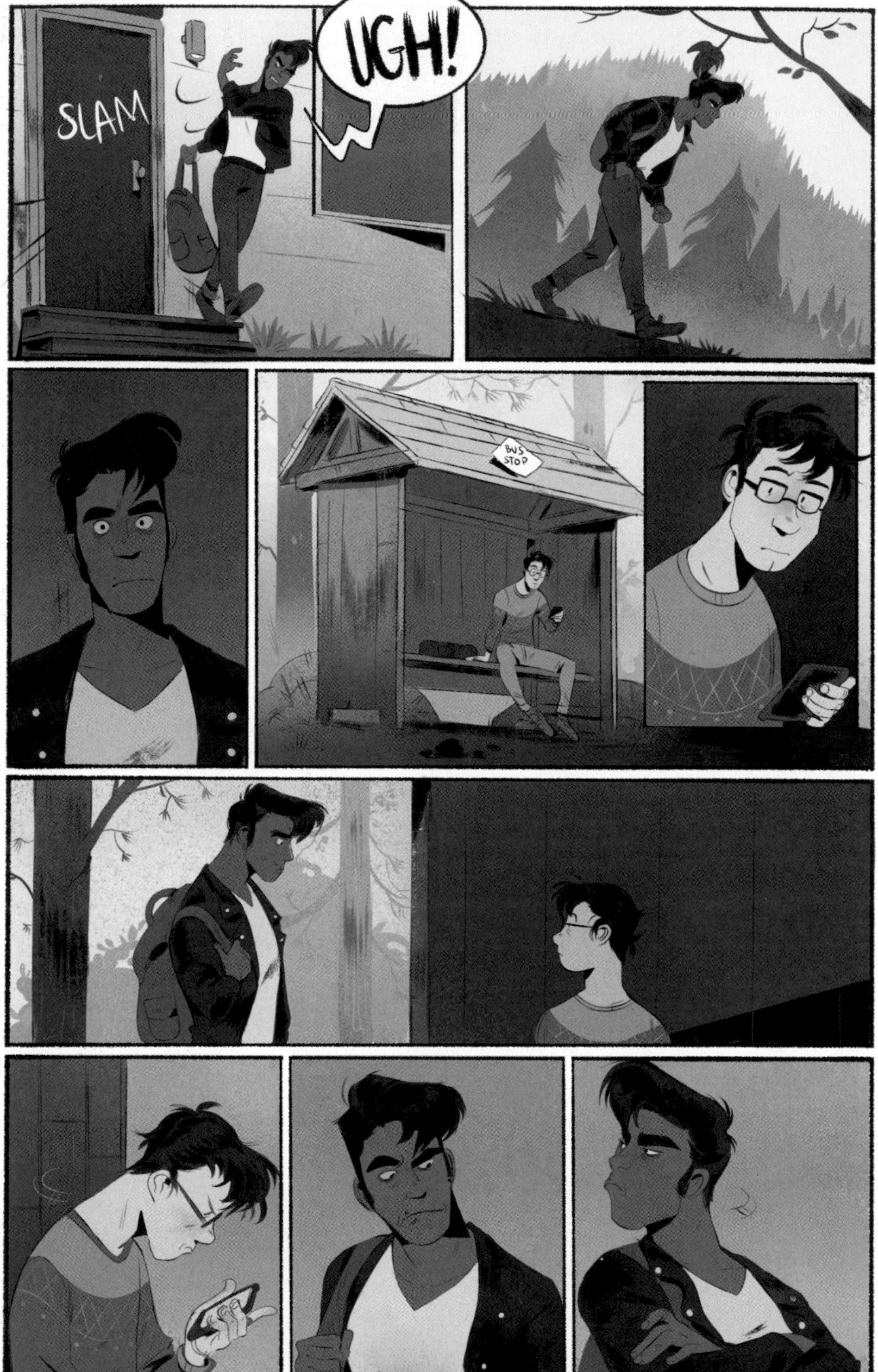
SLAM
UGH!
BUS STOP

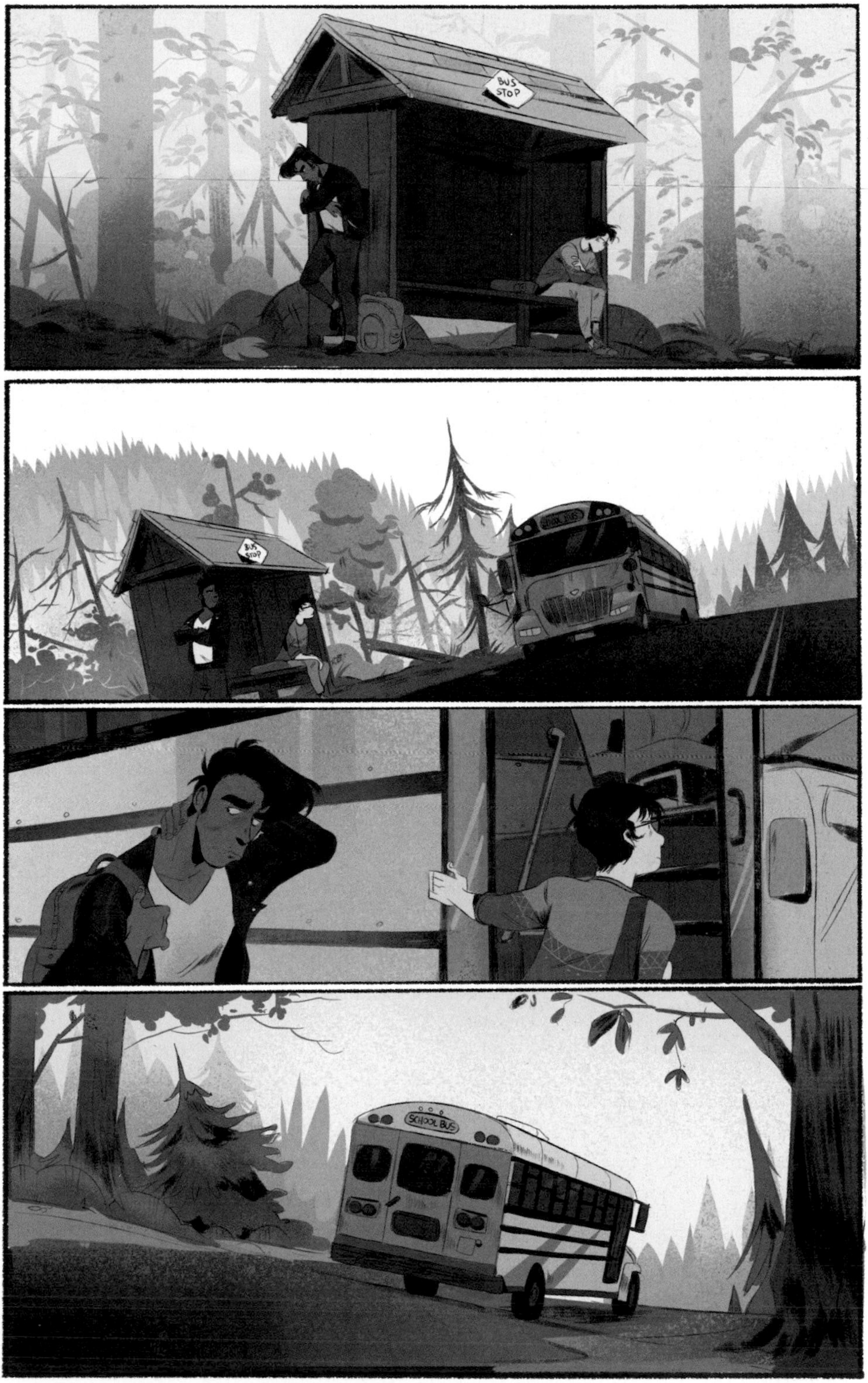
BUS STOP
BUS STOP
SCHOOL BUS

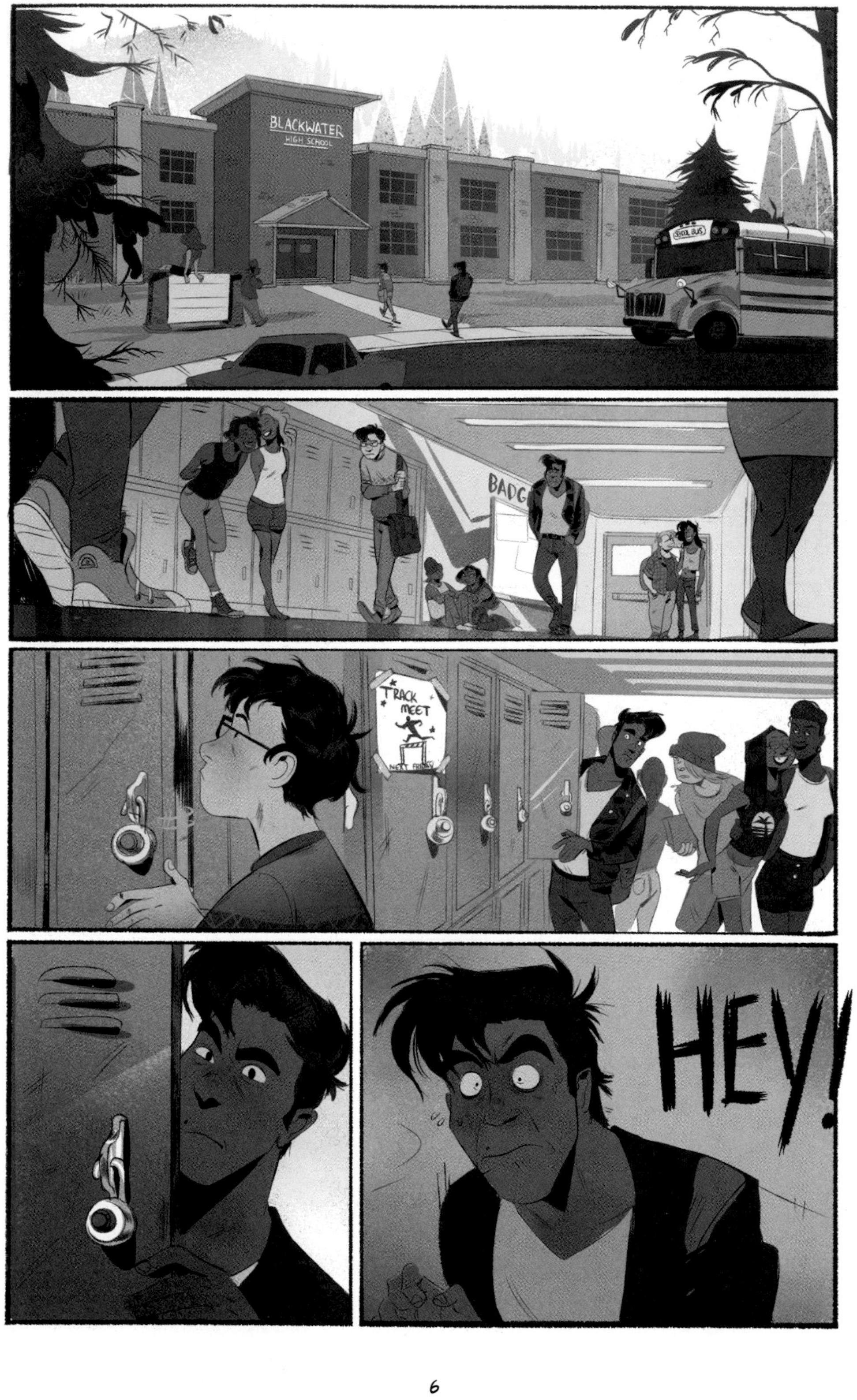
BLACKWATER
HIGH SCHOOL
BADG
TRACK MEET
NEXT FRIDAY
HEY!

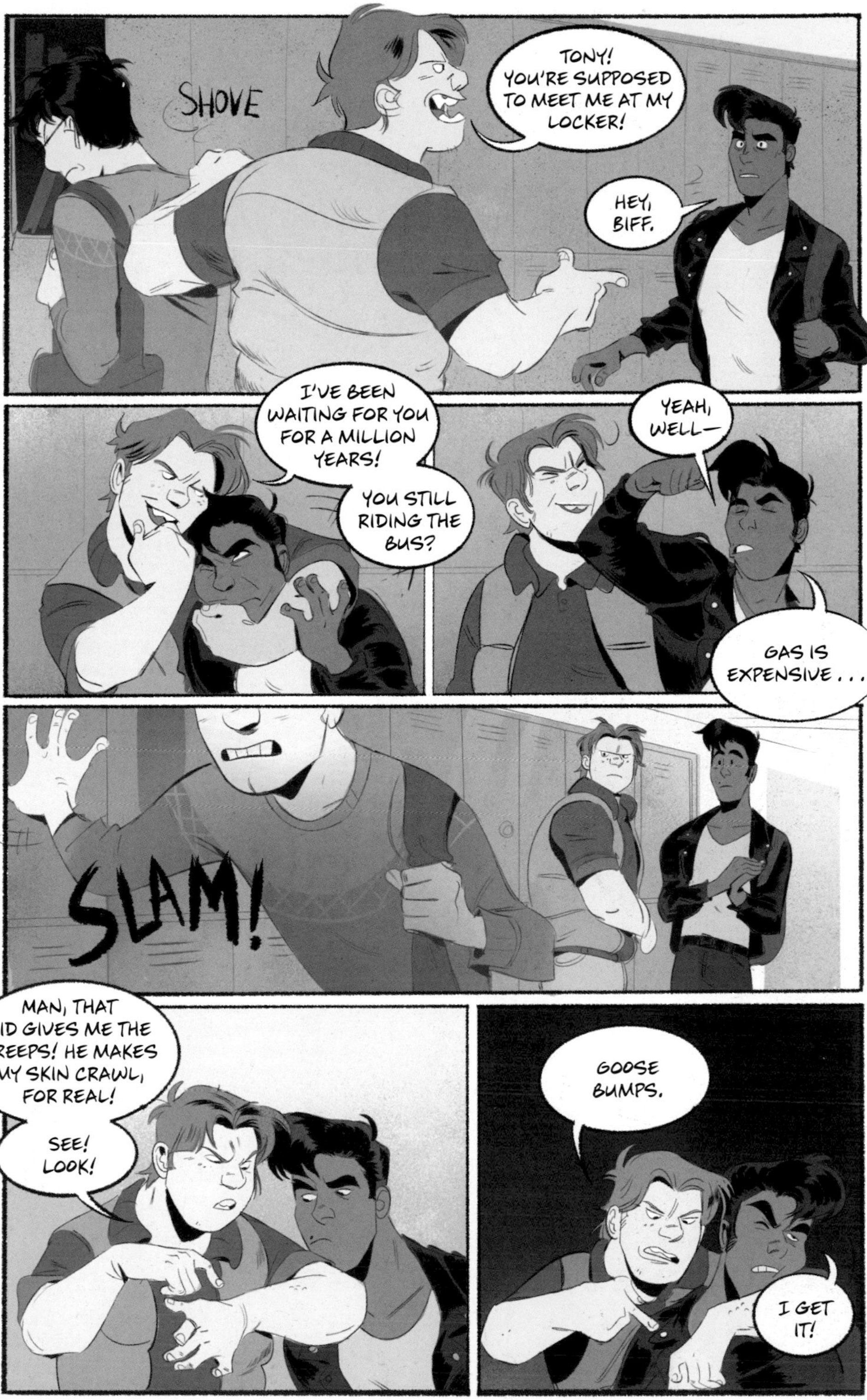
SHOVE
TONY! YOU'RE SUPPOSED TO MEET ME AT MY LOCKER!
HEY, BIFF.
I'VE BEEN WAITING FOR YOU FOR A MILLION YEARS!
YOU STILL RIDING THE BUS?
YEAH, WELL—
GAS IS EXPENSIVE . . .
SLAM!
MAN, THAT KID GIVES ME THE CREEPS! HE MAKES MY SKIN CRAWL, FOR REAL!
SEE! LOOK!
GOOSE BUMPS.
I GET IT!

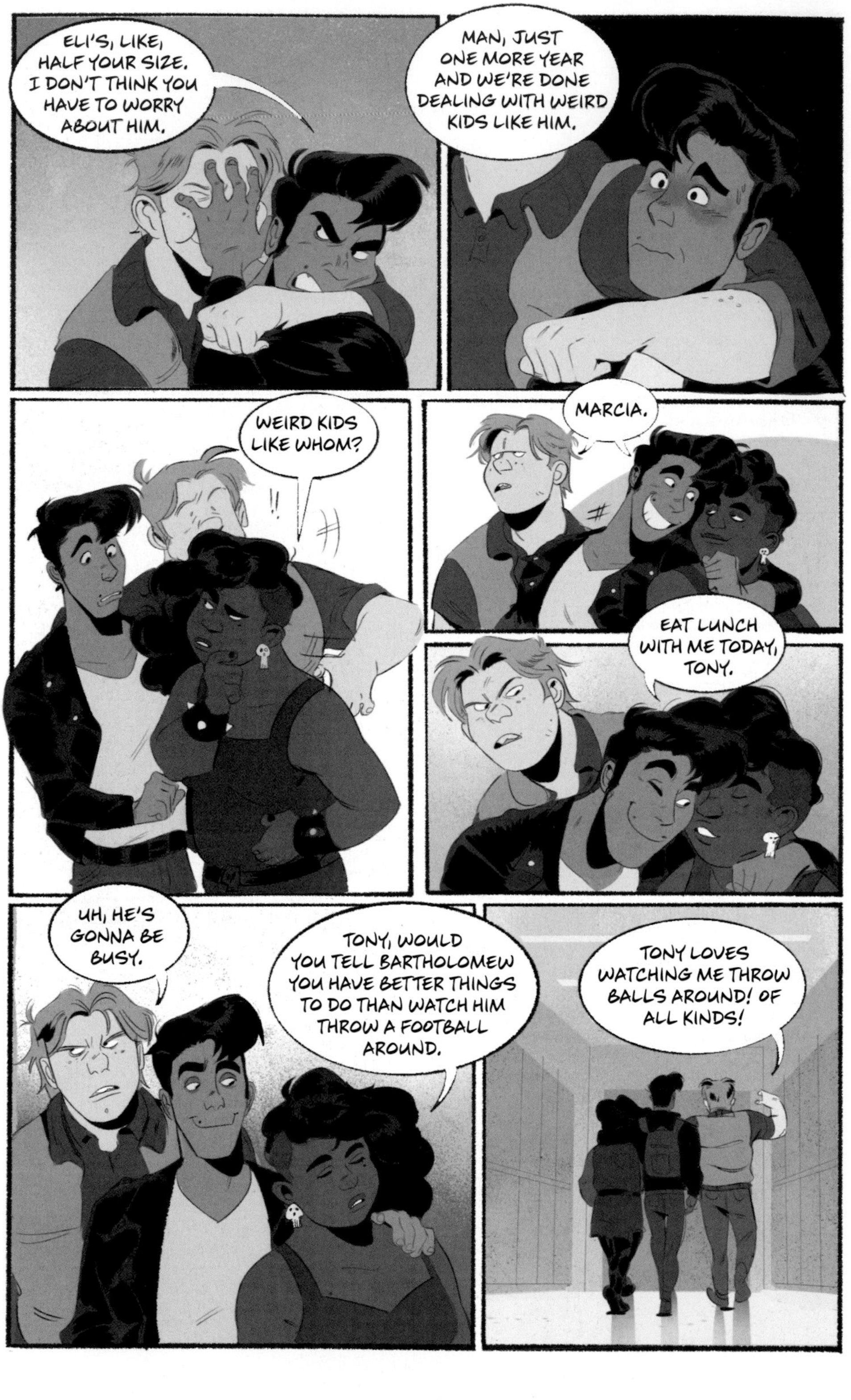
ELI'S, LIKE, HALF YOUR SIZE. I DON'T THINK YOU HAVE TO WORRY ABOUT HIM.
MAN, JUST ONE MORE YEAR AND WE'RE DONE DEALING WITH WEIRD KIDS LIKE HIM.
WEIRD KIDS LIKE WHOM?
!!
MARCIA.
EAT LUNCH WITH ME TODAY, TONY.
UH, HE'S GONNA BE BUSY.
TONY, WOULD YOU TELL BARTHOLOMEW YOU HAVE BETTER THINGS TO DO THAN WATCH HIM THROW A FOOTBALL AROUND.
TONY LOVES WATCHING ME THROW BALLS AROUND! OF ALL KINDS!

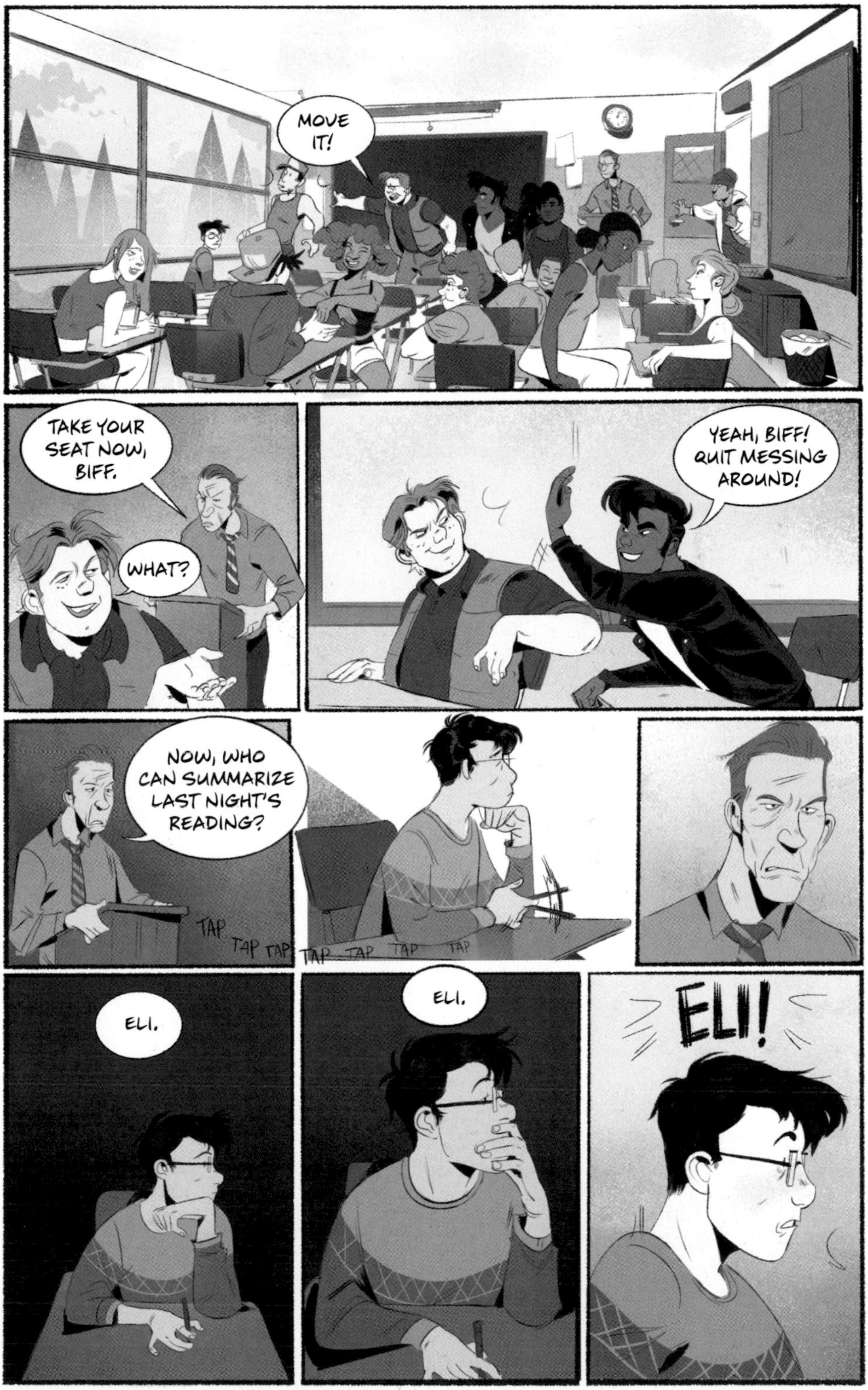
MOVE IT!
TAKE YOUR SEAT NOW, BIFF.
WHAT?
YEAH, BIFF! QUIT MESSING AROUND!
NOW, WHO CAN SUMMARIZE LAST NIGHT'S READING?
TAP TAP TAP TAP TAP TAP TAP
ELI.
ELI.
ELI!

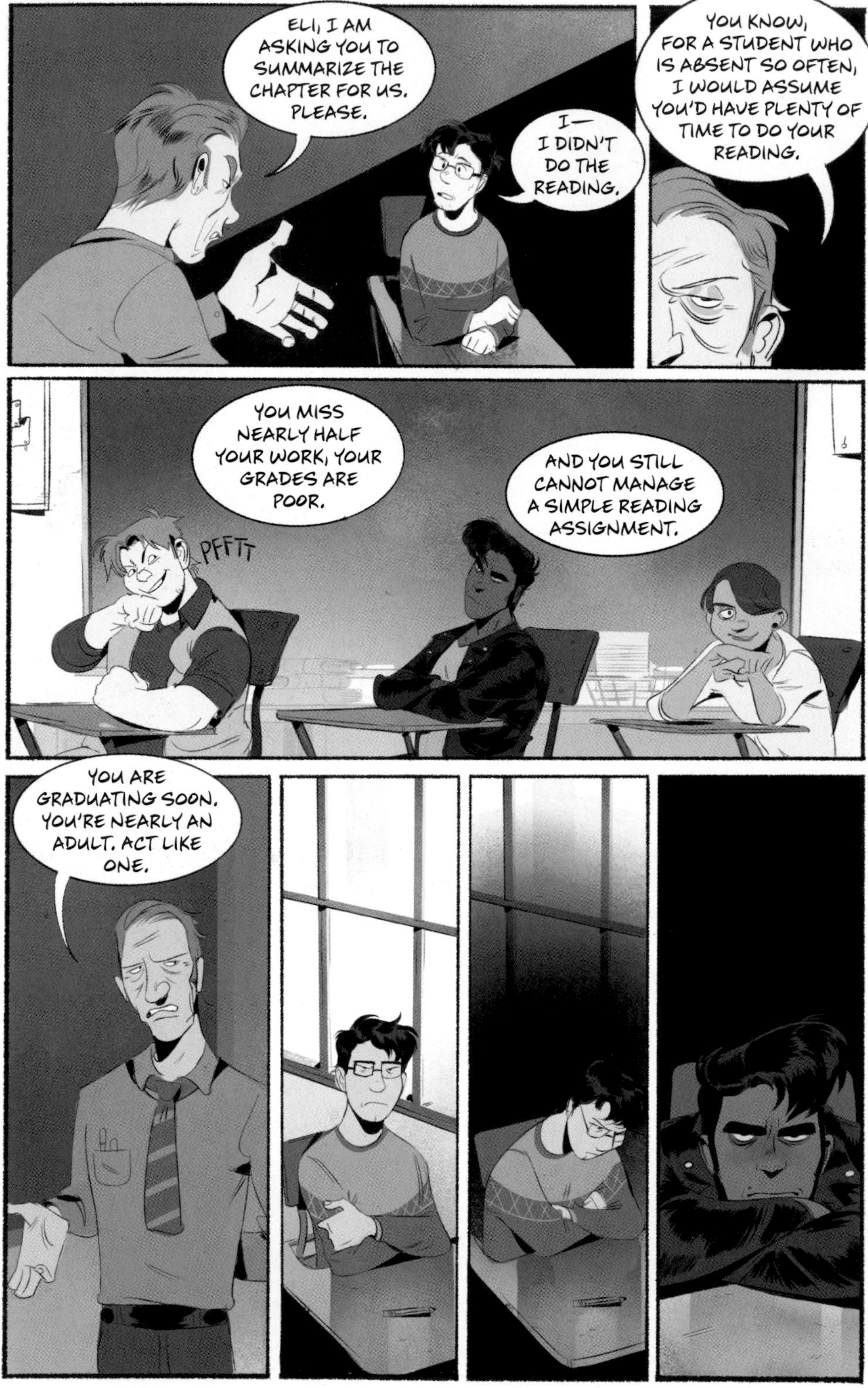
ELI, I AM ASKING YOU TO SUMMARIZE THE CHAPTER FOR US. PLEASE.
I— I DIDN'T DO THE READING.
YOU KNOW, FOR A STUDENT WHO IS ABSENT SO OFTEN, I WOULD ASSUME YOU'D HAVE PLENTY OF TIME TO DO YOUR READING.
YOU MISS NEARLY HALF YOUR WORK, YOUR GRADES ARE POOR.
AND YOU STILL CANNOT MANAGE A SIMPLE READING ASSIGNMENT.
PFFTT
YOU ARE GRADUATING SOON. YOU'RE NEARLY AN ADULT. ACT LIKE ONE.

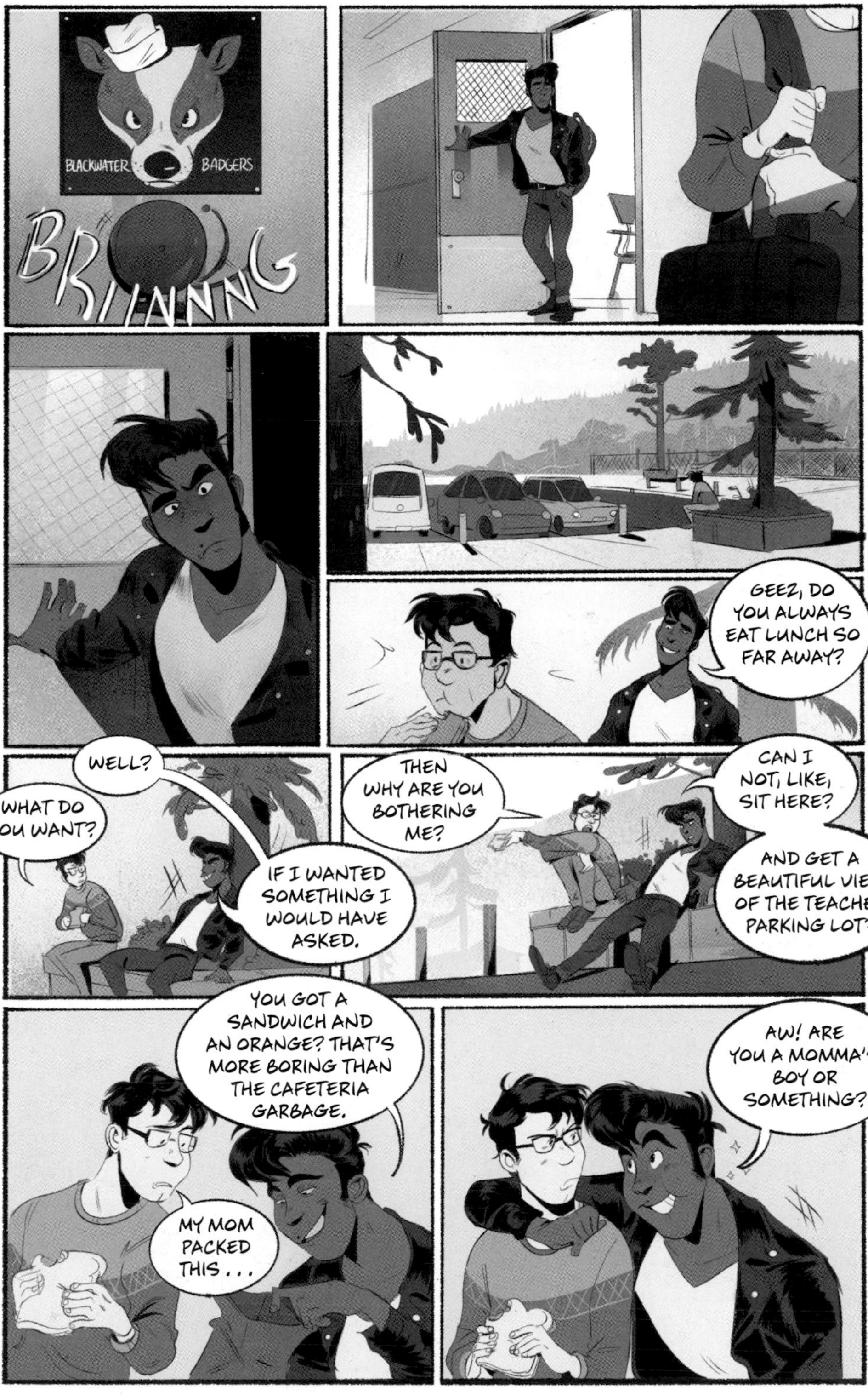
BLACKWATER BADGERS
BRIINNNG
GEEZ, DO YOU ALWAYS EAT LUNCH SO FAR AWAY?
WELL?
WHAT DO YOU WANT?
IF I WANTED SOMETHING I WOULD HAVE ASKED.
THEN WHY ARE YOU BOTHERING ME?
CAN I NOT, LIKE, SIT HERE?
AND GET A BEAUTIFUL VIEW OF THE TEACHER PARKING LOT?
YOU GOT A SANDWICH AND AN ORANGE? THAT'S MORE BORING THAN THE CAFETERIA GARBAGE.
MY MOM PACKED THIS . . .
AW! ARE YOU A MOMMA'S BOY OR SOMETHING?

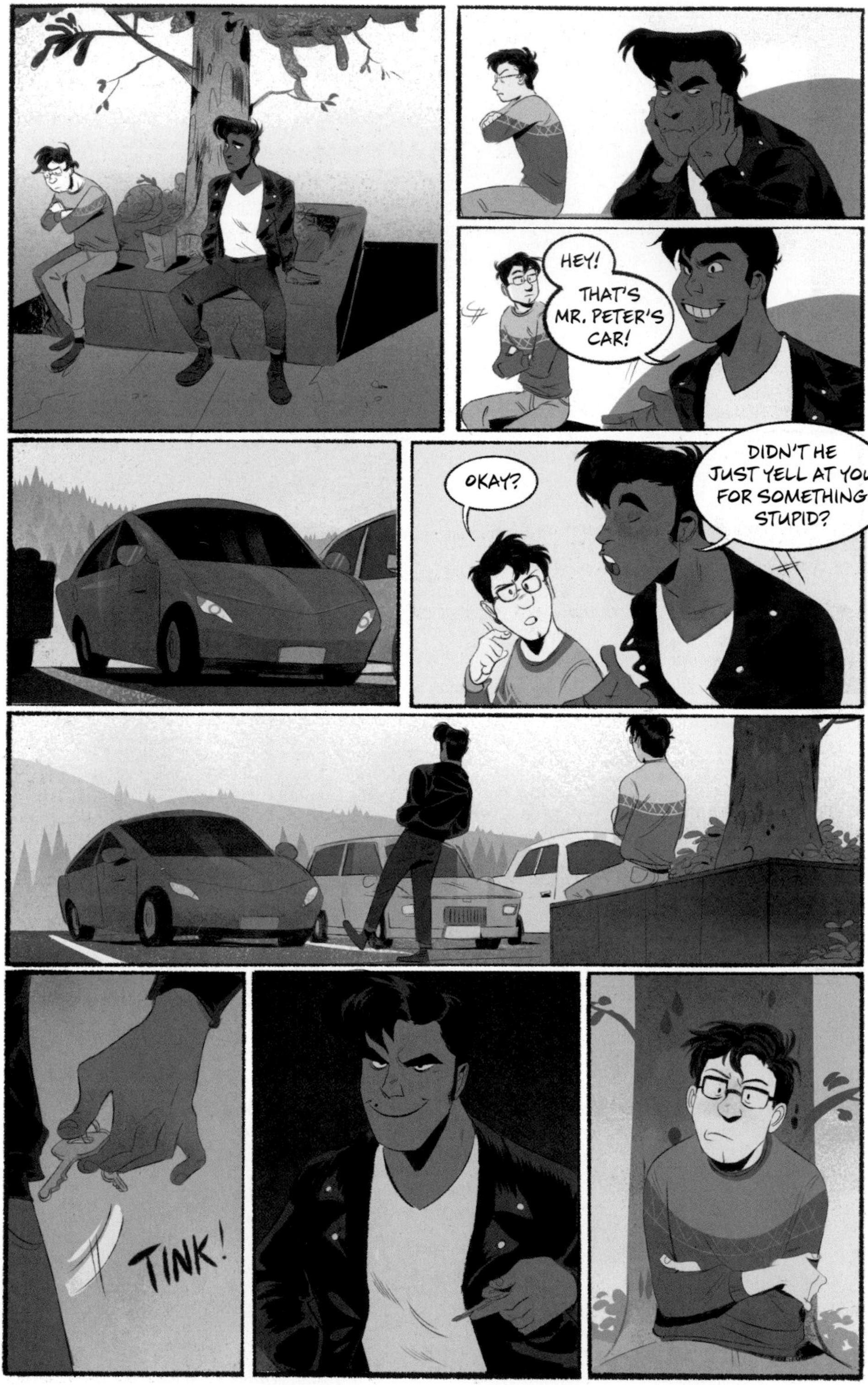

HEY!
THAT'S MR. PETER'S CAR!
OKAY?
DIDN'T HE JUST YELL AT YOU FOR SOMETHING STUPID?
TINK!

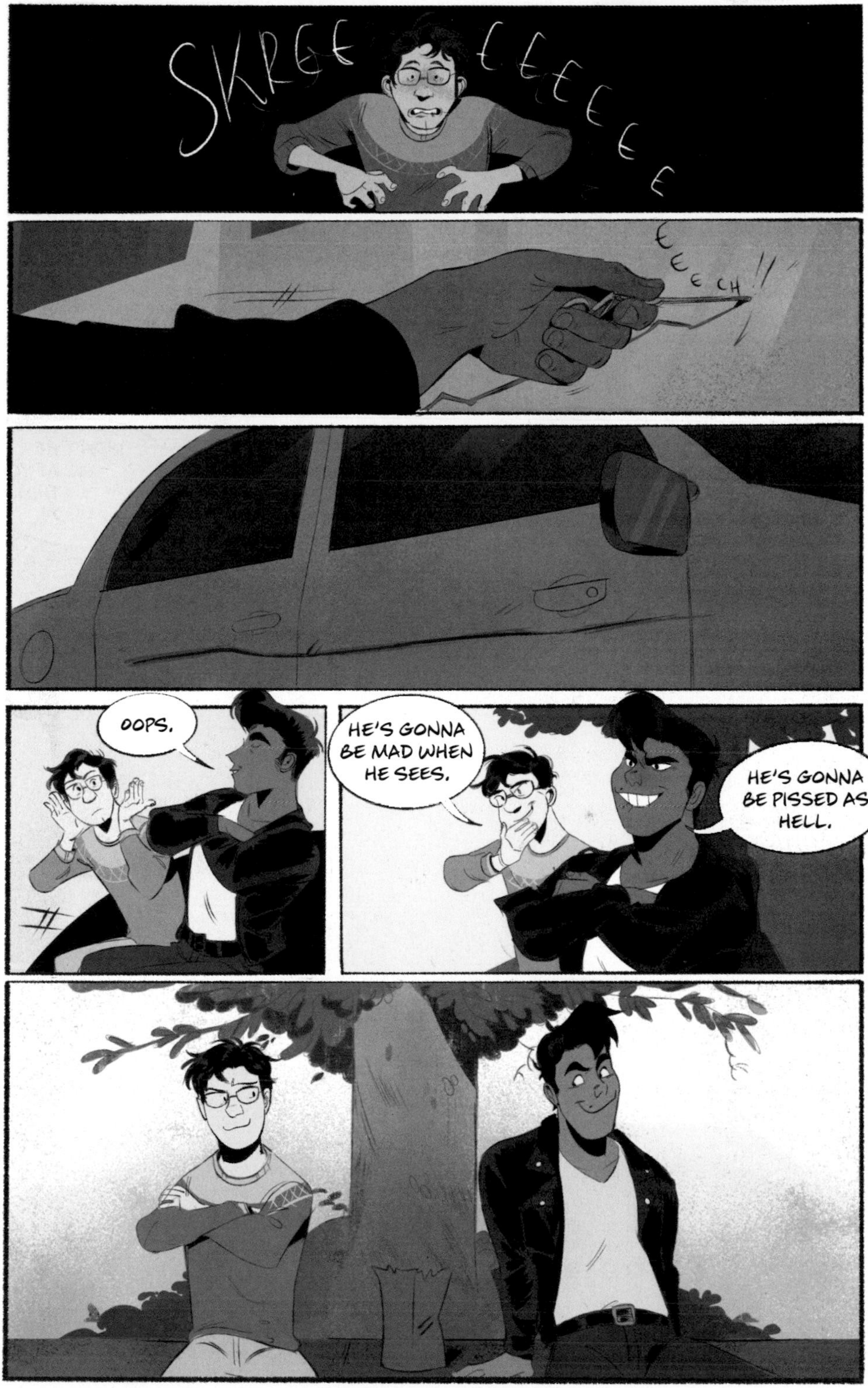
SKREEEEEEEEEE
EEECH!!
OOPS.
HE'S GONNA BE MAD WHEN HE SEES.
HE'S GONNA BE PISSED AS HELL.

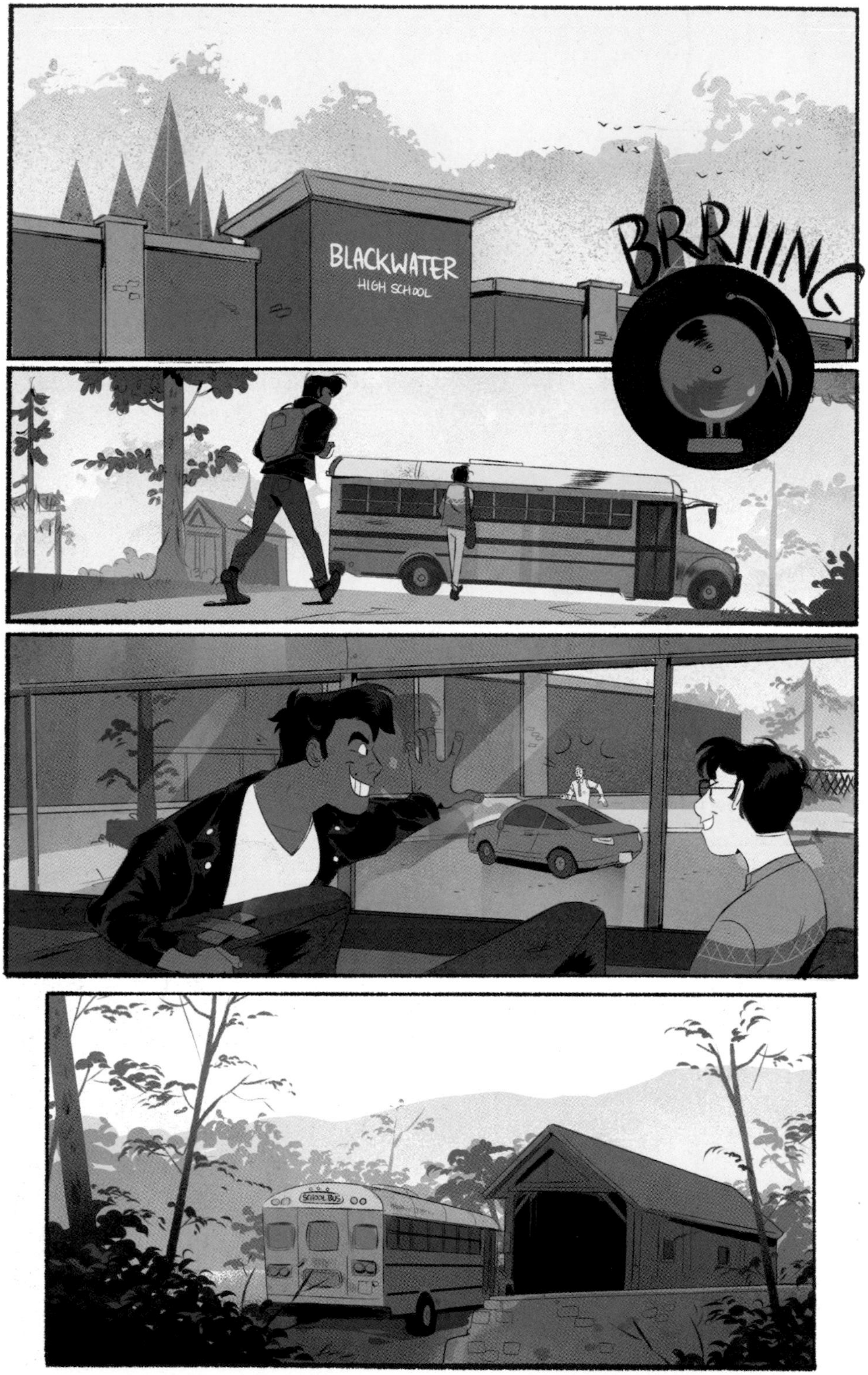
BLACKWATER
HIGH SCHOOL
BRRIIING
SCHOOL BUS

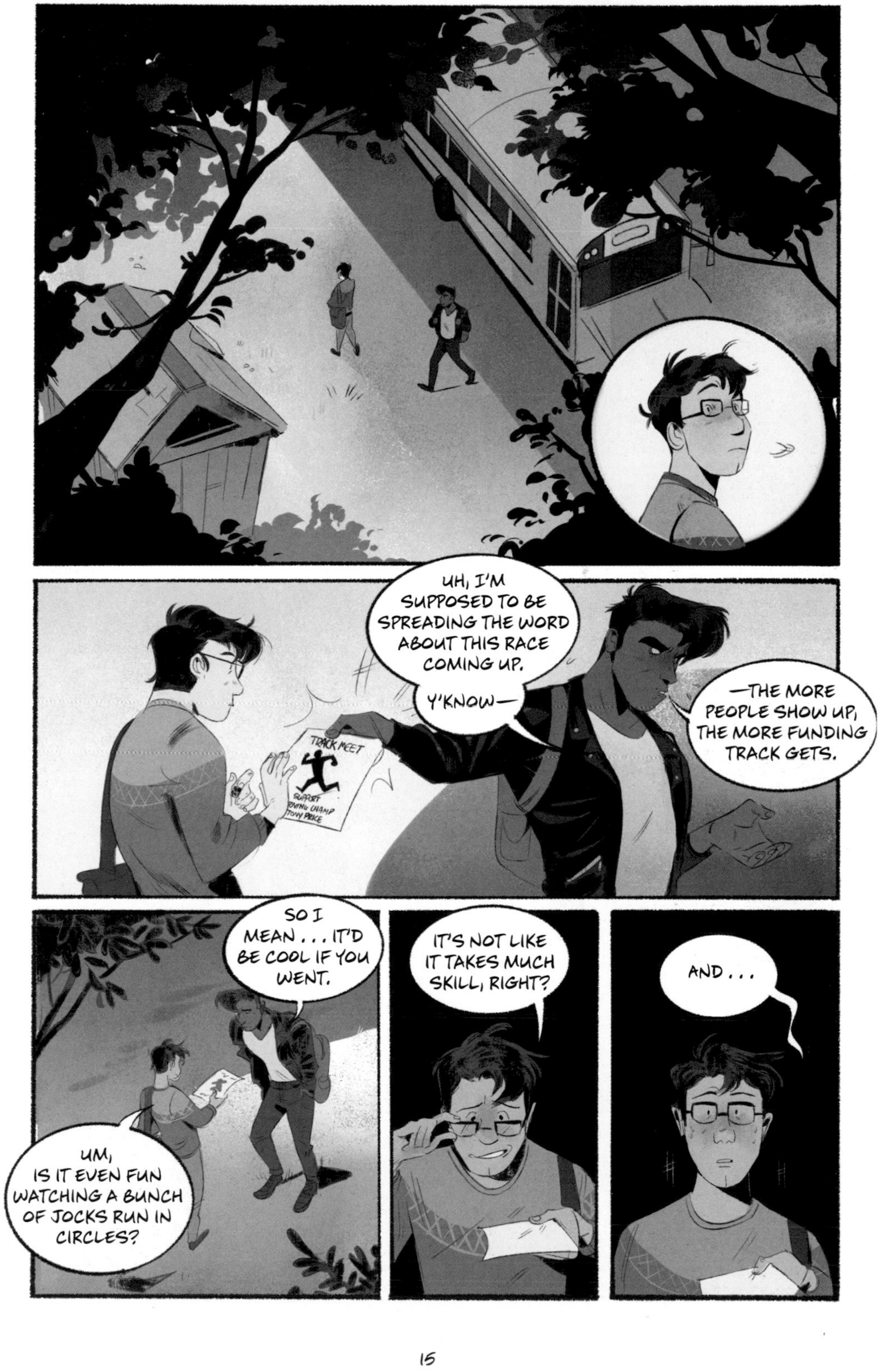
UH, I'M SUPPOSED TO BE SPREADING THE WORD ABOUT THIS RACE COMING UP.
Y'KNOW—
—THE MORE PEOPLE SHOW UP, THE MORE FUNDING TRACK GETS.
TRACK MEET
SO I MEAN . . . IT'D BE COOL IF YOU WENT.
UM, IS IT EVEN FUN WATCHING A BUNCH OF JOCKS RUN IN CIRCLES?
IT'S NOT LIKE IT TAKES MUCH SKILL, RIGHT?
AND . . .

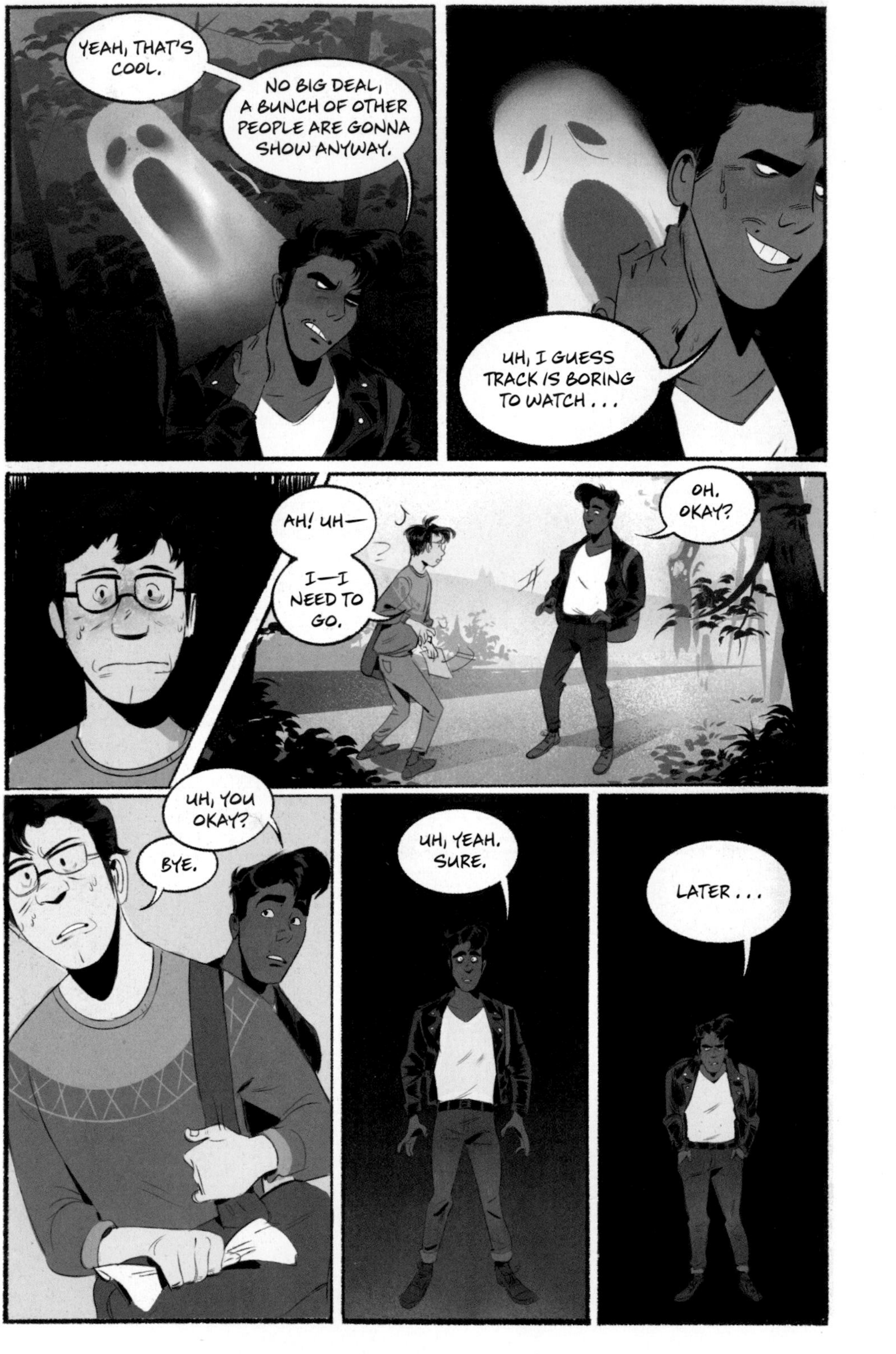
YEAH, THAT'S COOL.
NO BIG DEAL, A BUNCH OF OTHER PEOPLE ARE GONNA SHOW ANYWAY.
UH, I GUESS TRACK IS BORING TO WATCH . . .
AH! UH—
I—I NEED TO GO.
OH. OKAY?
UH, YOU OKAY?
BYE.
UH, YEAH. SURE.
LATER . . .

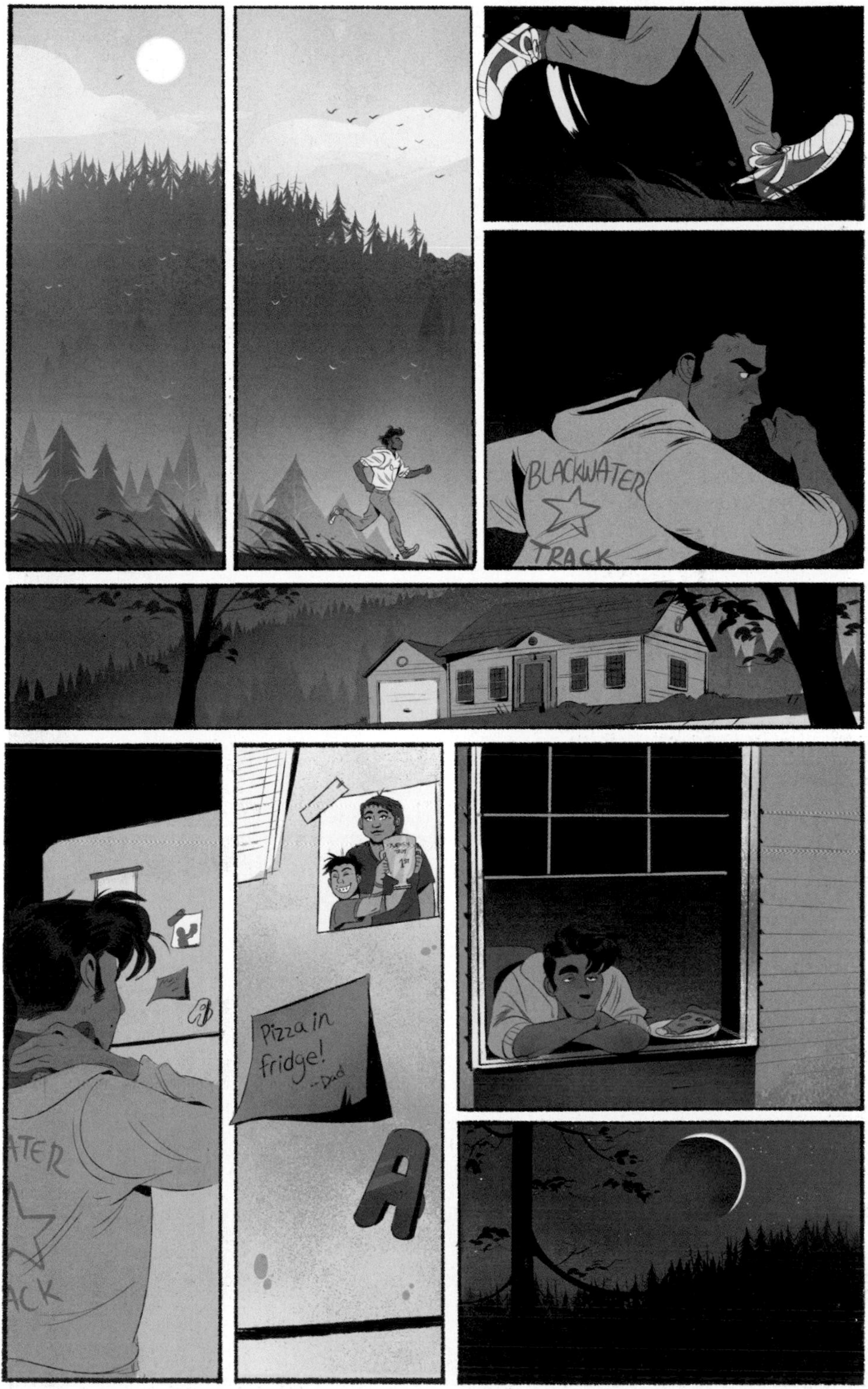

BLACKWATER
TRACK
Pizza in fridge!
--Dad

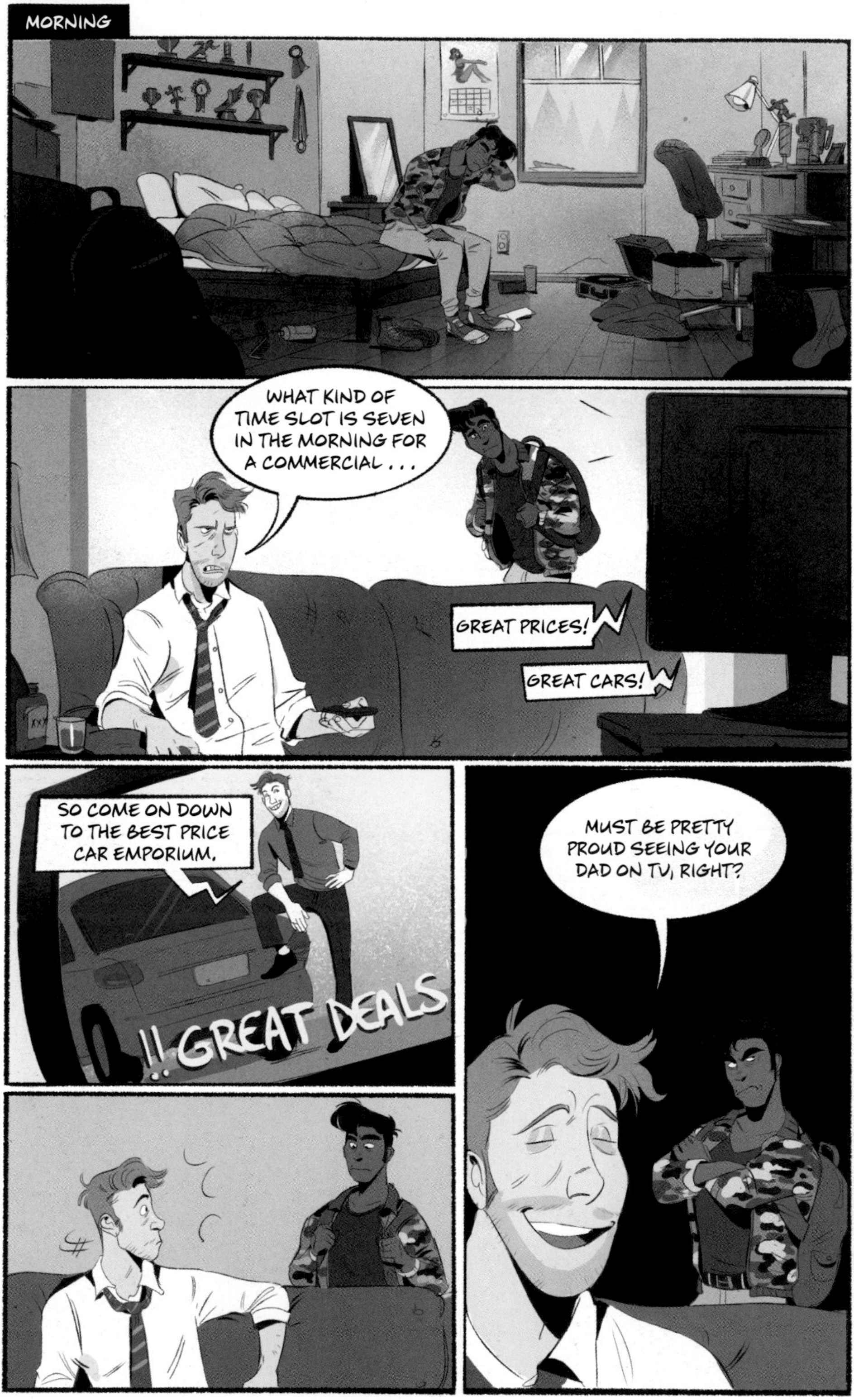
MORNING
WHAT KIND OF TIME SLOT IS SEVEN IN THE MORNING FOR A COMMERCIAL . . .
GREAT PRICES!
GREAT CARS!
SO COME ON DOWN TO THE BEST PRICE CAR EMPORIUM.
!! GREAT DEALS
MUST BE PRETTY PROUD SEEING YOUR DAD ON TV, RIGHT?

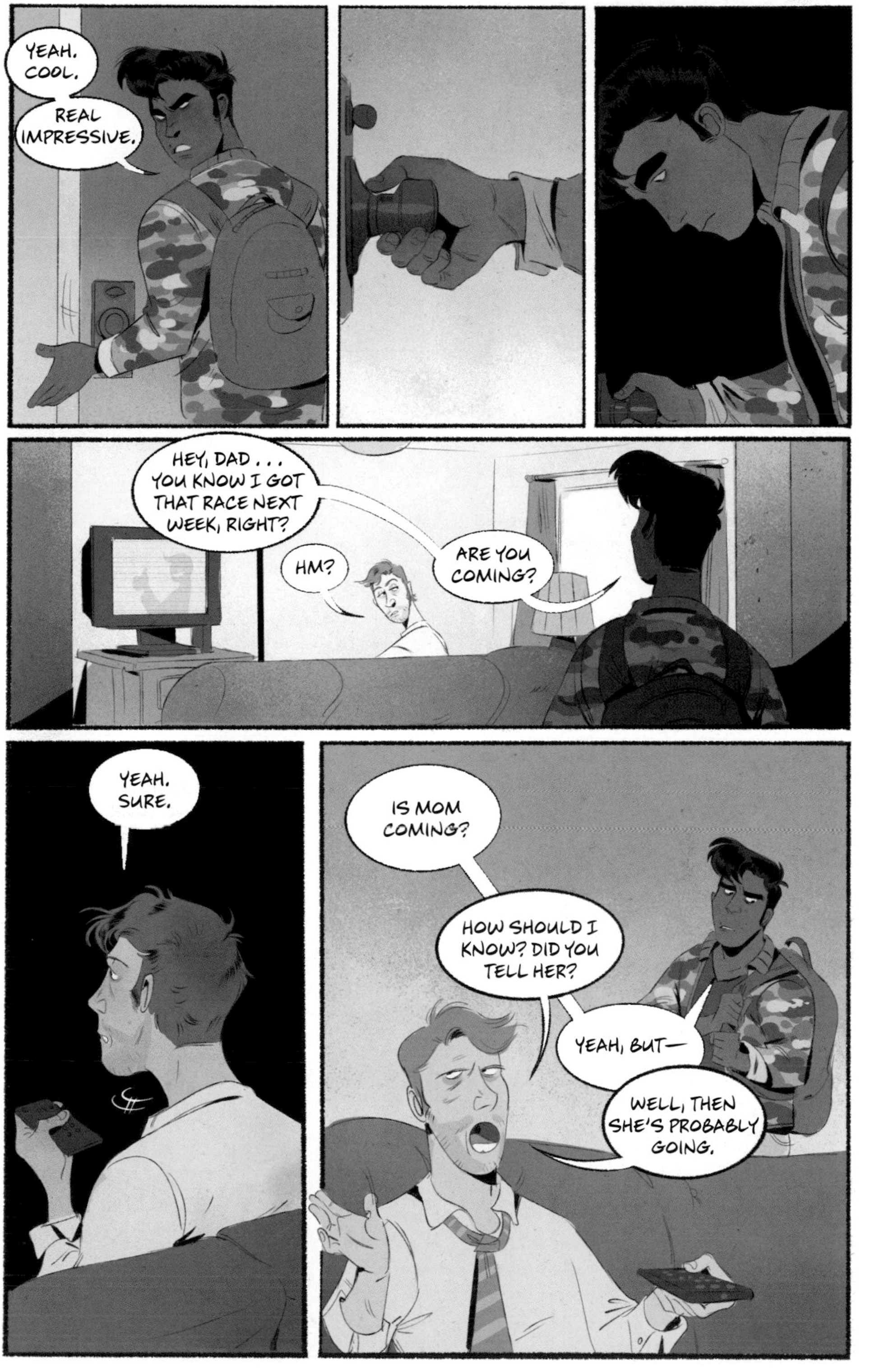
YEAH. COOL.
REAL IMPRESSIVE.
HEY, DAD . . . YOU KNOW I GOT THAT RACE NEXT WEEK, RIGHT?
HM?
ARE YOU COMING?
YEAH. SURE.
IS MOM COMING?
HOW SHOULD I KNOW? DID YOU TELL HER?
YEAH, BUT—
WELL, THEN SHE'S PROBABLY GOING.

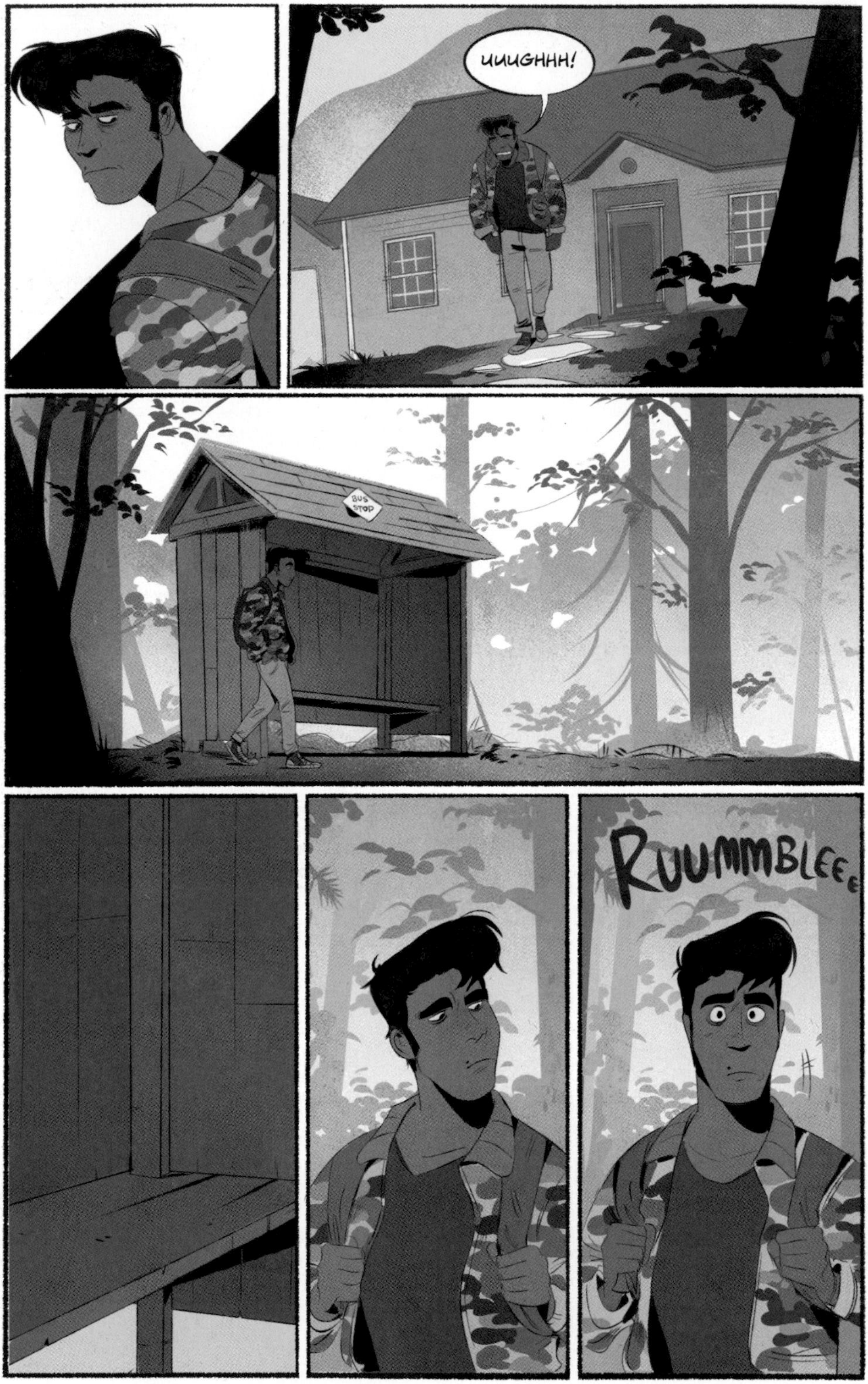
UUUGHHH!
BUS STOP
RUUMMBLEEE

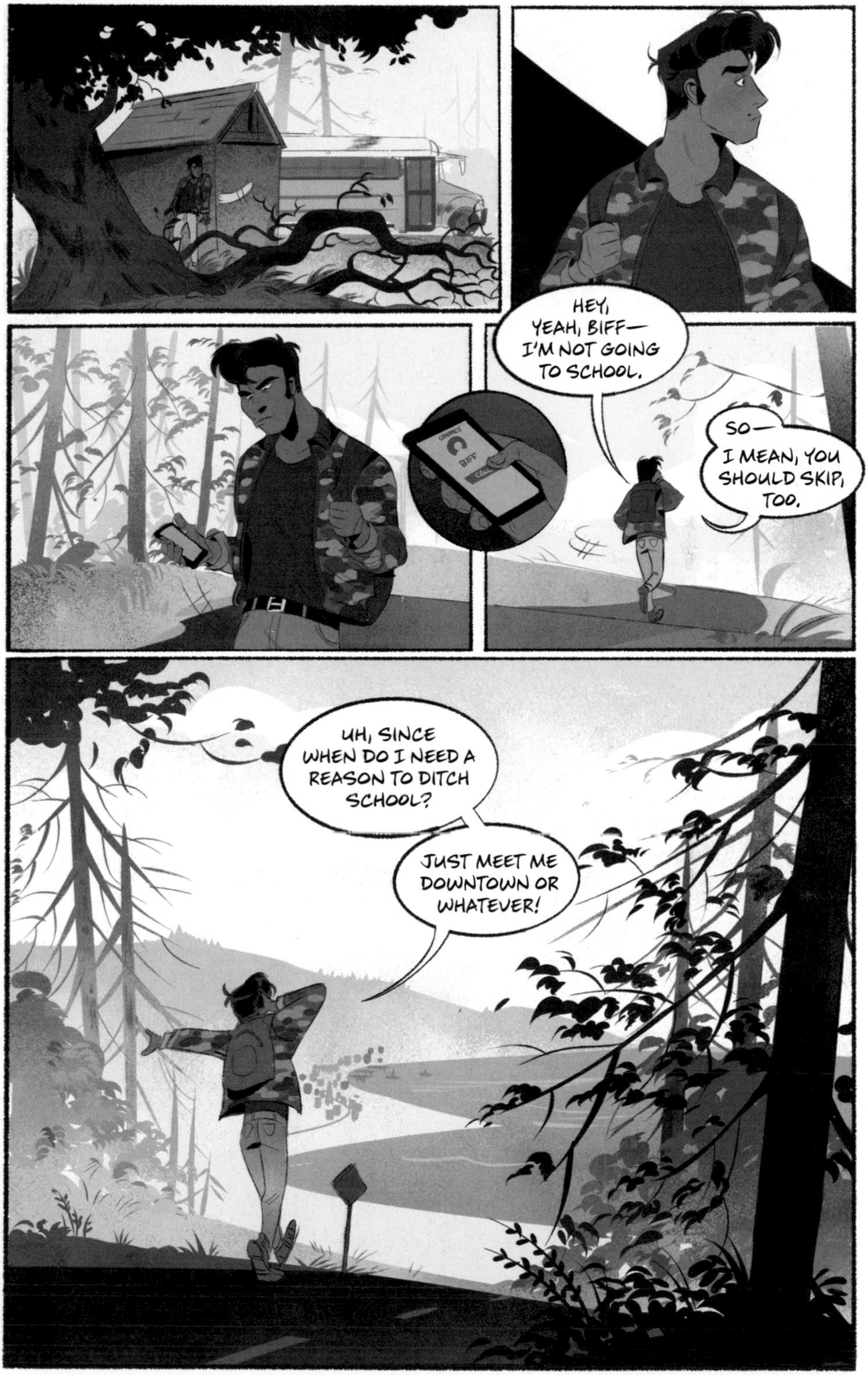
HEY, YEAH, BIFF— I'M NOT GOING TO SCHOOL.
SO— I MEAN, YOU SHOULD SKIP, TOO.
UH, SINCE WHEN DO I NEED A REASON TO DITCH SCHOOL?
JUST MEET ME DOWNTOWN OR WHATEVER!

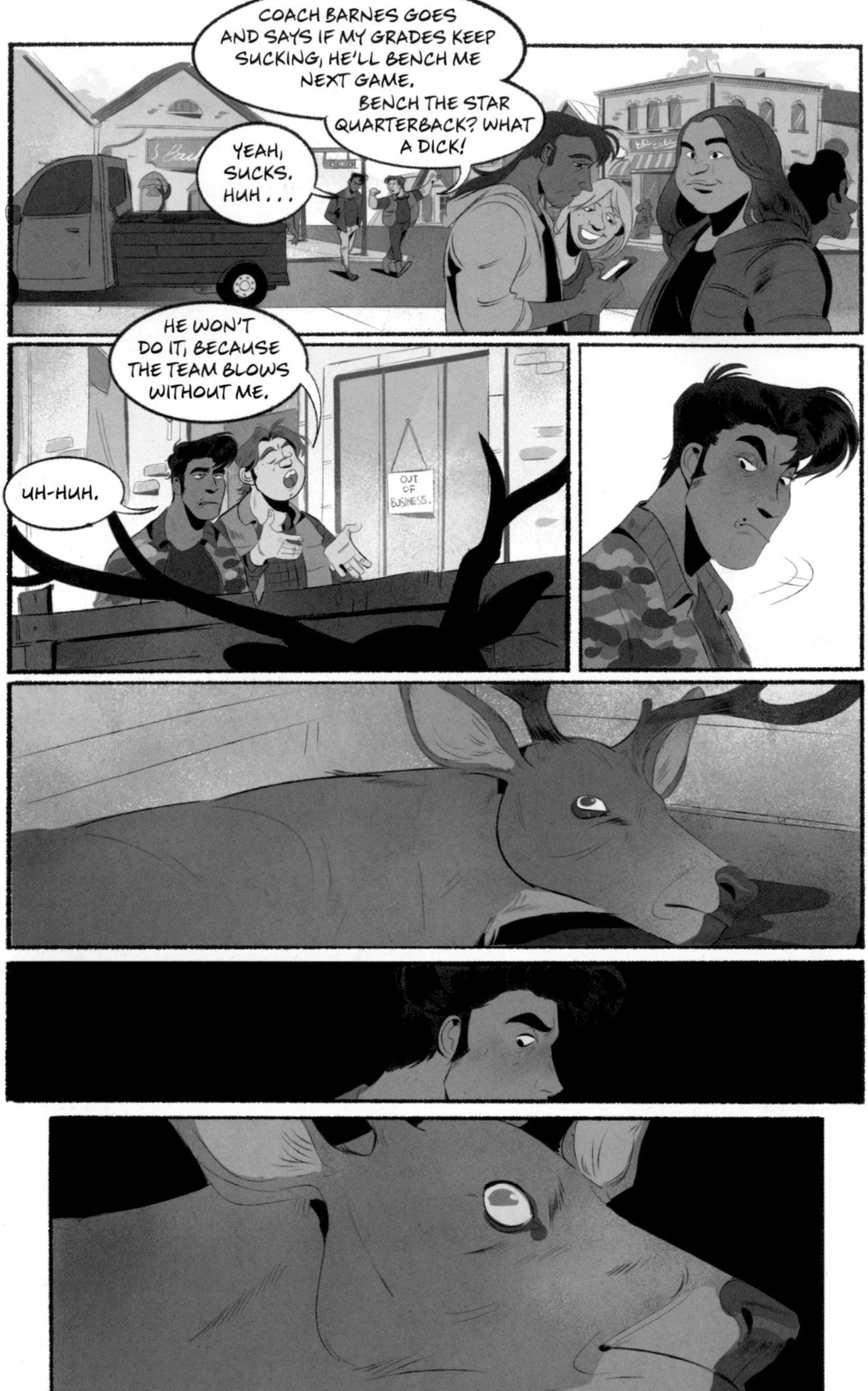
COACH BARNES GOES AND SAYS IF MY GRADES KEEP SUCKING, HE'LL BENCH ME NEXT GAME.
BENCH THE STAR QUARTERBACK? WHAT A DICK!
YEAH, SUCKS. HUH . . .
HE WON'T DO IT, BECAUSE THE TEAM BLOWS WITHOUT ME.
UH-HUH.
OUT OF BUSINESS.

TONY!!

YOU SCOPING THAT DEAD BUCK THERE OR SOMETHING?!

HEY! WE SHOULD GO HUNTING NEXT WEEKEND!

YOU TWO BOYS MIGHT WANT TO PUT A HOLD ON THAT.

BEEN HEARING FOLKS TALK ABOUT SEEING SOME ANIMAL WITH MANGE RUNNING LOOSE.

SOME SICK BEAR, MAYBE.

BULLSHIT.

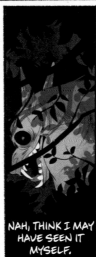

NAH, THINK I MAY HAVE SEEN IT MYSELF.

JUST A GLIMPSE. THE THING LOOKED GAUNT.

SUIT YOURSELVES IF YOU GO. I AIN'T YOUR BABYSITTER.

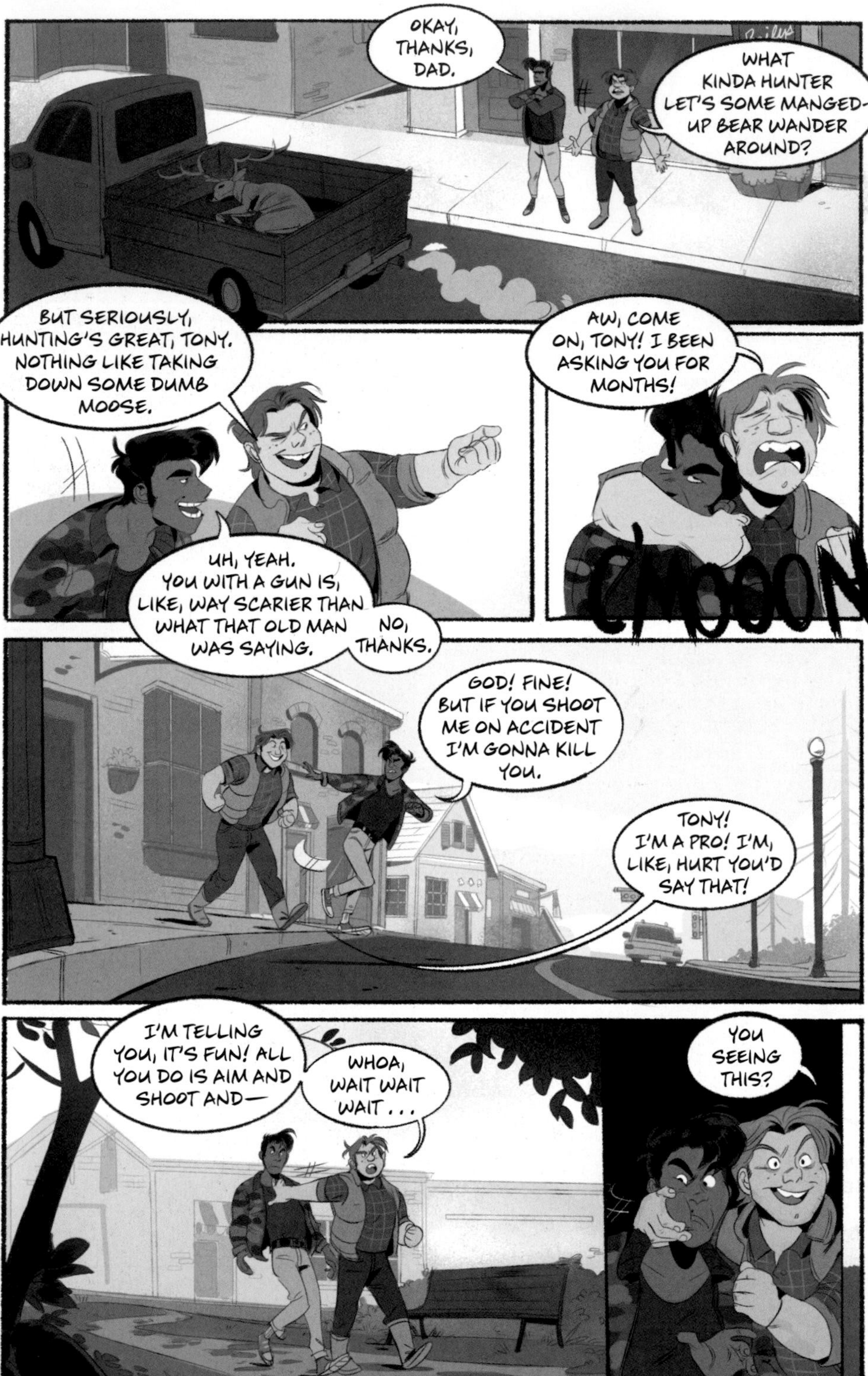
OKAY, THANKS, DAD.
WHAT KINDA HUNTER LET'S SOME MANGED-UP BEAR WANDER AROUND?
BUT SERIOUSLY, HUNTING'S GREAT, TONY. NOTHING LIKE TAKING DOWN SOME DUMB MOOSE.
UH, YEAH. YOU WITH A GUN IS, LIKE, WAY SCARIER THAN WHAT THAT OLD MAN WAS SAYING.
NO, THANKS.
AW, COME ON, TONY! I BEEN ASKING YOU FOR MONTHS!
C'MOOON
GOD! FINE! BUT IF YOU SHOOT ME ON ACCIDENT I'M GONNA KILL YOU.
TONY! I'M A PRO! I'M, LIKE, HURT YOU'D SAY THAT!
I'M TELLING YOU, IT'S FUN! ALL YOU DO IS AIM AND SHOOT AND—
WHOA, WAIT WAIT WAIT . . .
YOU SEEING THIS?

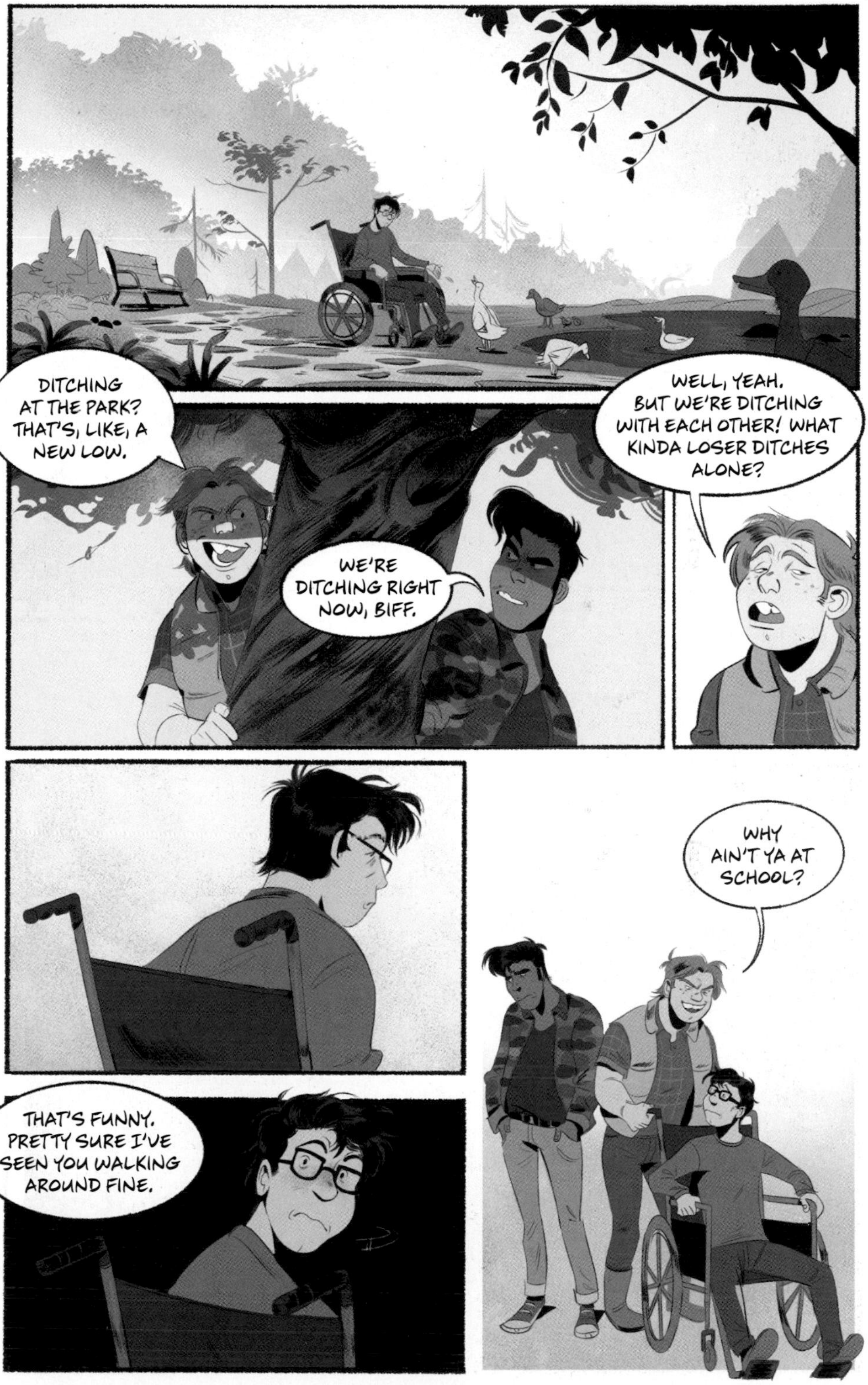
DITCHING AT THE PARK? THAT'S, LIKE, A NEW LOW.
WE'RE DITCHING RIGHT NOW, BIFF.
WELL, YEAH. BUT WE'RE DITCHING WITH EACH OTHER! WHAT KINDA LOSER DITCHES ALONE?
WHY AIN'T YA AT SCHOOL?
THAT'S FUNNY. PRETTY SURE I'VE SEEN YOU WALKING AROUND FINE.

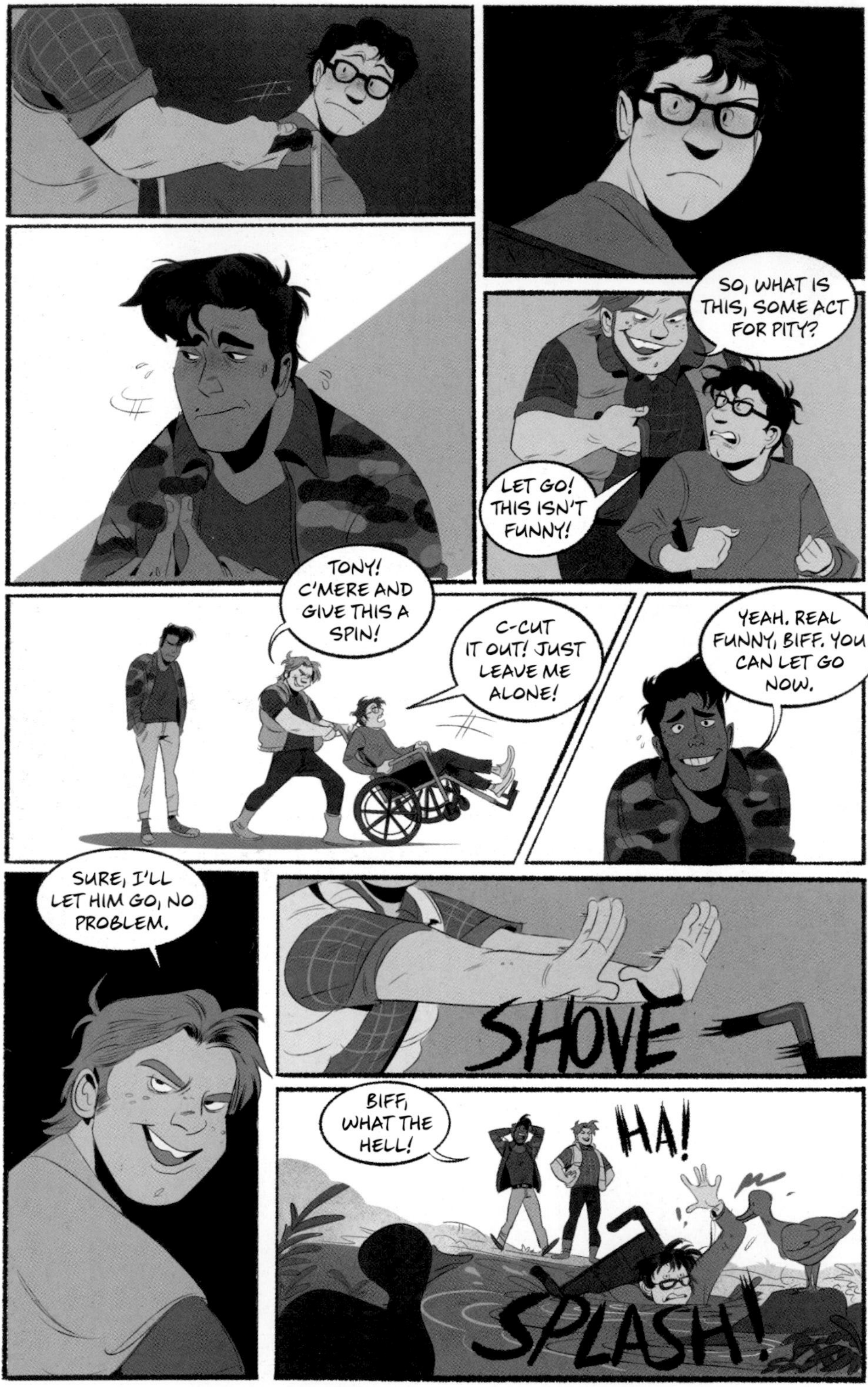

SO, WHAT IS THIS, SOME ACT FOR PITY?
LET GO! THIS ISN'T FUNNY!
TONY! C'MERE AND GIVE THIS A SPIN!
C-CUT IT OUT! JUST LEAVE ME ALONE!
YEAH. REAL FUNNY, BIFF. YOU CAN LET GO NOW.
SURE, I'LL LET HIM GO, NO PROBLEM.
SHOVE
BIFF, WHAT THE HELL!
HA!
SPLASH!

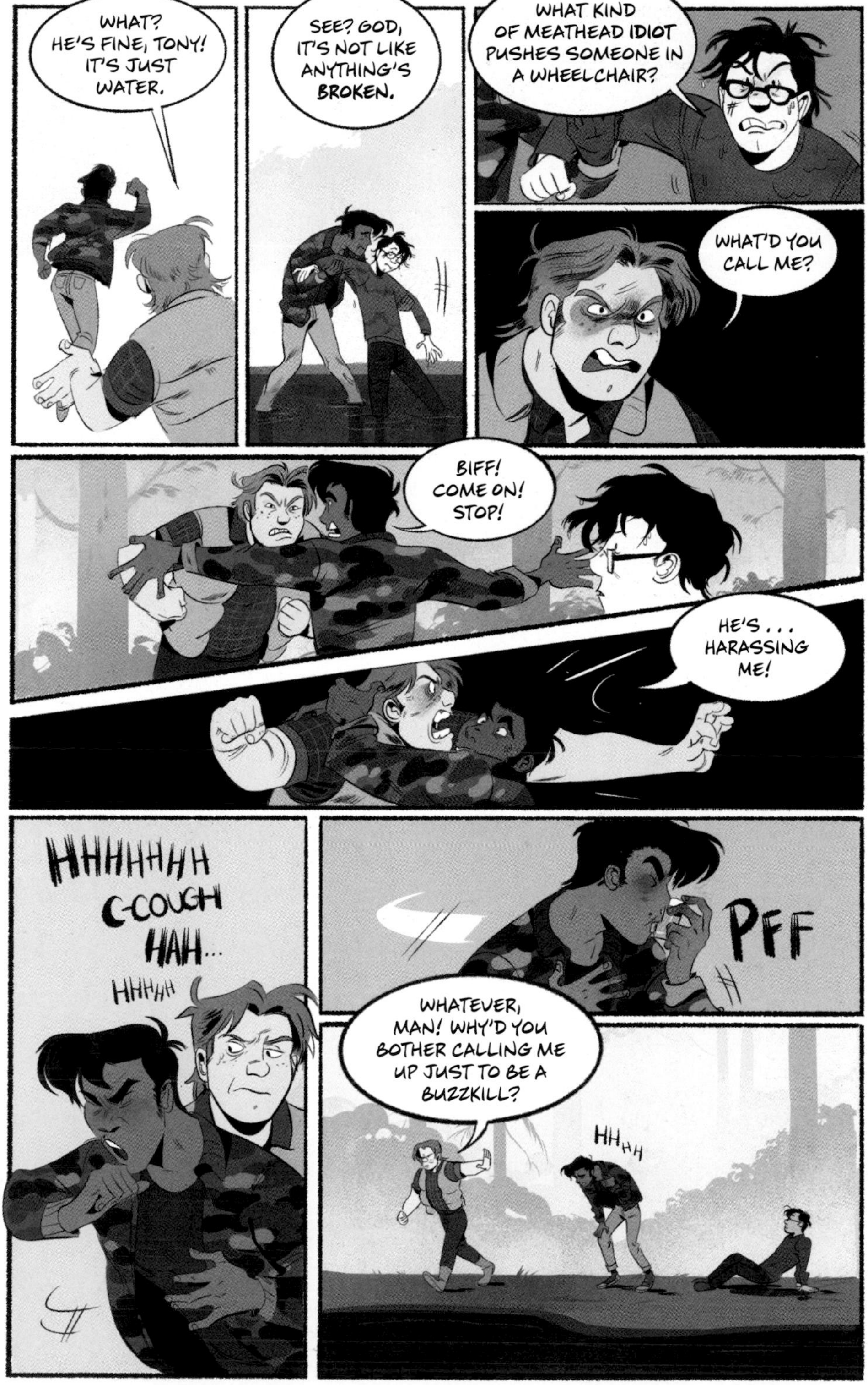
WHAT? HE'S FINE, TONY! IT'S JUST WATER.
SEE? GOD, IT'S NOT LIKE ANYTHING'S BROKEN.
WHAT KIND OF MEATHEAD IDIOT PUSHES SOMEONE IN A WHEELCHAIR?
WHAT'D YOU CALL ME?
BIFF! COME ON! STOP!
HE'S . . . HARASSING ME!
HHHHHHH
C-COUGH
HAH...
HHHHH
PFF
WHATEVER, MAN! WHY'D YOU BOTHER CALLING ME UP JUST TO BE A BUZZKILL?
HHHH

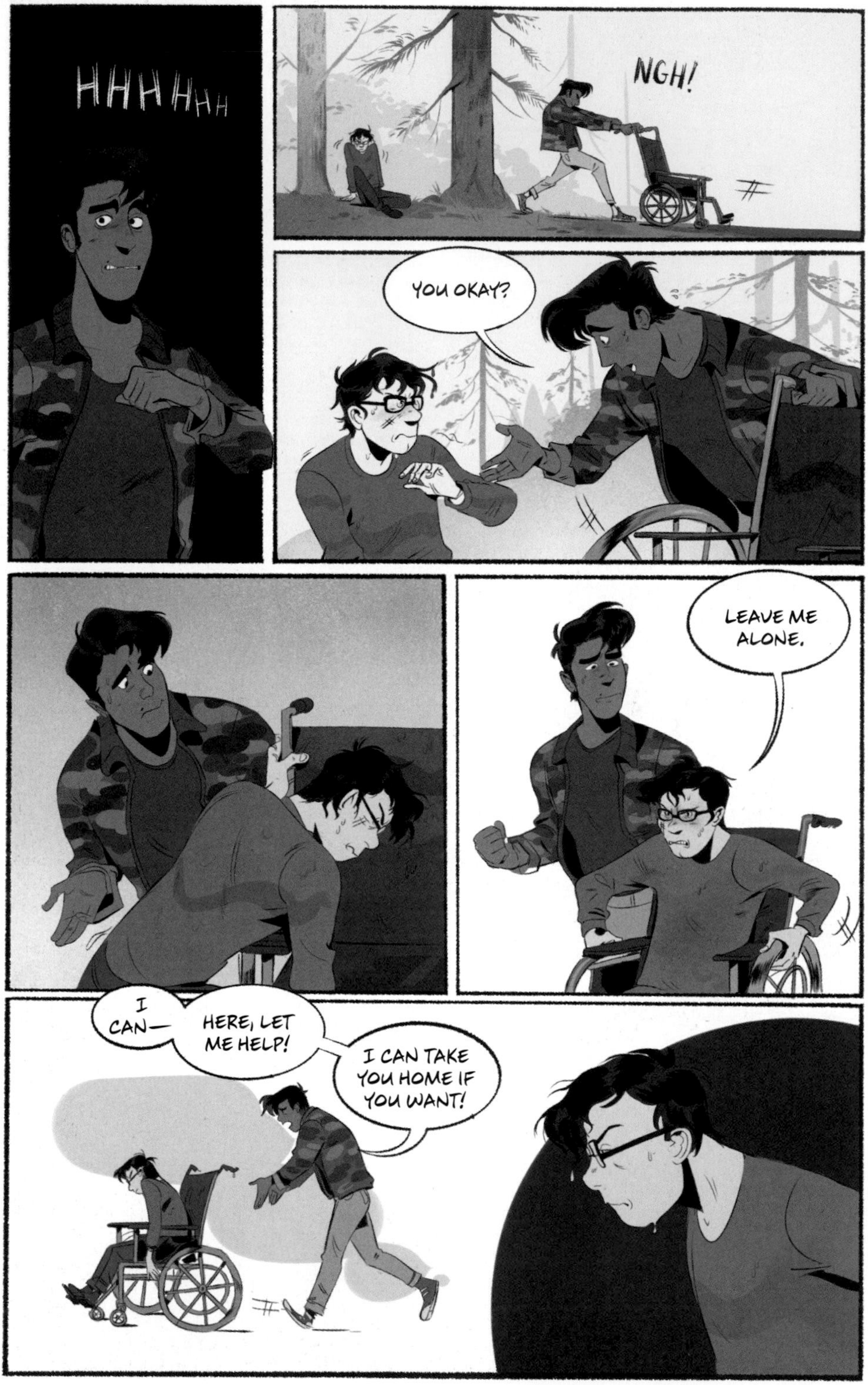
HHHHhhh
NGH!
YOU OKAY?
LEAVE ME ALONE.
I CAN—
HERE, LET ME HELP!
I CAN TAKE YOU HOME IF YOU WANT!

FINE.

UH, COULD YOU NOT TELL ANYONE ABOUT THE INHALER? NOBODY KNOWS ABOUT IT . . .

IT'S NOT A PROBLEM IF I USE IT BEFORE A RACE, SO . . .

UM, IT'S KINDA FUNNY—

ONCE I FORGOT MY INHALER BEFORE A RACE . . . I HAD TO PRETEND I GOT SICK SO I COULD FORFEIT.

WOW! I FEEL SO BAD FOR YOU!

THE POPULAR TRACK STAR HAD TO PRETEND TO BE SICK ONCE.

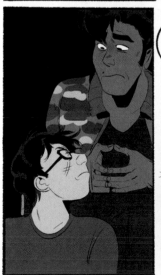

UH, I DON'T KNOW EXACTLY WHERE YOU LIVE, SO . . .

I CAN GO MYSELF.

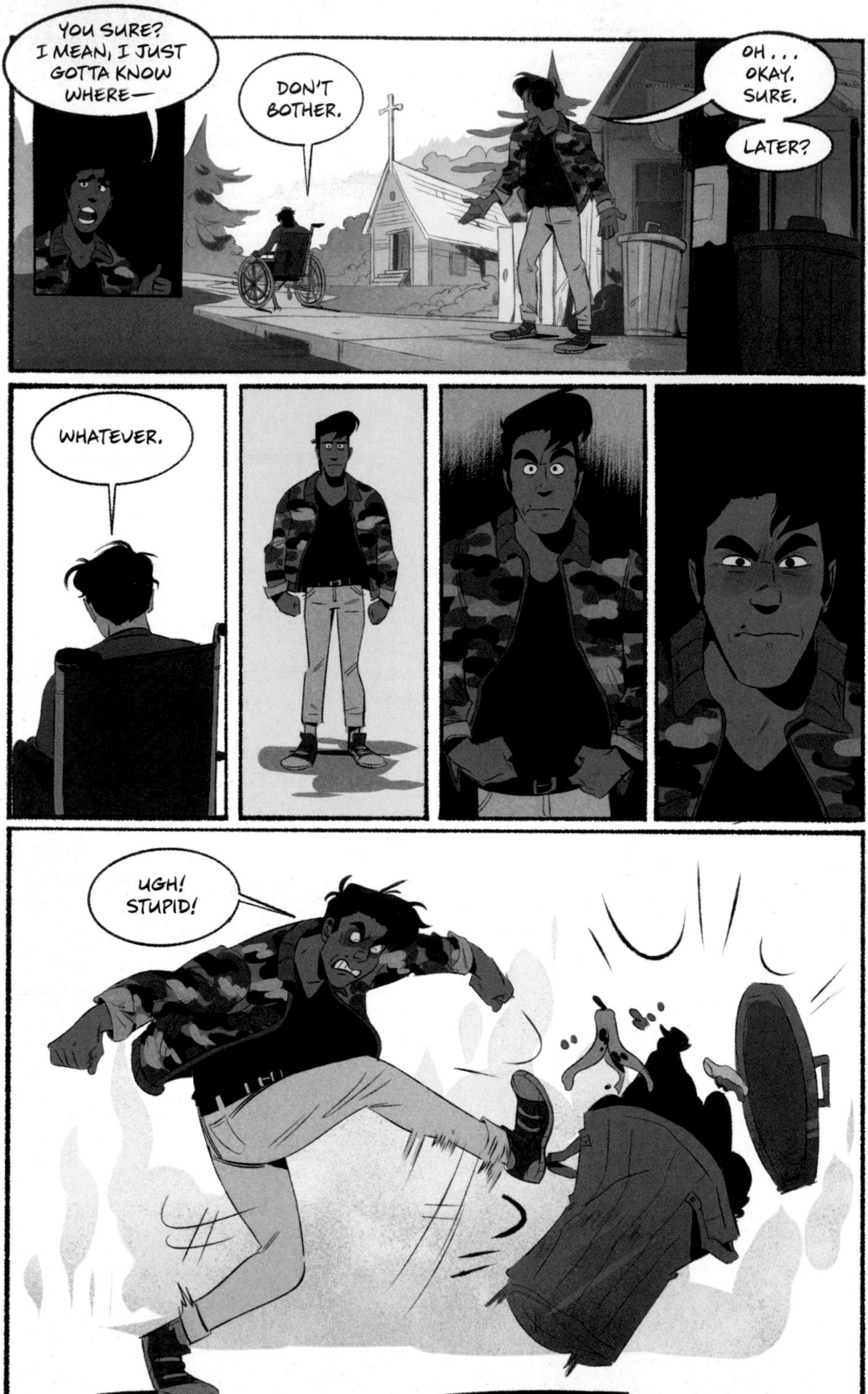
YOU SURE? I MEAN, I JUST GOTTA KNOW WHERE—
DON'T BOTHER.
OH . . . OKAY. SURE.
LATER?
WHATEVER.
UGH! STUPID!

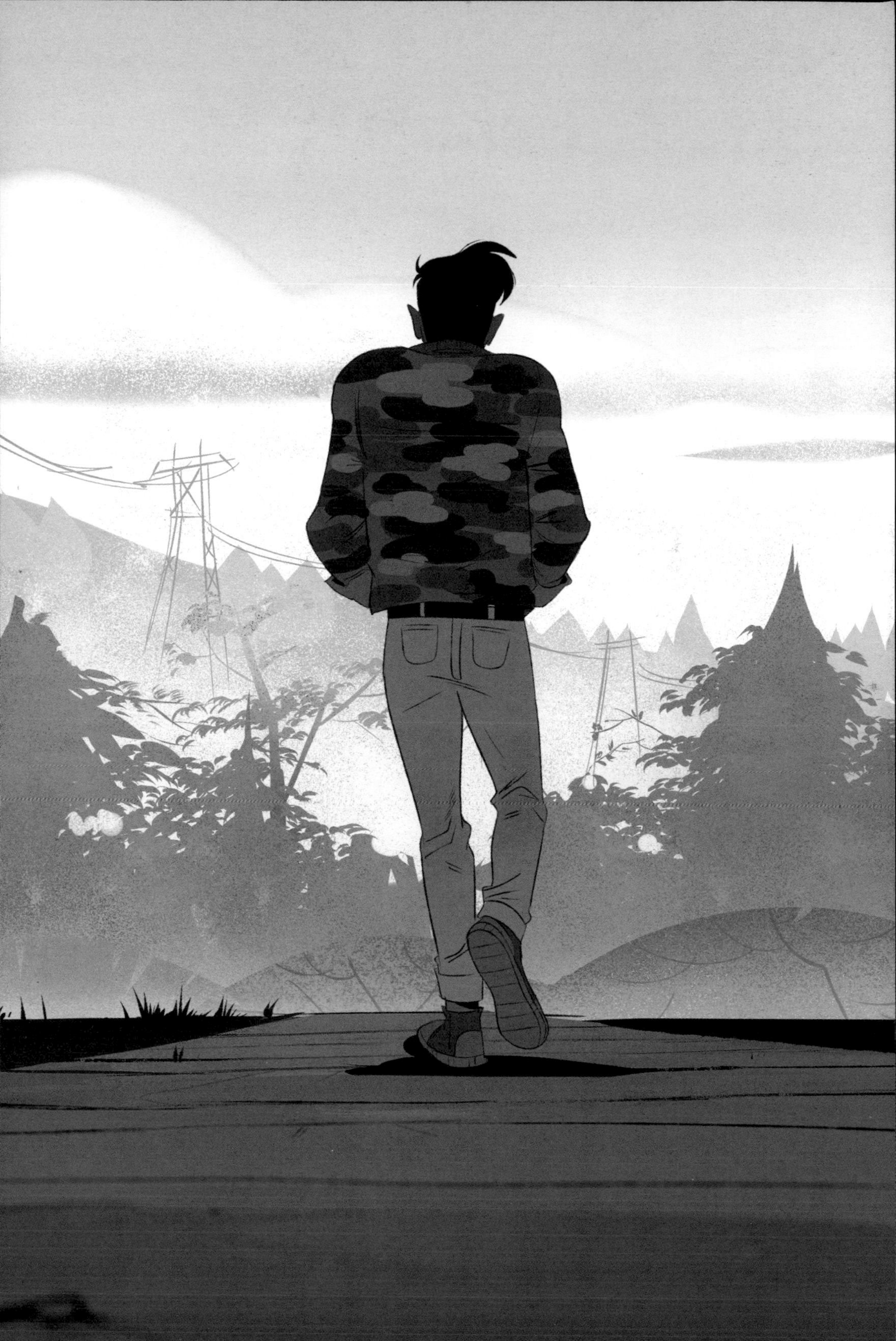

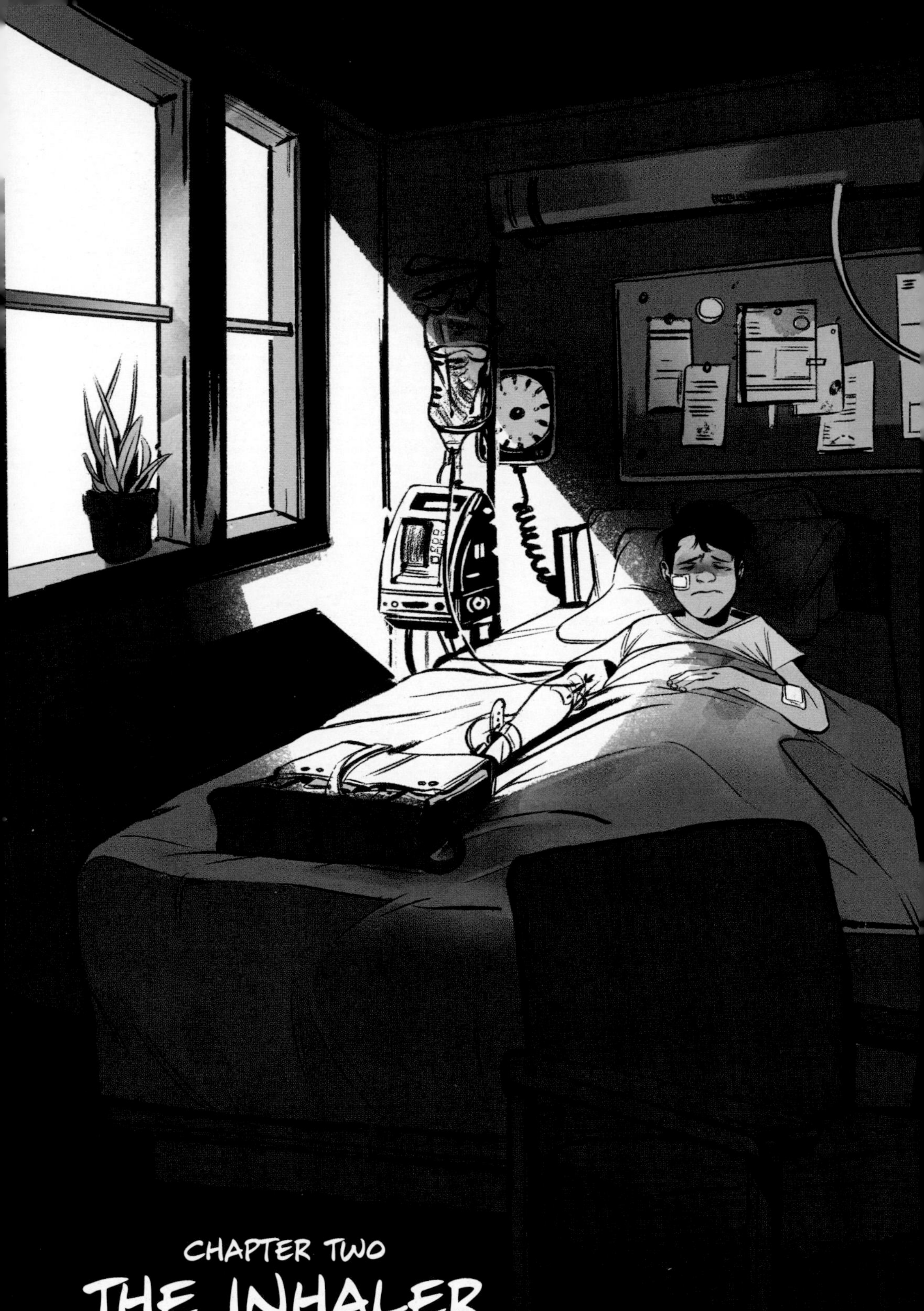

CHAPTER TWO

THE INHALER

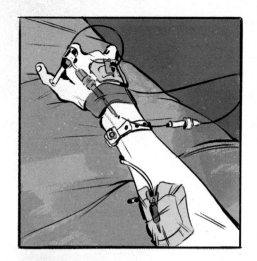
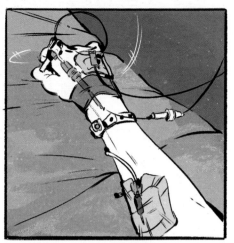

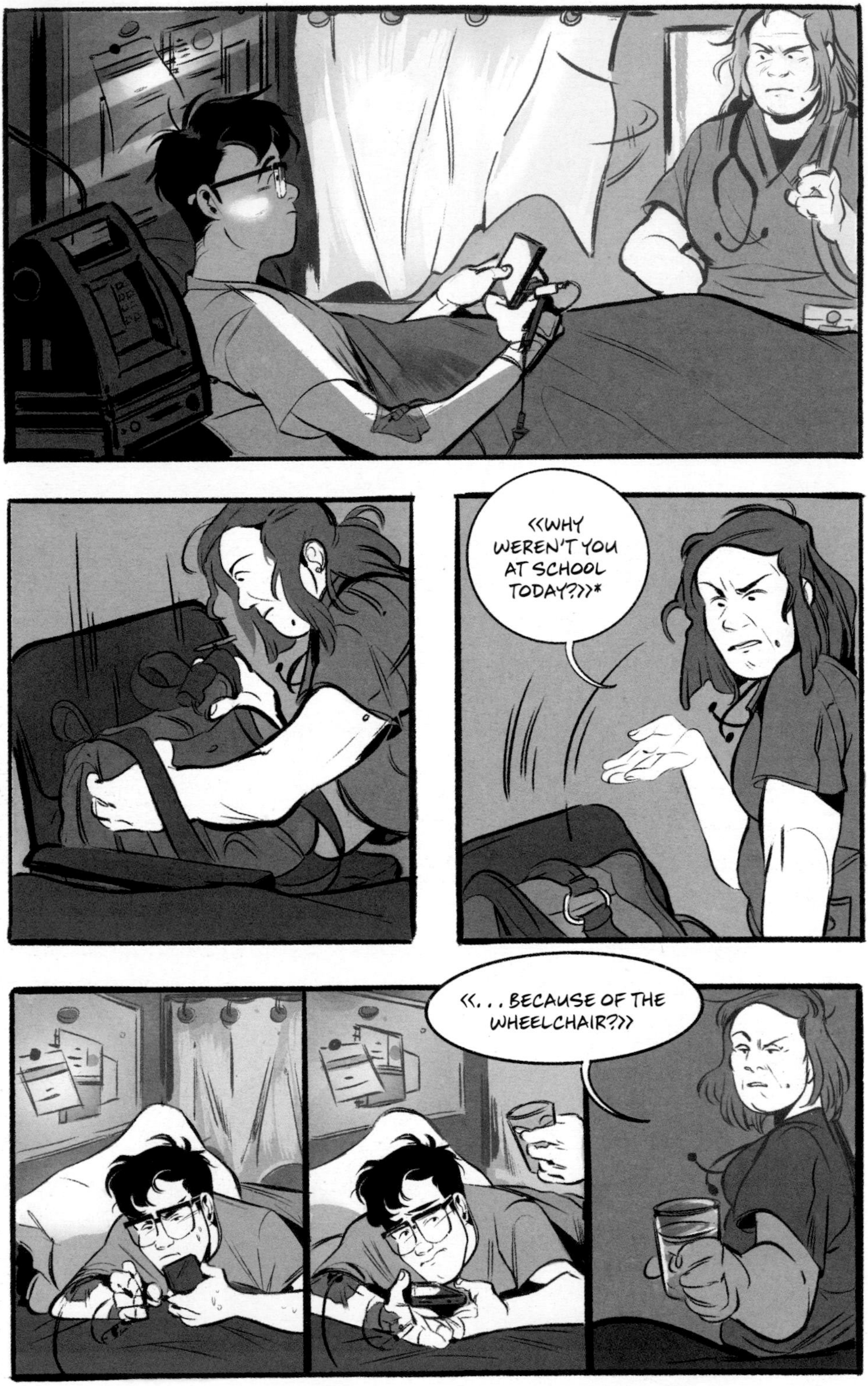
«WHY WEREN'T YOU AT SCHOOL TODAY?»*
«. . . BECAUSE OF THE WHEELCHAIR?»

*SPOKEN IN GERMAN

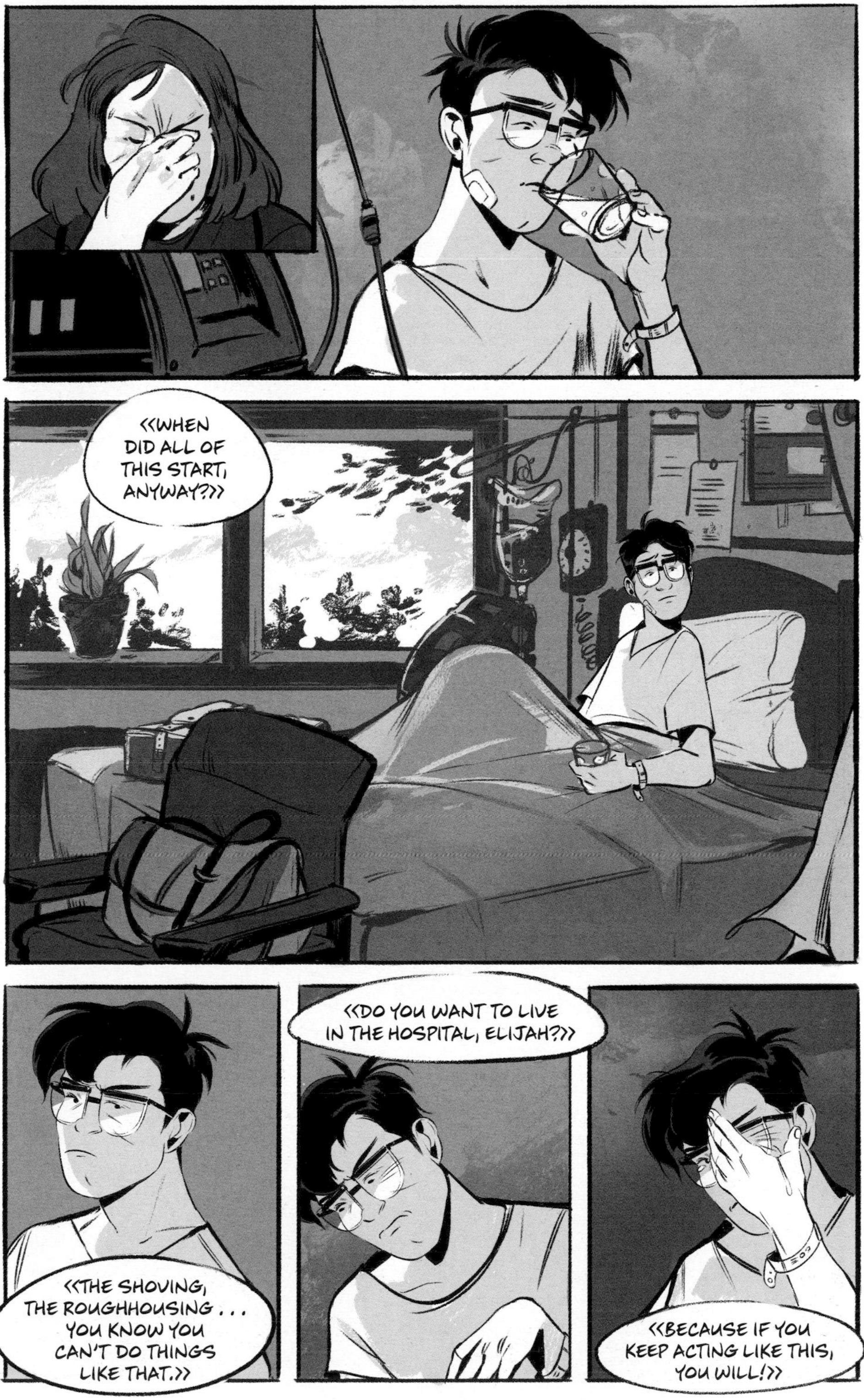

<<WHEN DID ALL OF THIS START, ANYWAY?>>
<<THE SHOVING, THE ROUGHHOUSING . . . YOU KNOW YOU CAN'T DO THINGS LIKE THAT.>>
<<DO YOU WANT TO LIVE IN THE HOSPITAL, ELIJAH?>>
<<BECAUSE IF YOU KEEP ACTING LIKE THIS, YOU WILL!>>

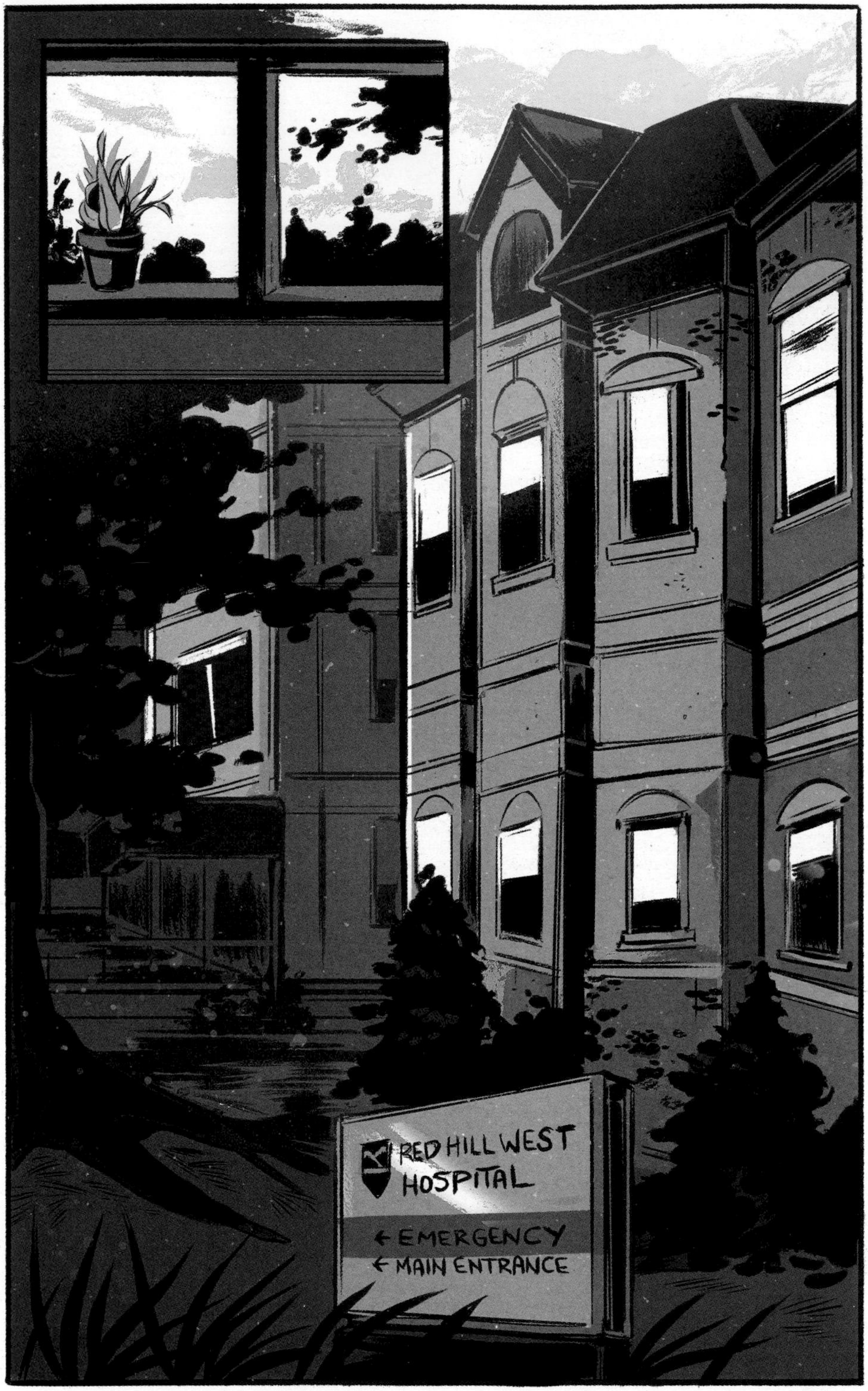
RED HILL WEST
HOSPITAL
← EMERGENCY
← MAIN ENTRANCE

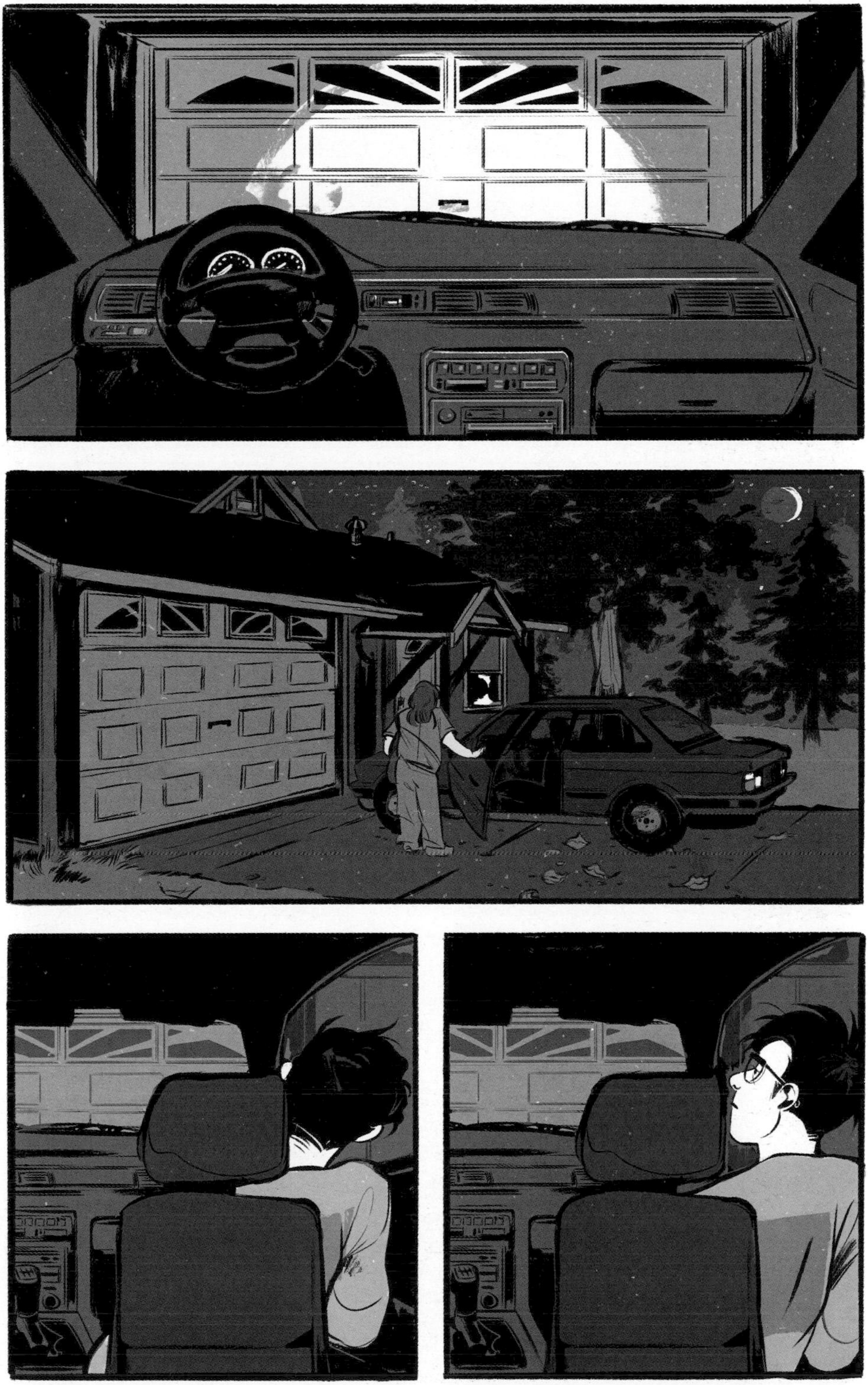

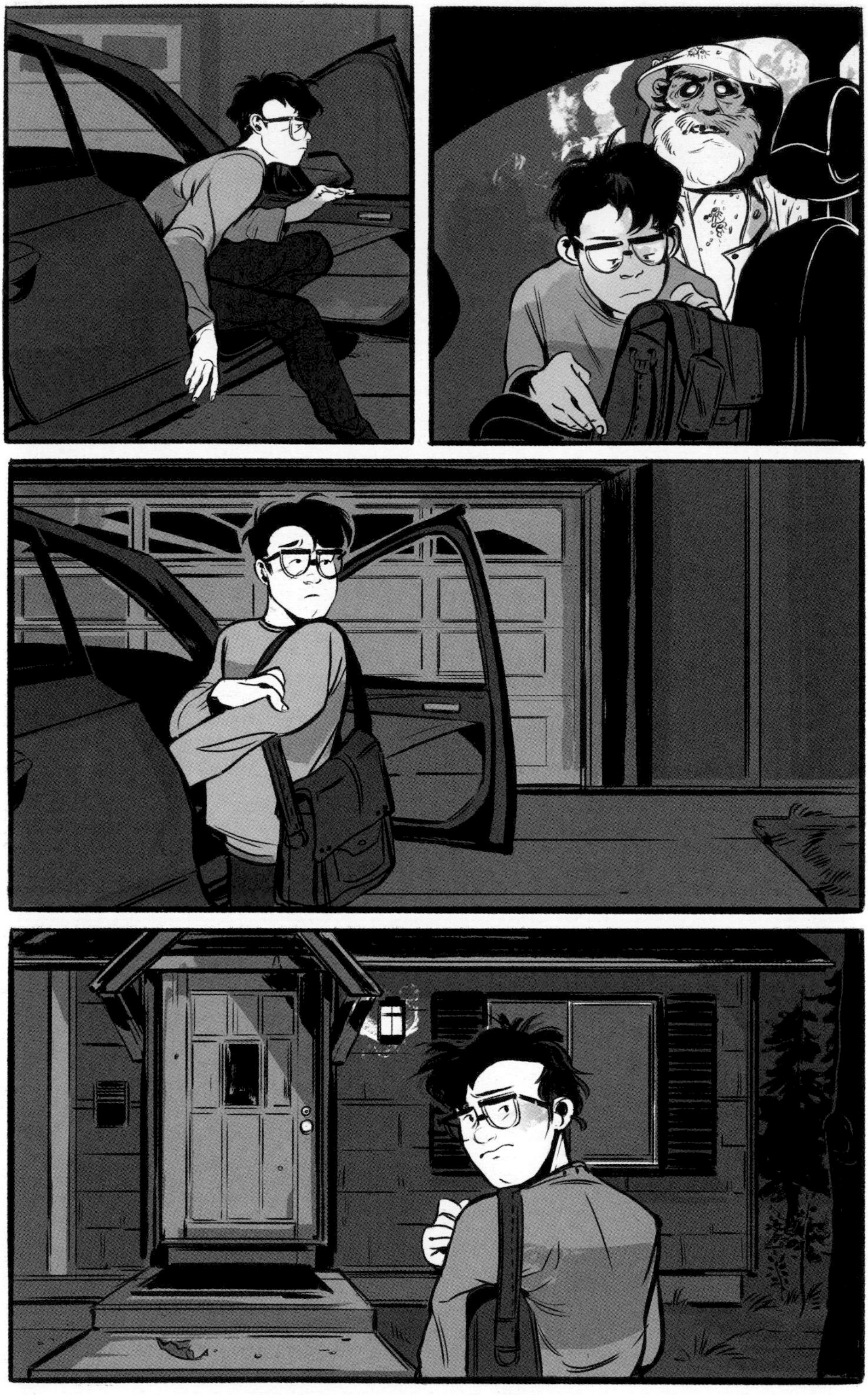

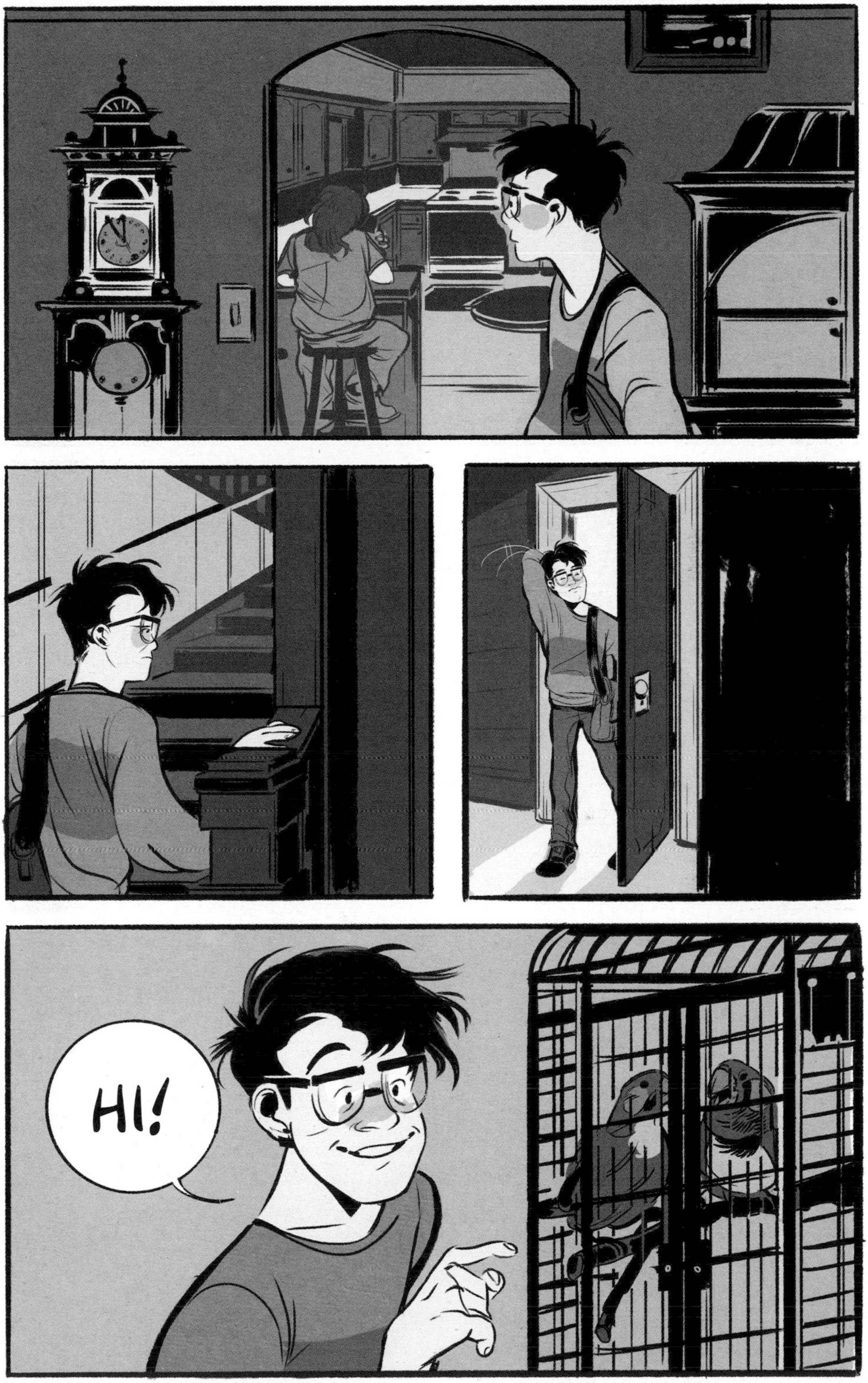
HI!

TRACK ME
SUPPORT
TRACK CHAMP
ONY PRICE
TRACK ME
SUPPORT*
TRACK CHAM
TONY P

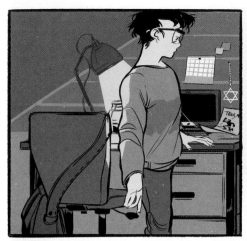

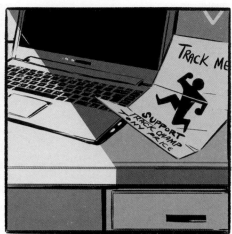

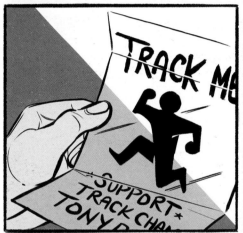

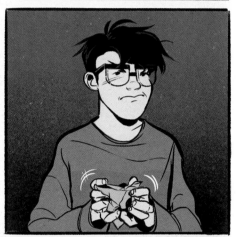

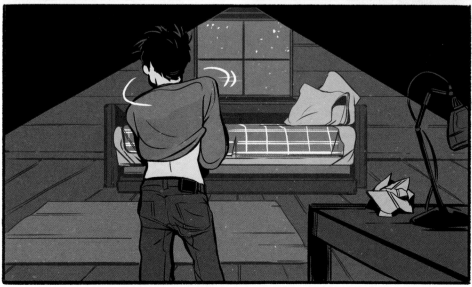

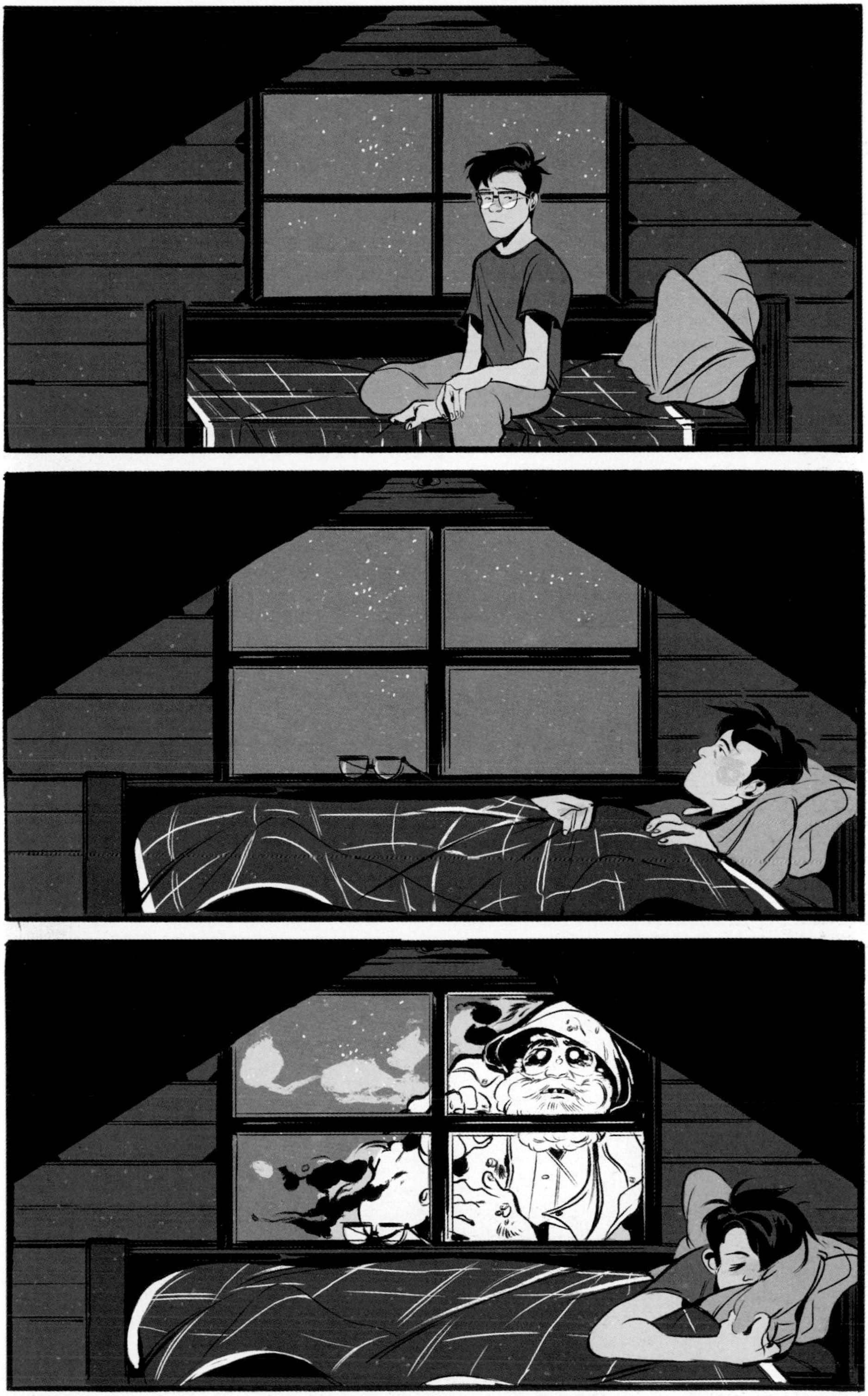

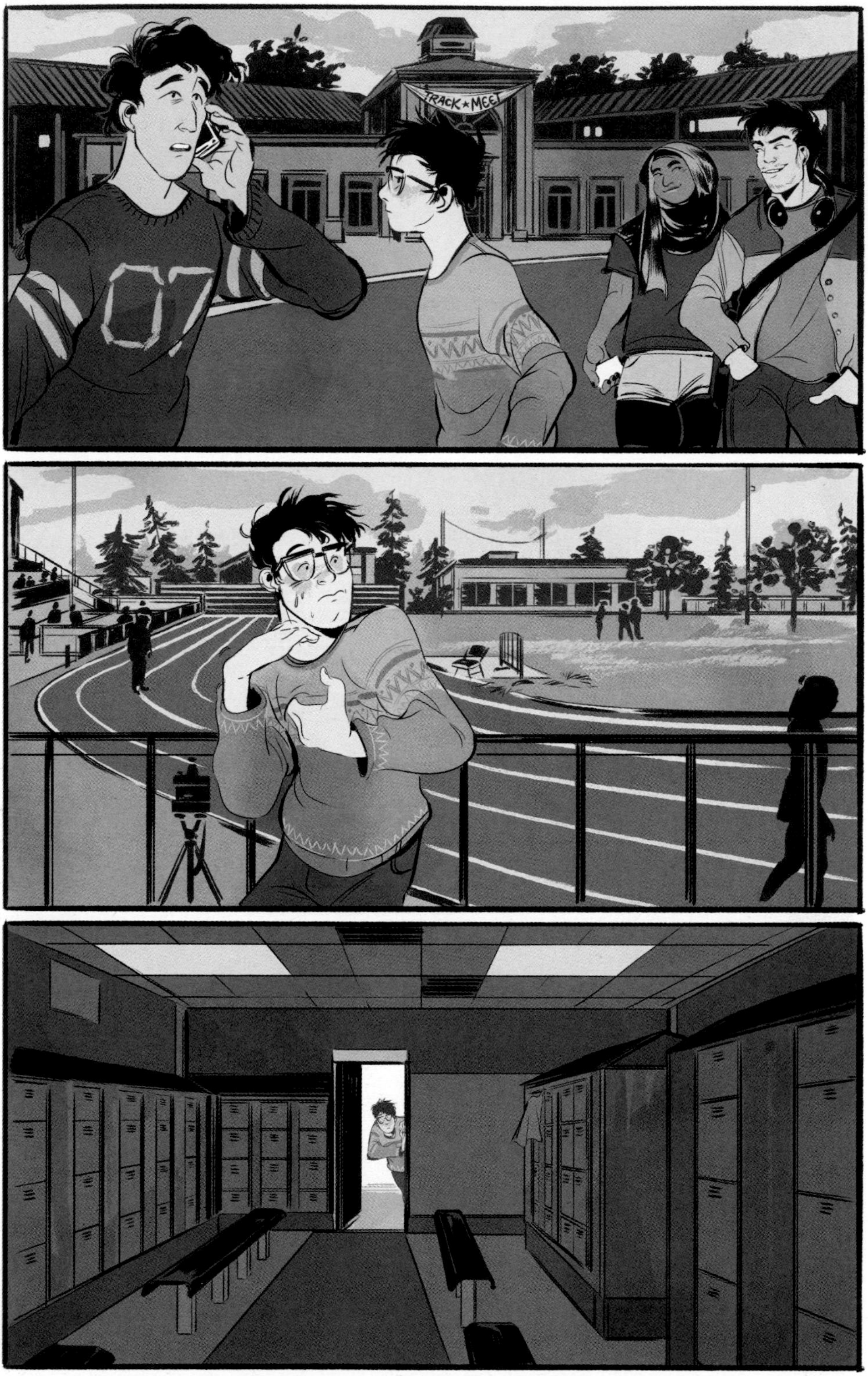
TRACK ★ MEET

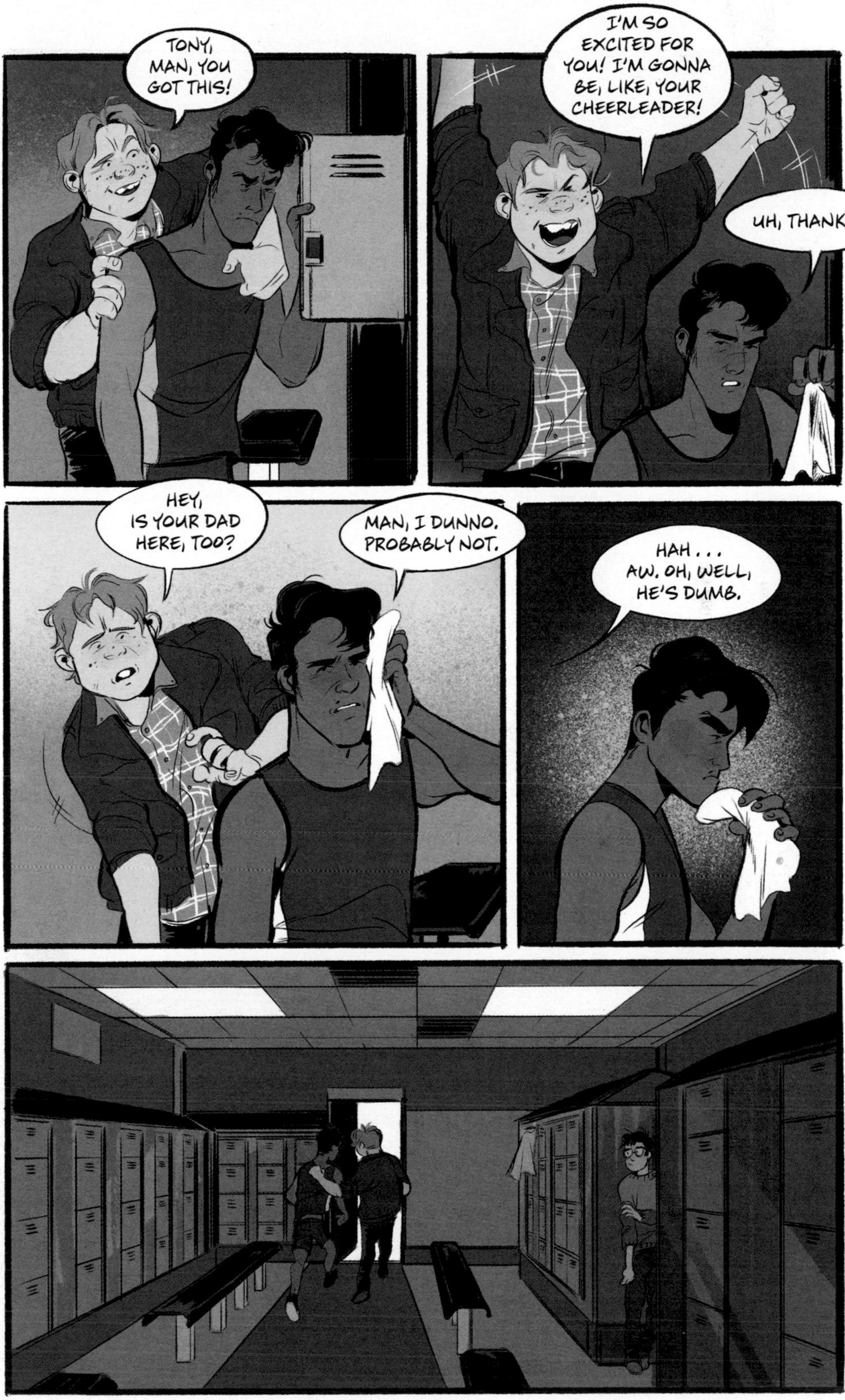
TONY, MAN, YOU GOT THIS!
I'M SO EXCITED FOR YOU! I'M GONNA BE, LIKE, YOUR CHEERLEADER!
UH, THANKS.
HEY, IS YOUR DAD HERE, TOO?
MAN, I DUNNO. PROBABLY NOT.
HAH . . . AW. OH, WELL, HE'S DUMB.

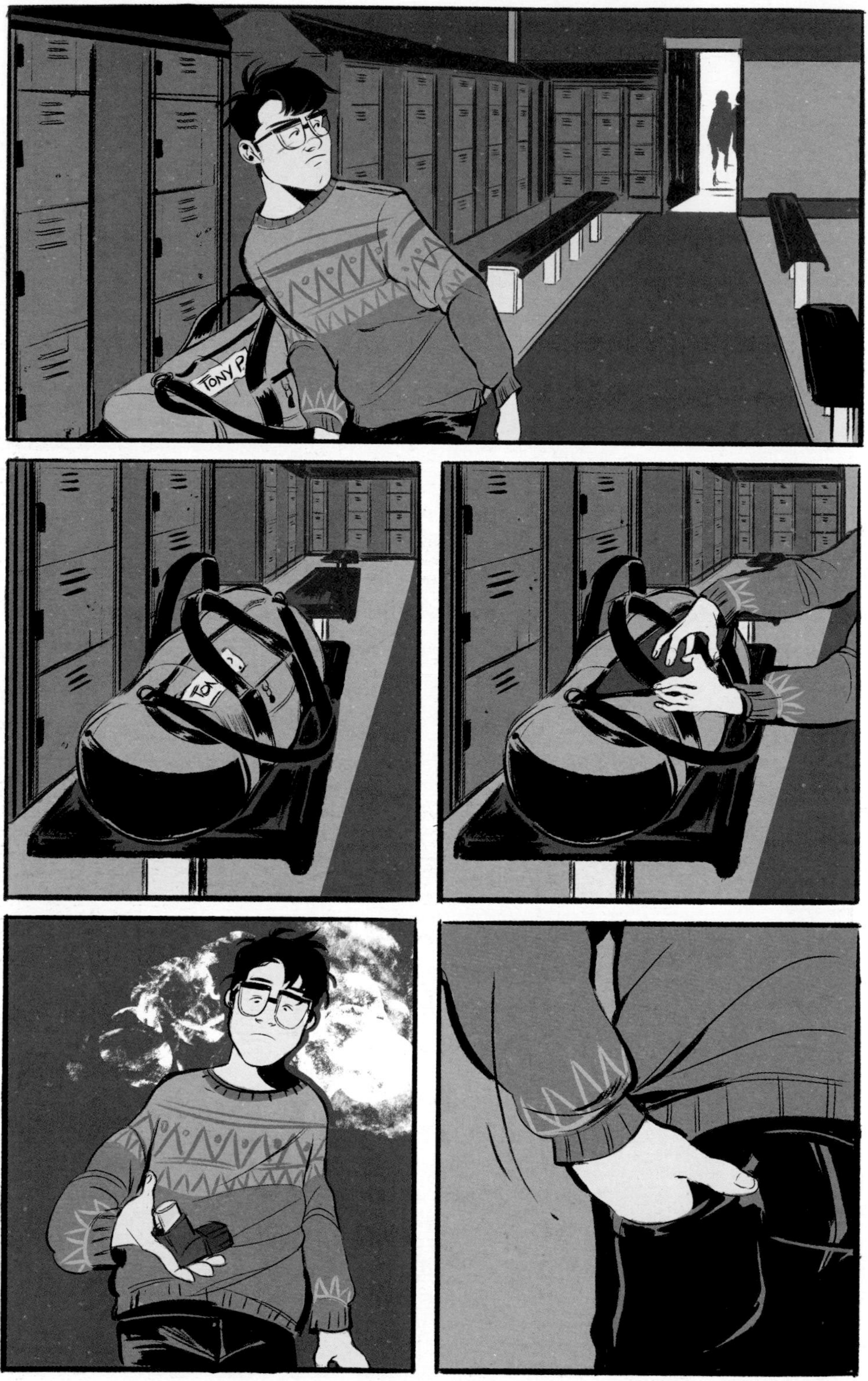
TONY P.

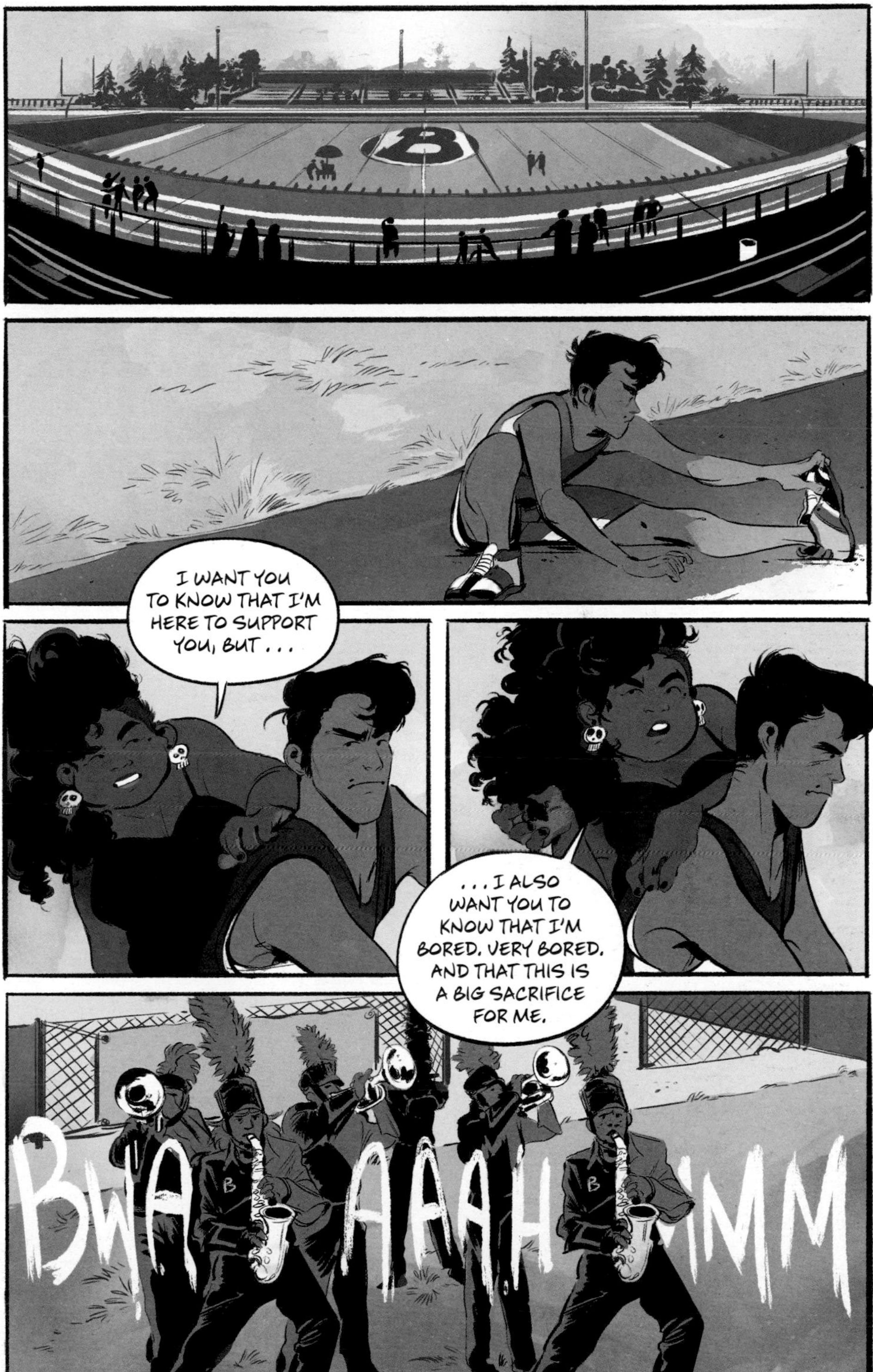
I WANT YOU TO KNOW THAT I'M HERE TO SUPPORT YOU, BUT . . .
. . . I ALSO WANT YOU TO KNOW THAT I'M BORED. VERY BORED. AND THAT THIS IS A BIG SACRIFICE FOR ME.
BWAAAAHMMM

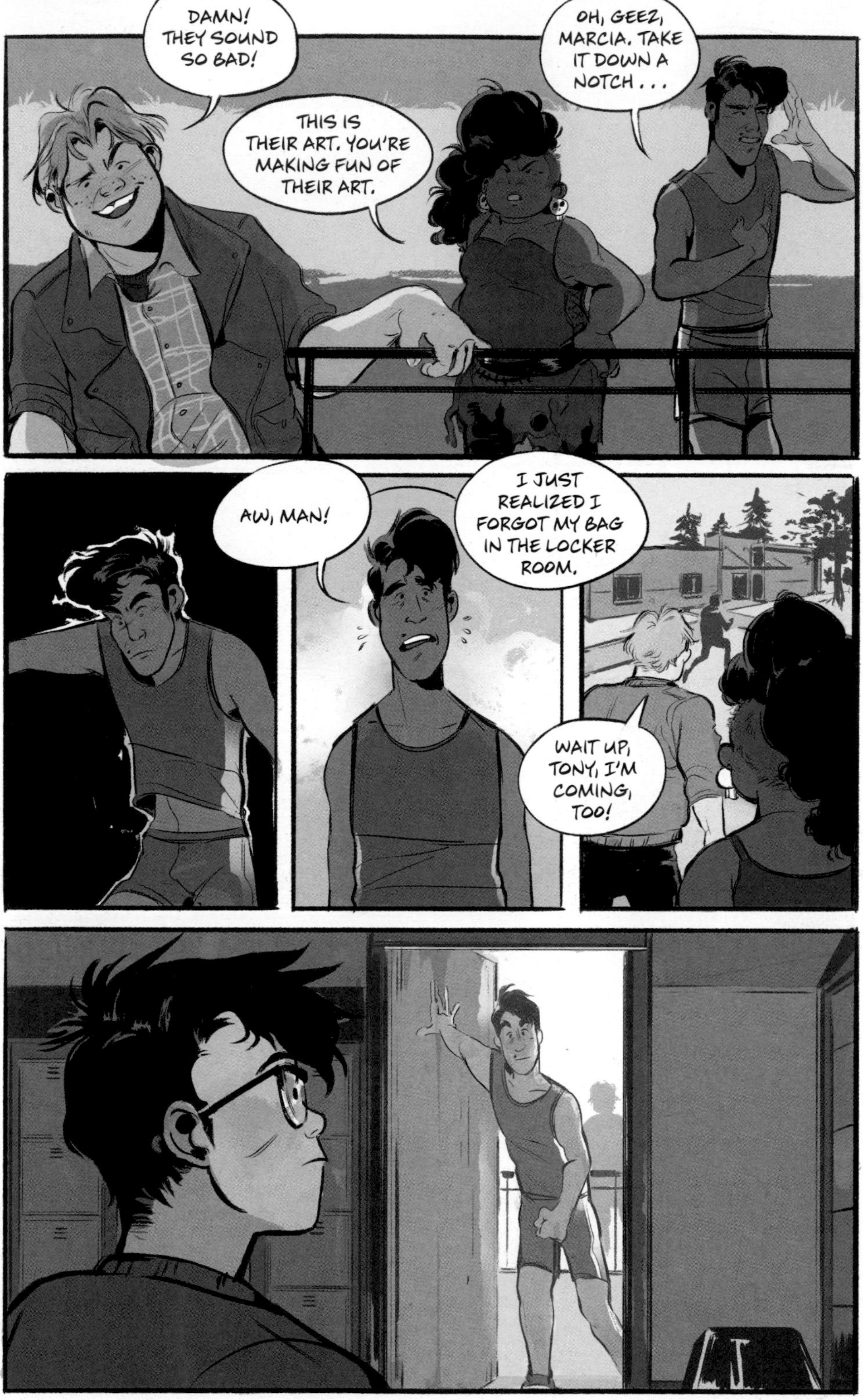
DAMN! THEY SOUND SO BAD!
THIS IS THEIR ART. YOU'RE MAKING FUN OF THEIR ART.
OH, GEEZ, MARCIA. TAKE IT DOWN A NOTCH . . .
AW, MAN!
I JUST REALIZED I FORGOT MY BAG IN THE LOCKER ROOM.
WAIT UP, TONY, I'M COMING, TOO!

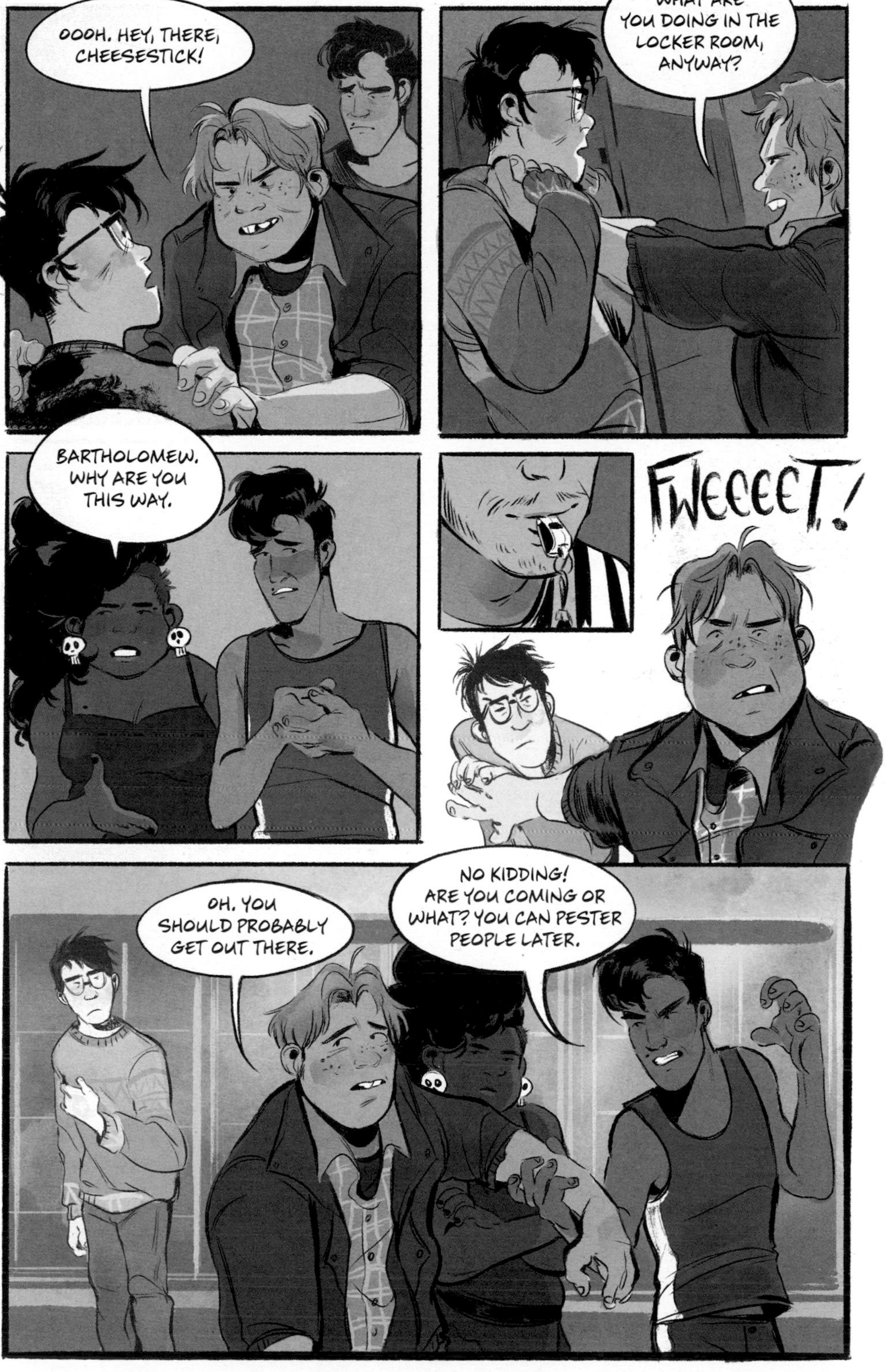
OOOH. HEY, THERE, CHEESESTICK!
WHAT ARE YOU DOING IN THE LOCKER ROOM, ANYWAY?
BARTHOLOMEW. WHY ARE YOU THIS WAY.
FWEEEET!
OH. YOU SHOULD PROBABLY GET OUT THERE.
NO KIDDING! ARE YOU COMING OR WHAT? YOU CAN PESTER PEOPLE LATER.

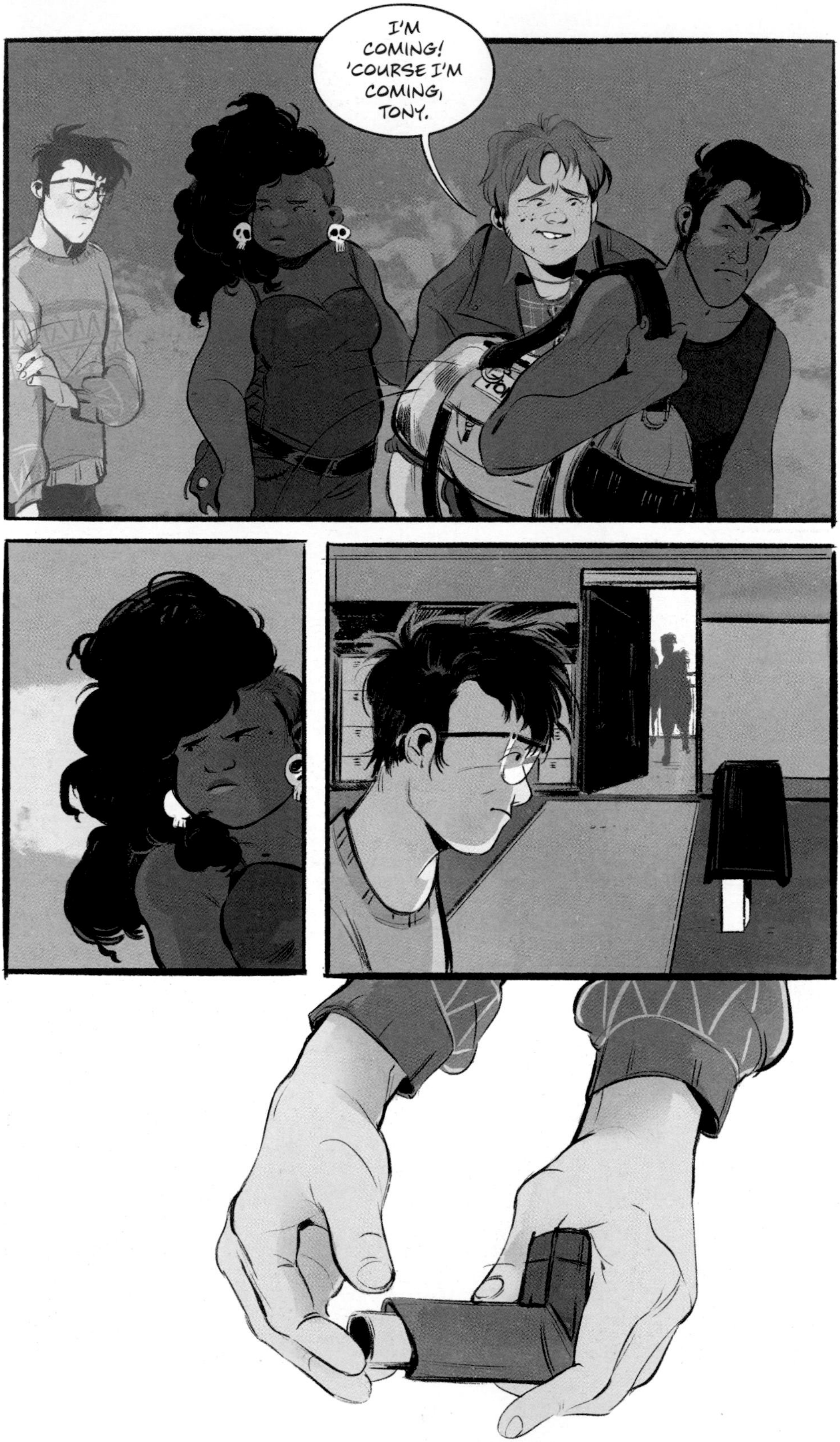
I'M COMING! 'COURSE I'M COMING, TONY.

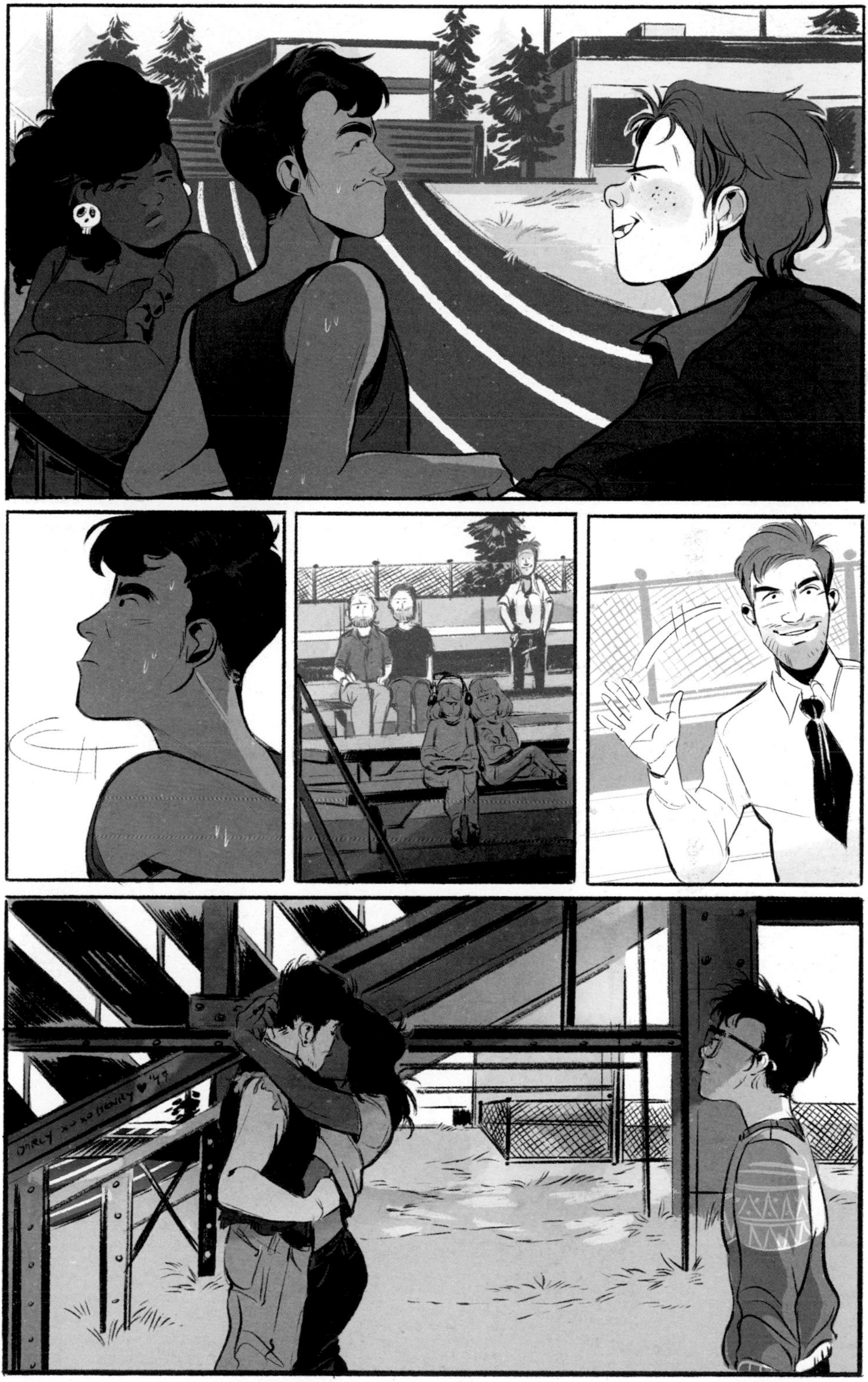

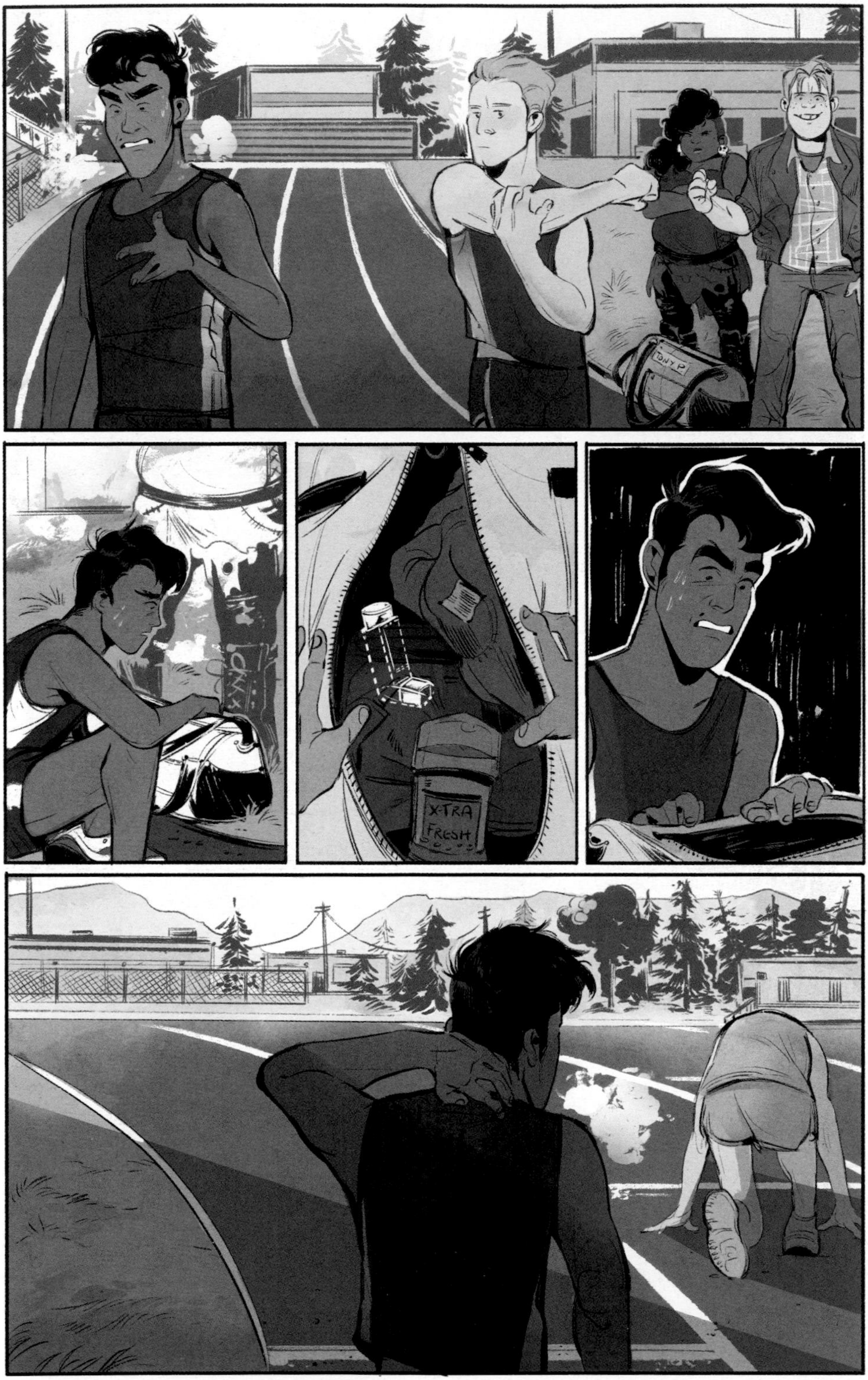
TONY P
X-TRA
FRESH

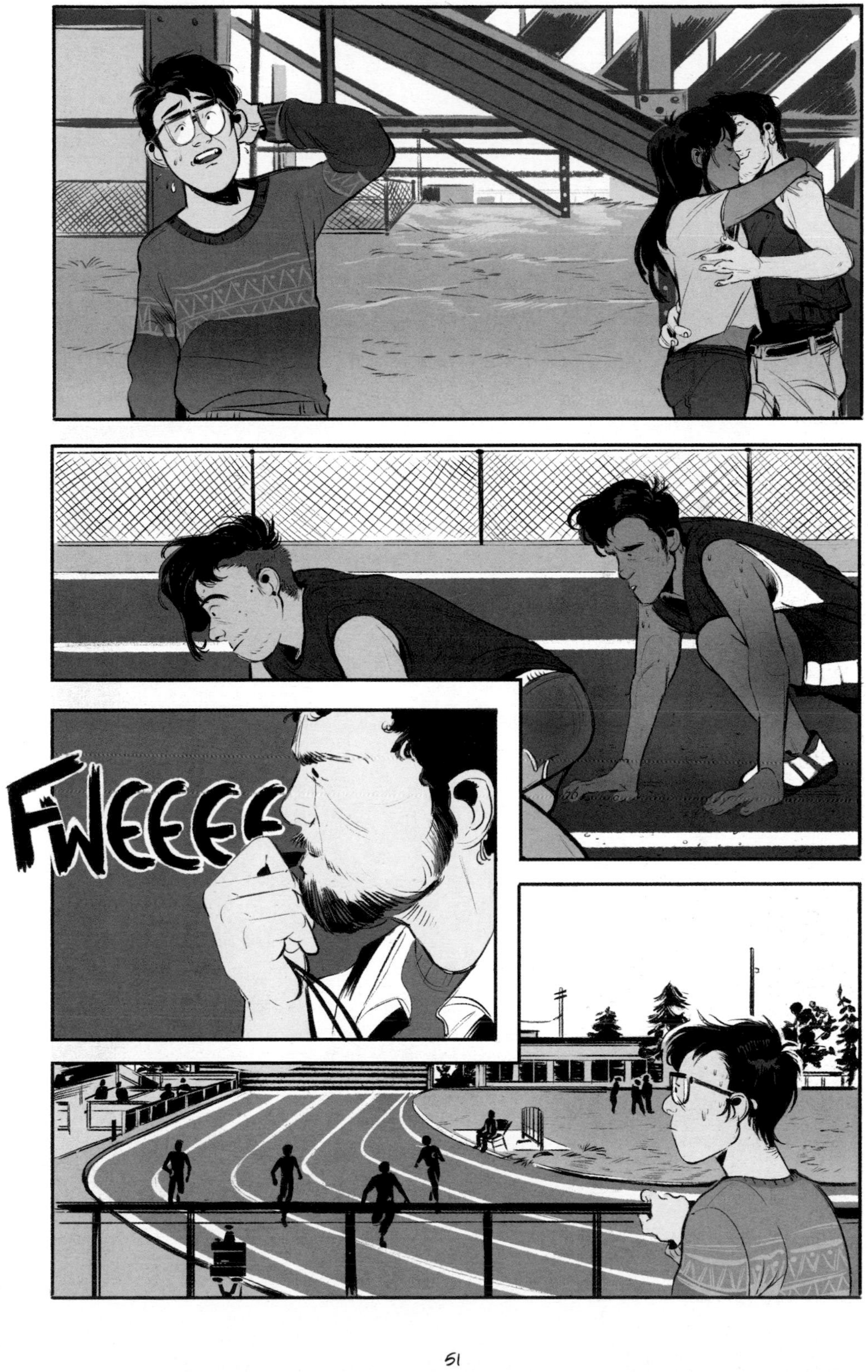
FWEEEE

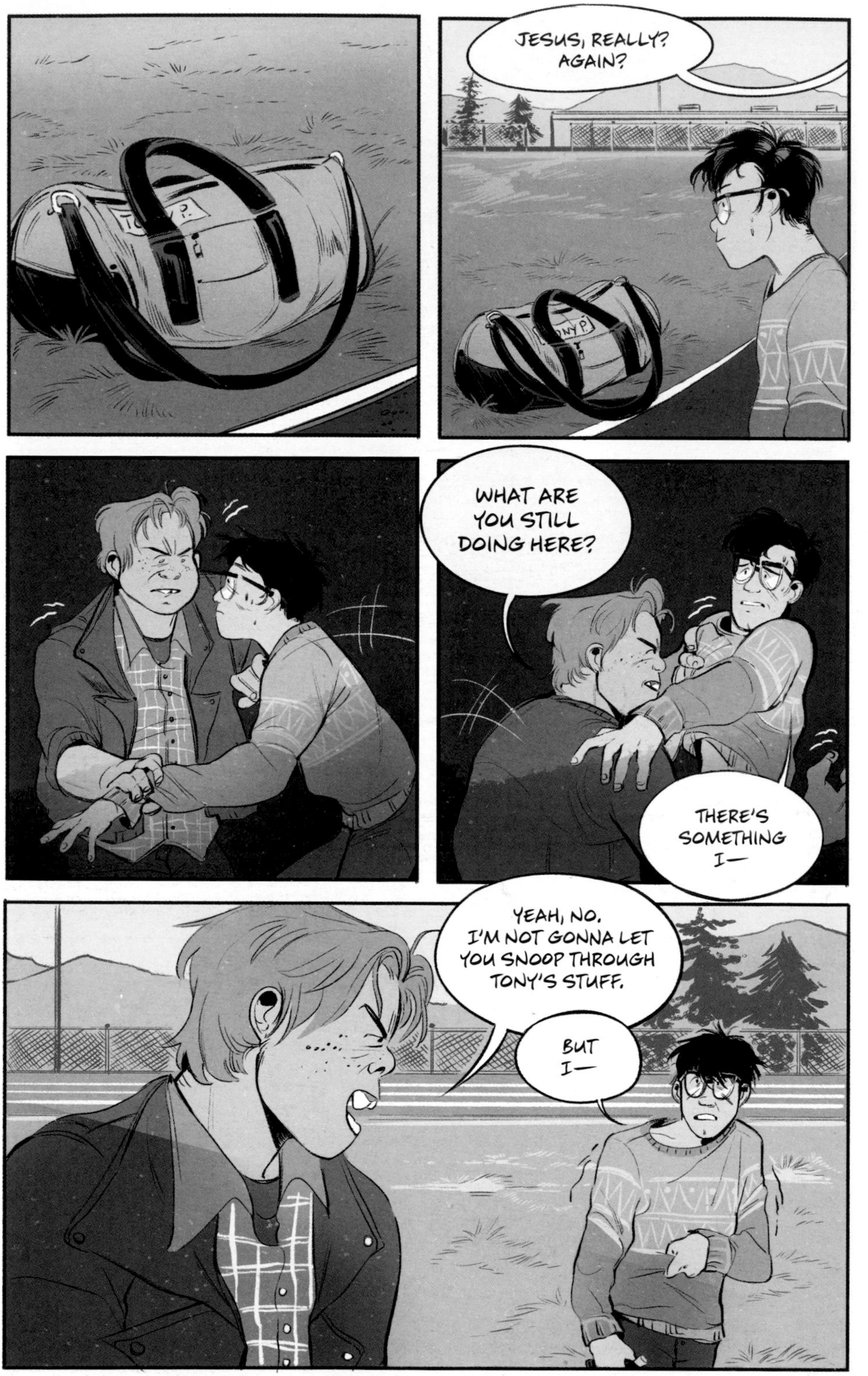
TONY P.
JESUS, REALLY? AGAIN?
TONY P.
WHAT ARE YOU STILL DOING HERE?
THERE'S SOMETHING I—
YEAH, NO. I'M NOT GONNA LET YOU SNOOP THROUGH TONY'S STUFF.
BUT I—

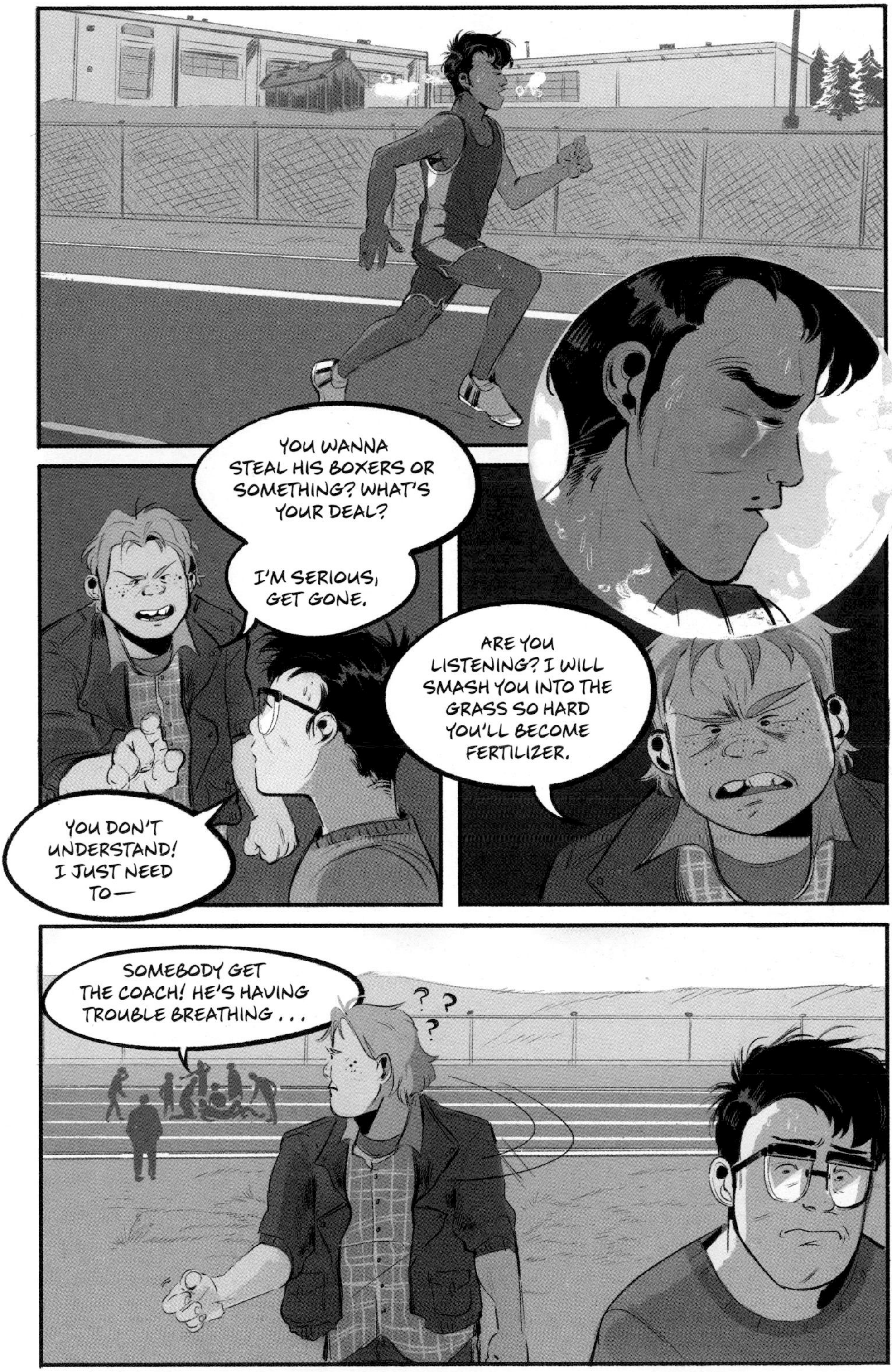
YOU WANNA STEAL HIS BOXERS OR SOMETHING? WHAT'S YOUR DEAL?
I'M SERIOUS, GET GONE.
YOU DON'T UNDERSTAND! I JUST NEED TO—
ARE YOU LISTENING? I WILL SMASH YOU INTO THE GRASS SO HARD YOU'LL BECOME FERTILIZER.
SOMEBODY GET THE COACH! HE'S HAVING TROUBLE BREATHING . . .
? ? ?

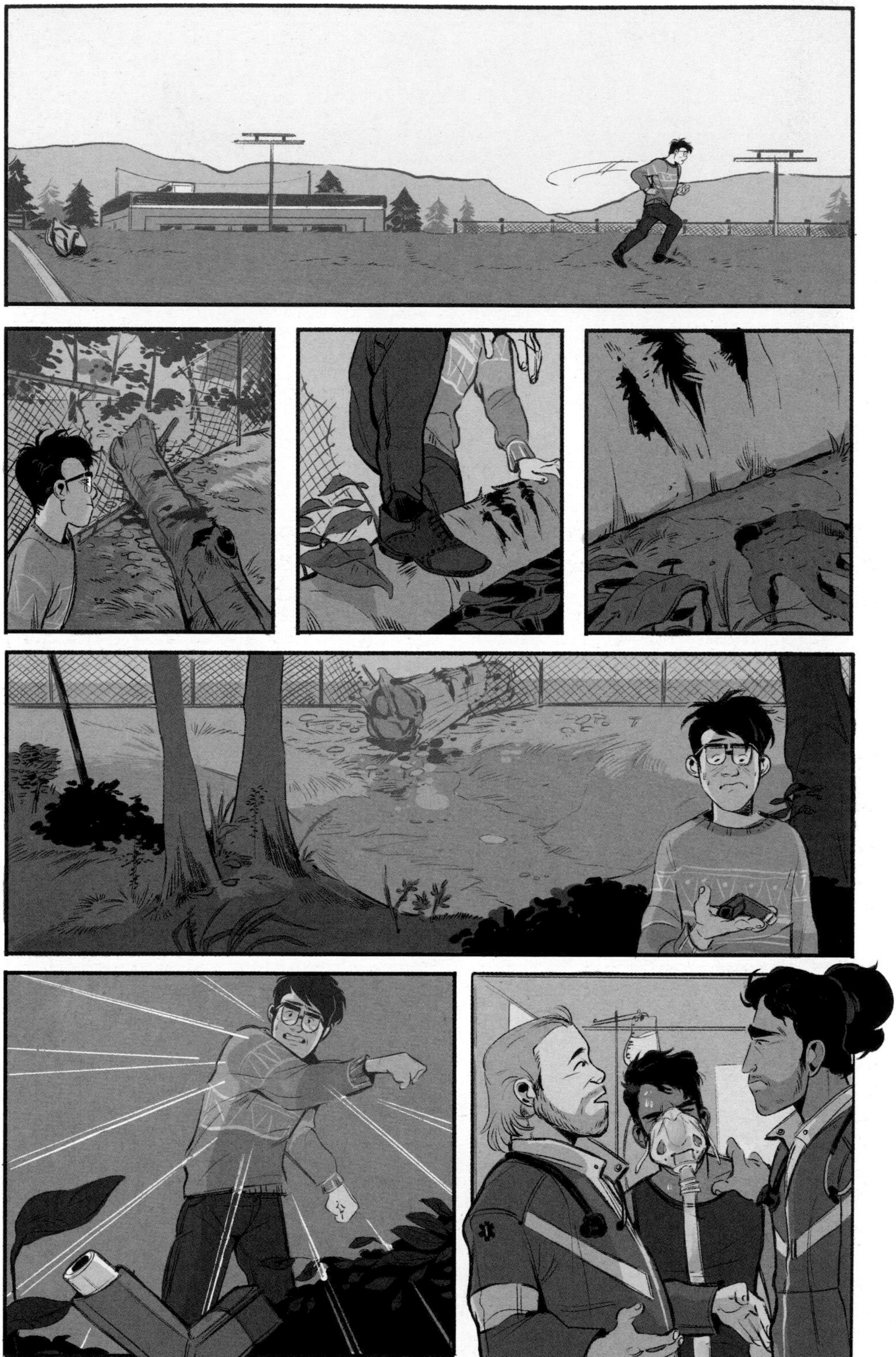

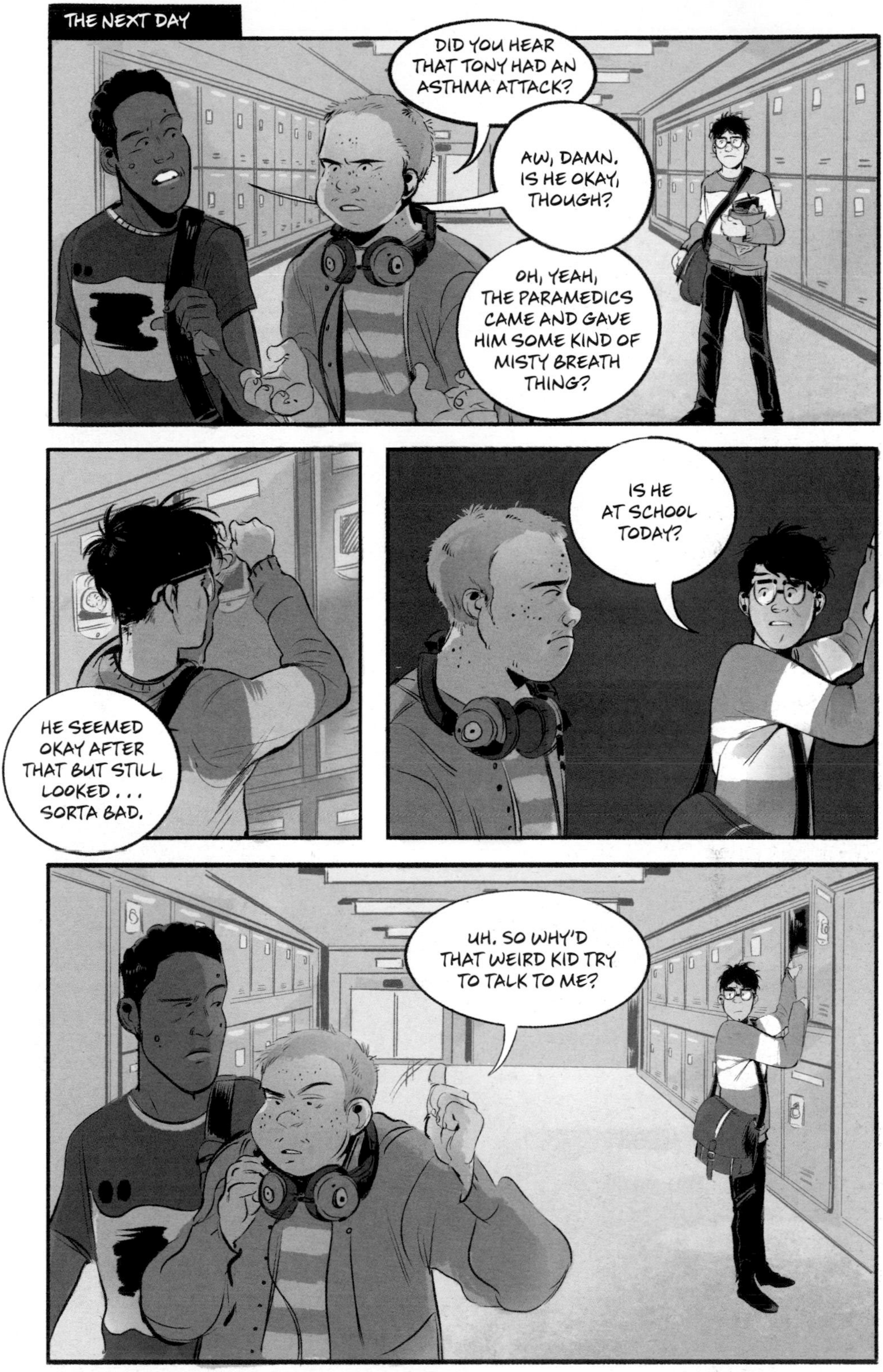
THE NEXT DAY
DID YOU HEAR THAT TONY HAD AN ASTHMA ATTACK?
AW, DAMN. IS HE OKAY, THOUGH?
OH, YEAH, THE PARAMEDICS CAME AND GAVE HIM SOME KIND OF MISTY BREATH THING?
HE SEEMED OKAY AFTER THAT BUT STILL LOOKED . . . SORTA BAD.
IS HE AT SCHOOL TODAY?
UH. SO WHY'D THAT WEIRD KID TRY TO TALK TO ME?

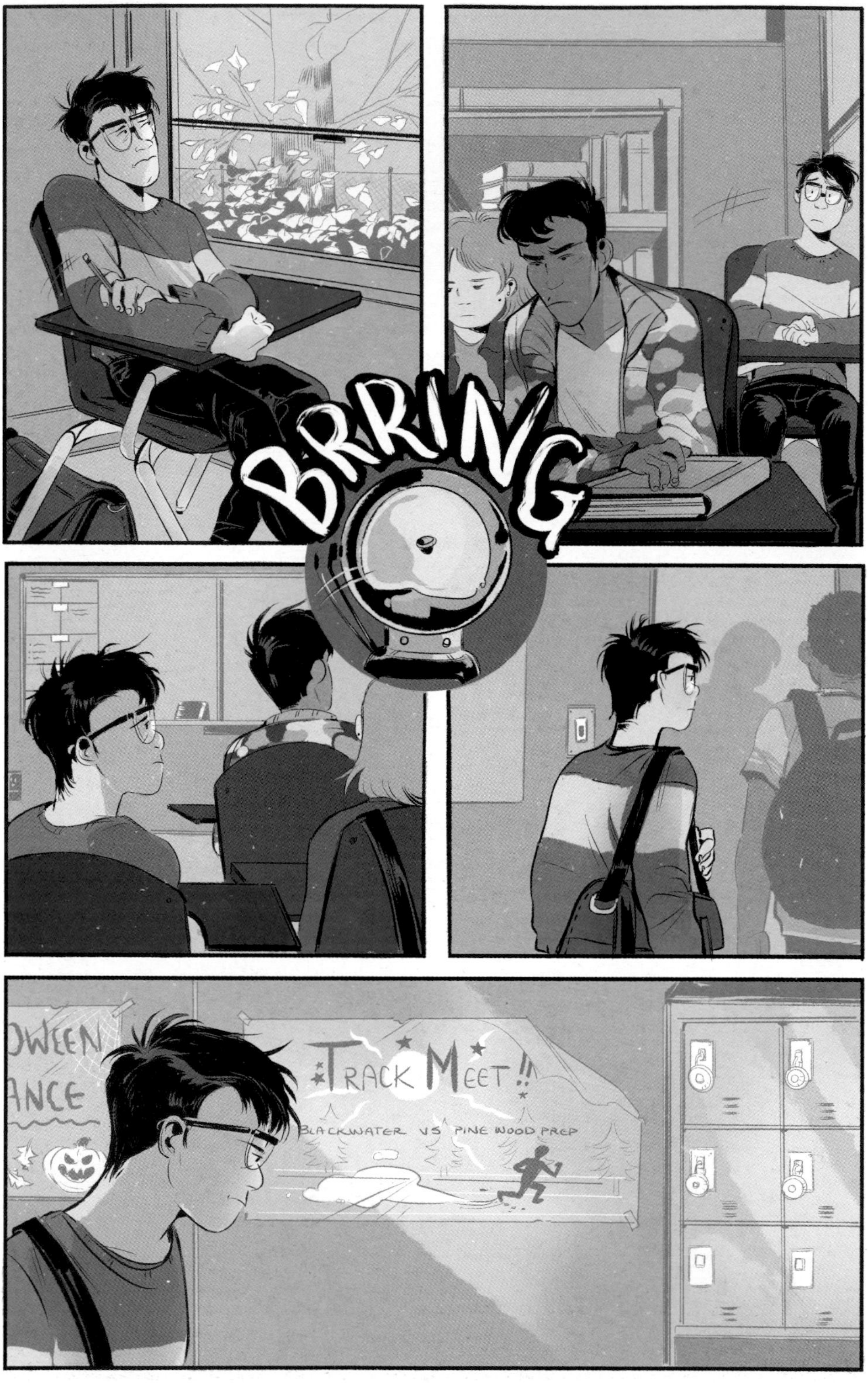
BRRING
OWEEN
ANCE
TRACK MEET!!
BLACKWATER VS PINE WOOD PREP

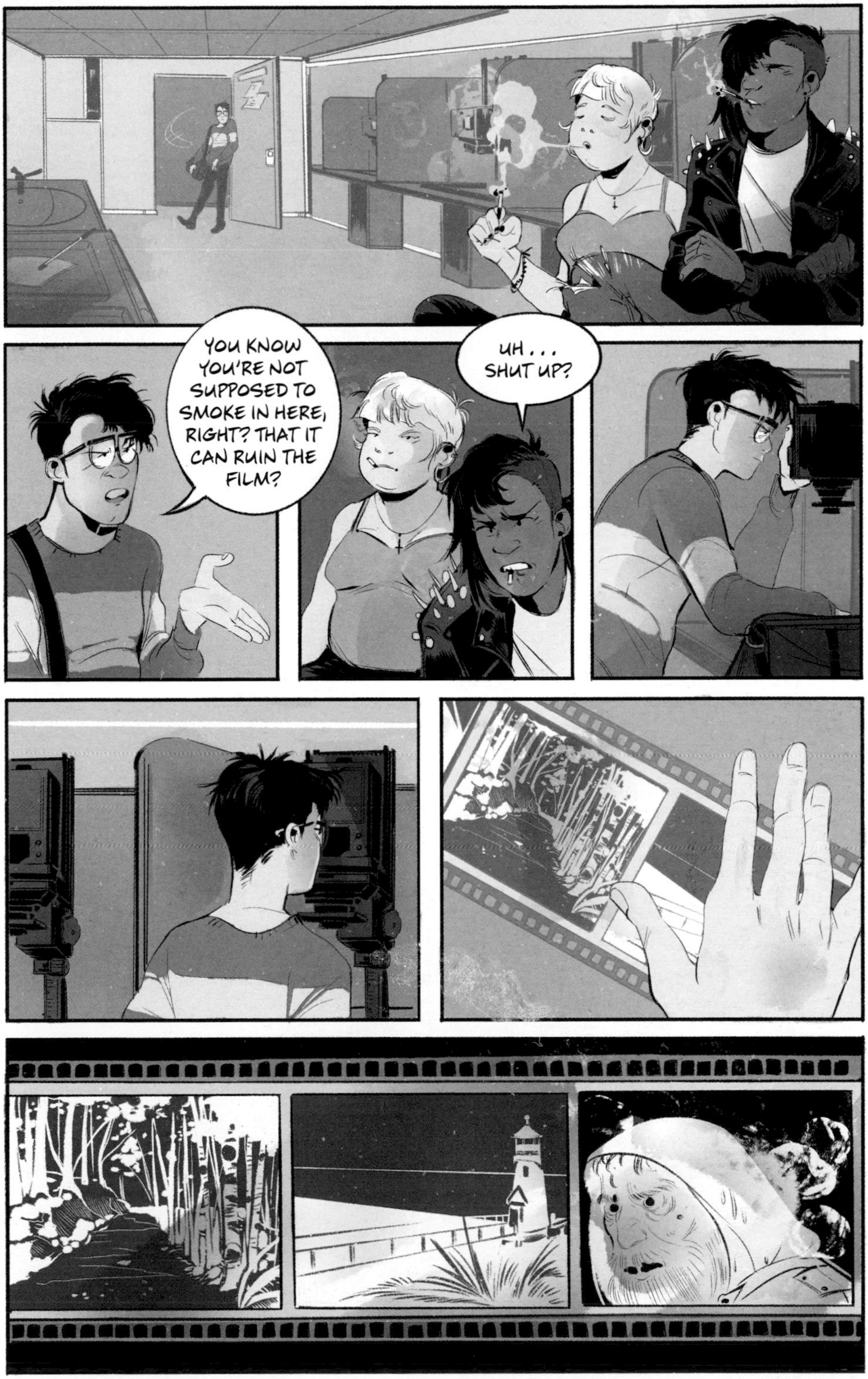
YOU KNOW YOU'RE NOT SUPPOSED TO SMOKE IN HERE, RIGHT? THAT IT CAN RUIN THE FILM?
UH . . . SHUT UP?

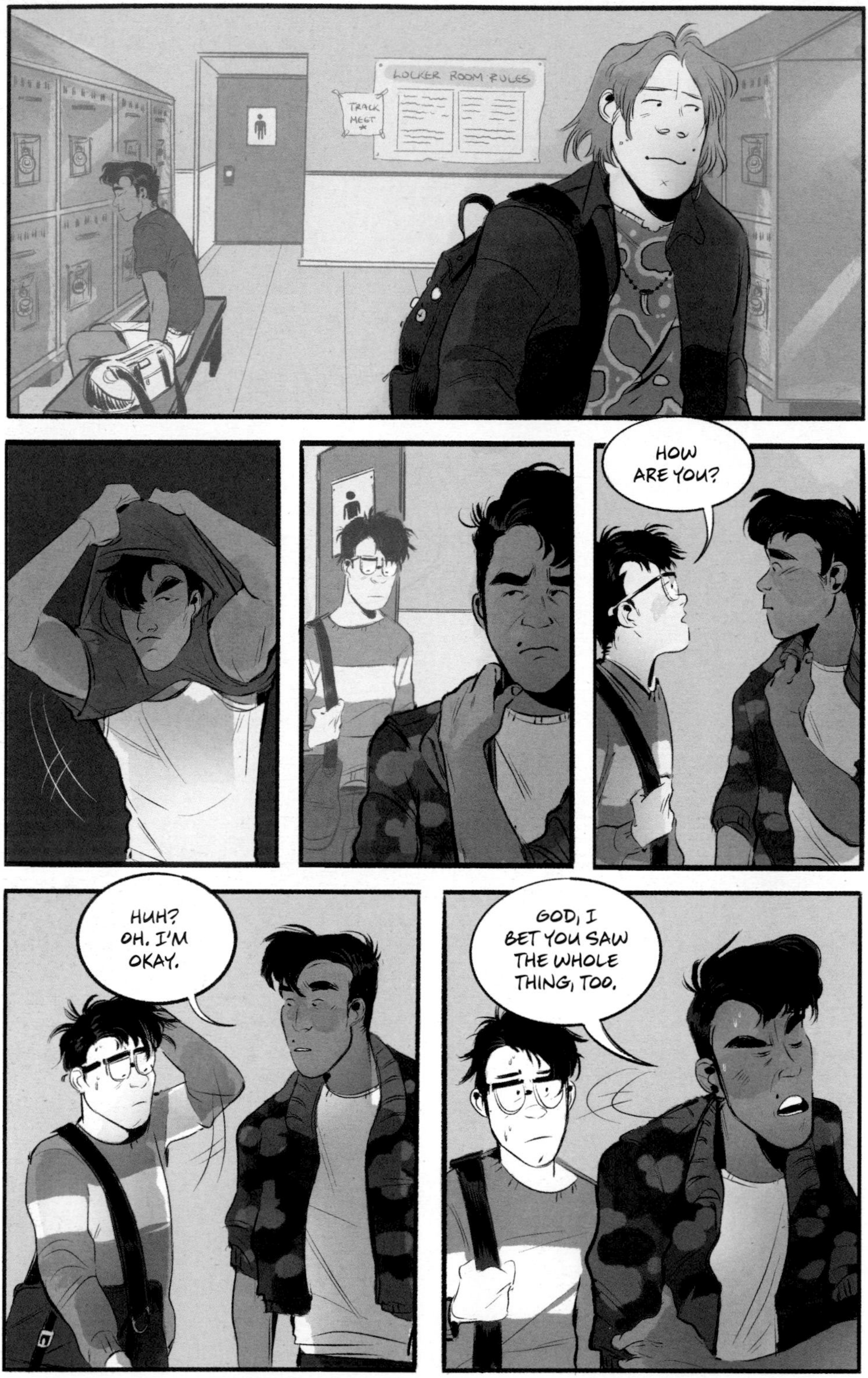
LOCKER ROOM RULES
TRACK MEET
HOW ARE YOU?
HUH? OH. I'M OKAY.
GOD, I BET YOU SAW THE WHOLE THING, TOO.

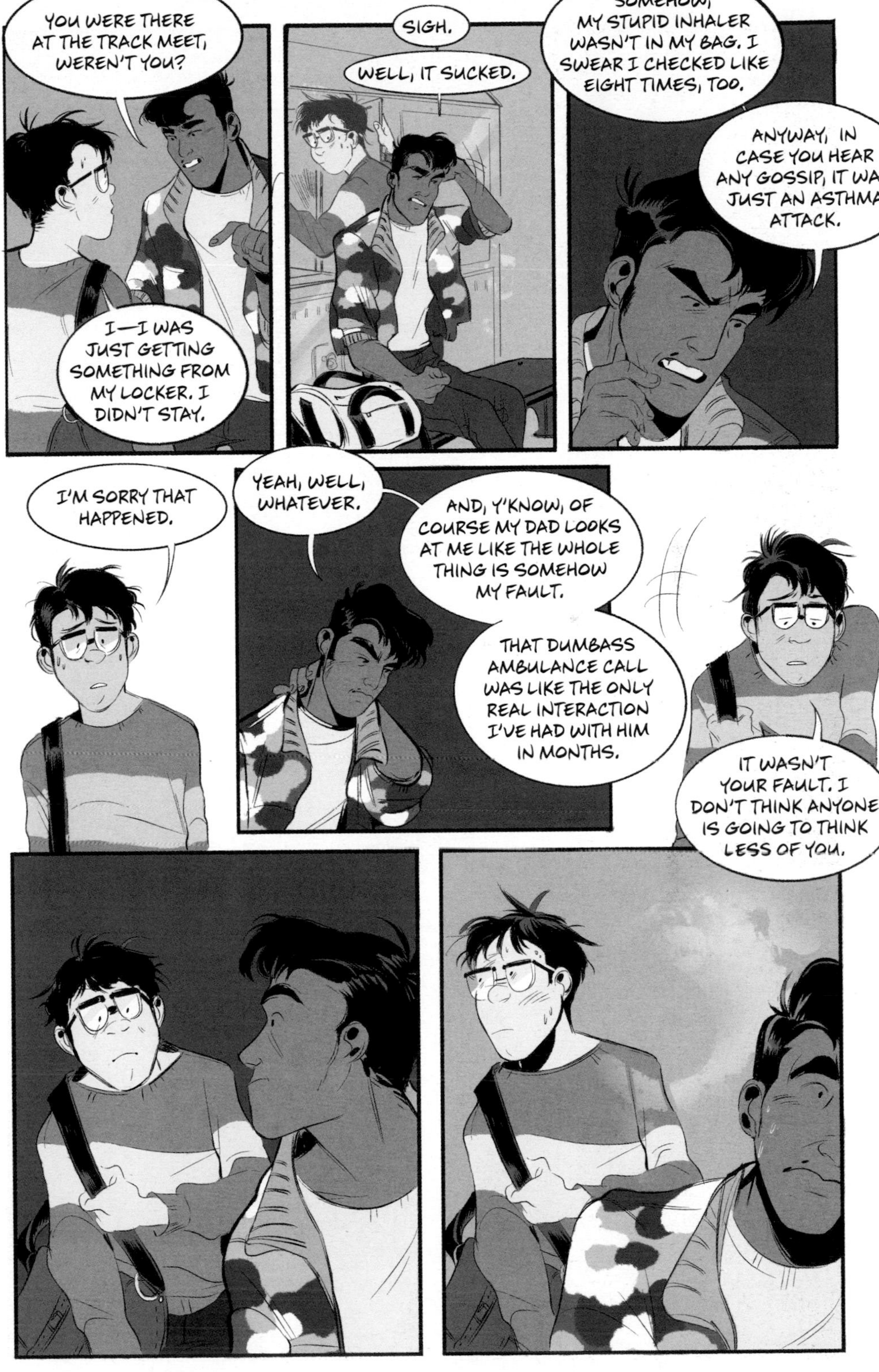
YOU WERE THERE AT THE TRACK MEET, WEREN'T YOU?
I—I WAS JUST GETTING SOMETHING FROM MY LOCKER. I DIDN'T STAY.
SIGH.
WELL, IT SUCKED.
SOMEHOW, MY STUPID INHALER WASN'T IN MY BAG. I SWEAR I CHECKED LIKE EIGHT TIMES, TOO.
ANYWAY, IN CASE YOU HEAR ANY GOSSIP, IT WAS JUST AN ASTHMA ATTACK.
I'M SORRY THAT HAPPENED.
YEAH, WELL, WHATEVER.
AND, Y'KNOW, OF COURSE MY DAD LOOKS AT ME LIKE THE WHOLE THING IS SOMEHOW MY FAULT.
THAT DUMBASS AMBULANCE CALL WAS LIKE THE ONLY REAL INTERACTION I'VE HAD WITH HIM IN MONTHS.
IT WASN'T YOUR FAULT. I DON'T THINK ANYONE IS GOING TO THINK LESS OF YOU.

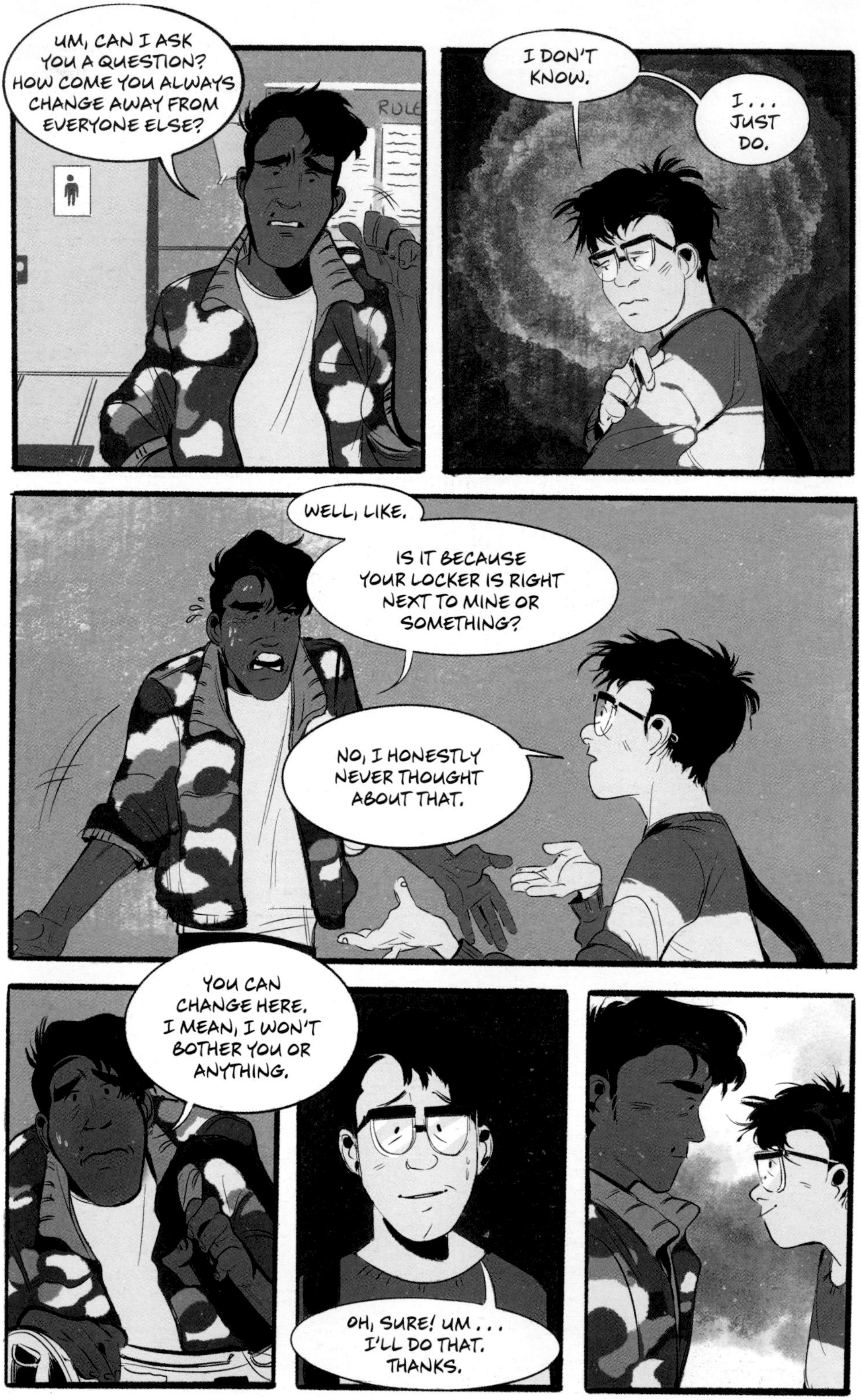
UM, CAN I ASK YOU A QUESTION? HOW COME YOU ALWAYS CHANGE AWAY FROM EVERYONE ELSE?
I DON'T KNOW.
I . . . JUST DO.
WELL, LIKE.
IS IT BECAUSE YOUR LOCKER IS RIGHT NEXT TO MINE OR SOMETHING?
NO, I HONESTLY NEVER THOUGHT ABOUT THAT.
YOU CAN CHANGE HERE. I MEAN, I WON'T BOTHER YOU OR ANYTHING.
OH, SURE! UM . . . I'LL DO THAT. THANKS.

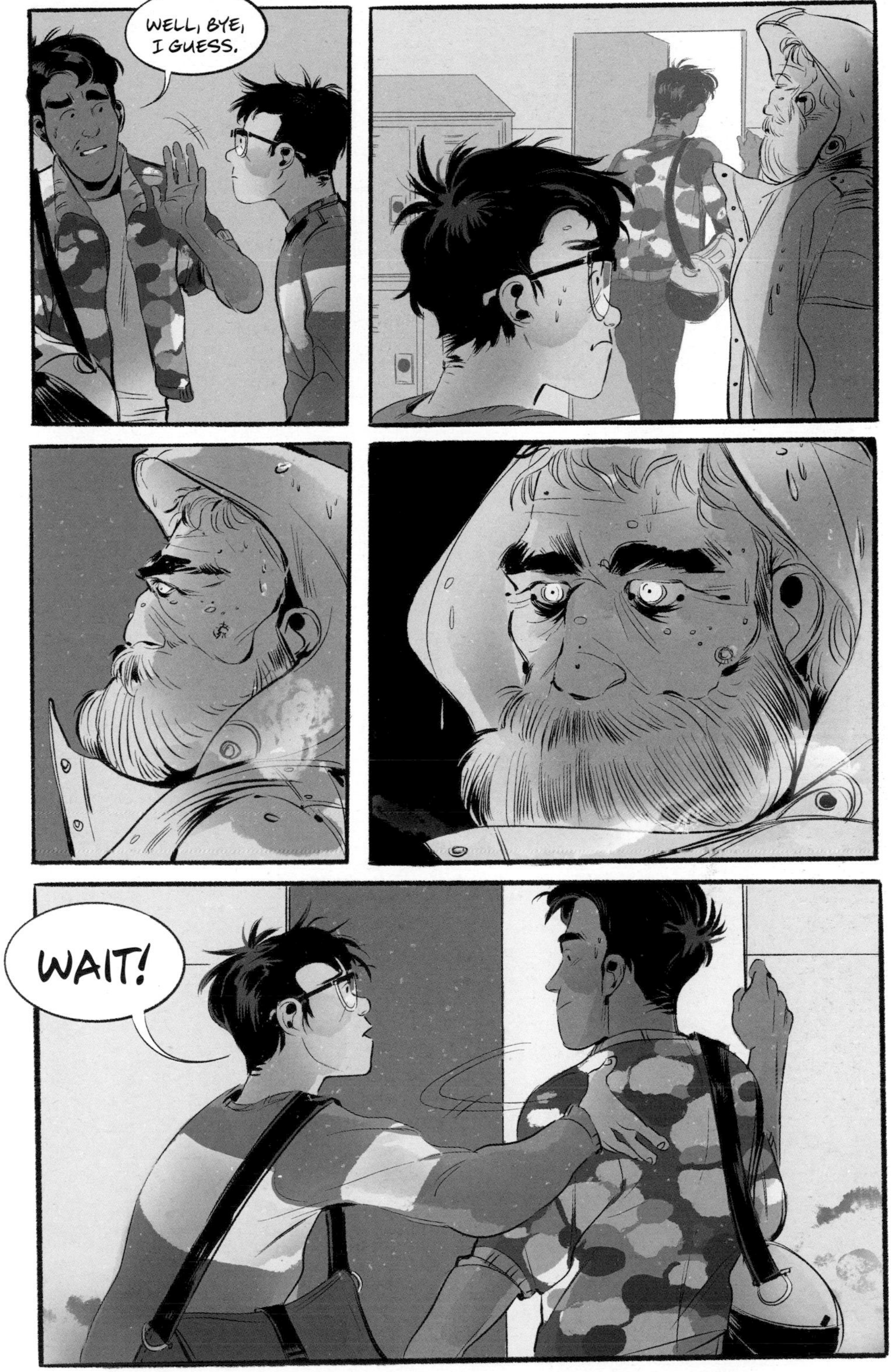
WELL, BYE, I GUESS.
WAIT!

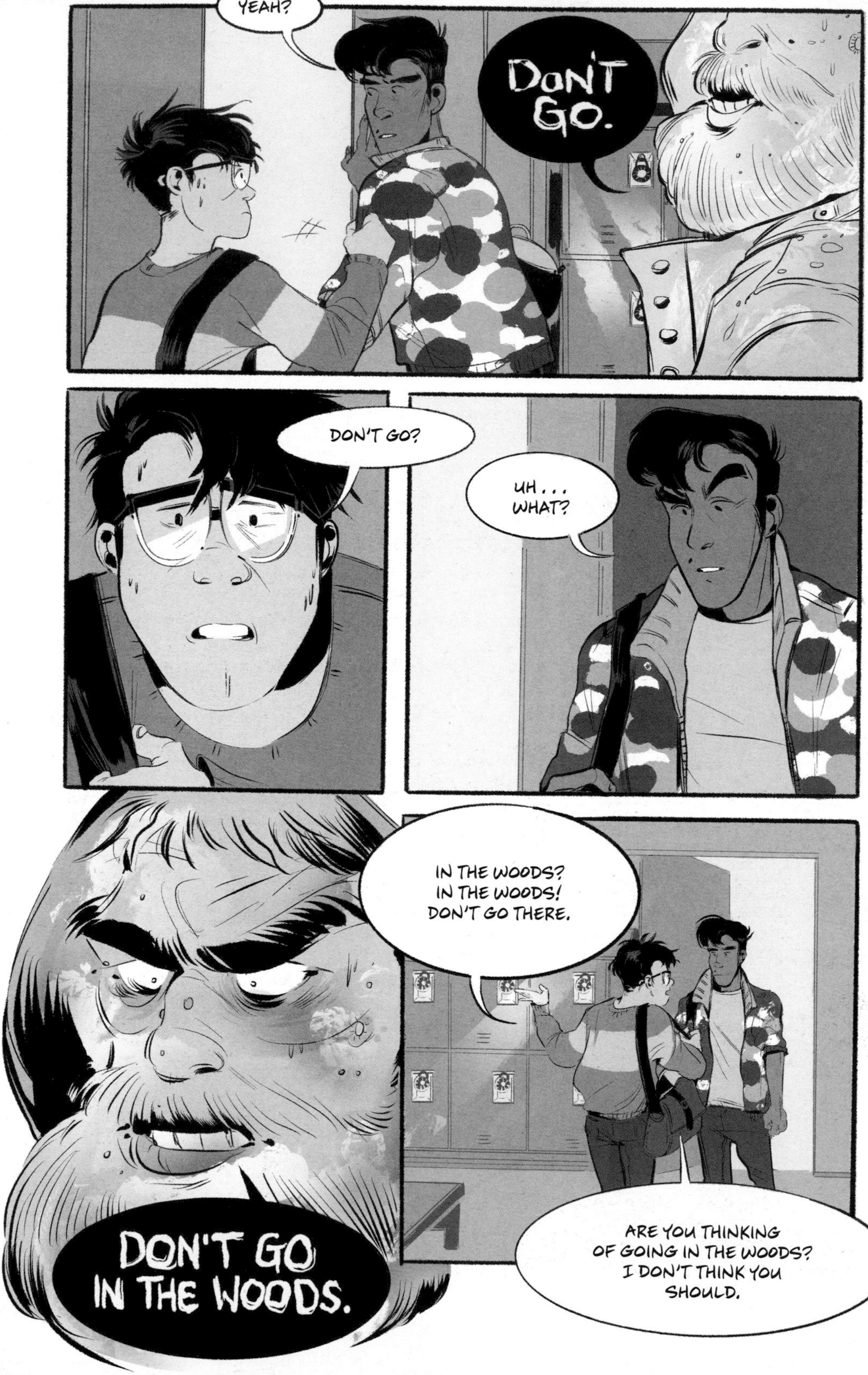
YEAH?
DON'T GO.
DON'T GO?
UH . . . WHAT?
IN THE WOODS? IN THE WOODS! DON'T GO THERE.
DON'T GO IN THE WOODS.
ARE YOU THINKING OF GOING IN THE WOODS? I DON'T THINK YOU SHOULD.

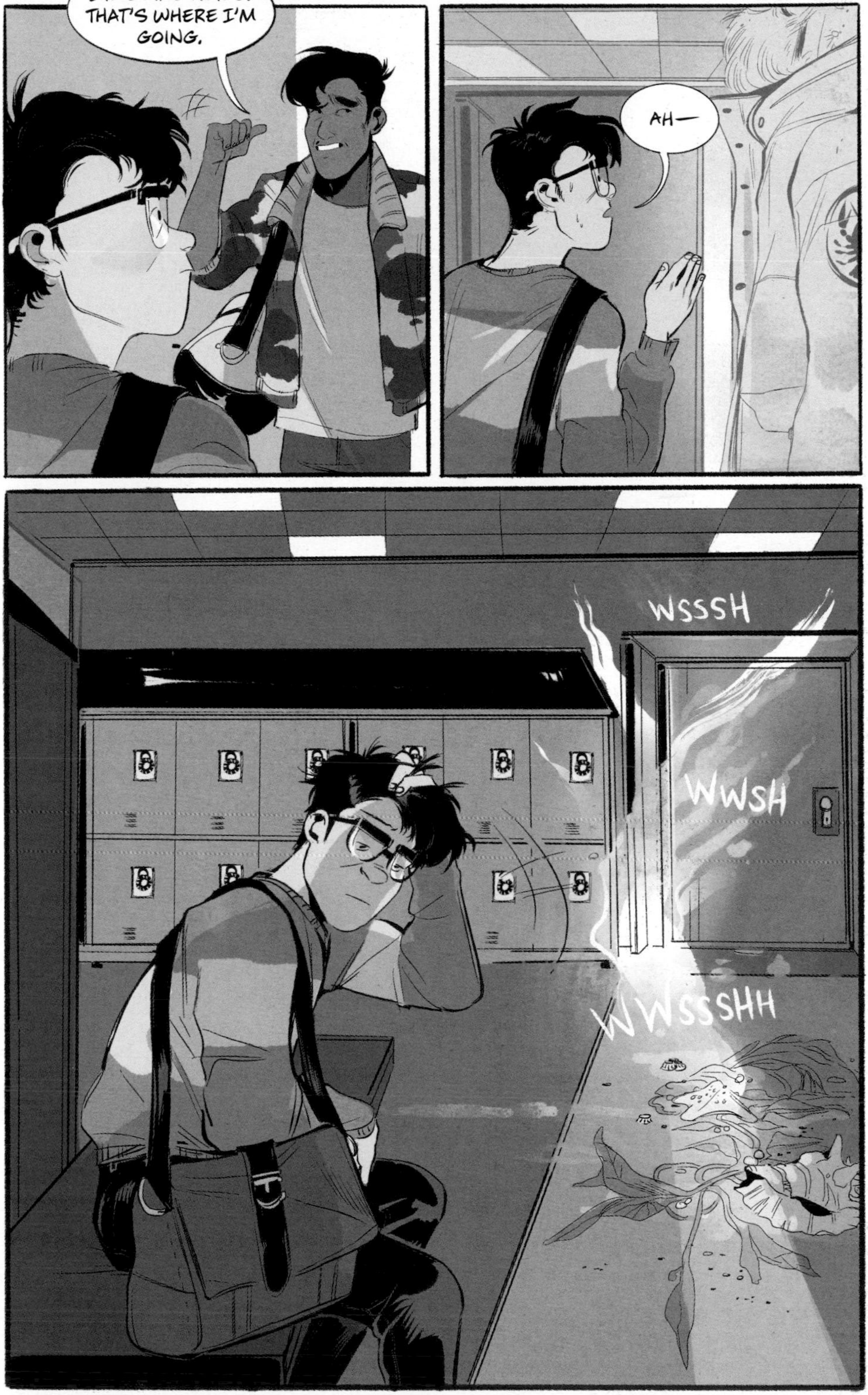
I'M GOING HOME. THAT'S WHERE I'M GOING.
AH—
WSSSH
WWSH
WWSSSHH

CHAPTER THREE

THE HUNTING TRIP

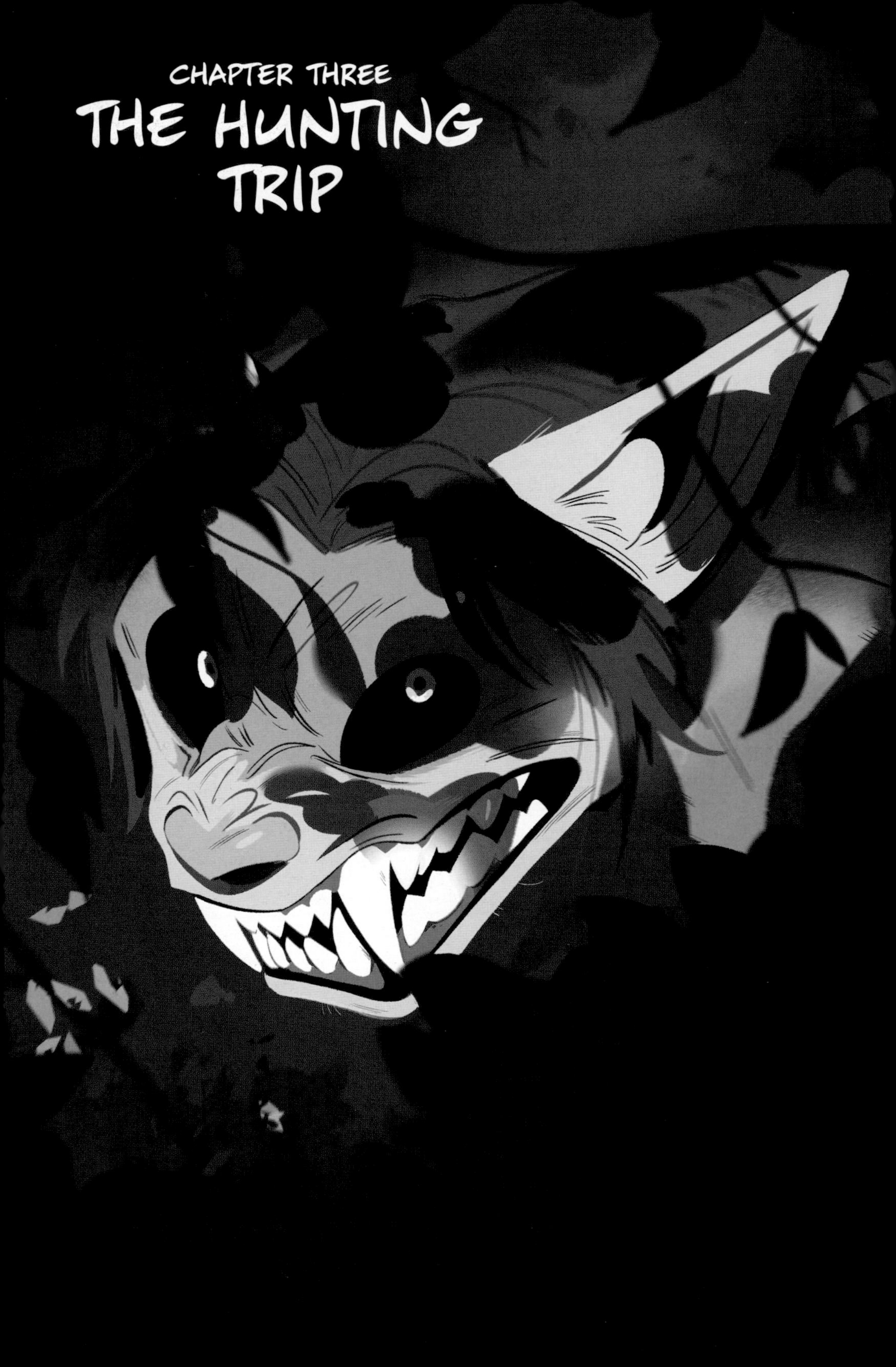

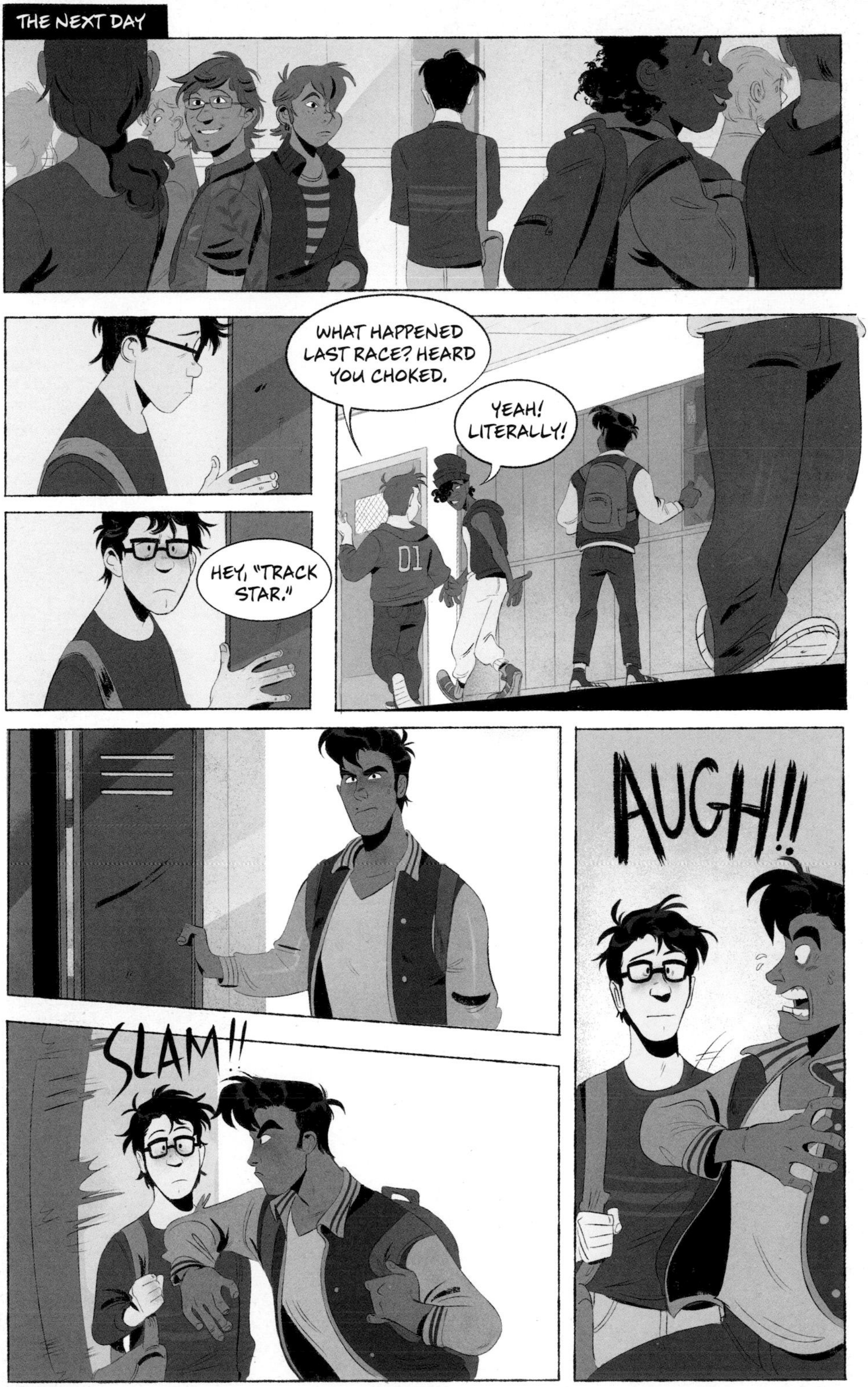
THE NEXT DAY
WHAT HAPPENED LAST RACE? HEARD YOU CHOKED.
YEAH! LITERALLY!
HEY, "TRACK STAR."
01
AUGH!!
SLAM!!

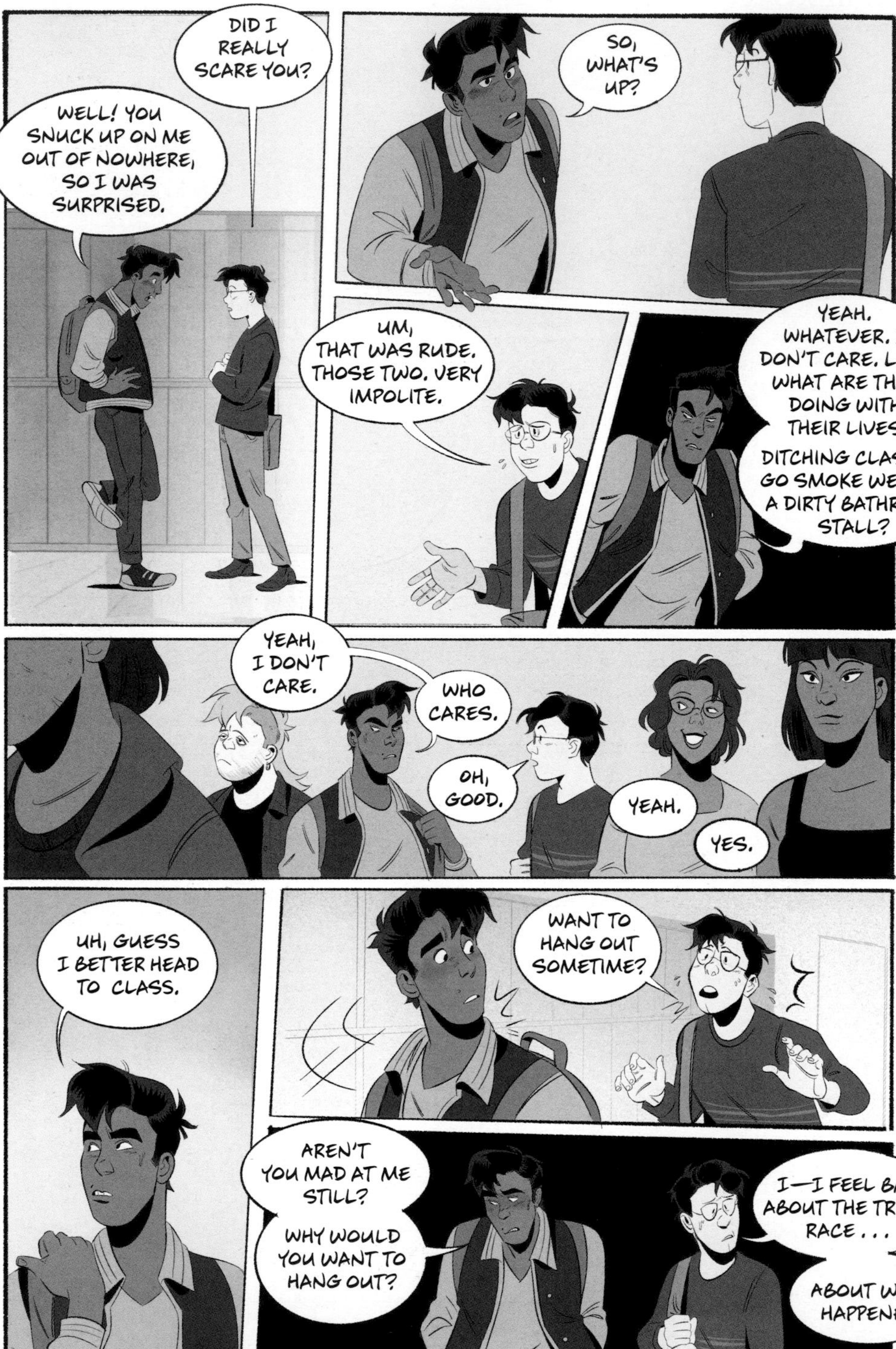
DID I REALLY SCARE YOU?
WELL! YOU SNUCK UP ON ME OUT OF NOWHERE, SO I WAS SURPRISED.
SO, WHAT'S UP?
UM, THAT WAS RUDE. THOSE TWO. VERY IMPOLITE.
YEAH. WHATEVER. I DON'T CARE. LIKE, WHAT ARE THEY DOING WITH THEIR LIVES?
DITCHING CLASS TO GO SMOKE WEED IN A DIRTY BATHROOM STALL?
YEAH, I DON'T CARE.
WHO CARES.
OH, GOOD.
YEAH.
YES.
UH, GUESS I BETTER HEAD TO CLASS.
WANT TO HANG OUT SOMETIME?
AREN'T YOU MAD AT ME STILL?
WHY WOULD YOU WANT TO HANG OUT?
I—I FEEL BAD ABOUT THE TRACK RACE . . .
ABOUT WHAT HAPPENED.

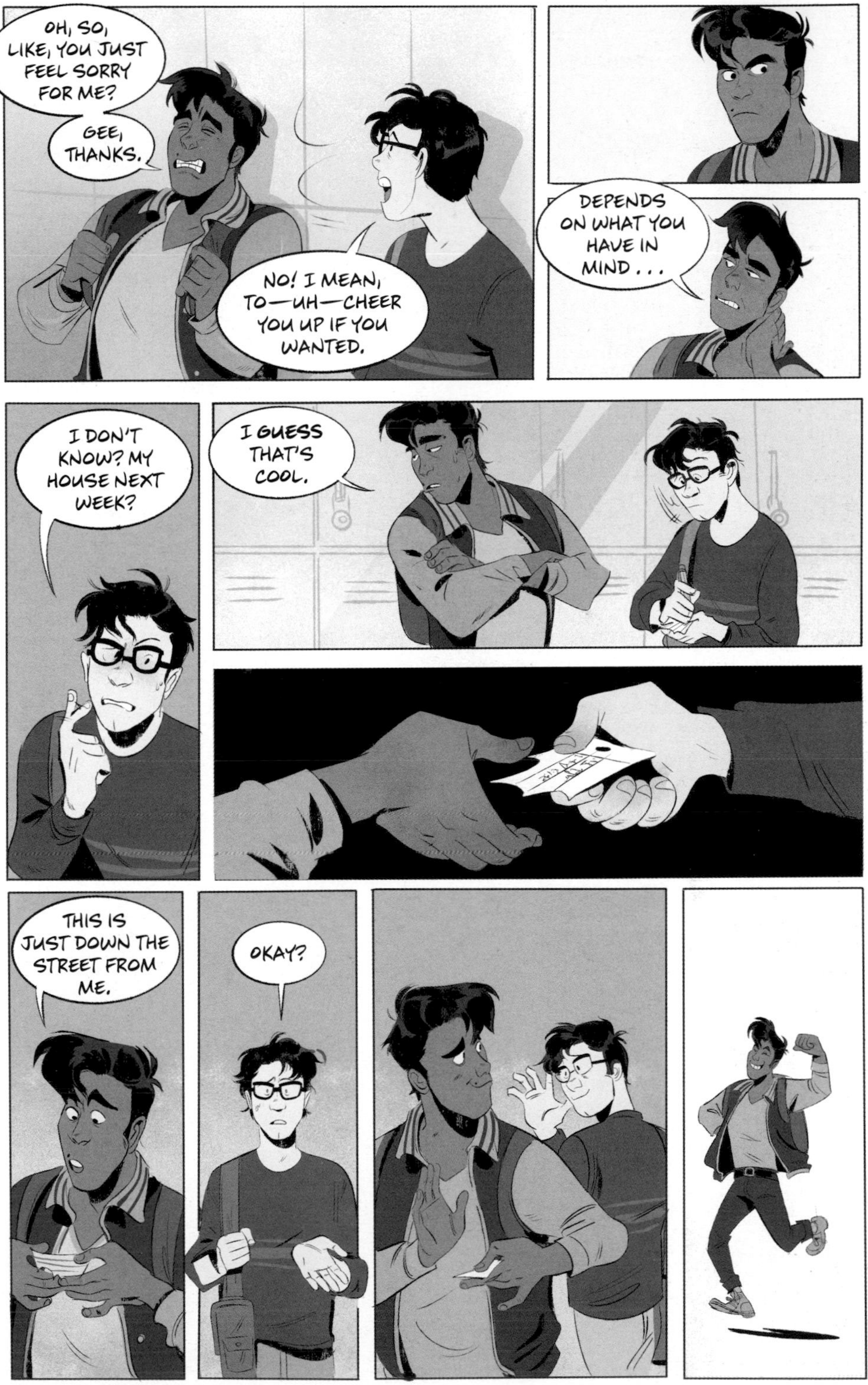
OH, SO, LIKE, YOU JUST FEEL SORRY FOR ME?
GEE, THANKS.
NO! I MEAN, TO—UH—CHEER YOU UP IF YOU WANTED.
DEPENDS ON WHAT YOU HAVE IN MIND . . .
I DON'T KNOW? MY HOUSE NEXT WEEK?
I GUESS THAT'S COOL.
THIS IS JUST DOWN THE STREET FROM ME.
OKAY?

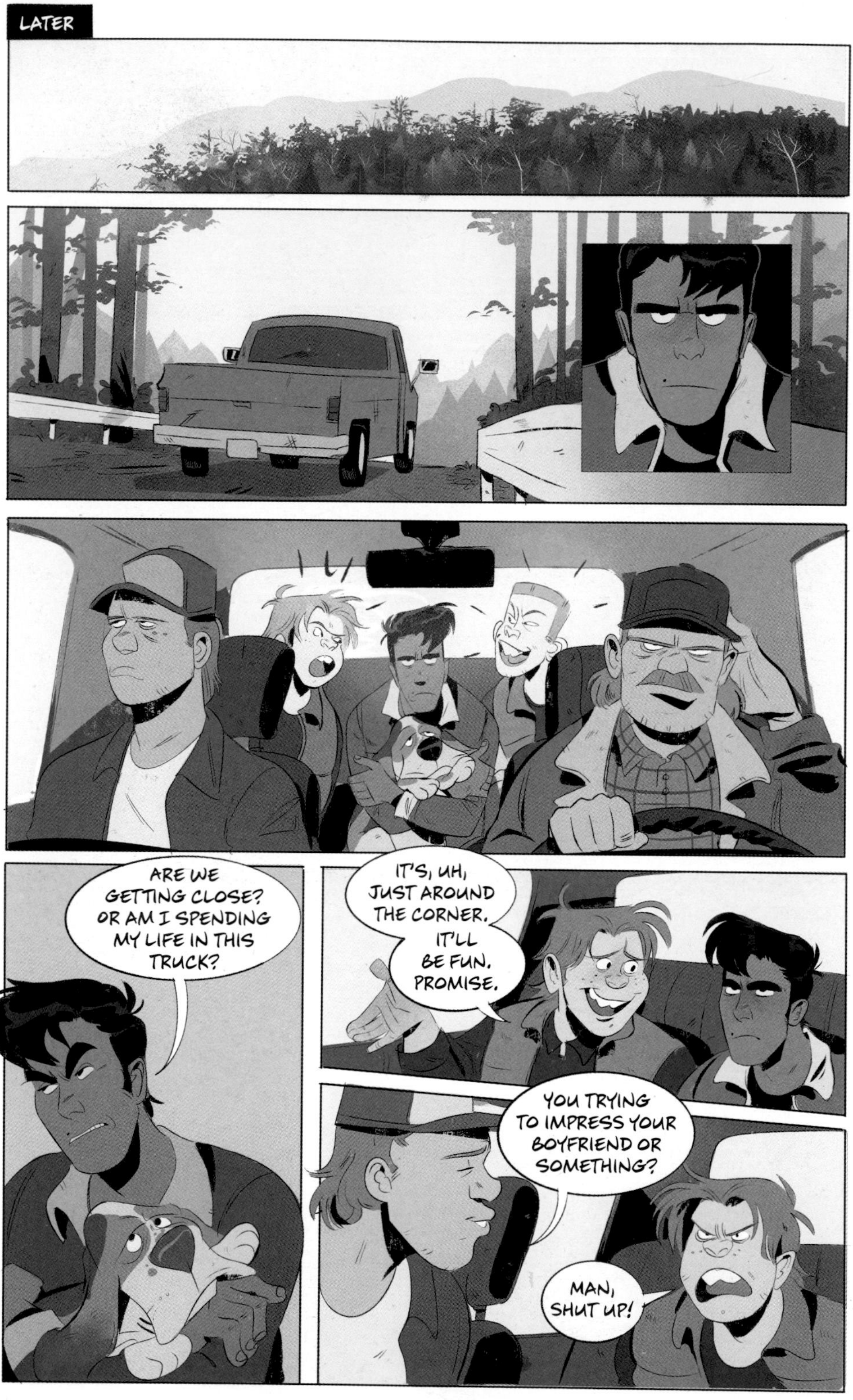
LATER
ARE WE GETTING CLOSE? OR AM I SPENDING MY LIFE IN THIS TRUCK?
IT'S, UH, JUST AROUND THE CORNER.
IT'LL BE FUN. PROMISE.
YOU TRYING TO IMPRESS YOUR BOYFRIEND OR SOMETHING?
MAN, SHUT UP!

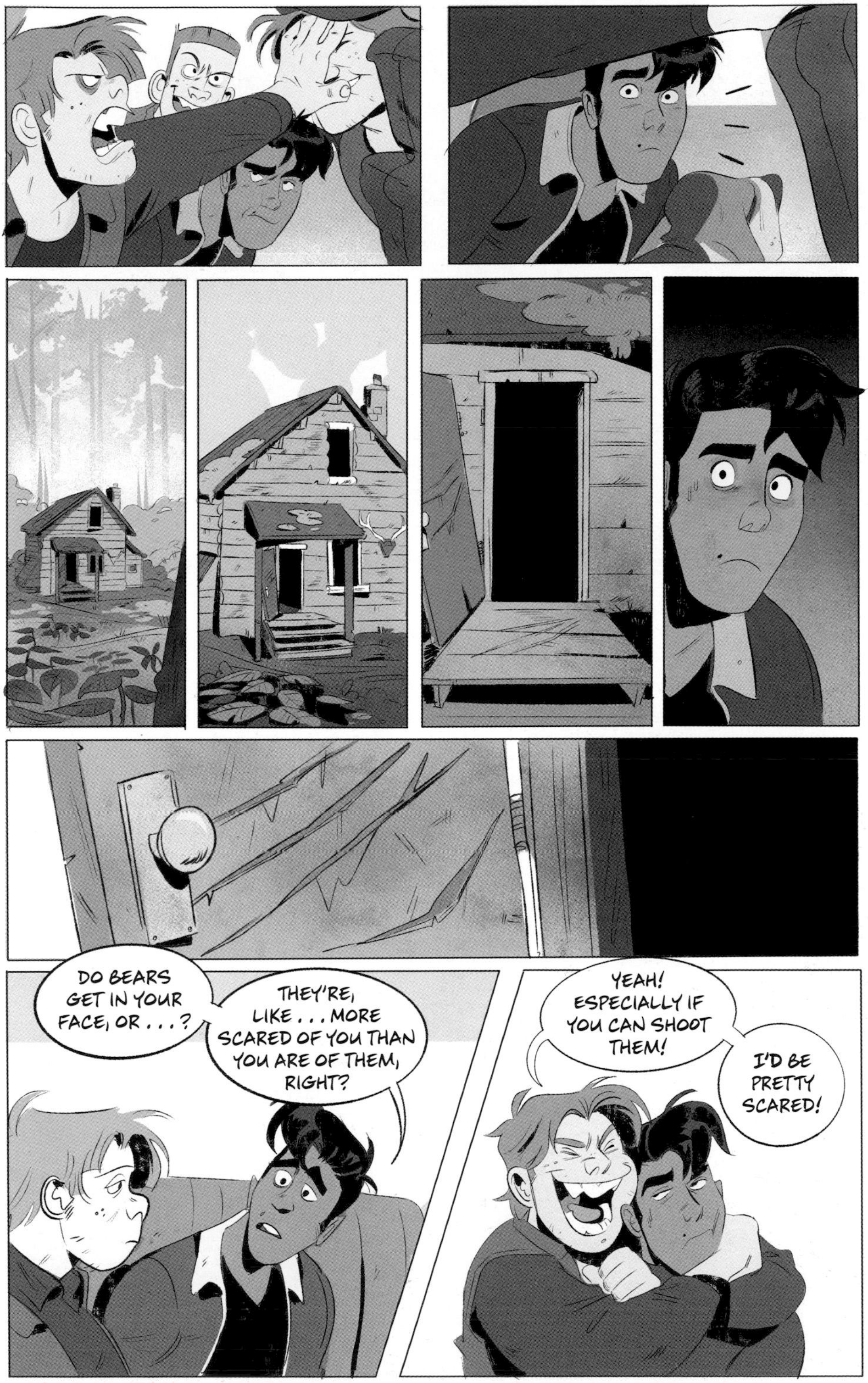
DO BEARS GET IN YOUR FACE, OR . . . ?
THEY'RE, LIKE . . . MORE SCARED OF YOU THAN YOU ARE OF THEM, RIGHT?
YEAH! ESPECIALLY IF YOU CAN SHOOT THEM!
I'D BE PRETTY SCARED!

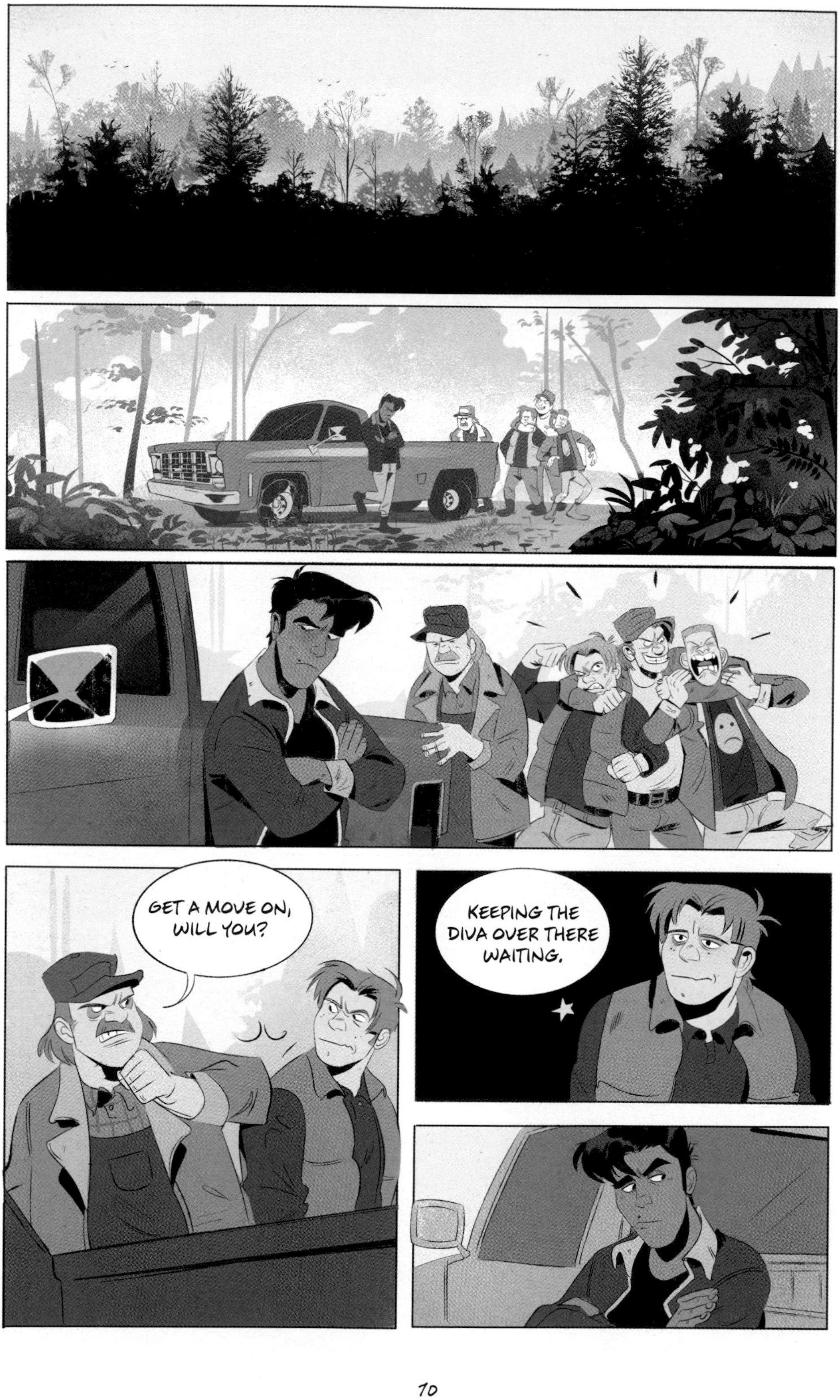
GET A MOVE ON, WILL YOU?
KEEPING THE DIVA OVER THERE WAITING.

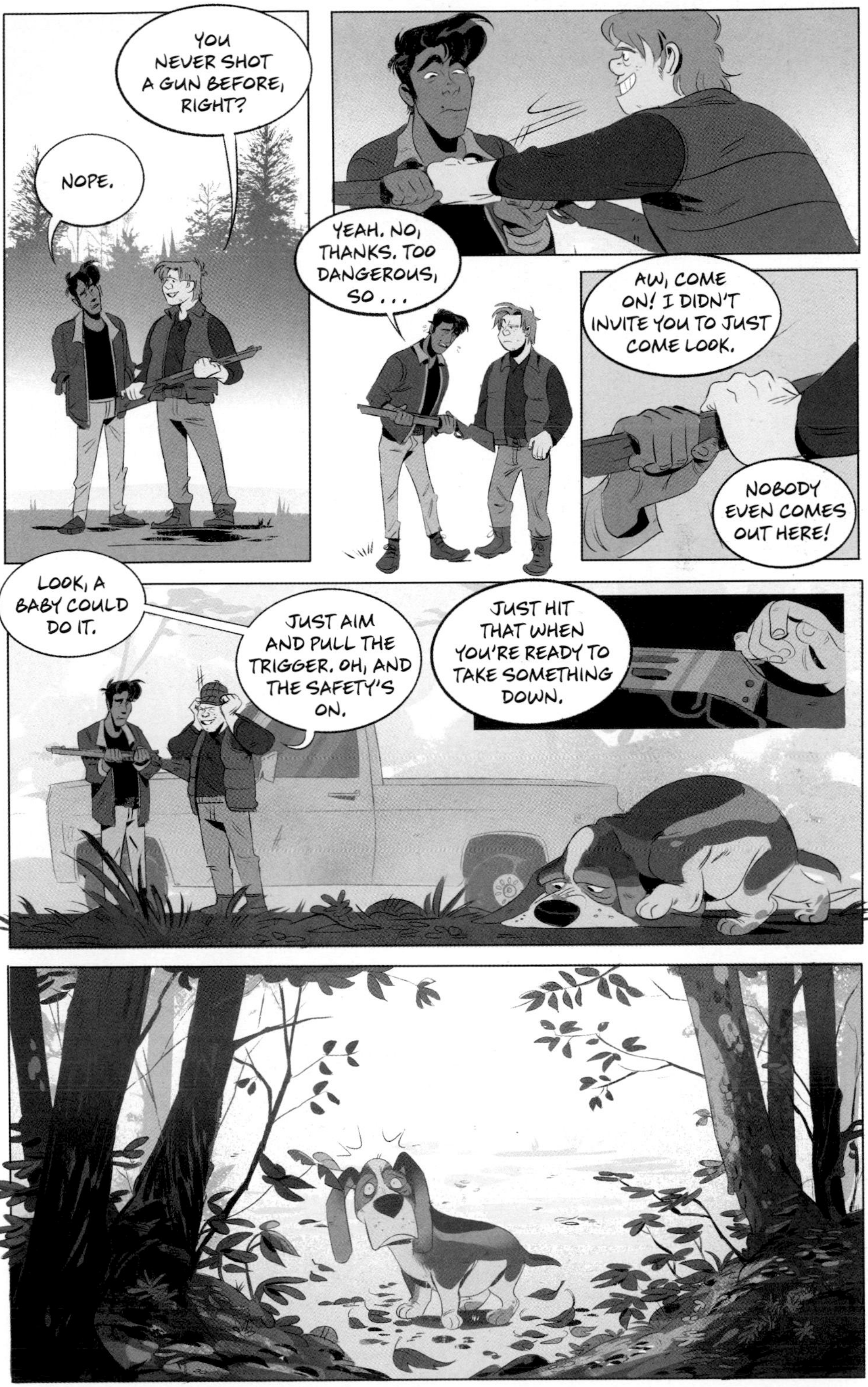
YOU NEVER SHOT A GUN BEFORE, RIGHT?
NOPE.
YEAH. NO, THANKS. TOO DANGEROUS, SO . . .
AW, COME ON! I DIDN'T INVITE YOU TO JUST COME LOOK.
NOBODY EVEN COMES OUT HERE!
LOOK, A BABY COULD DO IT.
JUST AIM AND PULL THE TRIGGER. OH, AND THE SAFETY'S ON.
JUST HIT THAT WHEN YOU'RE READY TO TAKE SOMETHING DOWN.

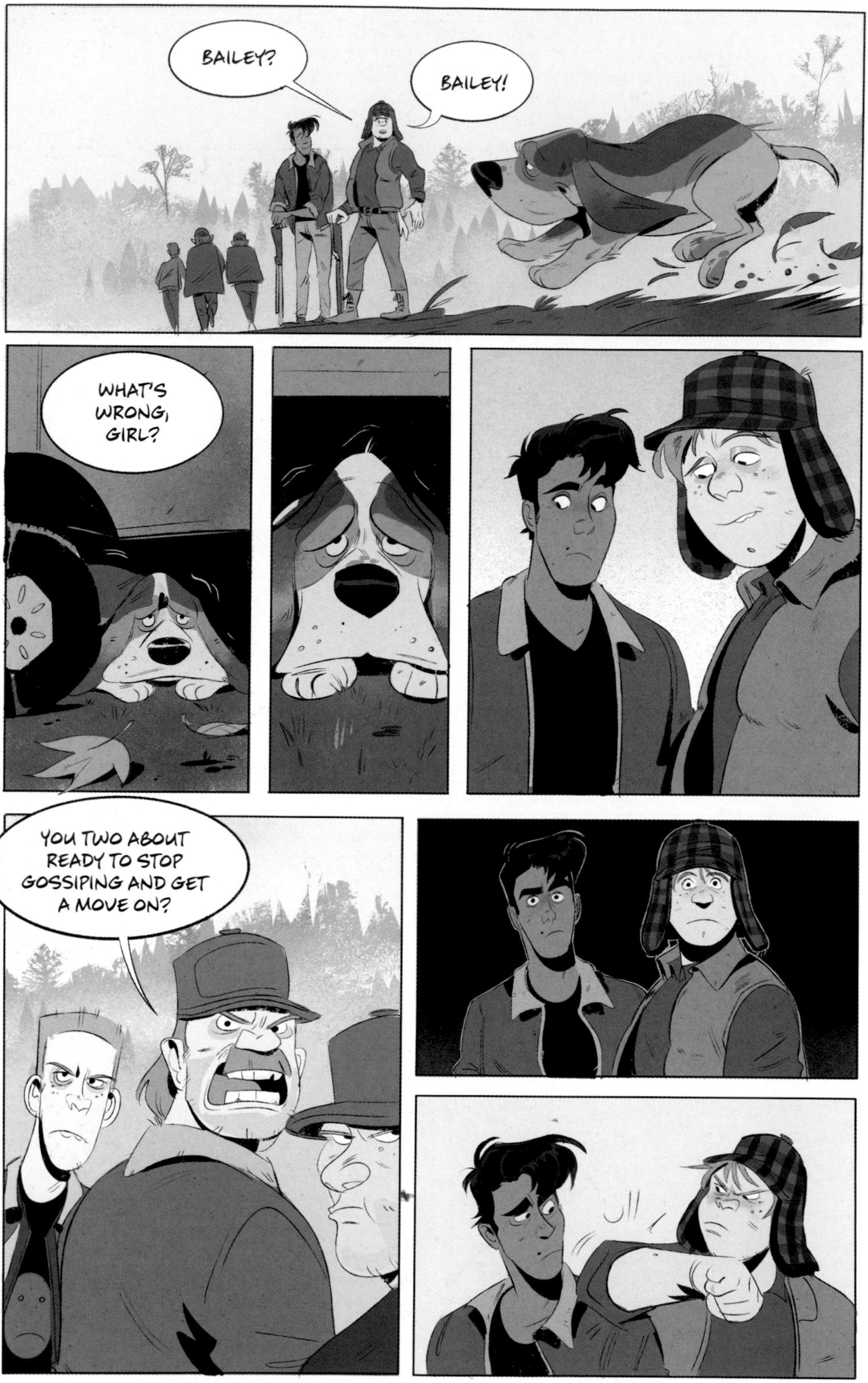
BAILEY?
BAILEY!
WHAT'S WRONG, GIRL?
YOU TWO ABOUT READY TO STOP GOSSIPING AND GET A MOVE ON?

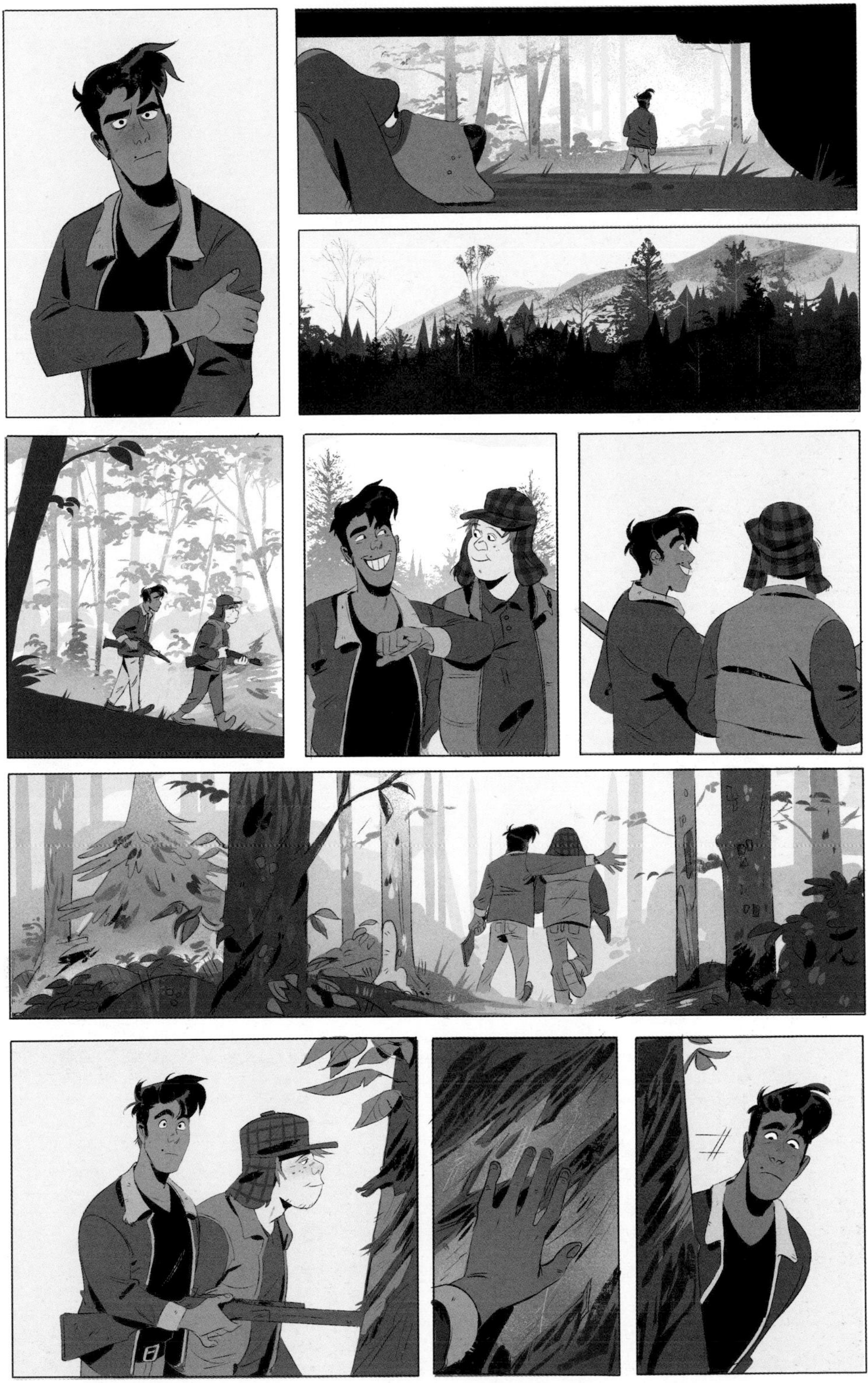

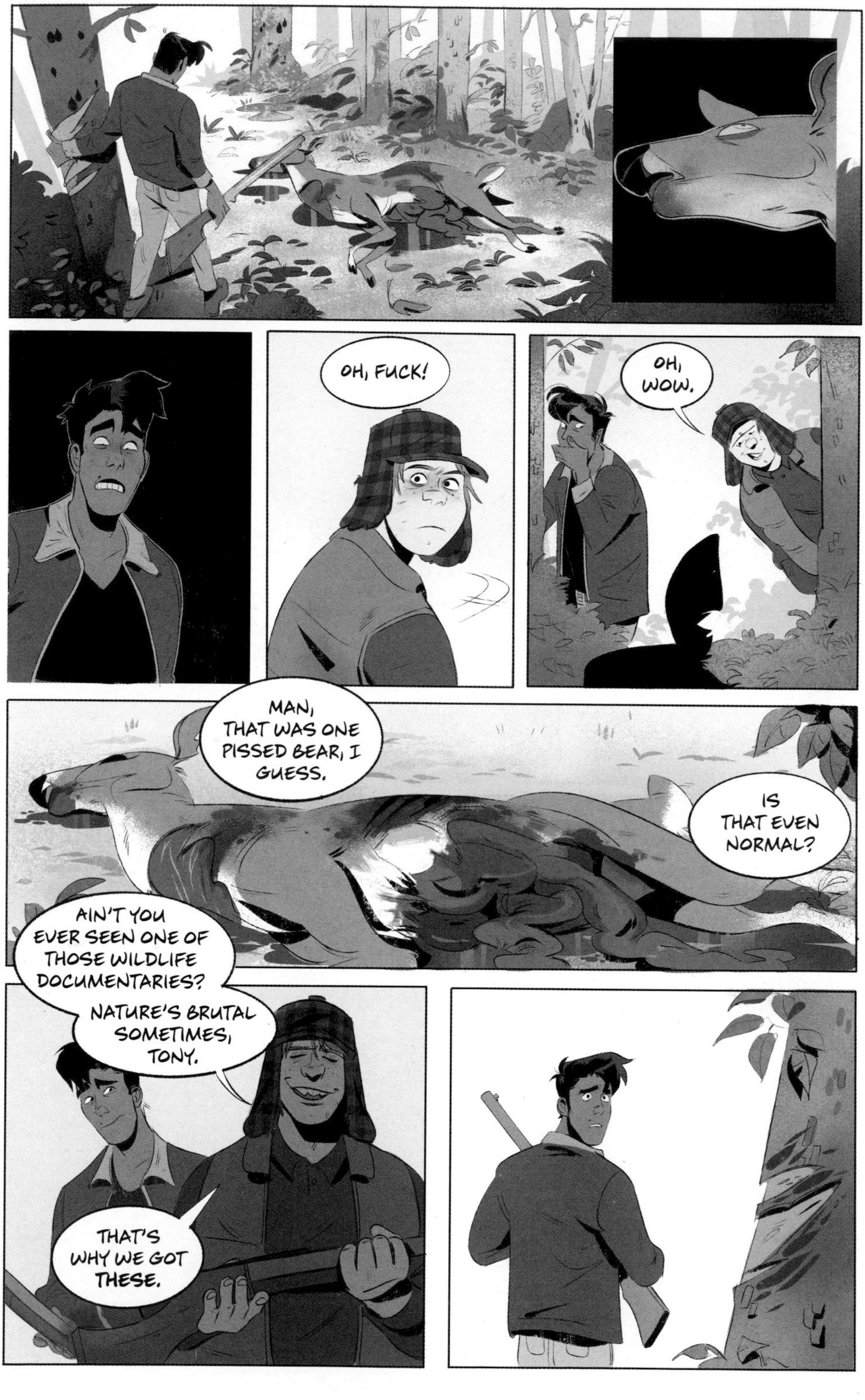
OH, FUCK!
OH, WOW.
MAN, THAT WAS ONE PISSED BEAR, I GUESS.
IS THAT EVEN NORMAL?
AIN'T YOU EVER SEEN ONE OF THOSE WILDLIFE DOCUMENTARIES?
NATURE'S BRUTAL SOMETIMES, TONY.
THAT'S WHY WE GOT THESE.

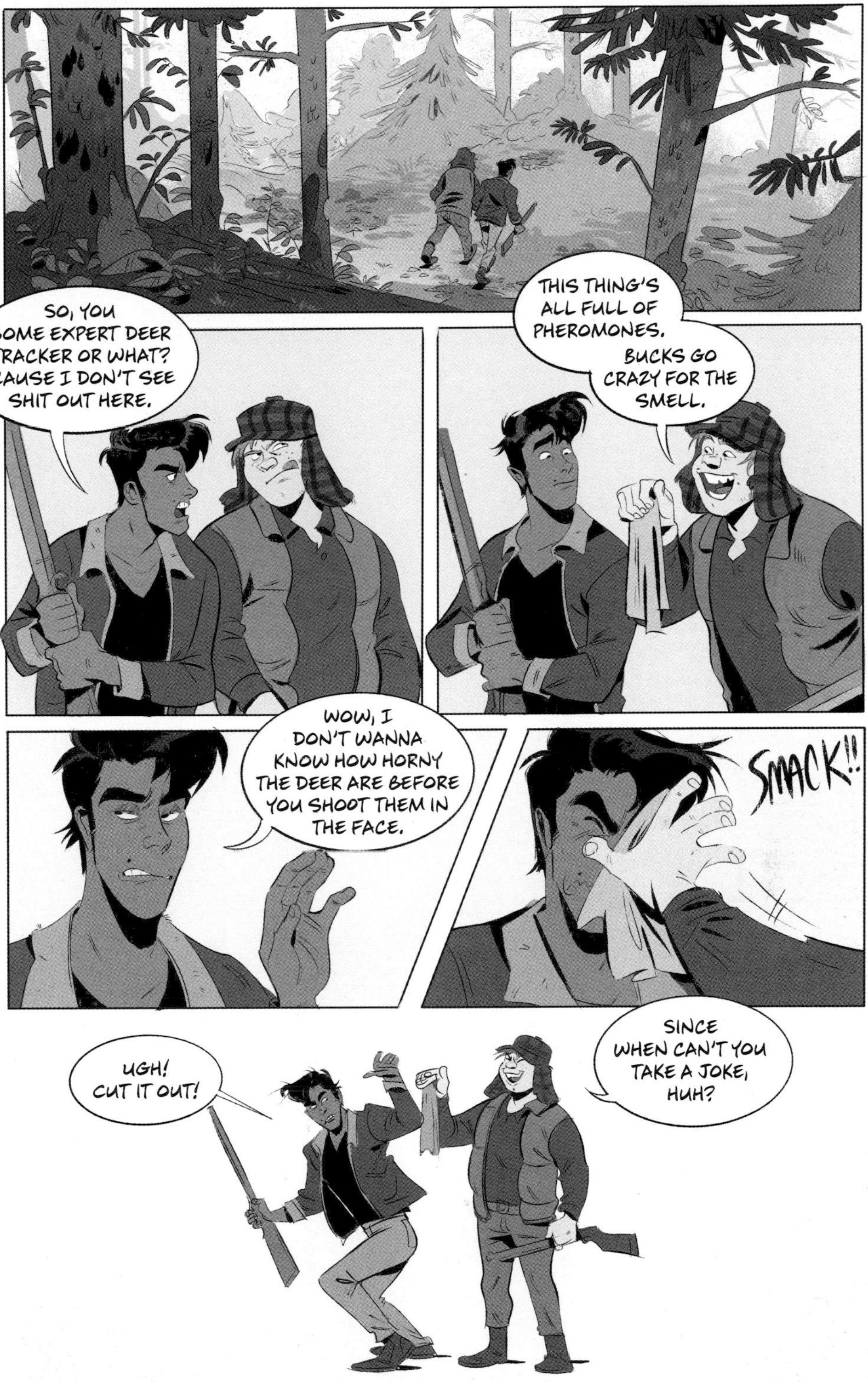
SO, YOU SOME EXPERT DEER TRACKER OR WHAT? 'CAUSE I DON'T SEE SHIT OUT HERE.
THIS THING'S ALL FULL OF PHEROMONES.
BUCKS GO CRAZY FOR THE SMELL.
WOW, I DON'T WANNA KNOW HOW HORNY THE DEER ARE BEFORE YOU SHOOT THEM IN THE FACE.
SMACK!!
UGH! CUT IT OUT!
SINCE WHEN CAN'T YOU TAKE A JOKE, HUH?

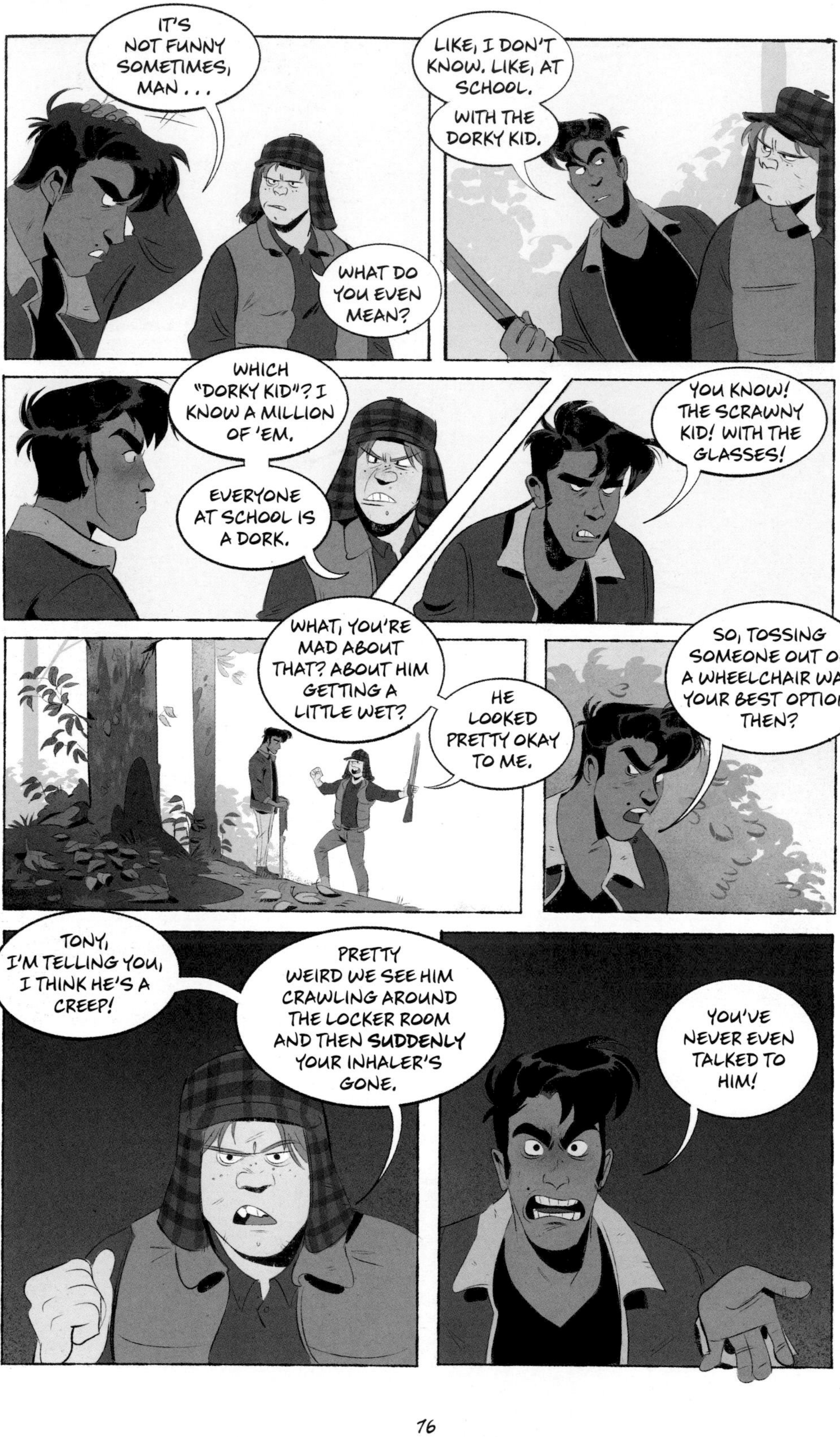
IT'S NOT FUNNY SOMETIMES, MAN . . .
WHAT DO YOU EVEN MEAN?
LIKE, I DON'T KNOW. LIKE, AT SCHOOL.
WITH THE DORKY KID.
WHICH "DORKY KID"? I KNOW A MILLION OF 'EM.
EVERYONE AT SCHOOL IS A DORK.
YOU KNOW! THE SCRAWNY KID! WITH THE GLASSES!
WHAT, YOU'RE MAD ABOUT THAT? ABOUT HIM GETTING A LITTLE WET?
HE LOOKED PRETTY OKAY TO ME.
SO, TOSSING SOMEONE OUT OF A WHEELCHAIR WAS YOUR BEST OPTION, THEN?
TONY, I'M TELLING YOU, I THINK HE'S A CREEP!
PRETTY WEIRD WE SEE HIM CRAWLING AROUND THE LOCKER ROOM AND THEN SUDDENLY YOUR INHALER'S GONE.
YOU'VE NEVER EVEN TALKED TO HIM!

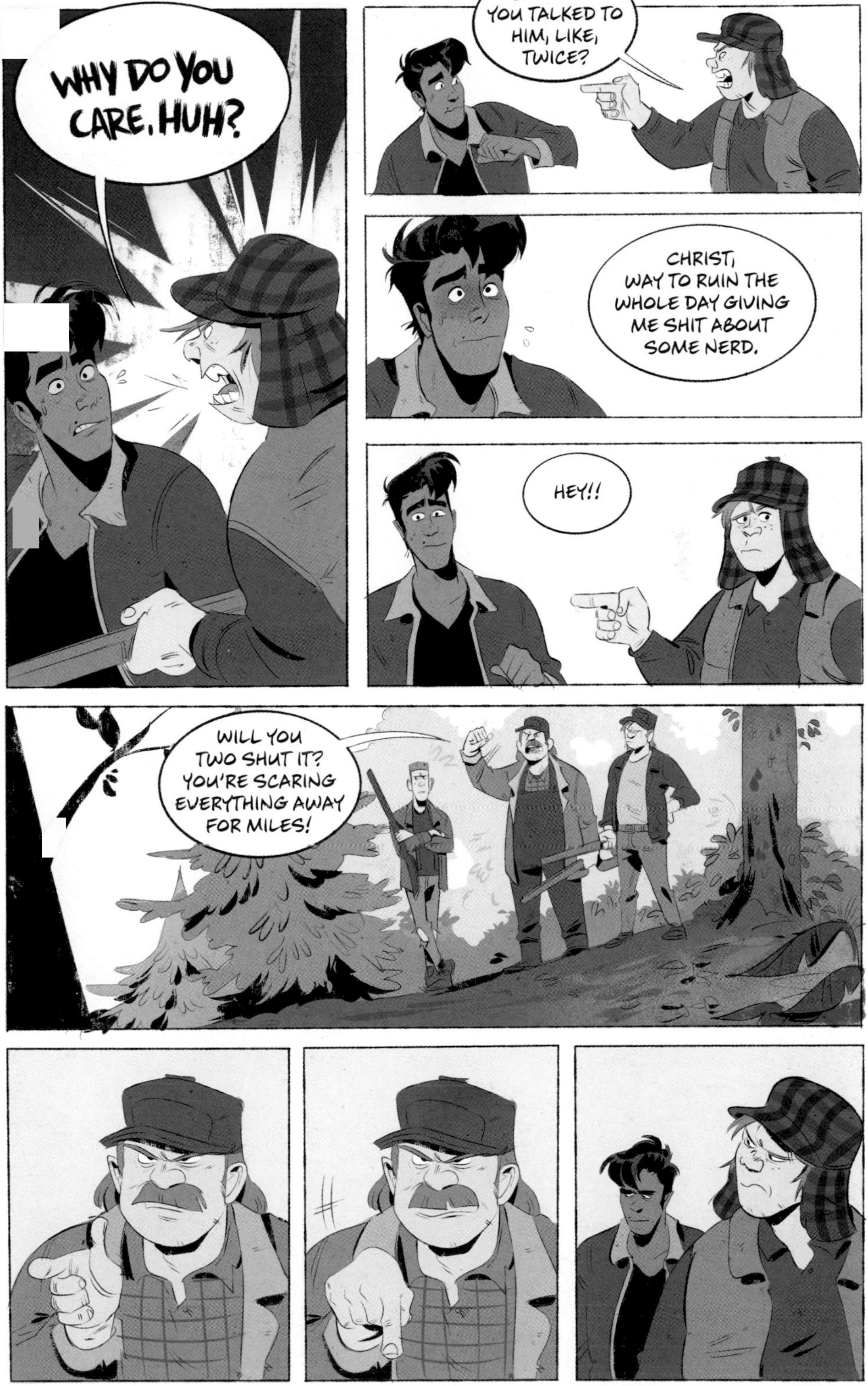
WHY DO YOU CARE, HUH?
BECAUSE YOU TALKED TO HIM, LIKE, TWICE?
CHRIST, WAY TO RUIN THE WHOLE DAY GIVING ME SHIT ABOUT SOME NERD.
HEY!!
WILL YOU TWO SHUT IT? YOU'RE SCARING EVERYTHING AWAY FOR MILES!

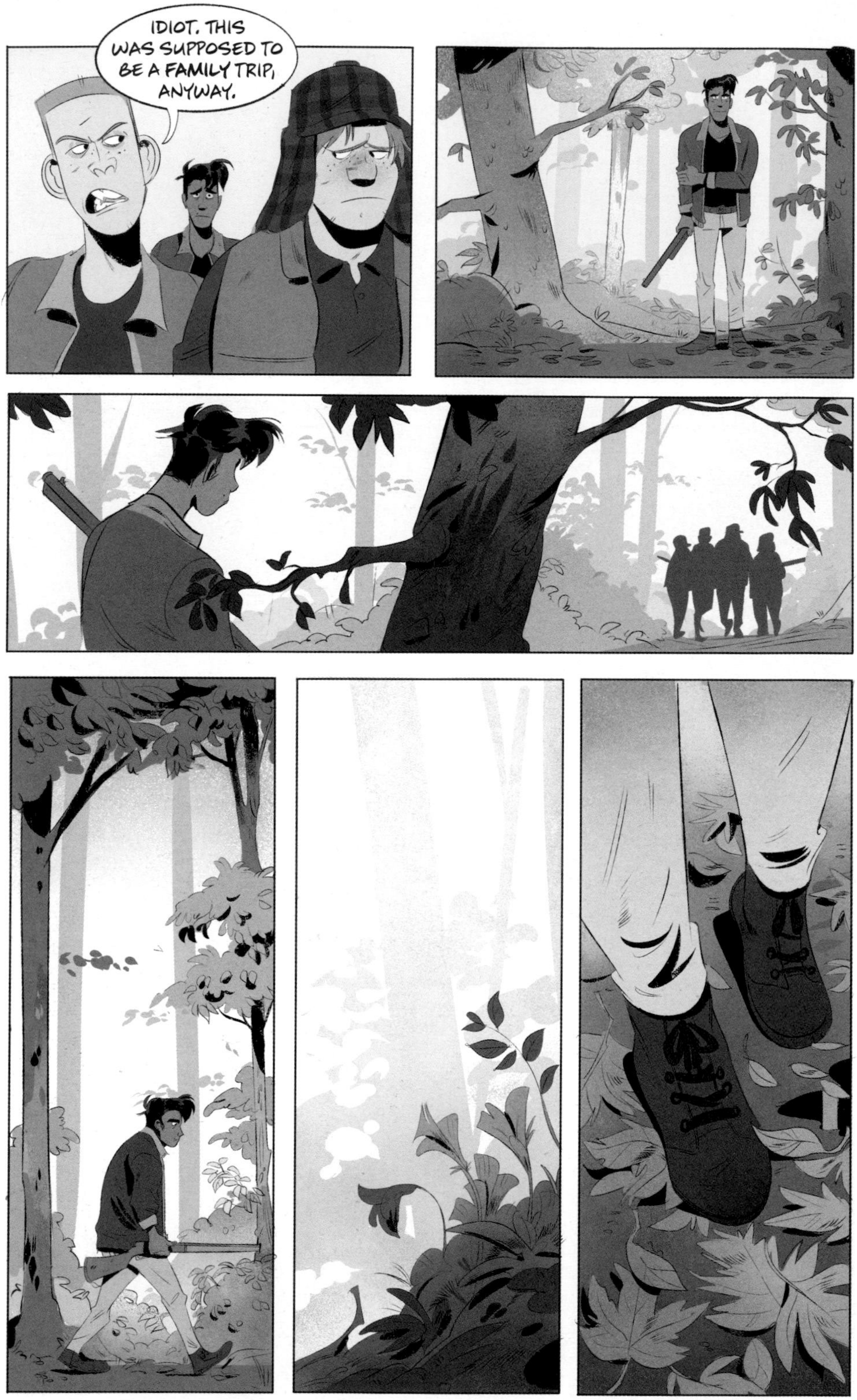
IDIOT. THIS WAS SUPPOSED TO BE A FAMILY TRIP, ANYWAY.

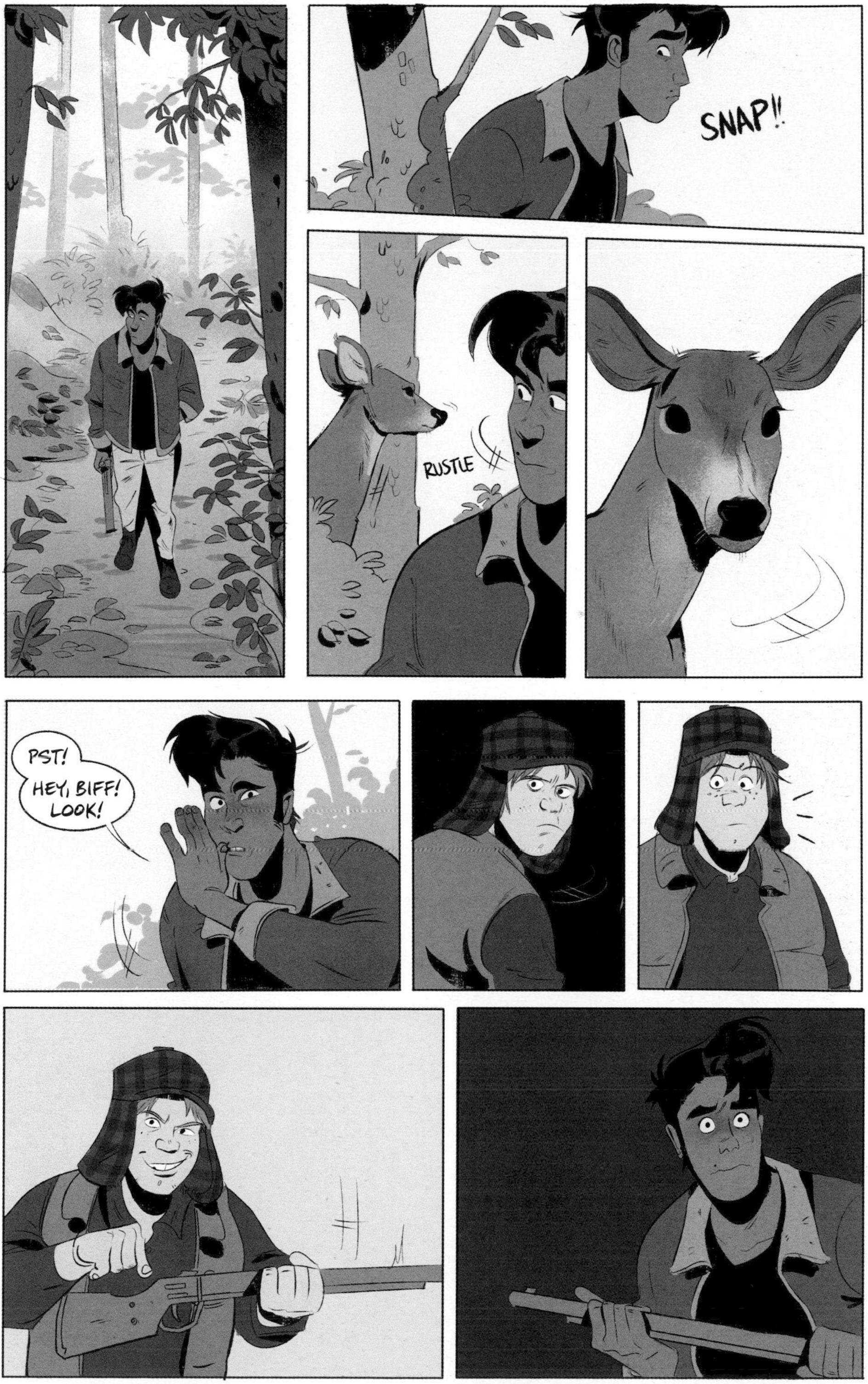
SNAP!!
RUSTLE
PST!
HEY, BIFF! LOOK!

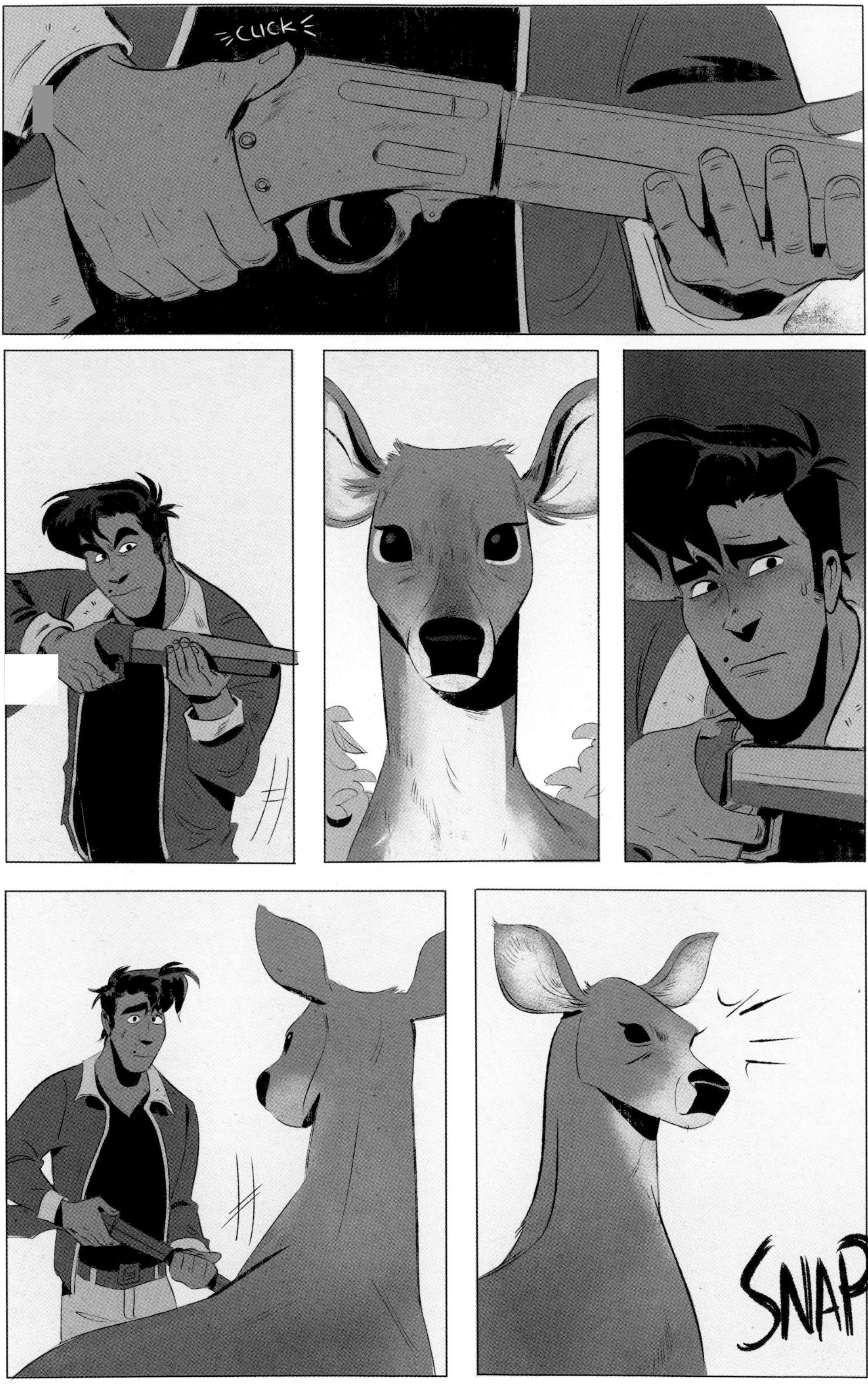
CLICK
SNAP

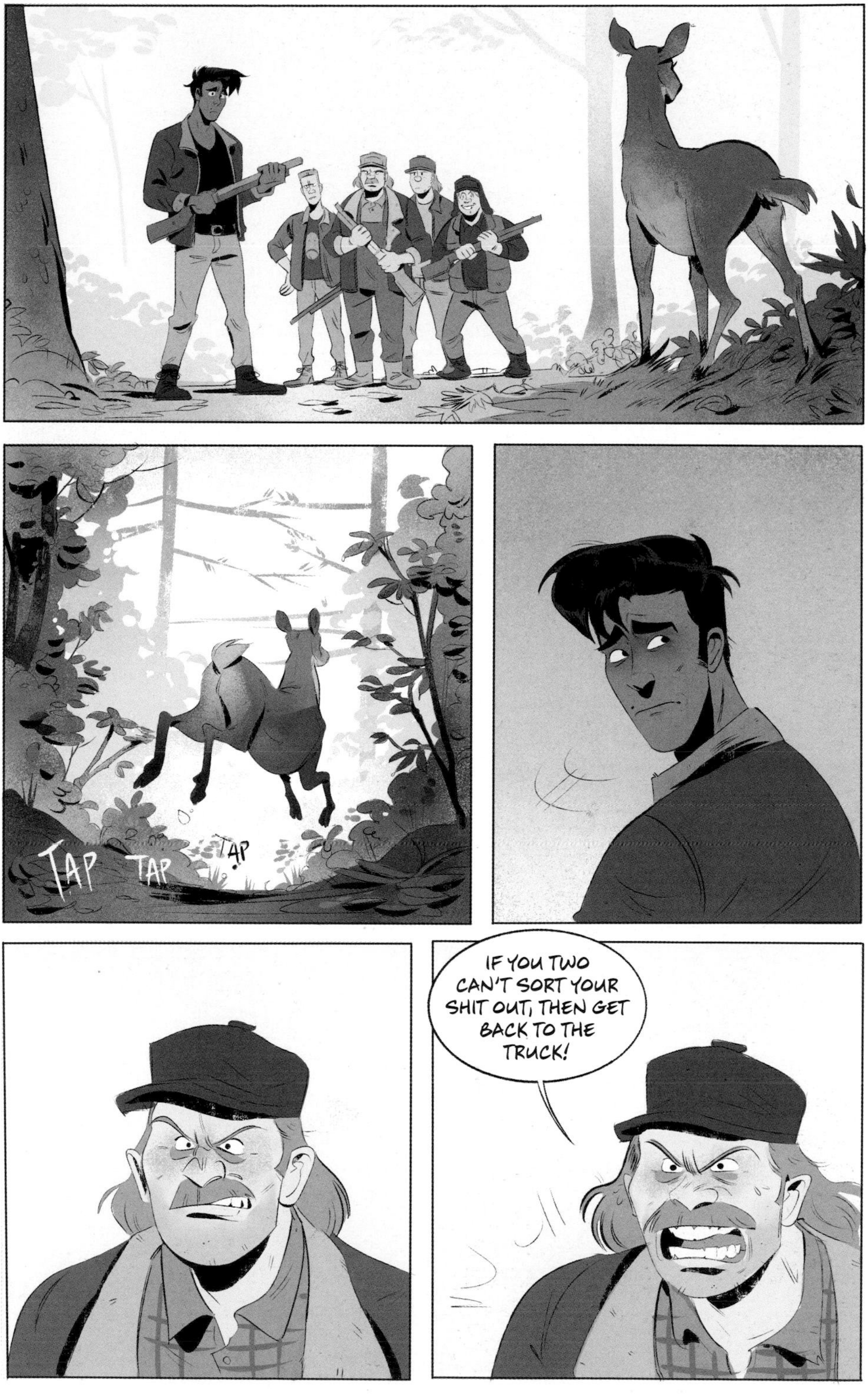
TAP TAP TAP
IF YOU TWO CAN'T SORT YOUR SHIT OUT, THEN GET BACK TO THE TRUCK!

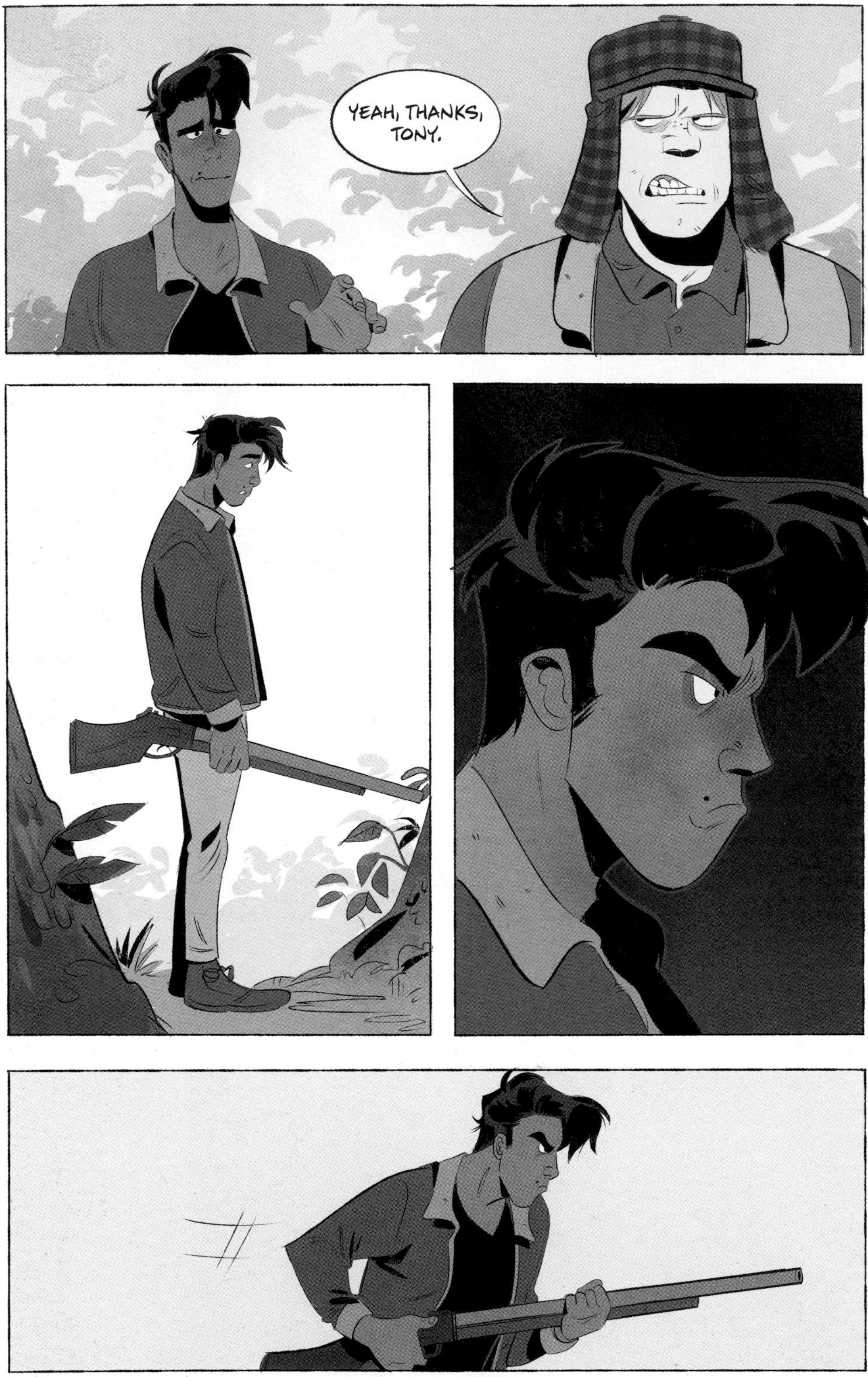
YEAH, THANKS, TONY.

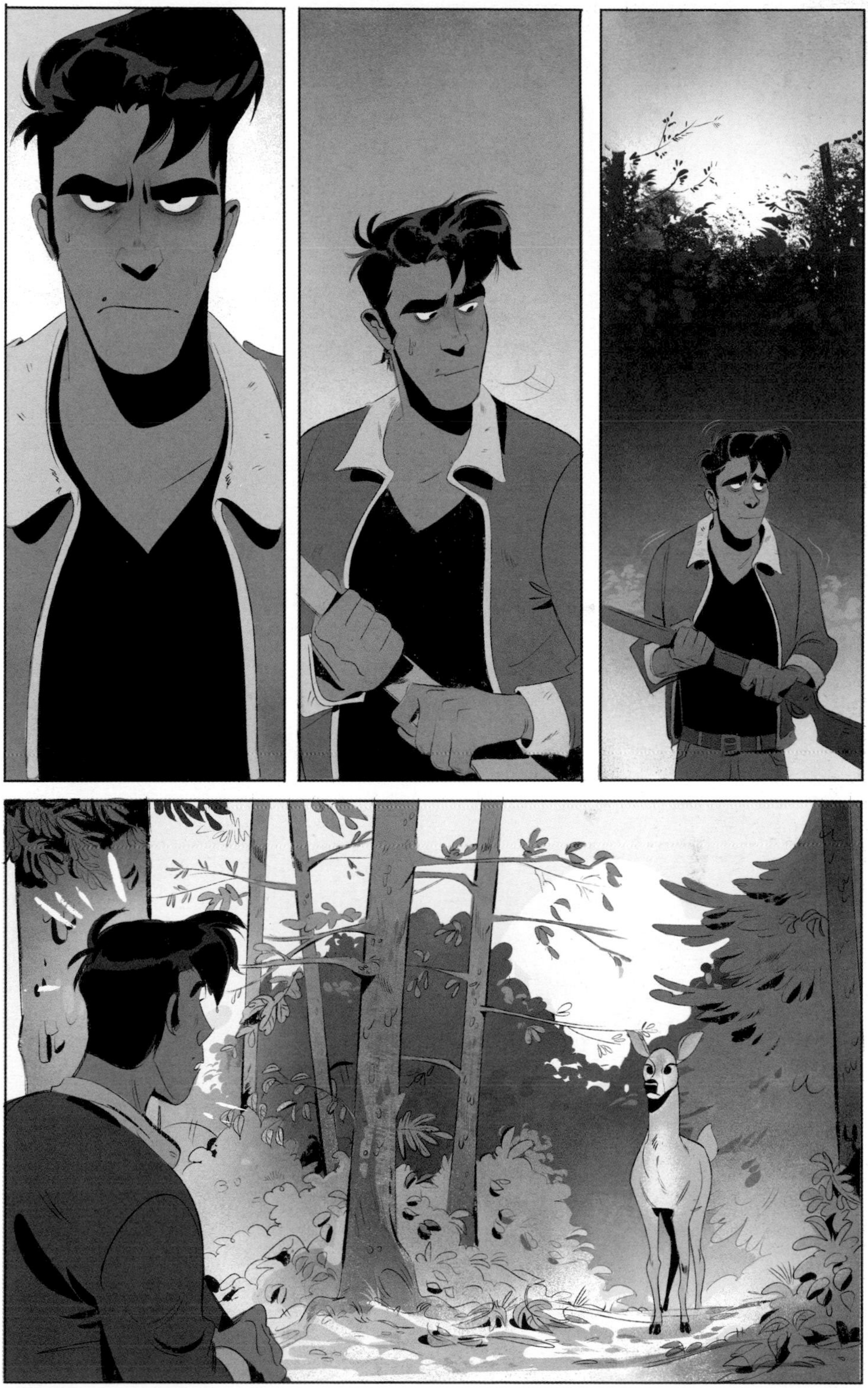

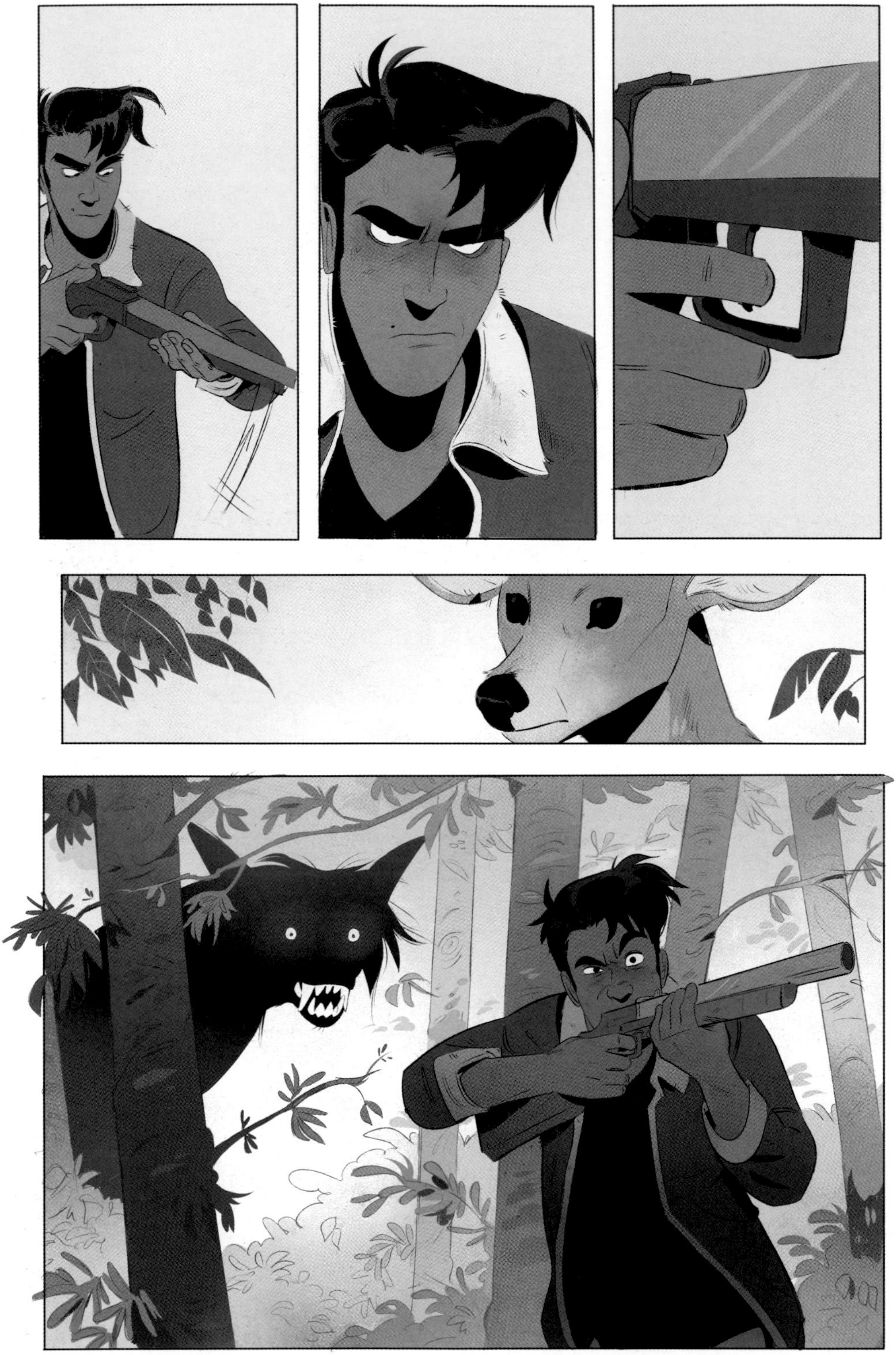

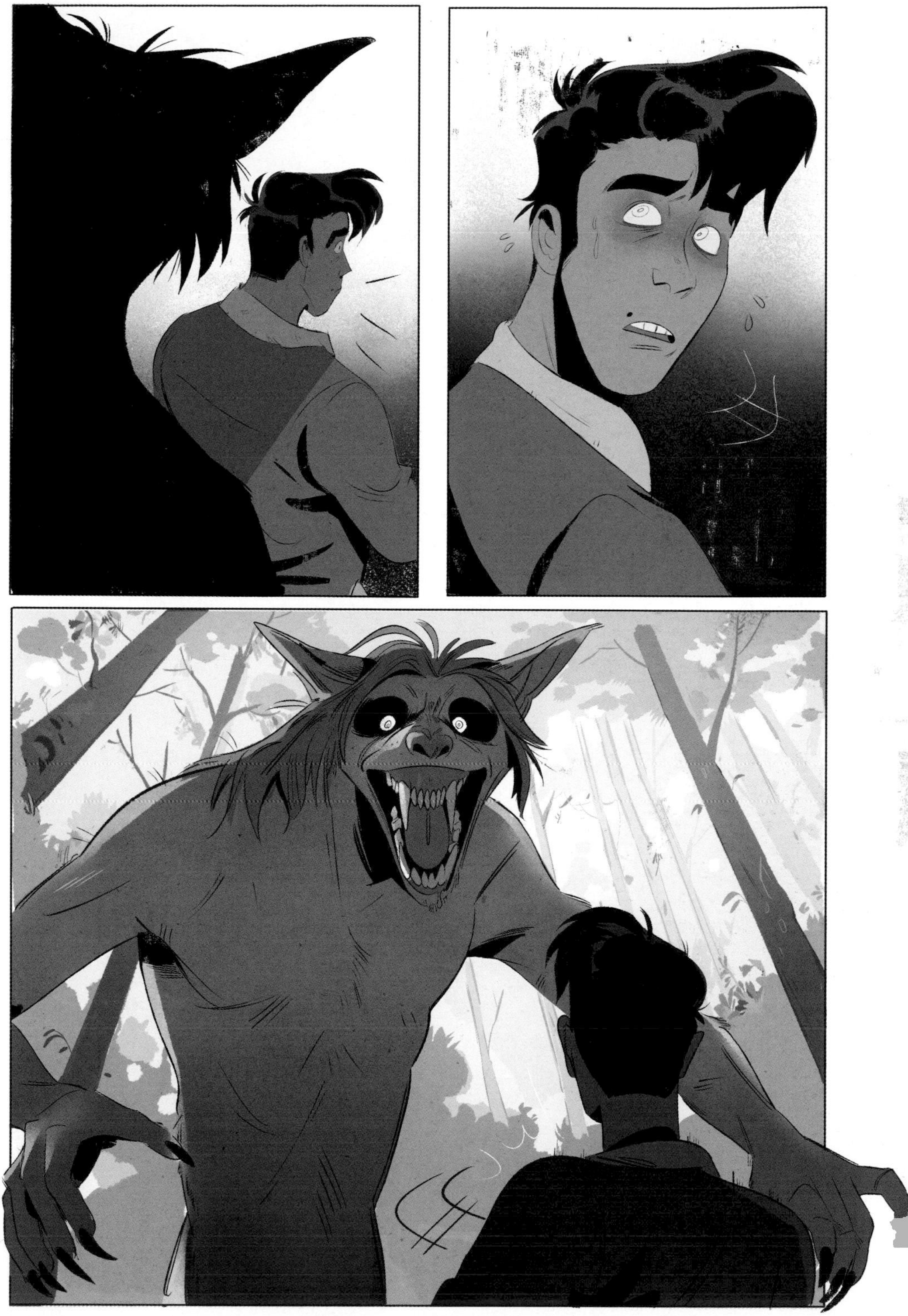

WHUMP!

CLICK!

RAAAAHH!!

BANG!!

AAAUUUGGHH

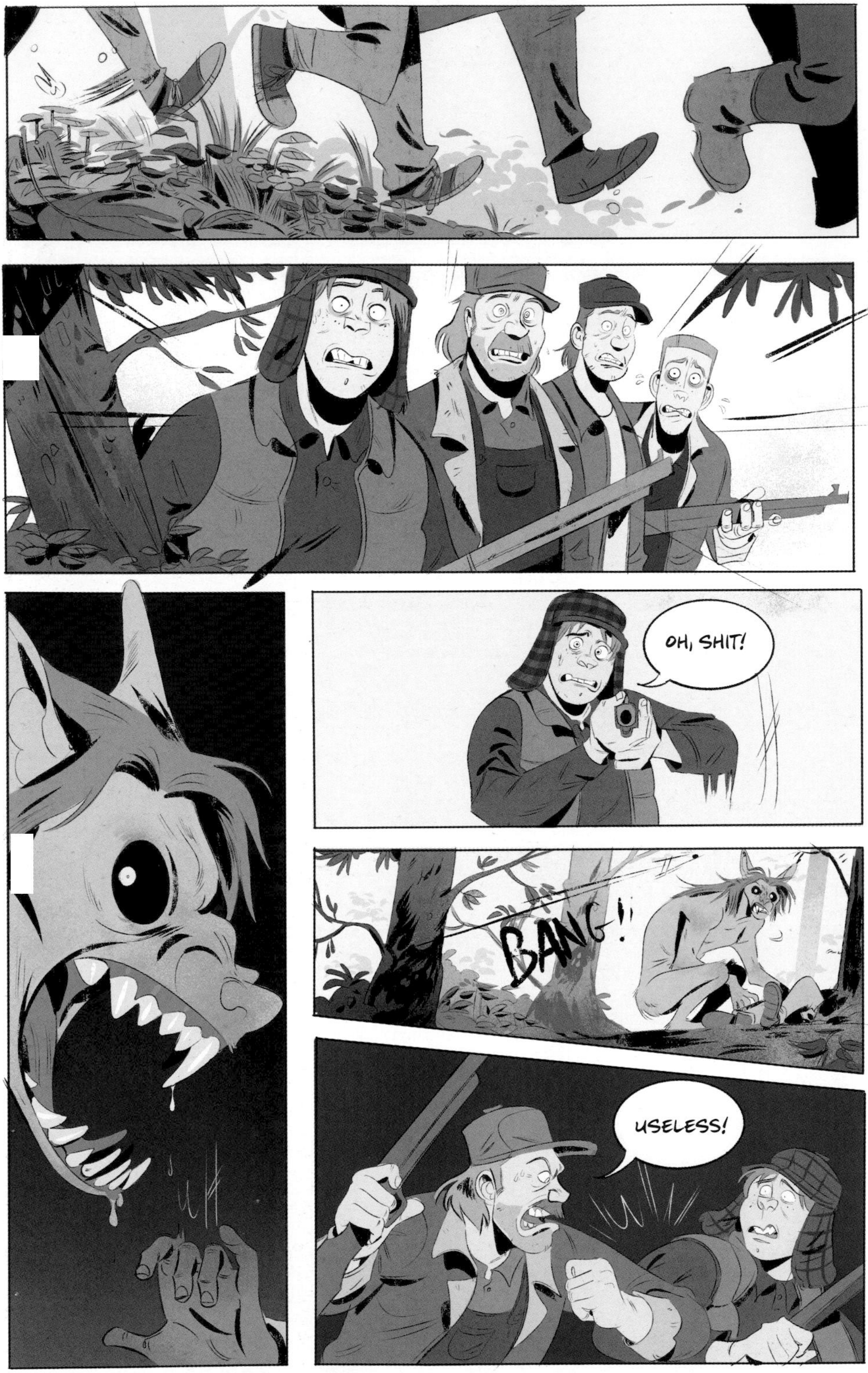
OH, SHIT!
BANG!
USELESS!

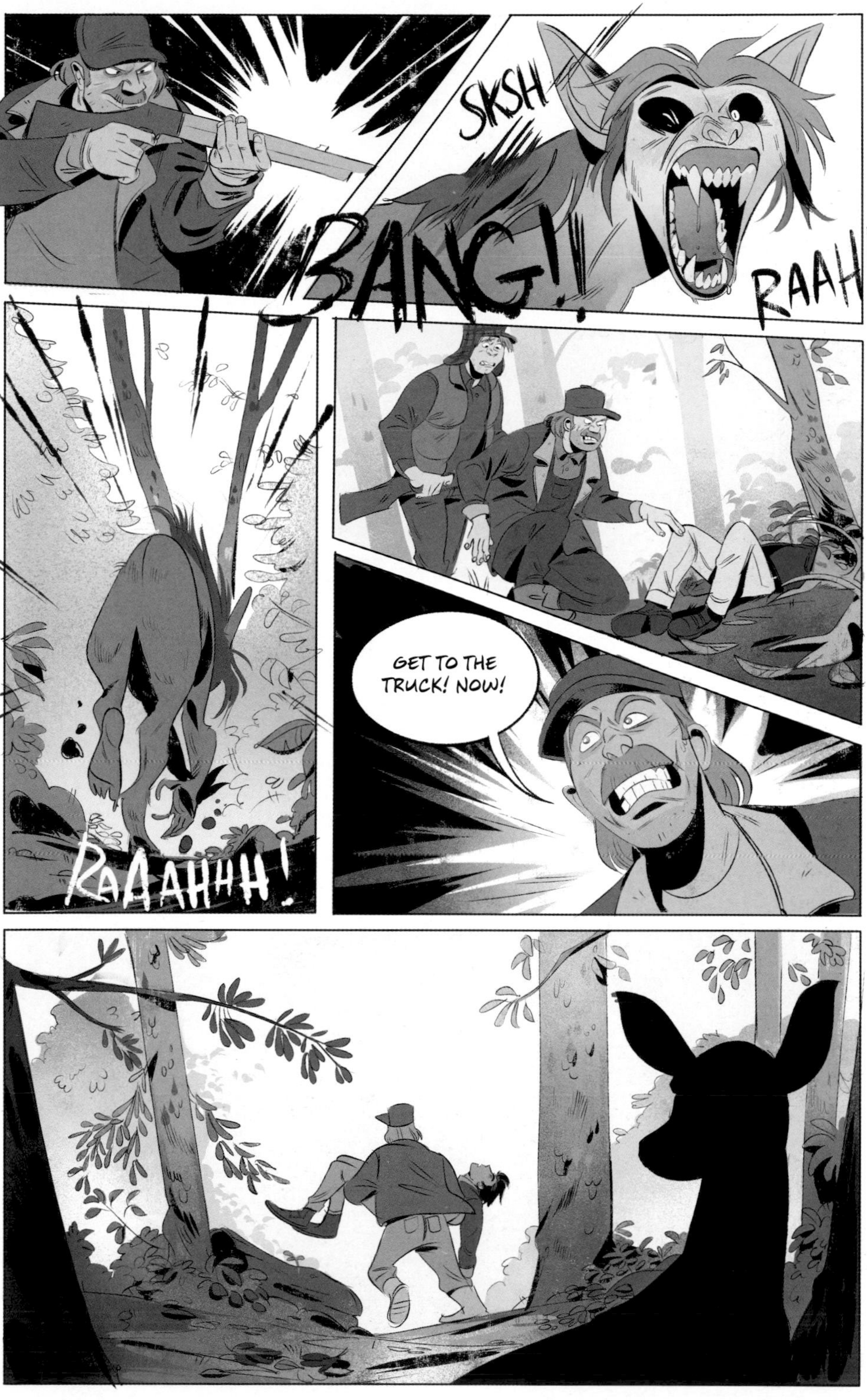
SKSH
BANG!!
RAAH!
RAAHHH!
GET TO THE TRUCK! NOW!

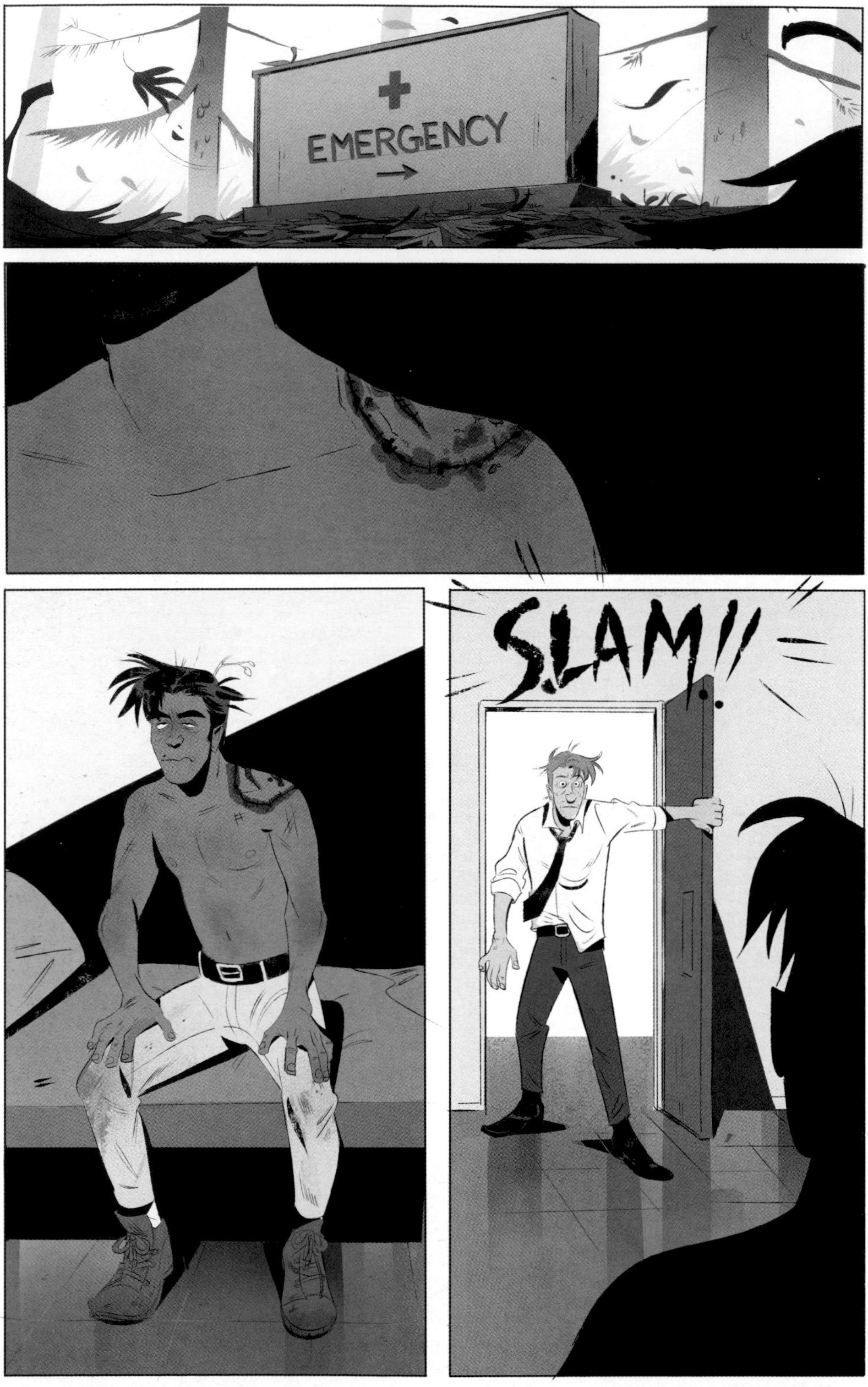
EMERGENCY
SLAM!!

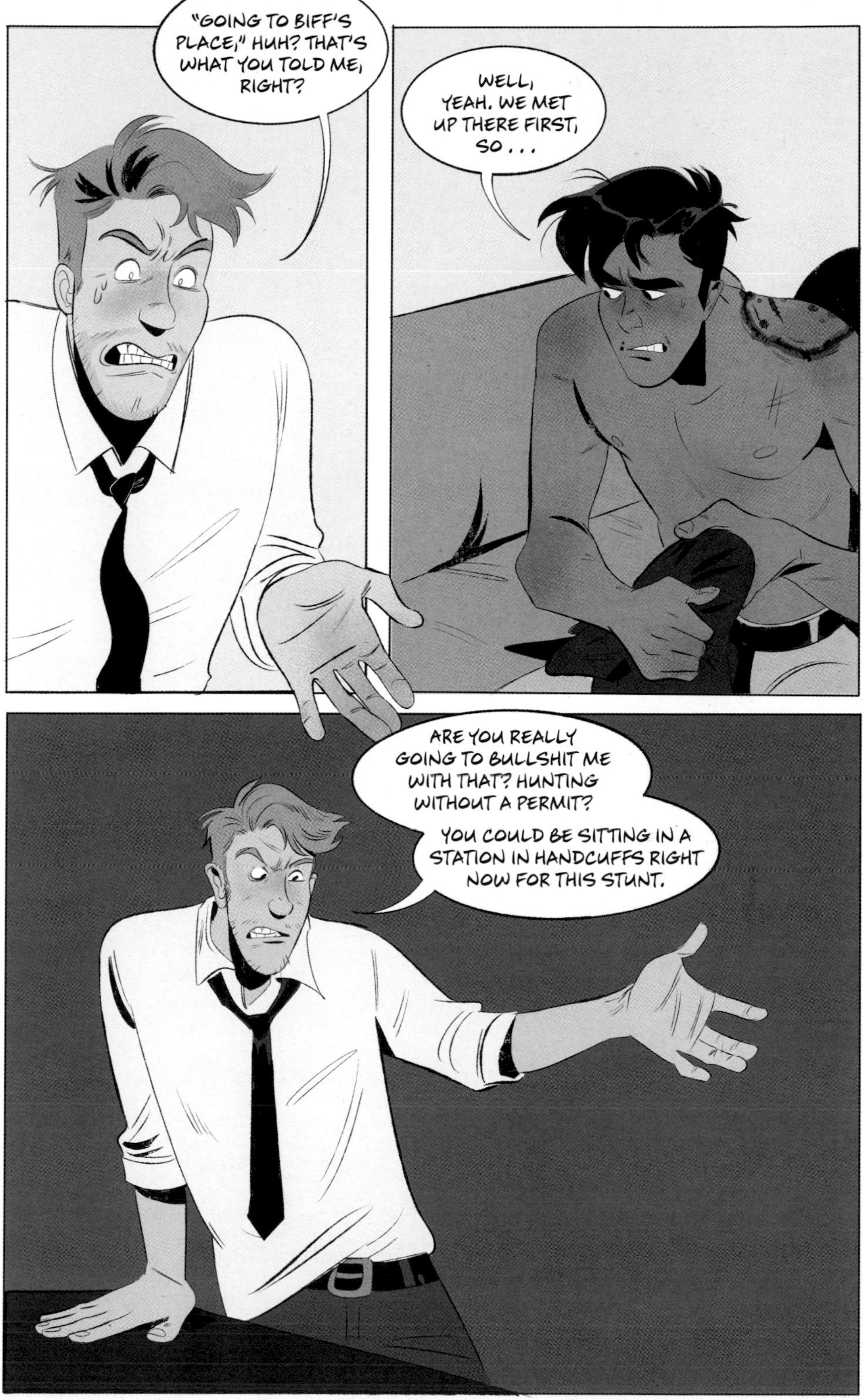
"GOING TO BIFF'S PLACE," HUH? THAT'S WHAT YOU TOLD ME, RIGHT?
WELL, YEAH. WE MET UP THERE FIRST, SO . . .
ARE YOU REALLY GOING TO BULLSHIT ME WITH THAT? HUNTING WITHOUT A PERMIT?
YOU COULD BE SITTING IN A STATION IN HANDCUFFS RIGHT NOW FOR THIS STUNT.

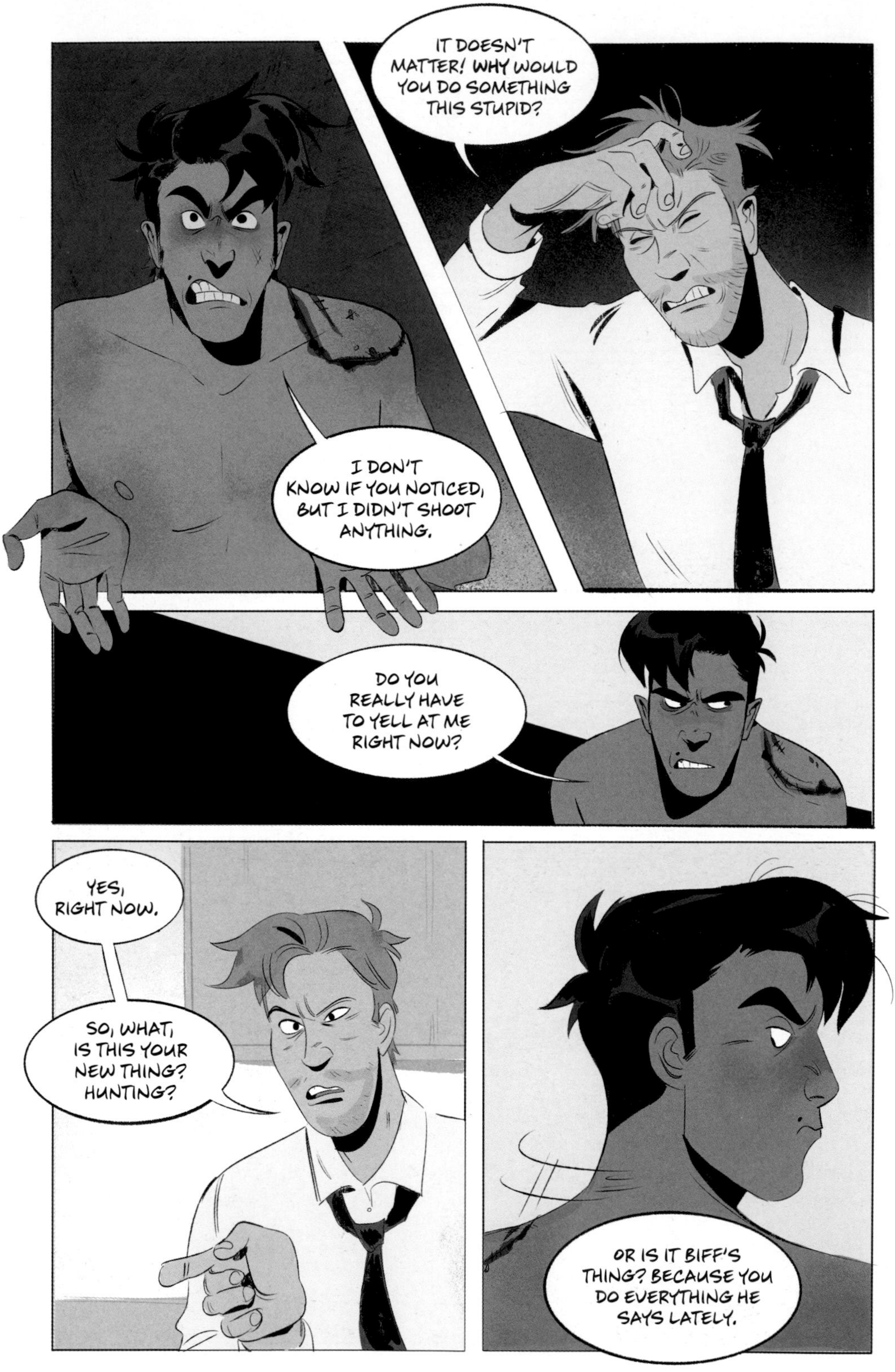
IT DOESN'T MATTER! WHY WOULD YOU DO SOMETHING THIS STUPID?
I DON'T KNOW IF YOU NOTICED, BUT I DIDN'T SHOOT ANYTHING.
DO YOU REALLY HAVE TO YELL AT ME RIGHT NOW?
YES, RIGHT NOW.
SO, WHAT, IS THIS YOUR NEW THING? HUNTING?
OR IS IT BIFF'S THING? BECAUSE YOU DO EVERYTHING HE SAYS LATELY.

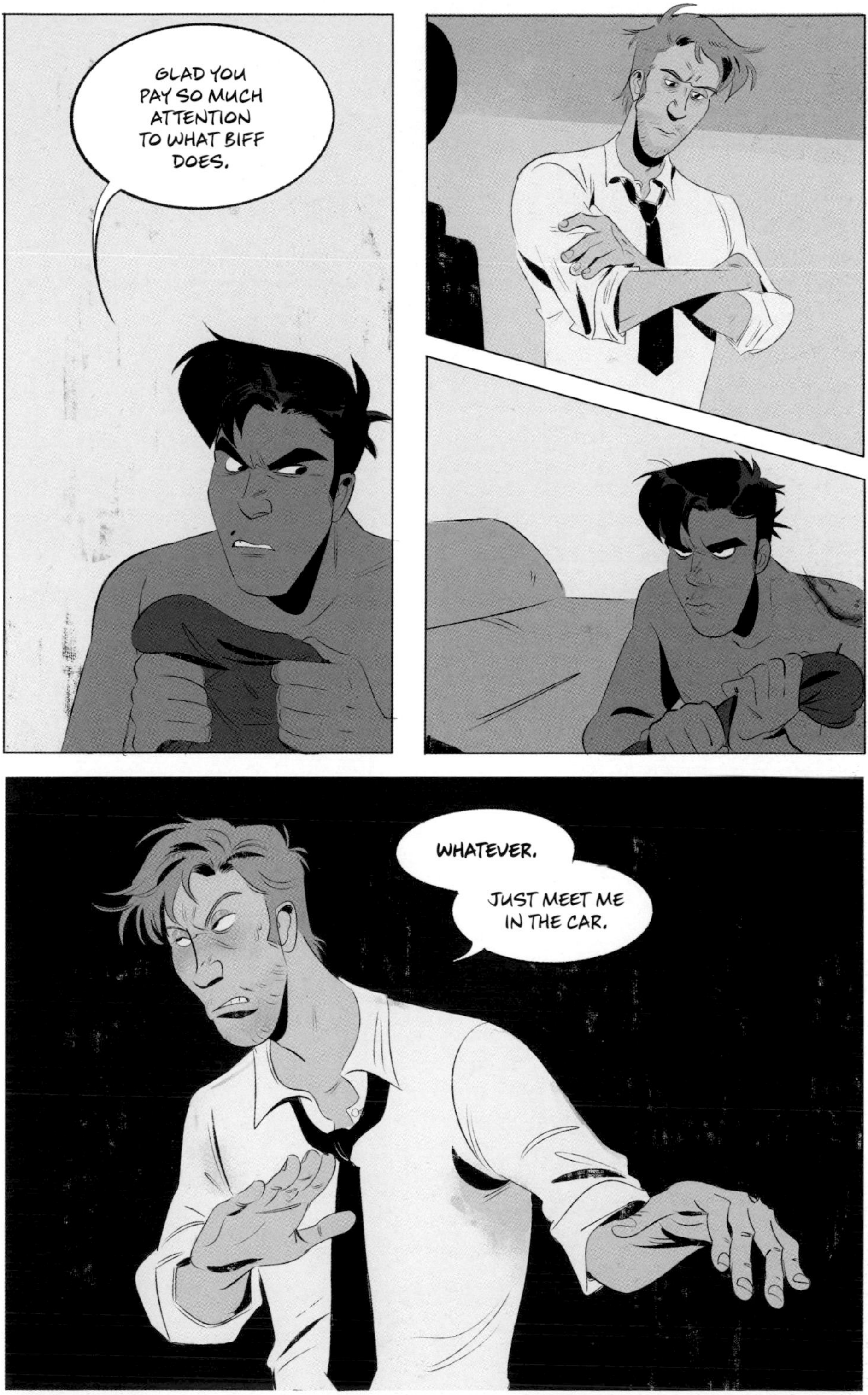
GLAD YOU PAY SO MUCH ATTENTION TO WHAT BIFF DOES.
WHATEVER.
JUST MEET ME IN THE CAR.

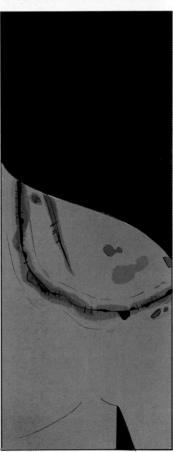

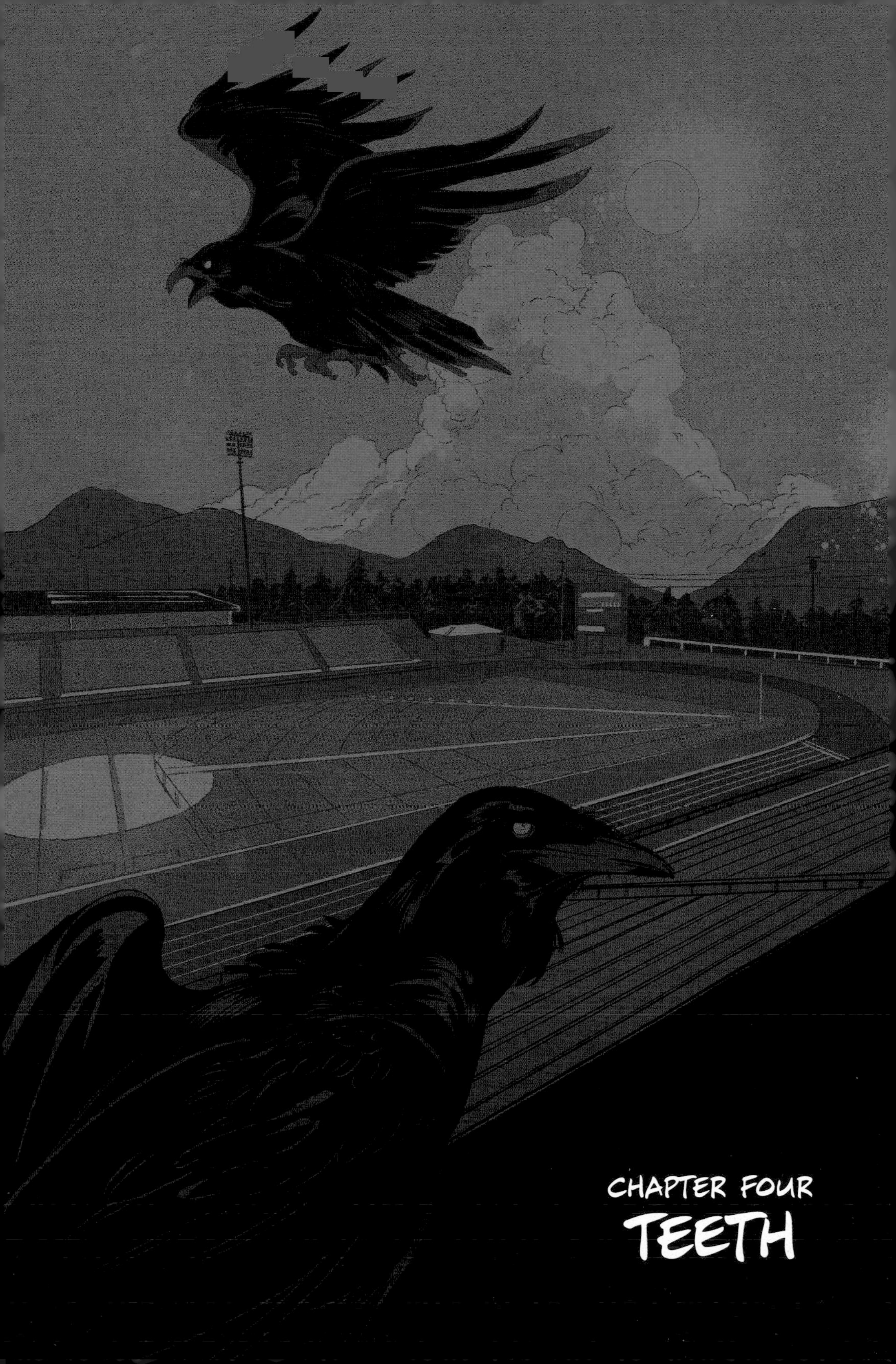

CHAPTER FOUR
TEETH

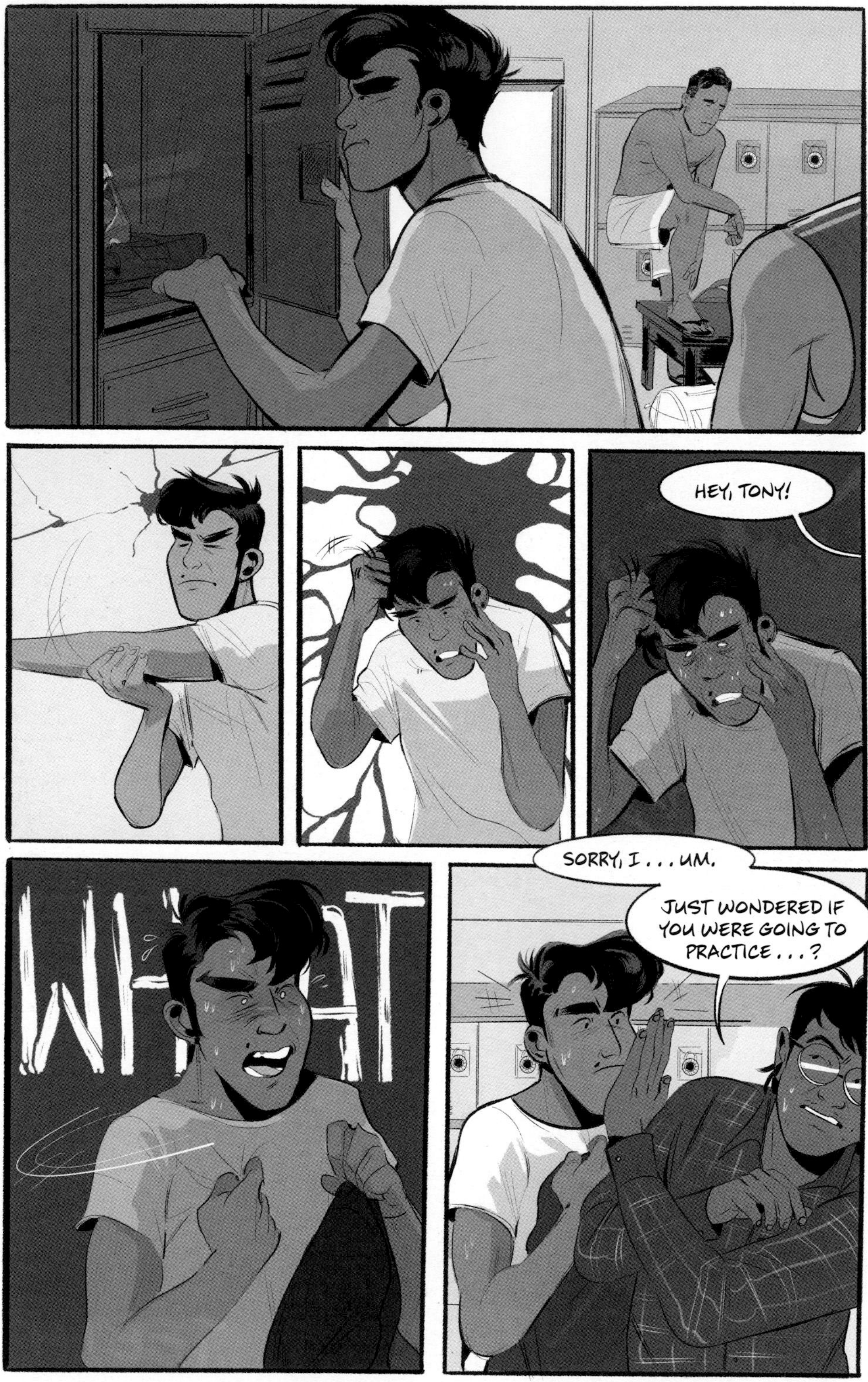
HEY, TONY!
WHAT
SORRY, I . . . UM.
JUST WONDERED IF YOU WERE GOING TO PRACTICE . . . ?

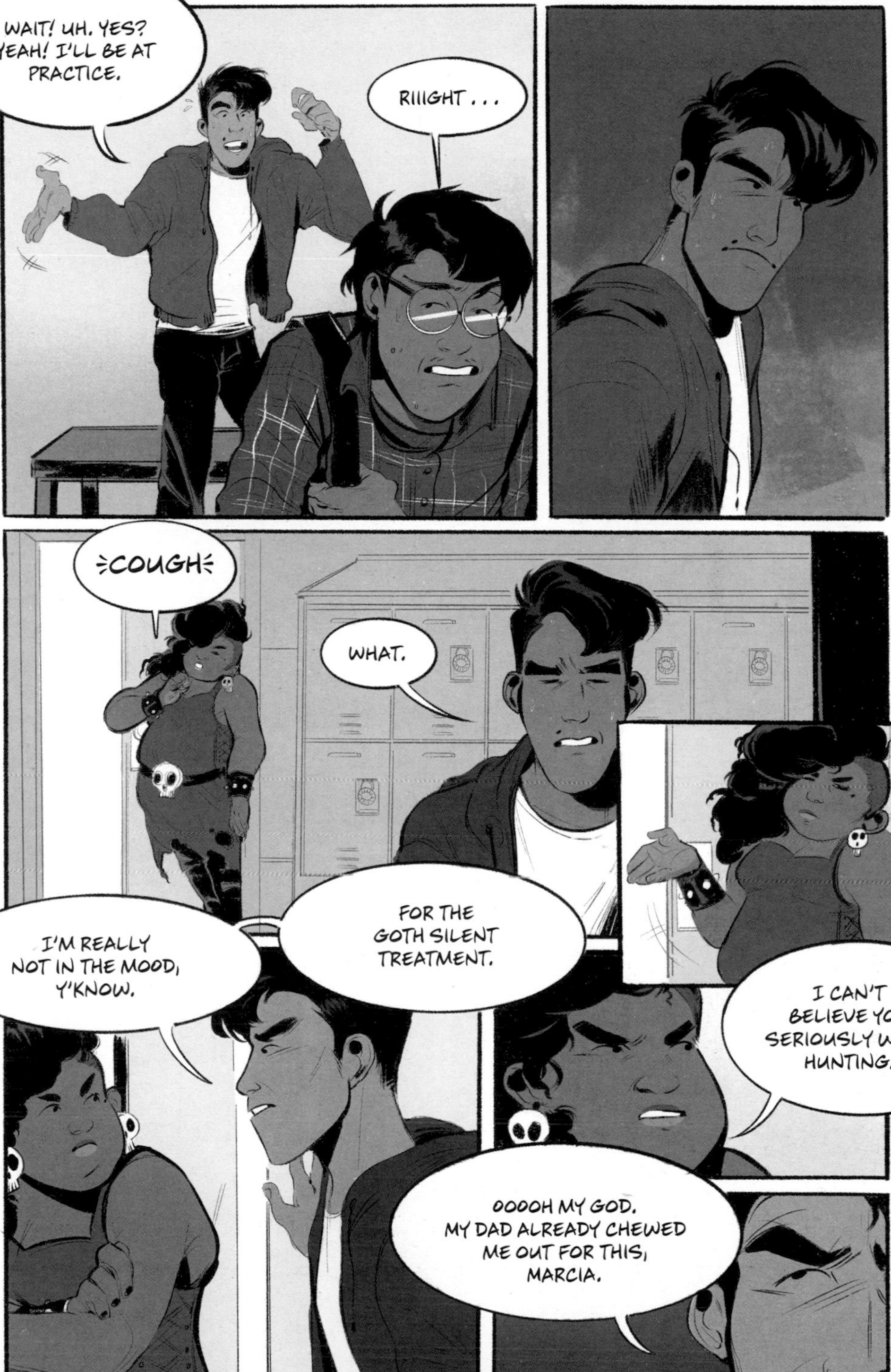
WAIT! UH. YES? YEAH! I'LL BE AT PRACTICE.
RIIIGHT . . .
COUGH
WHAT.
FOR THE GOTH SILENT TREATMENT.
I'M REALLY NOT IN THE MOOD, Y'KNOW.
I CAN'T BELIEVE YOU SERIOUSLY WENT HUNTING.
OOOOH MY GOD. MY DAD ALREADY CHEWED ME OUT FOR THIS, MARCIA.

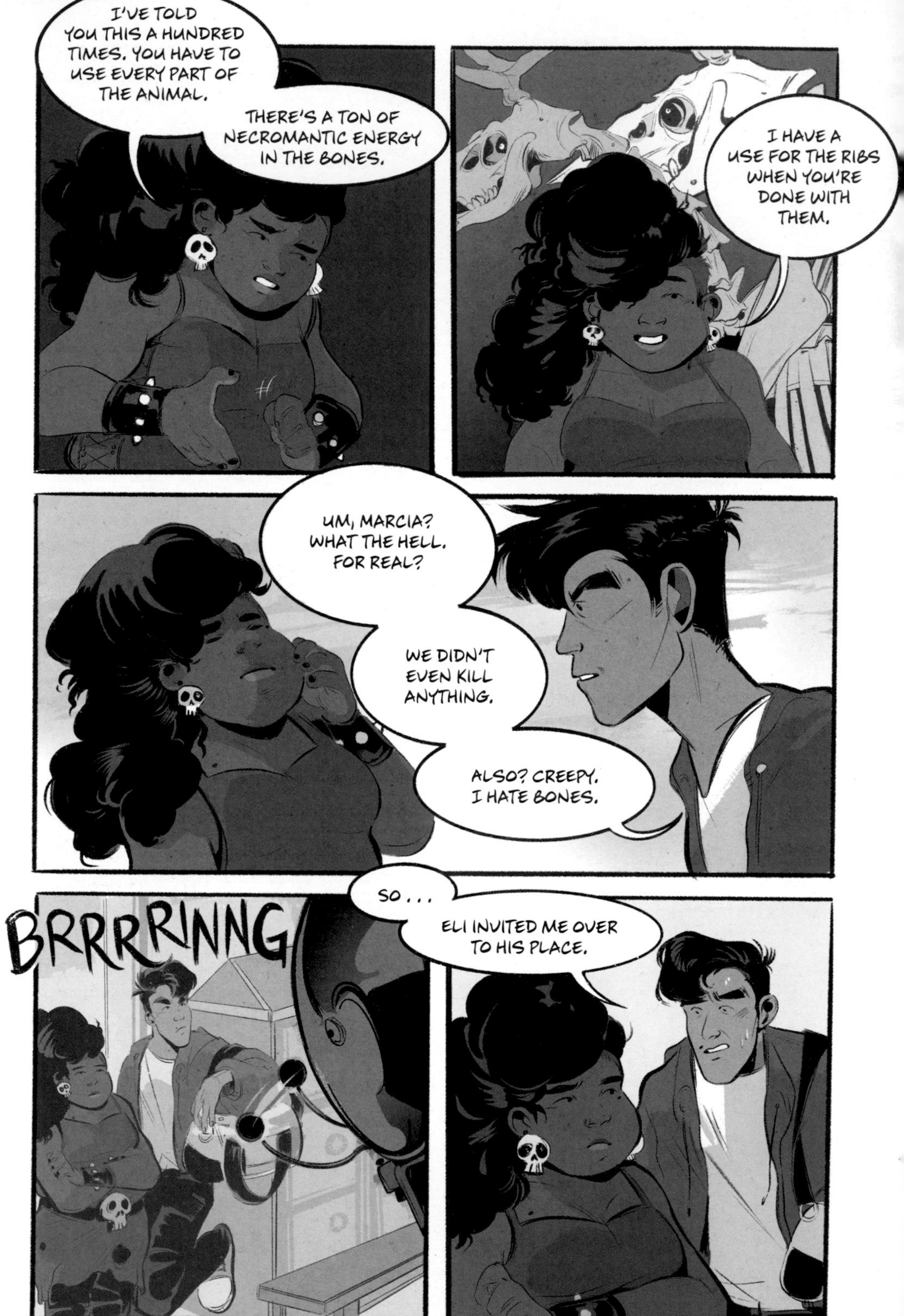

I'VE TOLD YOU THIS A HUNDRED TIMES. YOU HAVE TO USE EVERY PART OF THE ANIMAL.
THERE'S A TON OF NECROMANTIC ENERGY IN THE BONES.
I HAVE A USE FOR THE RIBS WHEN YOU'RE DONE WITH THEM.
UM, MARCIA? WHAT THE HELL. FOR REAL?
WE DIDN'T EVEN KILL ANYTHING.
ALSO? CREEPY. I HATE BONES.
BRRRRINNG
SO . . .
ELI INVITED ME OVER TO HIS PLACE.

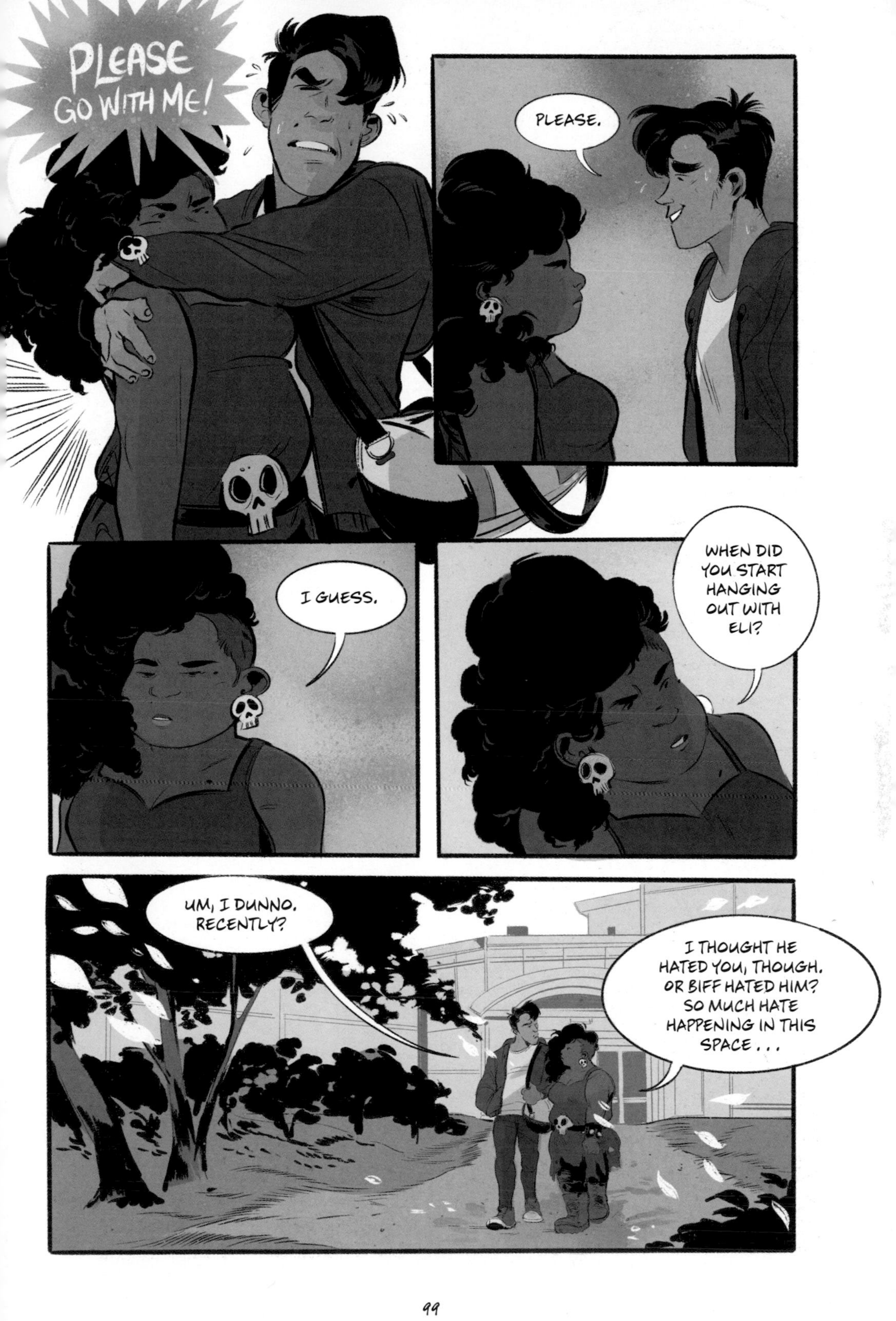
PLEASE GO WITH ME!
PLEASE.
I GUESS.
WHEN DID YOU START HANGING OUT WITH ELI?
UM, I DUNNO. RECENTLY?
I THOUGHT HE HATED YOU, THOUGH. OR BIFF HATED HIM? SO MUCH HATE HAPPENING IN THIS SPACE . . .

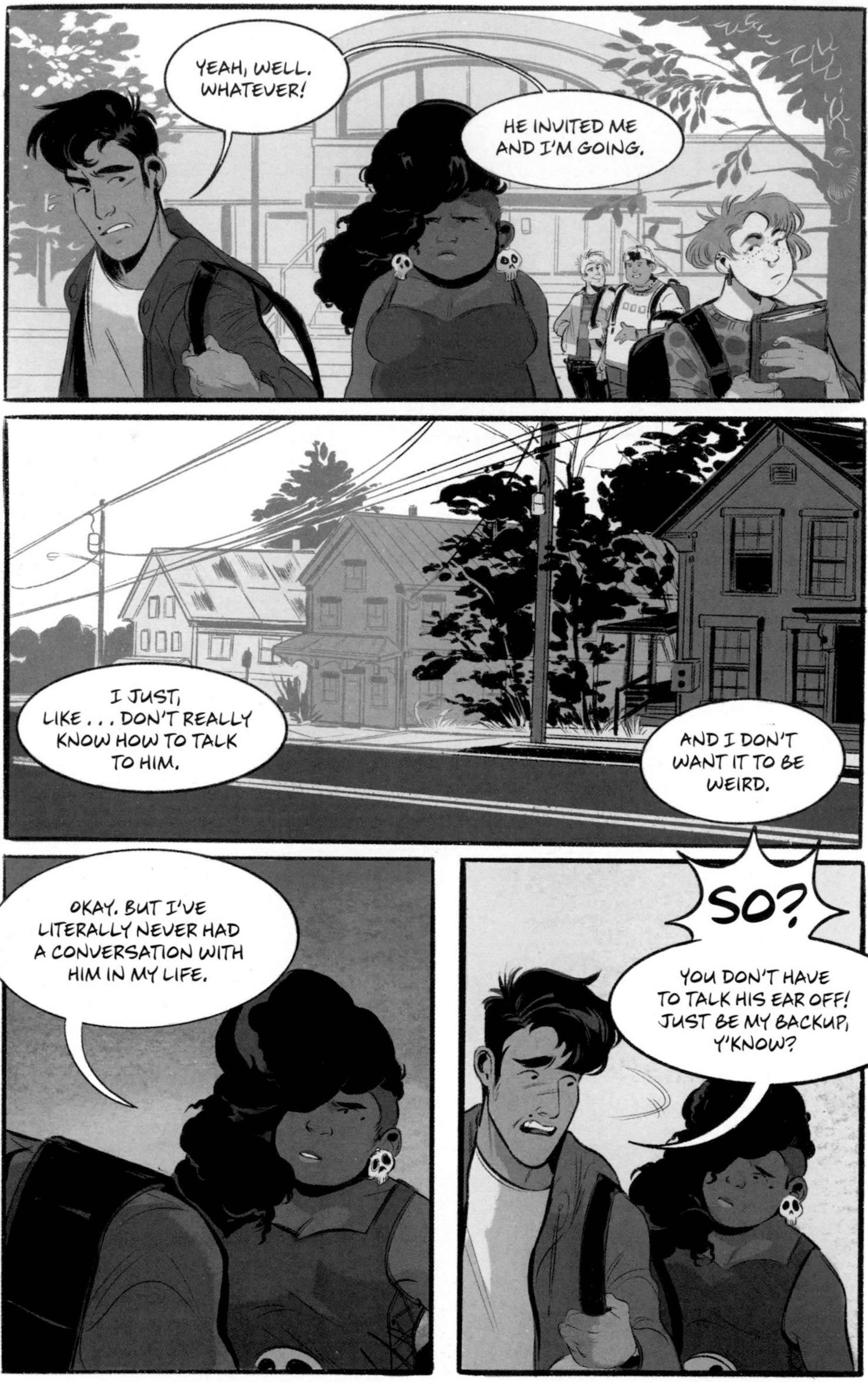
YEAH, WELL. WHATEVER!
HE INVITED ME AND I'M GOING.
I JUST, LIKE . . . DON'T REALLY KNOW HOW TO TALK TO HIM.
AND I DON'T WANT IT TO BE WEIRD.
OKAY. BUT I'VE LITERALLY NEVER HAD A CONVERSATION WITH HIM IN MY LIFE.
SO?
YOU DON'T HAVE TO TALK HIS EAR OFF! JUST BE MY BACKUP, Y'KNOW?

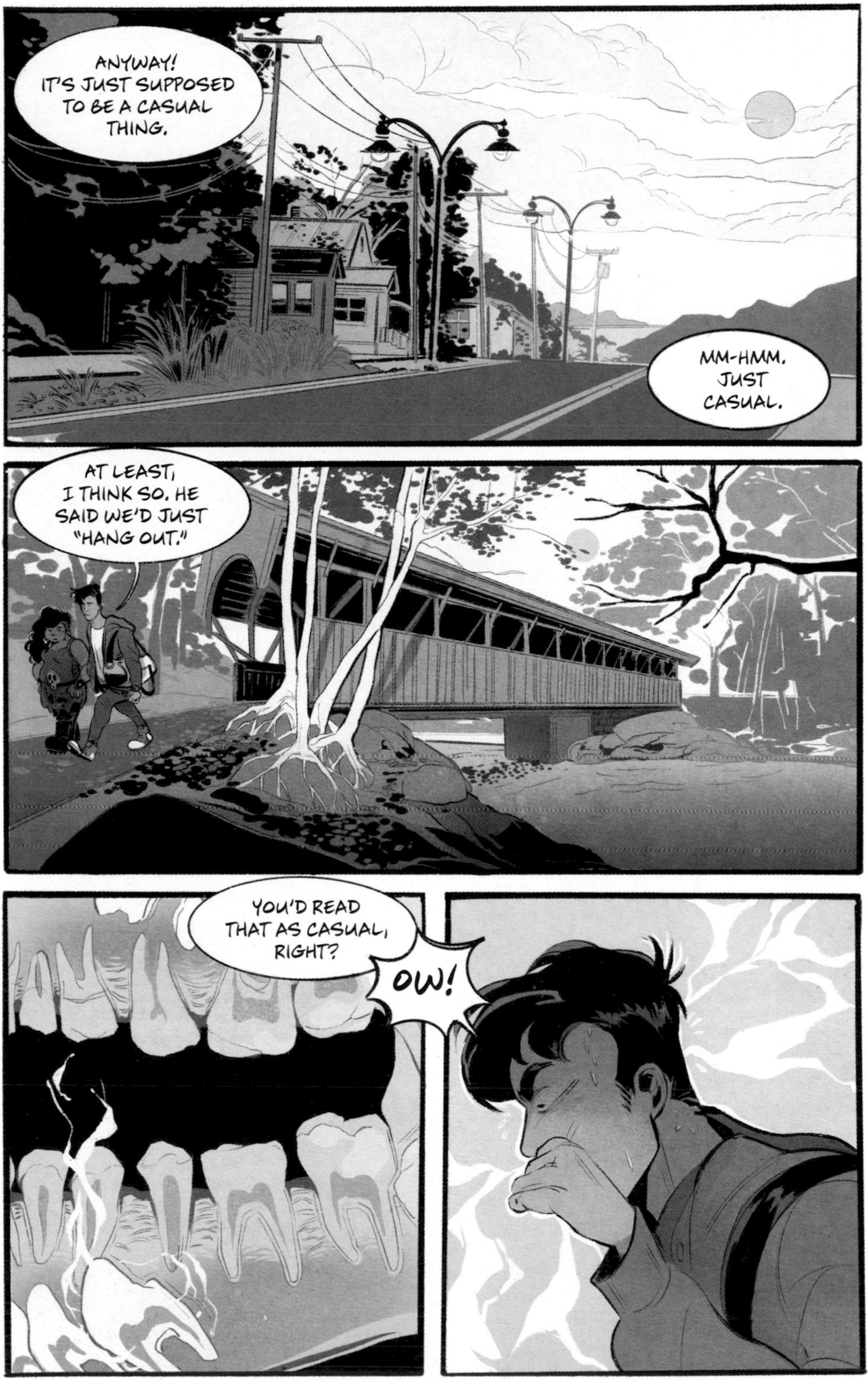
ANYWAY! IT'S JUST SUPPOSED TO BE A CASUAL THING.
MM-HMM. JUST CASUAL.
AT LEAST, I THINK SO. HE SAID WE'D JUST "HANG OUT."
YOU'D READ THAT AS CASUAL, RIGHT?
OW!

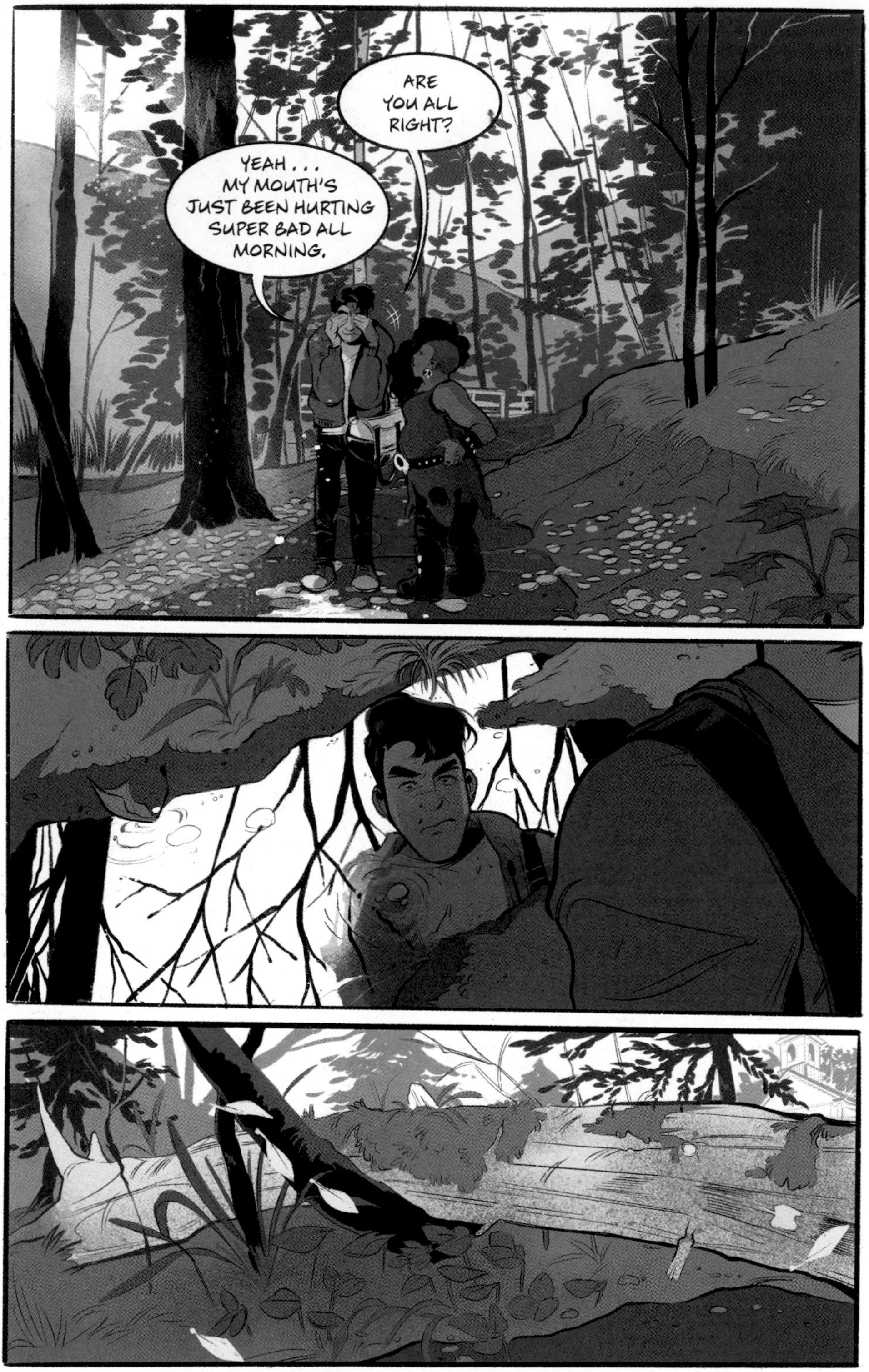
ARE YOU ALL RIGHT?
YEAH . . . MY MOUTH'S JUST BEEN HURTING SUPER BAD ALL MORNING.

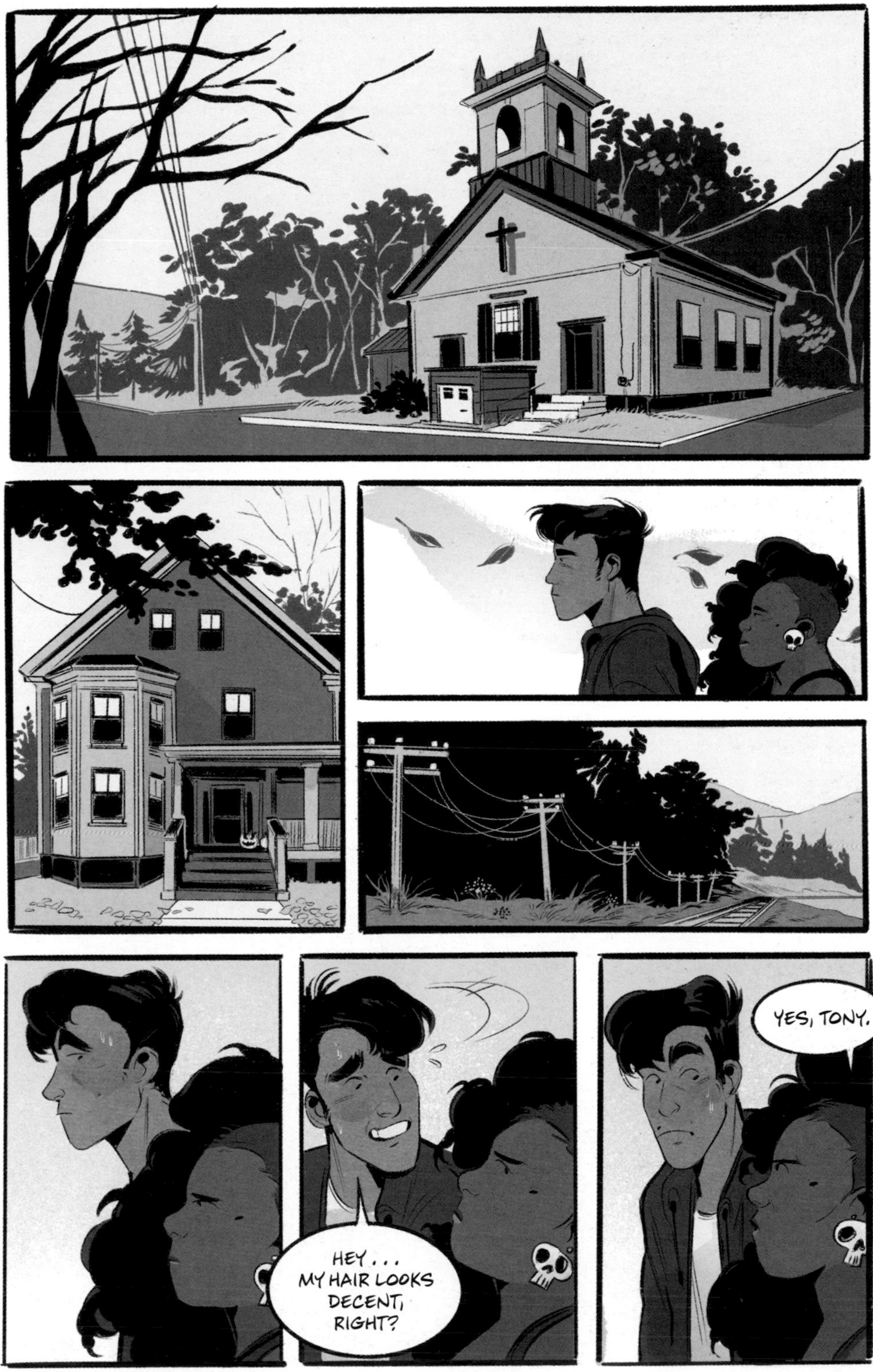
HEY . . . MY HAIR LOOKS DECENT, RIGHT?
YES, TONY.

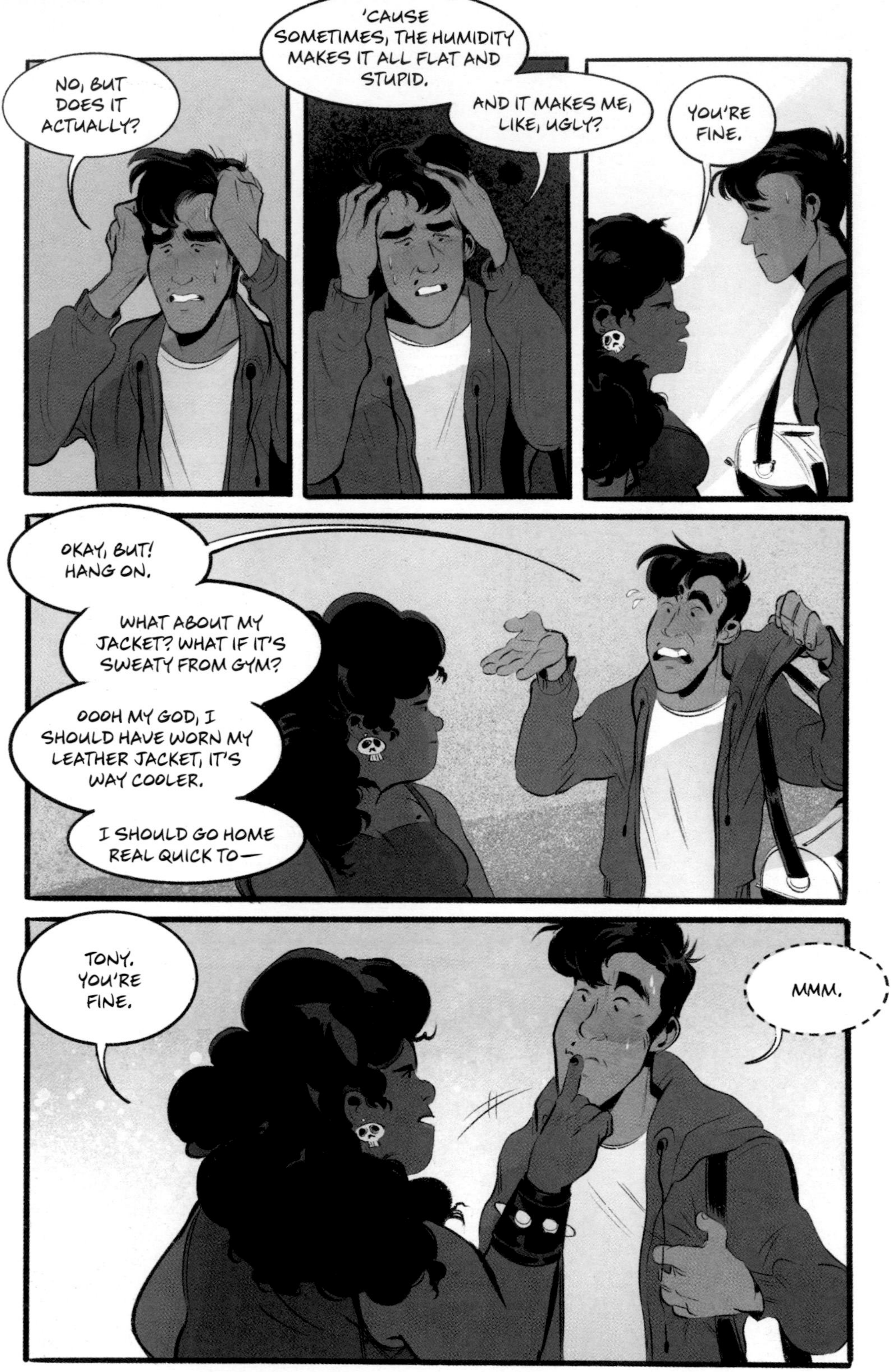
NO, BUT DOES IT ACTUALLY?
'CAUSE SOMETIMES, THE HUMIDITY MAKES IT ALL FLAT AND STUPID.
AND IT MAKES ME, LIKE, UGLY?
YOU'RE FINE.
OKAY, BUT! HANG ON.
WHAT ABOUT MY JACKET? WHAT IF IT'S SWEATY FROM GYM?
OOOH MY GOD, I SHOULD HAVE WORN MY LEATHER JACKET, IT'S WAY COOLER.
I SHOULD GO HOME REAL QUICK TO—
TONY. YOU'RE FINE.
MMM.

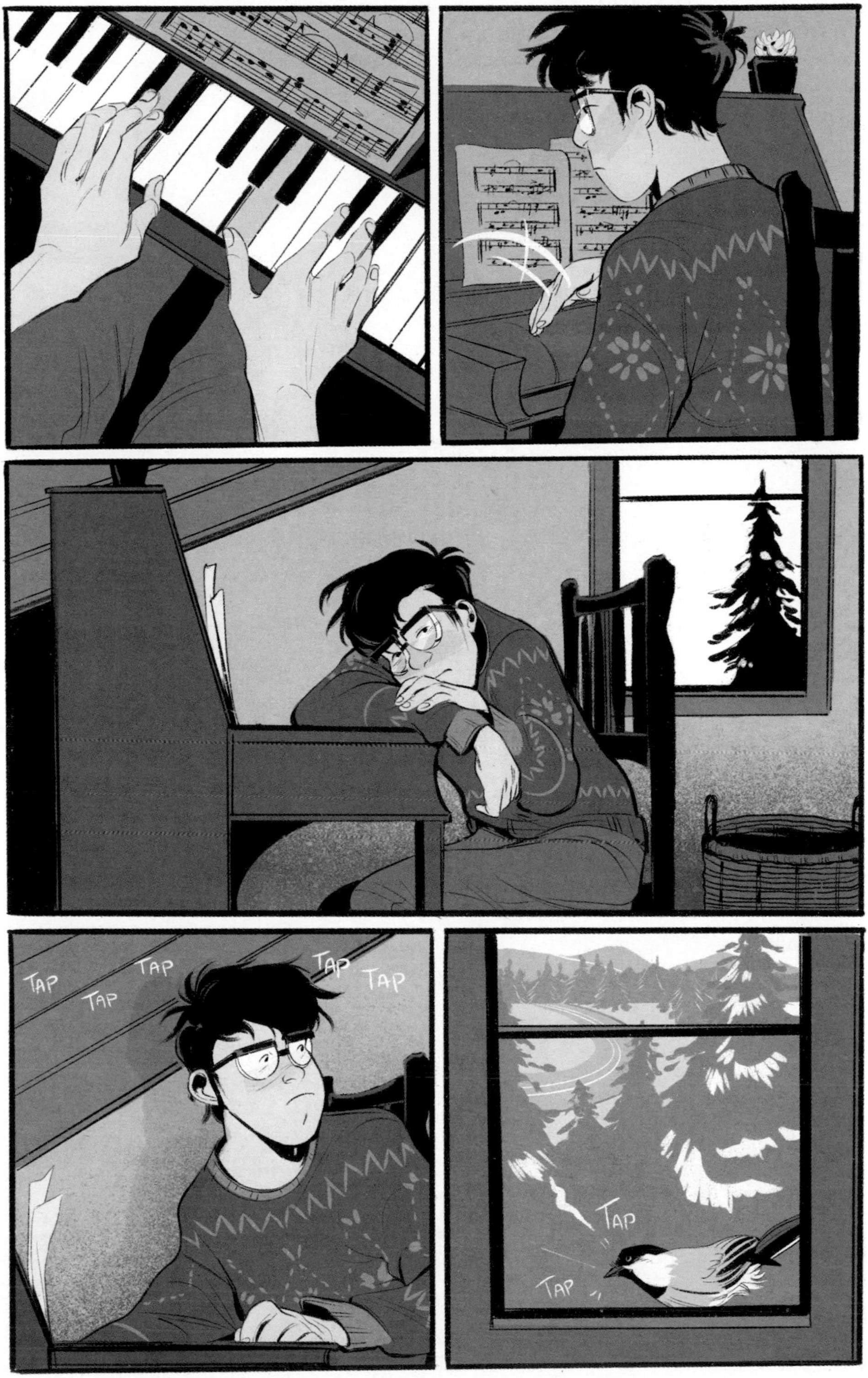
TAP
TAP
TAP
TAP
TAP
TAP
TAP

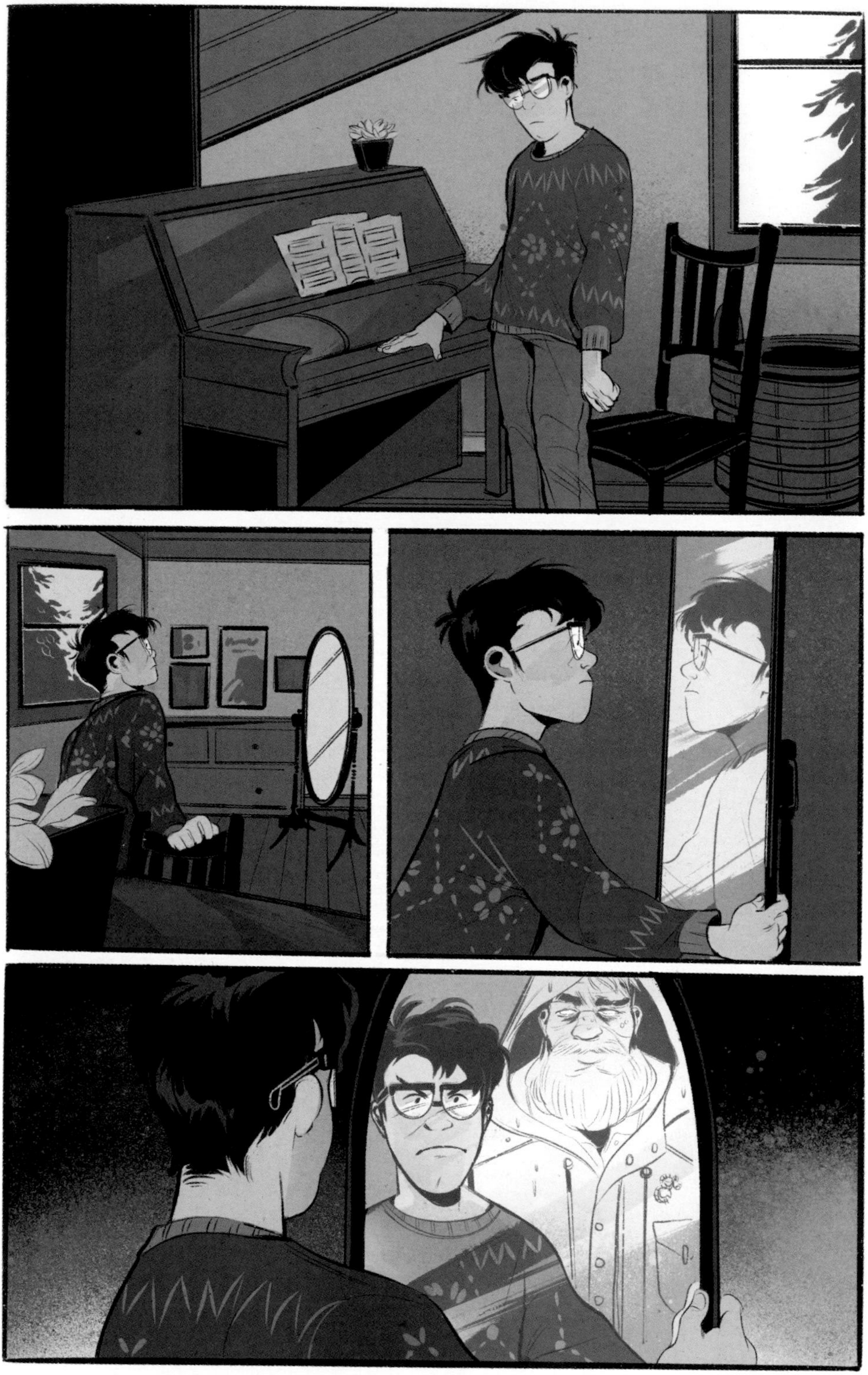

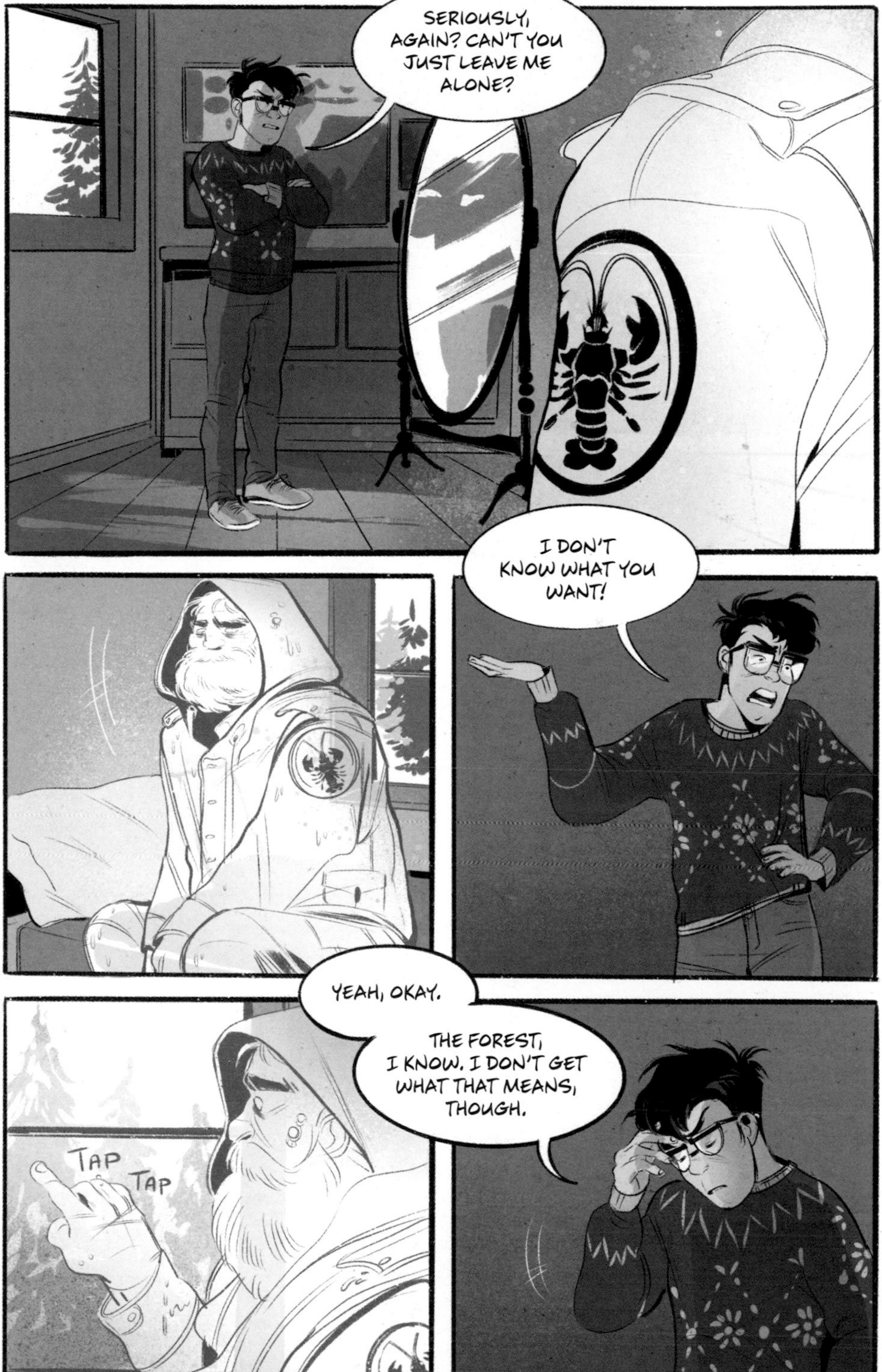
SERIOUSLY, AGAIN? CAN'T YOU JUST LEAVE ME ALONE?
I DON'T KNOW WHAT YOU WANT!
YEAH, OKAY.
TAP TAP
THE FOREST, I KNOW. I DON'T GET WHAT THAT MEANS, THOUGH.

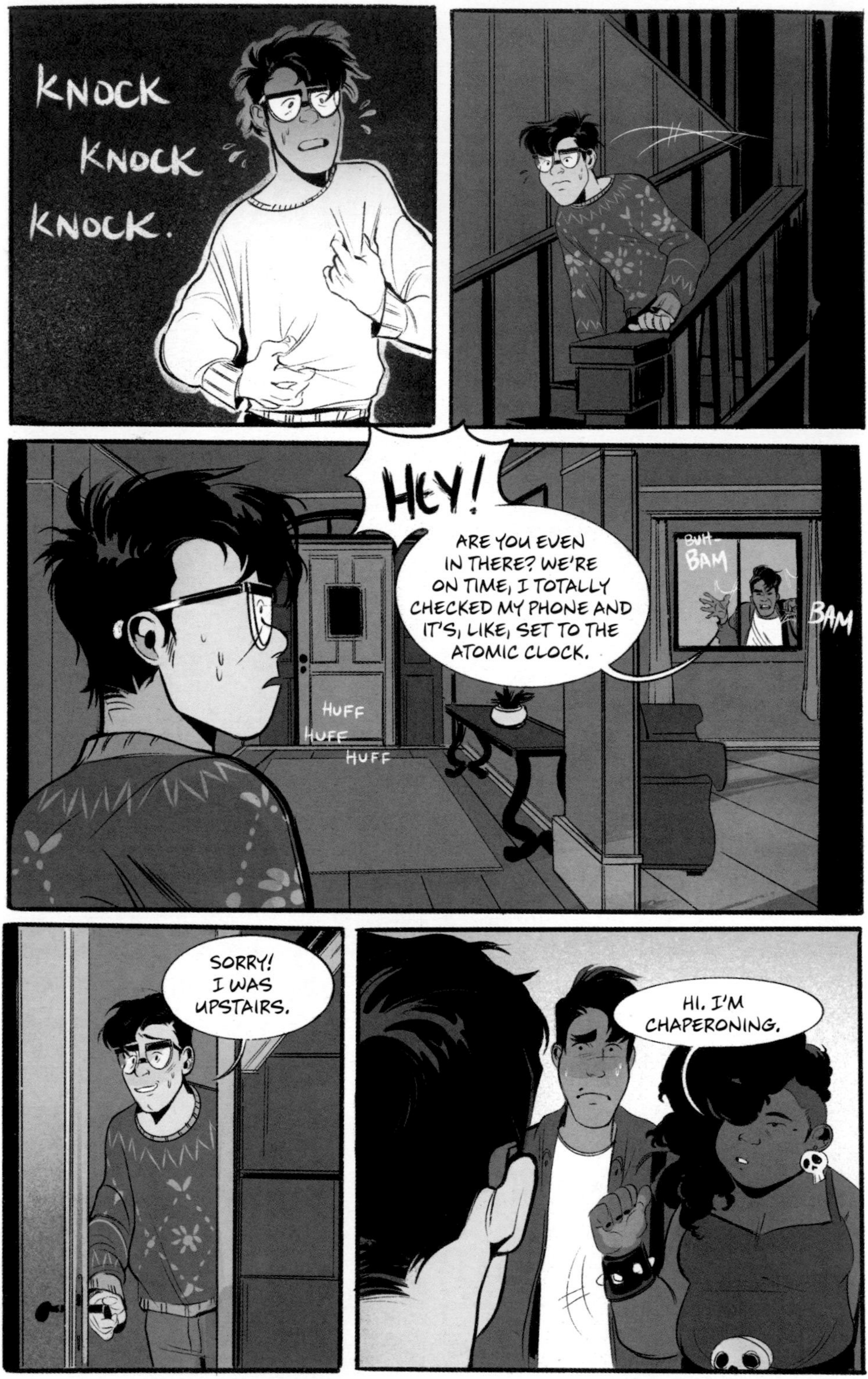
KNOCK
KNOCK
KNOCK.
HEY!
ARE YOU EVEN IN THERE? WE'RE ON TIME, I TOTALLY CHECKED MY PHONE AND IT'S, LIKE, SET TO THE ATOMIC CLOCK.
BUH-BAM
BAM
HUFF
HUFF
HUFF
SORRY! I WAS UPSTAIRS.
HI. I'M CHAPERONING.

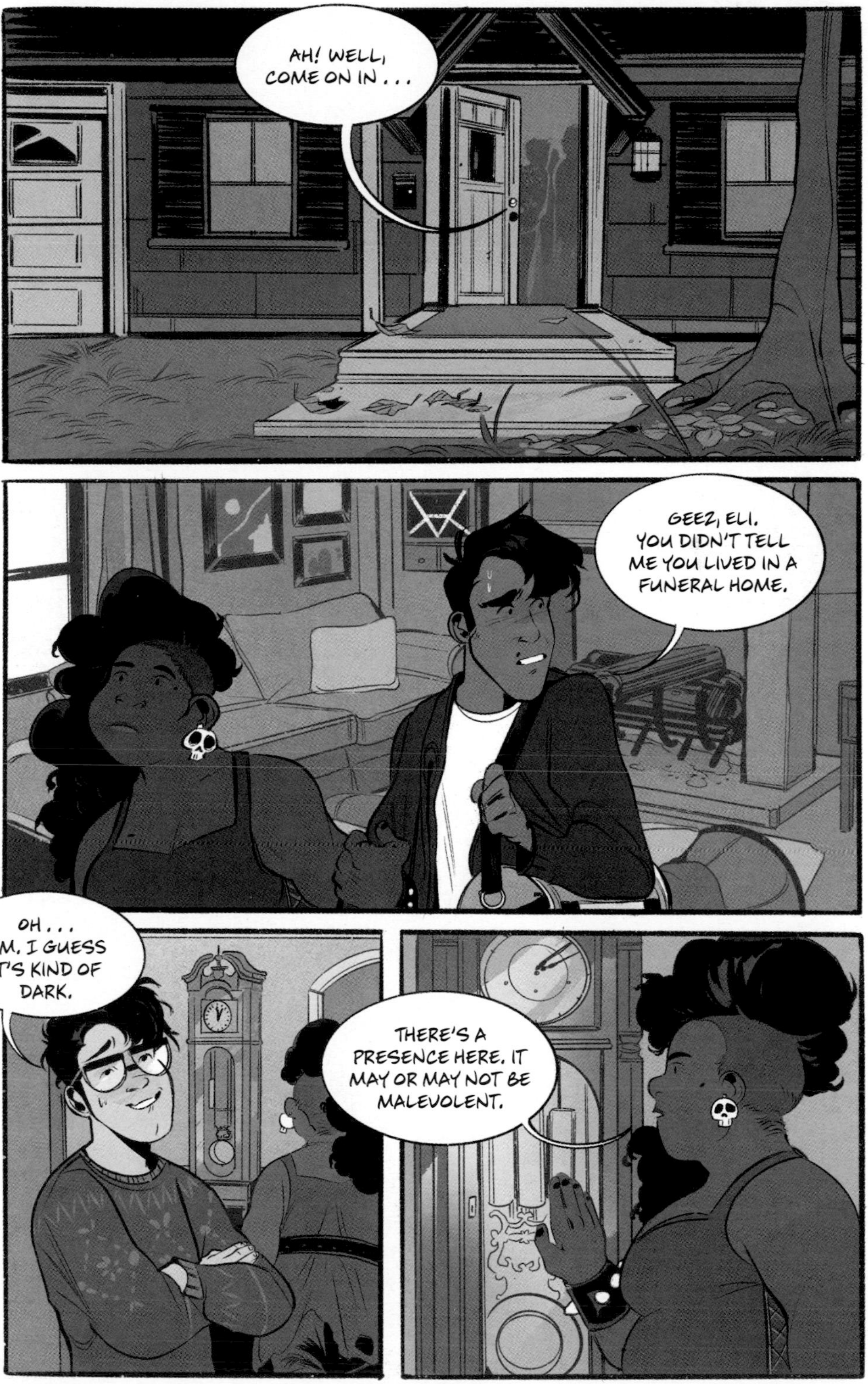
AH! WELL, COME ON IN . . .
GEEZ, ELI. YOU DIDN'T TELL ME YOU LIVED IN A FUNERAL HOME.
OH . . . UM. I GUESS IT'S KIND OF DARK.
THERE'S A PRESENCE HERE. IT MAY OR MAY NOT BE MALEVOLENT.

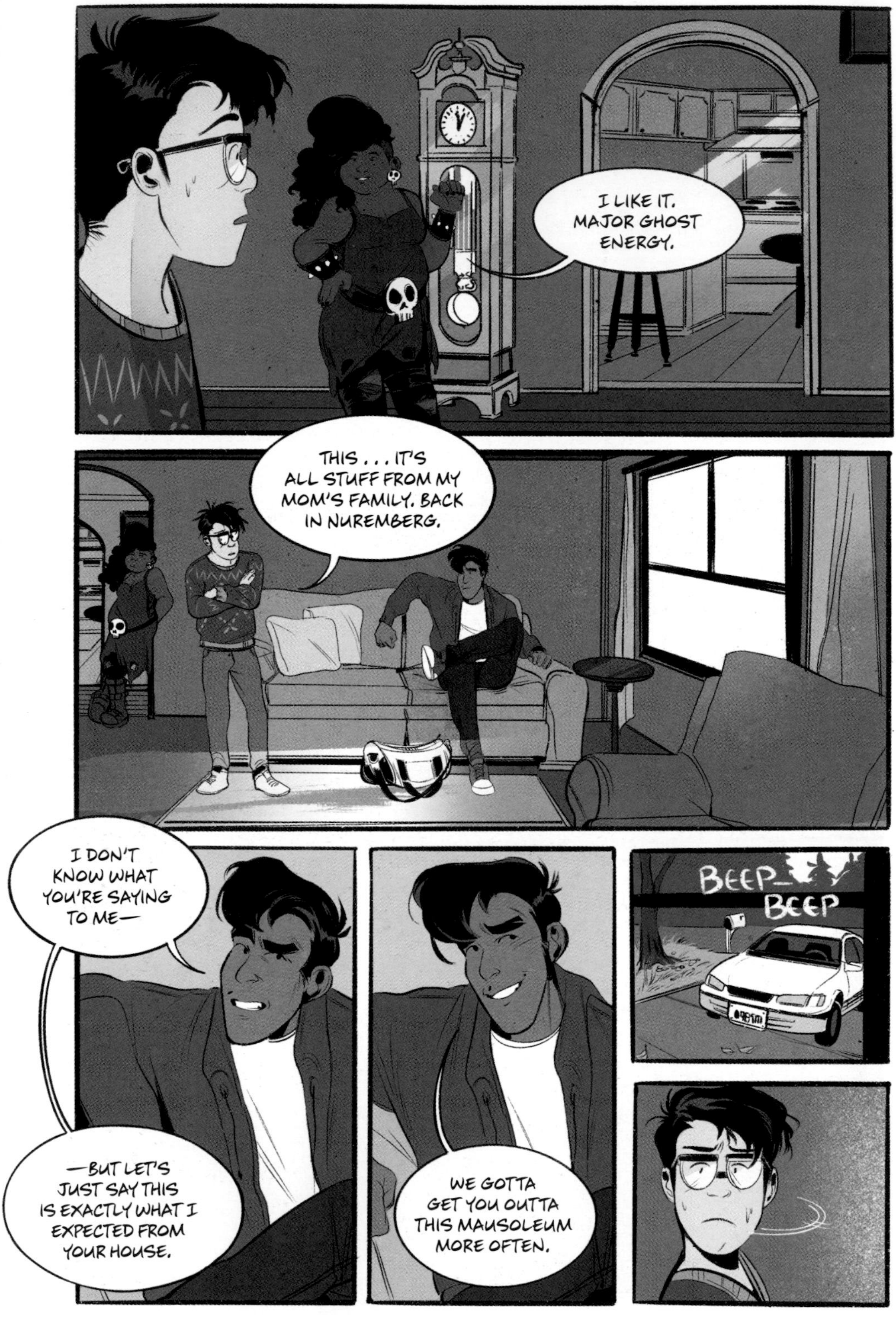
I LIKE IT. MAJOR GHOST ENERGY.
THIS . . . IT'S ALL STUFF FROM MY MOM'S FAMILY. BACK IN NUREMBERG.
I DON'T KNOW WHAT YOU'RE SAYING TO ME—
—BUT LET'S JUST SAY THIS IS EXACTLY WHAT I EXPECTED FROM YOUR HOUSE.
WE GOTTA GET YOU OUTTA THIS MAUSOLEUM MORE OFTEN.
BEEP_ BEEP

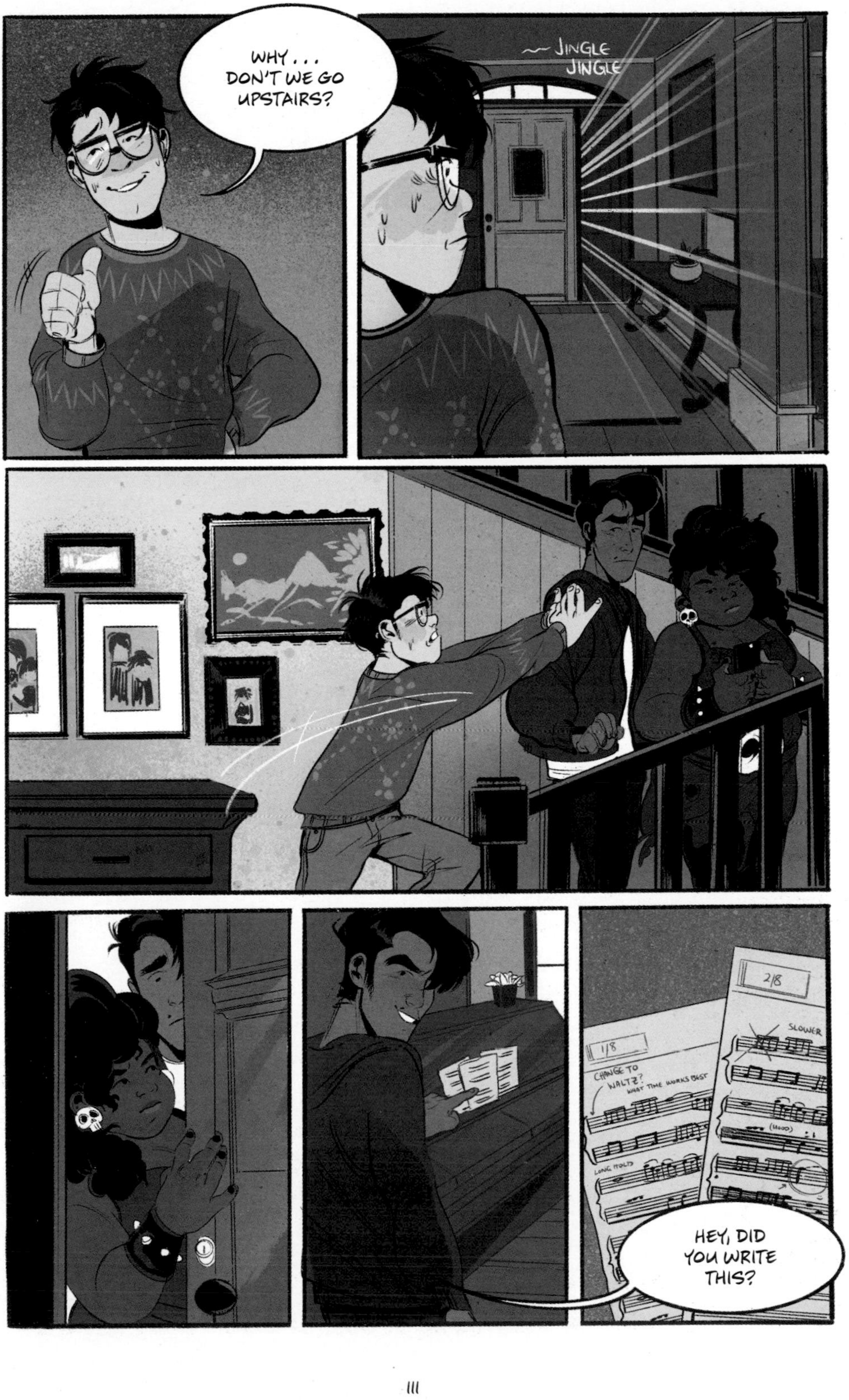
WHY . . . DON'T WE GO UPSTAIRS?
JINGLE JINGLE
1/8
CHANGE TO WALTZ?
WHAT TIME WORKS BEST
2/8
SLOWER
HEY, DID YOU WRITE THIS?

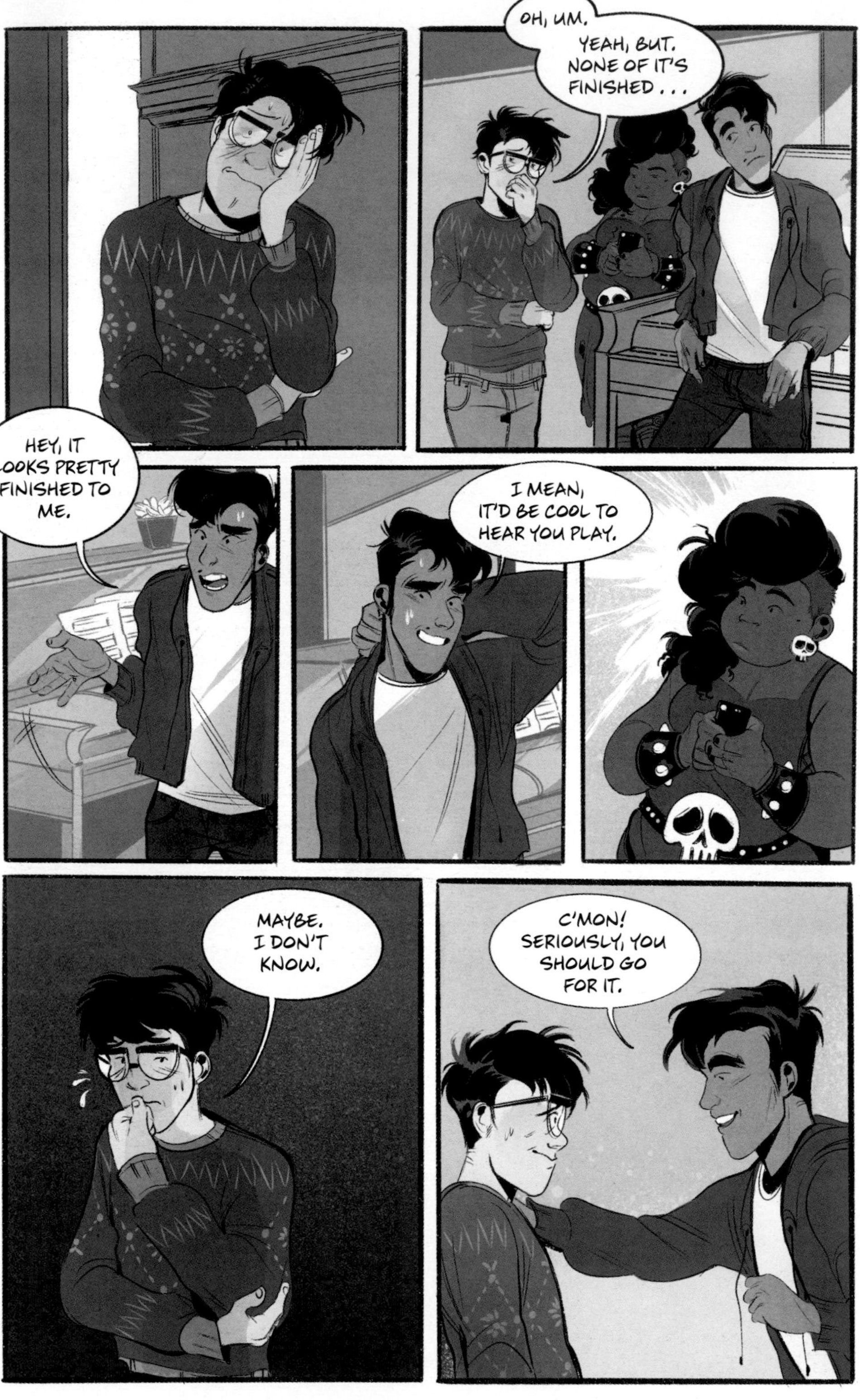
OH, UM.
YEAH, BUT. NONE OF IT'S FINISHED . . .
HEY, IT LOOKS PRETTY FINISHED TO ME.
I MEAN, IT'D BE COOL TO HEAR YOU PLAY.
MAYBE. I DON'T KNOW.
C'MON! SERIOUSLY, YOU SHOULD GO FOR IT.

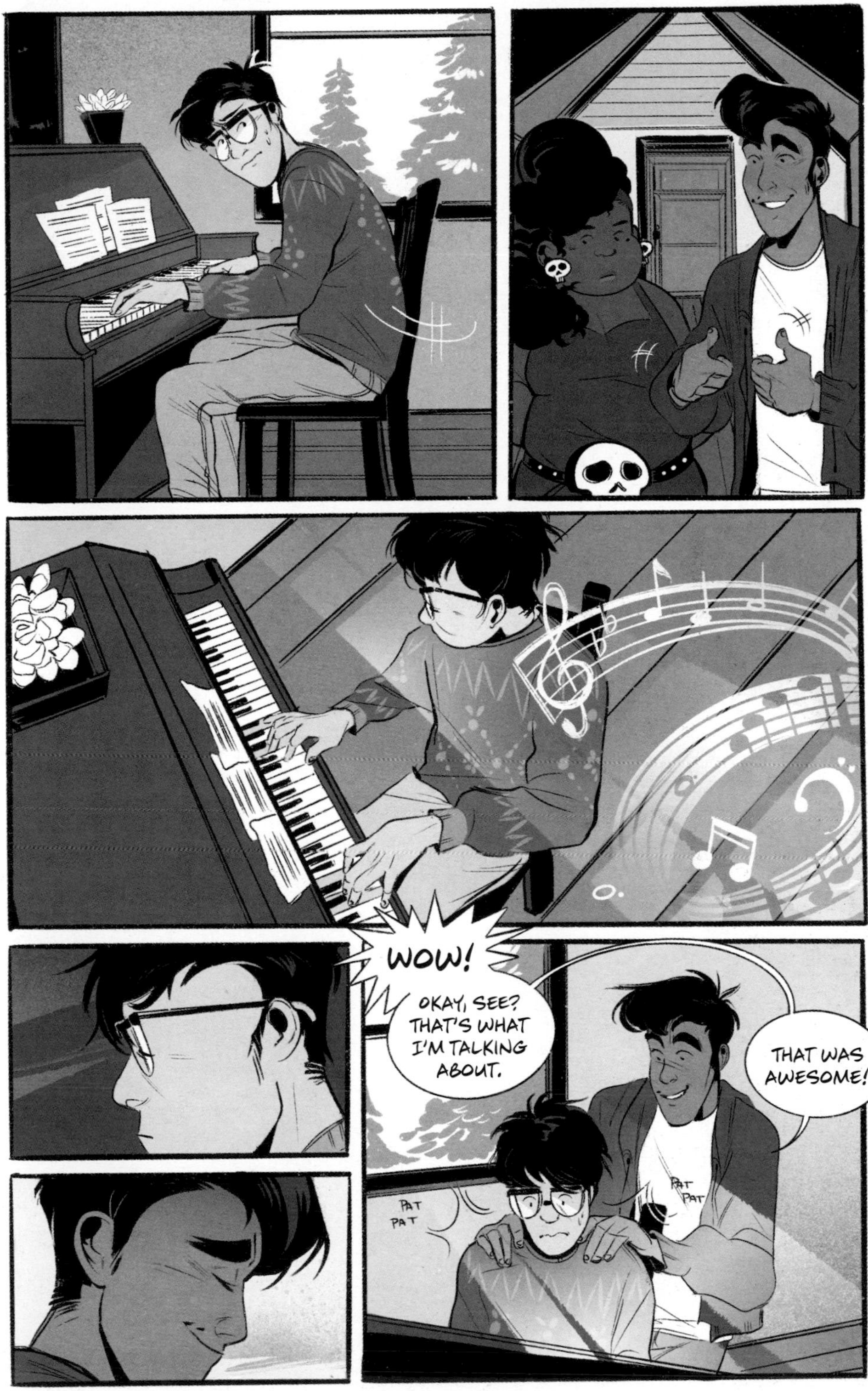
WOW!
OKAY, SEE? THAT'S WHAT I'M TALKING ABOUT.
THAT WAS AWESOME!
PAT PAT
PAT PAT

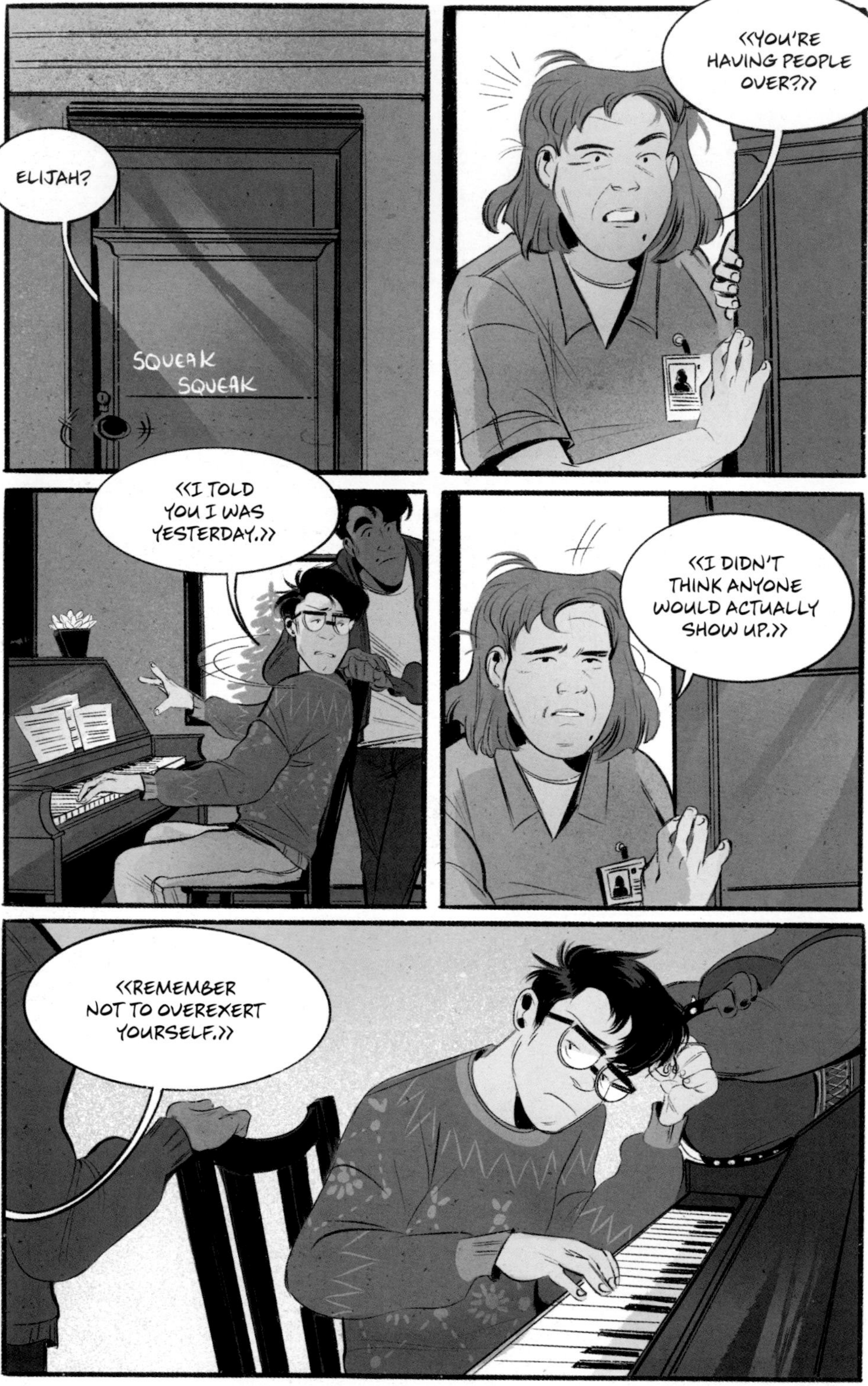
ELIJAH?
SQUEAK SQUEAK
<<YOU'RE HAVING PEOPLE OVER?>>
<<I TOLD YOU I WAS YESTERDAY.>>
<<I DIDN'T THINK ANYONE WOULD ACTUALLY SHOW UP.>>
<<REMEMBER NOT TO OVEREXERT YOURSELF.>>

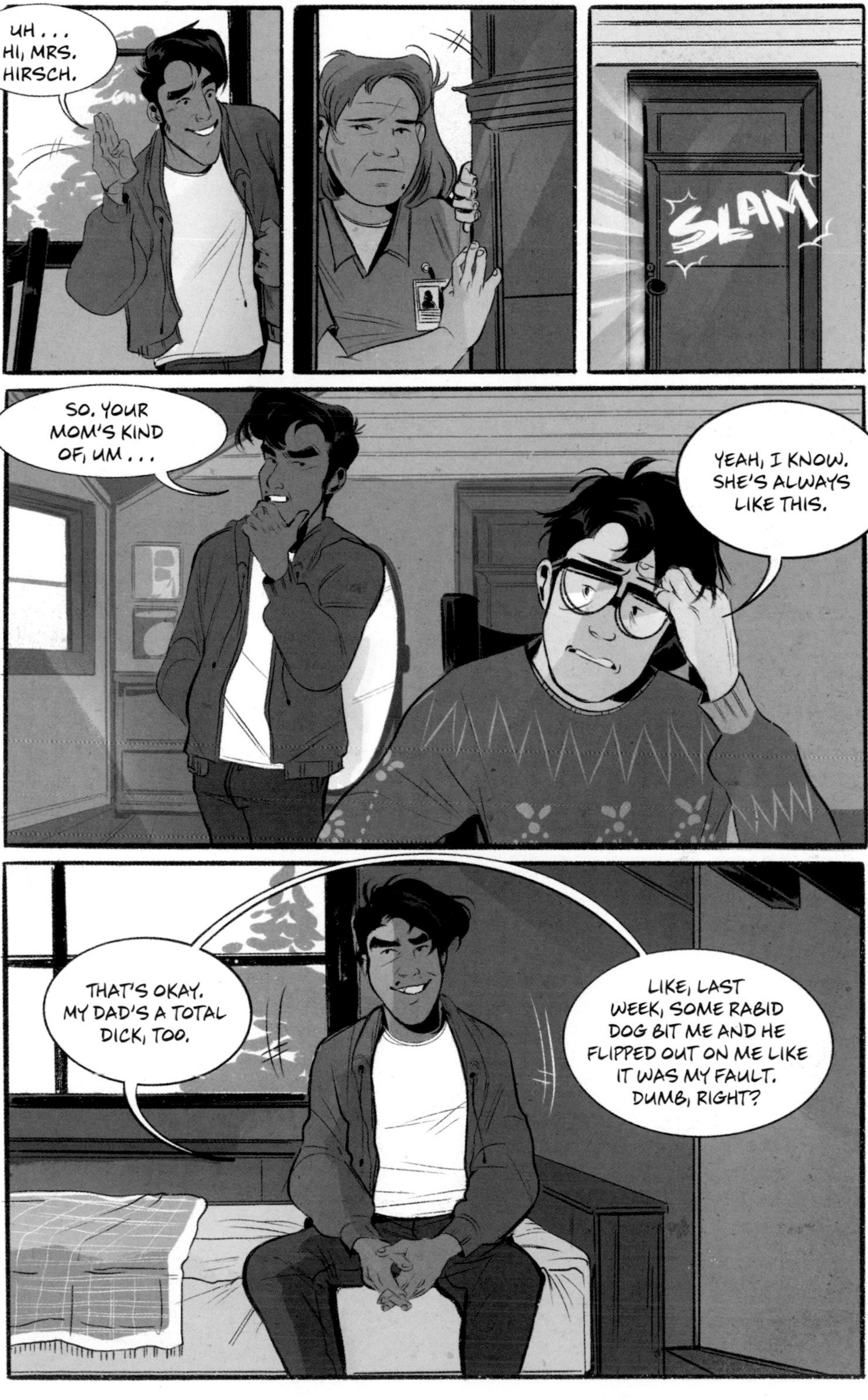
UH . . . HI, MRS. HIRSCH.
SLAM
SO. YOUR MOM'S KIND OF, UM . . .
YEAH, I KNOW. SHE'S ALWAYS LIKE THIS.
THAT'S OKAY. MY DAD'S A TOTAL DICK, TOO.
LIKE, LAST WEEK, SOME RABID DOG BIT ME AND HE FLIPPED OUT ON ME LIKE IT WAS MY FAULT. DUMB, RIGHT?

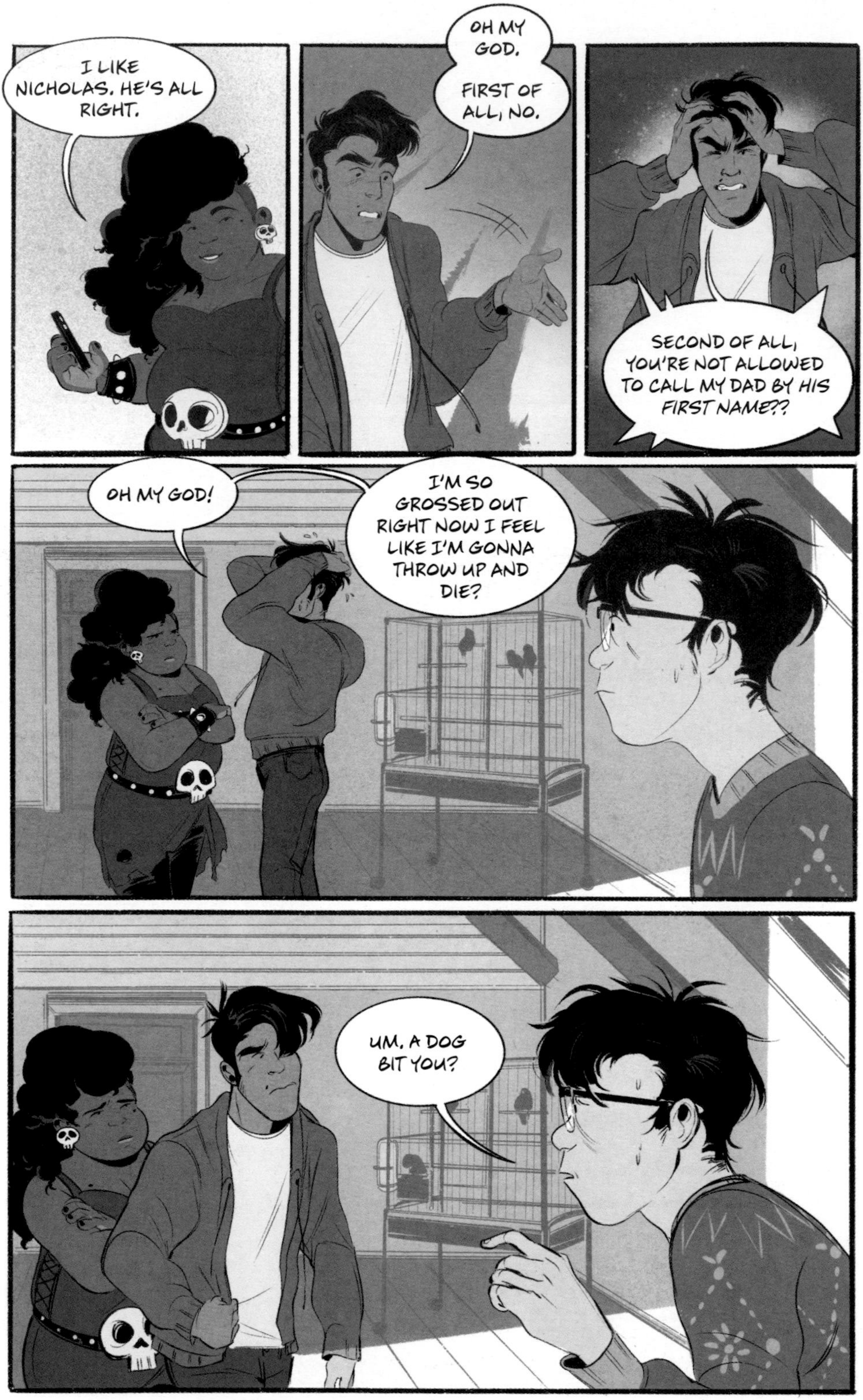
I LIKE NICHOLAS. HE'S ALL RIGHT.
OH MY GOD.
FIRST OF ALL, NO.
SECOND OF ALL, YOU'RE NOT ALLOWED TO CALL MY DAD BY HIS FIRST NAME??
OH MY GOD!
I'M SO GROSSED OUT RIGHT NOW I FEEL LIKE I'M GONNA THROW UP AND DIE?
UM. A DOG BIT YOU?

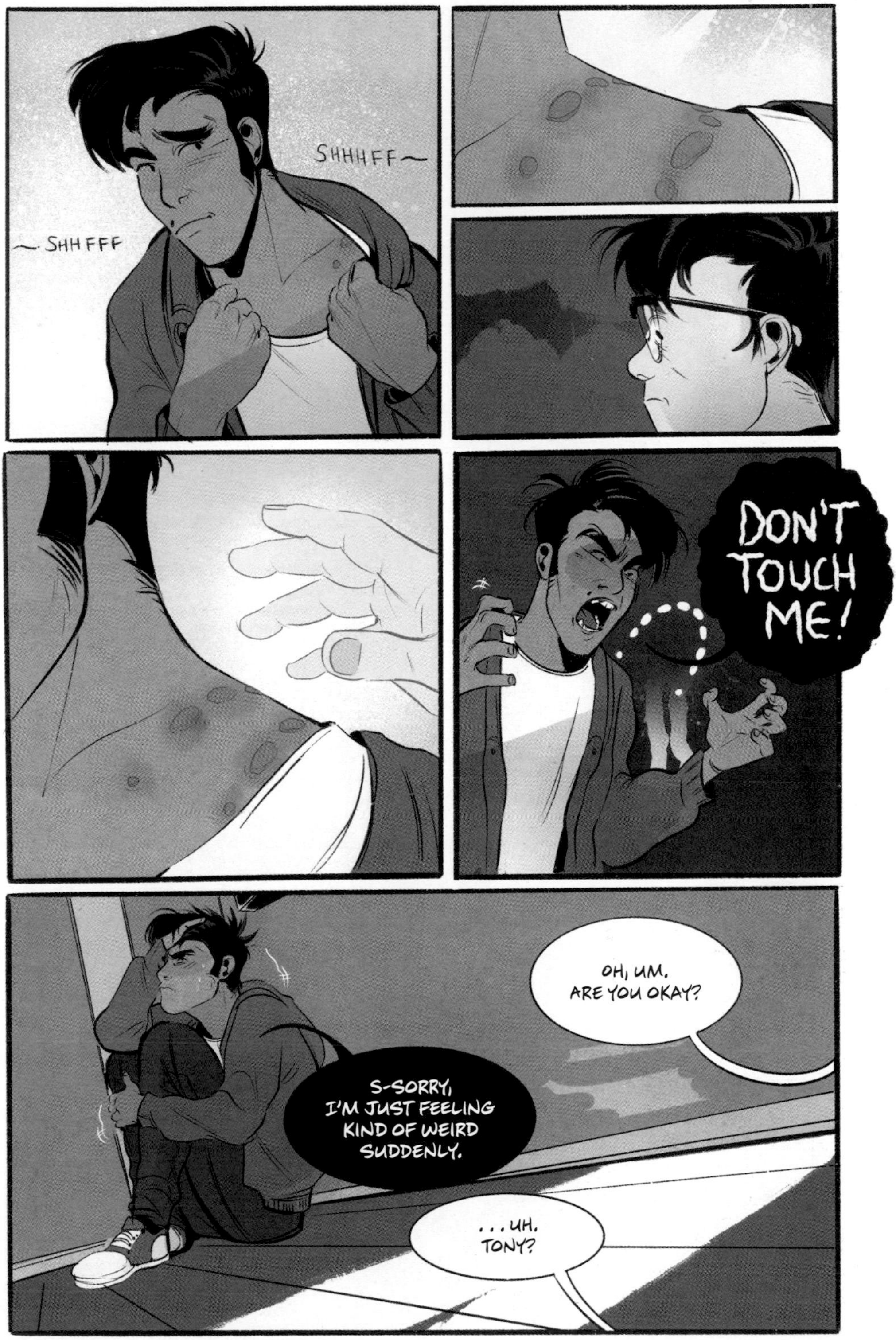
SHHHFF~
~SHHFFF
DON'T TOUCH ME!
OH, UM. ARE YOU OKAY?
S-SORRY, I'M JUST FEELING KIND OF WEIRD SUDDENLY.
...UH. TONY?

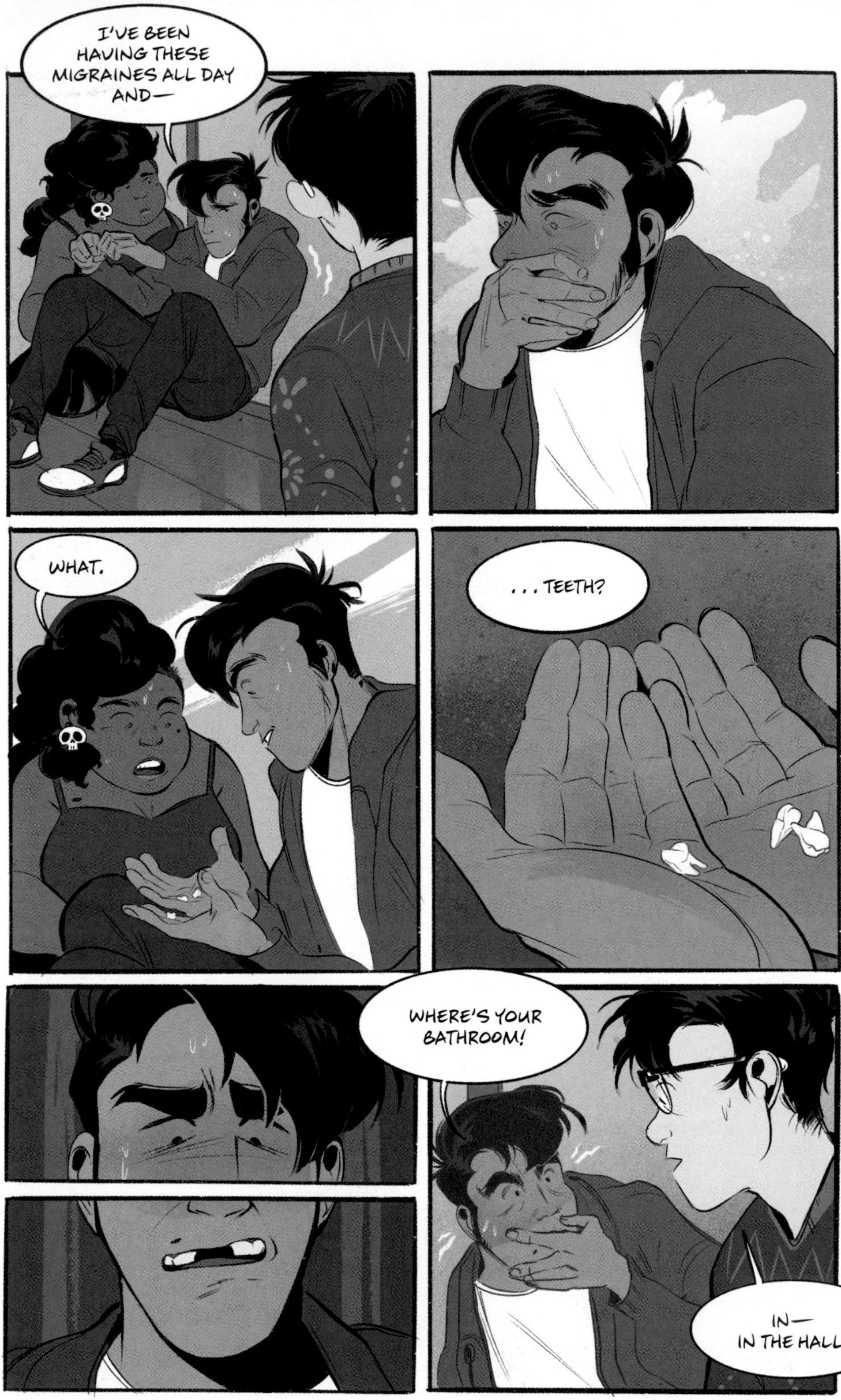
I'VE BEEN HAVING THESE MIGRAINES ALL DAY AND—
WHAT.
. . . TEETH?
WHERE'S YOUR BATHROOM!
IN—
IN THE HALL.

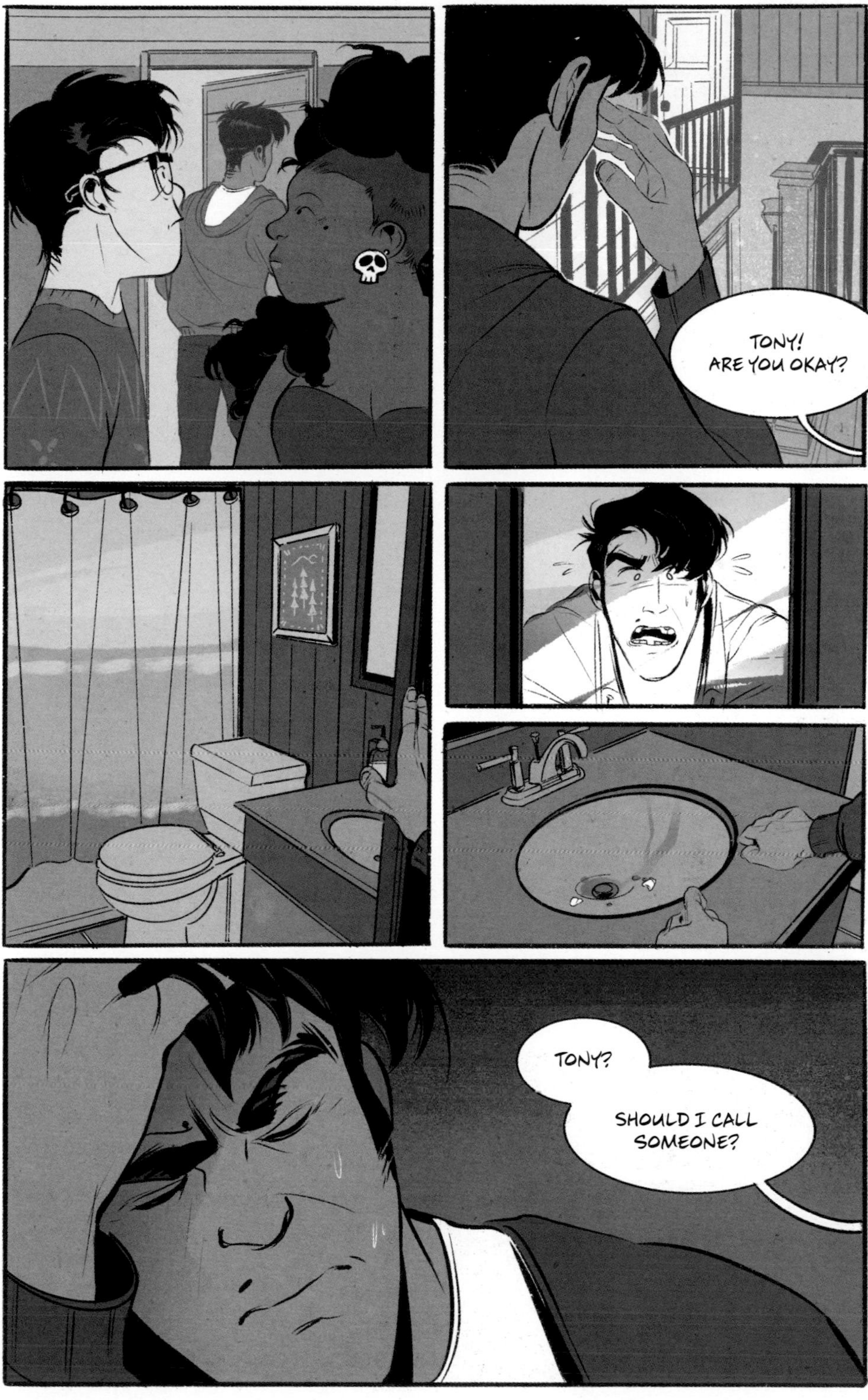
TONY!
ARE YOU OKAY?
TONY?
SHOULD I CALL SOMEONE?

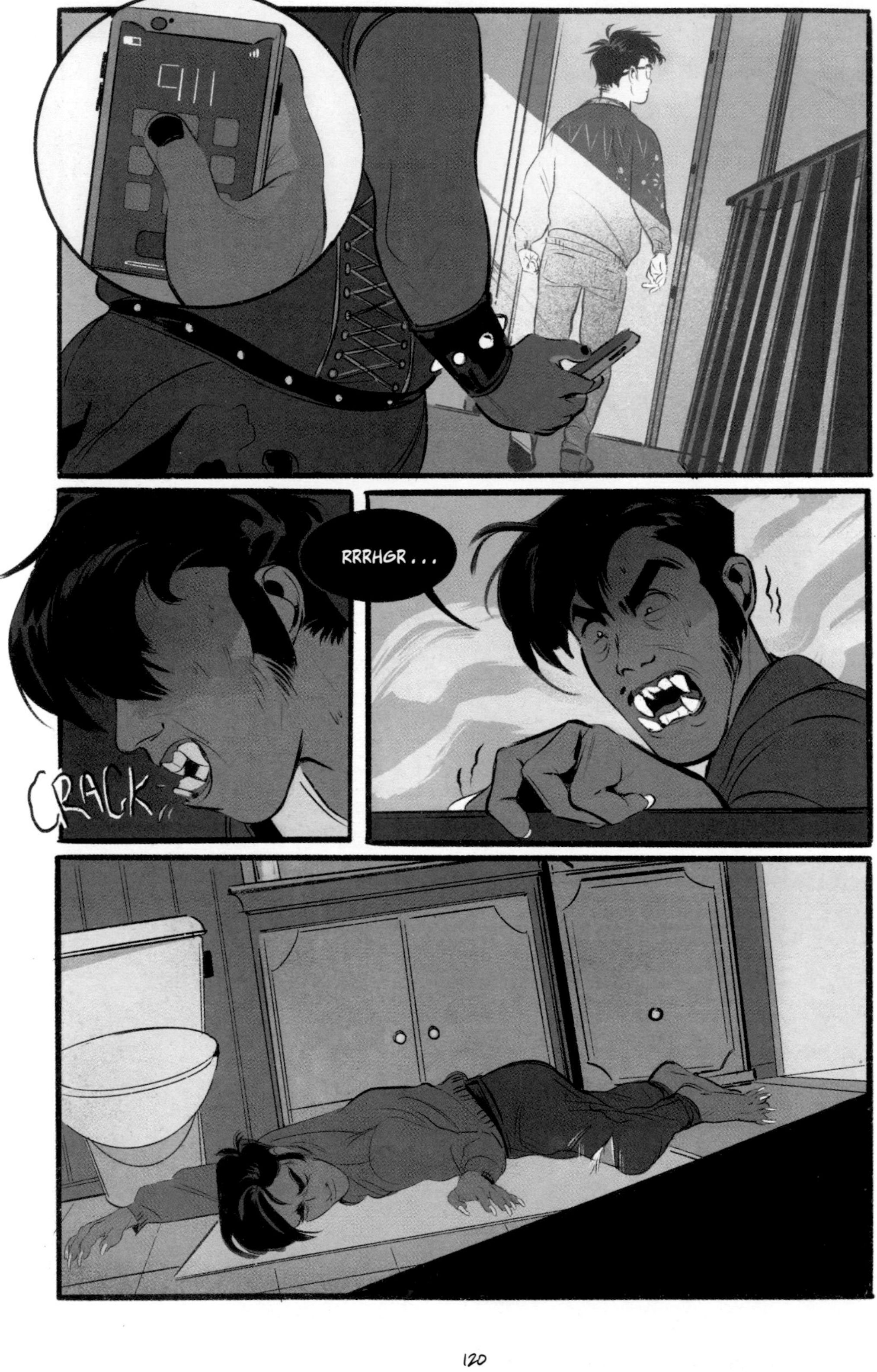
911
RRRHGR . . .
CRACK

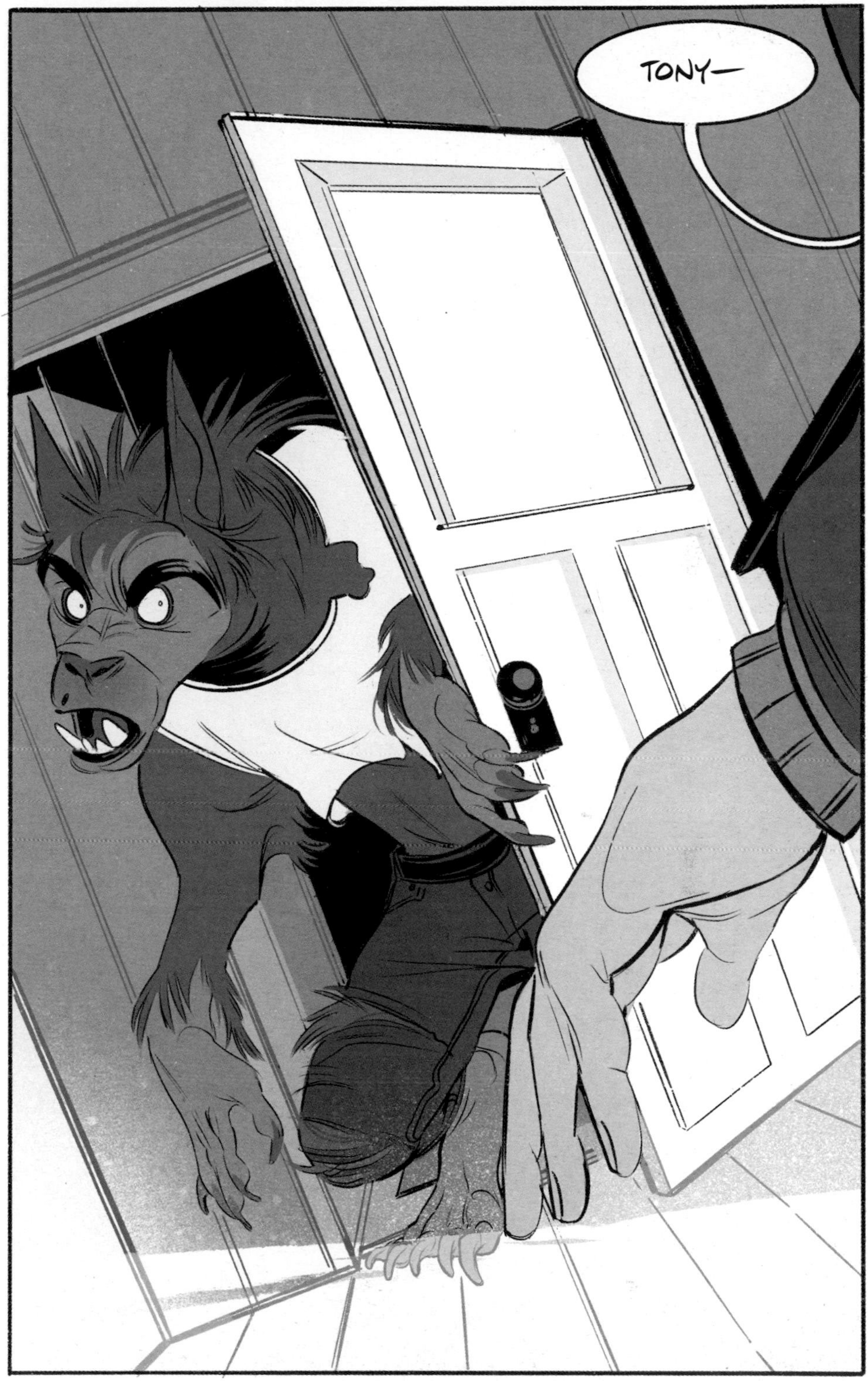
TONY—

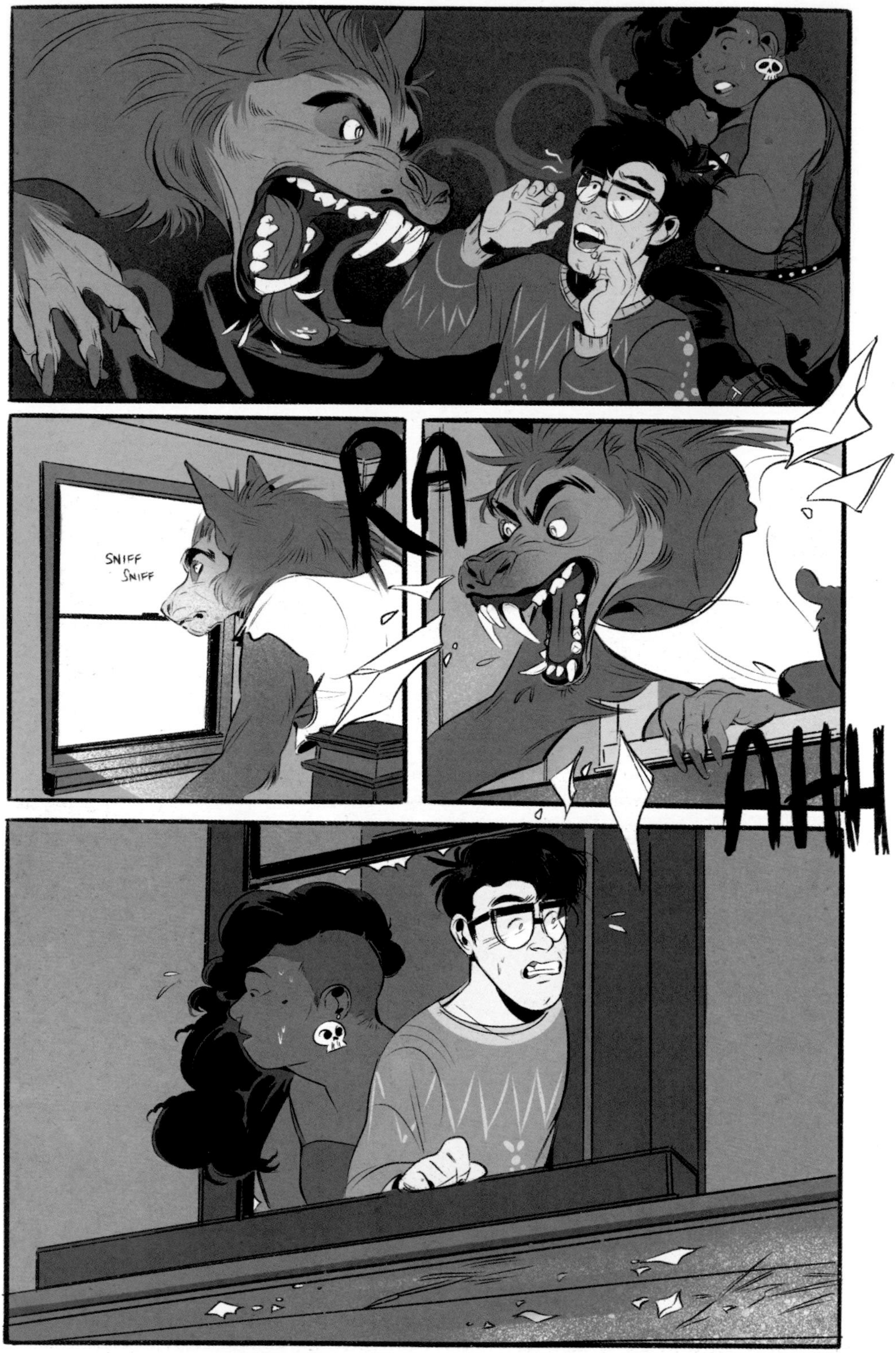
SNIFF
SNIFF
RA
AHH

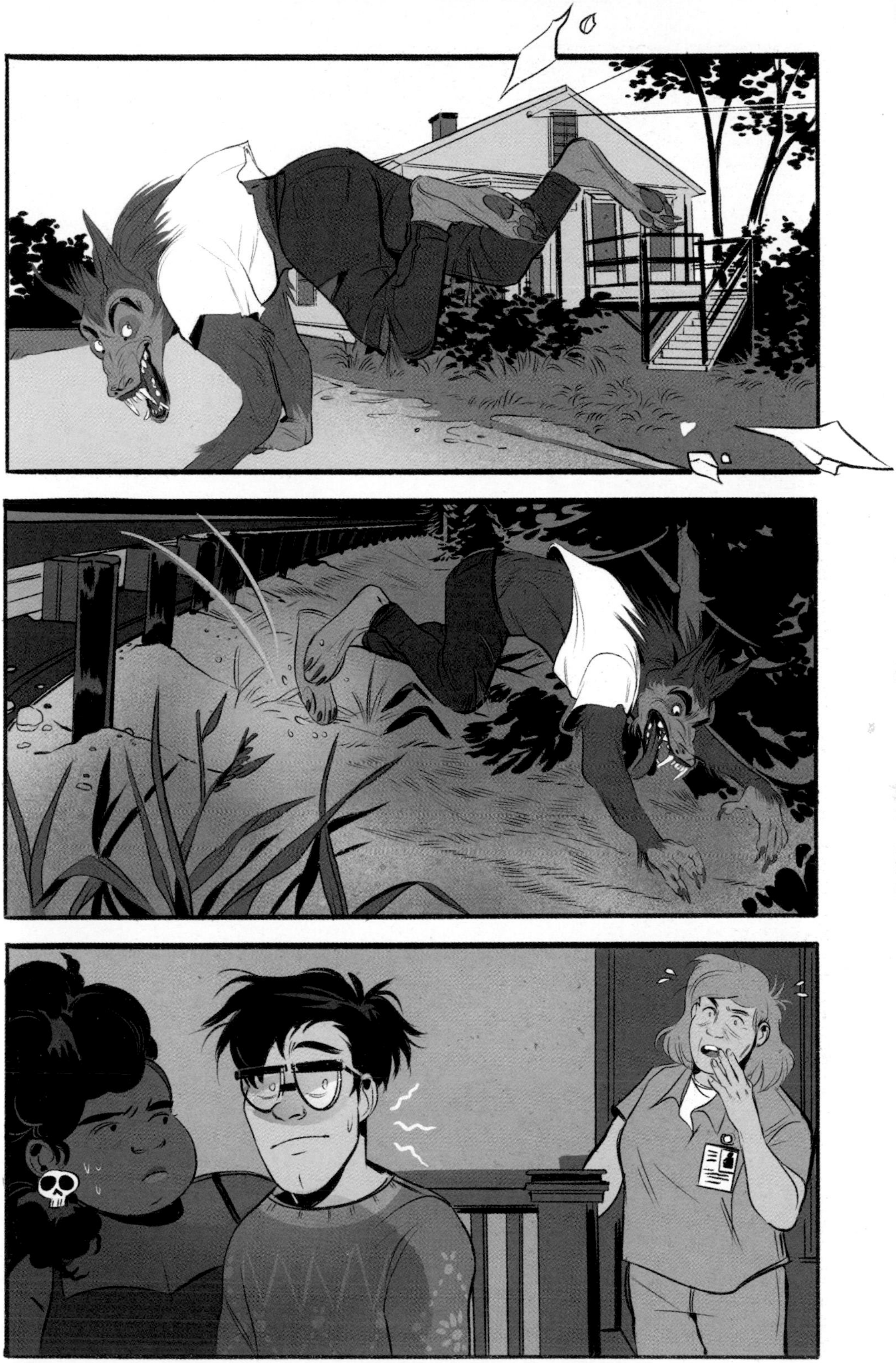

CHAPTER FIVE
THE CABIN

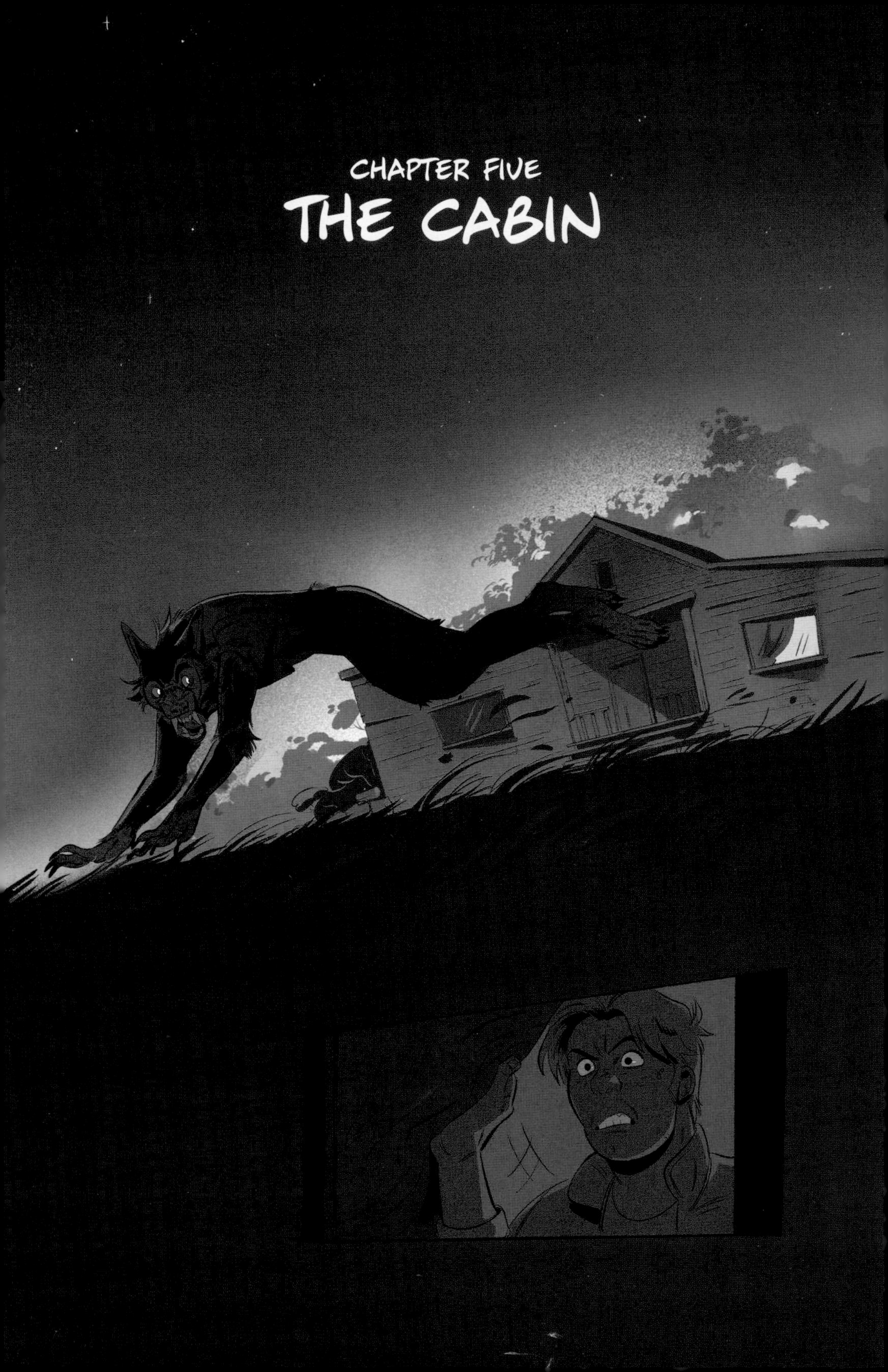

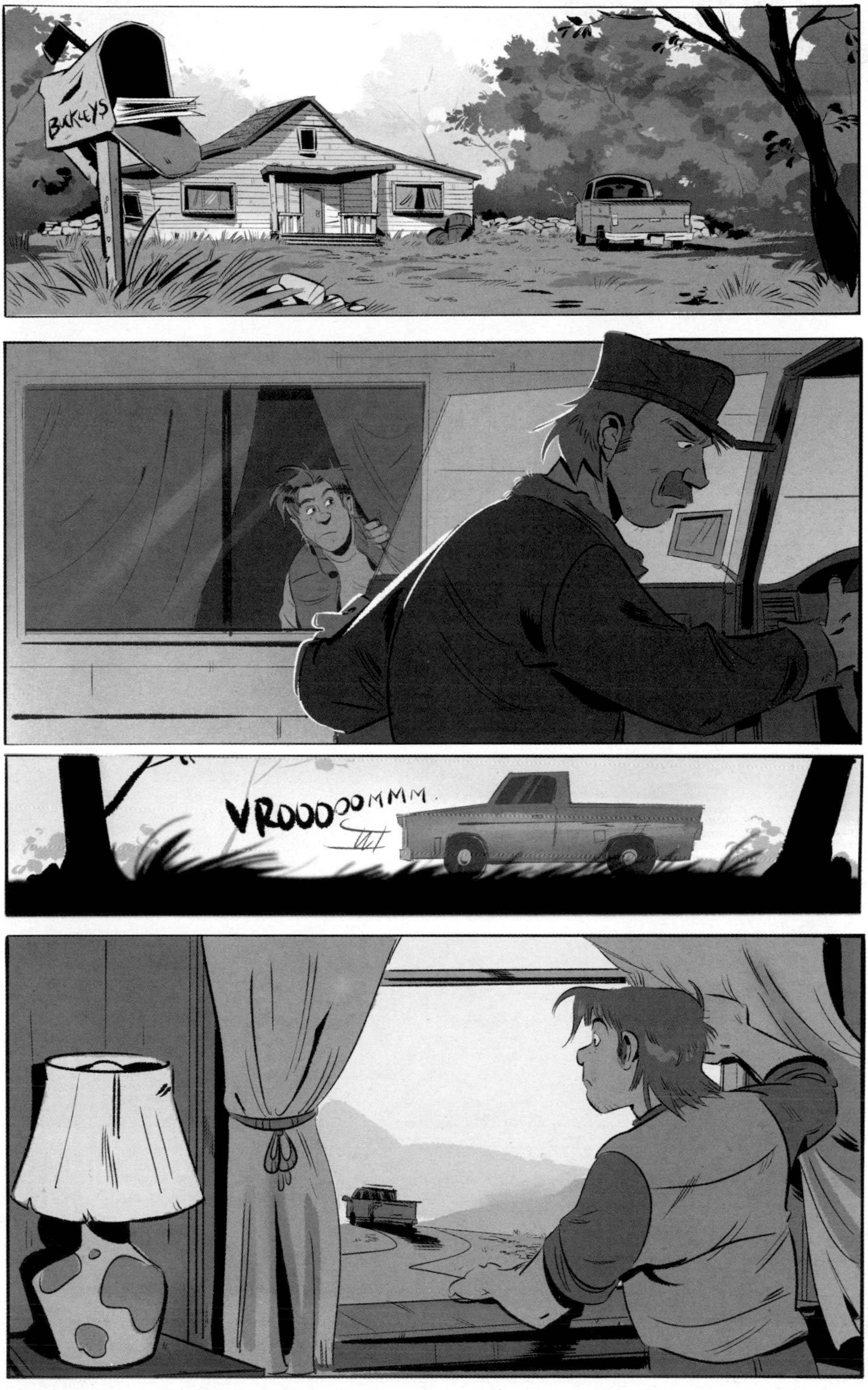
BUCKLEYS
VROOOOOMMM

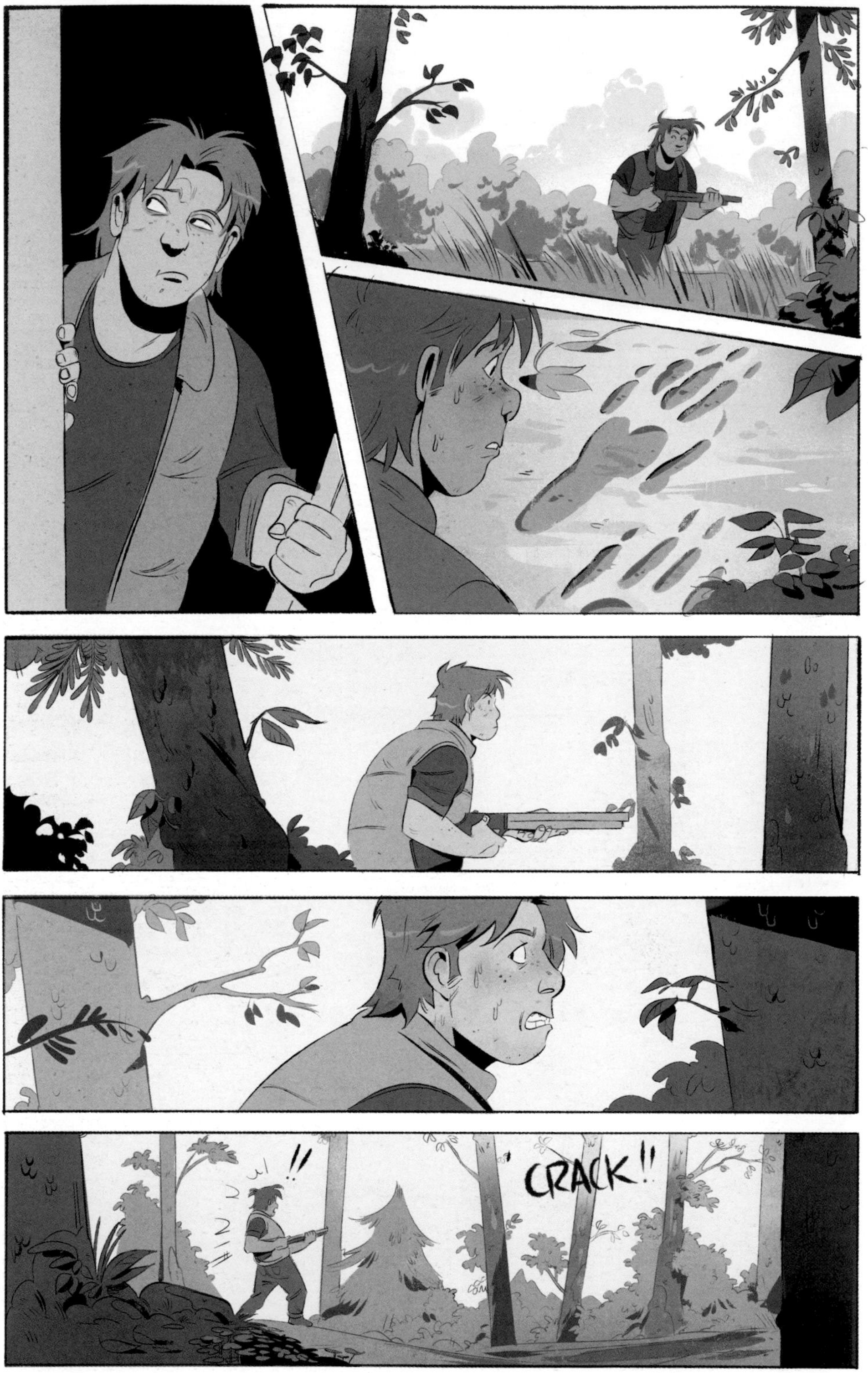
!!
CRACK!!

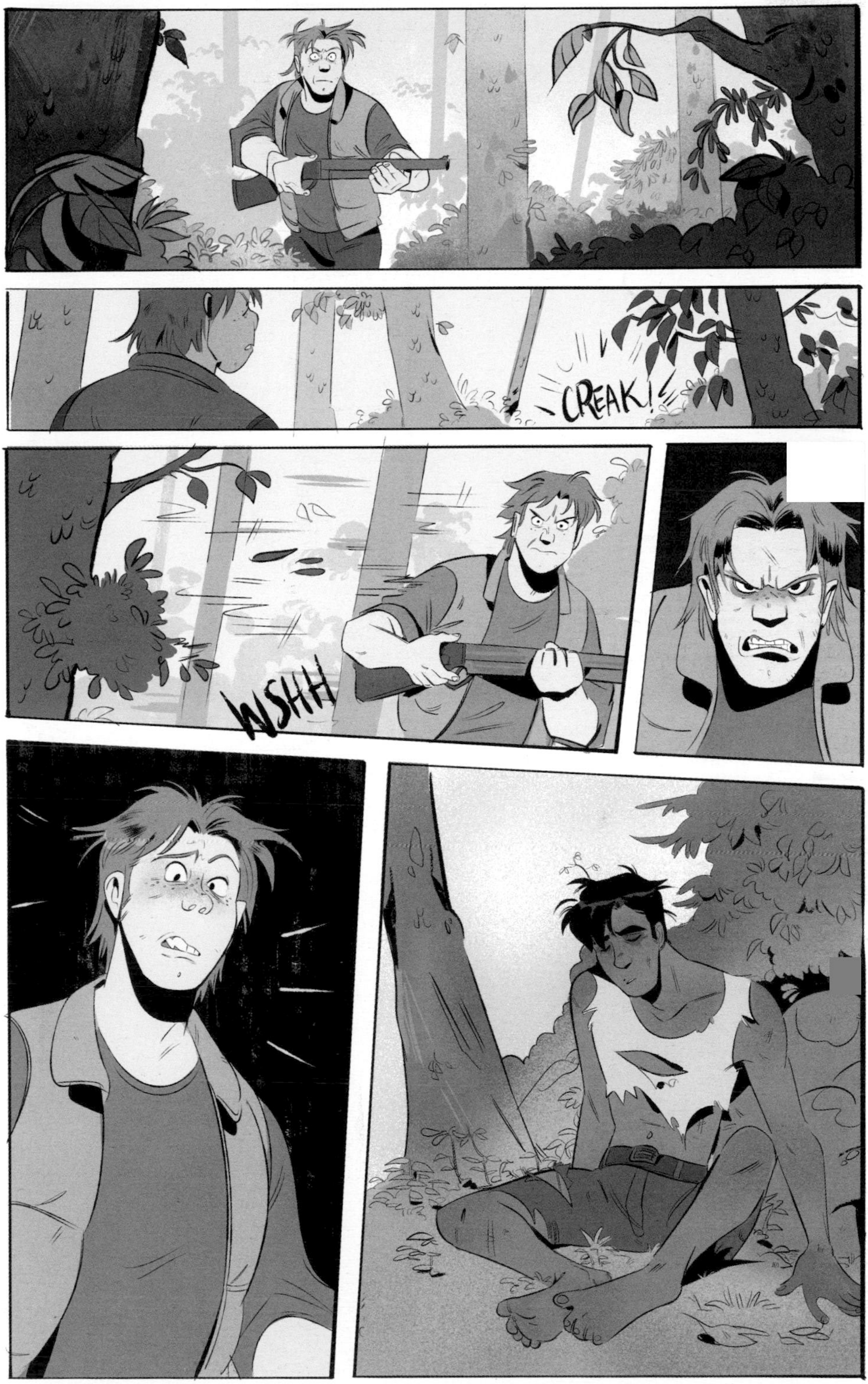
CREAK!
WSHH

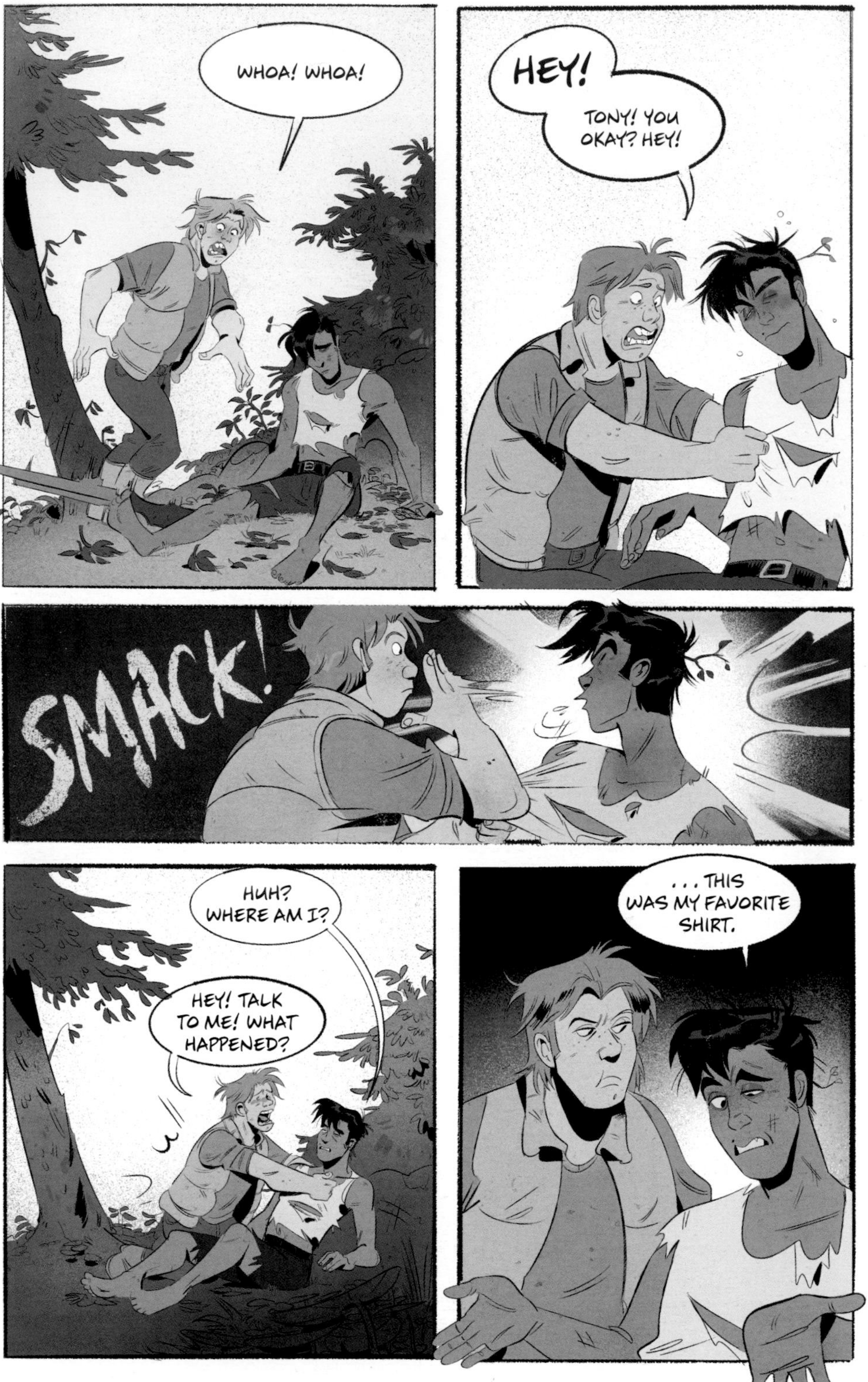
WHOA! WHOA!
HEY!
TONY! YOU OKAY? HEY!
SMACK!
HUH? WHERE AM I?
HEY! TALK TO ME! WHAT HAPPENED?
. . . THIS WAS MY FAVORITE SHIRT.

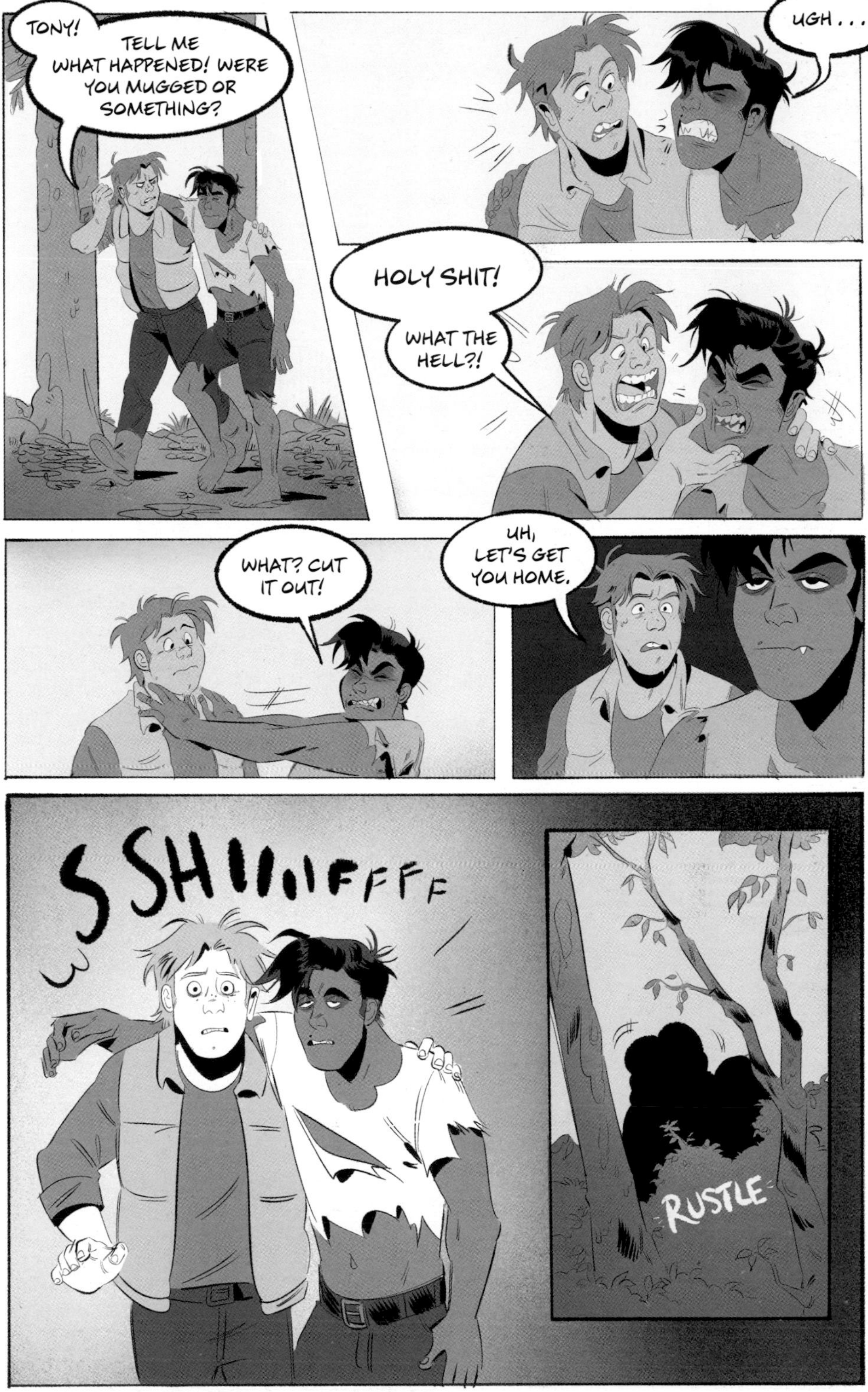
TONY!
TELL ME WHAT HAPPENED! WERE YOU MUGGED OR SOMETHING?
UGH . . .
HOLY SHIT!
WHAT THE HELL?!
WHAT? CUT IT OUT!
UH, LET'S GET YOU HOME.
SSHIIIIFFFF
RUSTLE

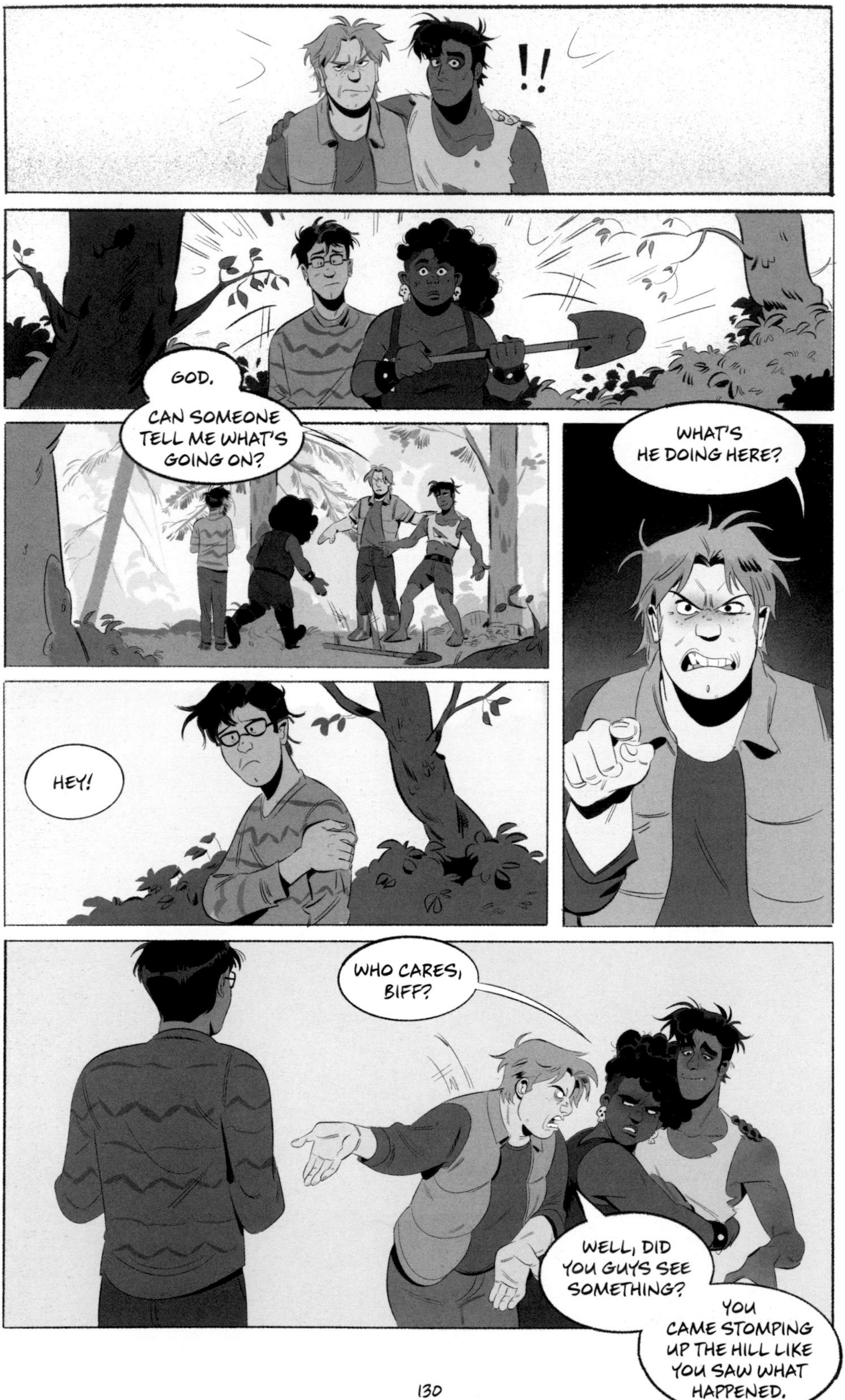
!!
GOD.
CAN SOMEONE TELL ME WHAT'S GOING ON?
WHAT'S HE DOING HERE?
HEY!
WHO CARES, BIFF?
WELL, DID YOU GUYS SEE SOMETHING?
YOU CAME STOMPING UP THE HILL LIKE YOU SAW WHAT HAPPENED.

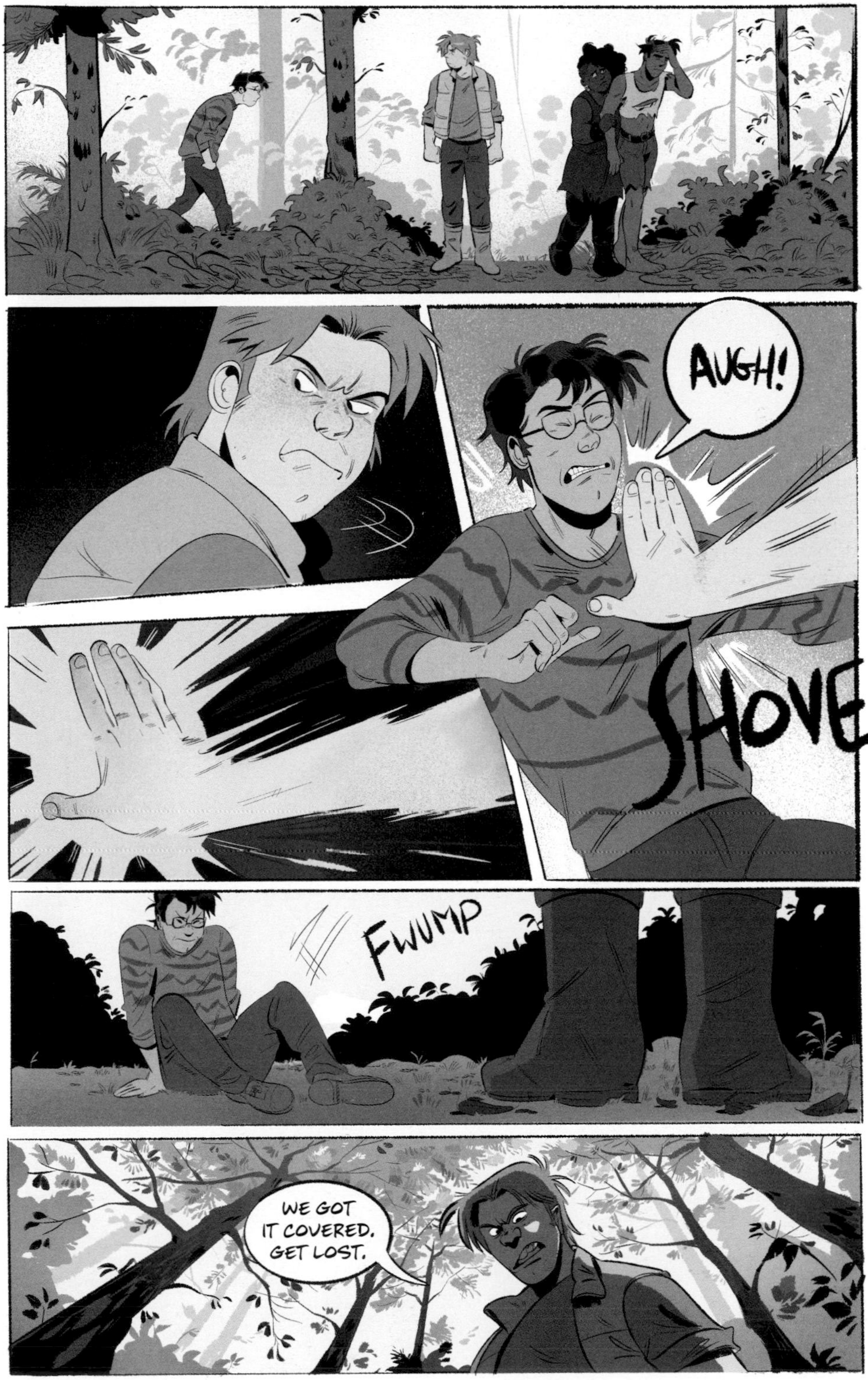
AUGH!
SHOVE
FWUMP
WE GOT IT COVERED. GET LOST.

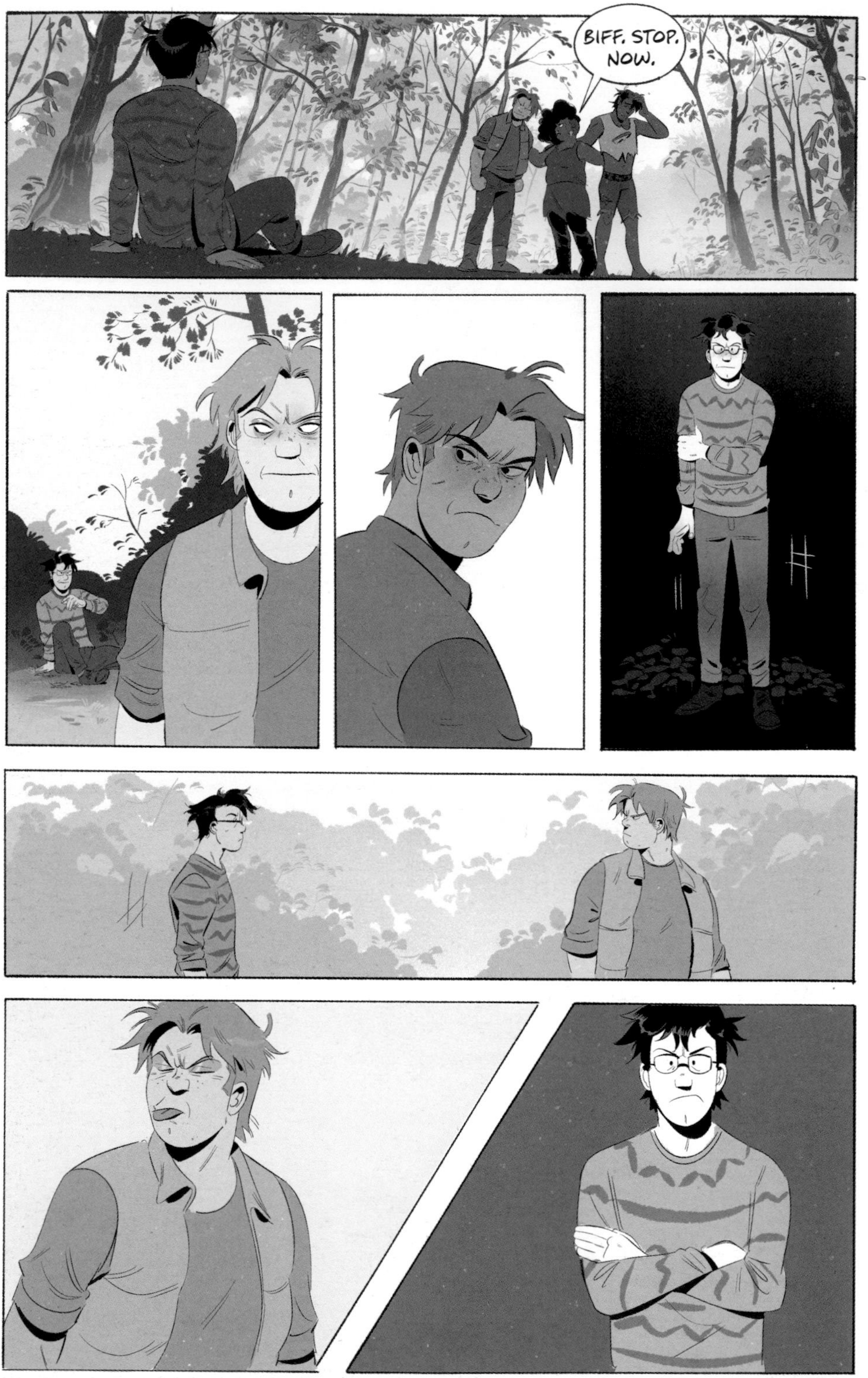
BIFF. STOP. NOW.

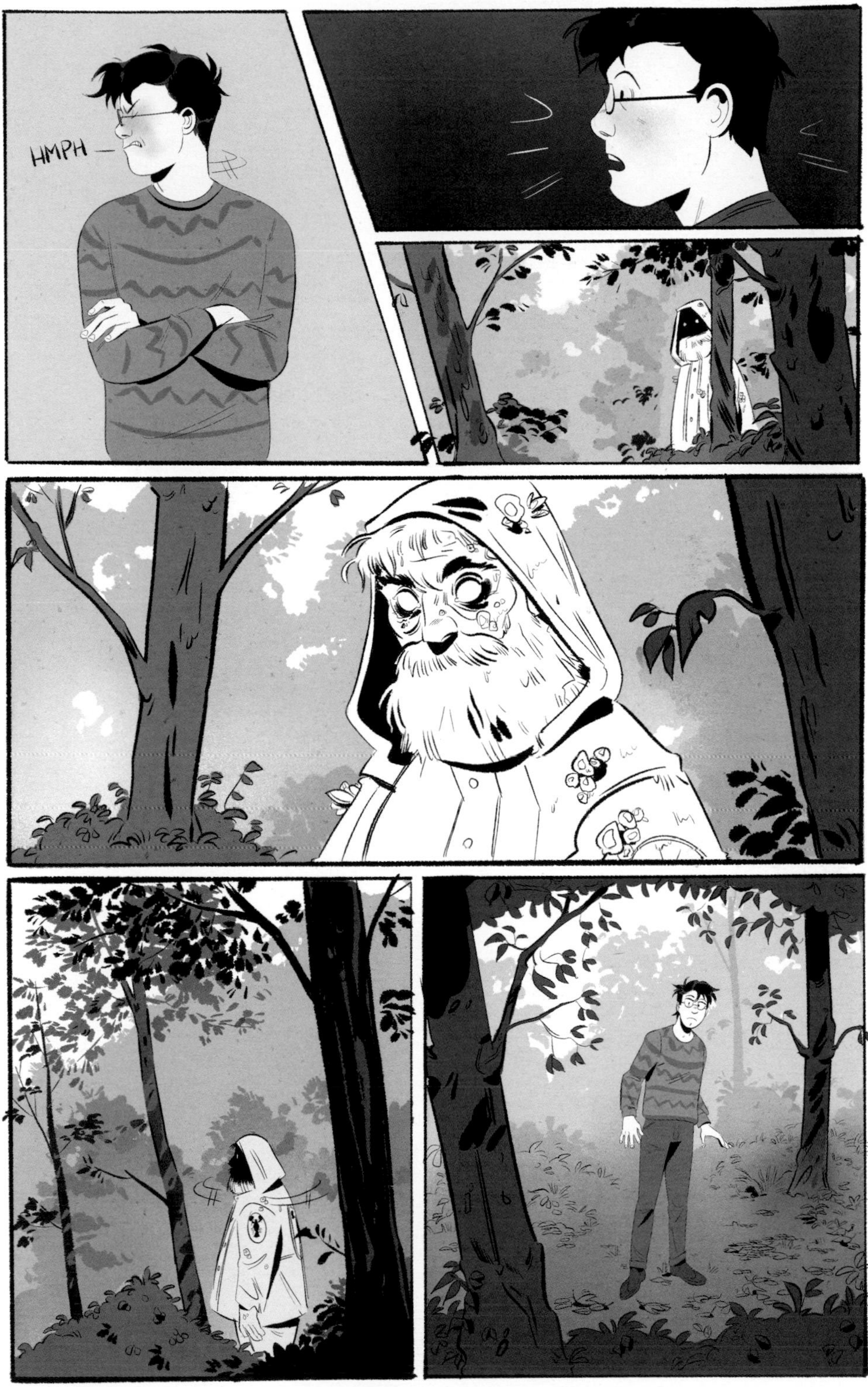
HMPH

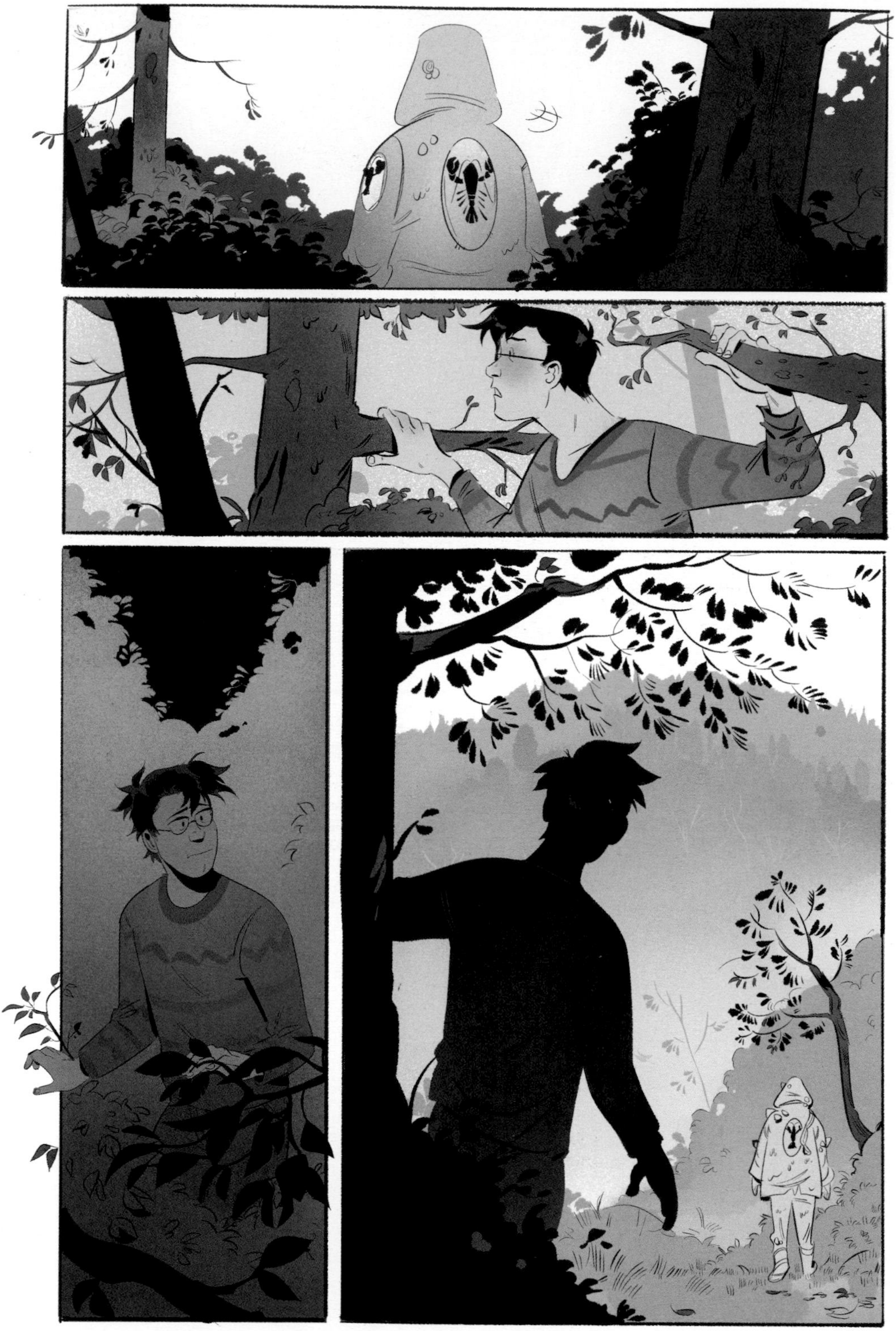

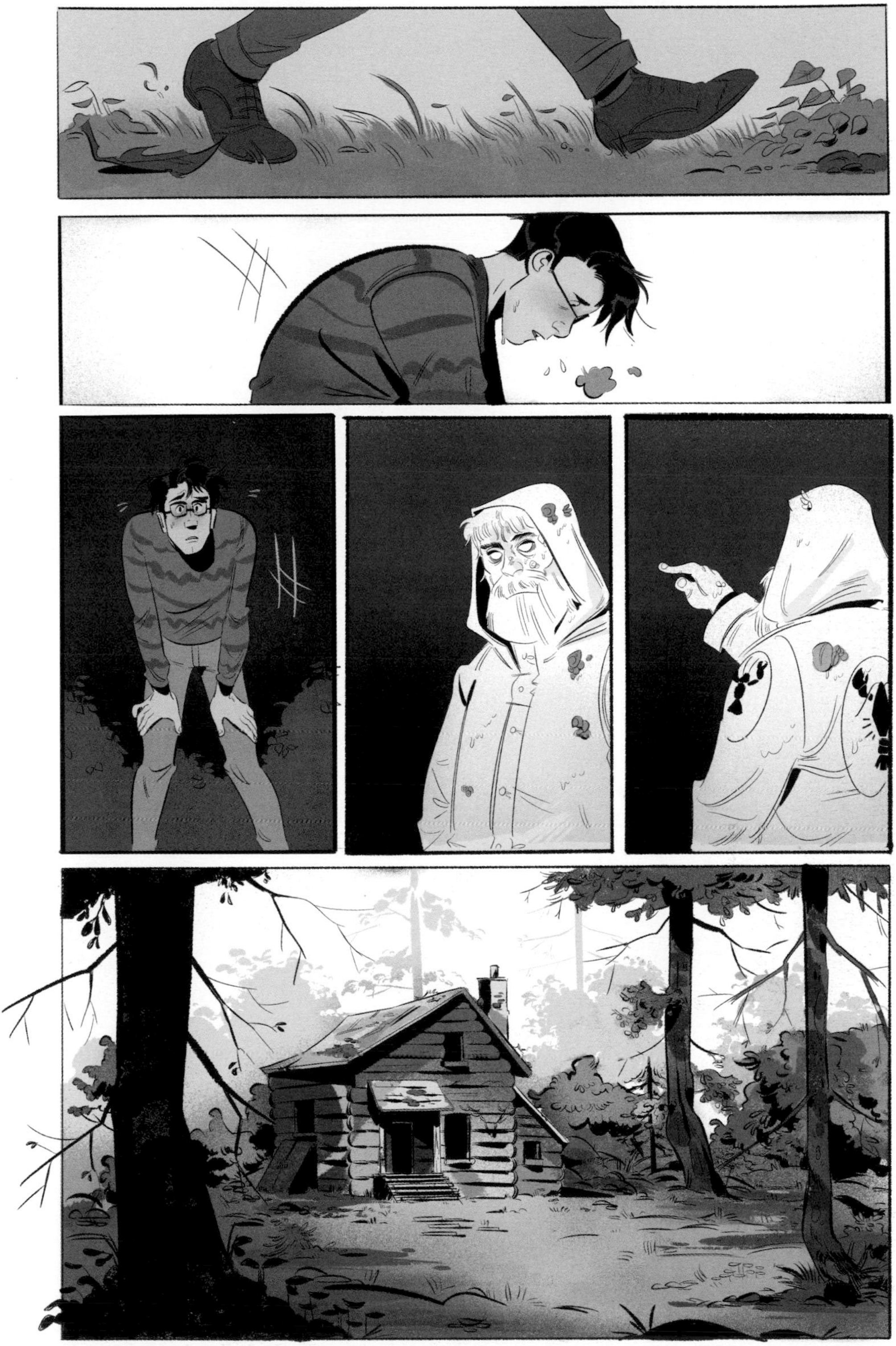

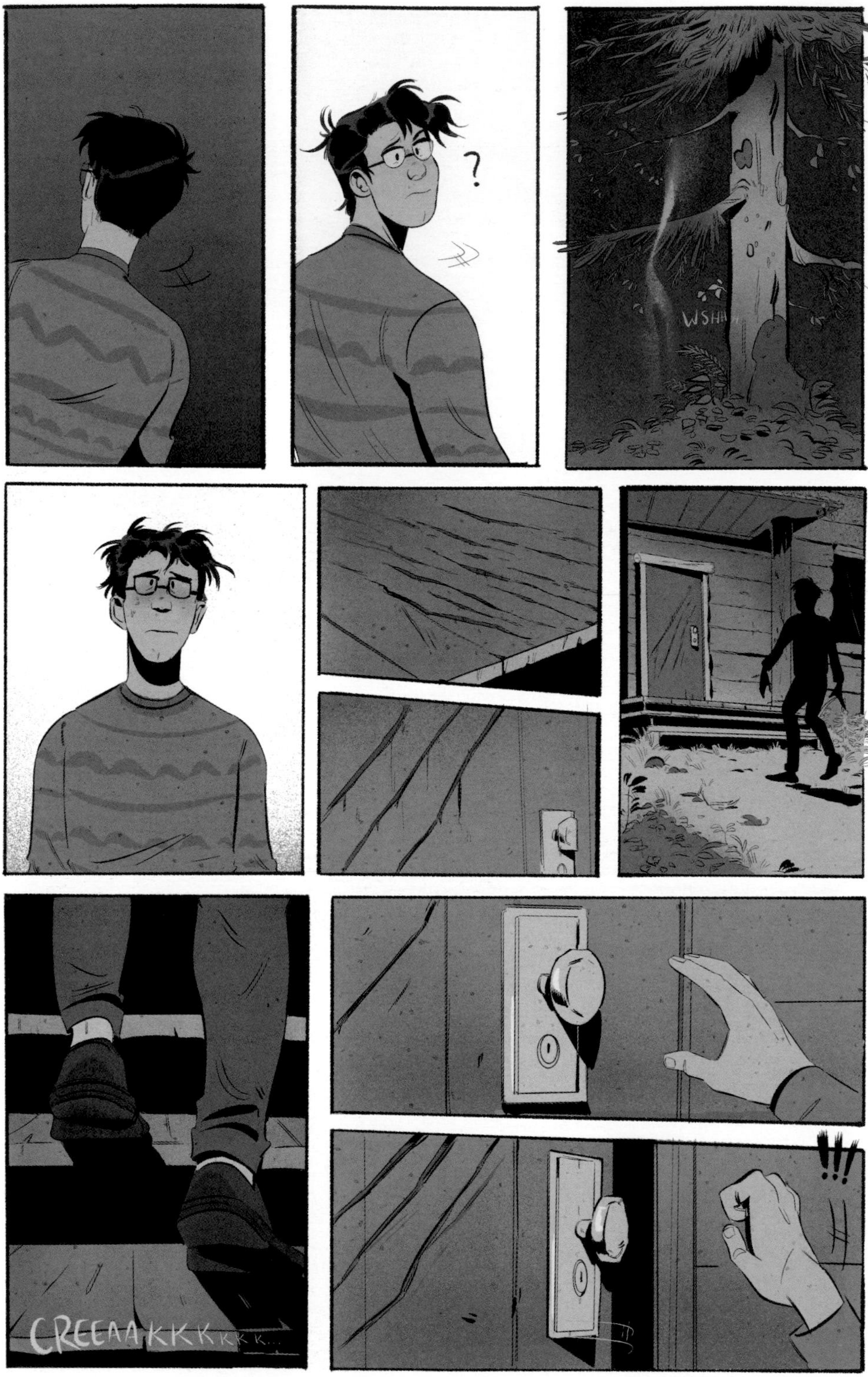
?
WSHHH
CREEAAKKKkkk...
!!!

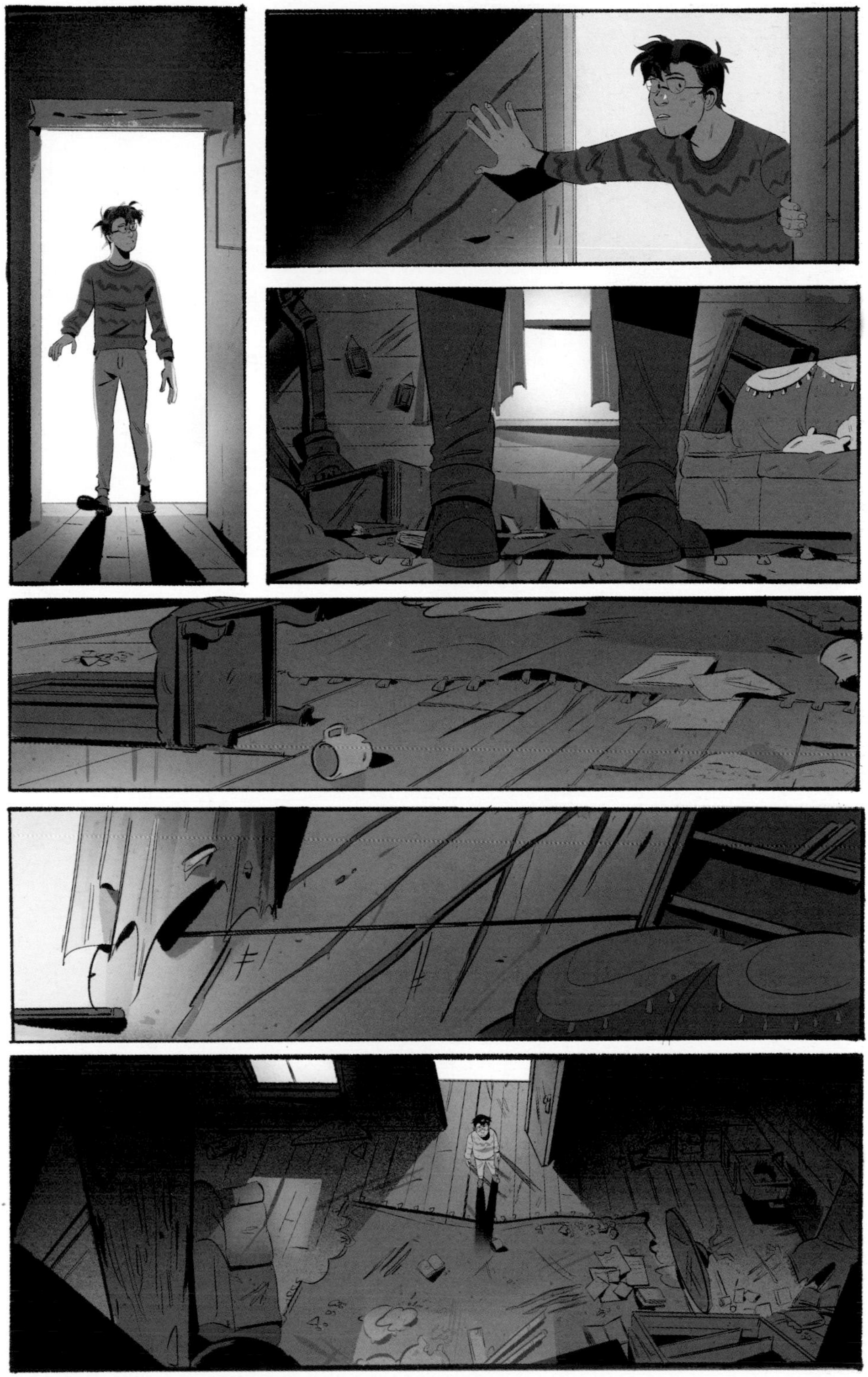

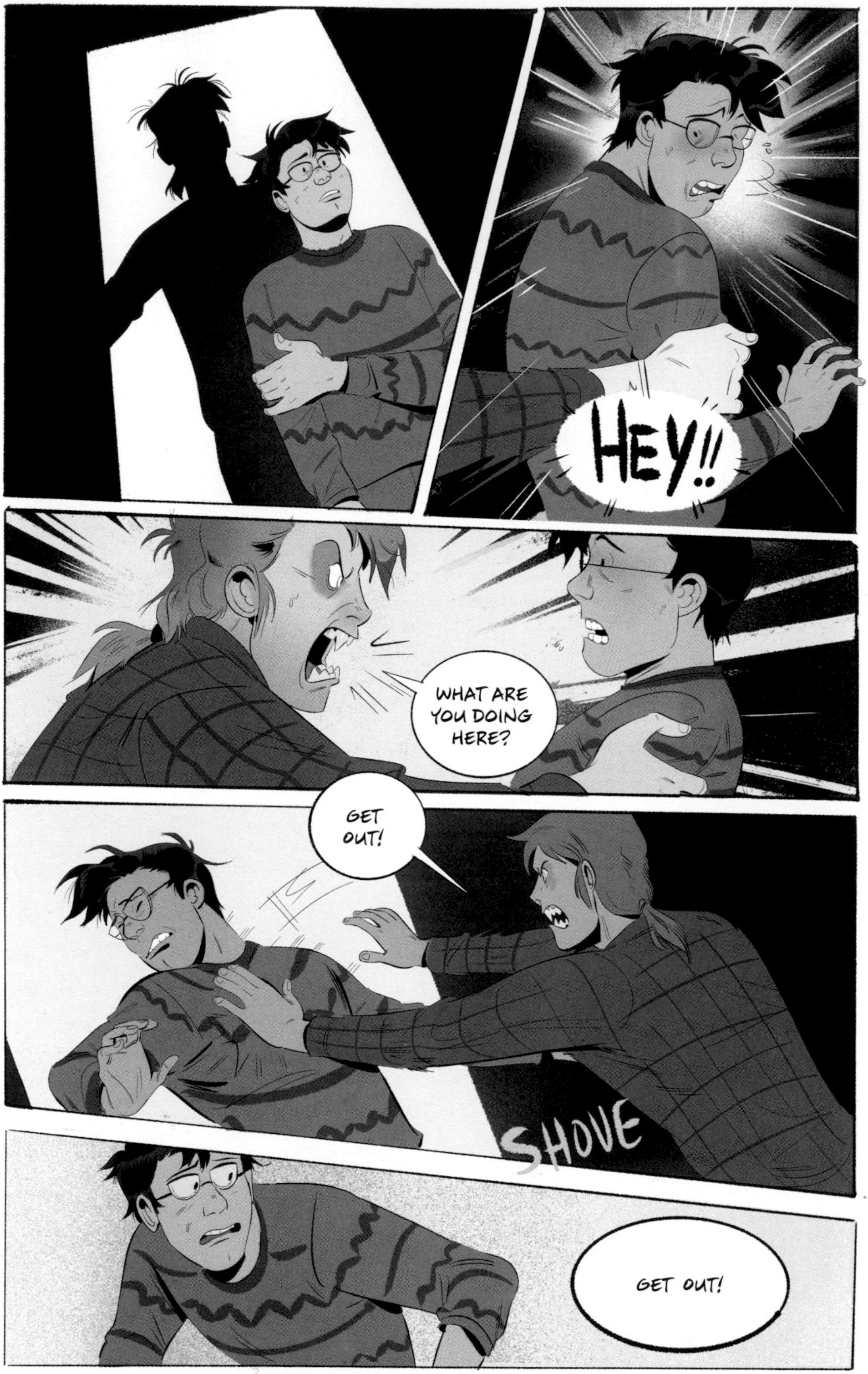
HEY!!
WHAT ARE YOU DOING HERE?
GET OUT!
SHOVE
GET OUT!

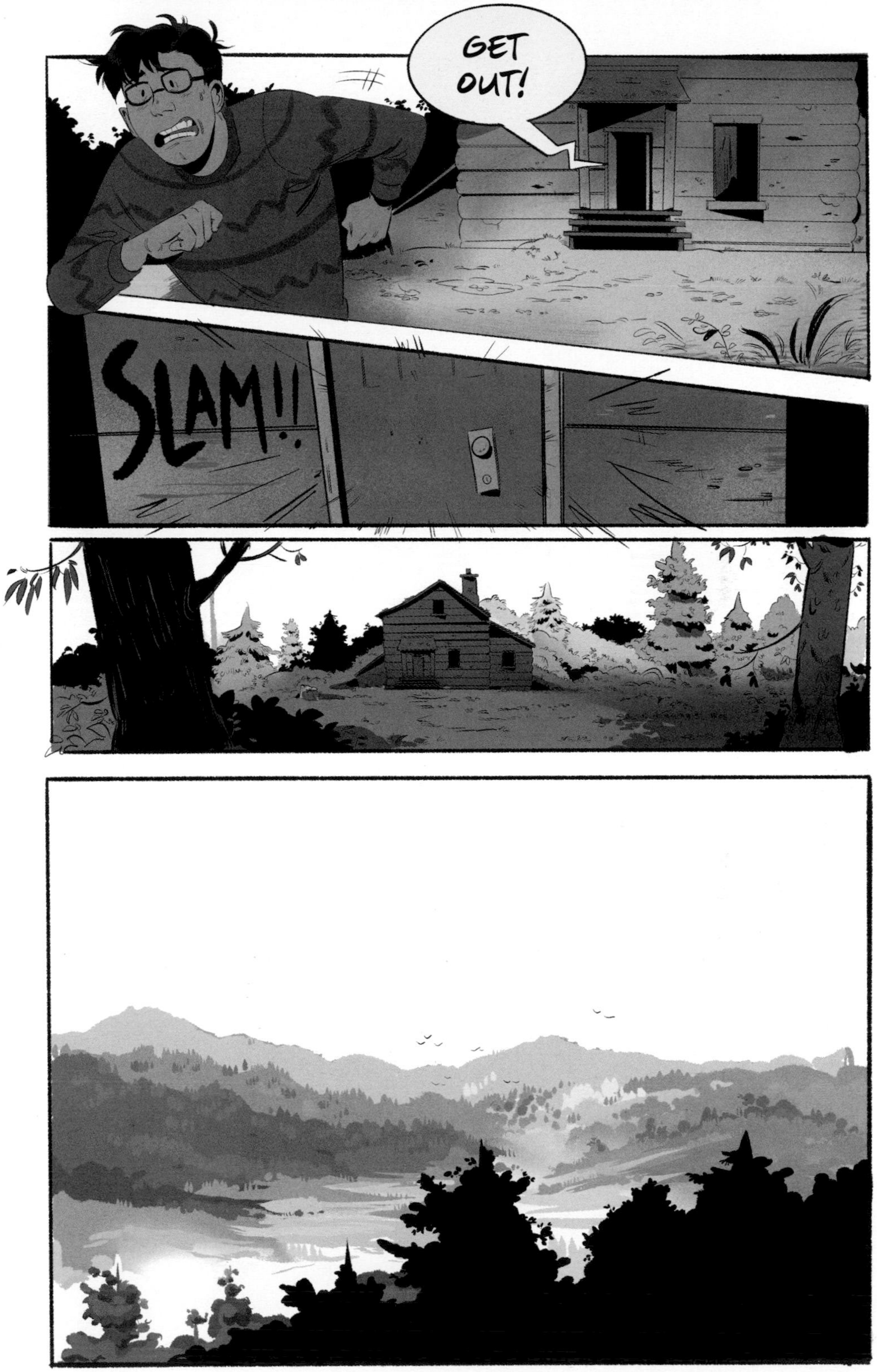
GET OUT!
SLAM!!

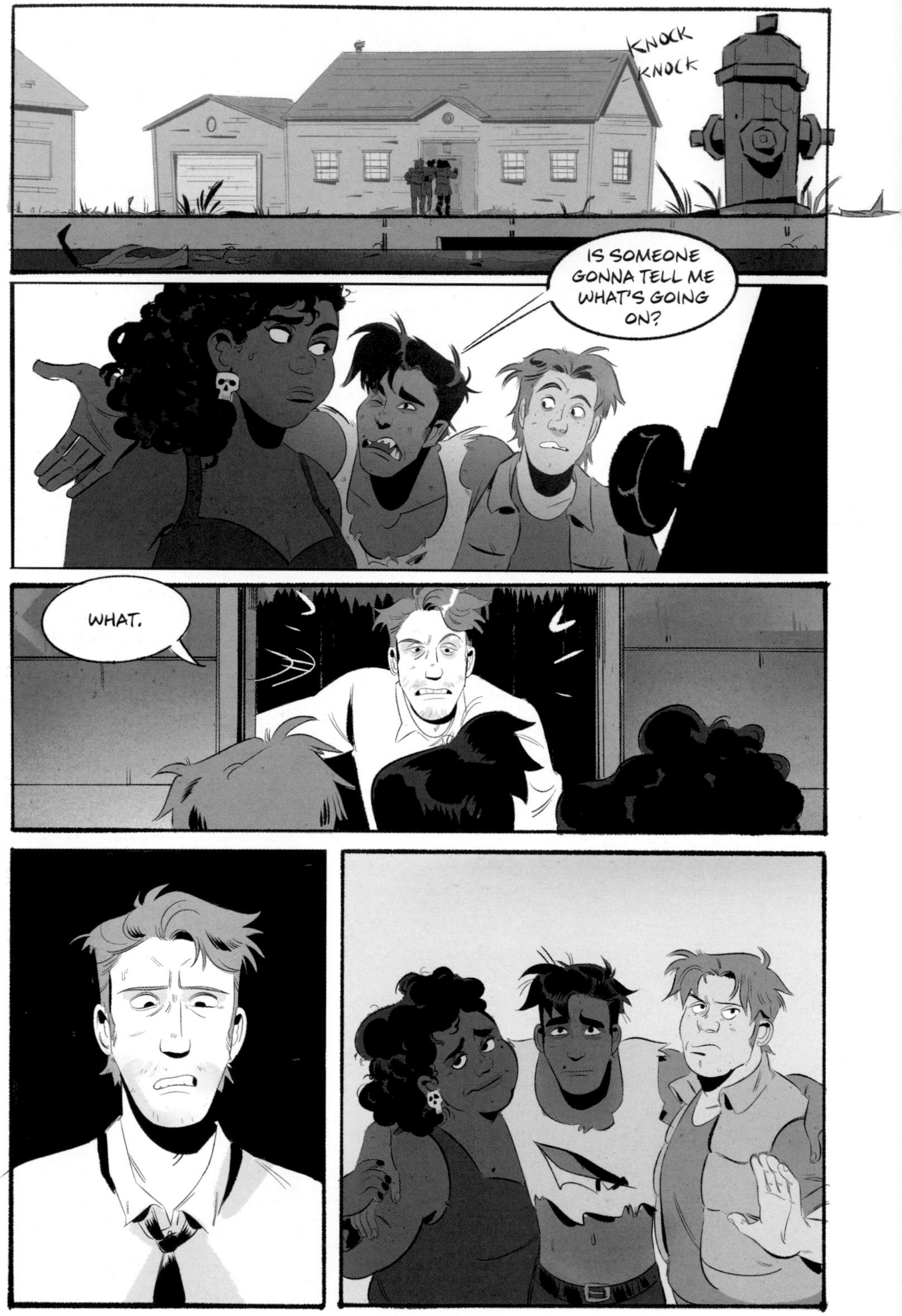
KNOCK
KNOCK
IS SOMEONE GONNA TELL ME WHAT'S GOING ON?
WHAT.

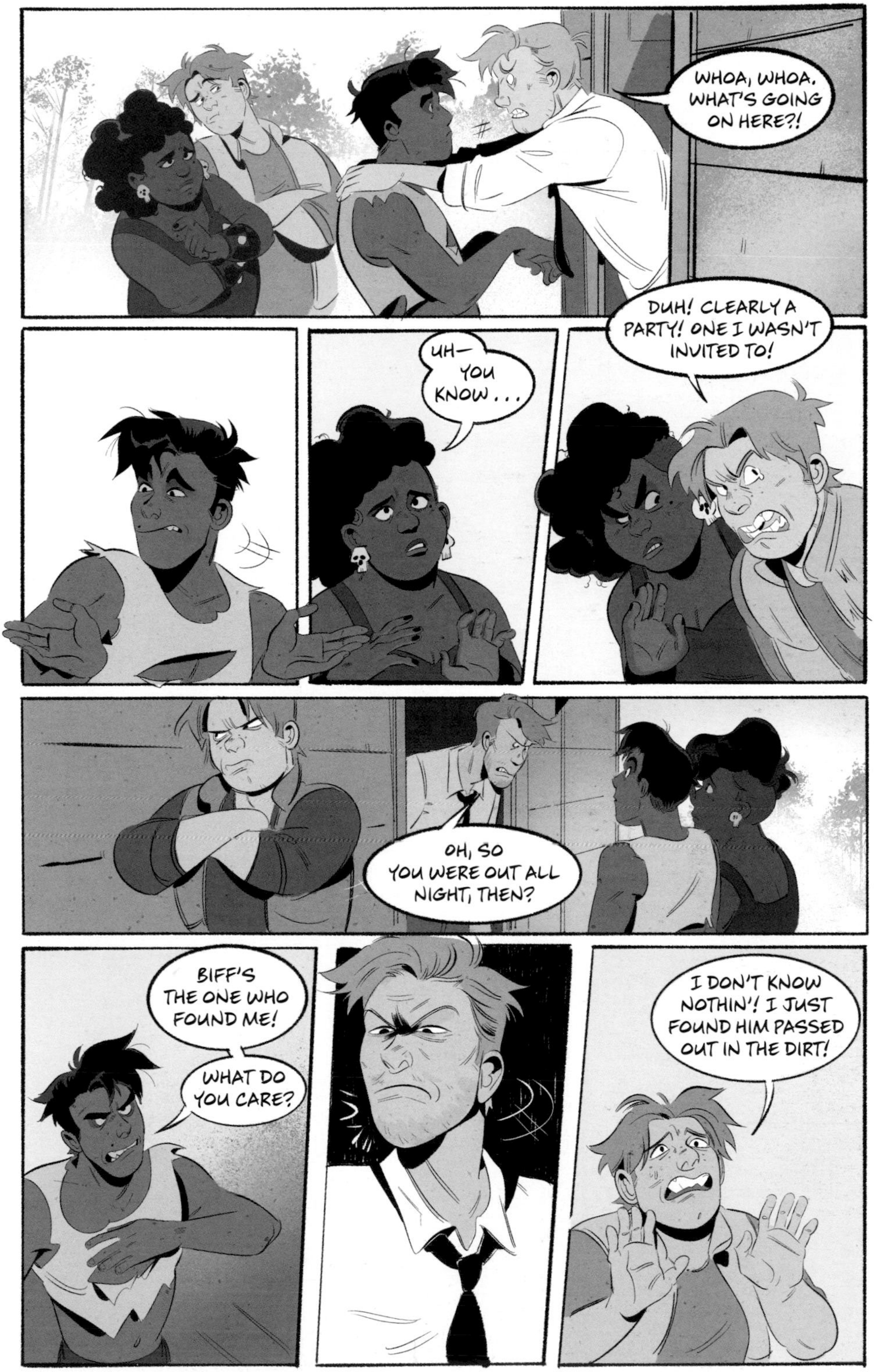
WHOA, WHOA. WHAT'S GOING ON HERE?!
UH— YOU KNOW . . .
DUH! CLEARLY A PARTY! ONE I WASN'T INVITED TO!
OH, SO YOU WERE OUT ALL NIGHT, THEN?
BIFF'S THE ONE WHO FOUND ME!
WHAT DO YOU CARE?
I DON'T KNOW NOTHIN'! I JUST FOUND HIM PASSED OUT IN THE DIRT!

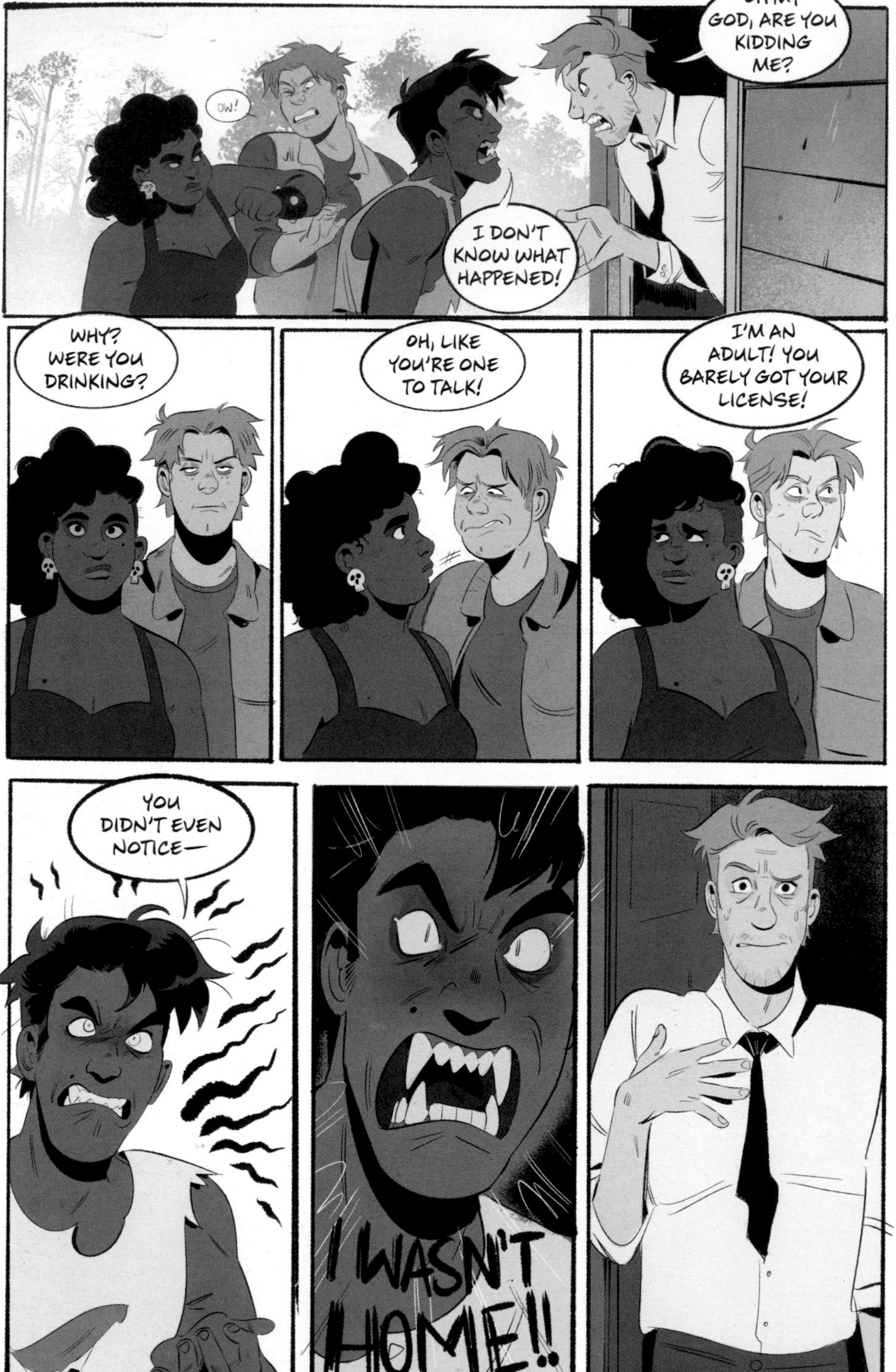
OH MY GOD, ARE YOU KIDDING ME?
OW!
I DON'T KNOW WHAT HAPPENED!
WHY? WERE YOU DRINKING?
OH, LIKE YOU'RE ONE TO TALK!
I'M AN ADULT! YOU BARELY GOT YOUR LICENSE!
YOU DIDN'T EVEN NOTICE—
I WASN'T HOME!!

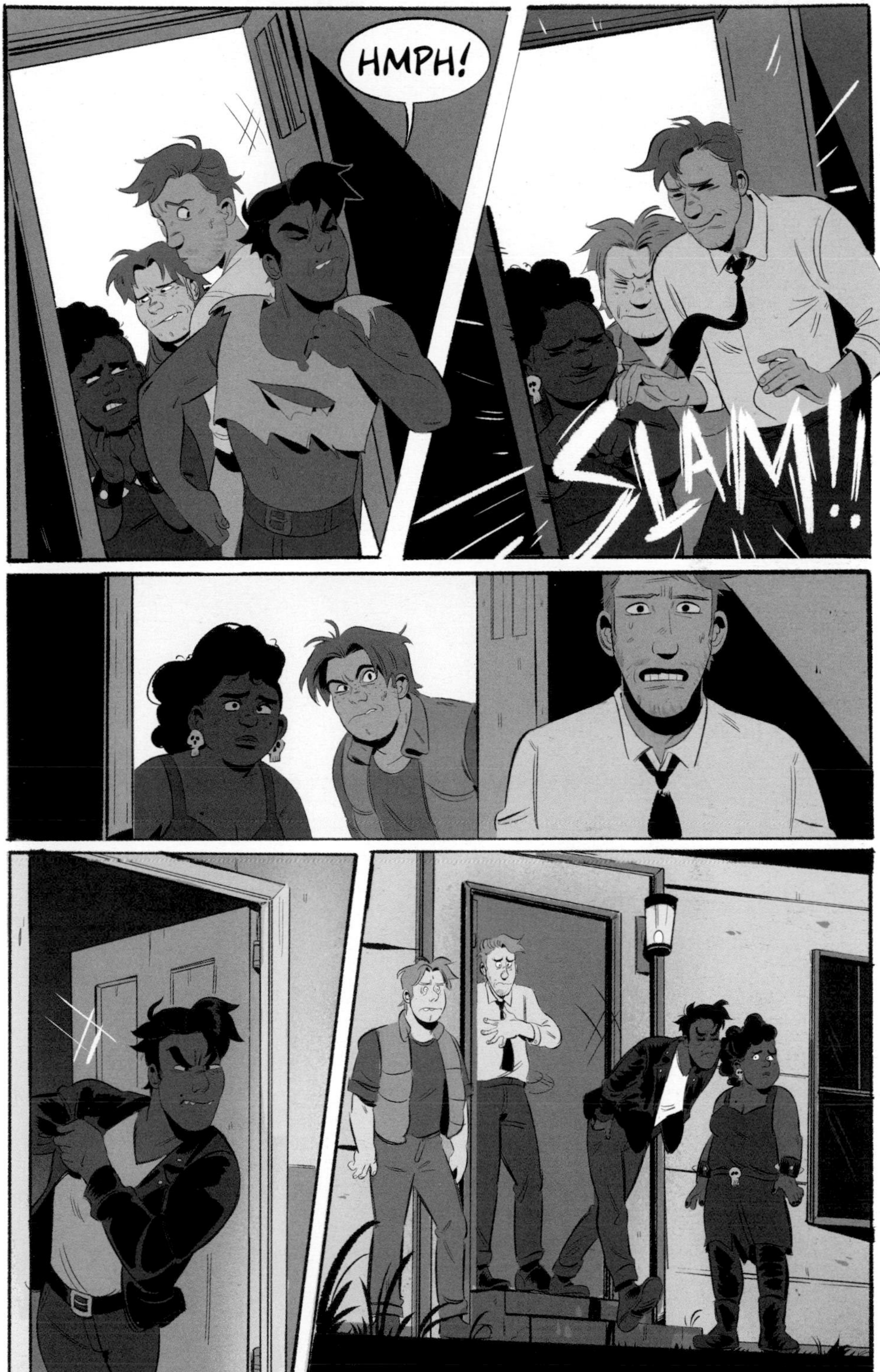
HMPH!
SLAM!!

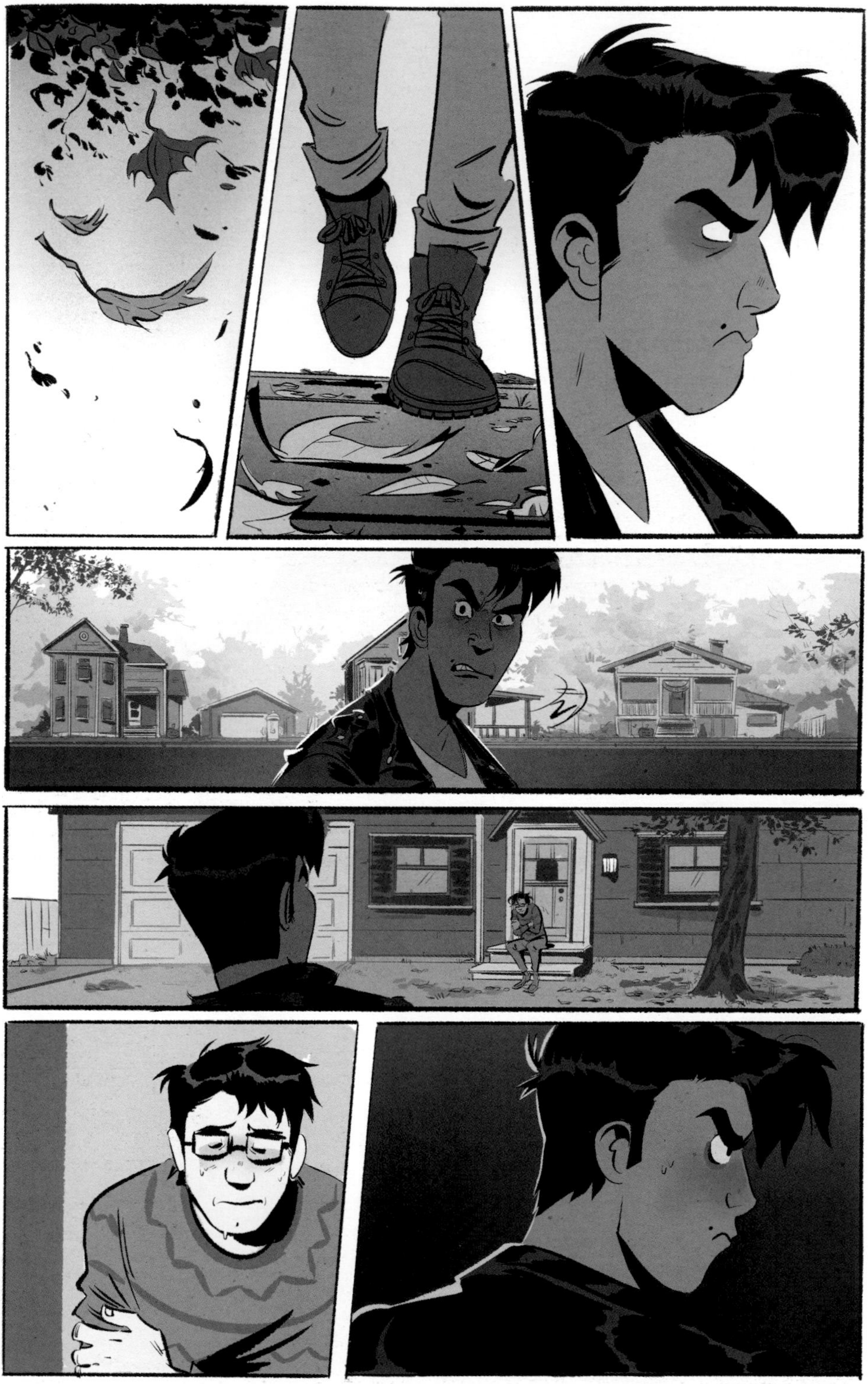

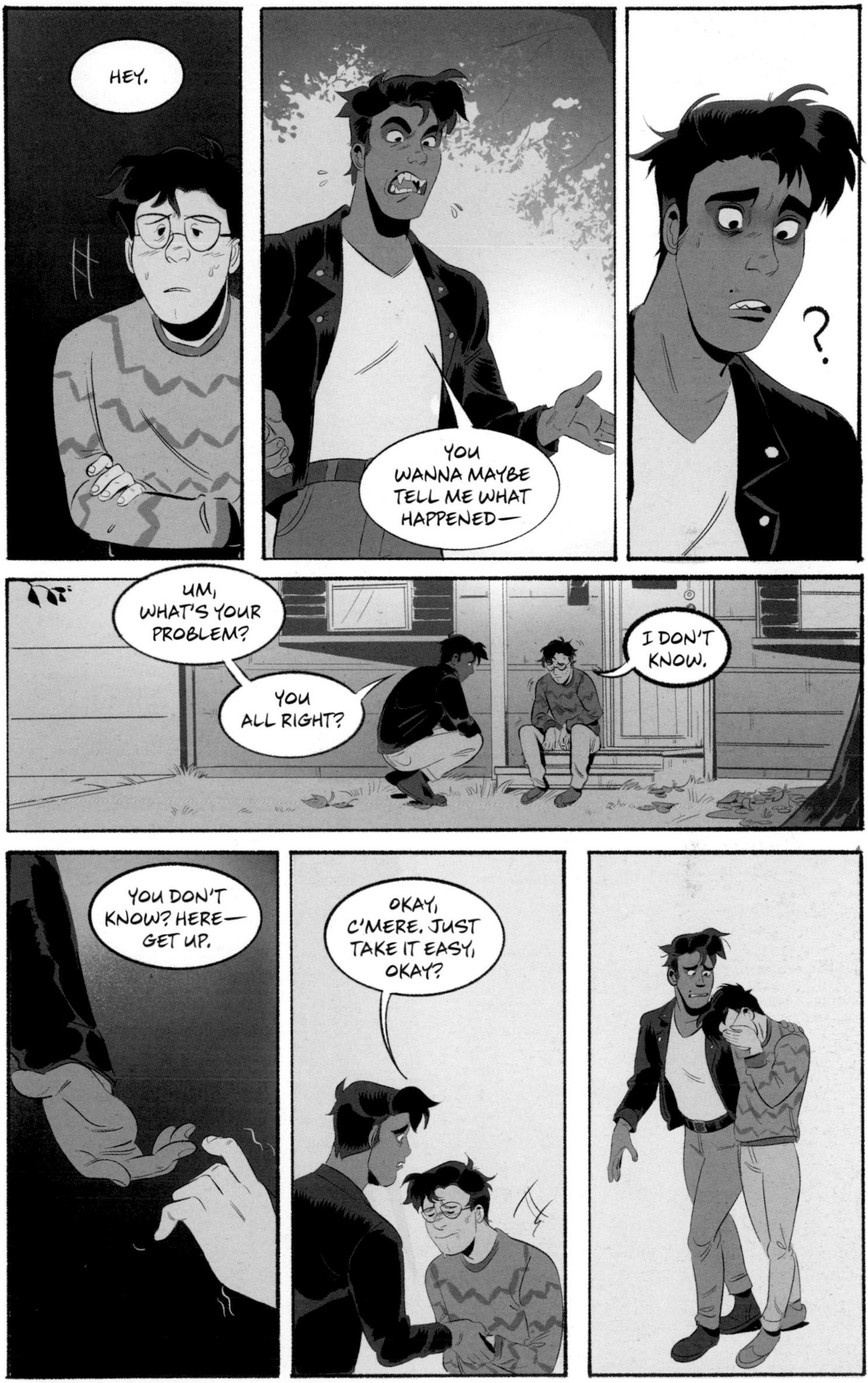
HEY.
YOU WANNA MAYBE TELL ME WHAT HAPPENED—
?
UM, WHAT'S YOUR PROBLEM?
YOU ALL RIGHT?
I DON'T KNOW.
YOU DON'T KNOW? HERE— GET UP.
OKAY, C'MERE. JUST TAKE IT EASY, OKAY?

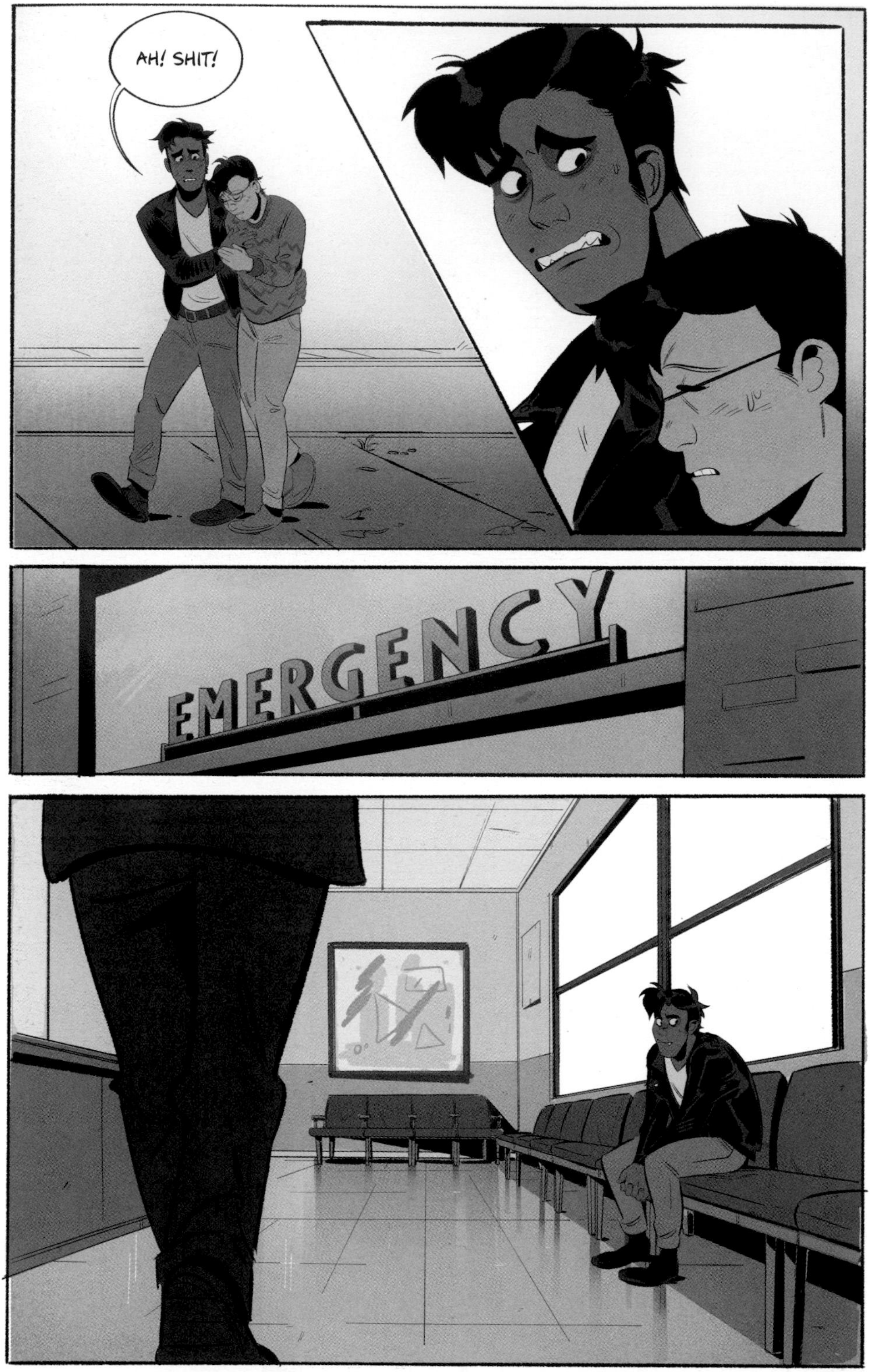
AH! SHIT!
EMERGENCY

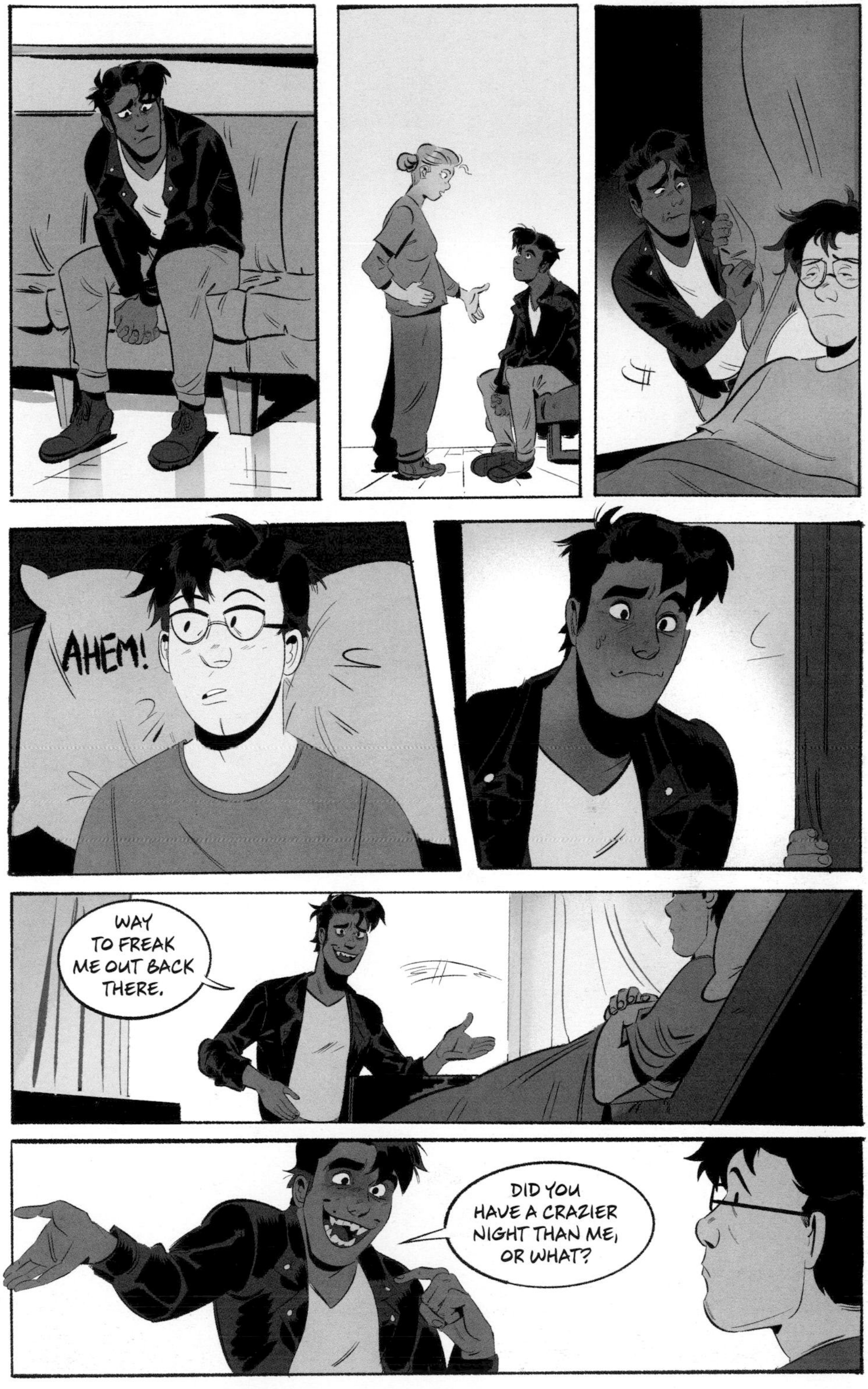
AHEM!
WAY TO FREAK ME OUT BACK THERE.
DID YOU HAVE A CRAZIER NIGHT THAN ME, OR WHAT?

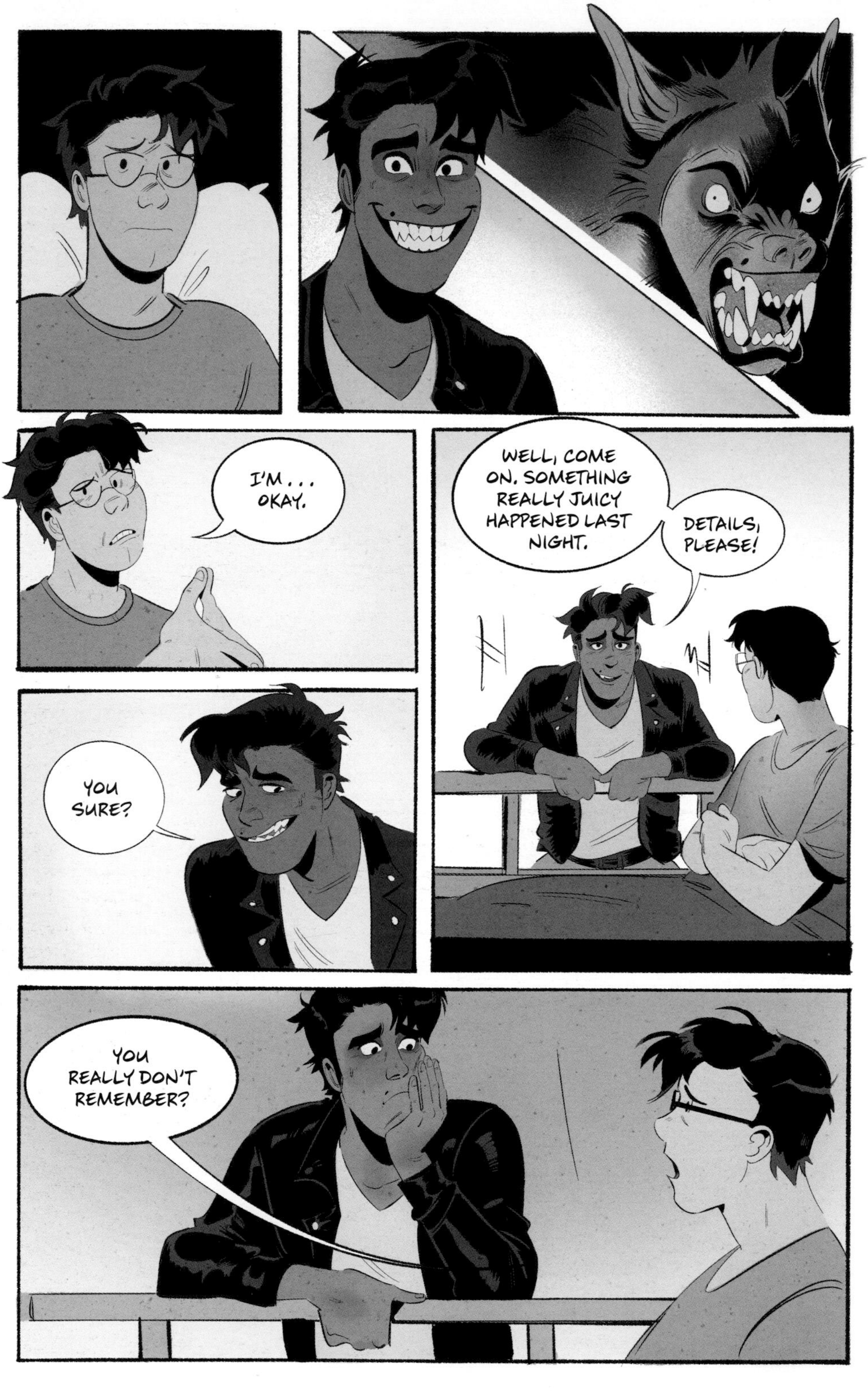
I'M . . . OKAY.
WELL, COME ON. SOMETHING REALLY JUICY HAPPENED LAST NIGHT.
DETAILS, PLEASE!
YOU SURE?
YOU REALLY DON'T REMEMBER?

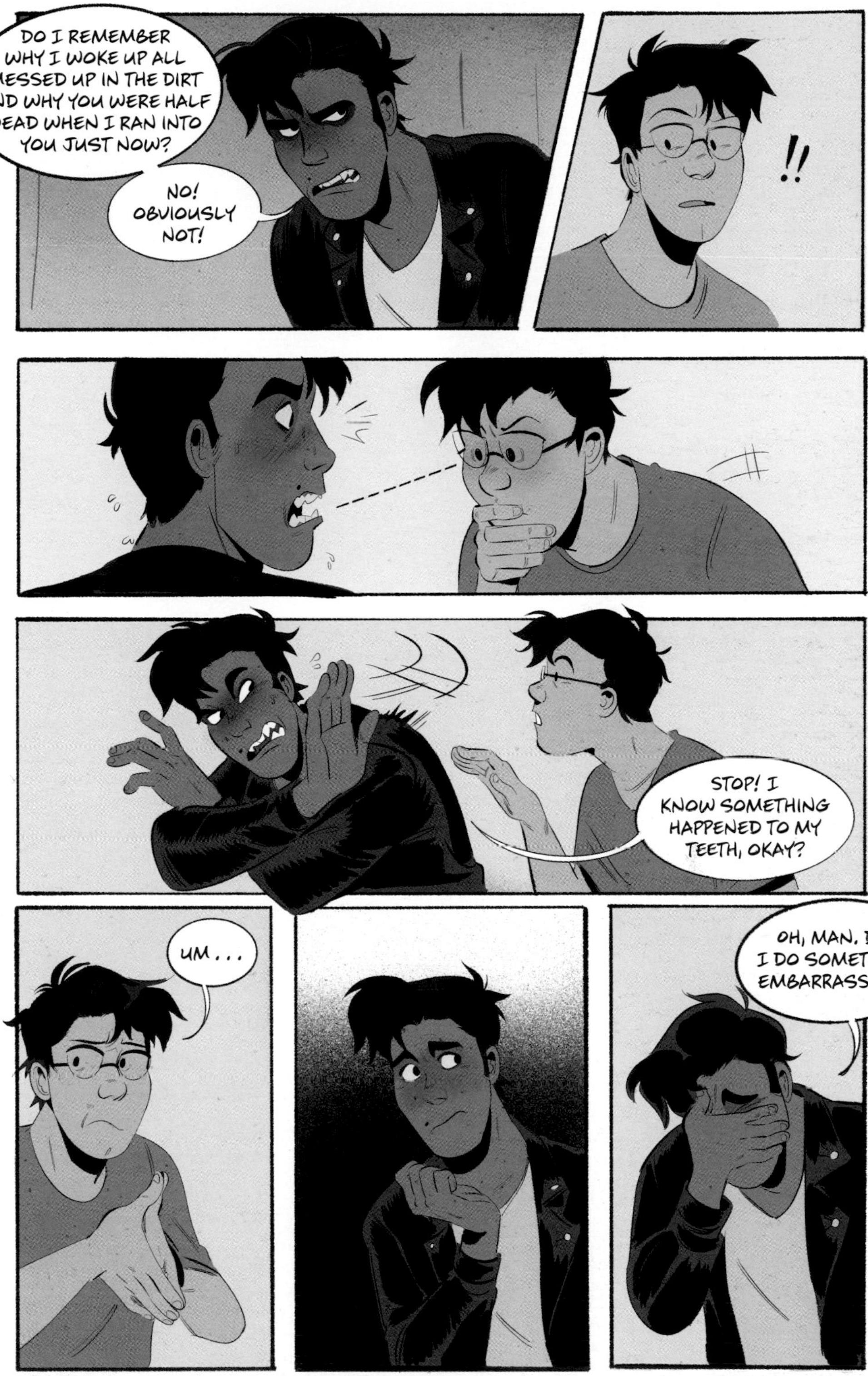
DO I REMEMBER WHY I WOKE UP ALL MESSED UP IN THE DIRT AND WHY YOU WERE HALF DEAD WHEN I RAN INTO YOU JUST NOW?
NO! OBVIOUSLY NOT!
!!
STOP! I KNOW SOMETHING HAPPENED TO MY TEETH, OKAY?
UM . . .
OH, MAN. DID I DO SOMETHING EMBARRASSING?

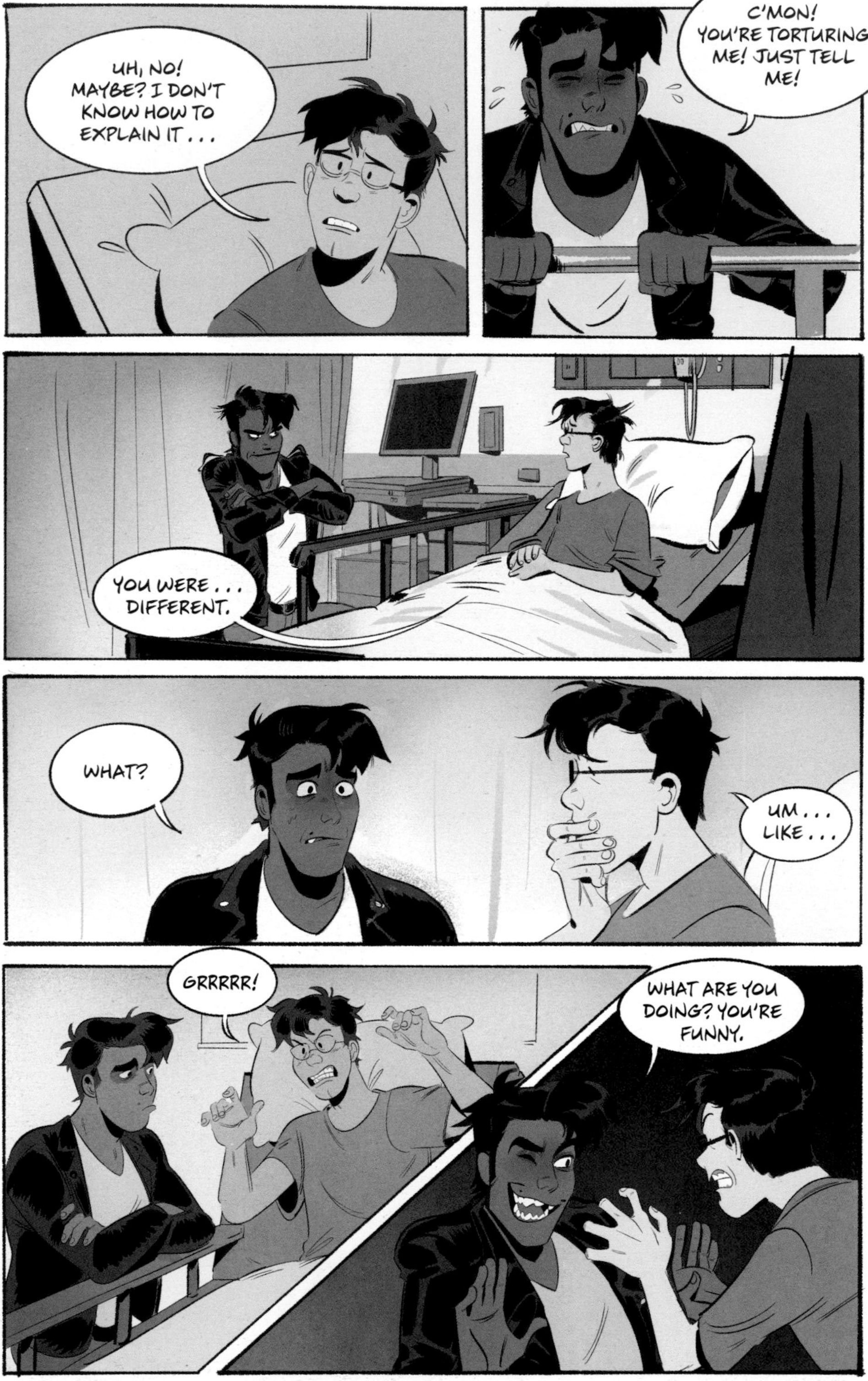
UH, NO!
MAYBE? I DON'T KNOW HOW TO EXPLAIN IT . . .
C'MON! YOU'RE TORTURING ME! JUST TELL ME!
YOU WERE . . . DIFFERENT.
WHAT?
UM . . . LIKE . . .
GRRRRR!
WHAT ARE YOU DOING? YOU'RE FUNNY.

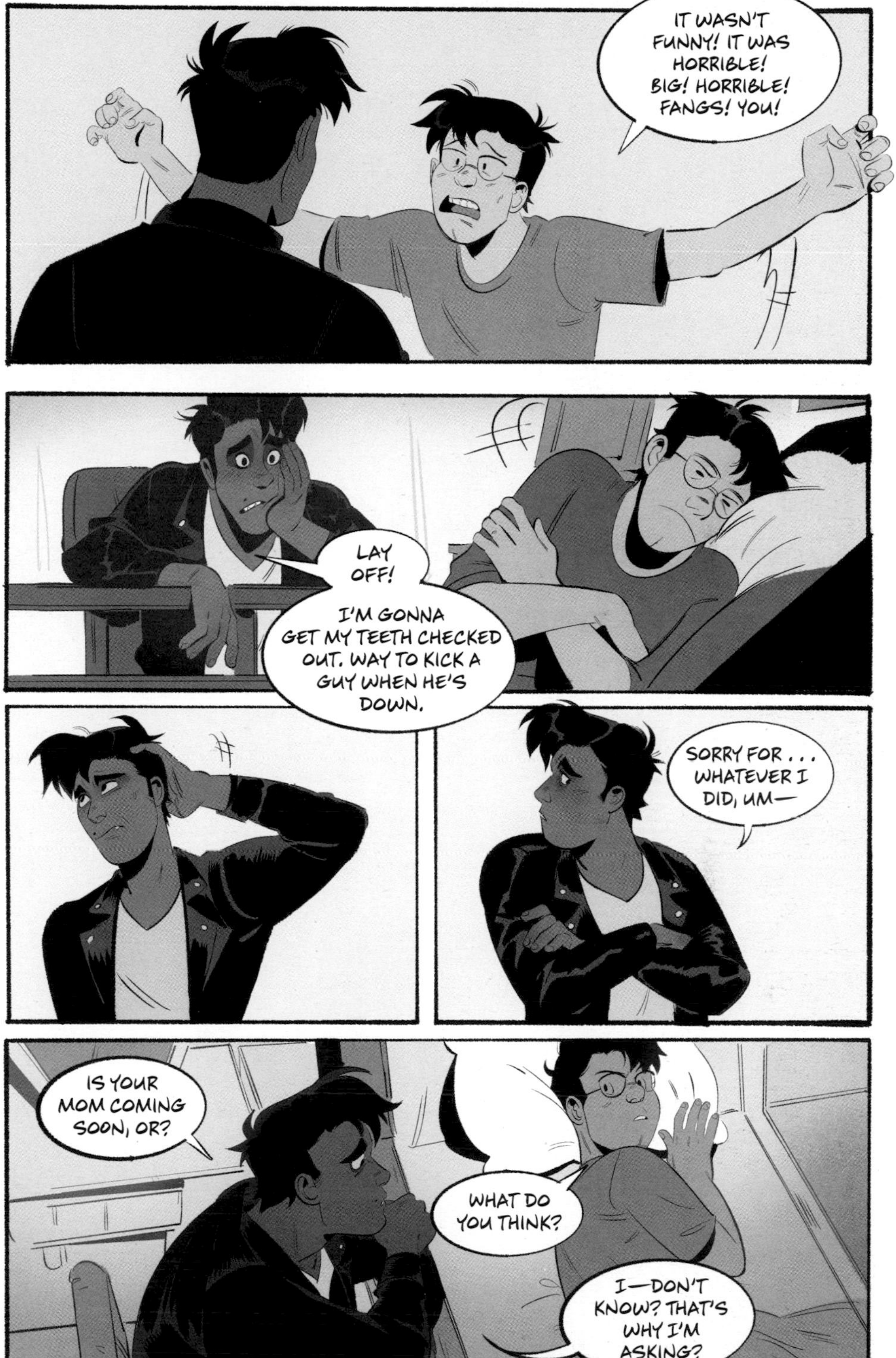
IT WASN'T FUNNY! IT WAS HORRIBLE! BIG! HORRIBLE! FANGS! YOU!
LAY OFF!
I'M GONNA GET MY TEETH CHECKED OUT. WAY TO KICK A GUY WHEN HE'S DOWN.
SORRY FOR . . . WHATEVER I DID, UM—
IS YOUR MOM COMING SOON, OR?
WHAT DO YOU THINK?
I—DON'T KNOW? THAT'S WHY I'M ASKING?

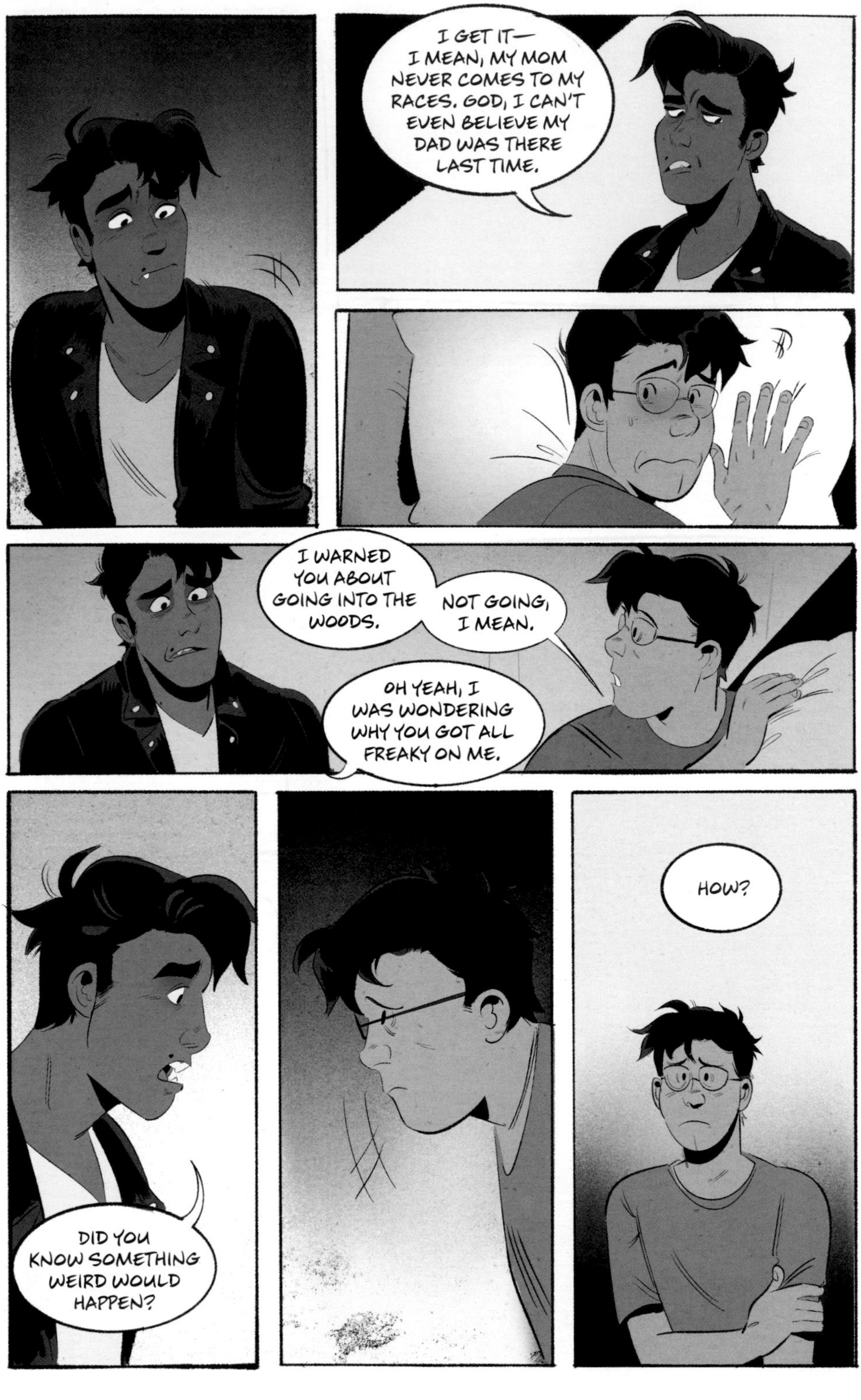
I GET IT— I MEAN, MY MOM NEVER COMES TO MY RACES. GOD, I CAN'T EVEN BELIEVE MY DAD WAS THERE LAST TIME.
I WARNED YOU ABOUT GOING INTO THE WOODS.
NOT GOING, I MEAN.
OH YEAH, I WAS WONDERING WHY YOU GOT ALL FREAKY ON ME.
DID YOU KNOW SOMETHING WEIRD WOULD HAPPEN?
HOW?

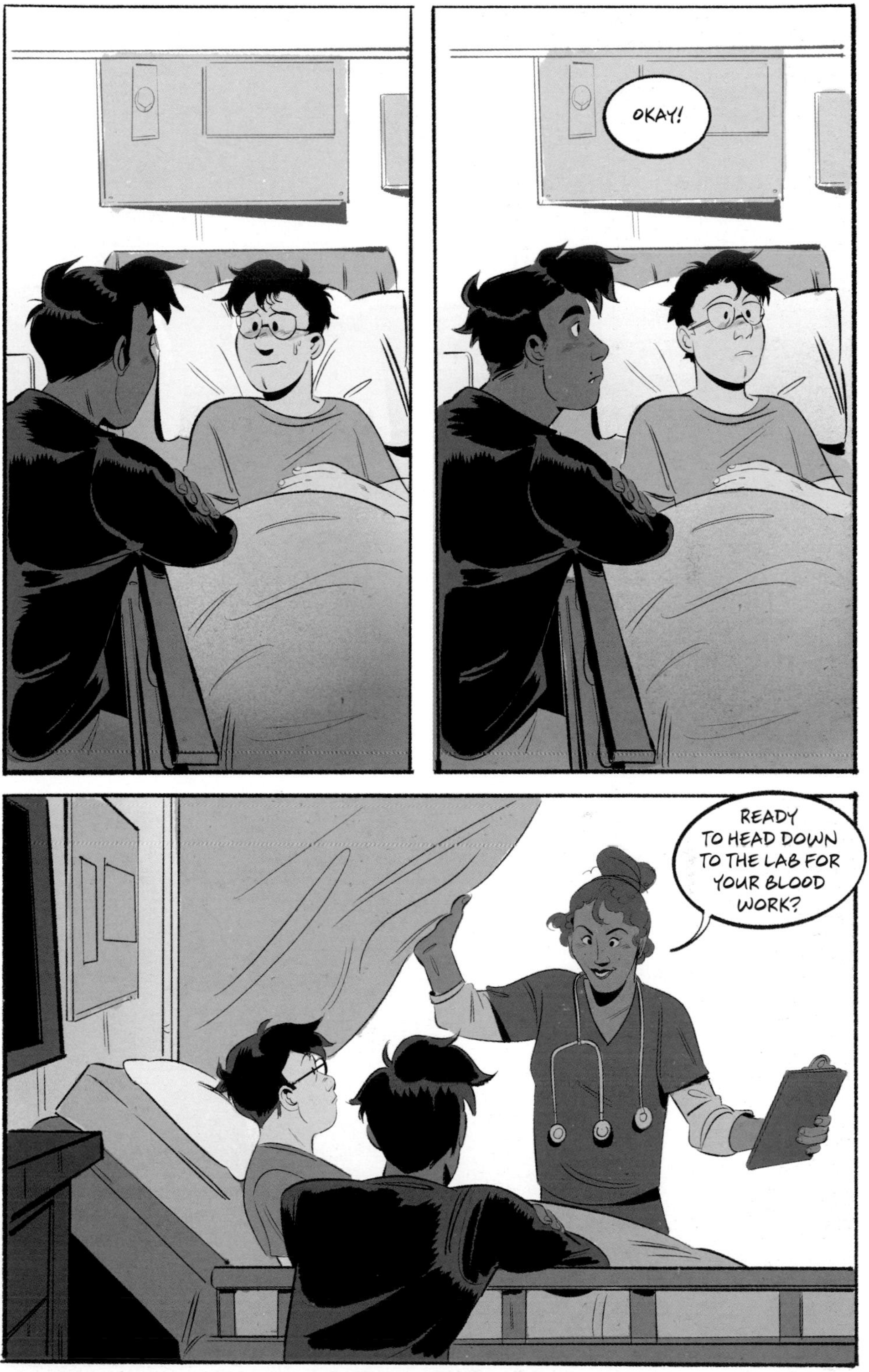
OKAY!
READY TO HEAD DOWN TO THE LAB FOR YOUR BLOOD WORK?

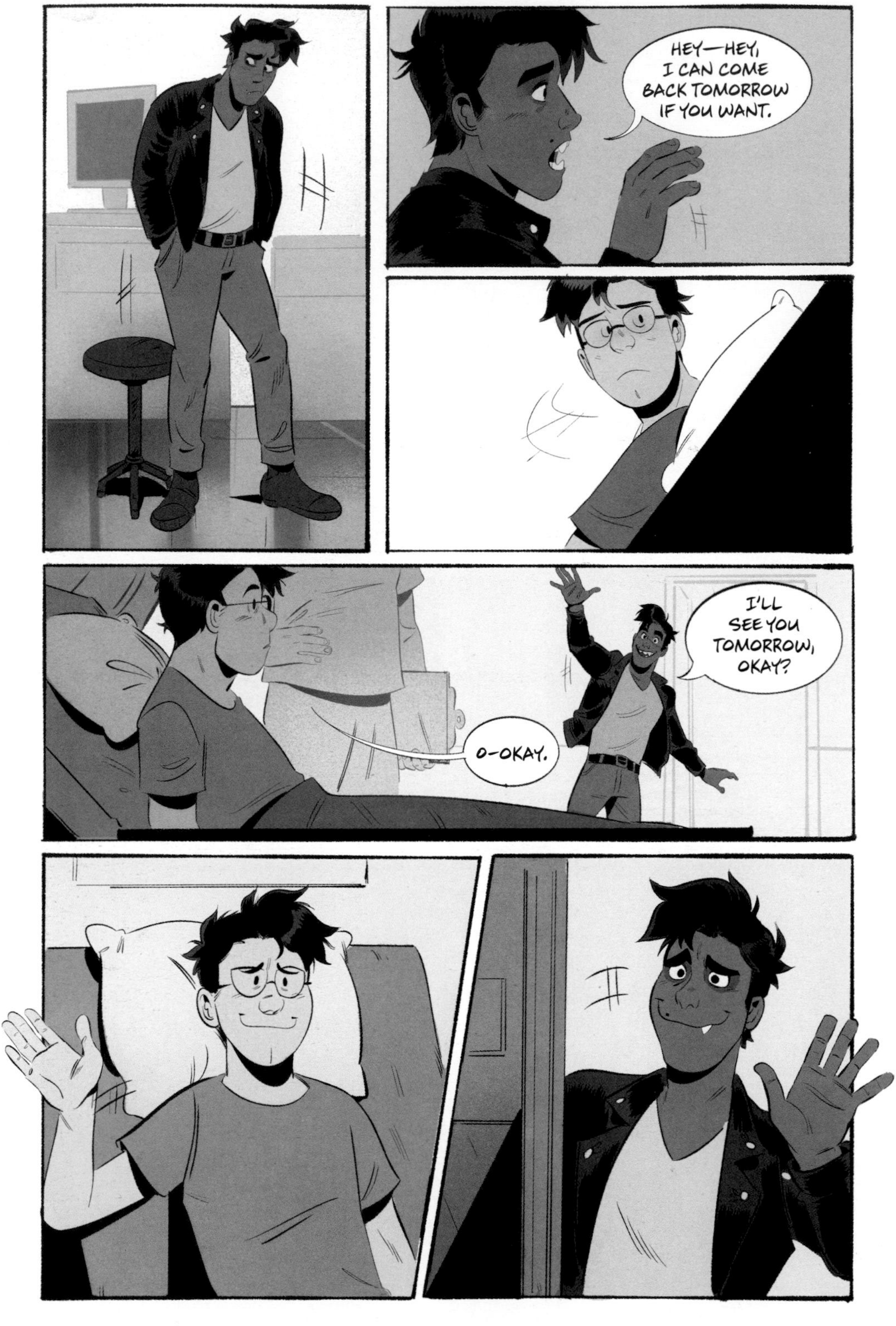
HEY—HEY, I CAN COME BACK TOMORROW IF YOU WANT.
I'LL SEE YOU TOMORROW, OKAY?
O-OKAY.

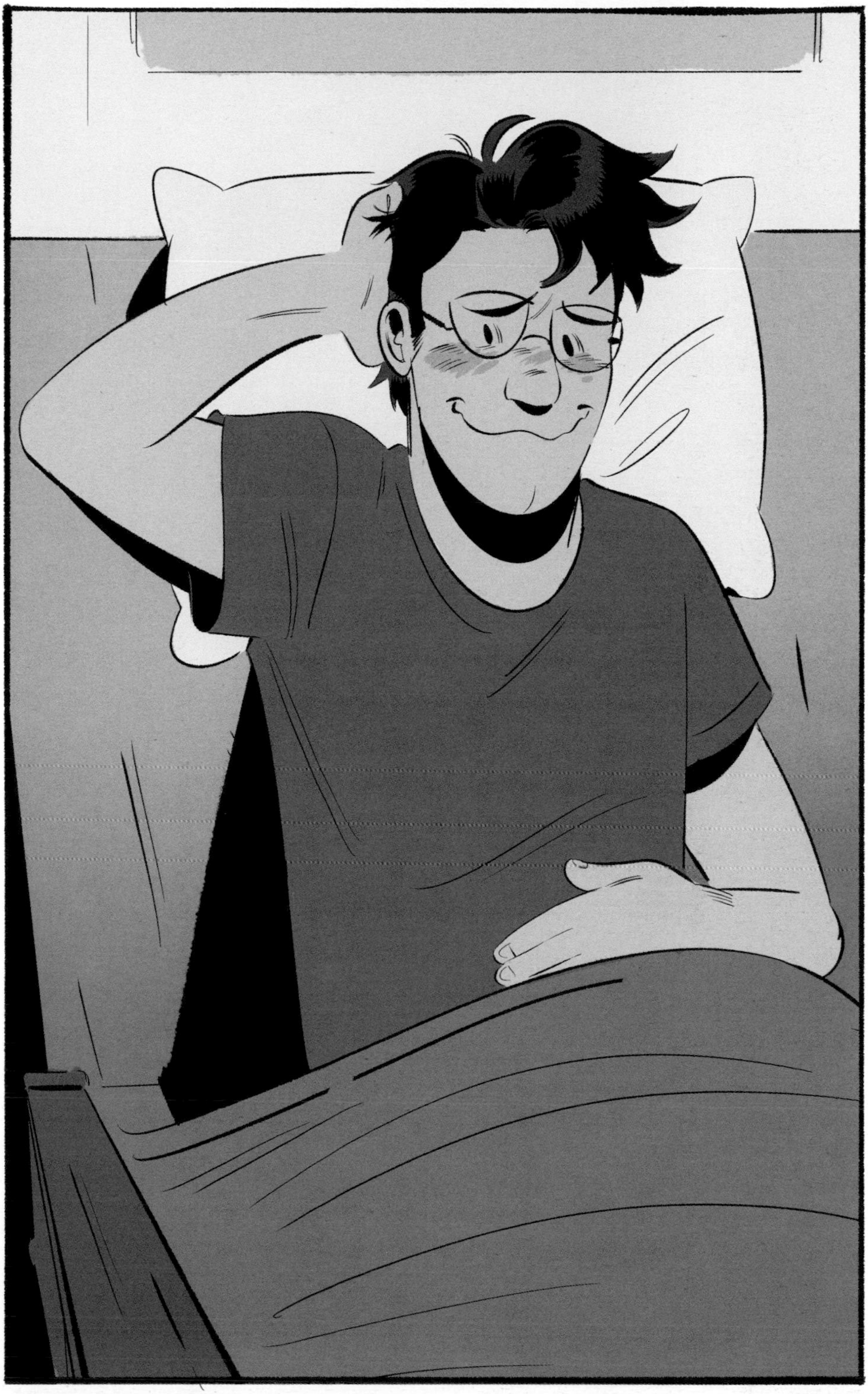

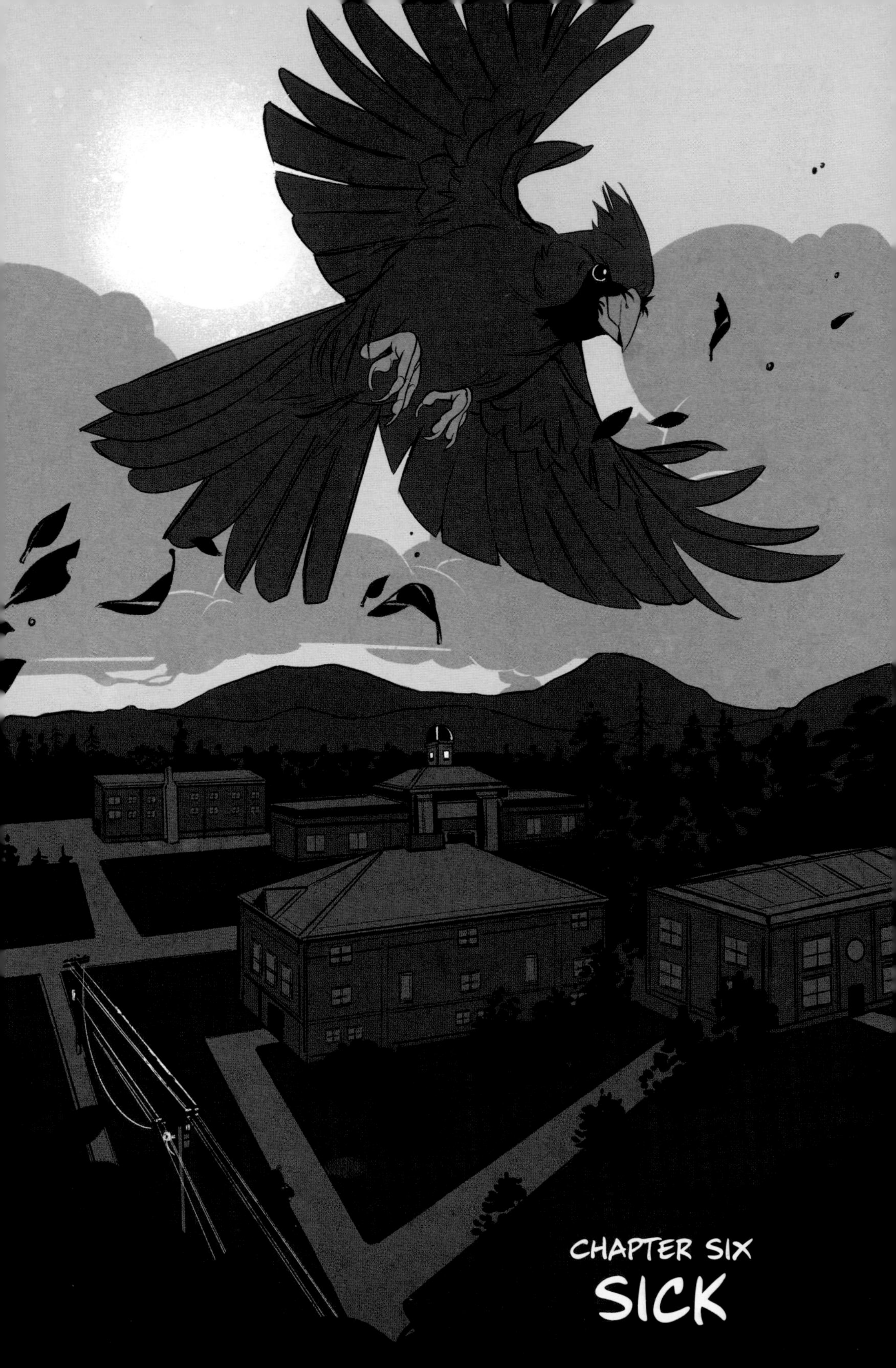
CHAPTER SIX
SICK

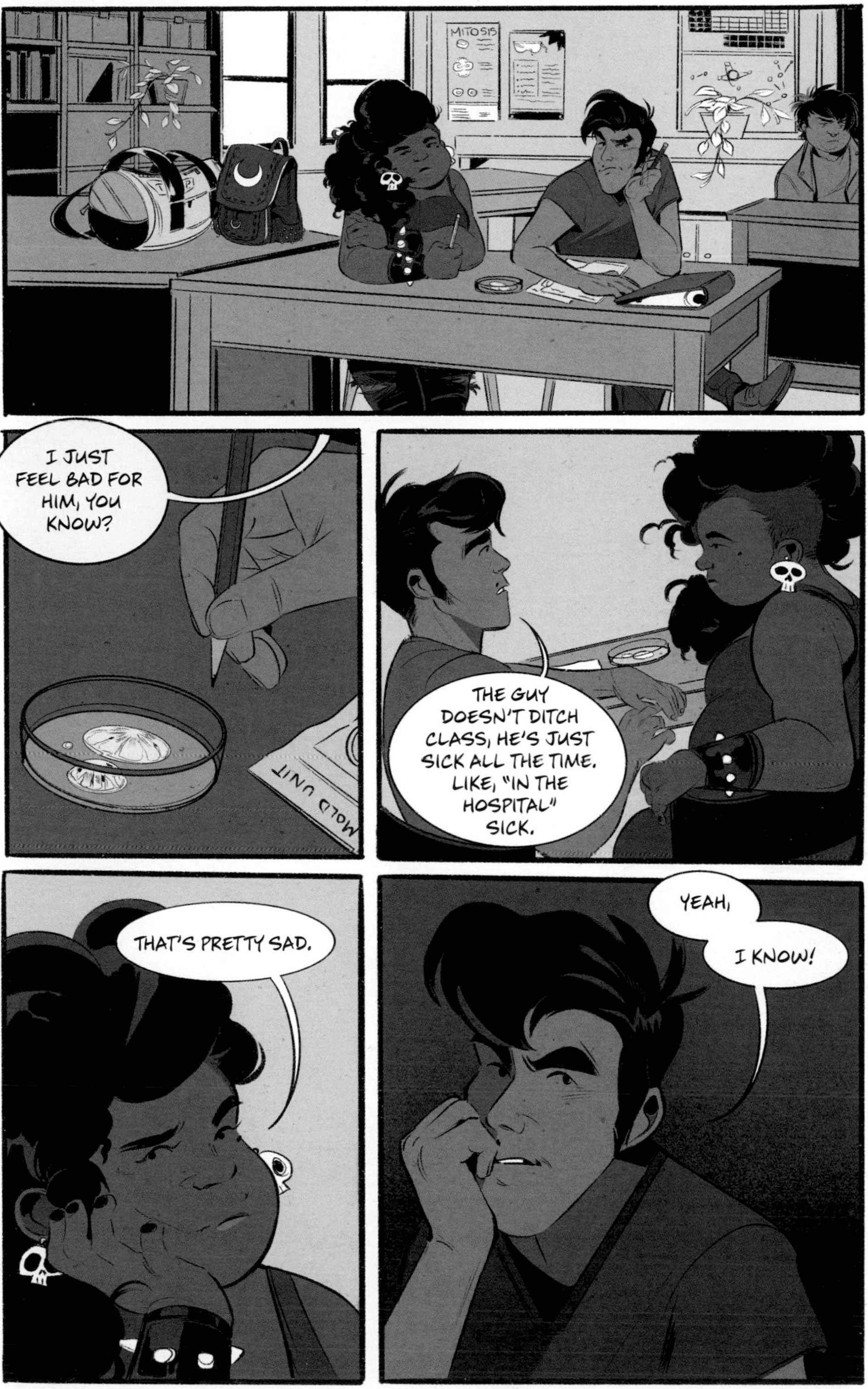
MITOSIS
I JUST FEEL BAD FOR HIM, YOU KNOW?
MOLD UNIT
THE GUY DOESN'T DITCH CLASS, HE'S JUST SICK ALL THE TIME. LIKE, "IN THE HOSPITAL" SICK.
THAT'S PRETTY SAD.
YEAH,
I KNOW!

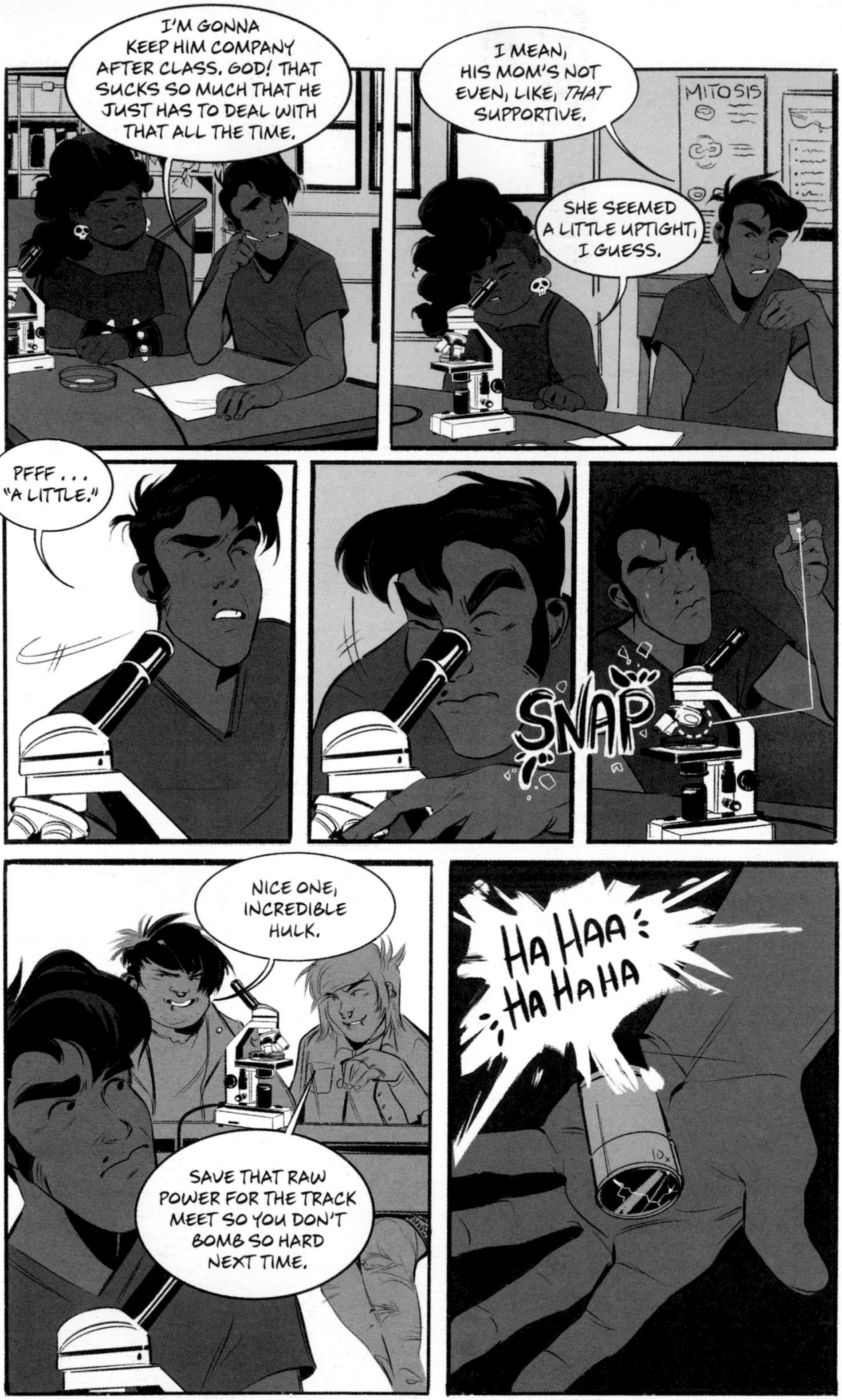
I'M GONNA KEEP HIM COMPANY AFTER CLASS. GOD! THAT SUCKS SO MUCH THAT HE JUST HAS TO DEAL WITH THAT ALL THE TIME.
I MEAN, HIS MOM'S NOT EVEN, LIKE, *THAT* SUPPORTIVE.
MITOSIS
SHE SEEMED A LITTLE UPTIGHT, I GUESS.
PFFF . . . "A LITTLE."
SNAP
NICE ONE, INCREDIBLE HULK.
SAVE THAT RAW POWER FOR THE TRACK MEET SO YOU DON'T BOMB SO HARD NEXT TIME.
HA HAA HA HA HA
10x

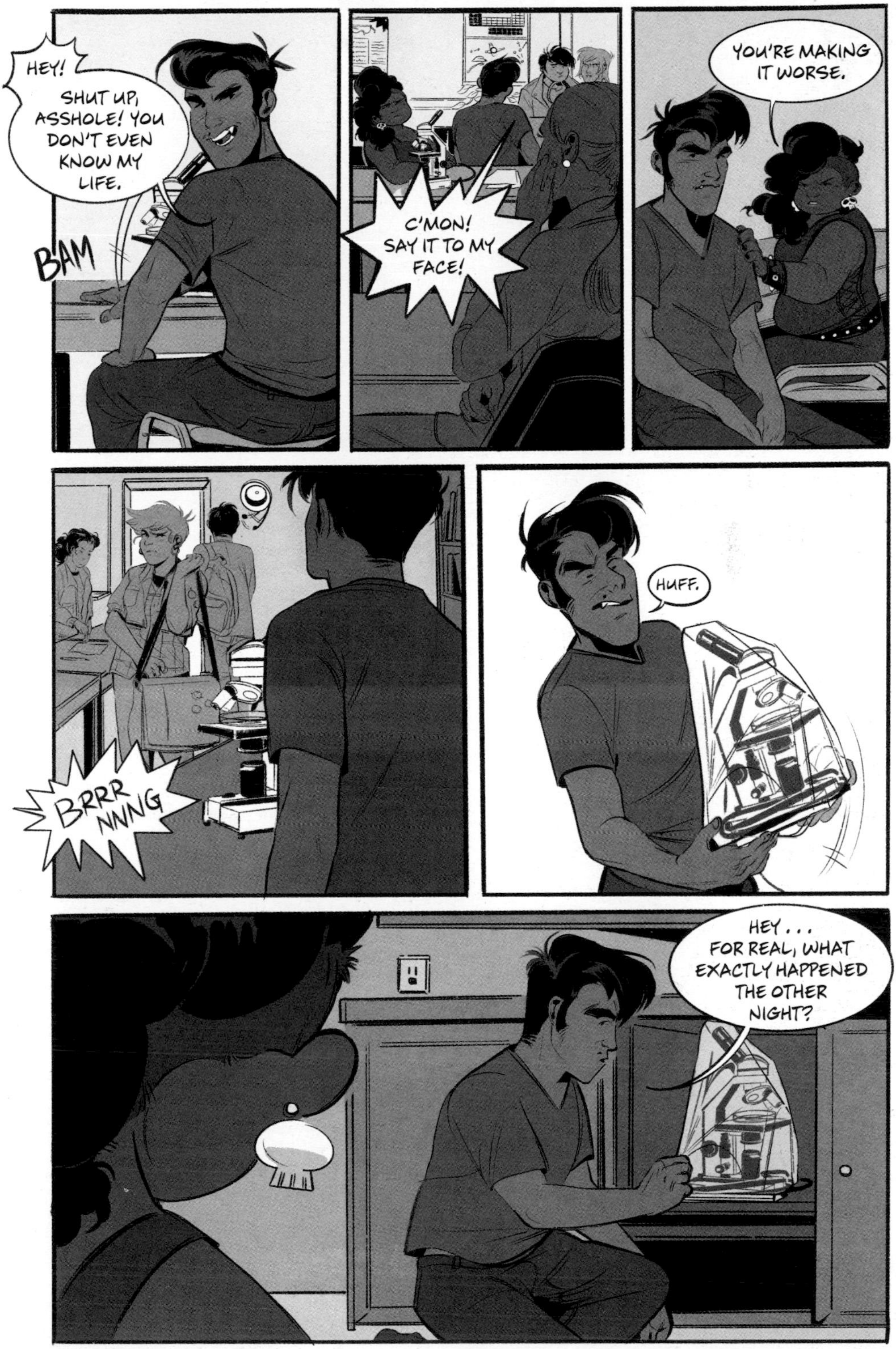
HEY!
SHUT UP, ASSHOLE! YOU DON'T EVEN KNOW MY LIFE.
BAM
C'MON! SAY IT TO MY FACE!
YOU'RE MAKING IT WORSE.
BRRR NNNG
HUFF.
HEY . . . FOR REAL, WHAT EXACTLY HAPPENED THE OTHER NIGHT?

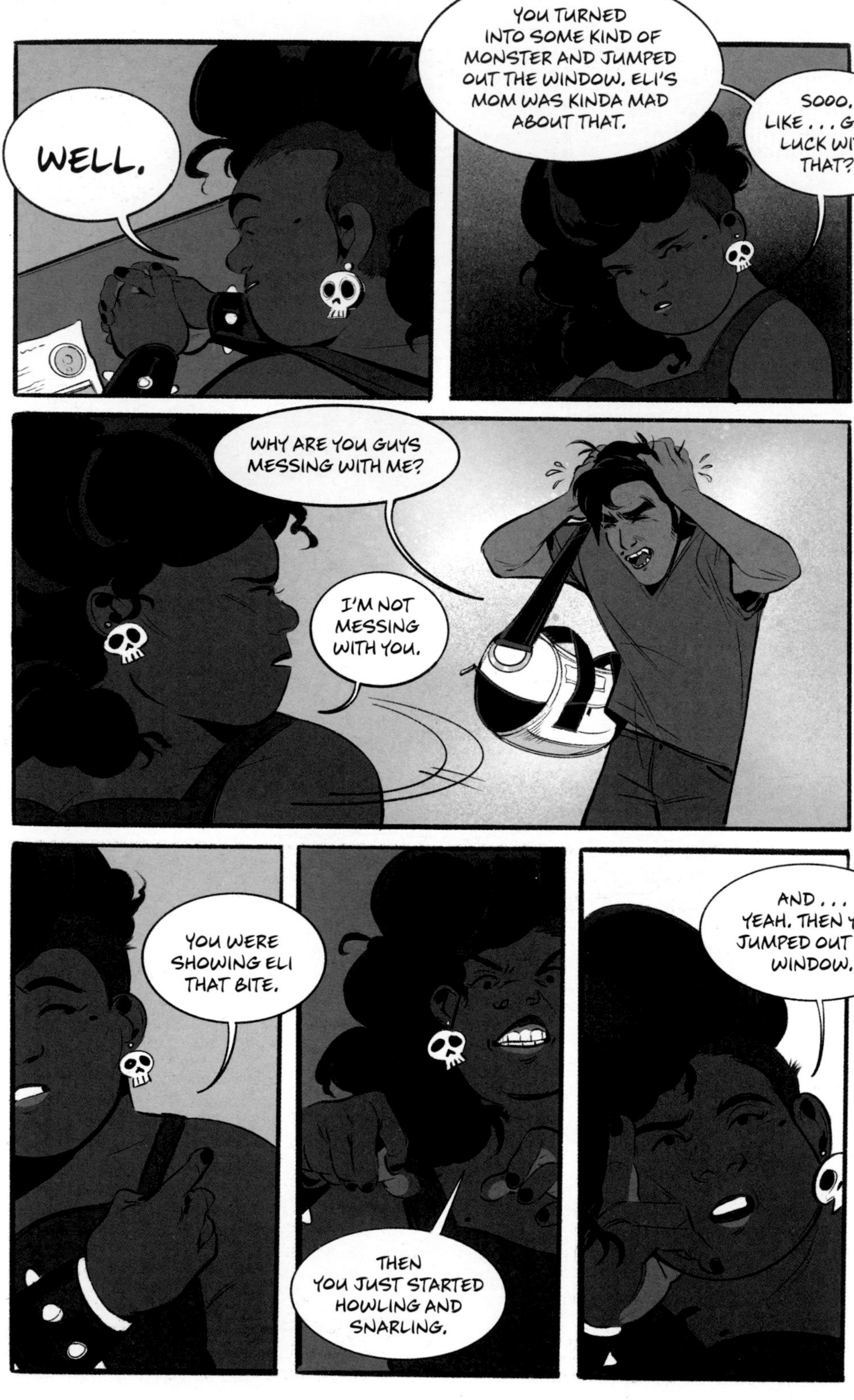
WELL.
YOU TURNED INTO SOME KIND OF MONSTER AND JUMPED OUT THE WINDOW. ELI'S MOM WAS KINDA MAD ABOUT THAT.
SOOO. LIKE . . . GOOD LUCK WITH THAT?
WHY ARE YOU GUYS MESSING WITH ME?
I'M NOT MESSING WITH YOU.
YOU WERE SHOWING ELI THAT BITE.
THEN YOU JUST STARTED HOWLING AND SNARLING.
AND . . . YEAH. THEN YOU JUMPED OUT THE WINDOW.

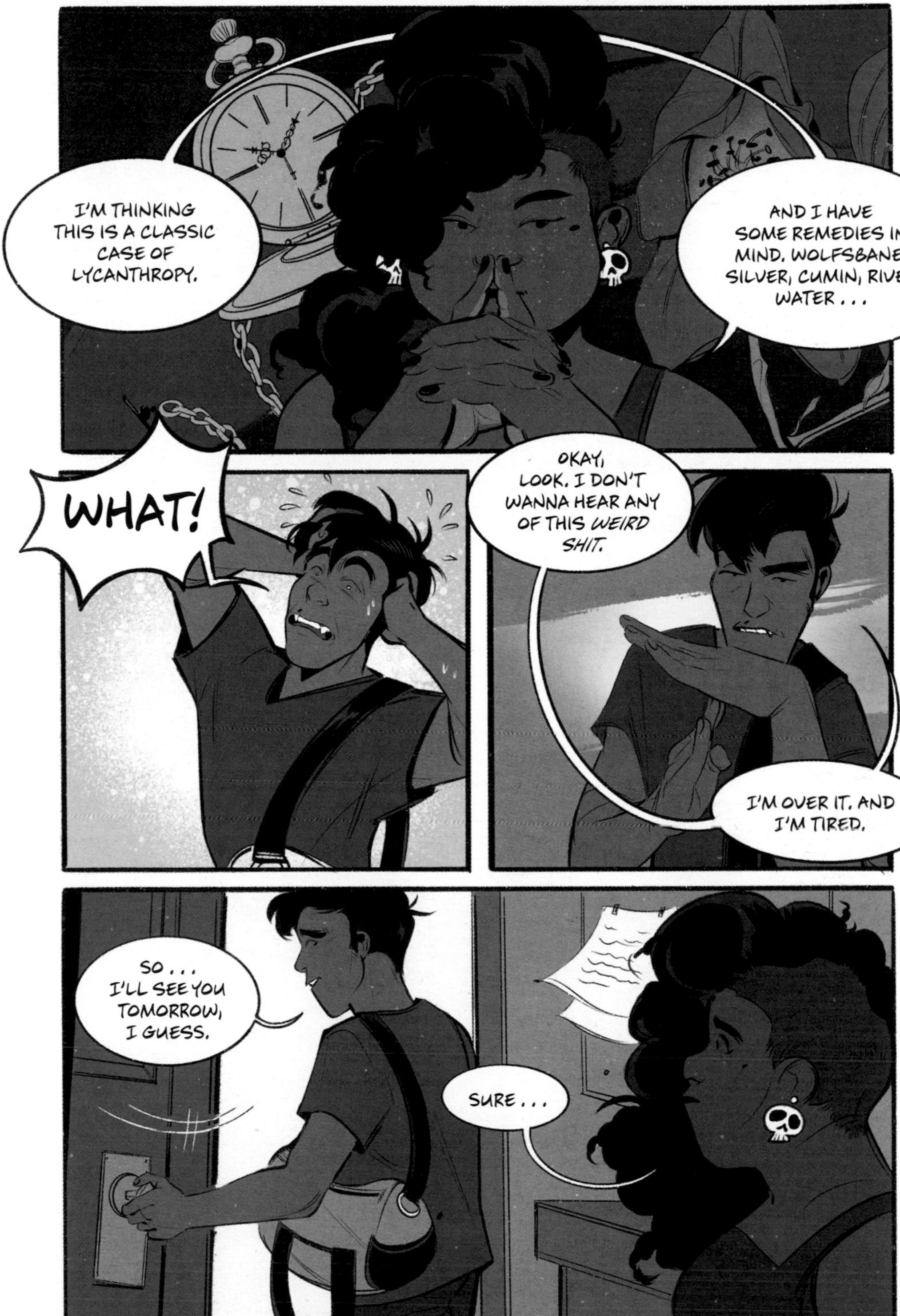
I'M THINKING THIS IS A CLASSIC CASE OF LYCANTHROPY.
AND I HAVE SOME REMEDIES IN MIND. WOLFSBANE, SILVER, CUMIN, RIVER WATER . . .
WHAT!
OKAY, LOOK. I DON'T WANNA HEAR ANY OF THIS *WEIRD* SHIT.
I'M OVER IT. AND I'M TIRED.
SO . . . I'LL SEE YOU TOMORROW, I GUESS.
SURE . . .

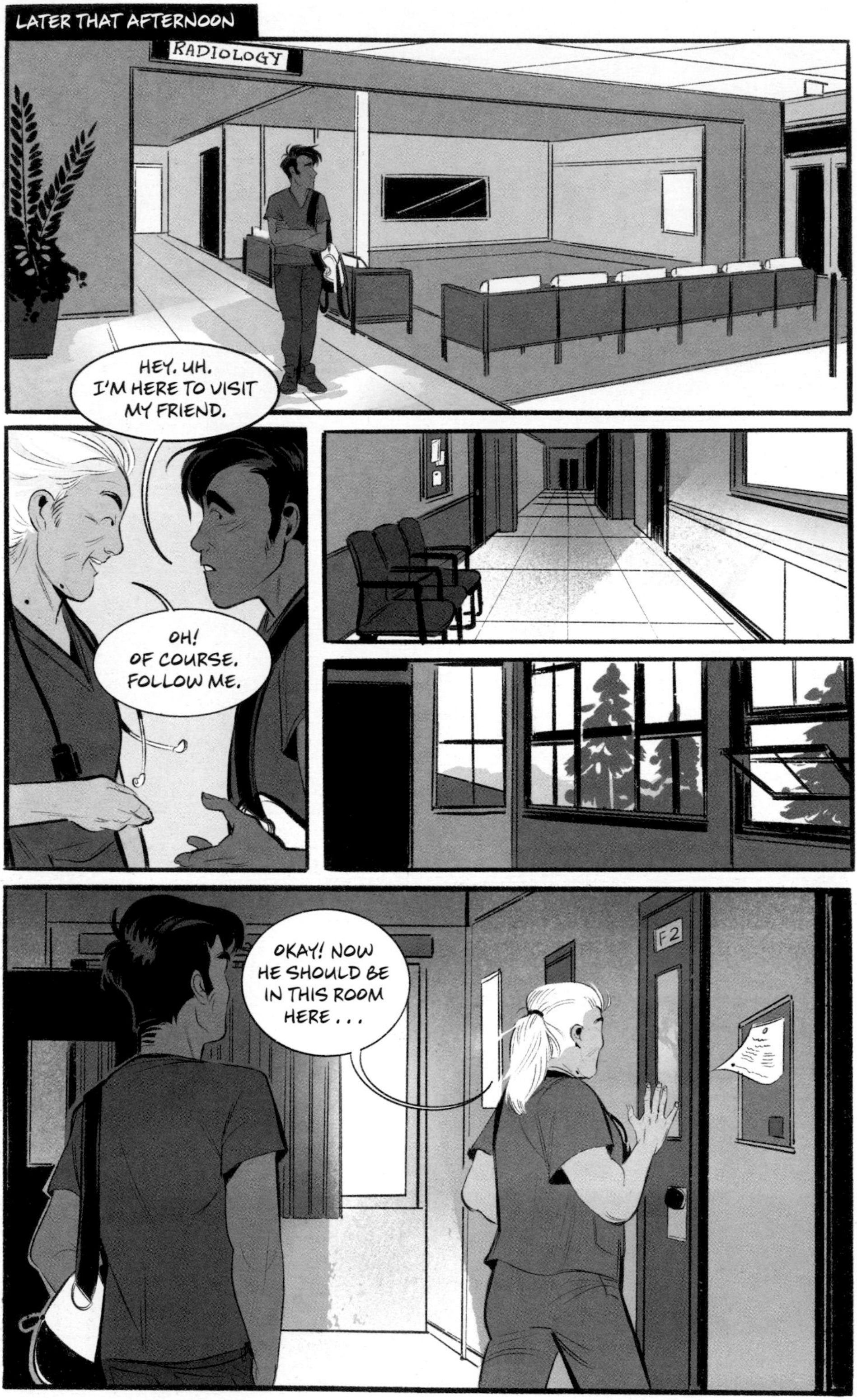
LATER THAT AFTERNOON
RADIOLOGY
HEY. UH. I'M HERE TO VISIT MY FRIEND.
OH! OF COURSE. FOLLOW ME.
F2
OKAY! NOW HE SHOULD BE IN THIS ROOM HERE . . .

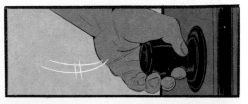

HIT THE CALL BUTTON IF YOU NEED ANYTHING.

HEY, UH. CAME BY AGAIN TODAY. TOLD YA I WOULD!

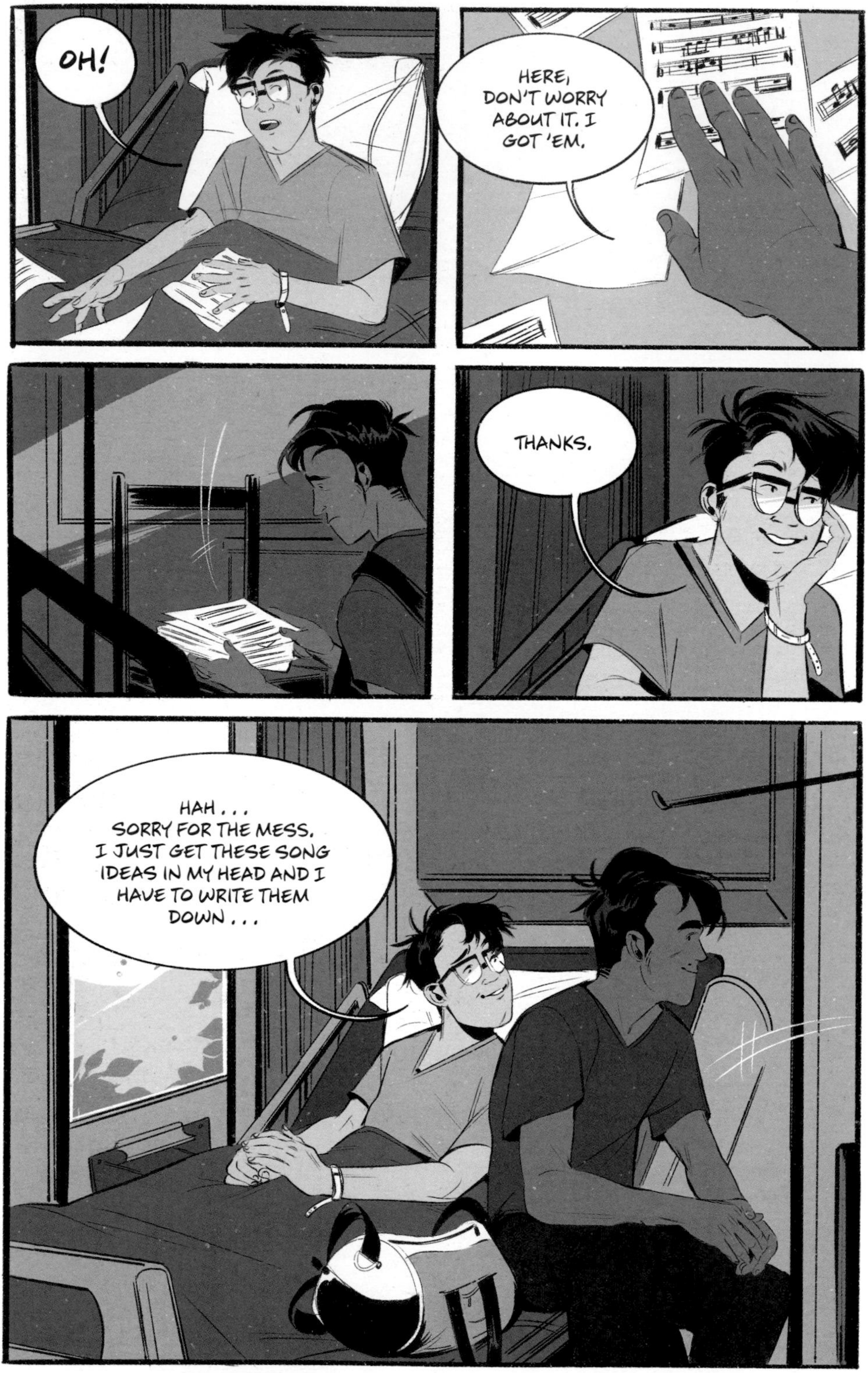
OH!
HERE, DON'T WORRY ABOUT IT. I GOT 'EM.
THANKS.
HAH . . . SORRY FOR THE MESS. I JUST GET THESE SONG IDEAS IN MY HEAD AND I HAVE TO WRITE THEM DOWN . . .

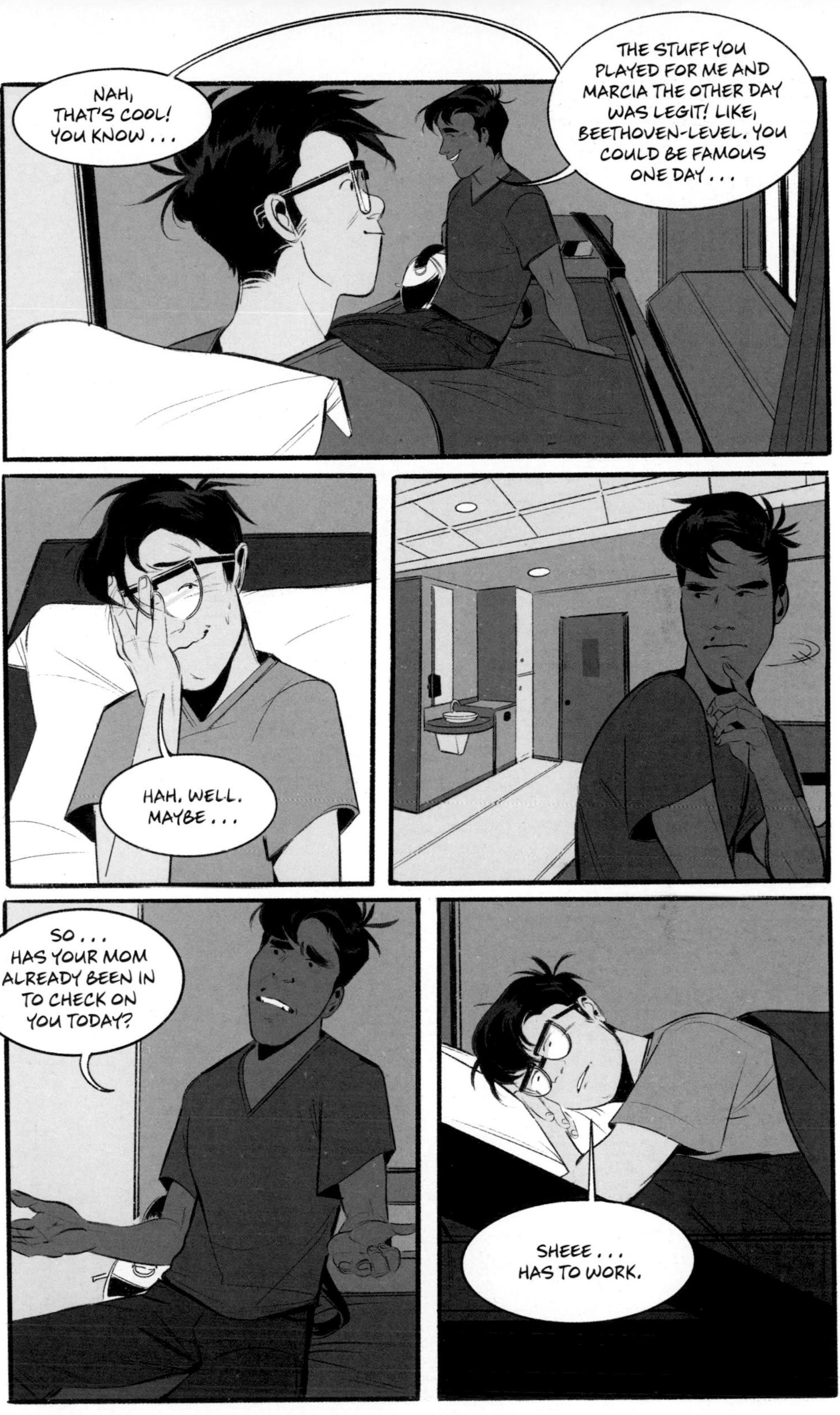
NAH, THAT'S COOL! YOU KNOW . . .
THE STUFF YOU PLAYED FOR ME AND MARCIA THE OTHER DAY WAS LEGIT! LIKE, BEETHOVEN-LEVEL. YOU COULD BE FAMOUS ONE DAY . . .
HAH. WELL. MAYBE . . .
SO . . . HAS YOUR MOM ALREADY BEEN IN TO CHECK ON YOU TODAY?
SHEEE . . . HAS TO WORK.

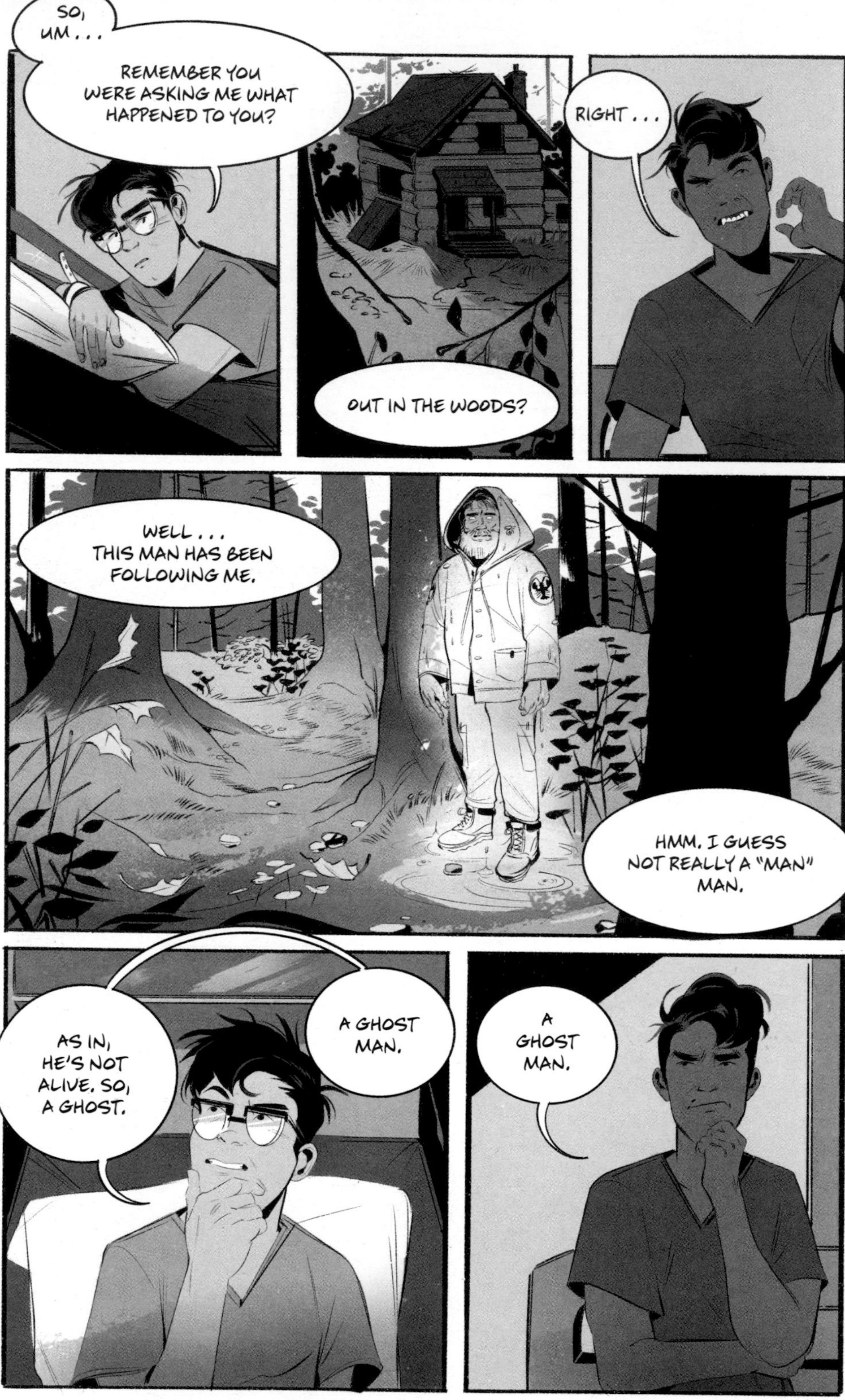
SO, UM . . .
REMEMBER YOU WERE ASKING ME WHAT HAPPENED TO YOU?
OUT IN THE WOODS?
RIGHT . . .
WELL . . . THIS MAN HAS BEEN FOLLOWING ME.
HMM. I GUESS NOT REALLY A "MAN" MAN.
AS IN, HE'S NOT ALIVE. SO, A GHOST.
A GHOST MAN.
A GHOST MAN.

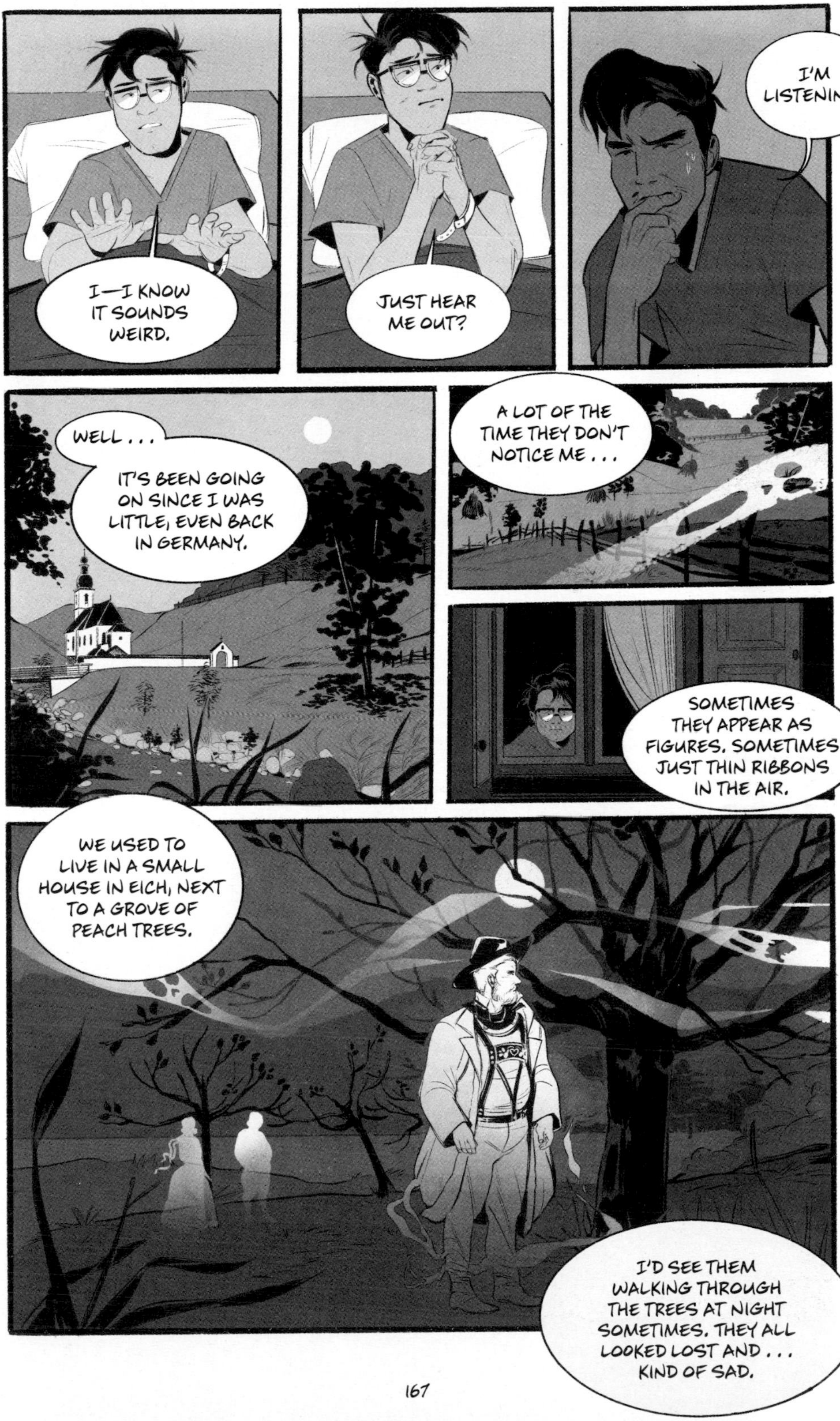

I—I KNOW IT SOUNDS WEIRD.
JUST HEAR ME OUT?
I'M LISTENING.
WELL . . .
IT'S BEEN GOING ON SINCE I WAS LITTLE, EVEN BACK IN GERMANY.
A LOT OF THE TIME THEY DON'T NOTICE ME . . .
SOMETIMES THEY APPEAR AS FIGURES. SOMETIMES JUST THIN RIBBONS IN THE AIR.
WE USED TO LIVE IN A SMALL HOUSE IN EICH, NEXT TO A GROVE OF PEACH TREES.
I'D SEE THEM WALKING THROUGH THE TREES AT NIGHT SOMETIMES. THEY ALL LOOKED LOST AND . . . KIND OF SAD.

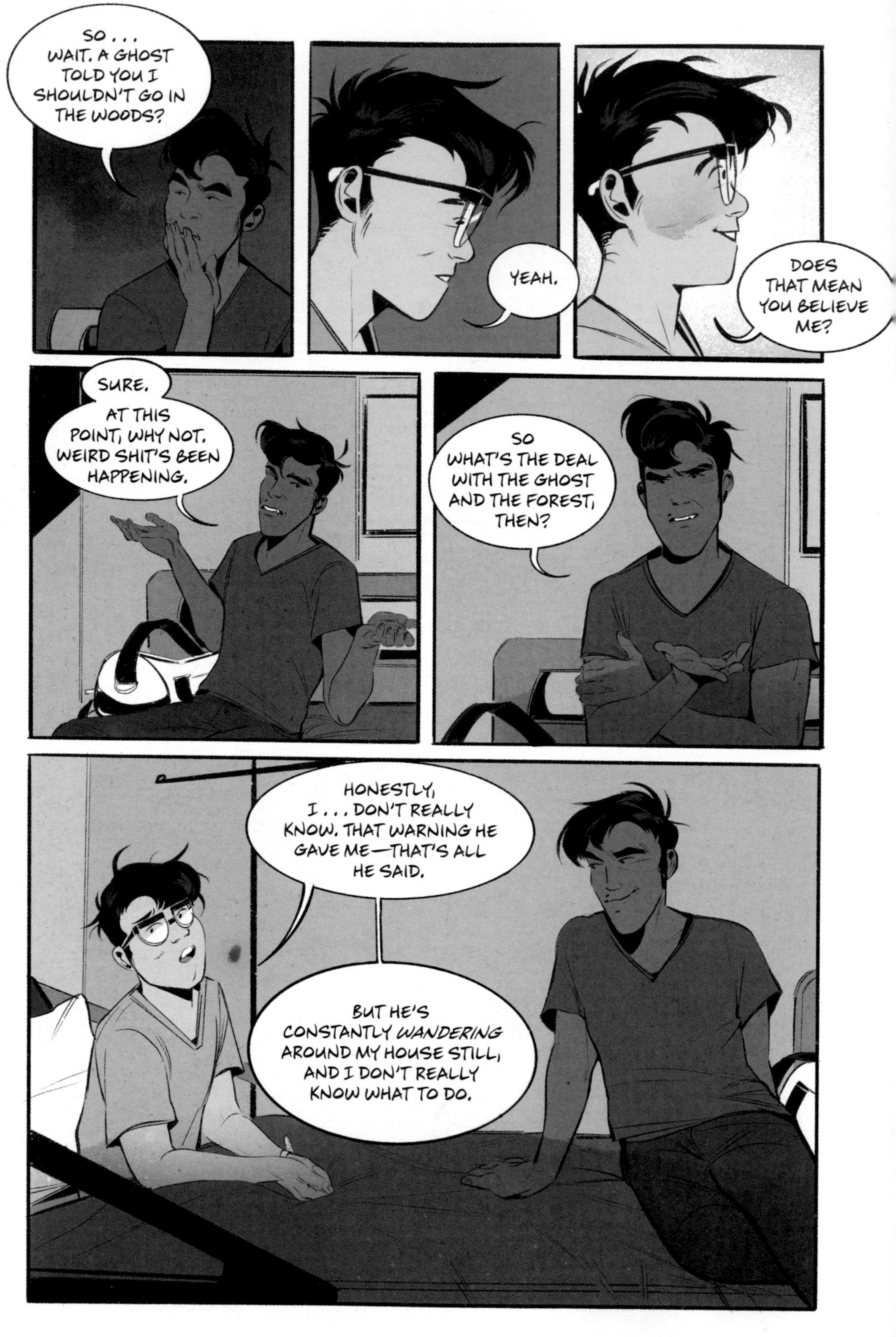
SO . . . WAIT. A GHOST TOLD YOU I SHOULDN'T GO IN THE WOODS?
YEAH.
DOES THAT MEAN YOU BELIEVE ME?
SURE.
AT THIS POINT, WHY NOT. WEIRD SHIT'S BEEN HAPPENING.
SO WHAT'S THE DEAL WITH THE GHOST AND THE FOREST, THEN?
HONESTLY, I . . . DON'T REALLY KNOW. THAT WARNING HE GAVE ME—THAT'S ALL HE SAID.
BUT HE'S CONSTANTLY *WANDERING* AROUND MY HOUSE STILL, AND I DON'T REALLY KNOW WHAT TO DO.

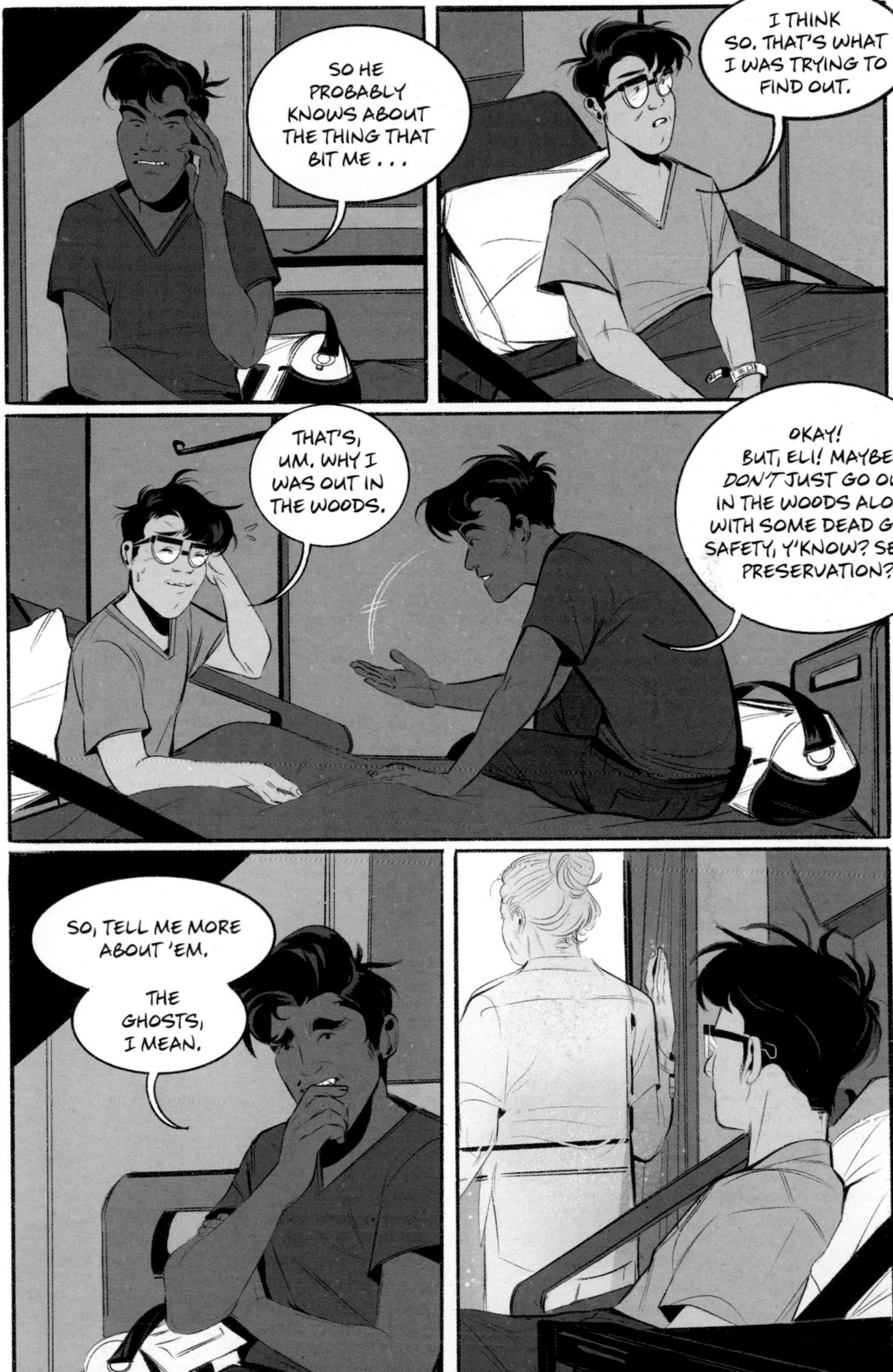
SO HE PROBABLY KNOWS ABOUT THE THING THAT BIT ME . . .
I THINK SO. THAT'S WHAT I WAS TRYING TO FIND OUT.
THAT'S, UM. WHY I WAS OUT IN THE WOODS.
OKAY! BUT, ELI! MAYBE *DON'T* JUST GO OUT IN THE WOODS ALONE WITH SOME DEAD GUY! SAFETY, Y'KNOW? SELF-PRESERVATION?
SO, TELL ME MORE ABOUT 'EM.
THE GHOSTS, I MEAN.

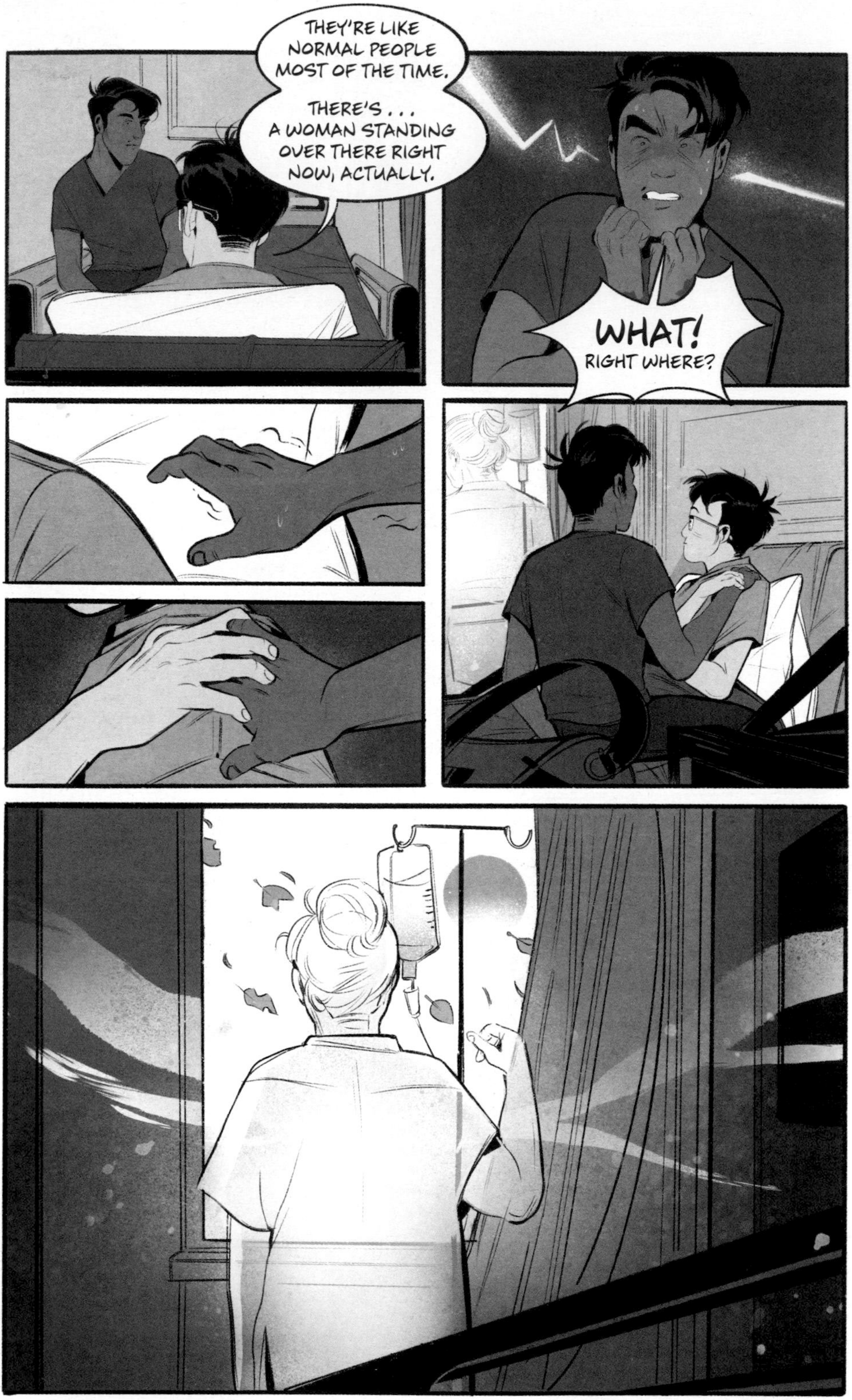
THEY'RE LIKE NORMAL PEOPLE MOST OF THE TIME.
THERE'S . . . A WOMAN STANDING OVER THERE RIGHT NOW, ACTUALLY.
WHAT! RIGHT WHERE?

WHAT THE HELL!

ELI! ELI, IF I'M TOUCHING YOU, I CAN SEE HER, TOO.

REALLY?

YEAH, MAN! YOU DIDN'T KNOW?

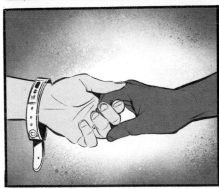

ELI HIRSCH?

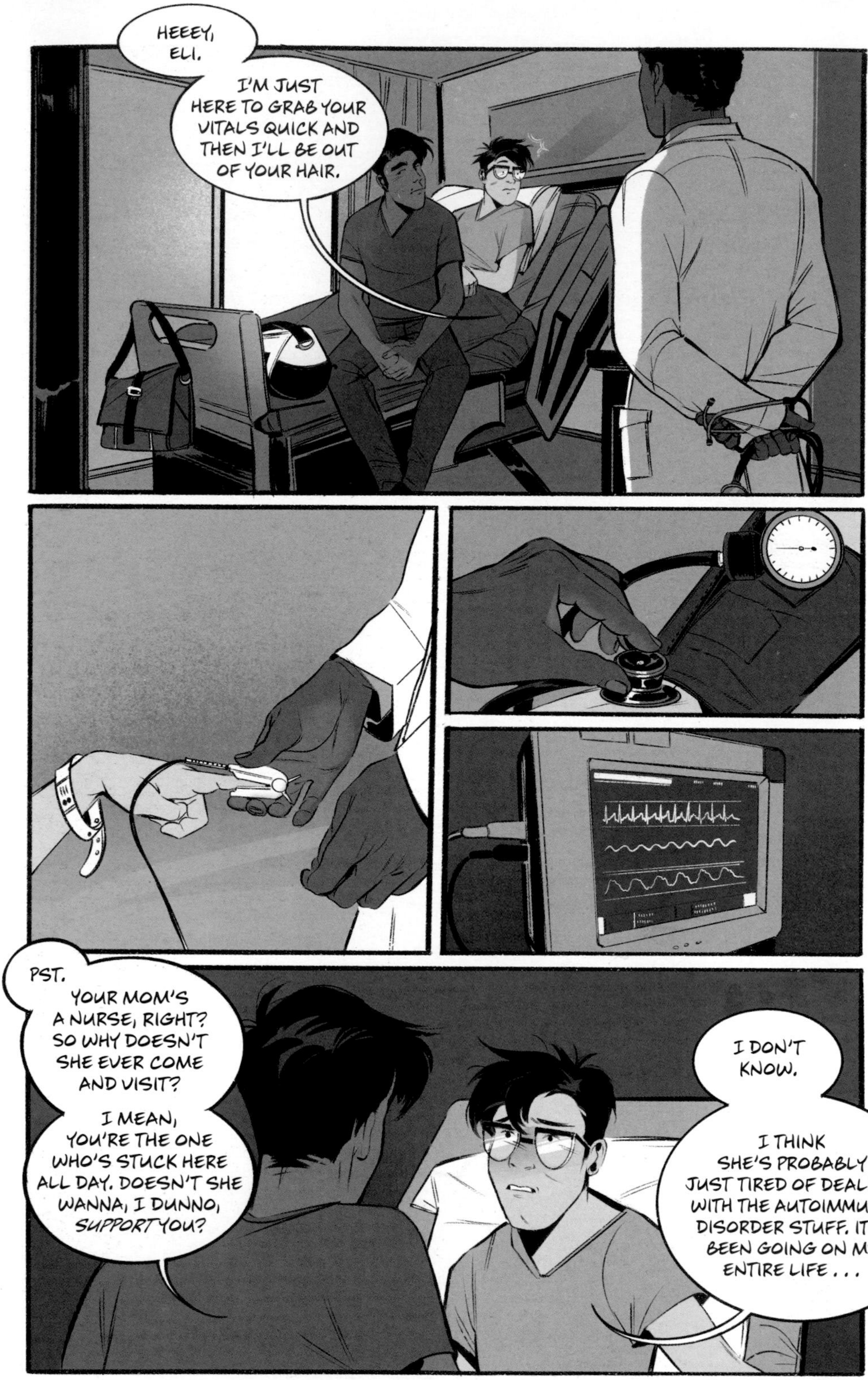
HEEEY, ELI.
I'M JUST HERE TO GRAB YOUR VITALS QUICK AND THEN I'LL BE OUT OF YOUR HAIR.
PST.
YOUR MOM'S A NURSE, RIGHT? SO WHY DOESN'T SHE EVER COME AND VISIT?
I MEAN, YOU'RE THE ONE WHO'S STUCK HERE ALL DAY. DOESN'T SHE WANNA, I DUNNO, *SUPPORT* YOU?
I DON'T KNOW.
I THINK SHE'S PROBABLY JUST TIRED OF DEALING WITH THE AUTOIMMUNE DISORDER STUFF. IT'S BEEN GOING ON MY ENTIRE LIFE . . .

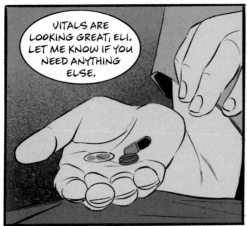

VITALS ARE LOOKING GREAT, ELI. LET ME KNOW IF YOU NEED ANYTHING ELSE.

BUT SHE'S YOUR MOM, MAN. SHE SHOULD BE HERE.

LISTEN . . . I'M GONNA VISIT YOU EVERY SINGLE DAY YOU'RE STUCK HERE.

BECAUSE IT'S NOT HARD TO, LIKE, SIT IN A CHAIR AND BE PRESENT WHEN YOU'RE NOT FEELING WELL.

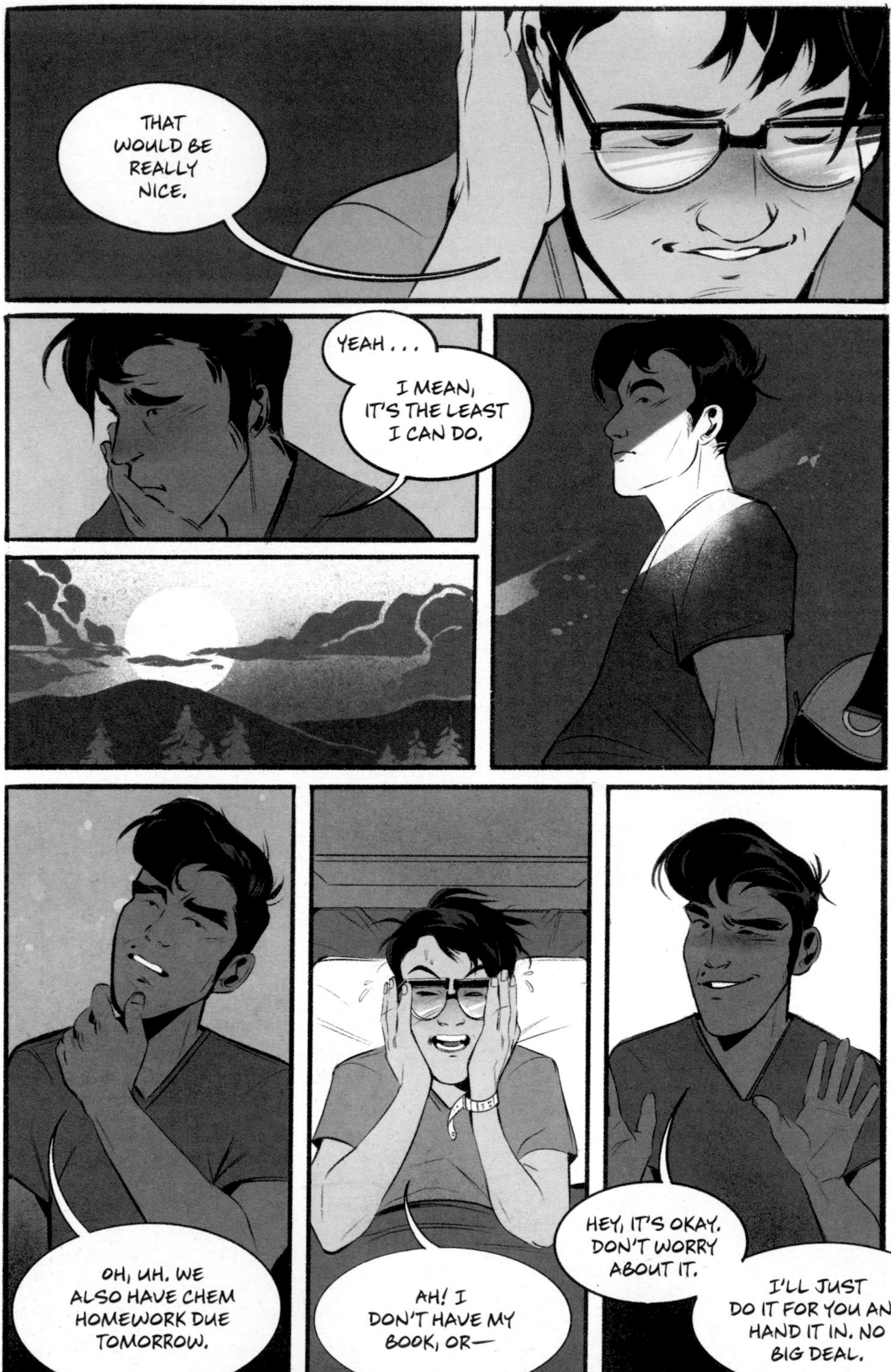
THAT WOULD BE REALLY NICE.
YEAH . . .
I MEAN, IT'S THE LEAST I CAN DO.
OH, UH. WE ALSO HAVE CHEM HOMEWORK DUE TOMORROW.
AH! I DON'T HAVE MY BOOK, OR—
HEY, IT'S OKAY. DON'T WORRY ABOUT IT.
I'LL JUST DO IT FOR YOU AND HAND IT IN. NO BIG DEAL.

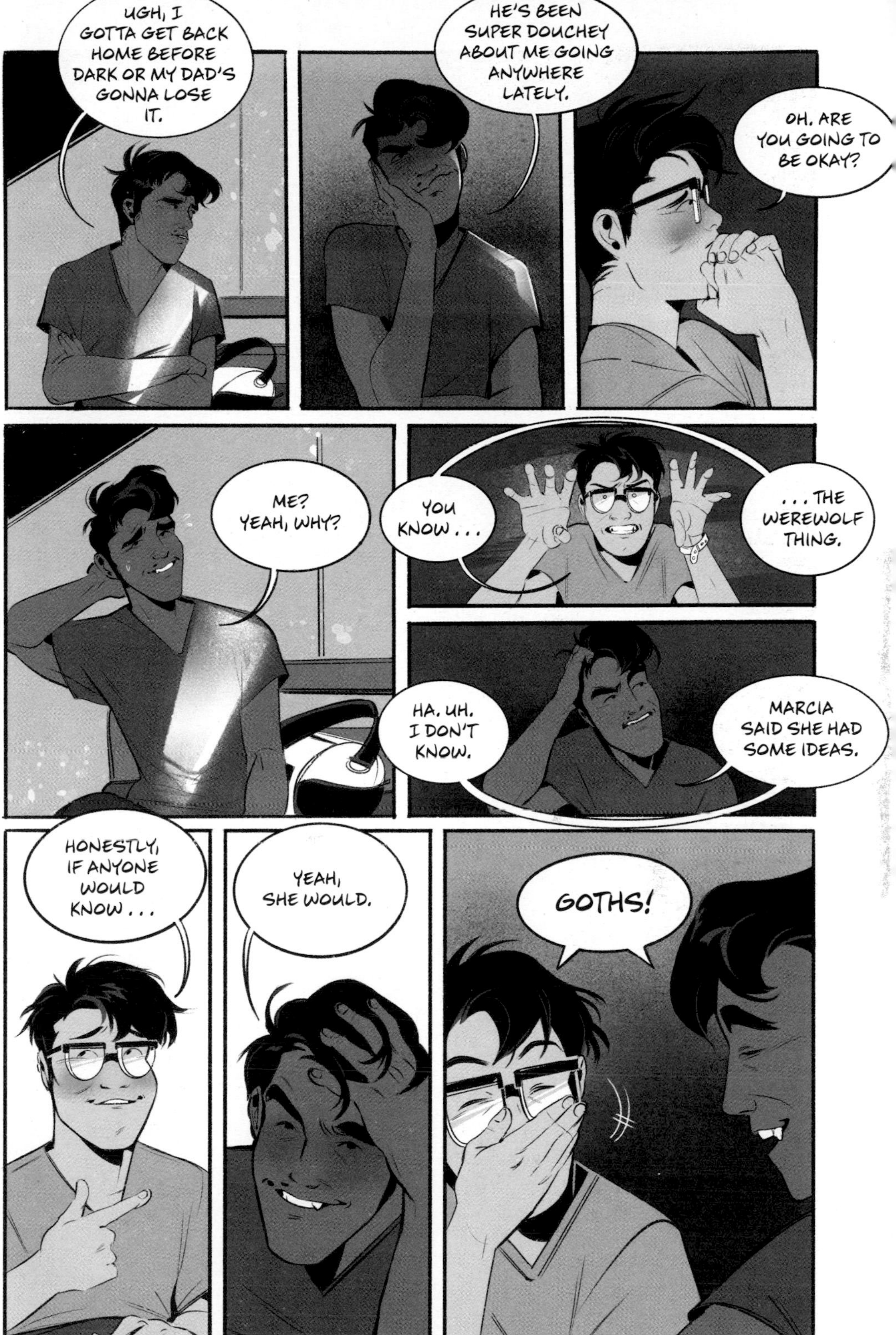
UGH, I GOTTA GET BACK HOME BEFORE DARK OR MY DAD'S GONNA LOSE IT.
HE'S BEEN SUPER DOUCHEY ABOUT ME GOING ANYWHERE LATELY.
OH. ARE YOU GOING TO BE OKAY?
ME? YEAH, WHY?
YOU KNOW . . .
. . . THE WEREWOLF THING.
HA. UH. I DON'T KNOW.
MARCIA SAID SHE HAD SOME IDEAS.
HONESTLY, IF ANYONE WOULD KNOW . . .
YEAH, SHE WOULD.
GOTHS!

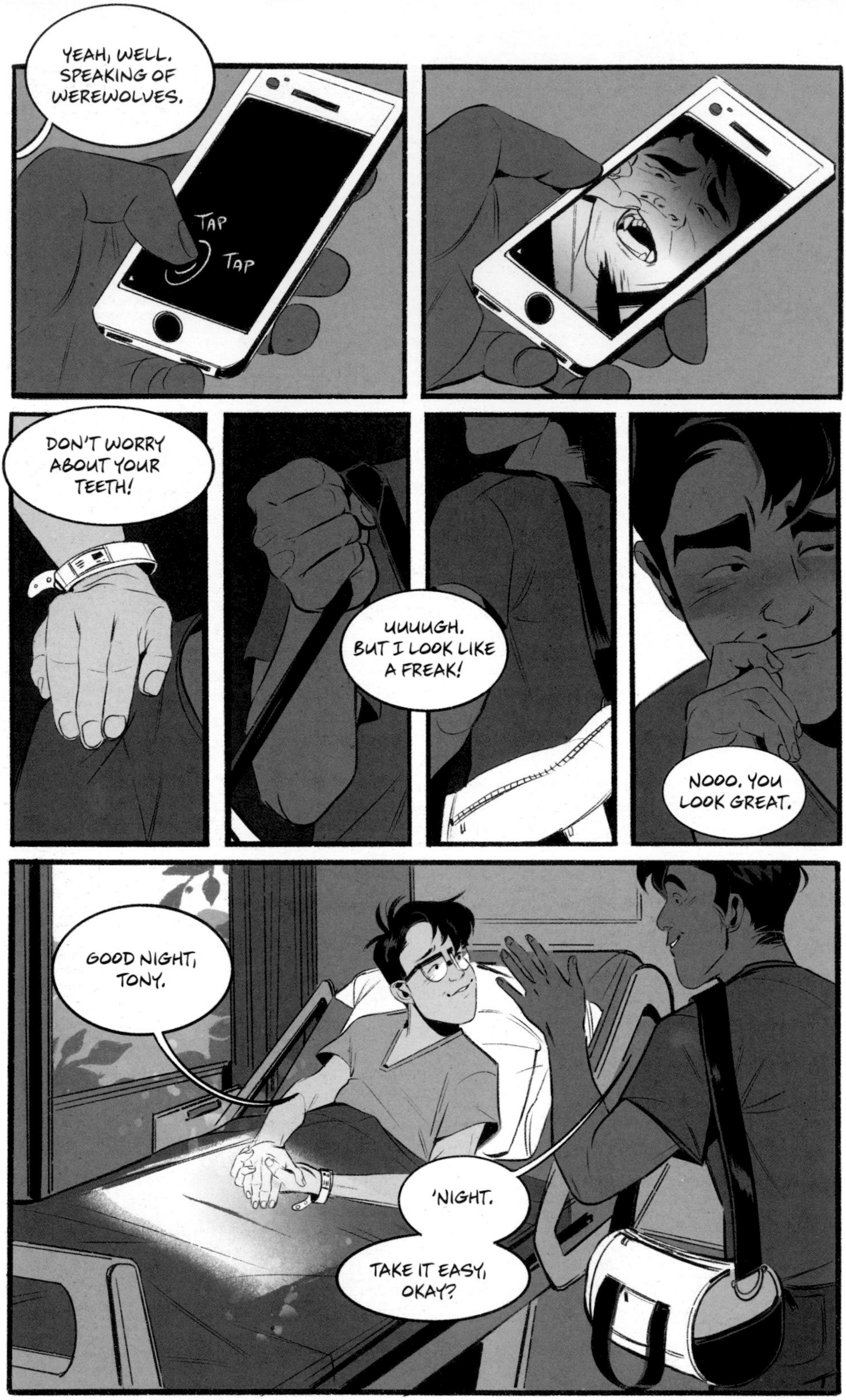
YEAH, WELL. SPEAKING OF WEREWOLVES.
TAP
TAP
DON'T WORRY ABOUT YOUR TEETH!
UUUUGH. BUT I LOOK LIKE A FREAK!
NOOO. YOU LOOK GREAT.
GOOD NIGHT, TONY.
'NIGHT.
TAKE IT EASY, OKAY?

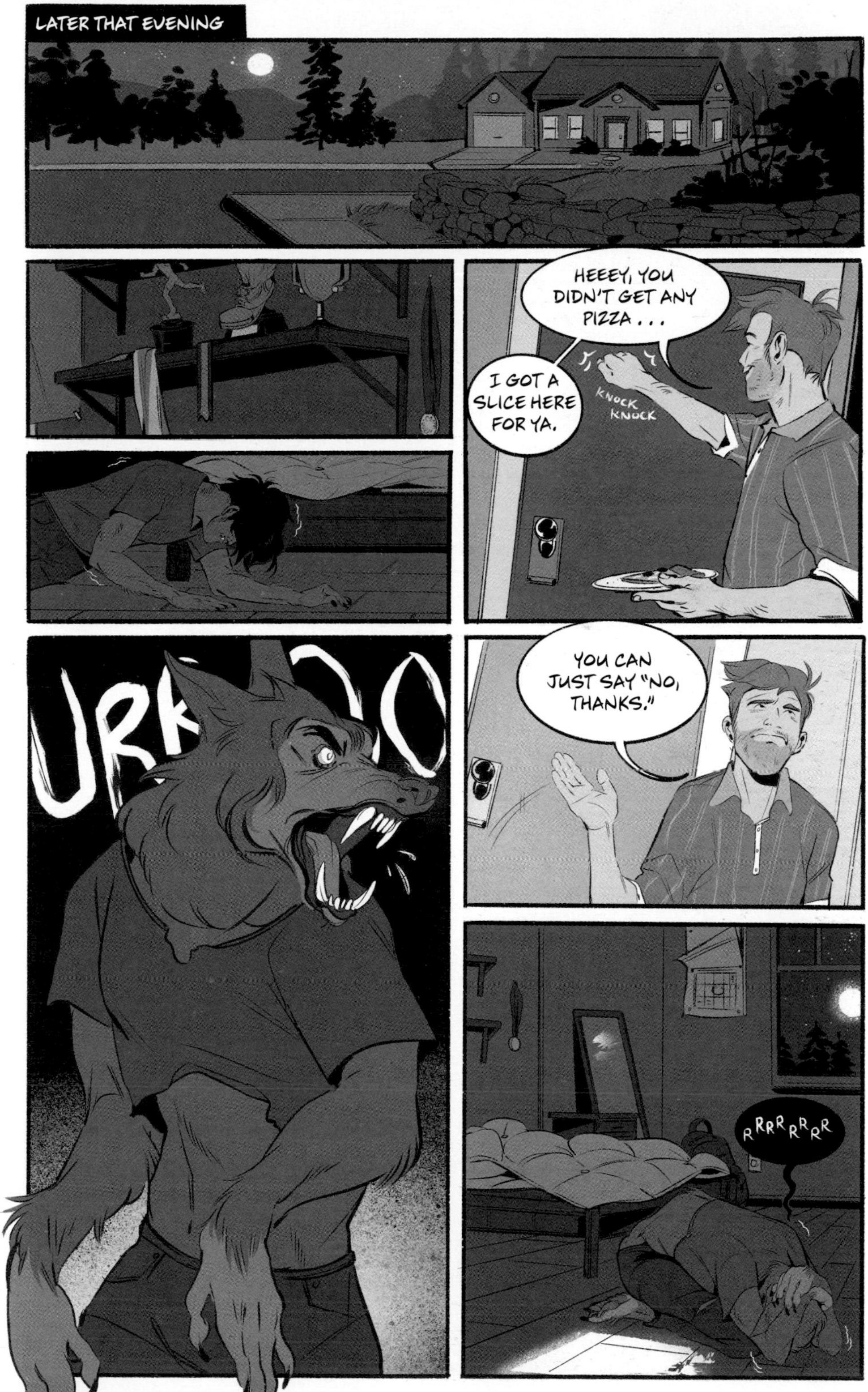
LATER THAT EVENING
HEEEY, YOU DIDN'T GET ANY PIZZA . . .
I GOT A SLICE HERE FOR YA.
KNOCK KNOCK
URK
YOU CAN JUST SAY "NO, THANKS."
RRRRRRRR

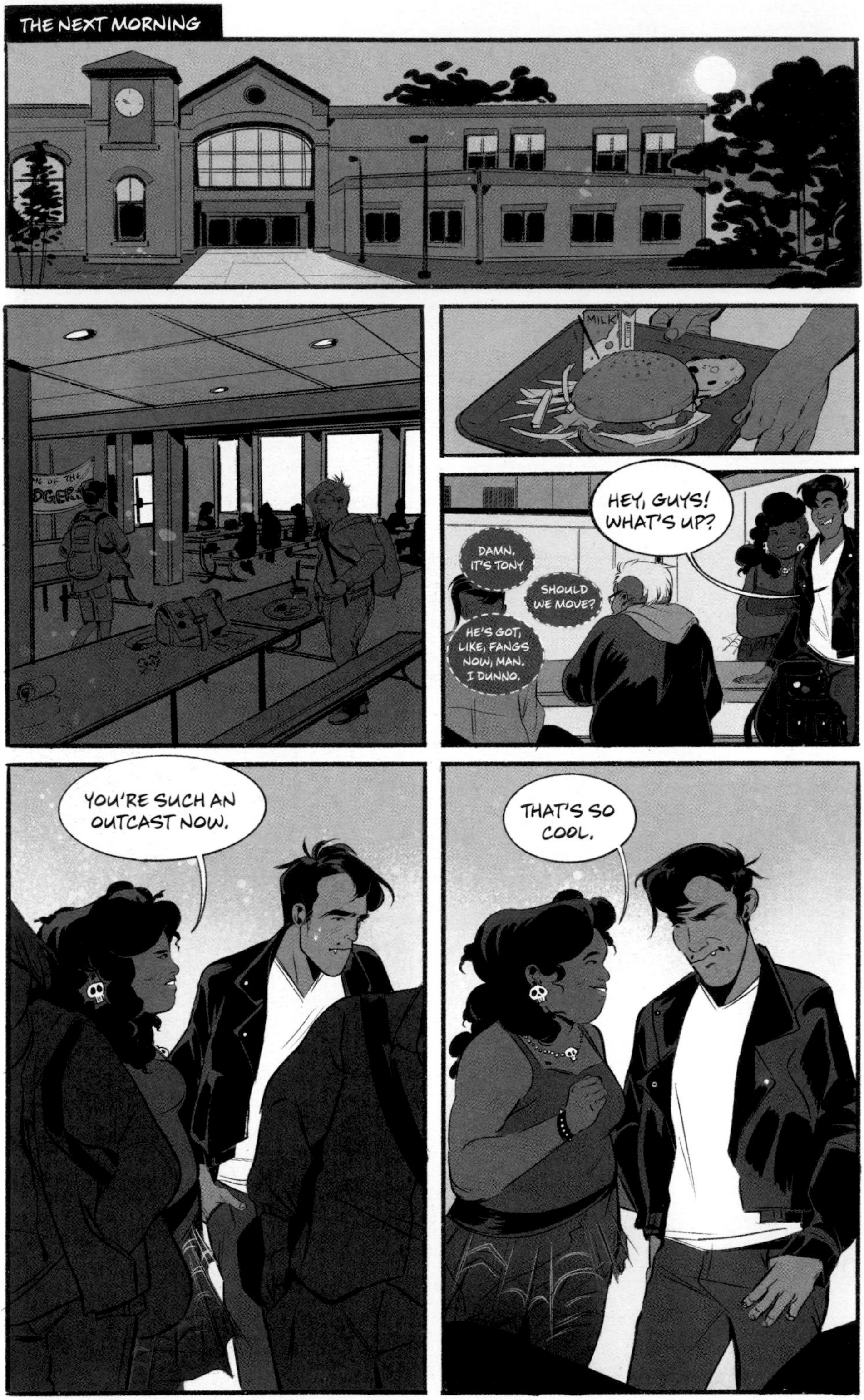
THE NEXT MORNING
MILK
HEY, GUYS! WHAT'S UP?
DAMN, IT'S TONY
SHOULD WE MOVE?
HE'S GOT, LIKE, FANGS NOW, MAN. I DUNNO.
YOU'RE SUCH AN OUTCAST NOW.
THAT'S SO COOL.

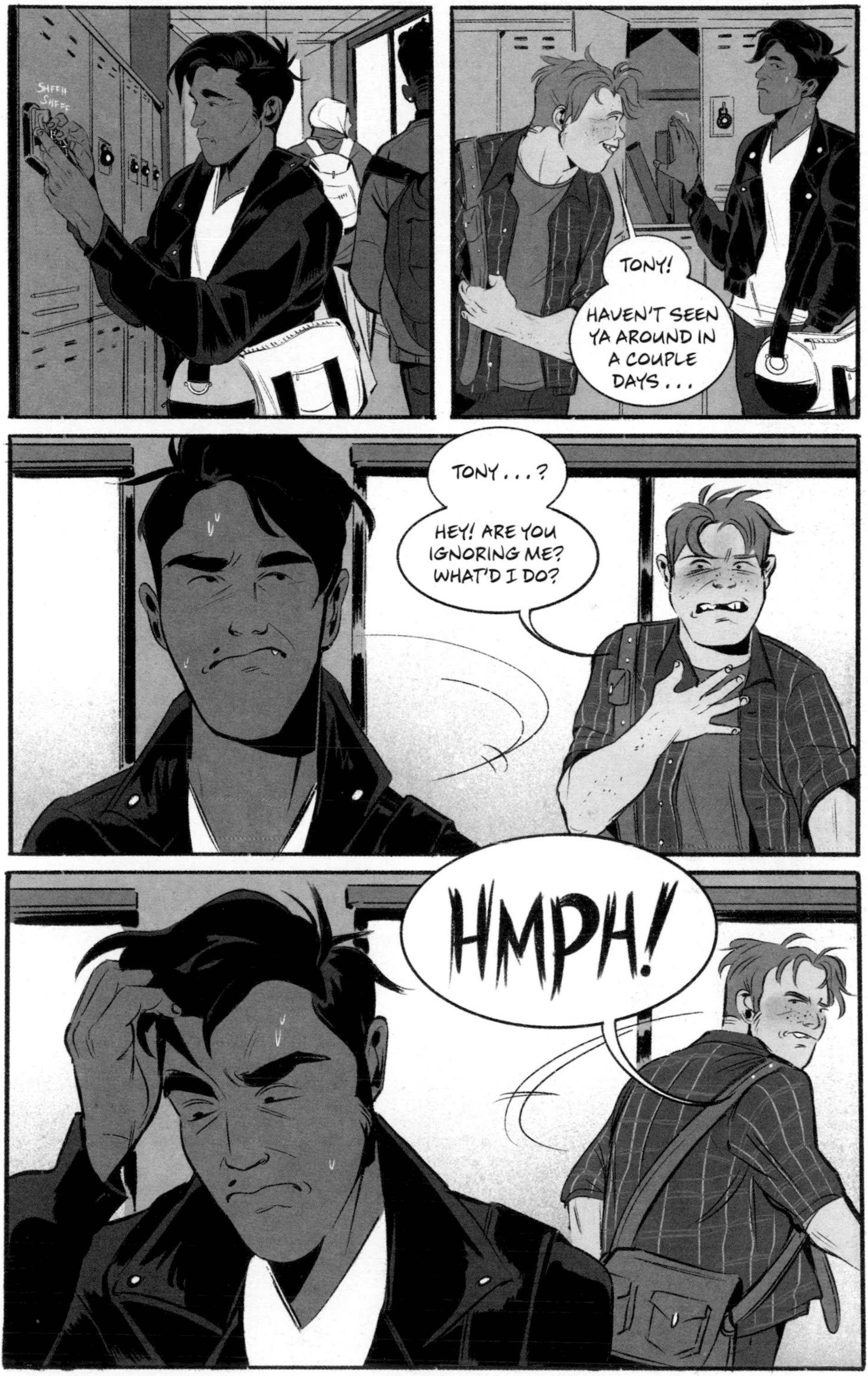
SHFFH SHFFF
TONY!
HAVEN'T SEEN YA AROUND IN A COUPLE DAYS . . .
TONY . . . ?
HEY! ARE YOU IGNORING ME? WHAT'D I DO?
HMPH!

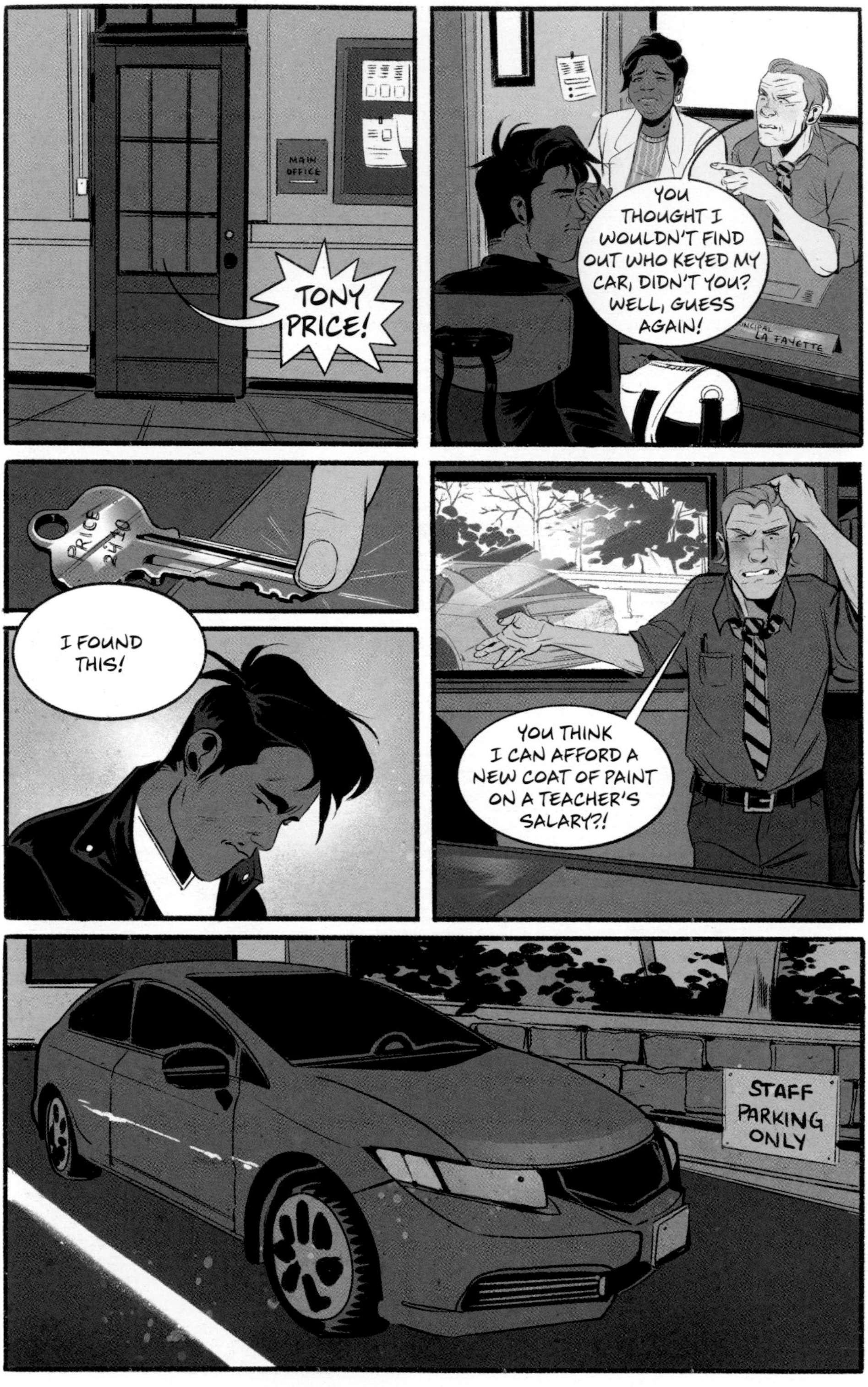
MAIN OFFICE
TONY PRICE!
YOU THOUGHT I WOULDN'T FIND OUT WHO KEYED MY CAR, DIDN'T YOU? WELL, GUESS AGAIN!
LA FAYETTE
PRICE 2410
I FOUND THIS!
YOU THINK I CAN AFFORD A NEW COAT OF PAINT ON A TEACHER'S SALARY?!
STAFF PARKING ONLY

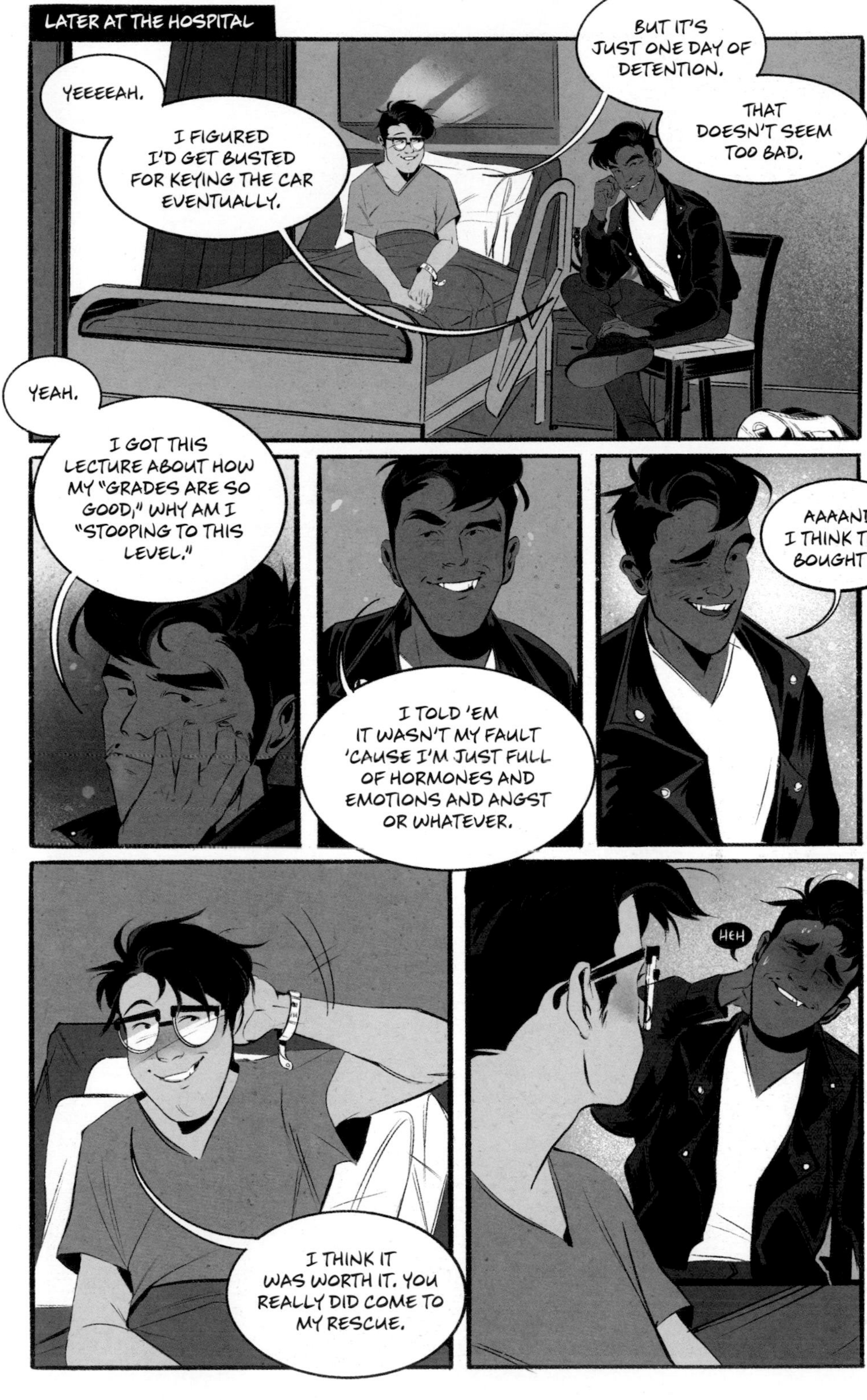
LATER AT THE HOSPITAL
YEEEEAH.
I FIGURED I'D GET BUSTED FOR KEYING THE CAR EVENTUALLY.
BUT IT'S JUST ONE DAY OF DETENTION.
THAT DOESN'T SEEM TOO BAD.
YEAH.
I GOT THIS LECTURE ABOUT HOW MY "GRADES ARE SO GOOD," WHY AM I "STOOPING TO THIS LEVEL."
I TOLD 'EM IT WASN'T MY FAULT 'CAUSE I'M JUST FULL OF HORMONES AND EMOTIONS AND ANGST OR WHATEVER.
AAAAND, I THINK THEY BOUGHT IT.
I THINK IT WAS WORTH IT. YOU REALLY DID COME TO MY RESCUE.
HEH

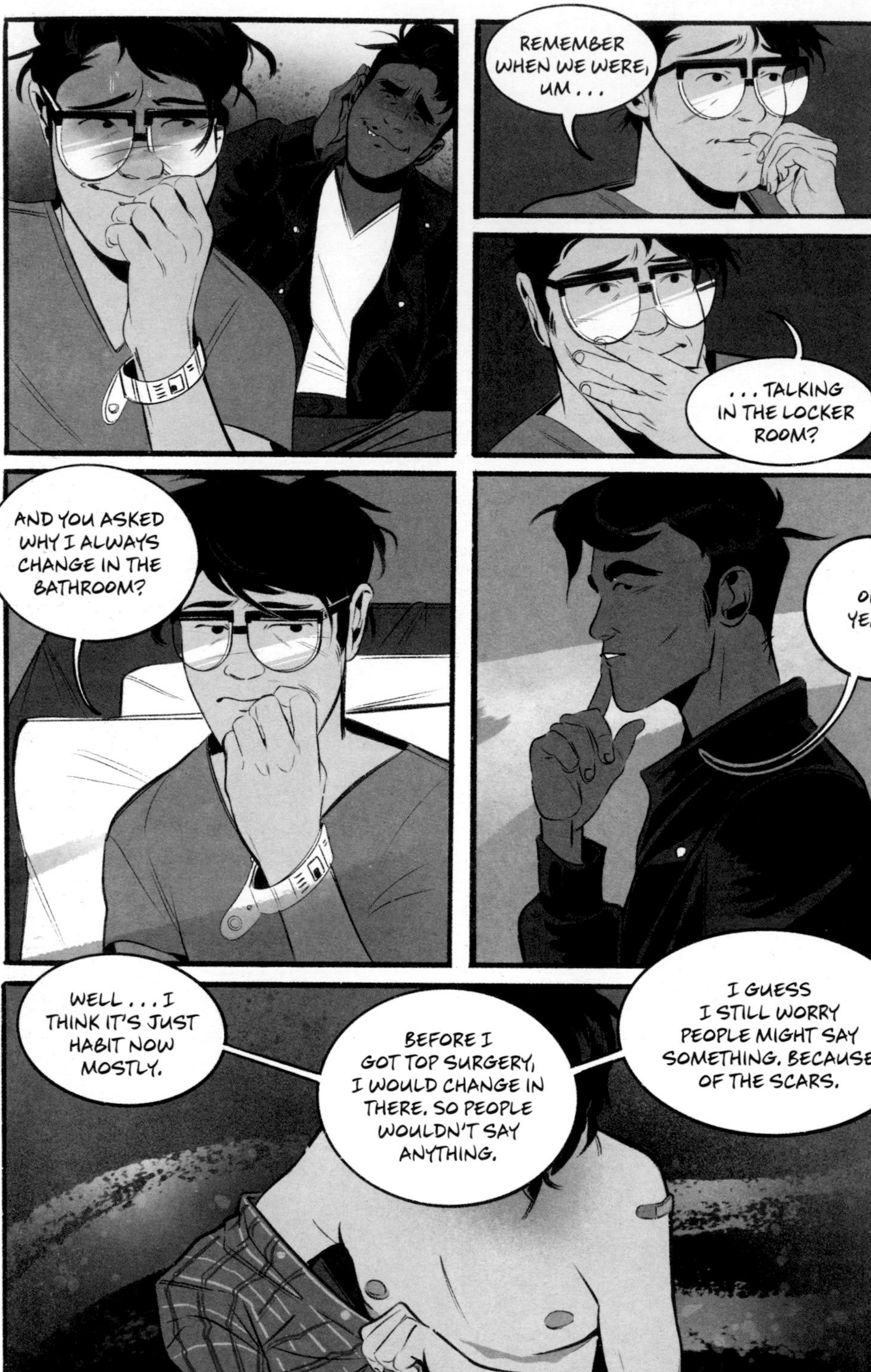
REMEMBER WHEN WE WERE, UM . . .
. . . TALKING IN THE LOCKER ROOM?
AND YOU ASKED WHY I ALWAYS CHANGE IN THE BATHROOM?
OH! YEAH.
WELL . . . I THINK IT'S JUST HABIT NOW MOSTLY.
BEFORE I GOT TOP SURGERY, I WOULD CHANGE IN THERE. SO PEOPLE WOULDN'T SAY ANYTHING.
I GUESS I STILL WORRY PEOPLE MIGHT SAY SOMETHING. BECAUSE OF THE SCARS.

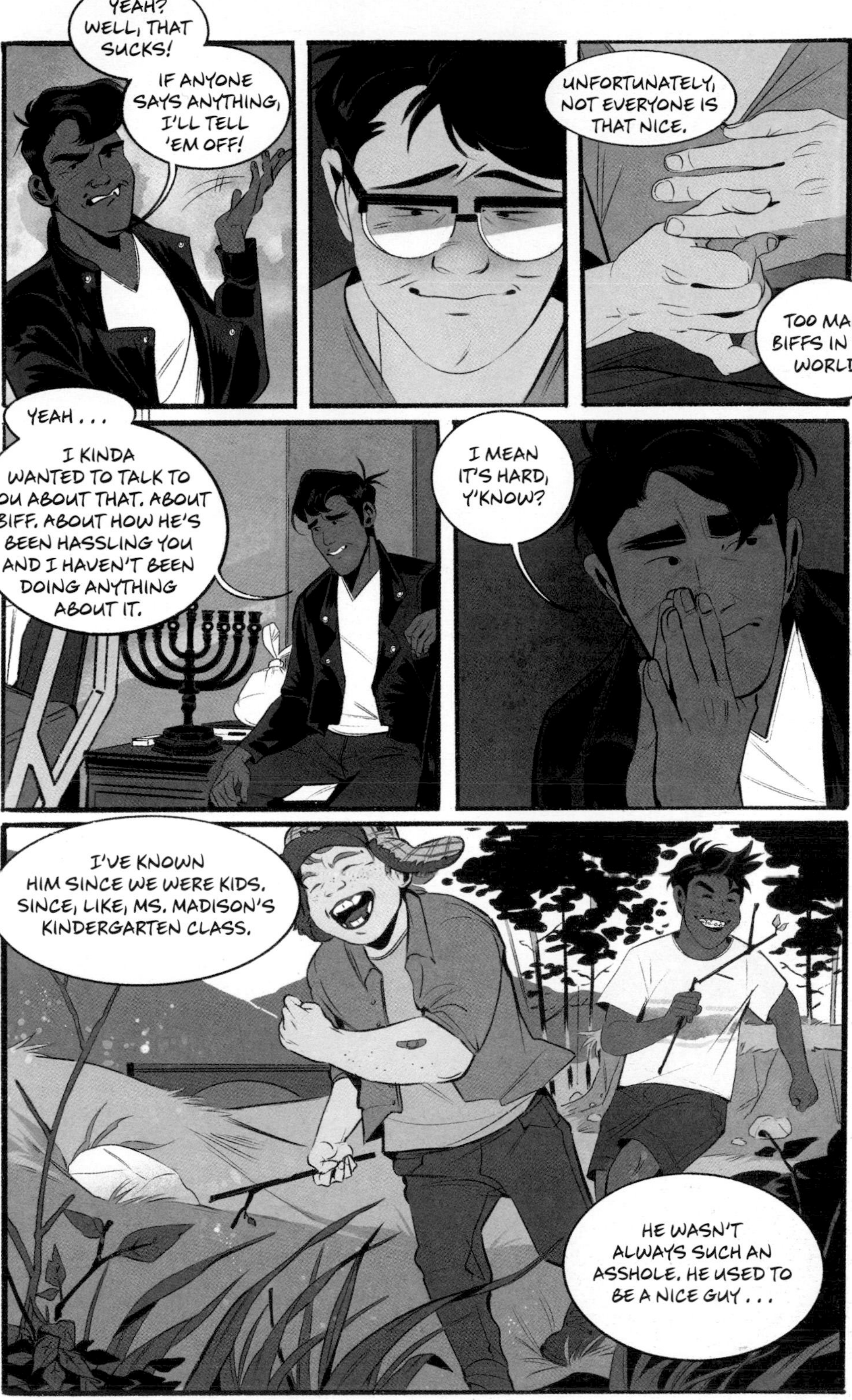
YEAH? WELL, THAT SUCKS!
IF ANYONE SAYS ANYTHING, I'LL TELL 'EM OFF!
UNFORTUNATELY, NOT EVERYONE IS THAT NICE.
TOO MANY BIFFS IN THE WORLD.
YEAH . . .
I KINDA WANTED TO TALK TO YOU ABOUT THAT. ABOUT BIFF. ABOUT HOW HE'S BEEN HASSLING YOU AND I HAVEN'T BEEN DOING ANYTHING ABOUT IT.
I MEAN IT'S HARD, Y'KNOW?
I'VE KNOWN HIM SINCE WE WERE KIDS. SINCE, LIKE, MS. MADISON'S KINDERGARTEN CLASS.
HE WASN'T ALWAYS SUCH AN ASSHOLE. HE USED TO BE A NICE GUY . . .

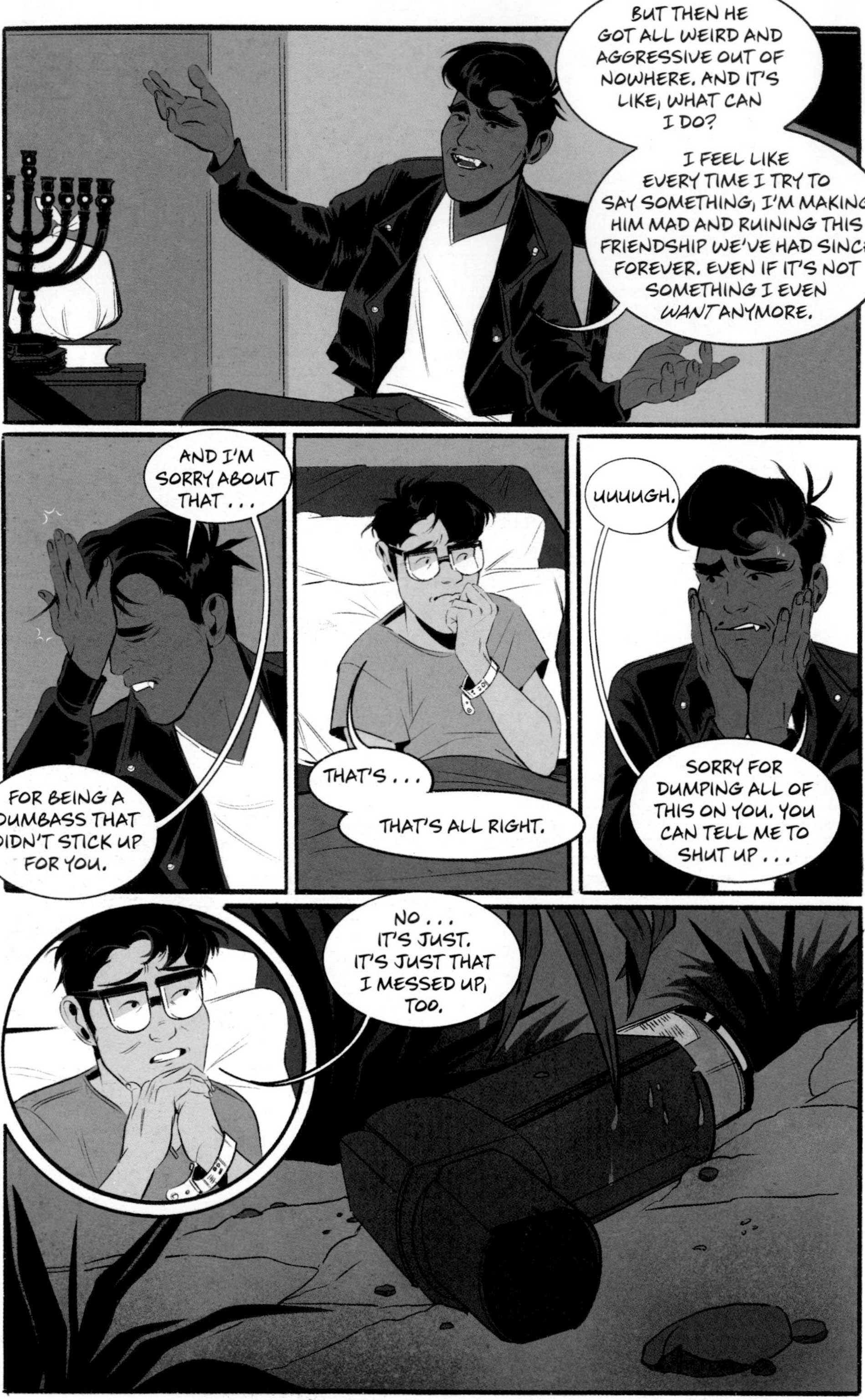
BUT THEN HE GOT ALL WEIRD AND AGGRESSIVE OUT OF NOWHERE. AND IT'S LIKE, WHAT CAN I DO?
I FEEL LIKE EVERY TIME I TRY TO SAY SOMETHING, I'M MAKING HIM MAD AND RUINING THIS FRIENDSHIP WE'VE HAD SINCE FOREVER. EVEN IF IT'S NOT SOMETHING I EVEN *WANT* ANYMORE.
AND I'M SORRY ABOUT THAT . . .
FOR BEING A DUMBASS THAT DIDN'T STICK UP FOR YOU.
THAT'S . . .
THAT'S ALL RIGHT.
UUUUGH.
SORRY FOR DUMPING ALL OF THIS ON YOU. YOU CAN TELL ME TO SHUT UP . . .
NO . . . IT'S JUST. IT'S JUST THAT I MESSED UP, TOO.

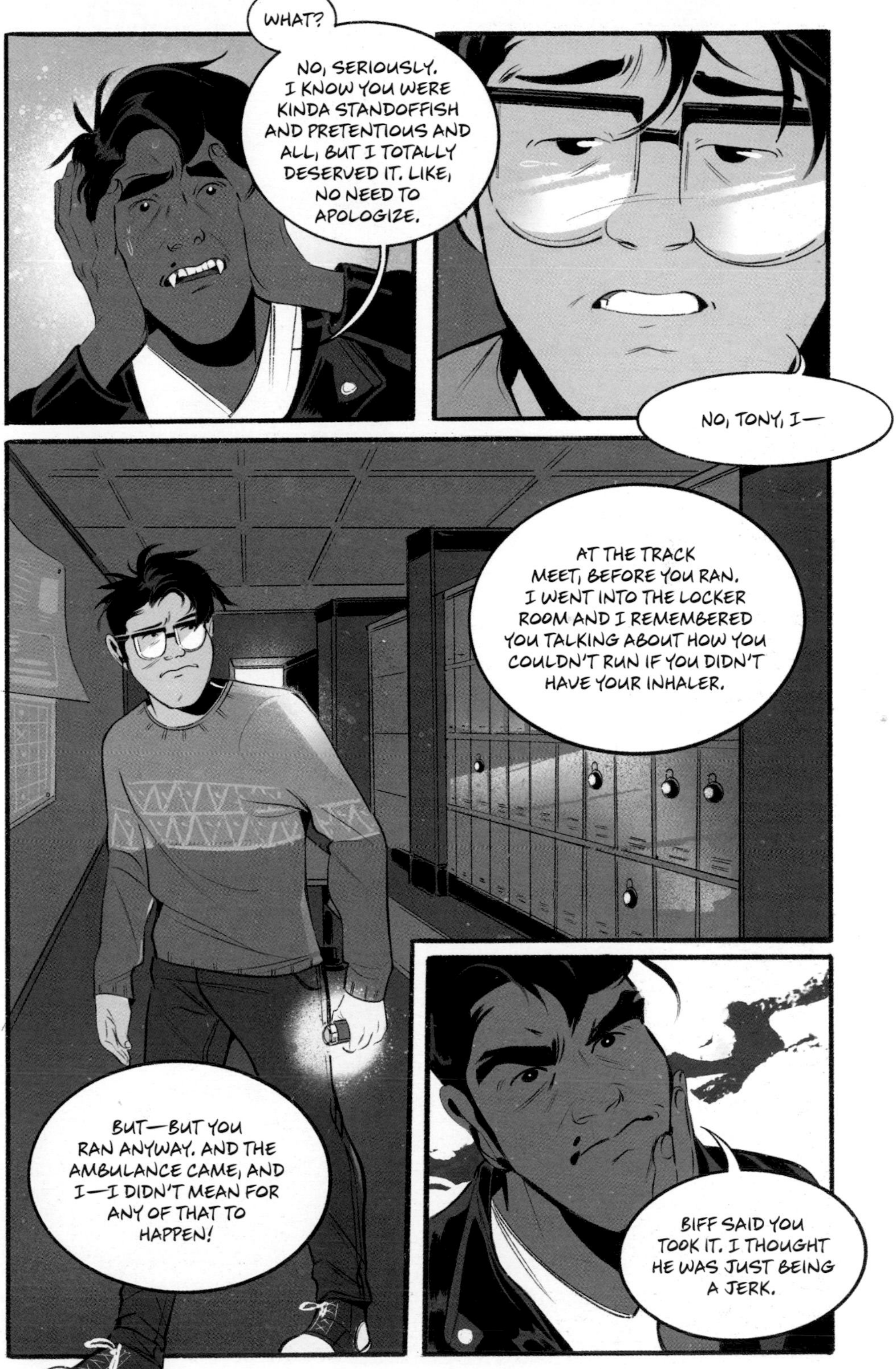
WHAT?
NO, SERIOUSLY. I KNOW YOU WERE KINDA STANDOFFISH AND PRETENTIOUS AND ALL, BUT I TOTALLY DESERVED IT. LIKE, NO NEED TO APOLOGIZE.
NO, TONY, I—
AT THE TRACK MEET, BEFORE YOU RAN. I WENT INTO THE LOCKER ROOM AND I REMEMBERED YOU TALKING ABOUT HOW YOU COULDN'T RUN IF YOU DIDN'T HAVE YOUR INHALER.
BUT—BUT YOU RAN ANYWAY. AND THE AMBULANCE CAME, AND I—I DIDN'T MEAN FOR ANY OF THAT TO HAPPEN!
BIFF SAID YOU TOOK IT. I THOUGHT HE WAS JUST BEING A JERK.

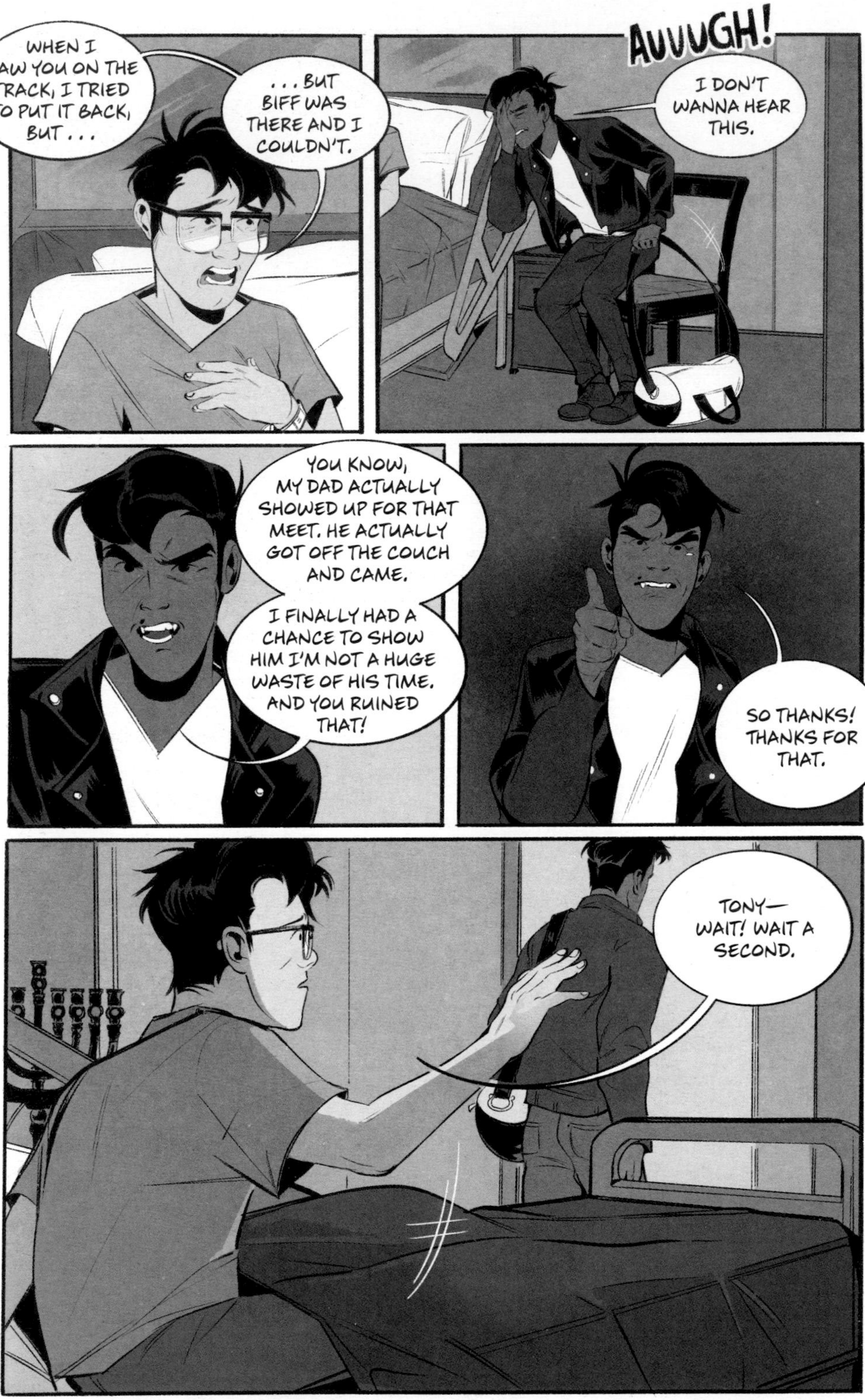
WHEN I SAW YOU ON THE TRACK, I TRIED TO PUT IT BACK, BUT . . .
. . . BUT BIFF WAS THERE AND I COULDN'T.
AUUUGH!
I DON'T WANNA HEAR THIS.
YOU KNOW, MY DAD ACTUALLY SHOWED UP FOR THAT MEET. HE ACTUALLY GOT OFF THE COUCH AND CAME.
I FINALLY HAD A CHANCE TO SHOW HIM I'M NOT A HUGE WASTE OF HIS TIME. AND YOU RUINED THAT!
SO THANKS! THANKS FOR THAT.
TONY— WAIT! WAIT A SECOND.

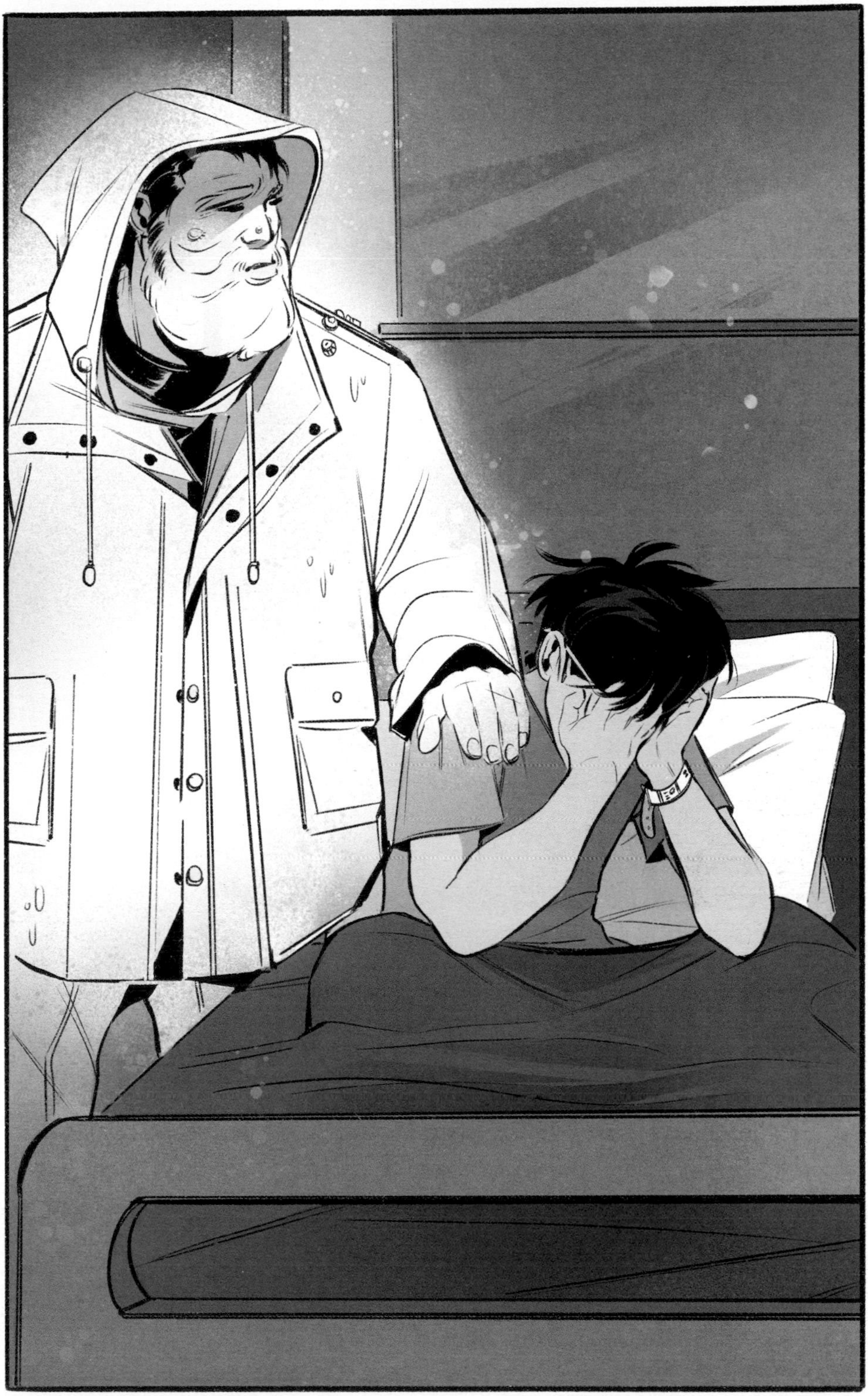

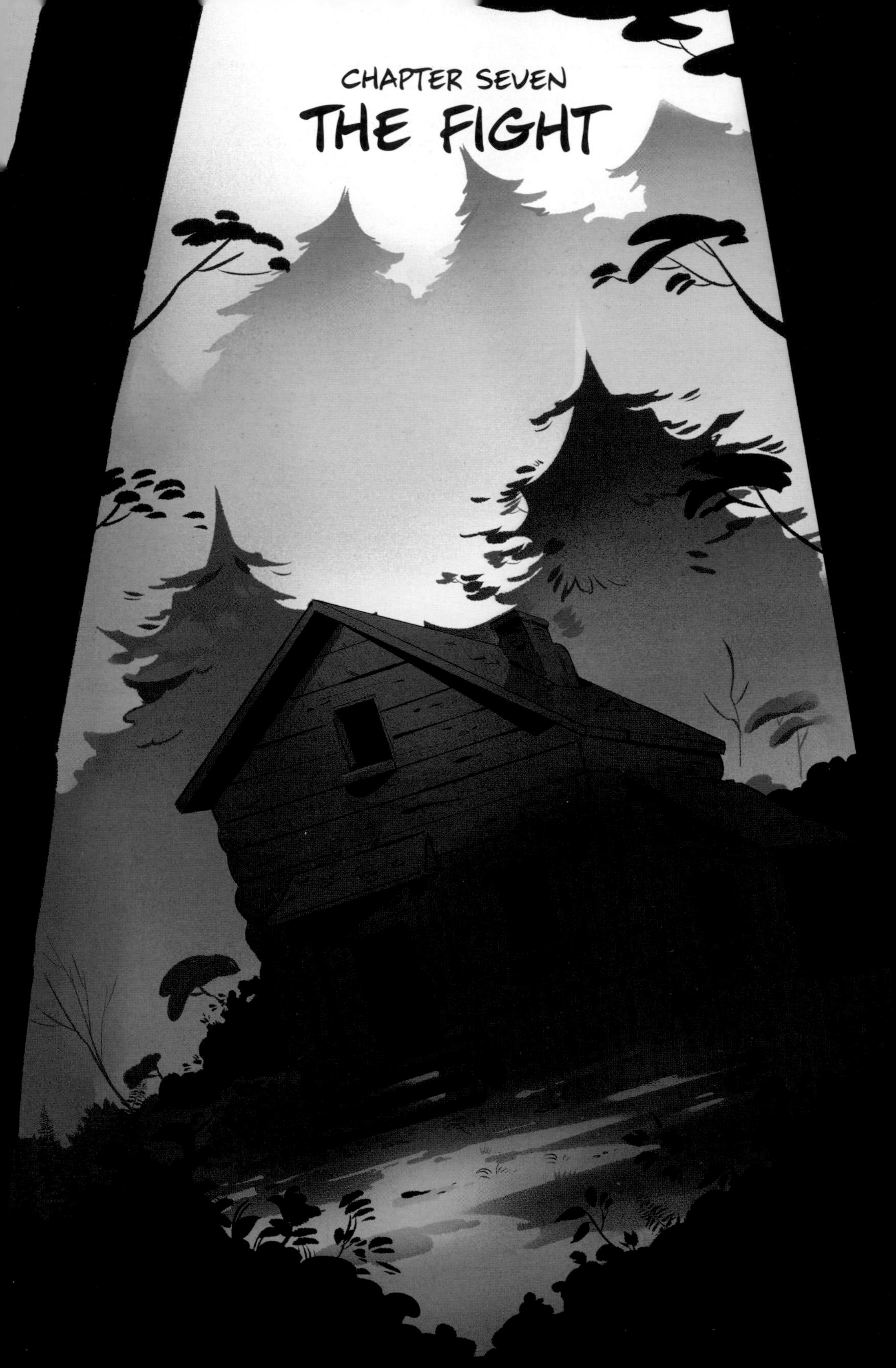
CHAPTER SEVEN
THE FIGHT

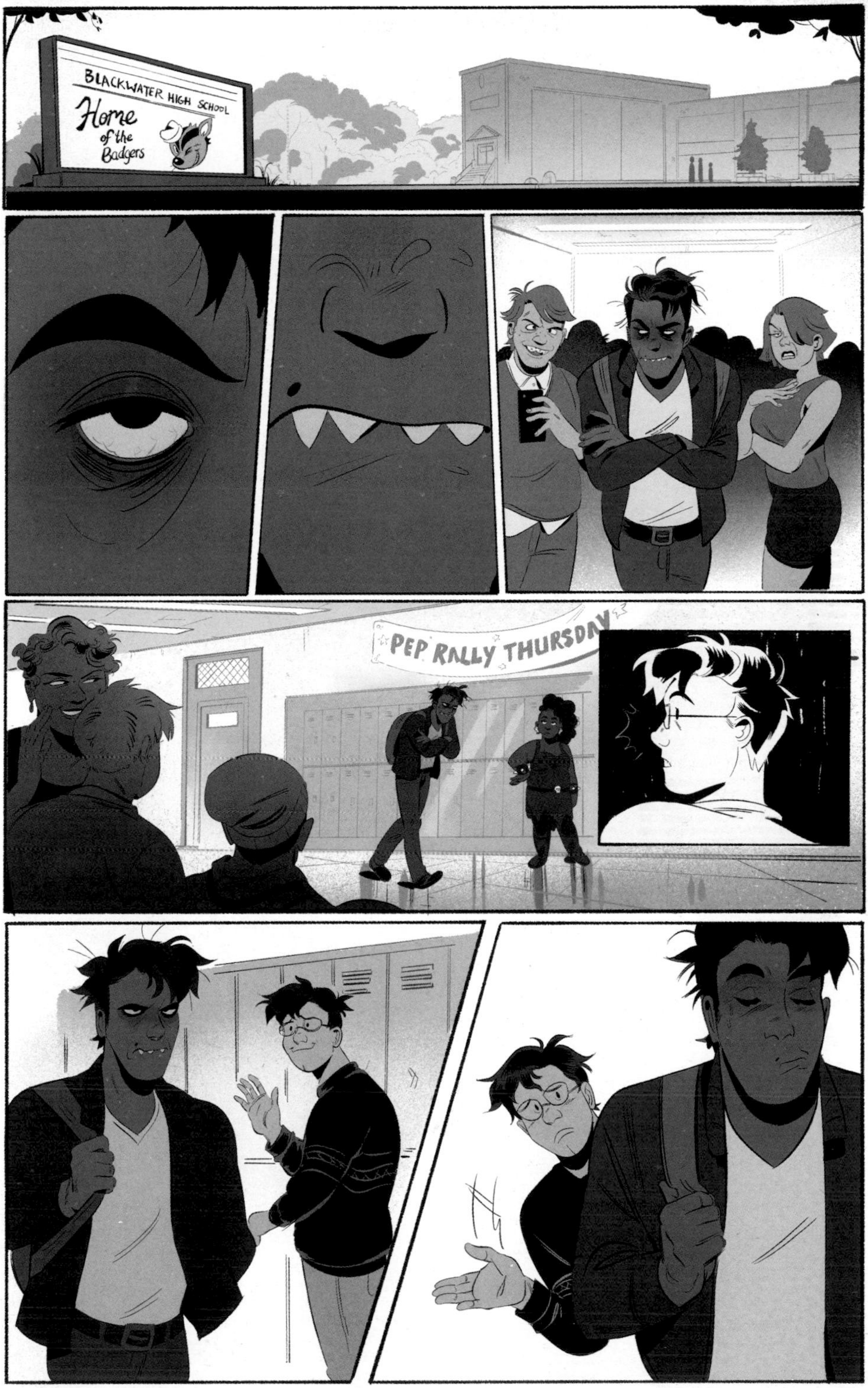
BLACKWATER HIGH SCHOOL
Home of the Badgers
PEP RALLY THURSDAY

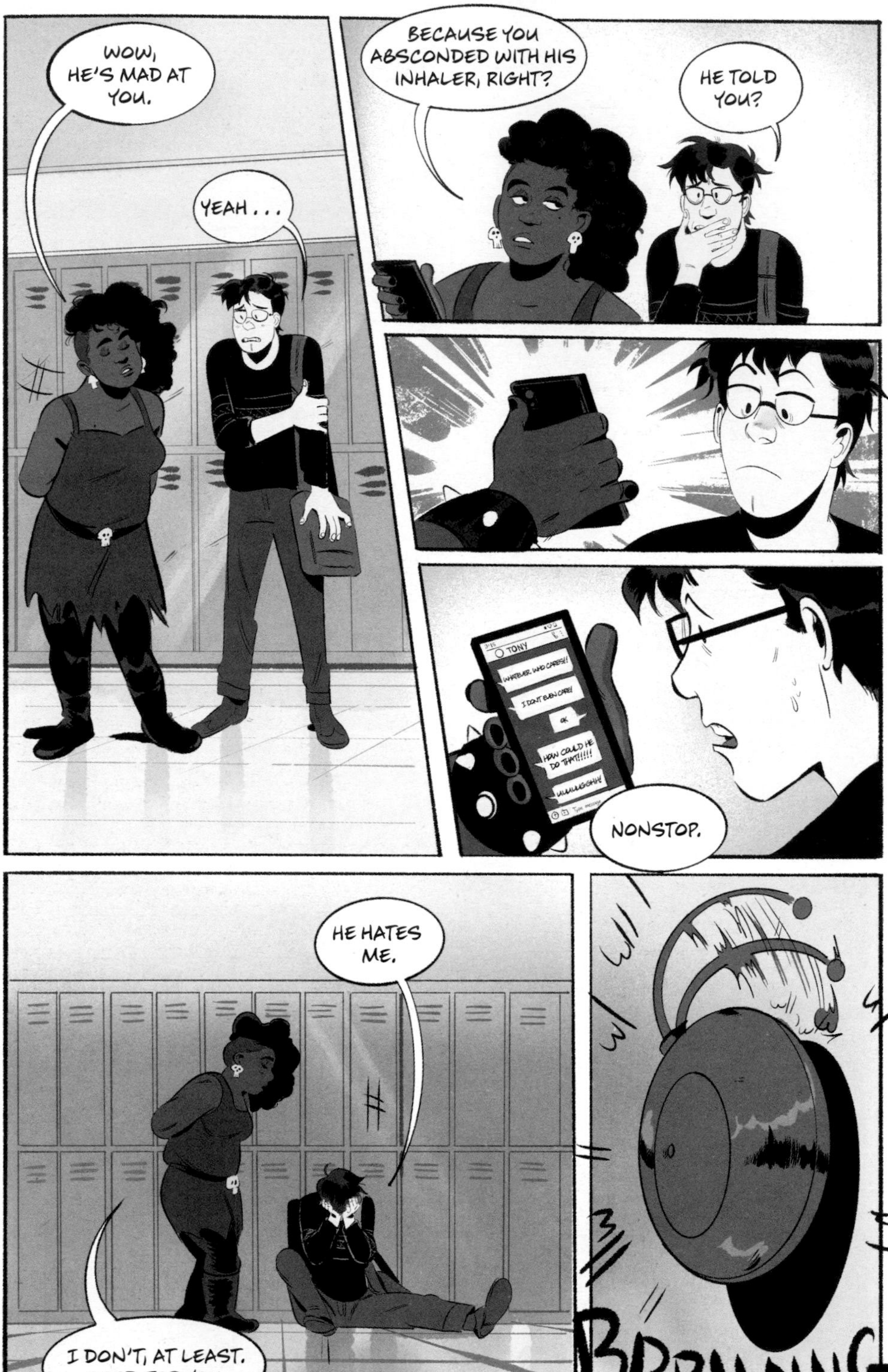
WOW, HE'S MAD AT YOU.
YEAH . . .
BECAUSE YOU ABSCONDED WITH HIS INHALER, RIGHT?
HE TOLD YOU?
TONY
WHATEVER WHO CARES!!
I DONT EVEN CARE!
OK
HOW COULD HE DO THAT!!!!!
UUUUUGGHH!
Type message
NONSTOP.
HE HATES ME.
I DON'T, AT LEAST. GOOD FOR YOU.
BRRIINNG

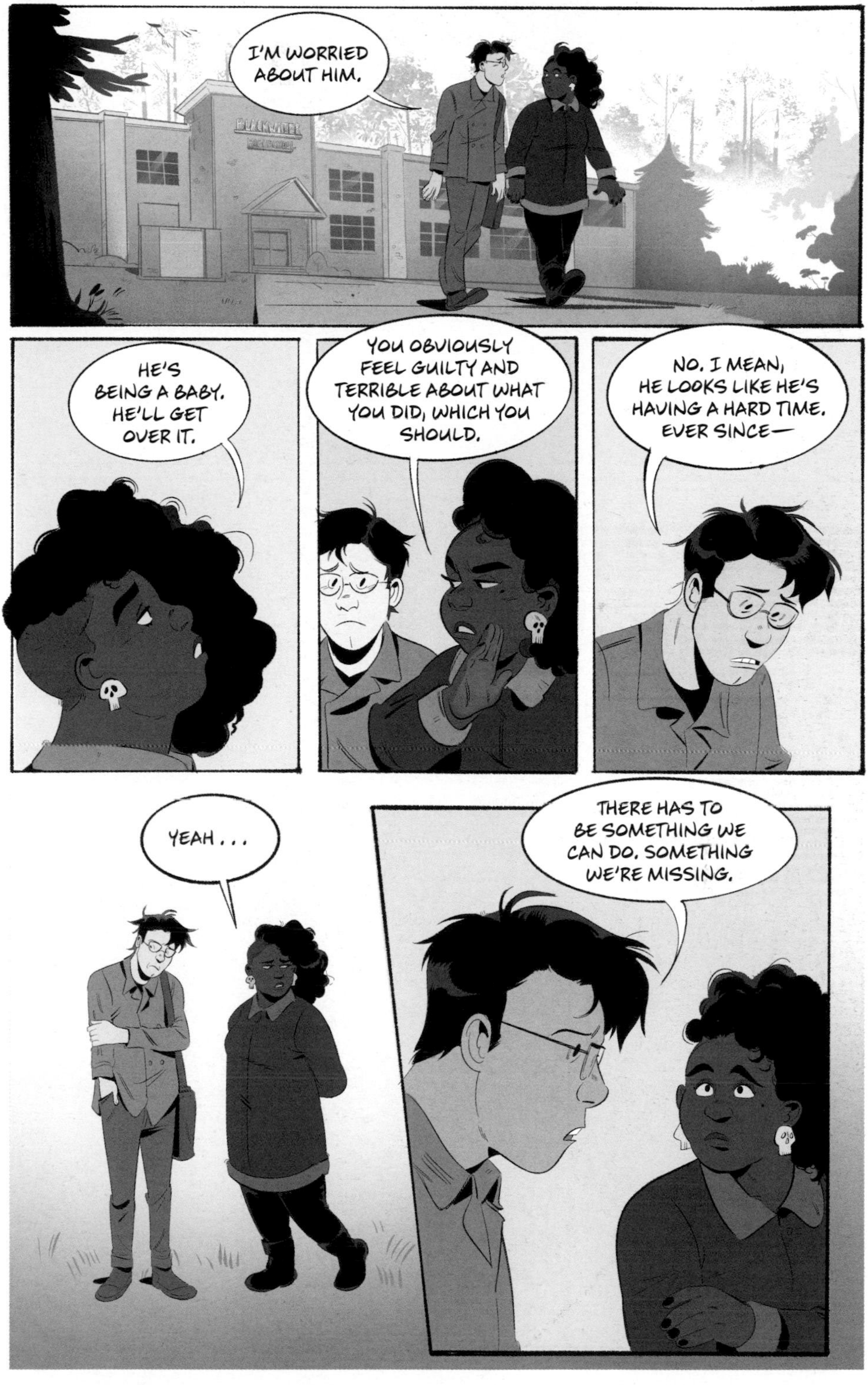
I'M WORRIED ABOUT HIM.
HE'S BEING A BABY. HE'LL GET OVER IT.
YOU OBVIOUSLY FEEL GUILTY AND TERRIBLE ABOUT WHAT YOU DID, WHICH YOU SHOULD.
NO. I MEAN, HE LOOKS LIKE HE'S HAVING A HARD TIME. EVER SINCE—
YEAH . . .
THERE HAS TO BE SOMETHING WE CAN DO. SOMETHING WE'RE MISSING.

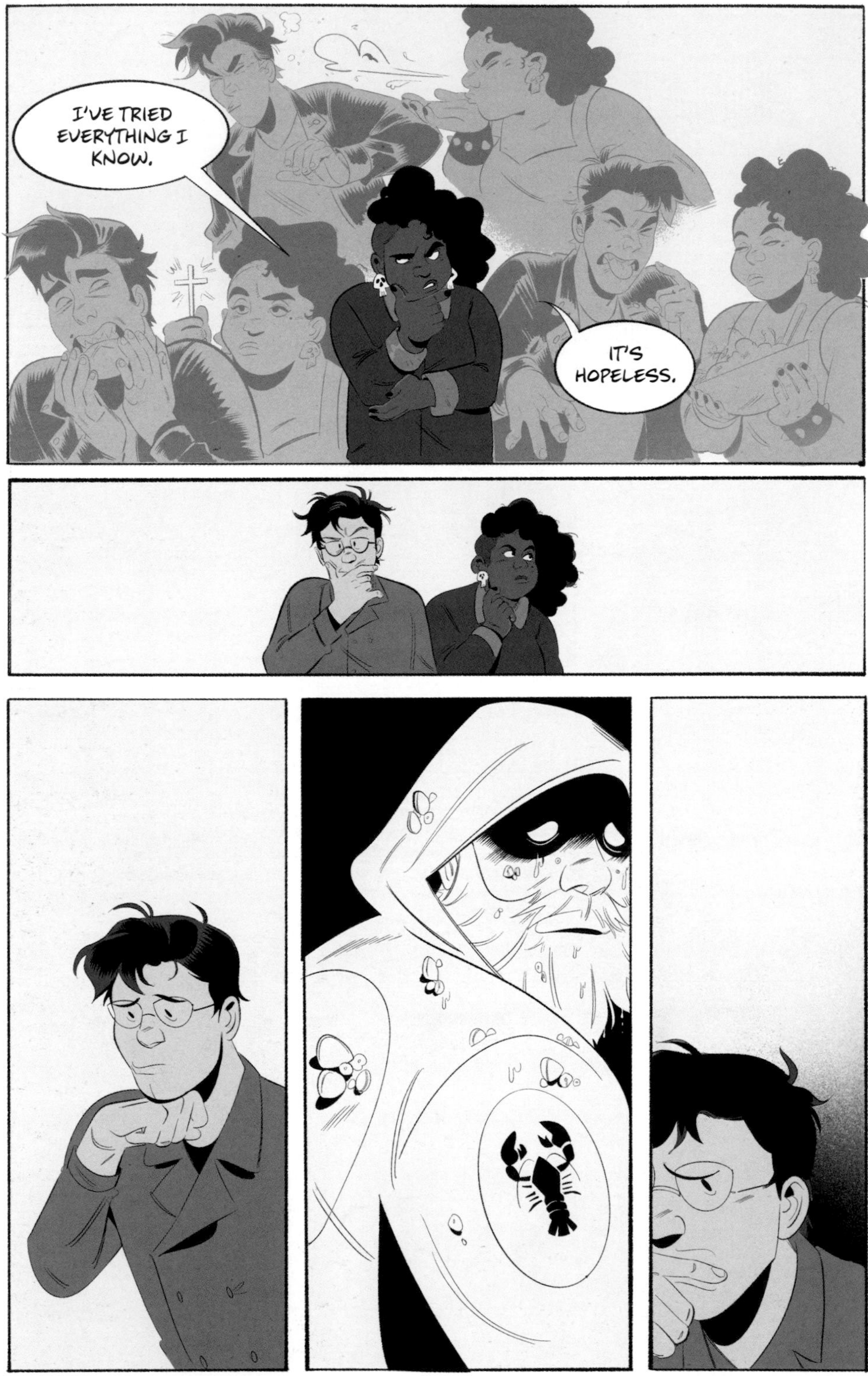
I'VE TRIED EVERYTHING I KNOW.
IT'S HOPELESS.

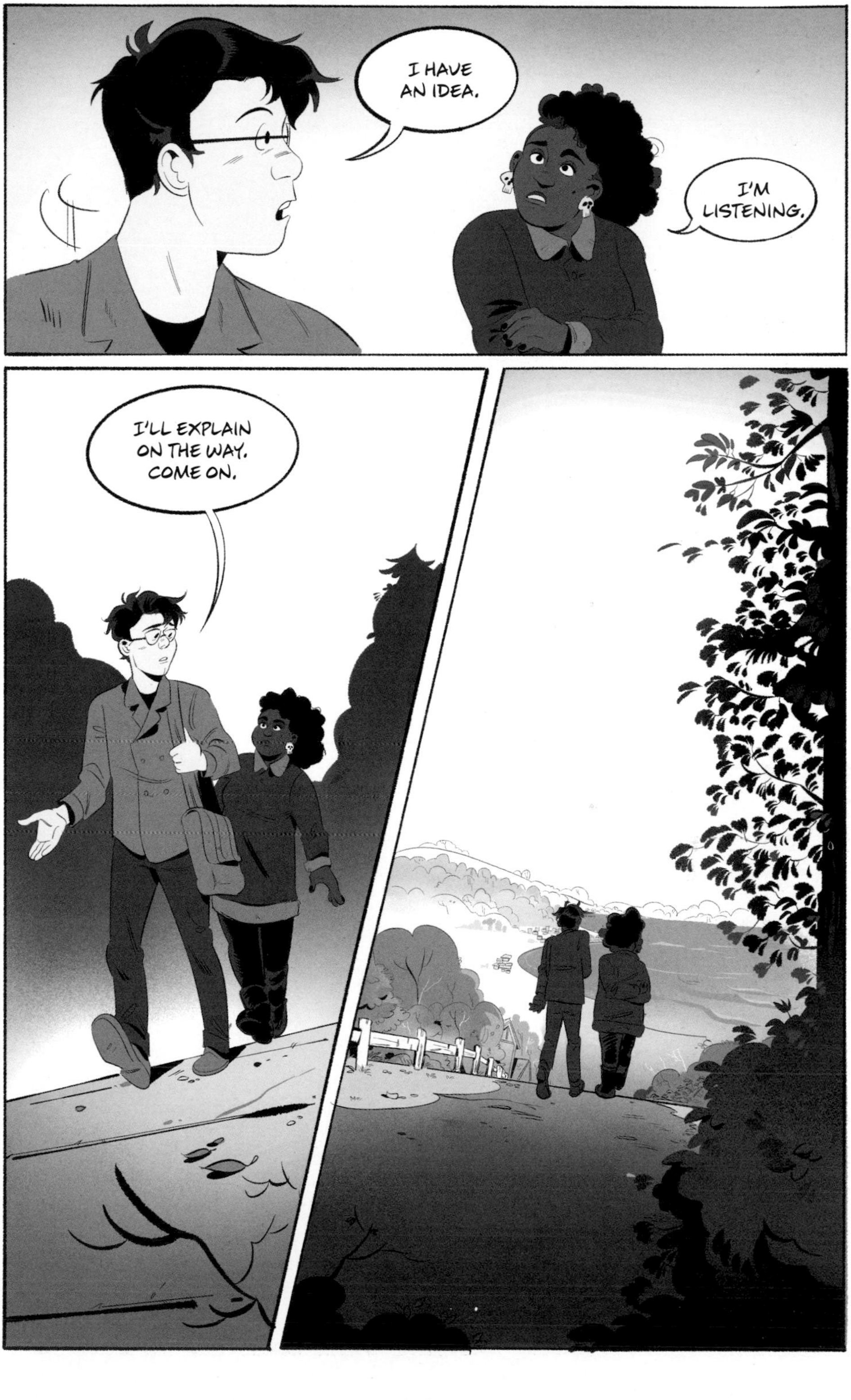
I HAVE AN IDEA.
I'M LISTENING.
I'LL EXPLAIN ON THE WAY. COME ON.

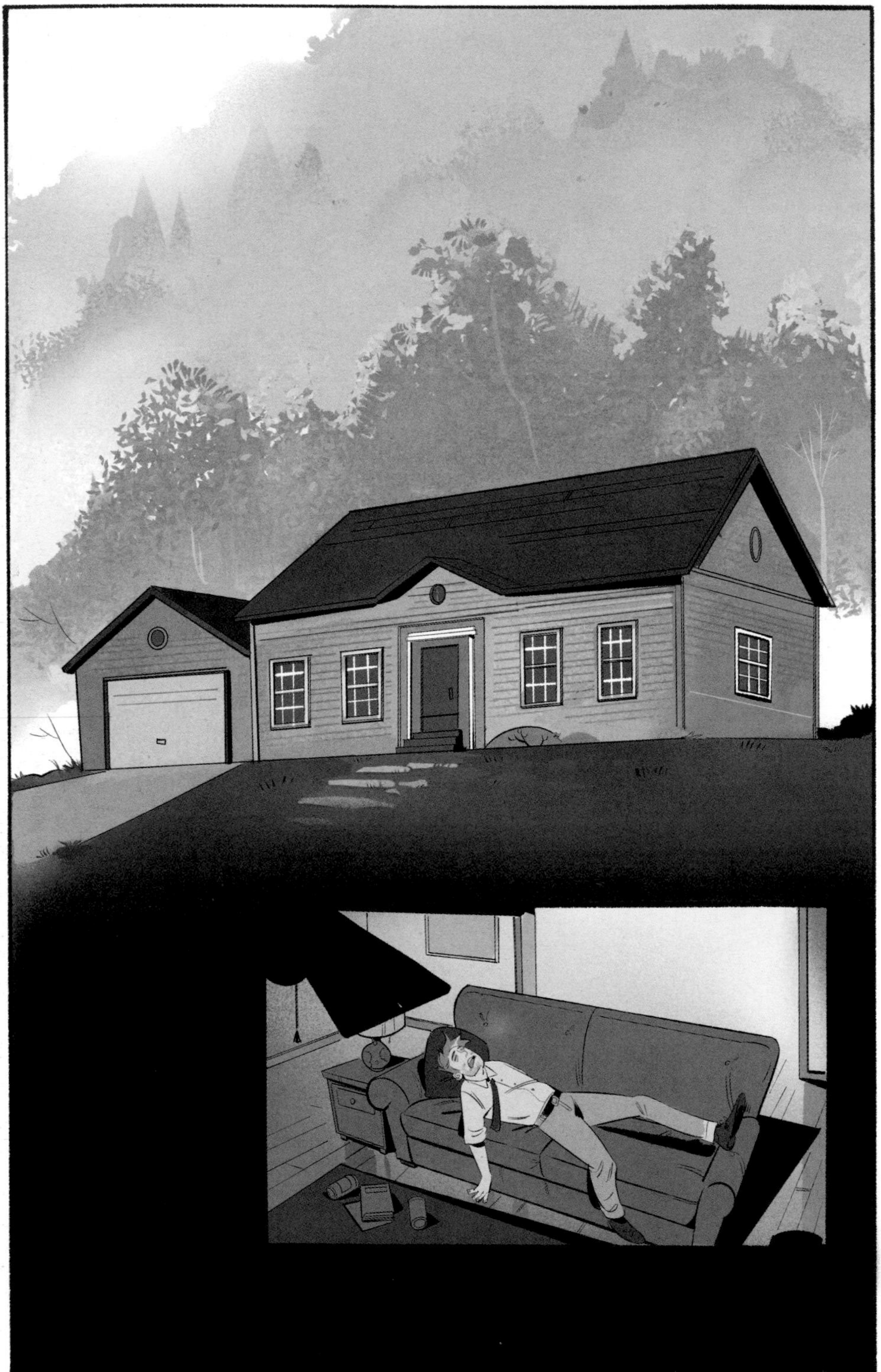

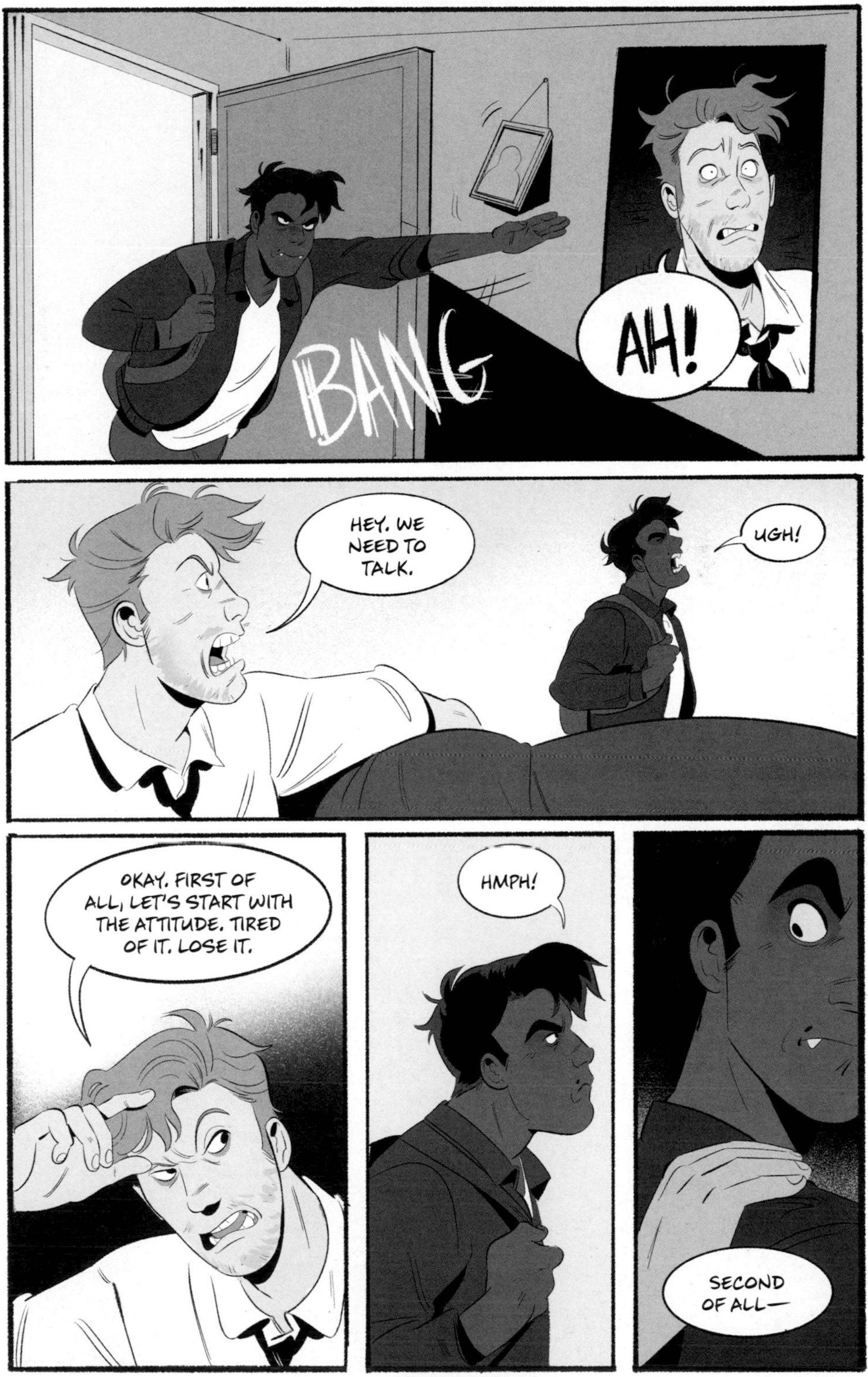
BANG
AH!
HEY. WE NEED TO TALK.
UGH!
OKAY. FIRST OF ALL, LET'S START WITH THE ATTITUDE. TIRED OF IT. LOSE IT.
HMPH!
SECOND OF ALL—

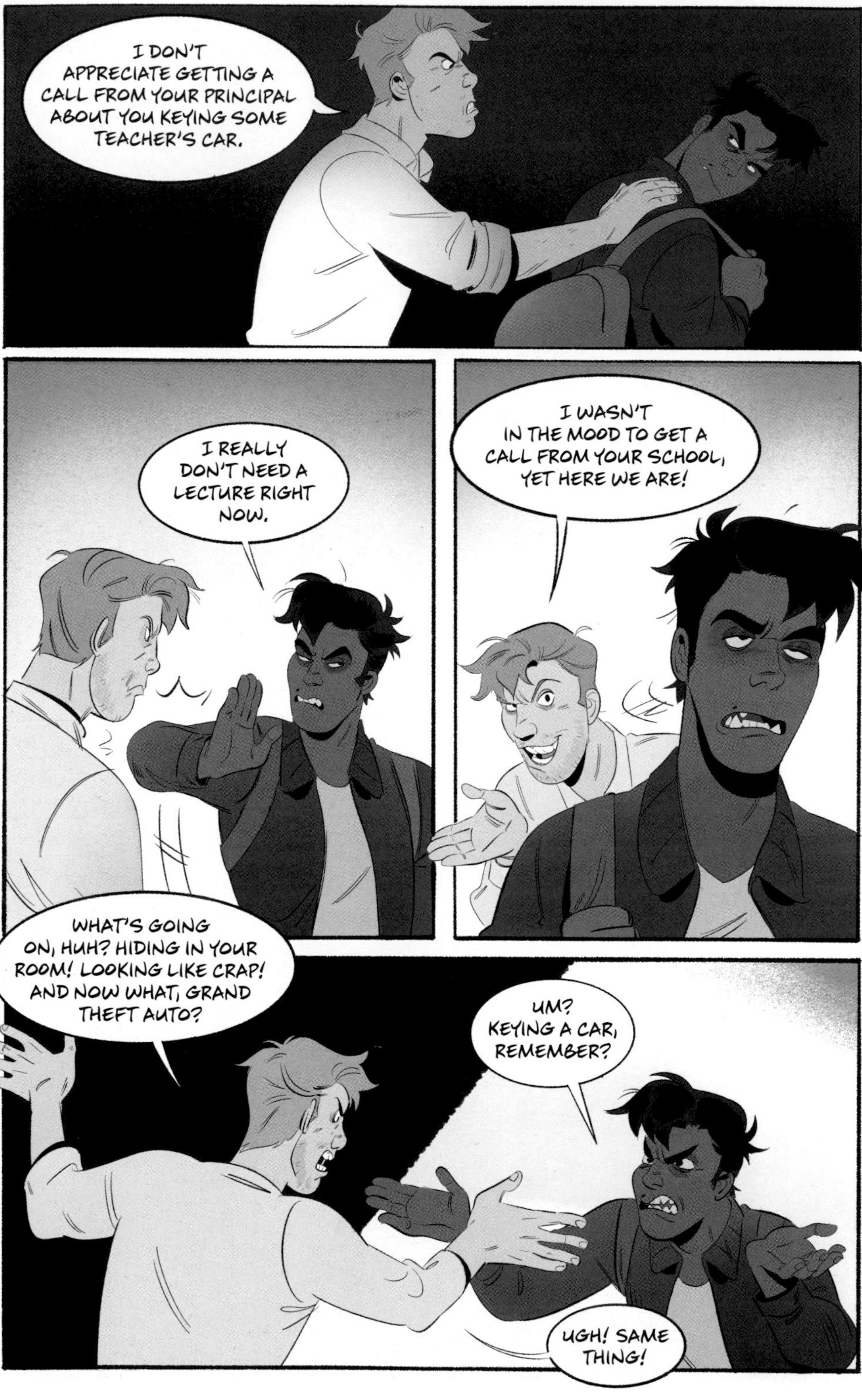
I DON'T APPRECIATE GETTING A CALL FROM YOUR PRINCIPAL ABOUT YOU KEYING SOME TEACHER'S CAR.
I REALLY DON'T NEED A LECTURE RIGHT NOW.
I WASN'T IN THE MOOD TO GET A CALL FROM YOUR SCHOOL, YET HERE WE ARE!
WHAT'S GOING ON, HUH? HIDING IN YOUR ROOM! LOOKING LIKE CRAP! AND NOW WHAT, GRAND THEFT AUTO?
UM? KEYING A CAR, REMEMBER?
UGH! SAME THING!

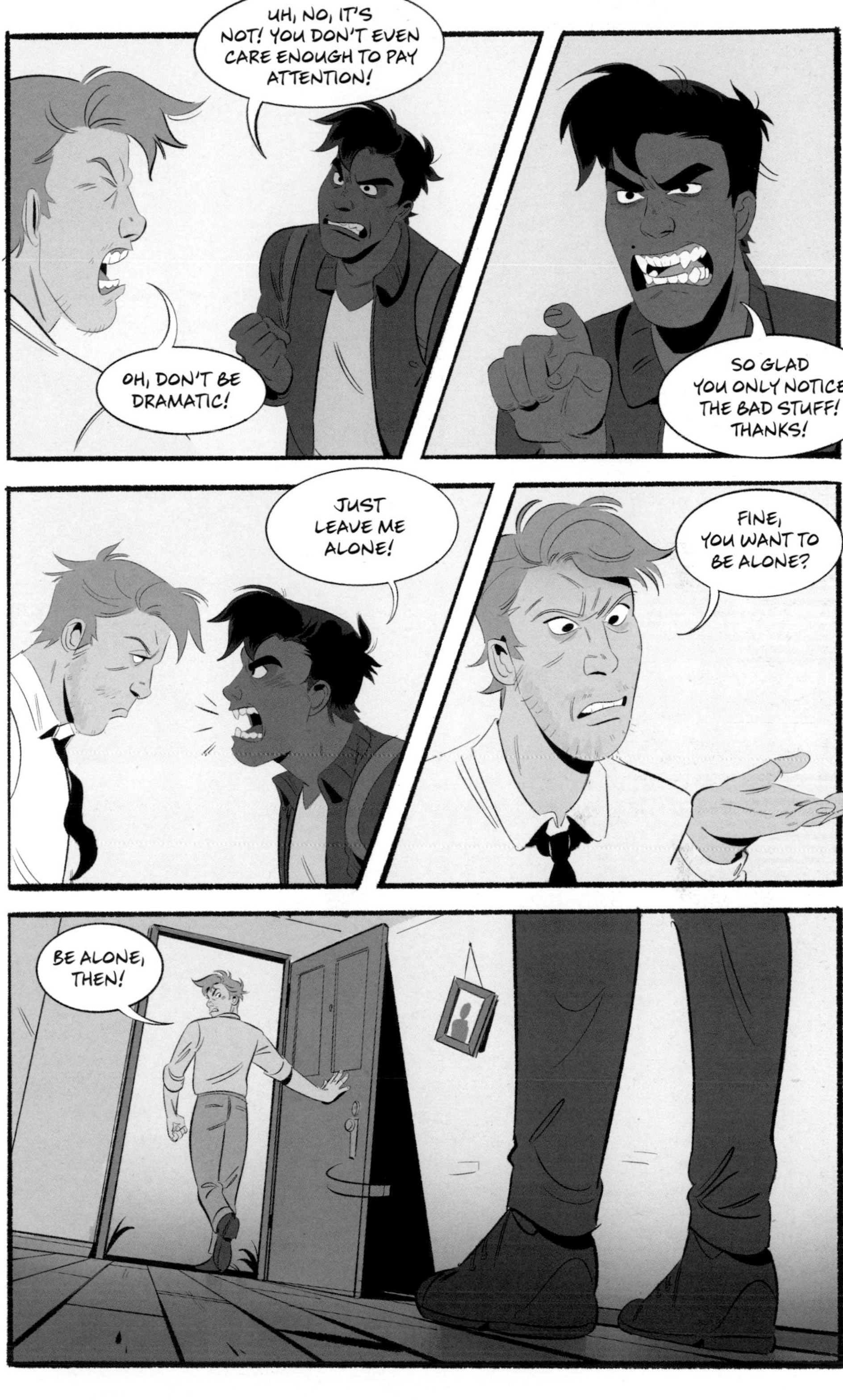
UH, NO, IT'S NOT! YOU DON'T EVEN CARE ENOUGH TO PAY ATTENTION!
OH, DON'T BE DRAMATIC!
SO GLAD YOU ONLY NOTICE THE BAD STUFF! THANKS!
JUST LEAVE ME ALONE!
FINE, YOU WANT TO BE ALONE?
BE ALONE, THEN!

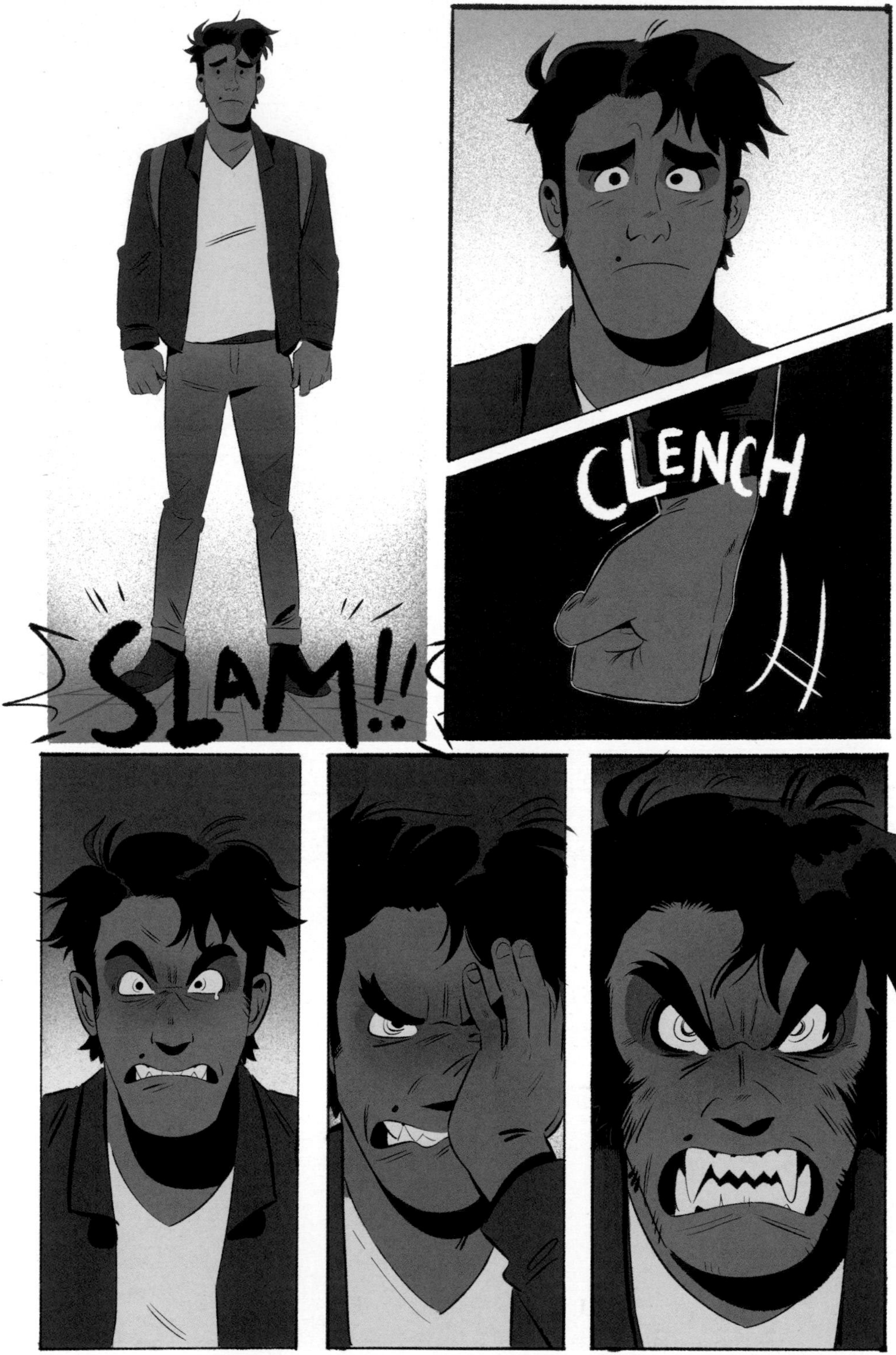
SLAM!!
CLENCH

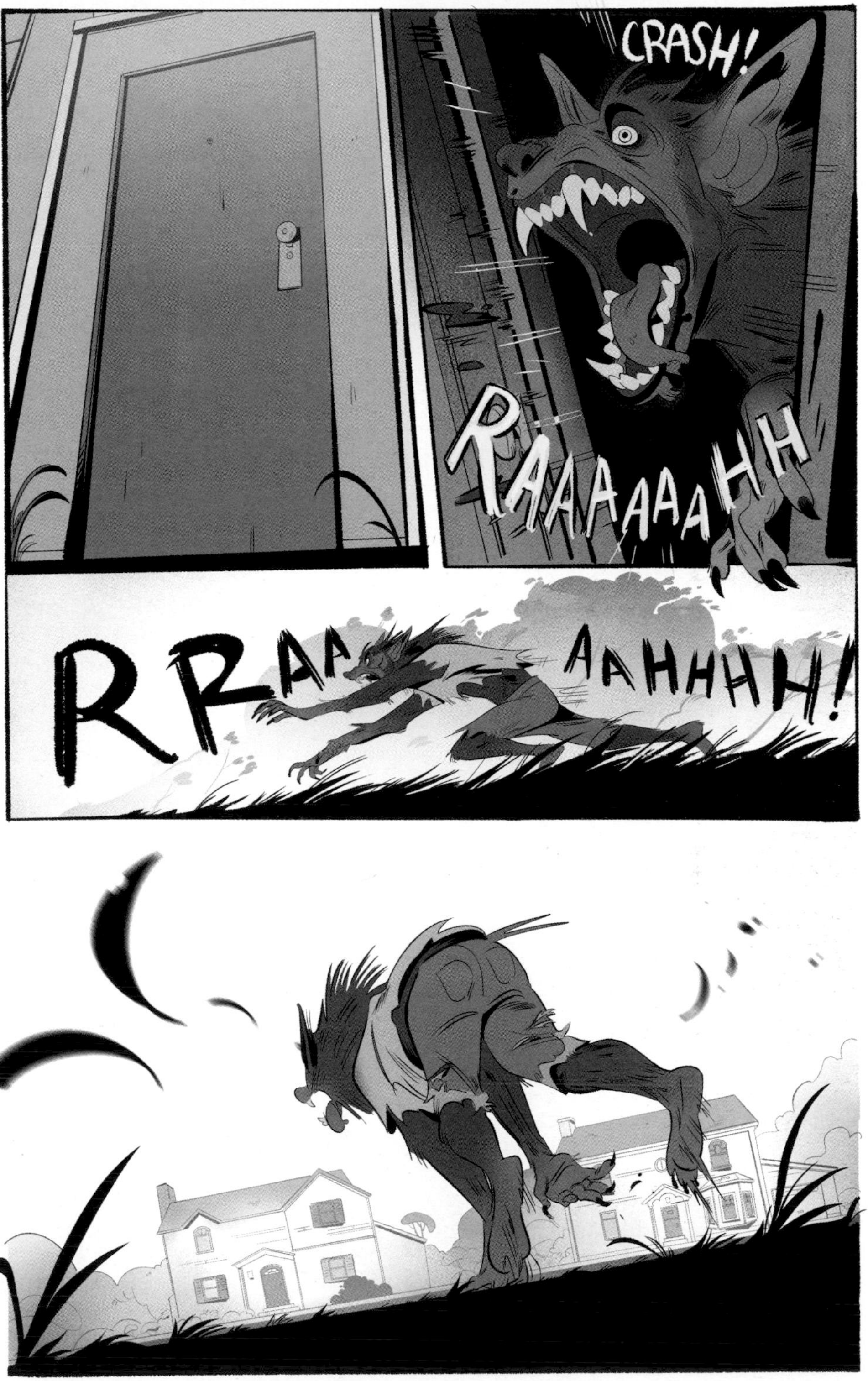
CRASH!
RAAAAAAHH
RRAAAAHHHH!

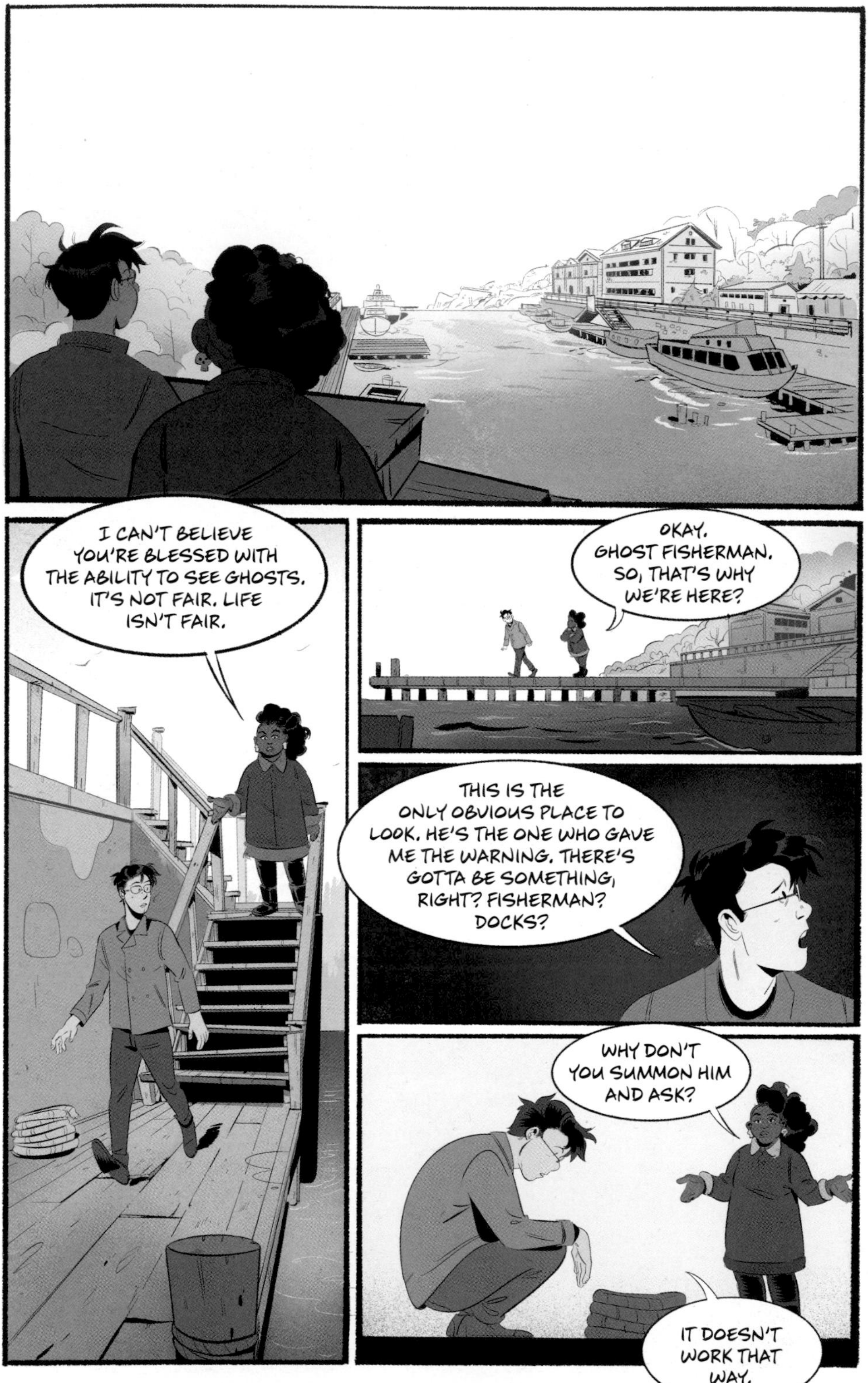
I CAN'T BELIEVE YOU'RE BLESSED WITH THE ABILITY TO SEE GHOSTS. IT'S NOT FAIR. LIFE ISN'T FAIR.
OKAY. GHOST FISHERMAN. SO, THAT'S WHY WE'RE HERE?
THIS IS THE ONLY OBVIOUS PLACE TO LOOK. HE'S THE ONE WHO GAVE ME THE WARNING. THERE'S GOTTA BE SOMETHING, RIGHT? FISHERMAN? DOCKS?
WHY DON'T YOU SUMMON HIM AND ASK?
IT DOESN'T WORK THAT WAY.

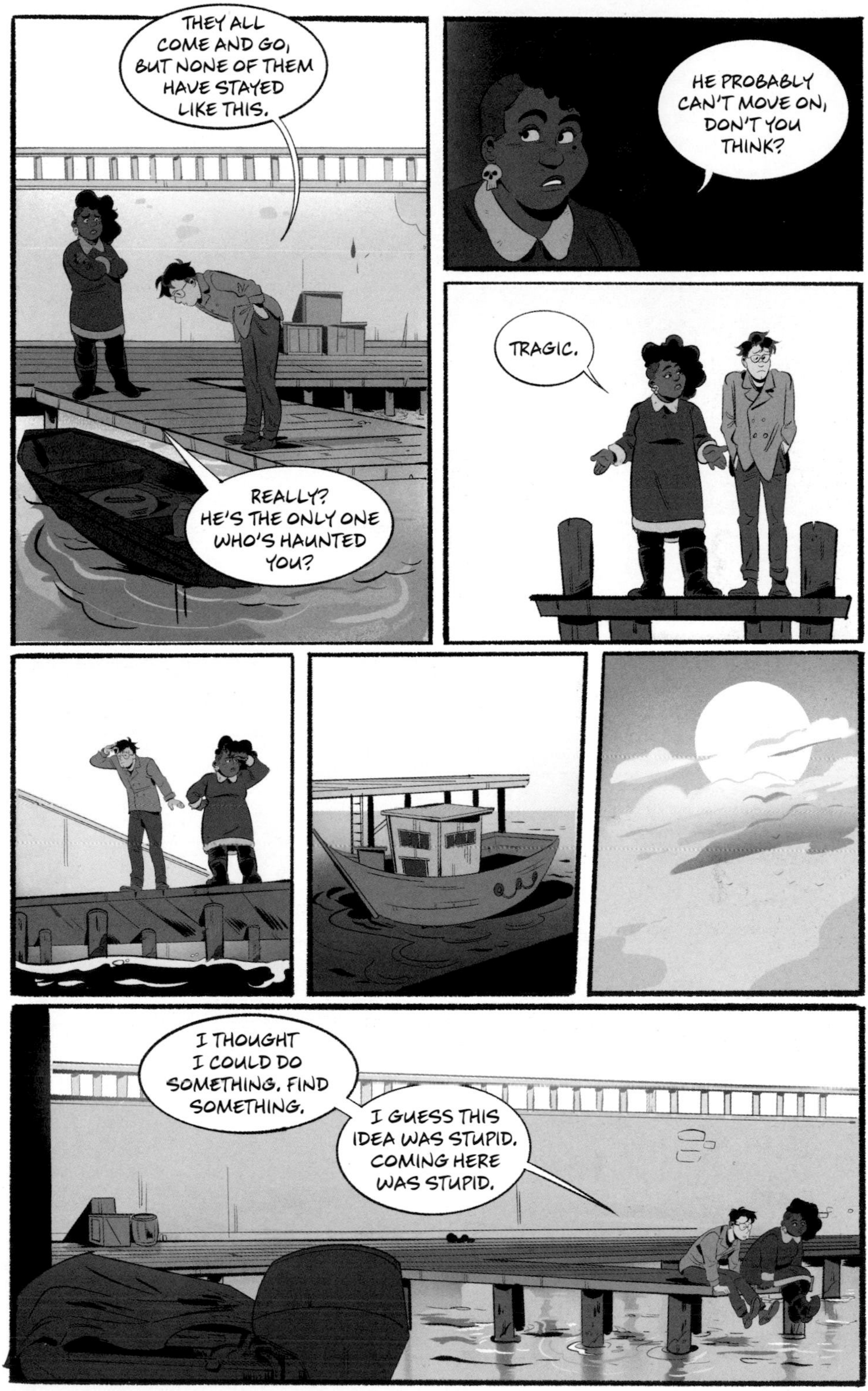
THEY ALL COME AND GO, BUT NONE OF THEM HAVE STAYED LIKE THIS.
REALLY? HE'S THE ONLY ONE WHO'S HAUNTED YOU?
HE PROBABLY CAN'T MOVE ON, DON'T YOU THINK?
TRAGIC.
I THOUGHT I COULD DO SOMETHING. FIND SOMETHING.
I GUESS THIS IDEA WAS STUPID. COMING HERE WAS STUPID.

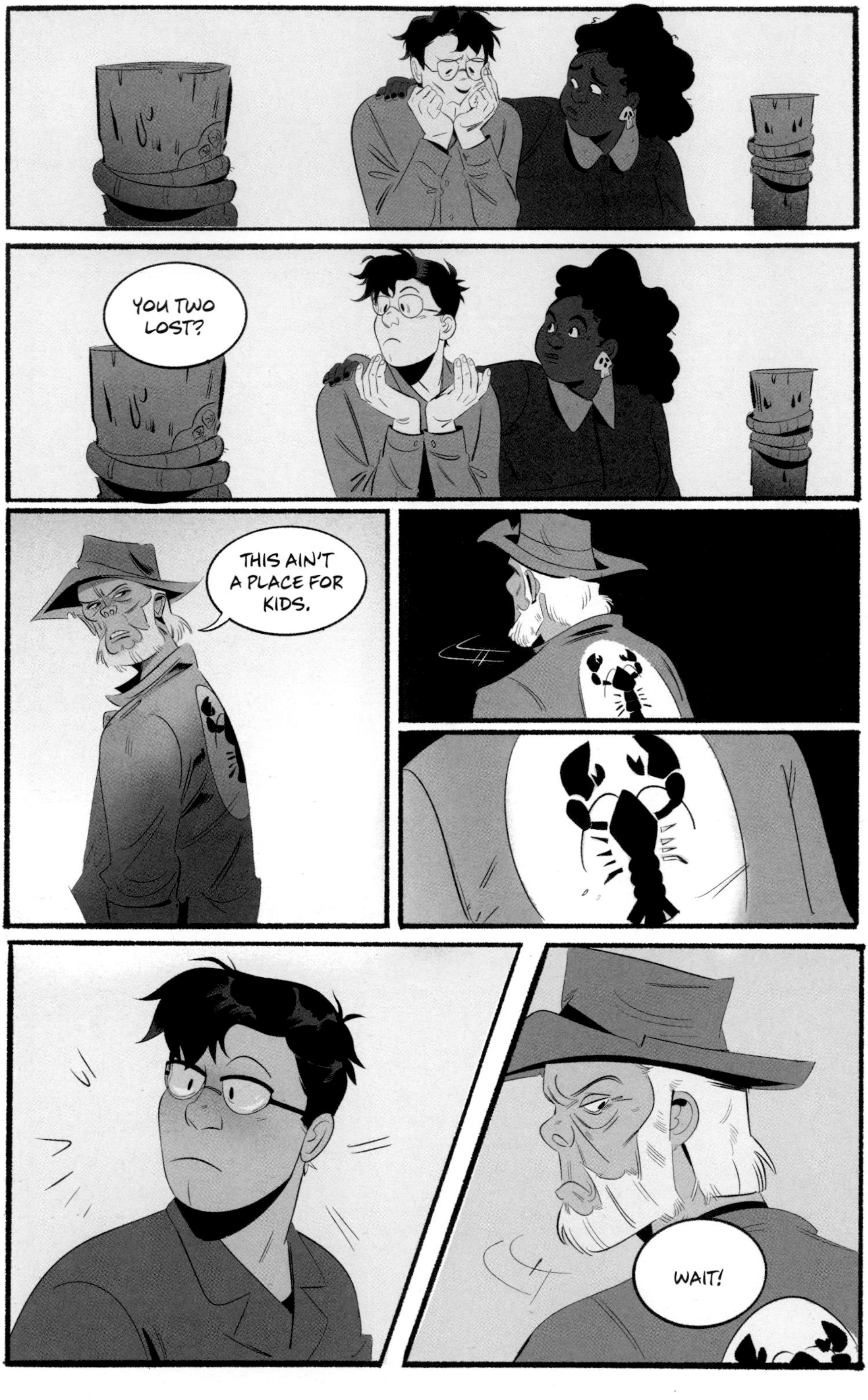
YOU TWO LOST?
THIS AIN'T A PLACE FOR KIDS.
WAIT!

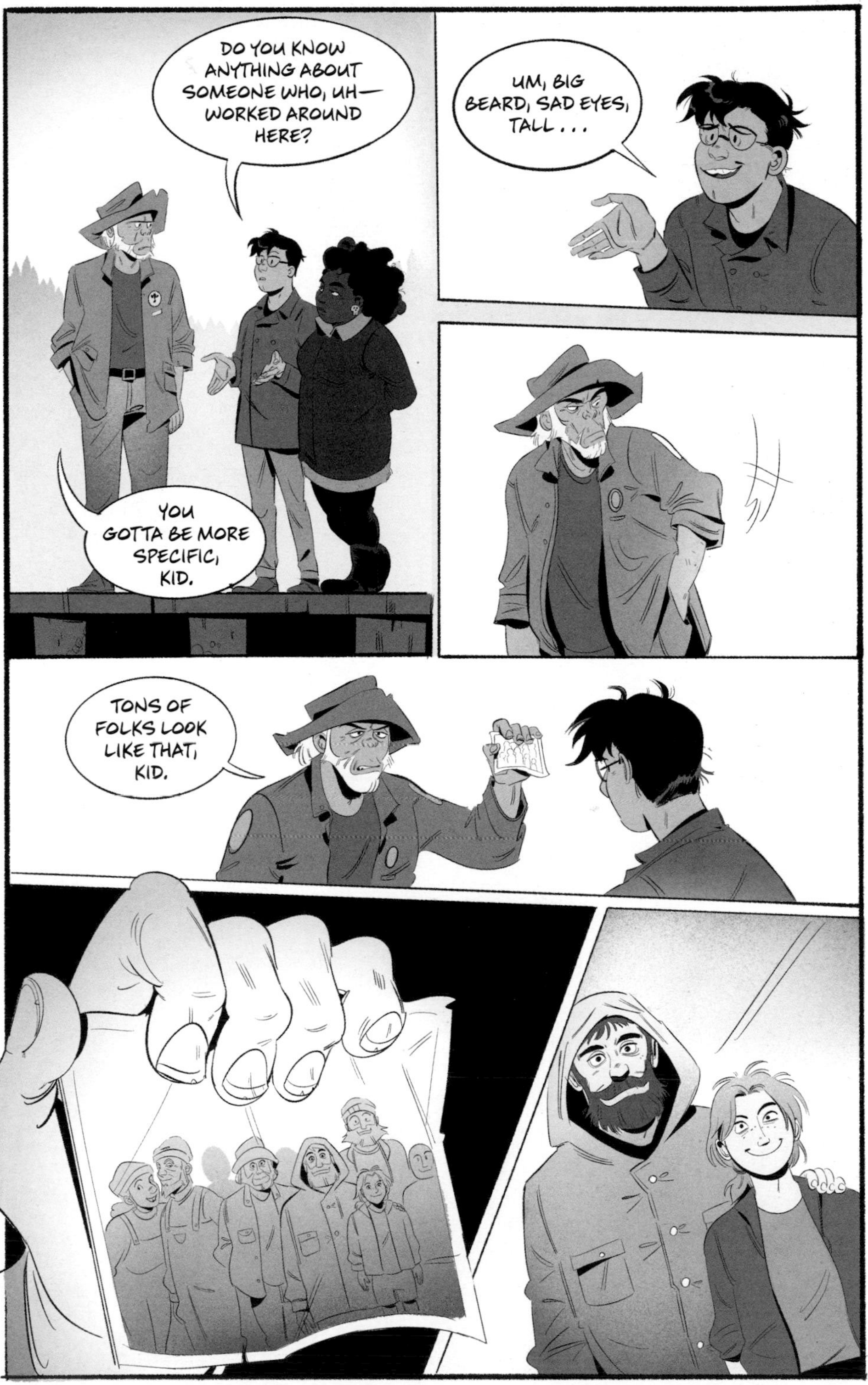
DO YOU KNOW ANYTHING ABOUT SOMEONE WHO, UH— WORKED AROUND HERE?
YOU GOTTA BE MORE SPECIFIC, KID.
UM, BIG BEARD, SAD EYES, TALL . . .
TONS OF FOLKS LOOK LIKE THAT, KID.

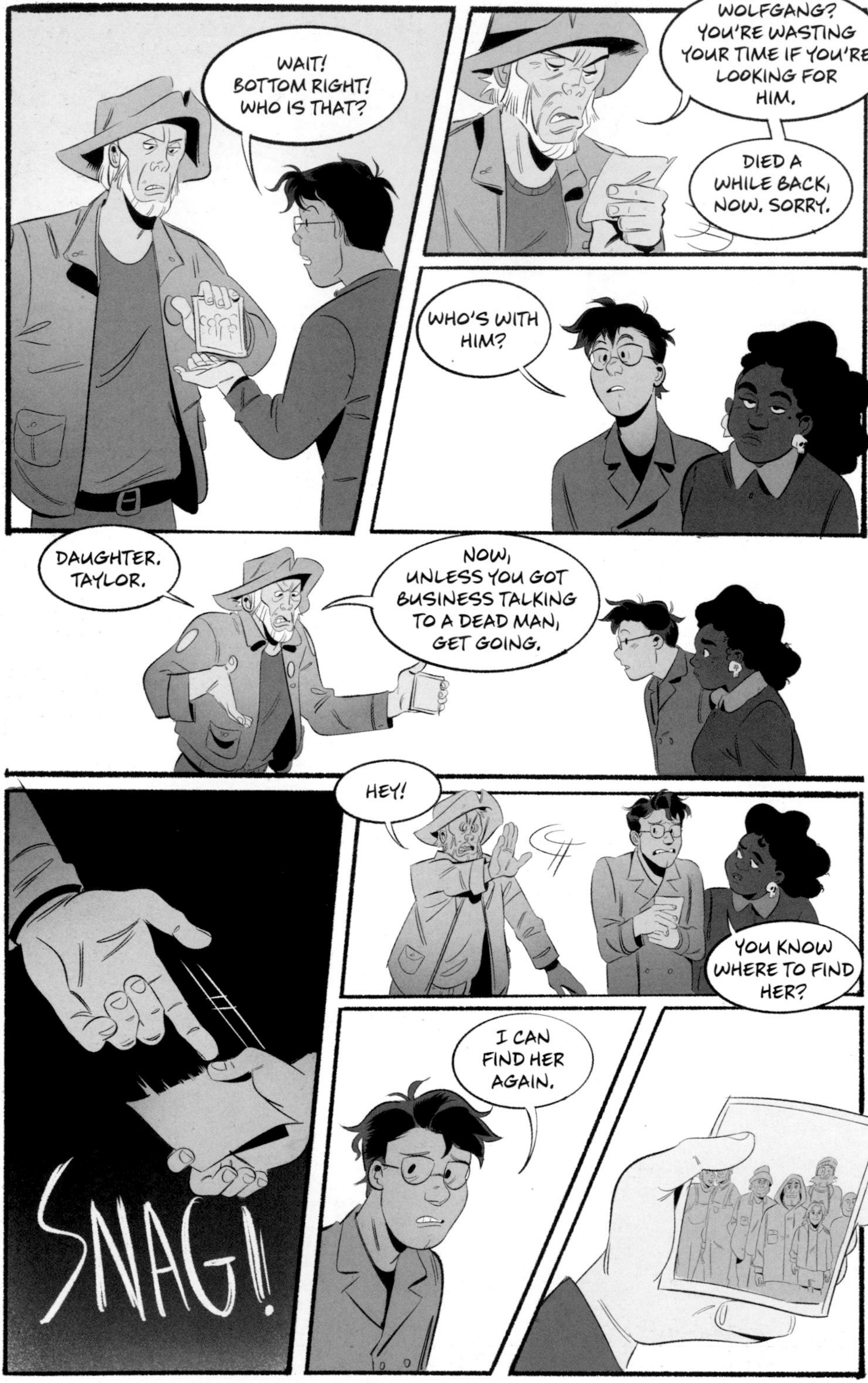
WAIT! BOTTOM RIGHT! WHO IS THAT?
WOLFGANG? YOU'RE WASTING YOUR TIME IF YOU'RE LOOKING FOR HIM.
DIED A WHILE BACK, NOW. SORRY.
WHO'S WITH HIM?
DAUGHTER. TAYLOR.
NOW, UNLESS YOU GOT BUSINESS TALKING TO A DEAD MAN, GET GOING.
SNAG!!
HEY!
YOU KNOW WHERE TO FIND HER?
I CAN FIND HER AGAIN.

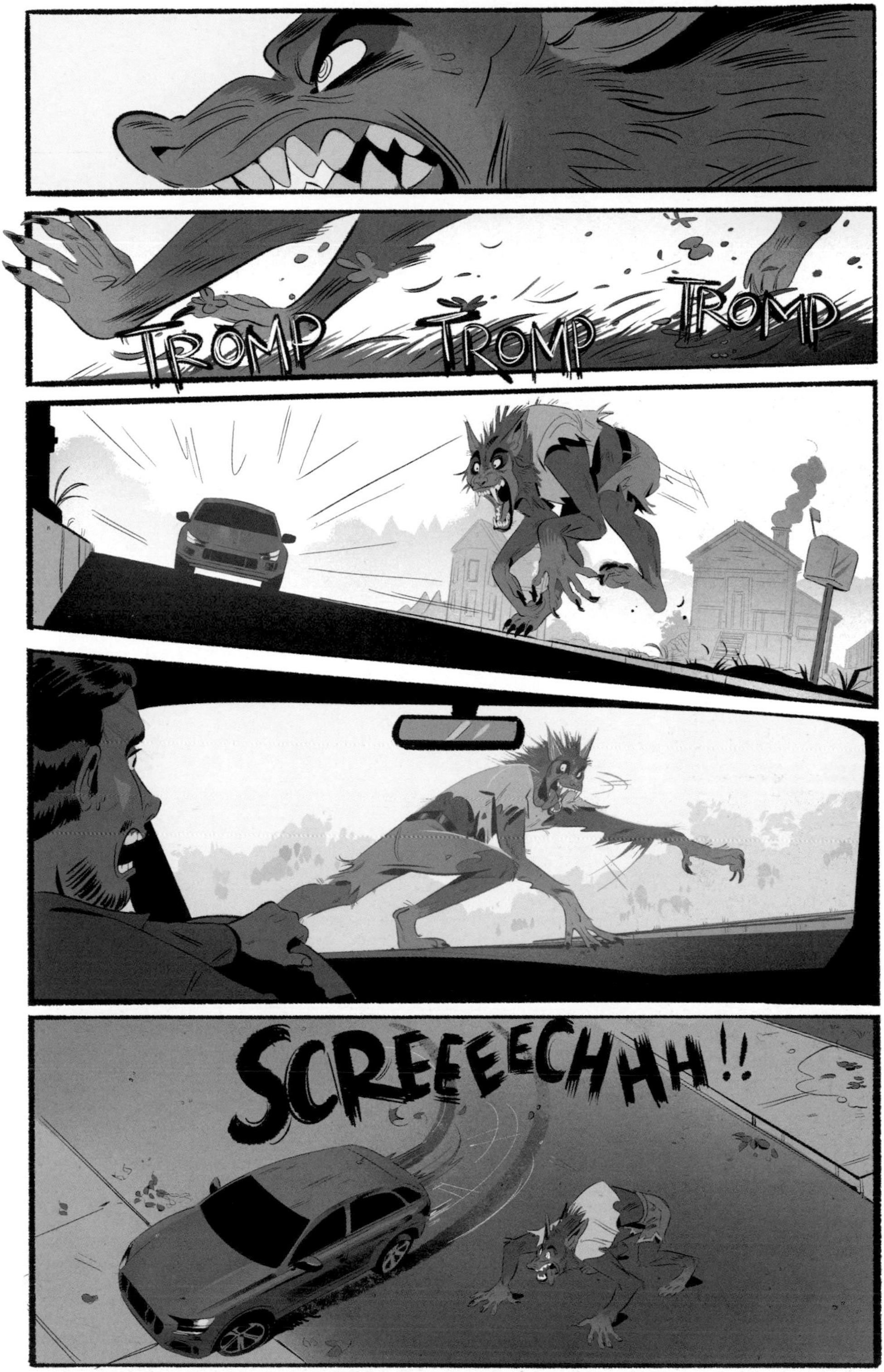
TROMP
TROMP
TROMP
SCREEEECHHH!!

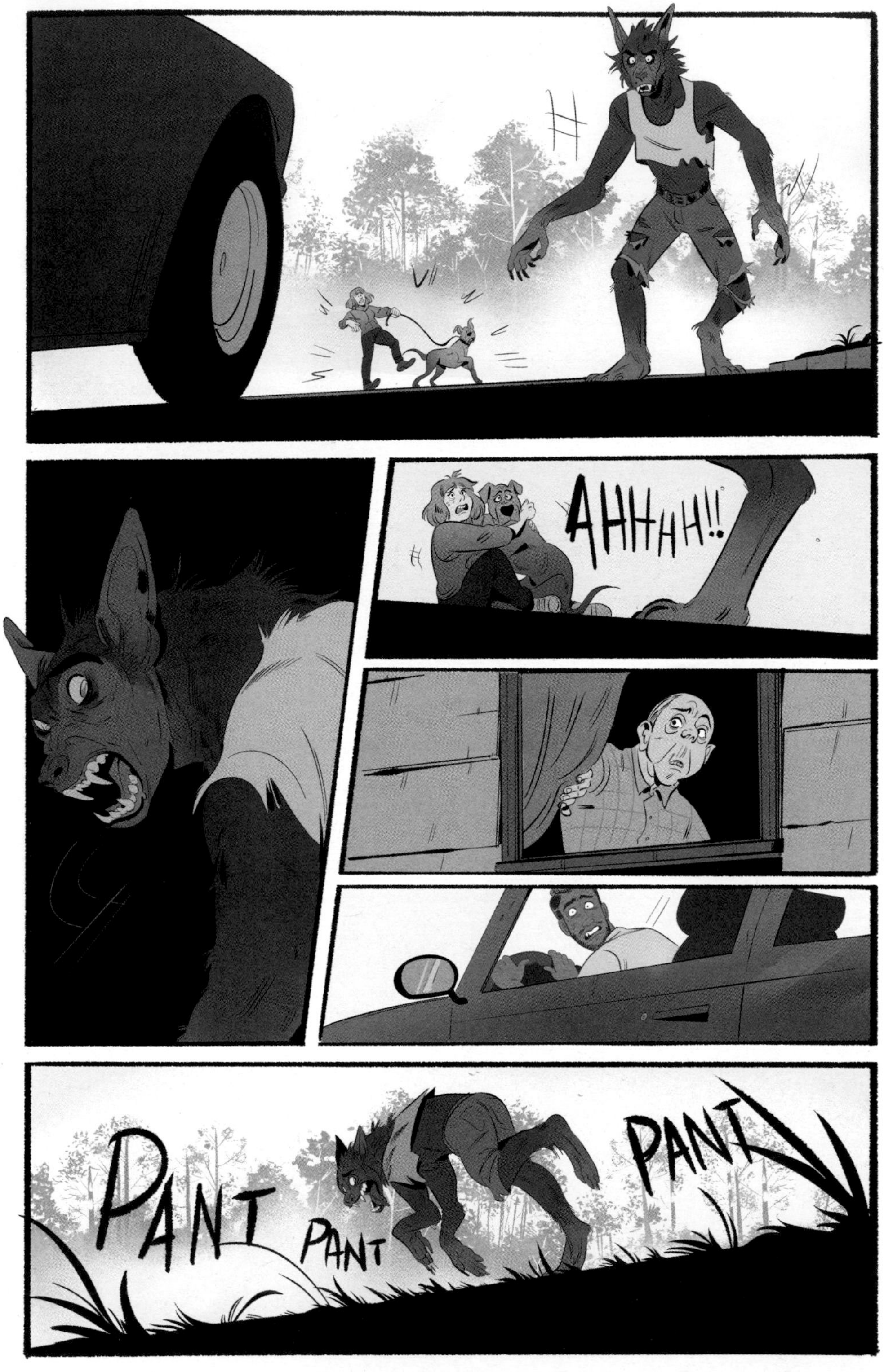
AHHHH!!
PANT
PANT
PANT

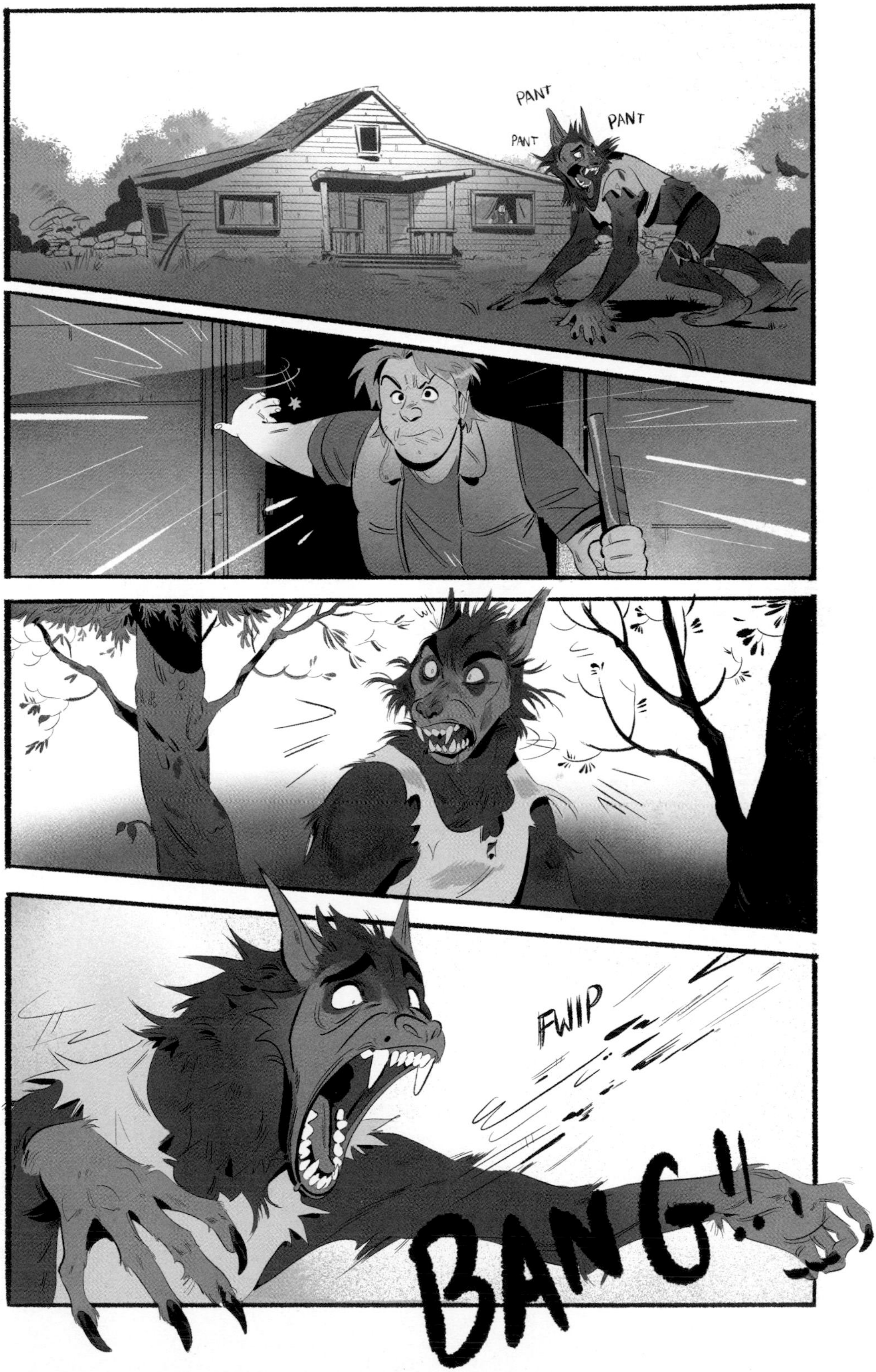
PANT
PANT
PANT
FWIP
BANG!!

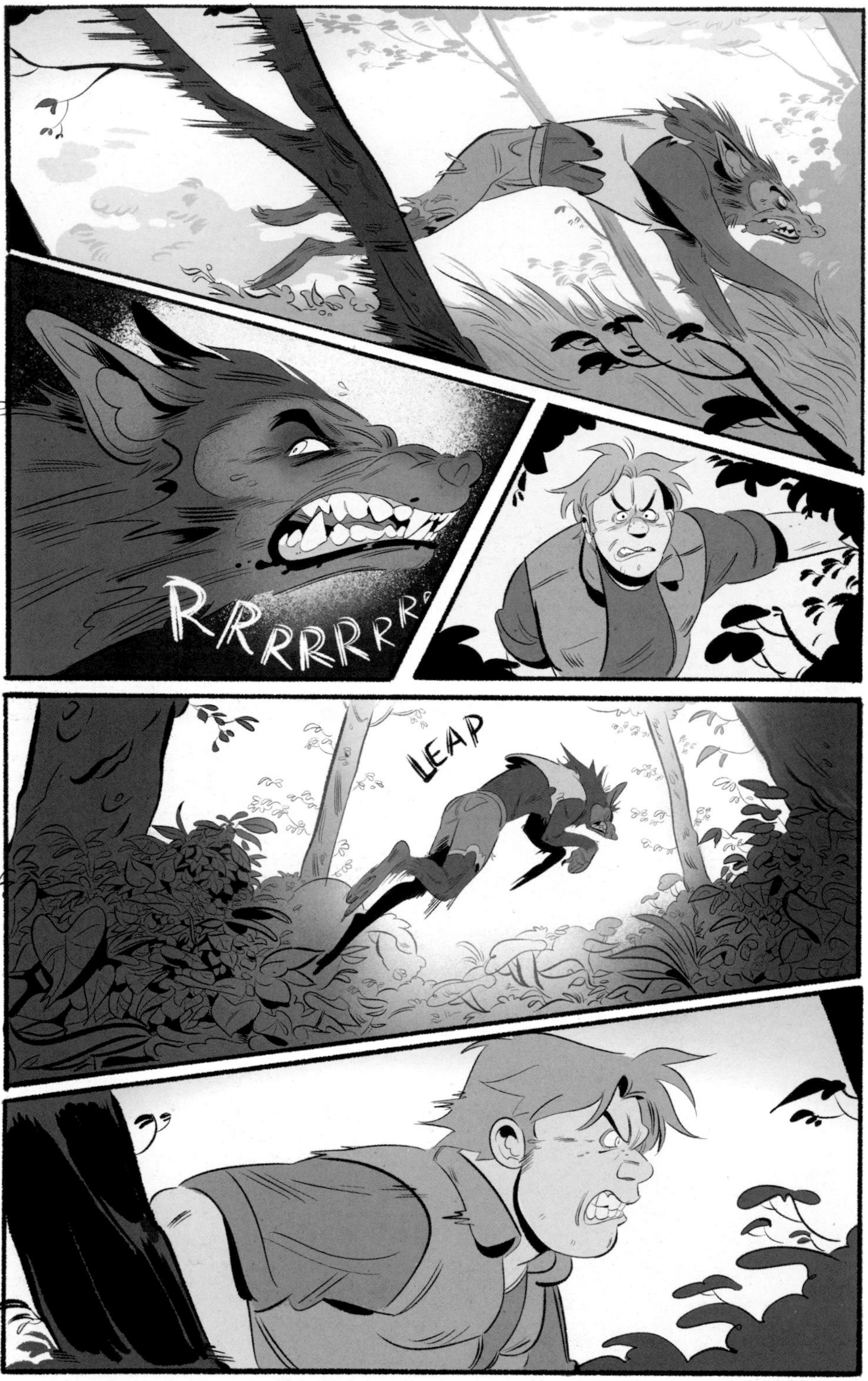
RRRRRRRR
LEAP

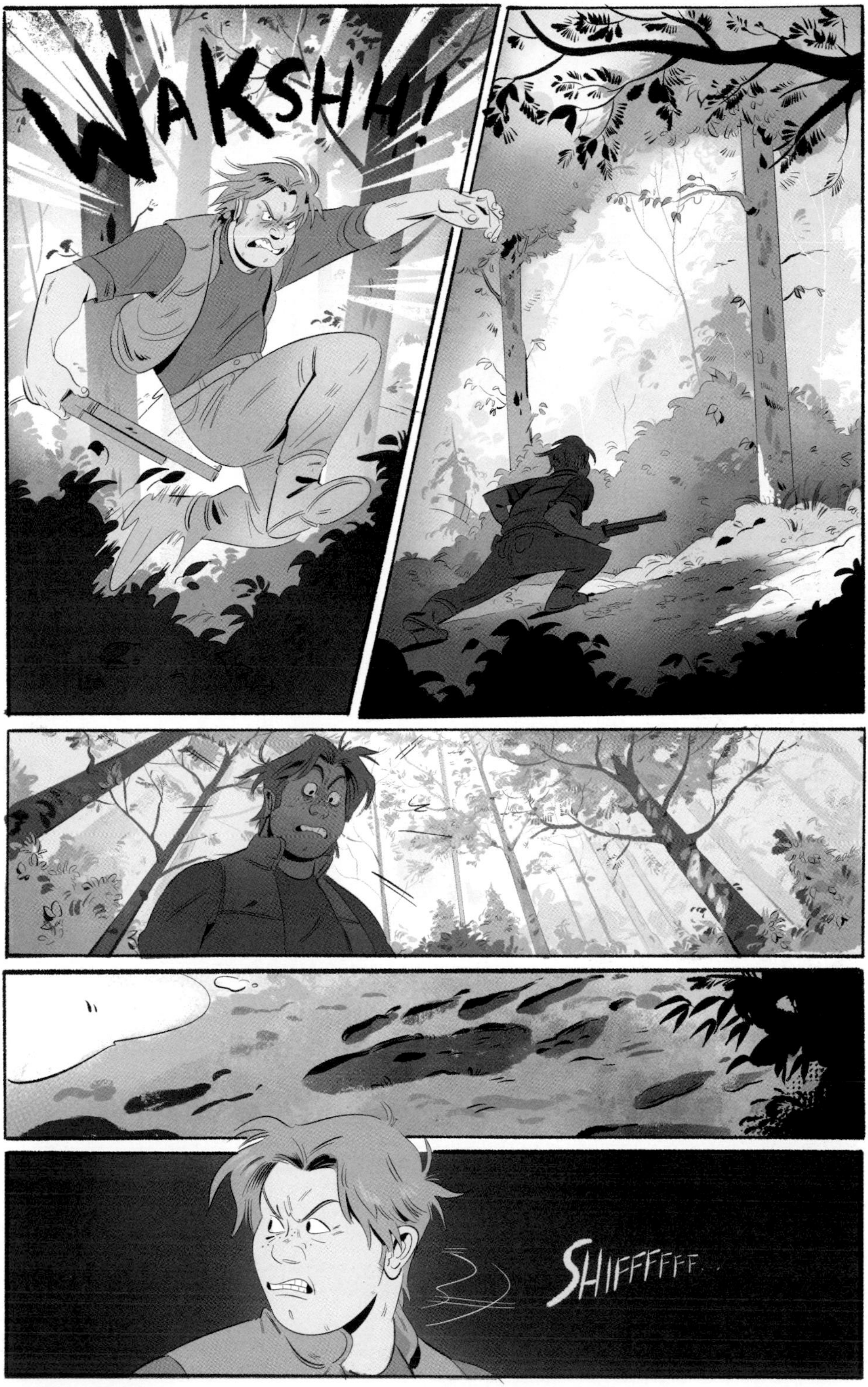
WAKSHH!
SHIFFFFFF...

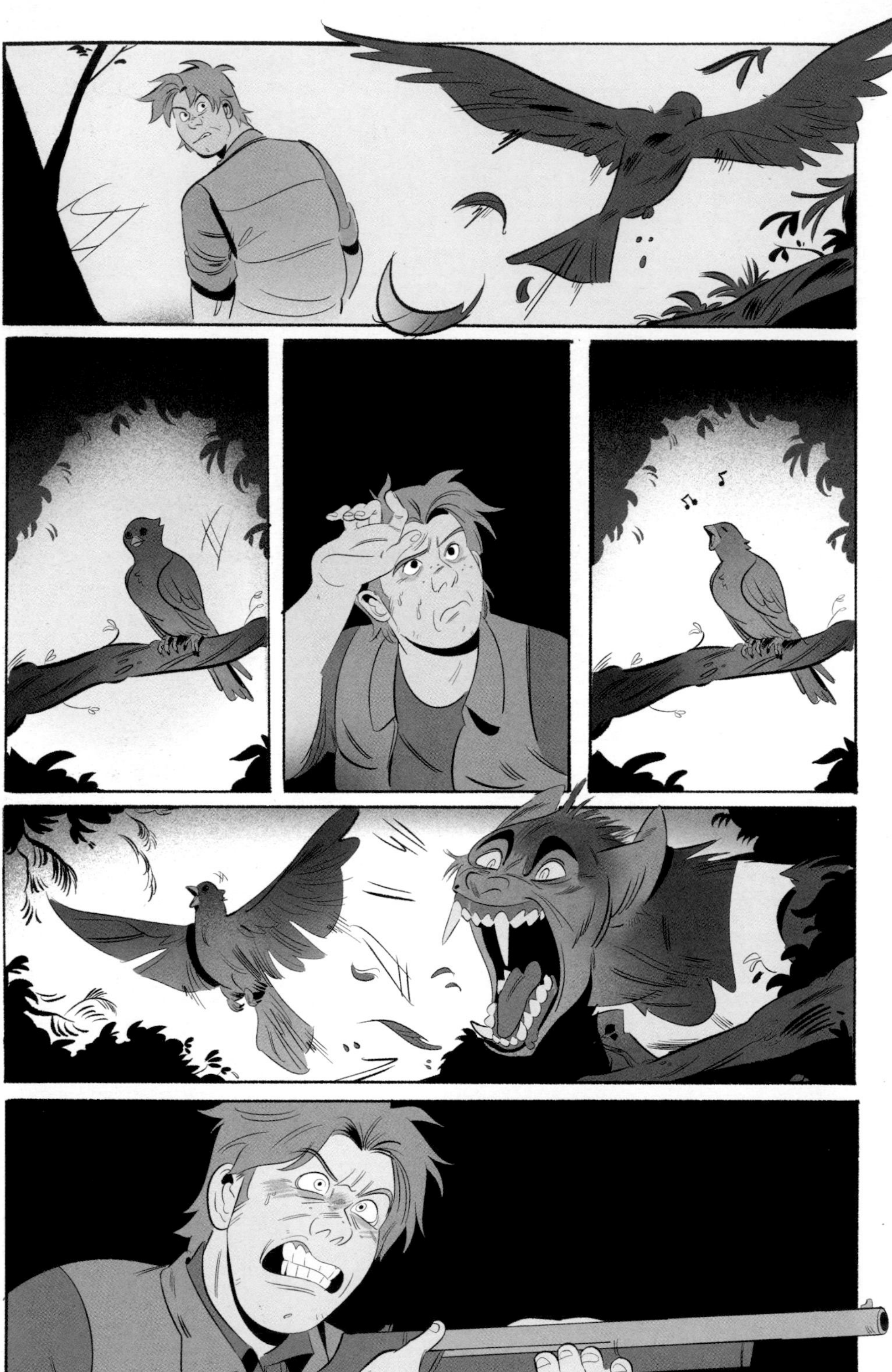

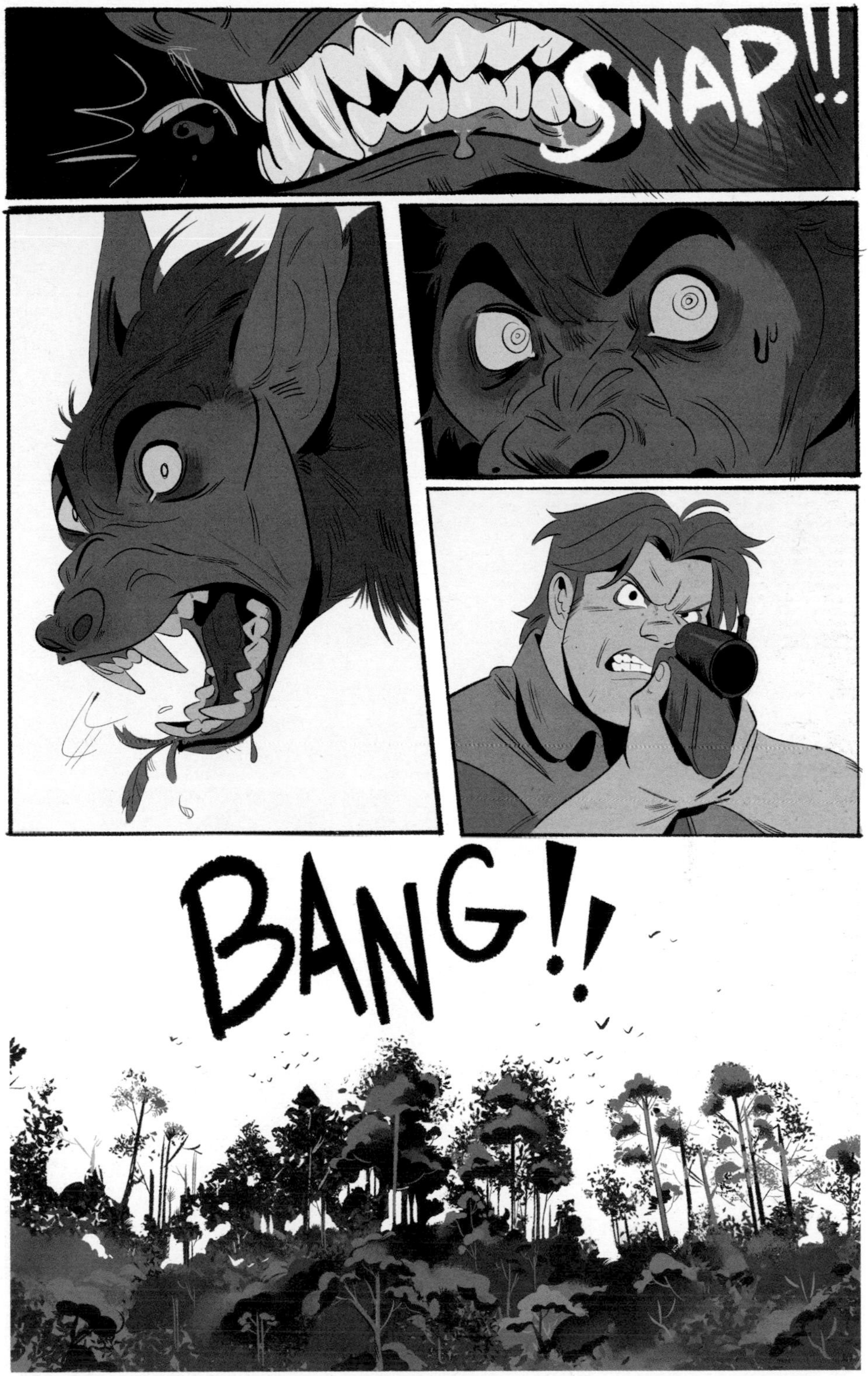
SNAP!!
BANG!!

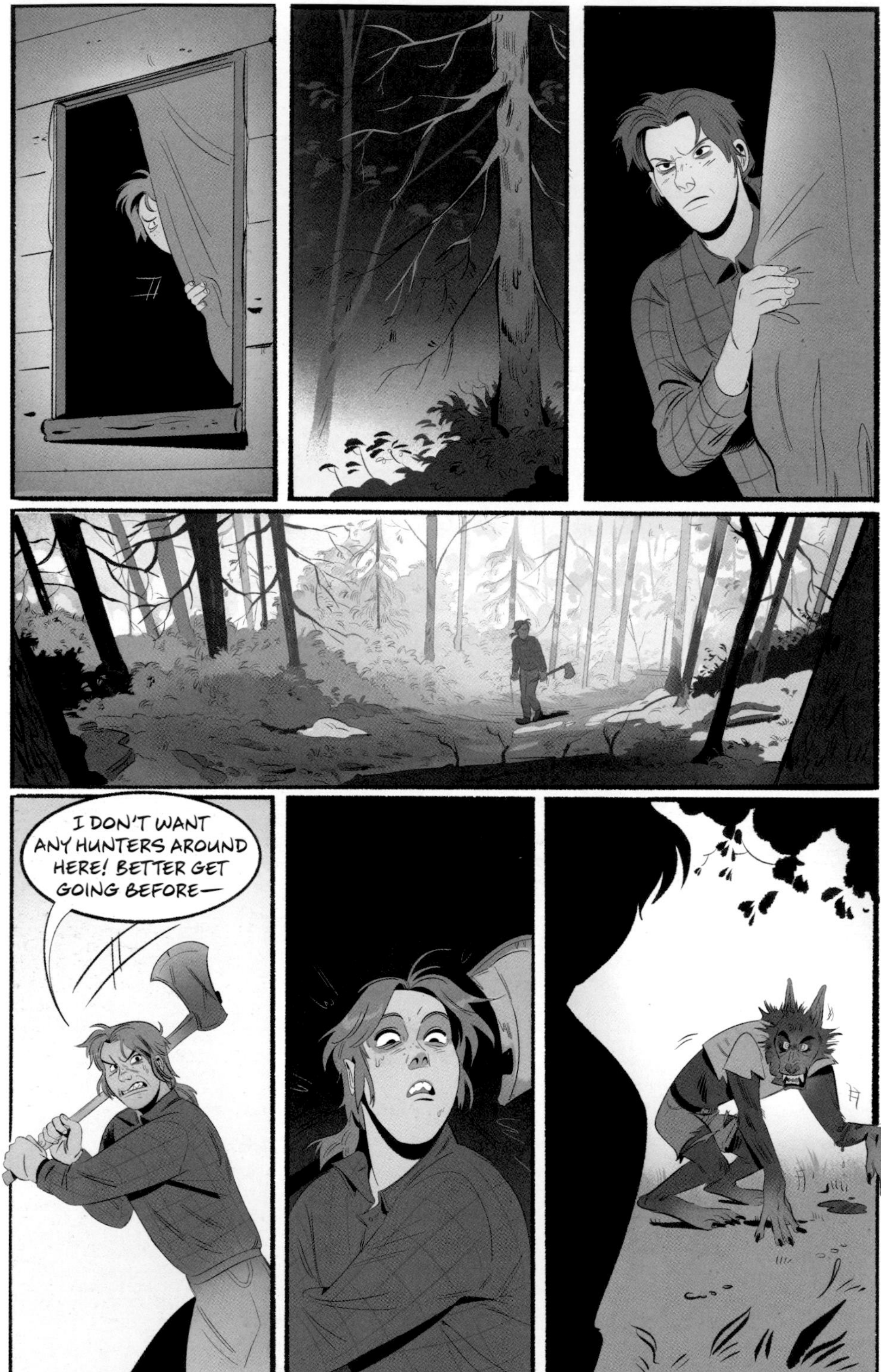
I DON'T WANT ANY HUNTERS AROUND HERE! BETTER GET GOING BEFORE—

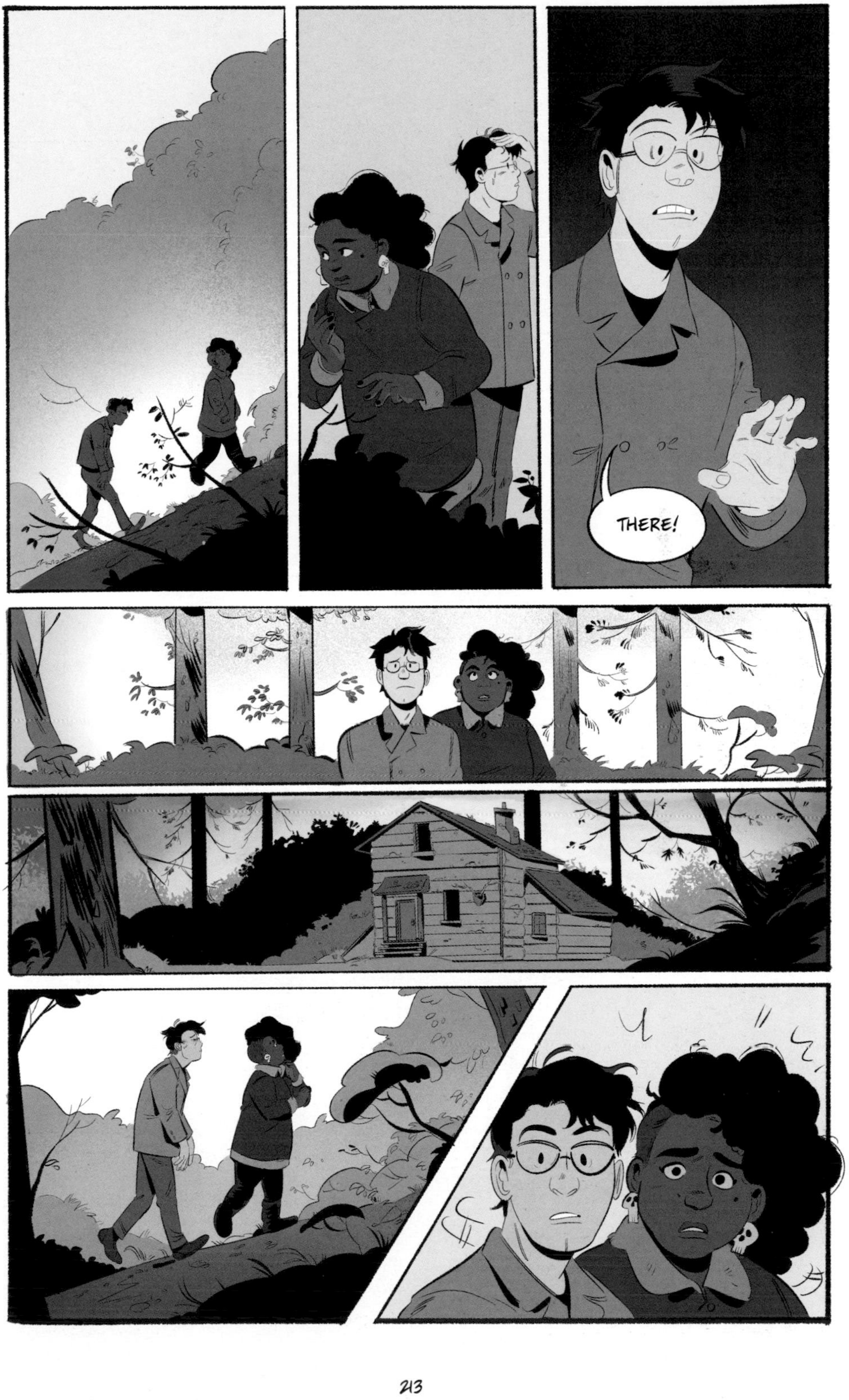
THERE!

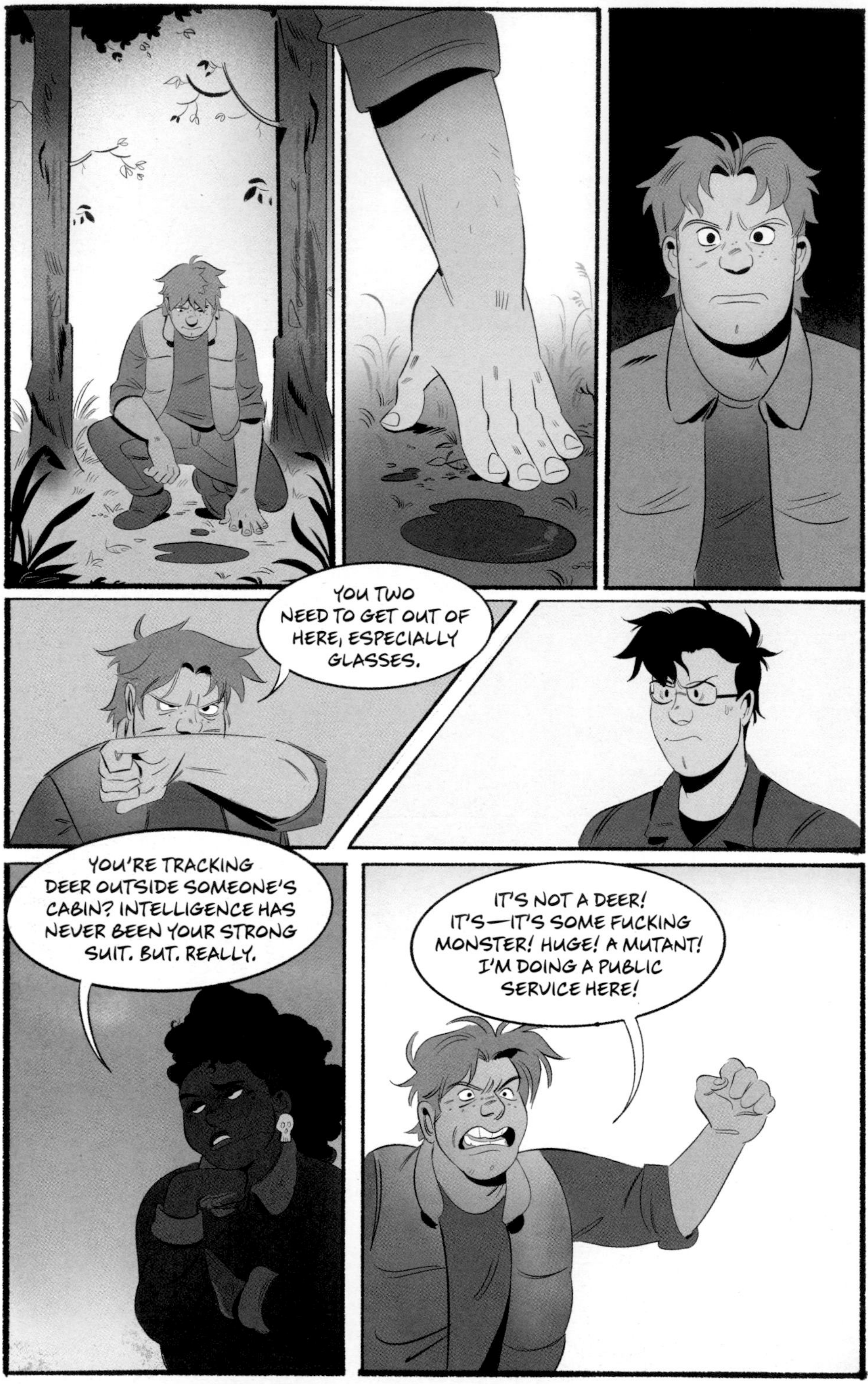

YOU TWO NEED TO GET OUT OF HERE, ESPECIALLY GLASSES.
YOU'RE TRACKING DEER OUTSIDE SOMEONE'S CABIN? INTELLIGENCE HAS NEVER BEEN YOUR STRONG SUIT. BUT. REALLY.
IT'S NOT A DEER! IT'S—IT'S SOME FUCKING MONSTER! HUGE! A MUTANT! I'M DOING A PUBLIC SERVICE HERE!

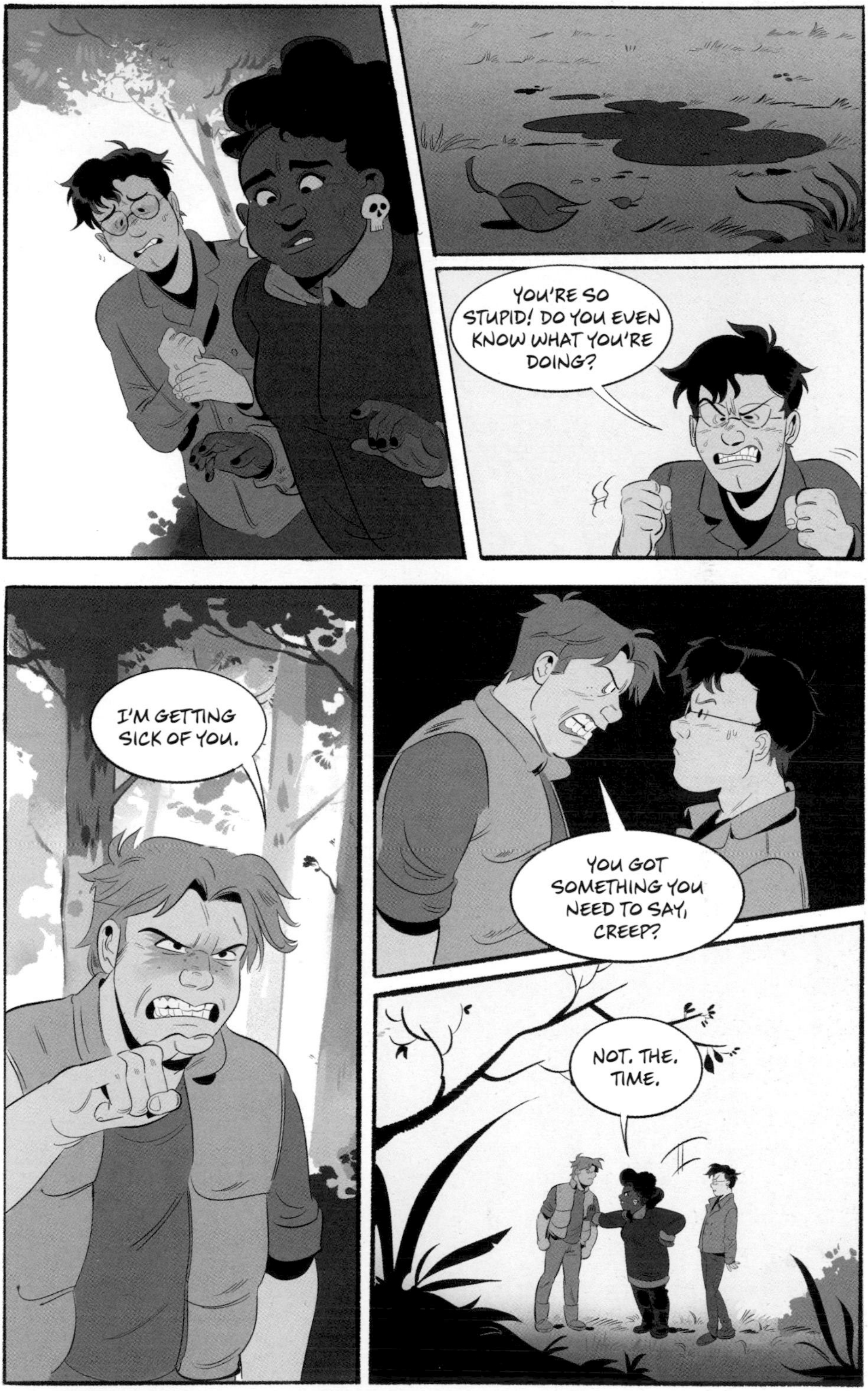
YOU'RE SO STUPID! DO YOU EVEN KNOW WHAT YOU'RE DOING?
I'M GETTING SICK OF YOU.
YOU GOT SOMETHING YOU NEED TO SAY, CREEP?
NOT. THE. TIME.

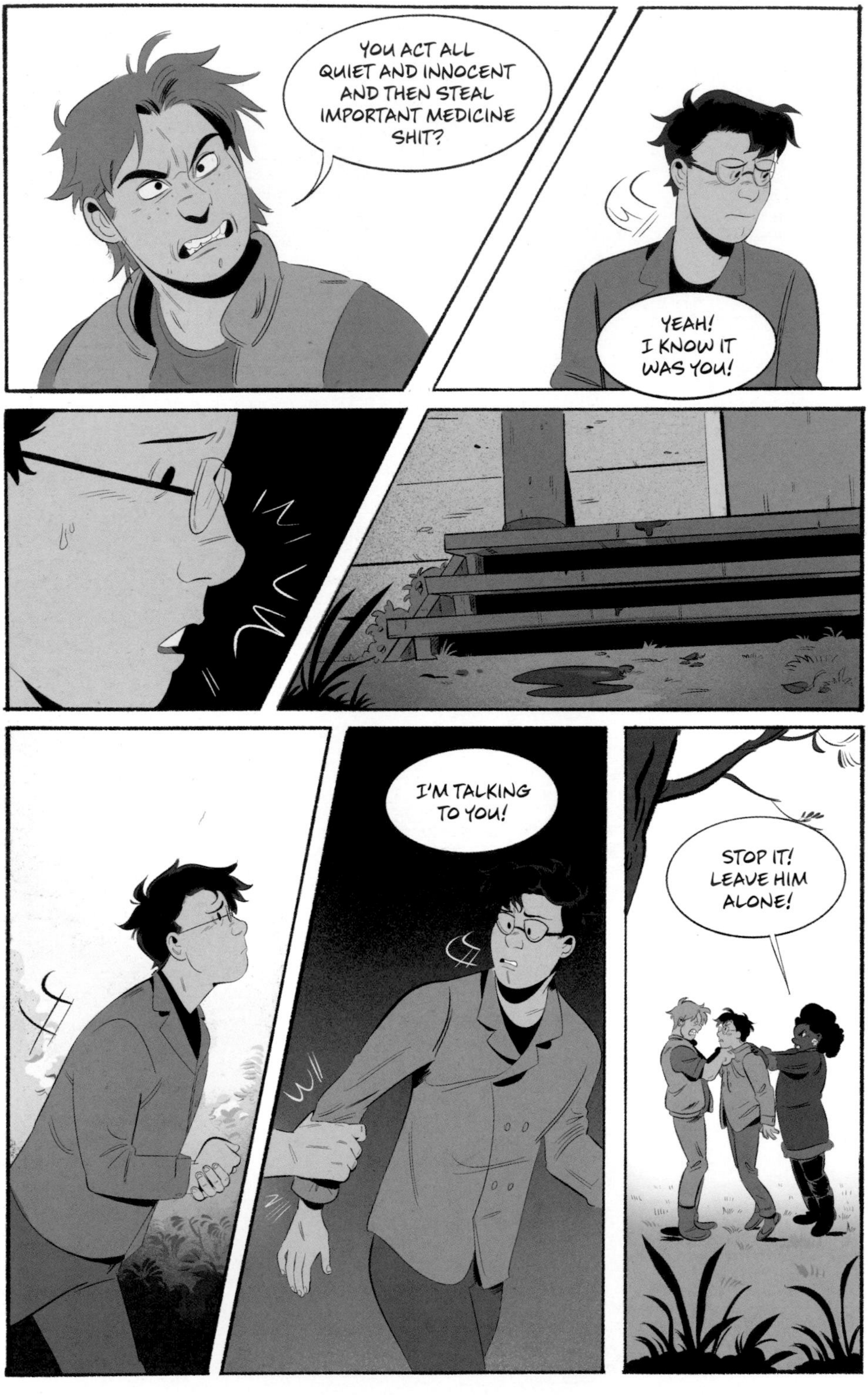
YOU ACT ALL QUIET AND INNOCENT AND THEN STEAL IMPORTANT MEDICINE SHIT?
YEAH! I KNOW IT WAS YOU!
I'M TALKING TO YOU!
STOP IT! LEAVE HIM ALONE!

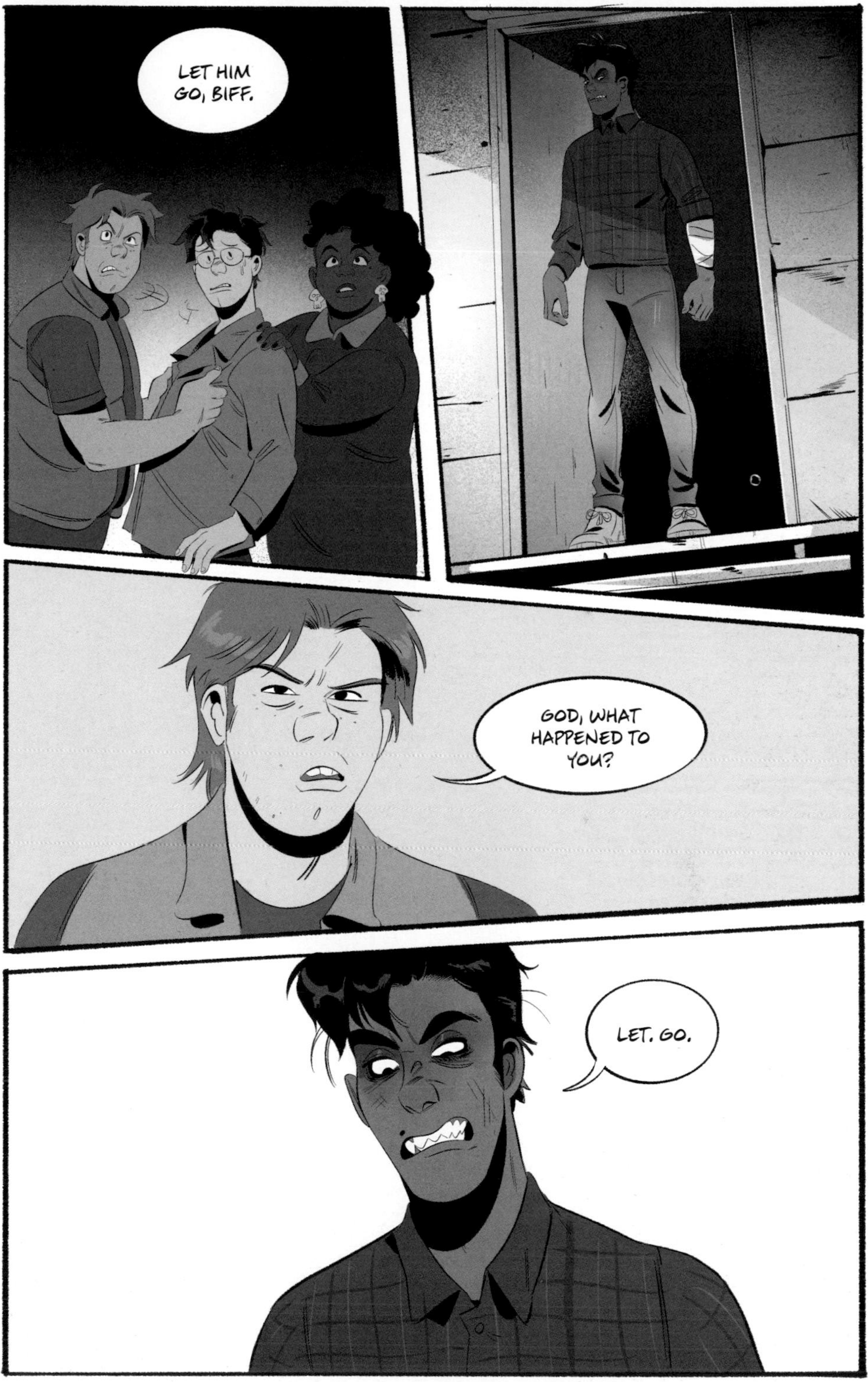
LET HIM GO, BIFF.
GOD, WHAT HAPPENED TO YOU?
LET. GO.

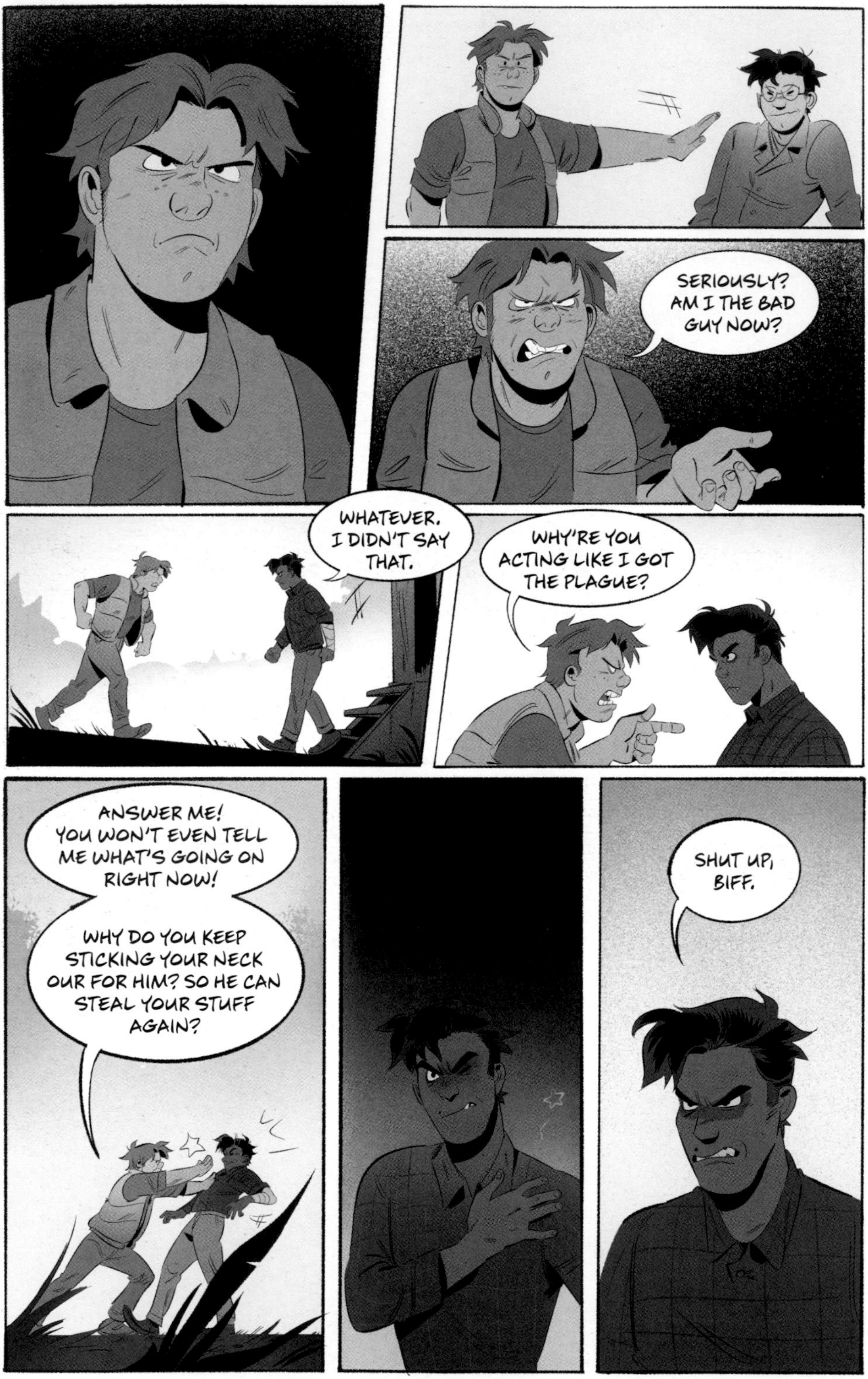
SERIOUSLY? AM I THE BAD GUY NOW?
WHATEVER. I DIDN'T SAY THAT.
WHY'RE YOU ACTING LIKE I GOT THE PLAGUE?
ANSWER ME! YOU WON'T EVEN TELL ME WHAT'S GOING ON RIGHT NOW!
WHY DO YOU KEEP STICKING YOUR NECK OUR FOR HIM? SO HE CAN STEAL YOUR STUFF AGAIN?
SHUT UP, BIFF.

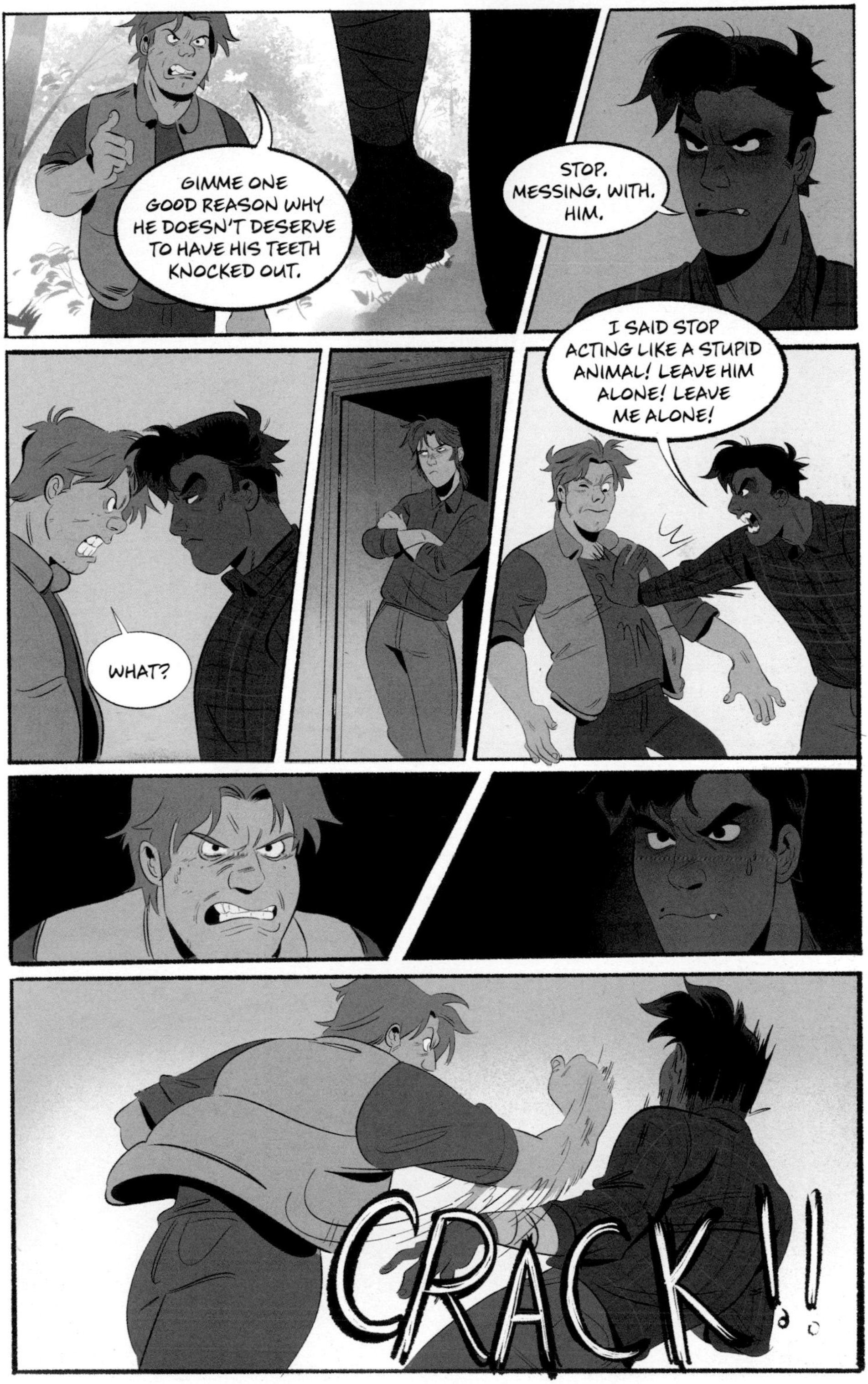
GIMME ONE GOOD REASON WHY HE DOESN'T DESERVE TO HAVE HIS TEETH KNOCKED OUT.
STOP. MESSING. WITH. HIM.
WHAT?
I SAID STOP ACTING LIKE A STUPID ANIMAL! LEAVE HIM ALONE! LEAVE ME ALONE!
CRACK!!

RRRGG

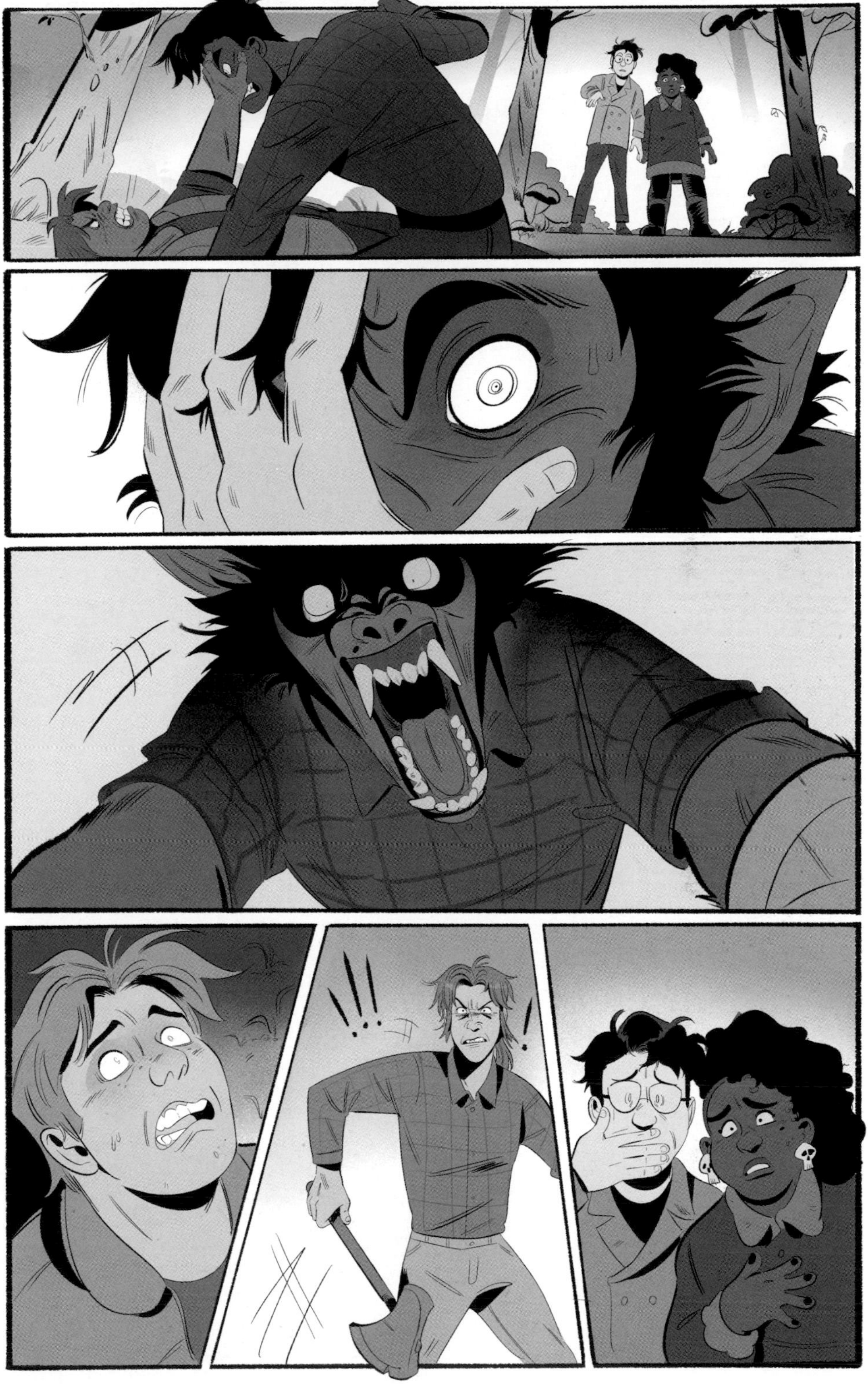
!!
!

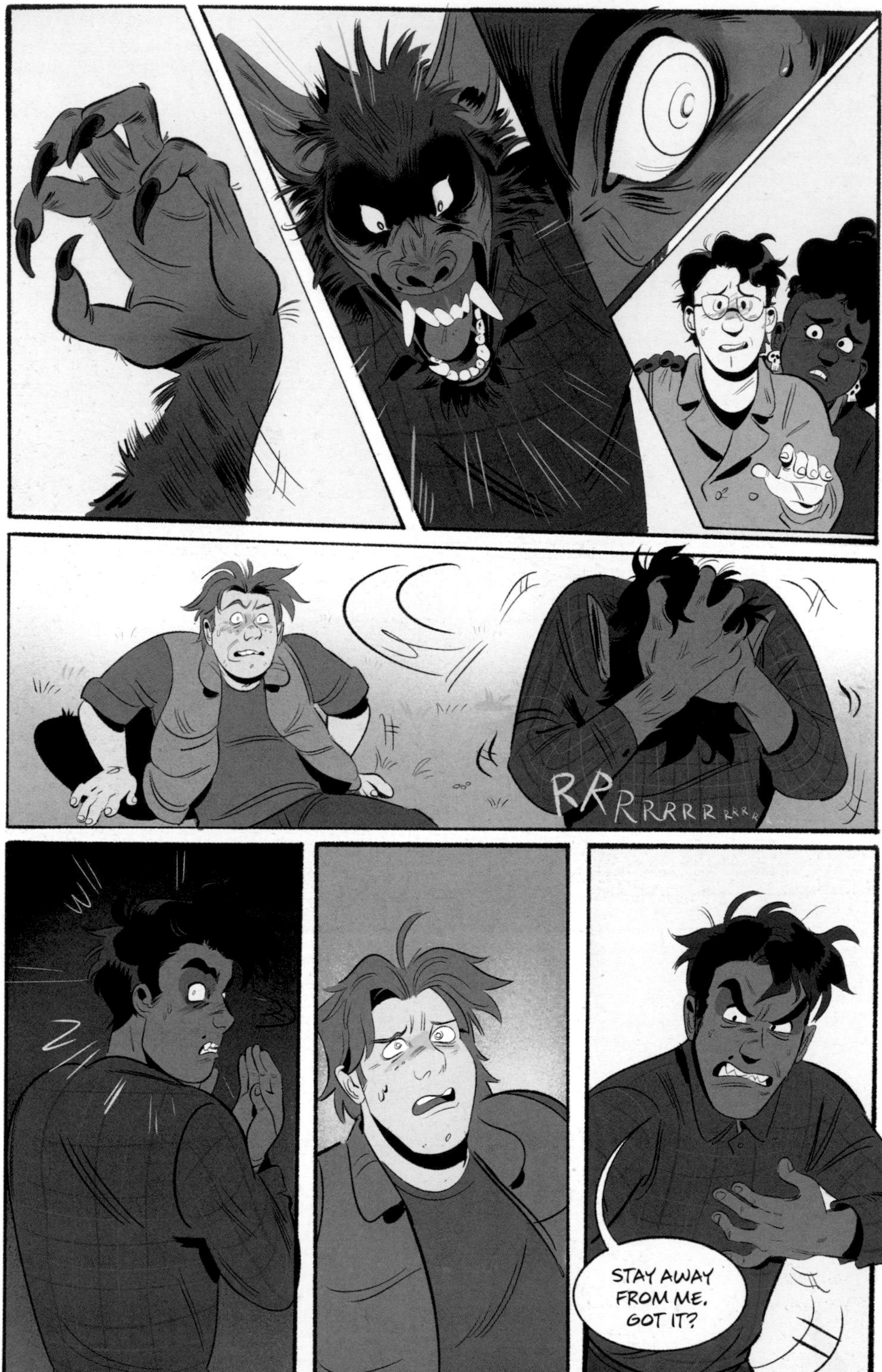
RRRRRRRRRR
STAY AWAY FROM ME. GOT IT?

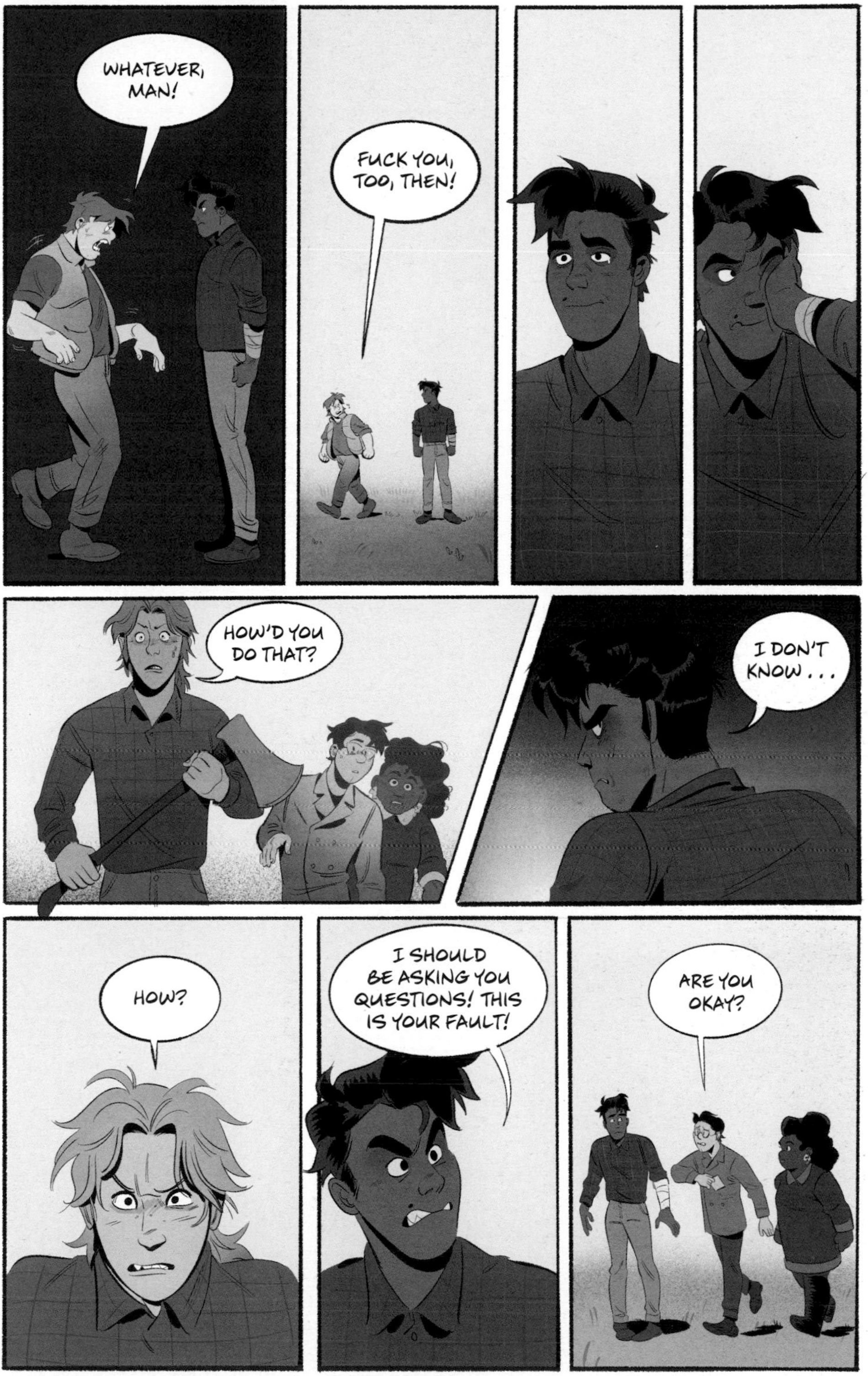
WHATEVER, MAN!
FUCK YOU, TOO, THEN!
HOW'D YOU DO THAT?
I DON'T KNOW . . .
HOW?
I SHOULD BE ASKING YOU QUESTIONS! THIS IS YOUR FAULT!
ARE YOU OKAY?

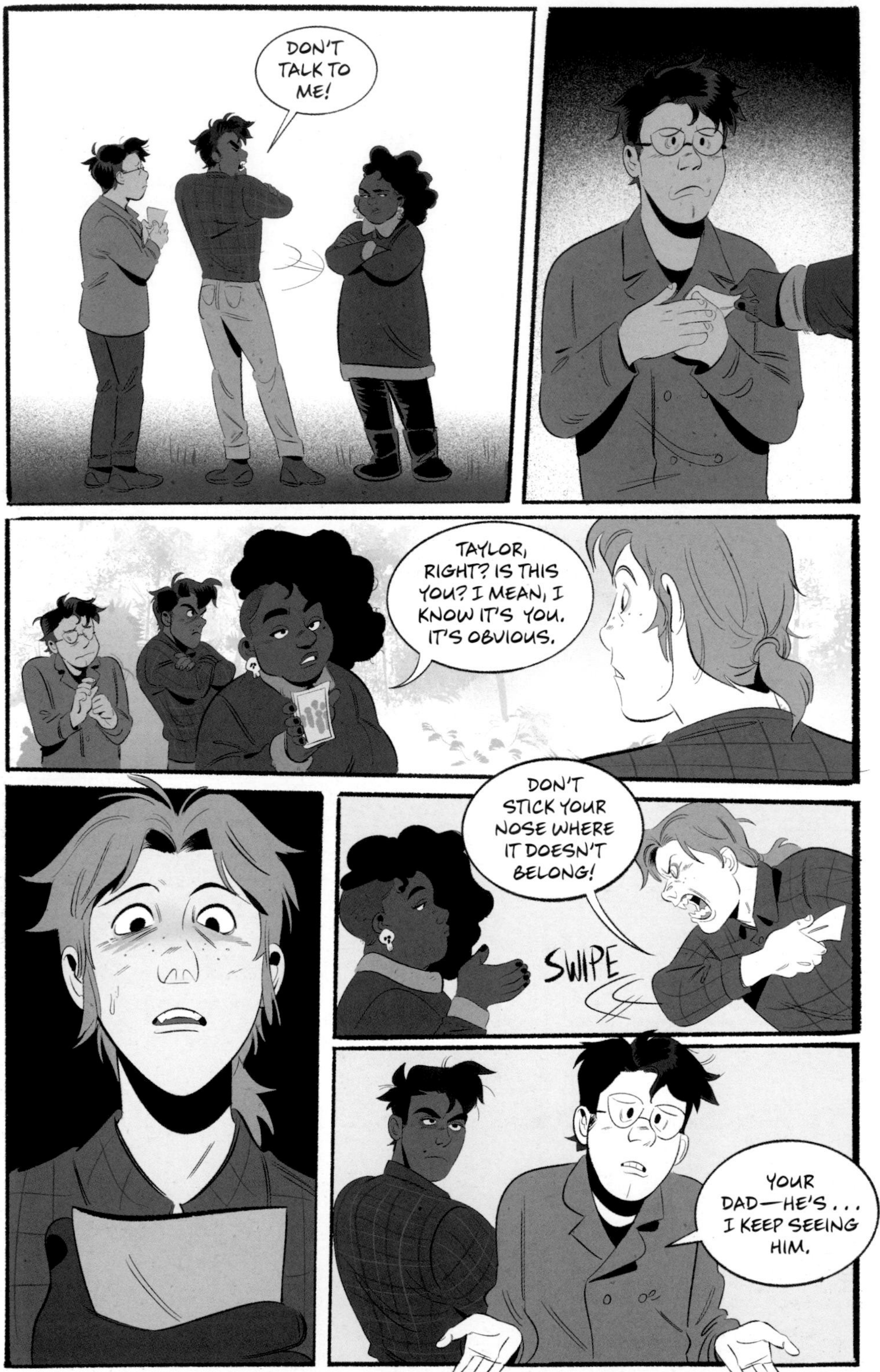
DON'T TALK TO ME!
TAYLOR, RIGHT? IS THIS YOU? I MEAN, I KNOW IT'S YOU. IT'S OBVIOUS.
DON'T STICK YOUR NOSE WHERE IT DOESN'T BELONG!
SWIPE
YOUR DAD—HE'S . . . I KEEP SEEING HIM.

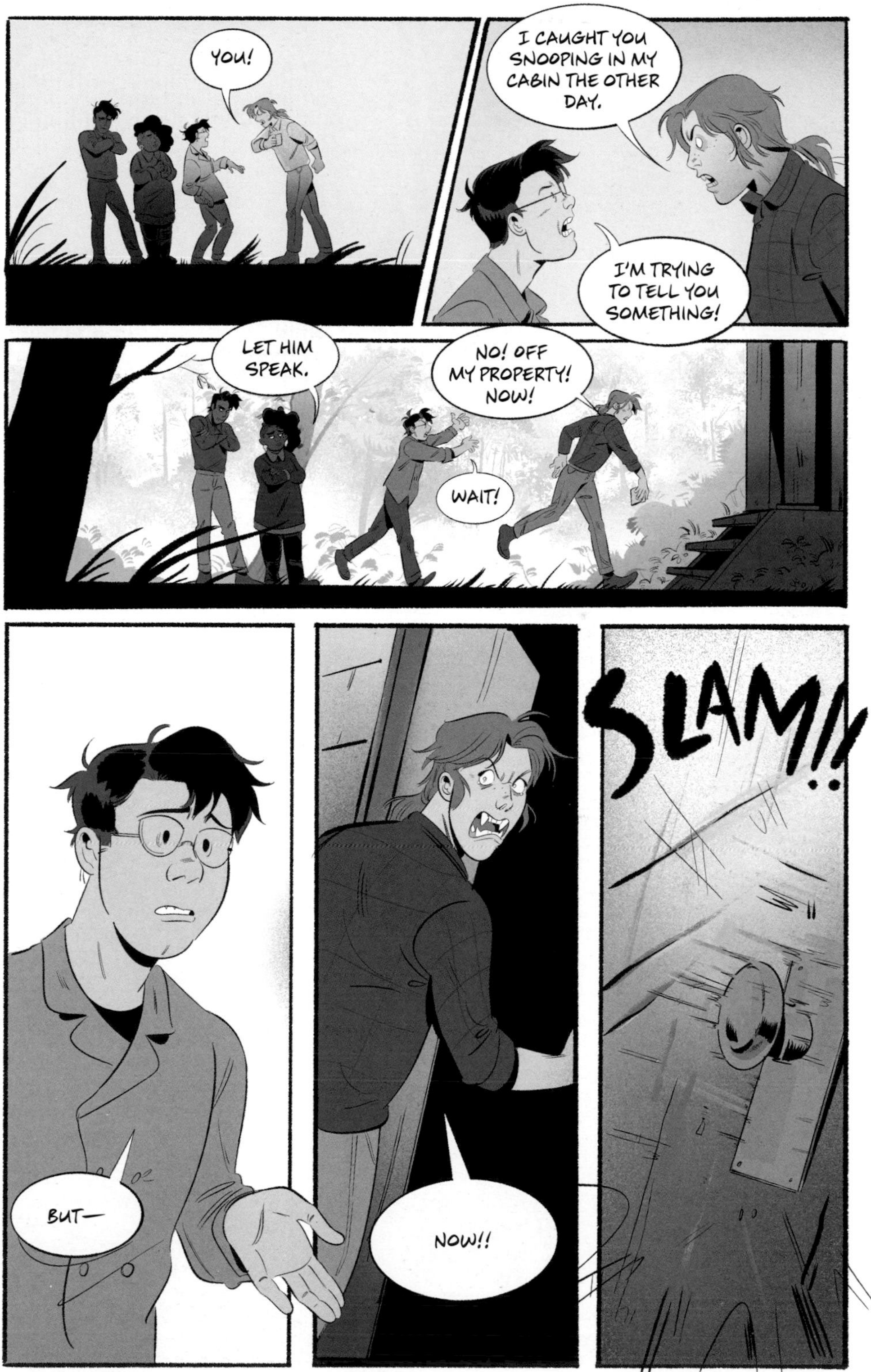
YOU!
I CAUGHT YOU SNOOPING IN MY CABIN THE OTHER DAY.
I'M TRYING TO TELL YOU SOMETHING!
LET HIM SPEAK.
NO! OFF MY PROPERTY! NOW!
WAIT!
BUT—
NOW!!
SLAM!!

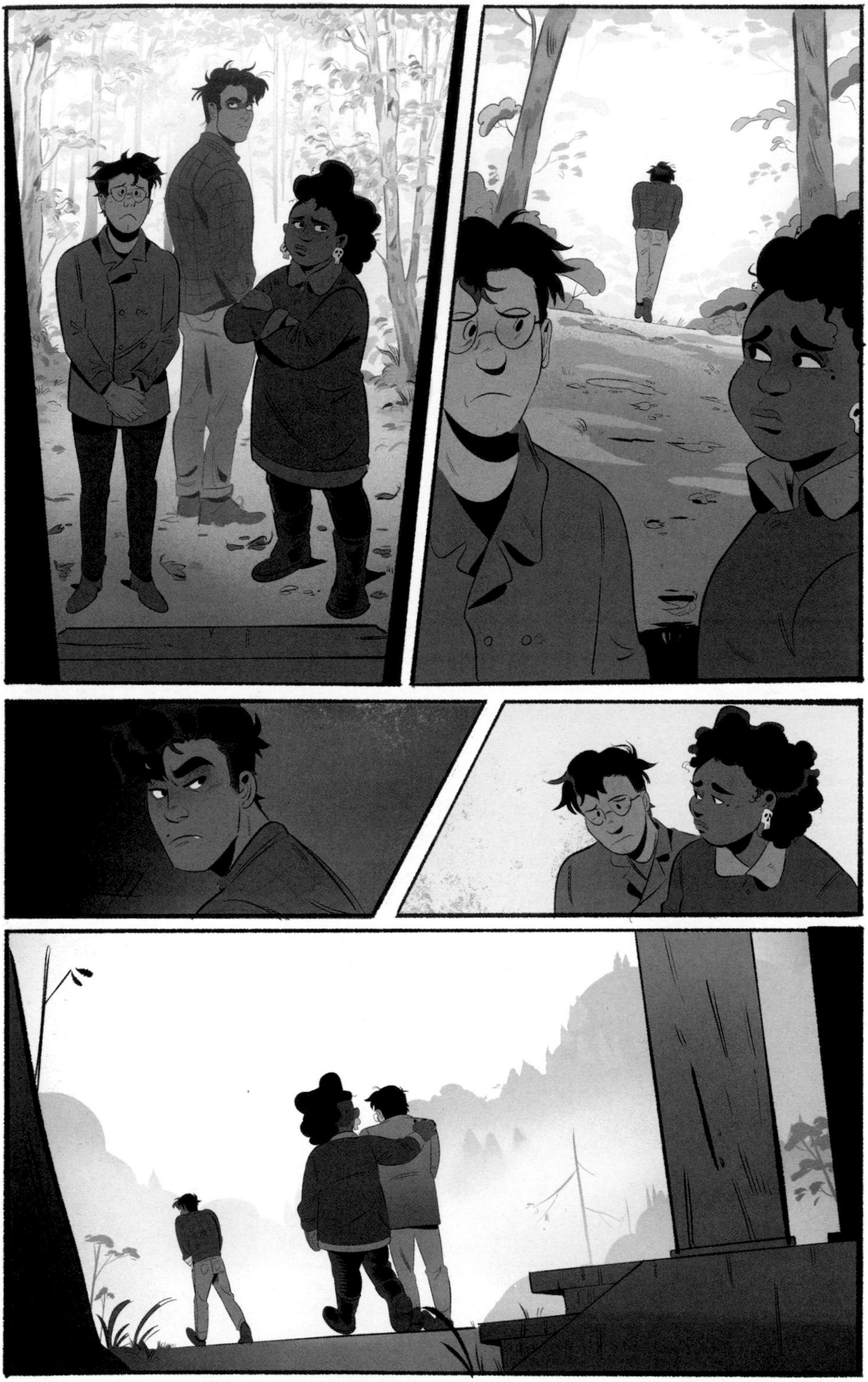

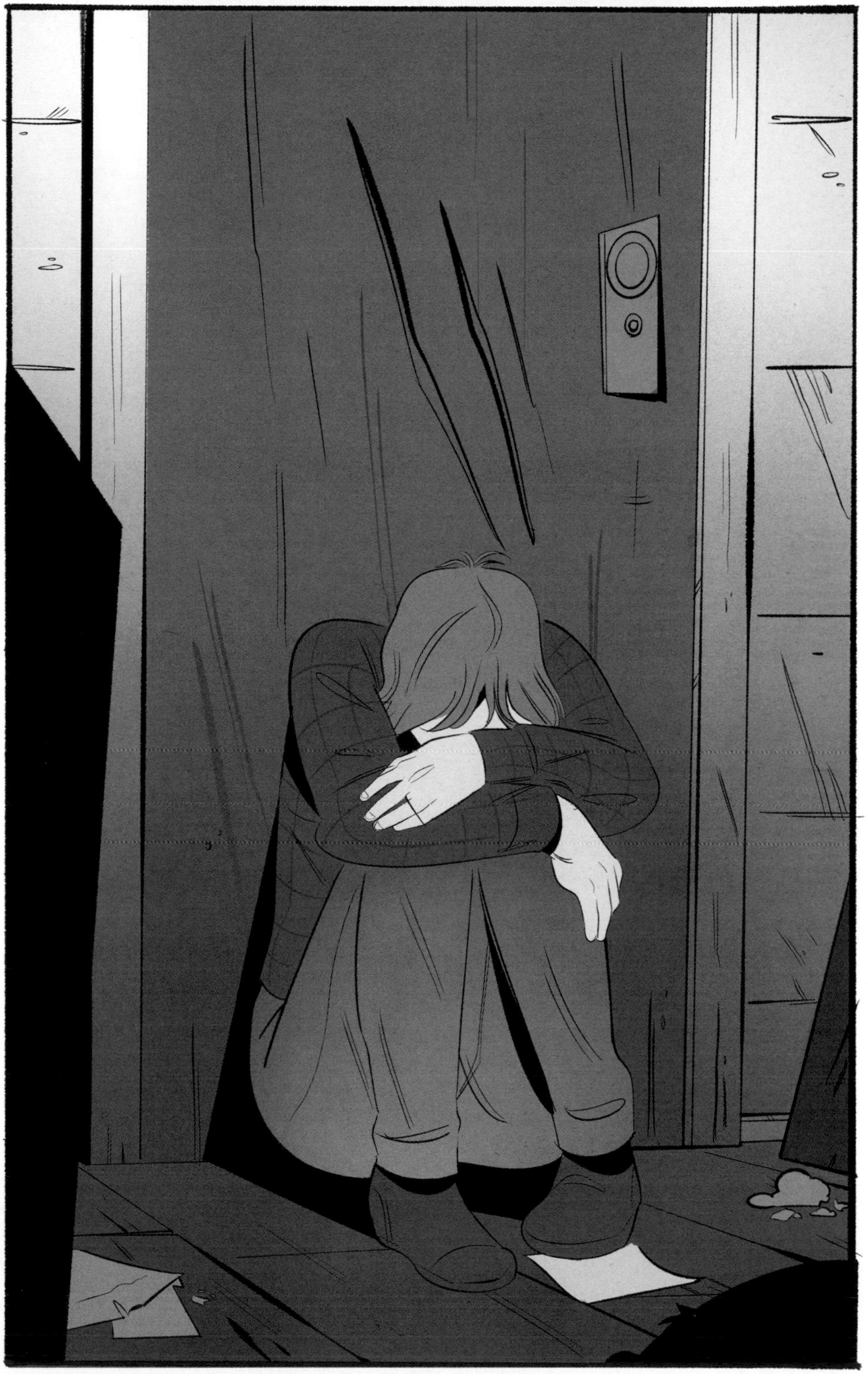

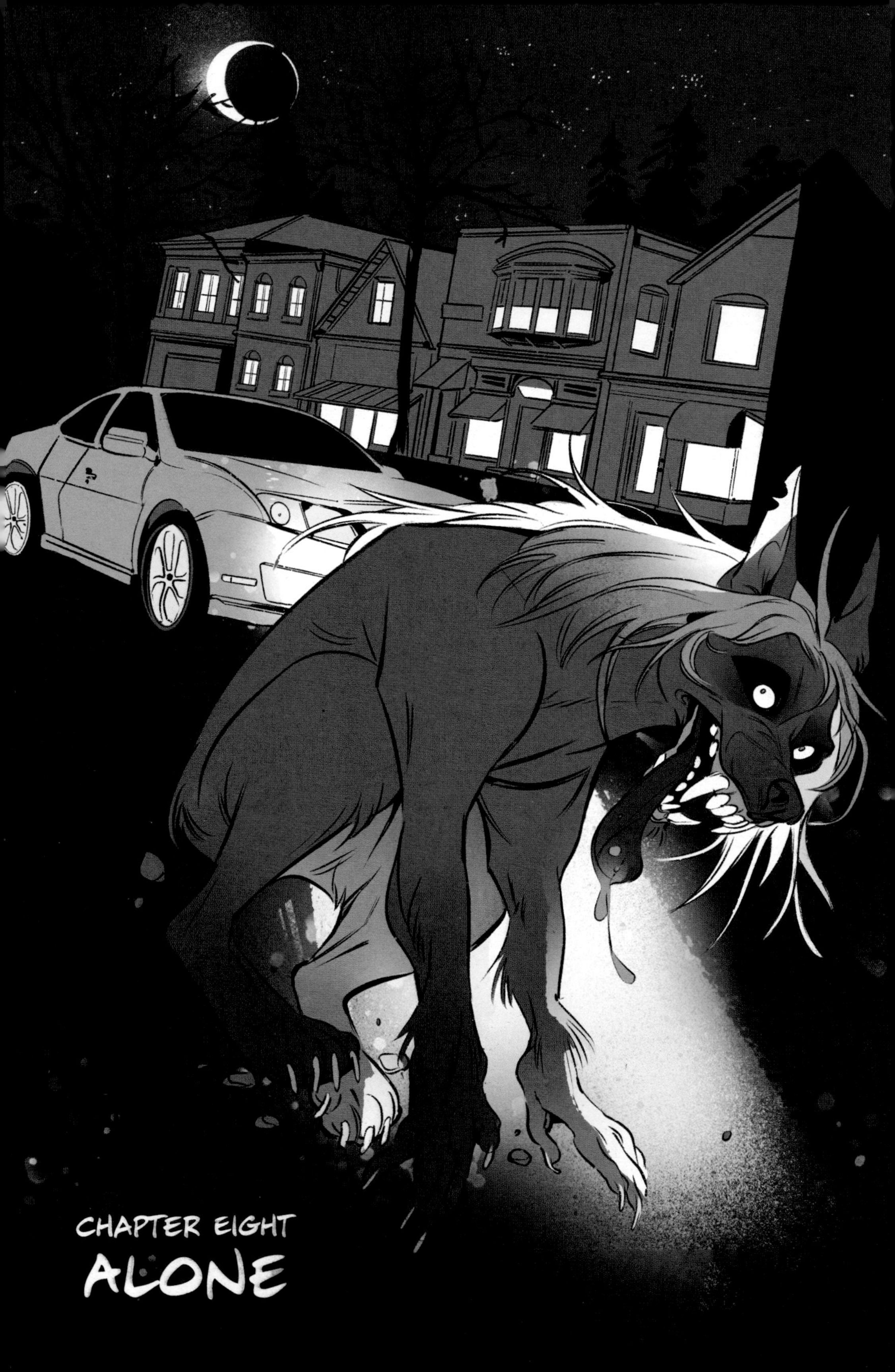

CHAPTER EIGHT
ALONE

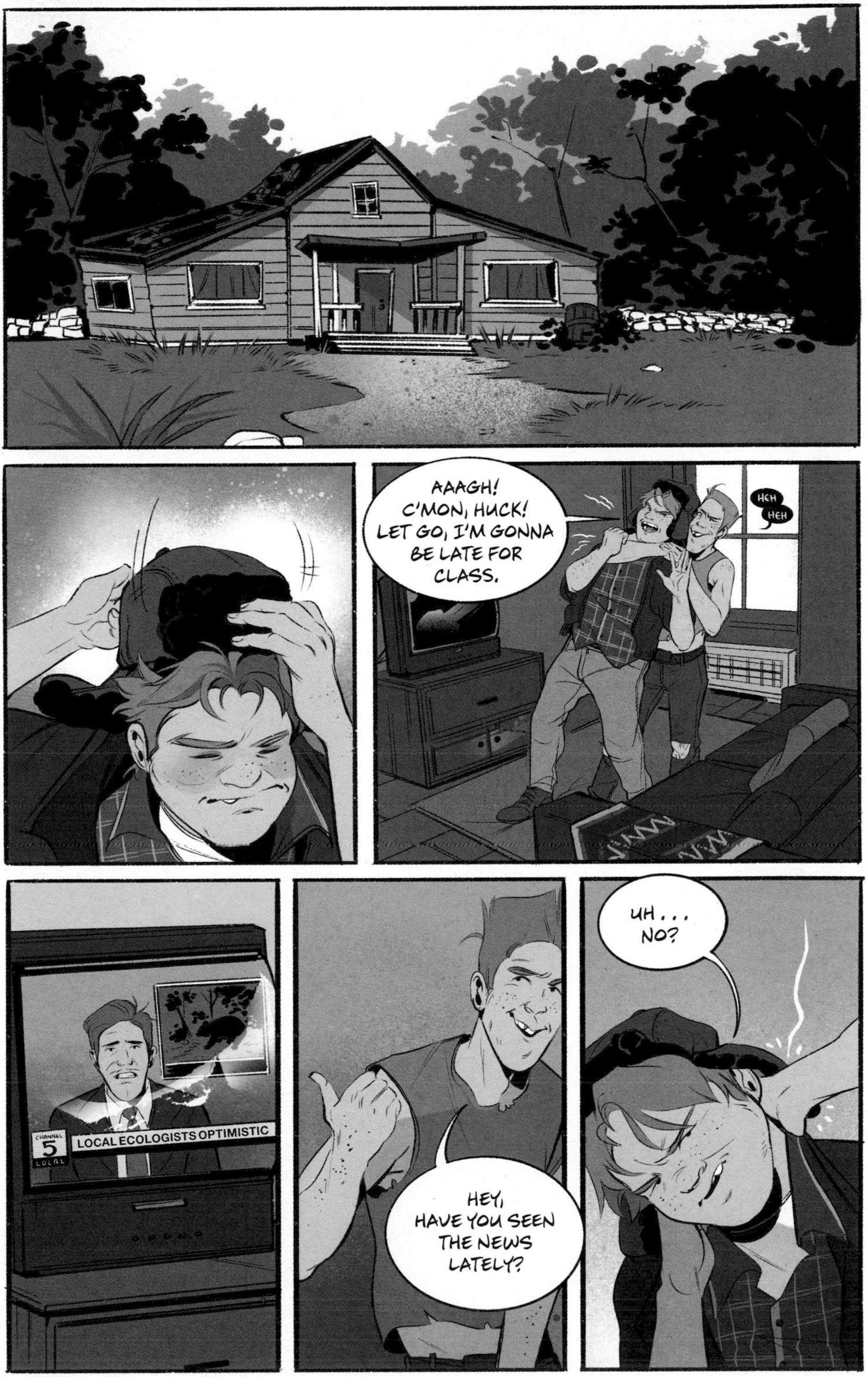

AAAGH! C'MON, HUCK! LET GO, I'M GONNA BE LATE FOR CLASS.
HEH HEH
CHANNEL 5 LOCAL
LOCAL ECOLOGISTS OPTIMISTIC
HEY, HAVE YOU SEEN THE NEWS LATELY?
UH . . . NO?

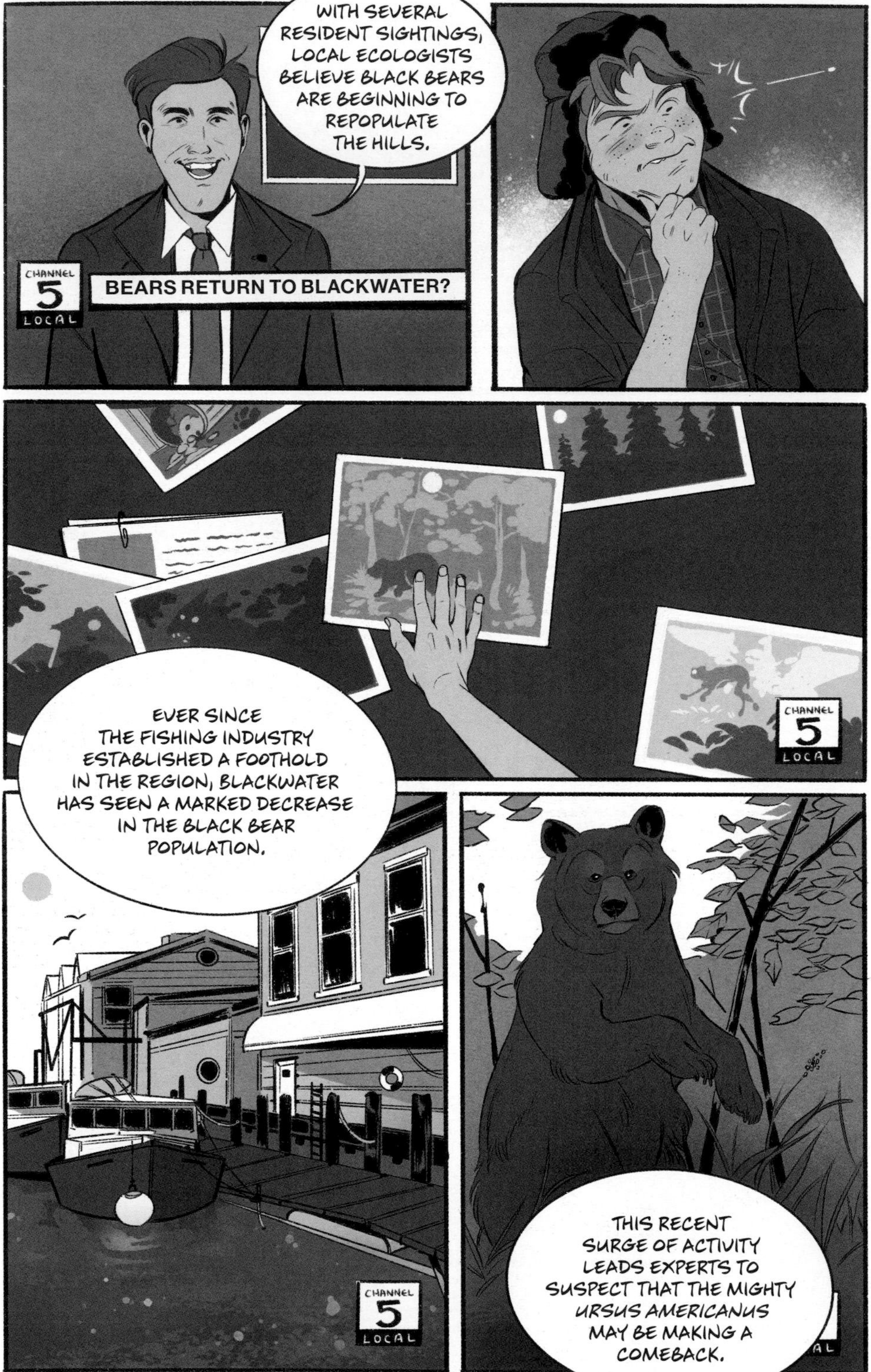
WITH SEVERAL RESIDENT SIGHTINGS, LOCAL ECOLOGISTS BELIEVE BLACK BEARS ARE BEGINNING TO REPOPULATE THE HILLS.
CHANNEL 5 LOCAL
BEARS RETURN TO BLACKWATER?
EVER SINCE THE FISHING INDUSTRY ESTABLISHED A FOOTHOLD IN THE REGION, BLACKWATER HAS SEEN A MARKED DECREASE IN THE BLACK BEAR POPULATION.
CHANNEL 5 LOCAL
CHANNEL 5 LOCAL
THIS RECENT SURGE OF ACTIVITY LEADS EXPERTS TO SUSPECT THAT THE MIGHTY URSUS AMERICANUS MAY BE MAKING A COMEBACK.

OW.

SCARED OF THE BEARS?

NUDGE

NUDGE

SOME LOCALS, ON THE OTHER HAND, HAVE TAKEN AN ENTIRELY DIFFERENT STANCE.

YEAH, SO MOST PEOPLE ARE UNDER THE IMPRESSION THAT BIGFOOT IS A WEST COAST PHENOMENON . . .

CHANNEL 5 LOCAL

BUT IN OUR COMMUNITY AND SEVERAL OTHERS NATIONWIDE, WE'VE BEEN SEEING REGION-SPECIFIC BIGFEET FACTIONS.

AND THE PUBLIC WILL REALIZE THAT, ONCE ALL THIS STUFF GETS DECLASSIFIED.

CHANNEL 5 LOCAL

HA! CRAZY STUFF, HUH? I TOLD YA!

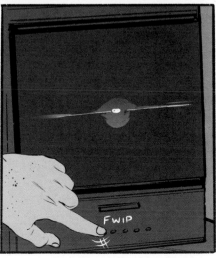

FWIP

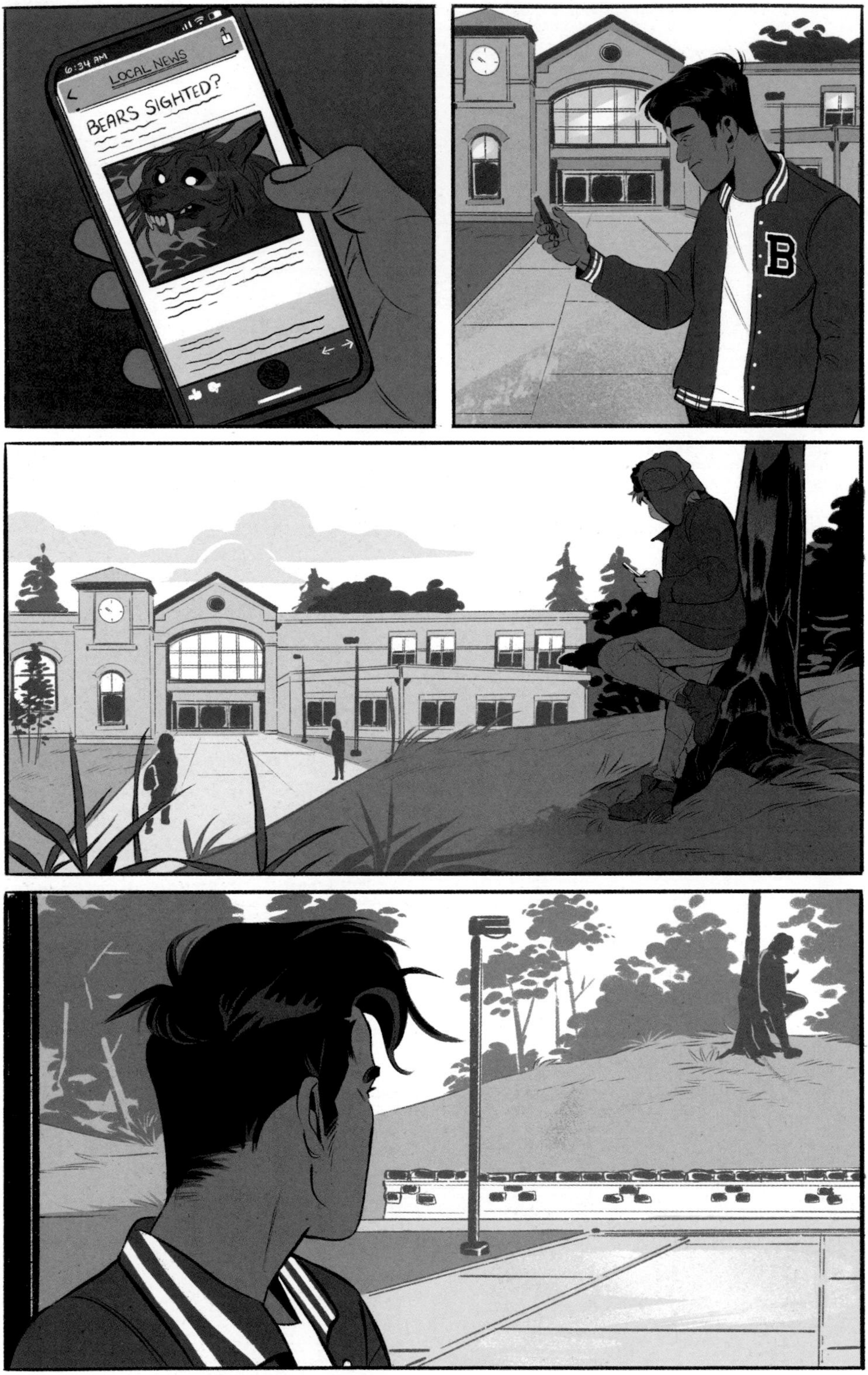
6:34 AM
LOCAL NEWS
BEARS SIGHTED?

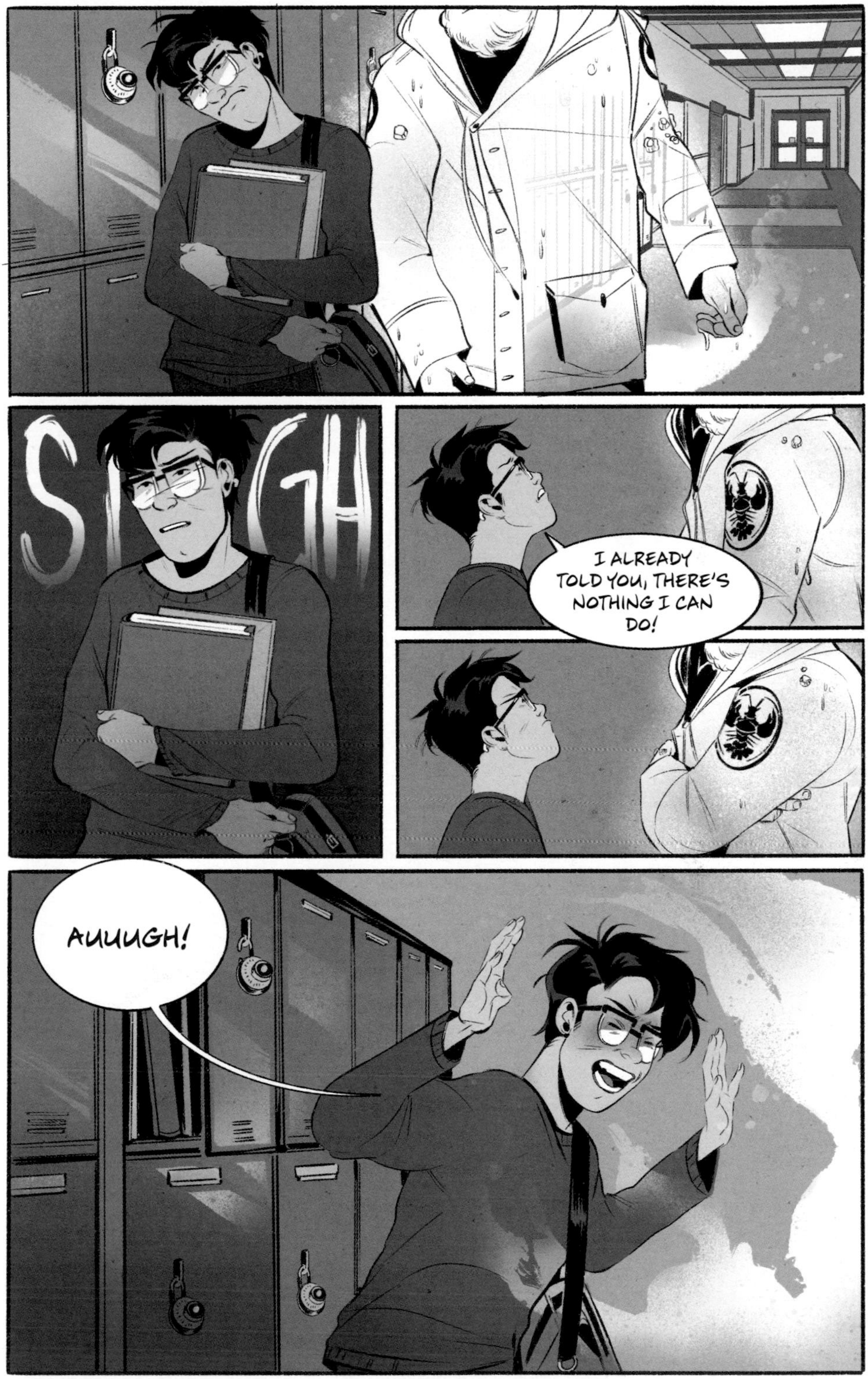
SIGH
I ALREADY TOLD YOU, THERE'S NOTHING I CAN DO!
AUUUGH!

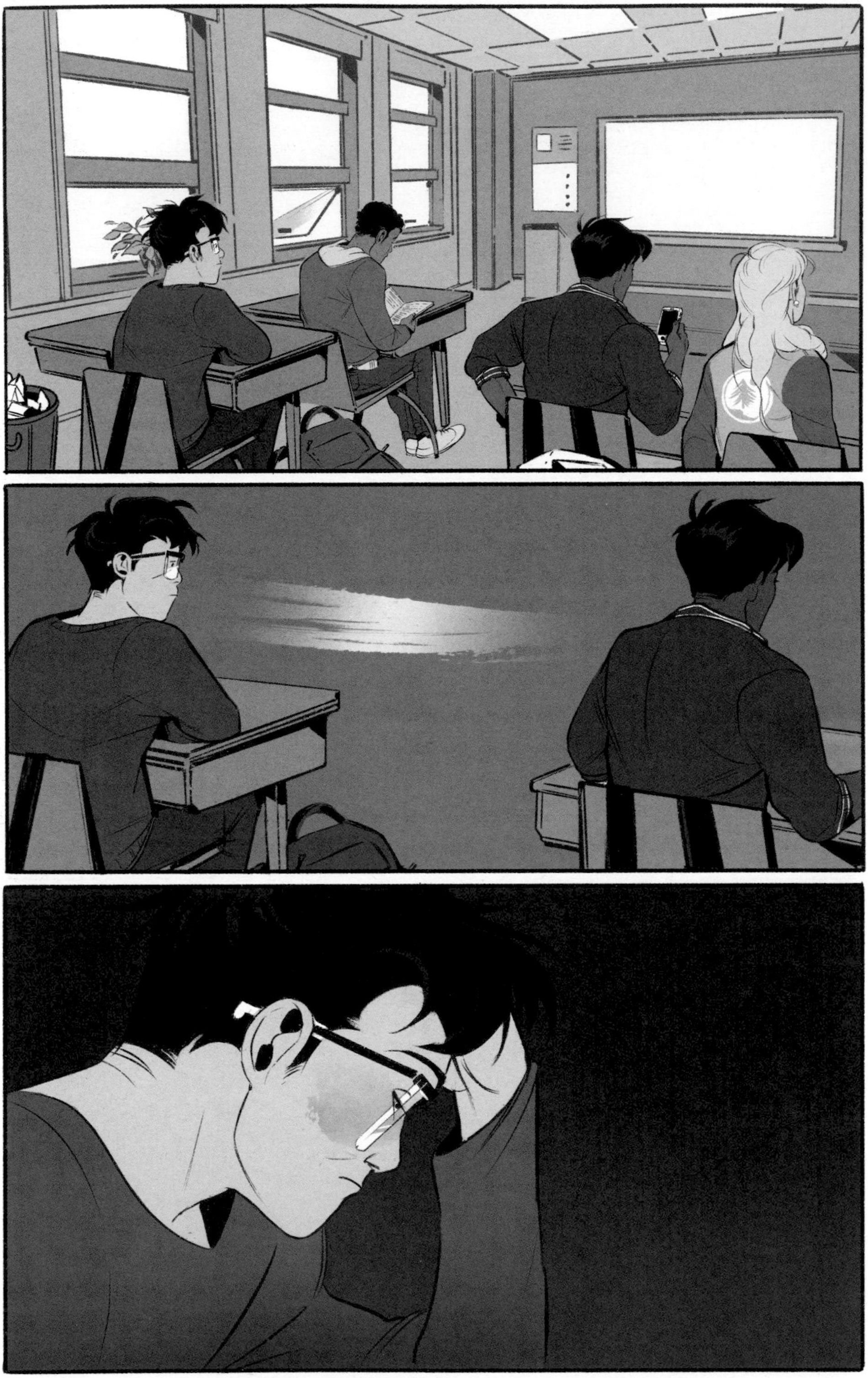

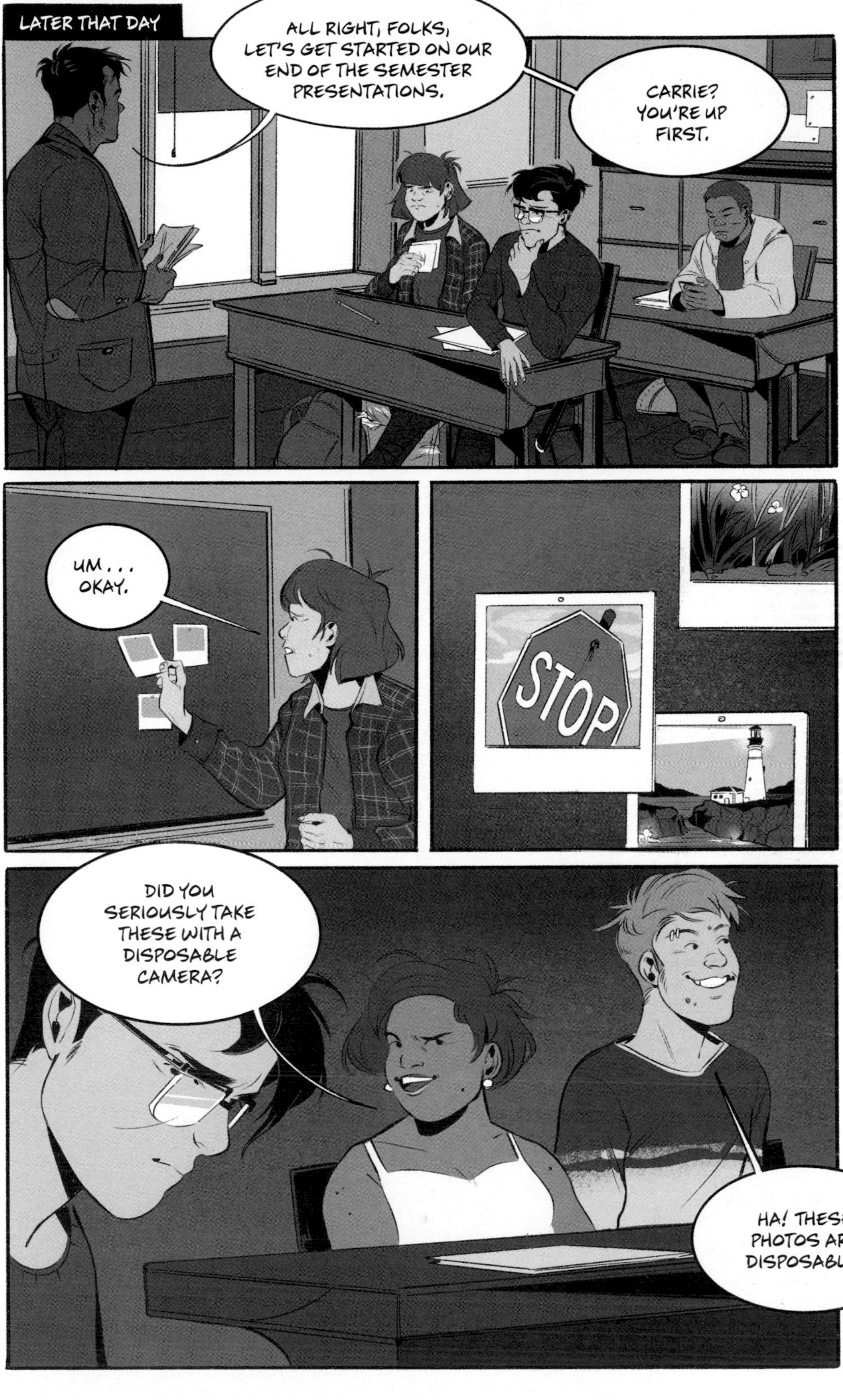

LATER THAT DAY
ALL RIGHT, FOLKS, LET'S GET STARTED ON OUR END OF THE SEMESTER PRESENTATIONS.
CARRIE? YOU'RE UP FIRST.
UM . . . OKAY.
STOP
DID YOU SERIOUSLY TAKE THESE WITH A DISPOSABLE CAMERA?
HA! THESE PHOTOS ARE DISPOSABLE.

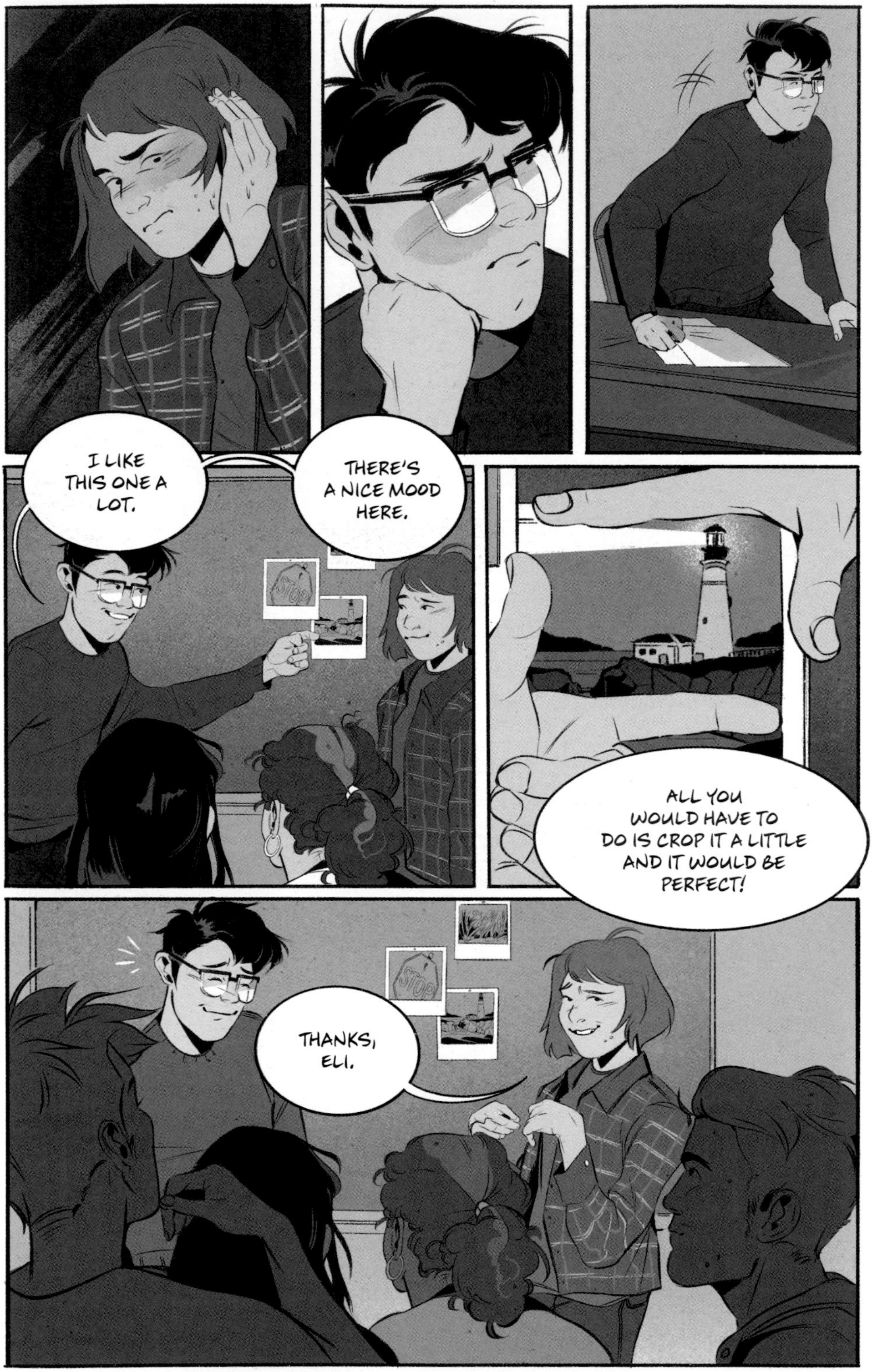
I LIKE THIS ONE A LOT.
THERE'S A NICE MOOD HERE.
ALL YOU WOULD HAVE TO DO IS CROP IT A LITTLE AND IT WOULD BE PERFECT!
THANKS, ELI.

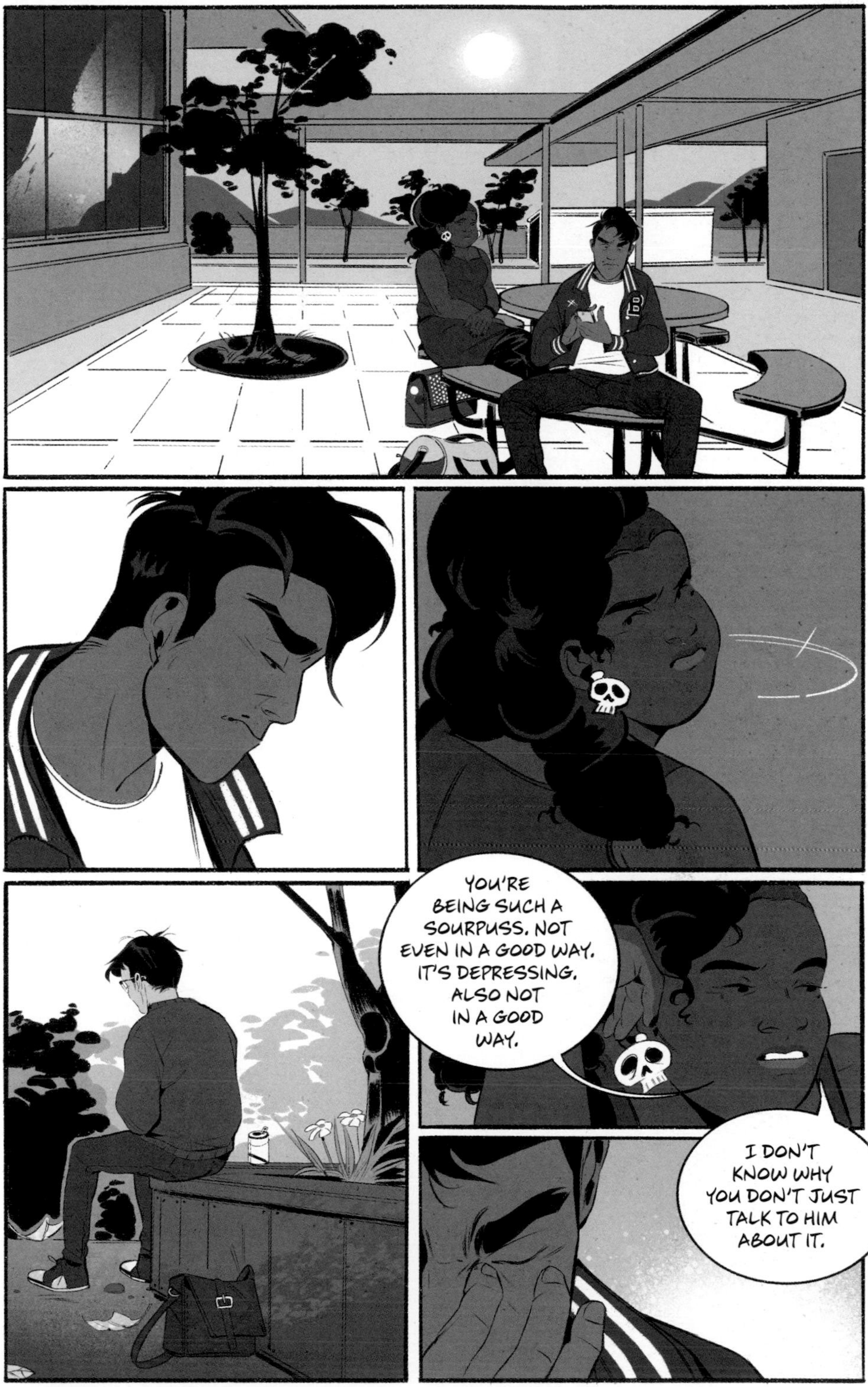
YOU'RE BEING SUCH A SOURPUSS. NOT EVEN IN A GOOD WAY. IT'S DEPRESSING. ALSO NOT IN A GOOD WAY.
I DON'T KNOW WHY YOU DON'T JUST TALK TO HIM ABOUT IT.

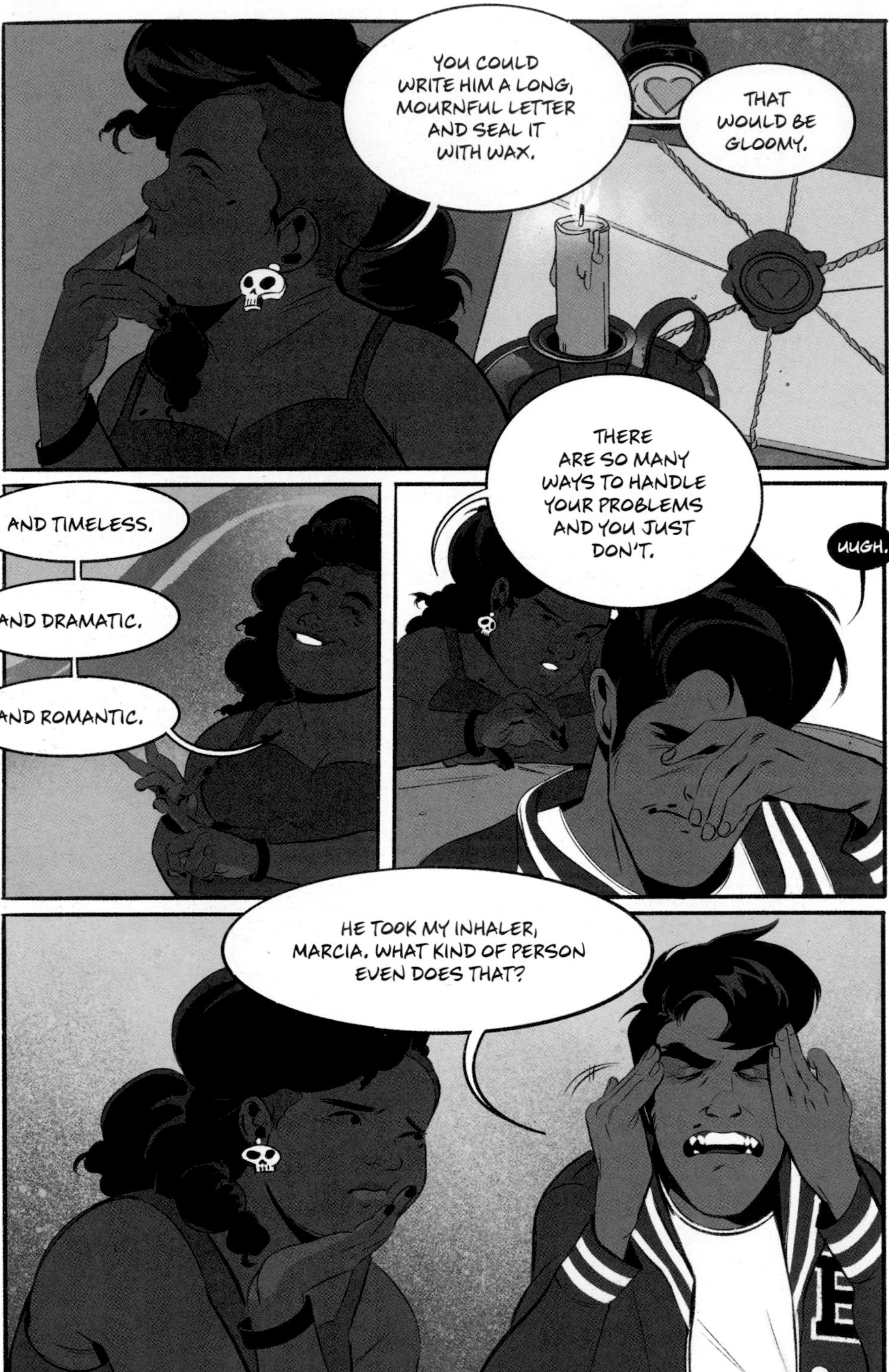
YOU COULD WRITE HIM A LONG, MOURNFUL LETTER AND SEAL IT WITH WAX.
THAT WOULD BE GLOOMY.
AND TIMELESS.
AND DRAMATIC.
AND ROMANTIC.
THERE ARE SO MANY WAYS TO HANDLE YOUR PROBLEMS AND YOU JUST DON'T.
UUGH.
HE TOOK MY INHALER, MARCIA. WHAT KIND OF PERSON EVEN DOES THAT?

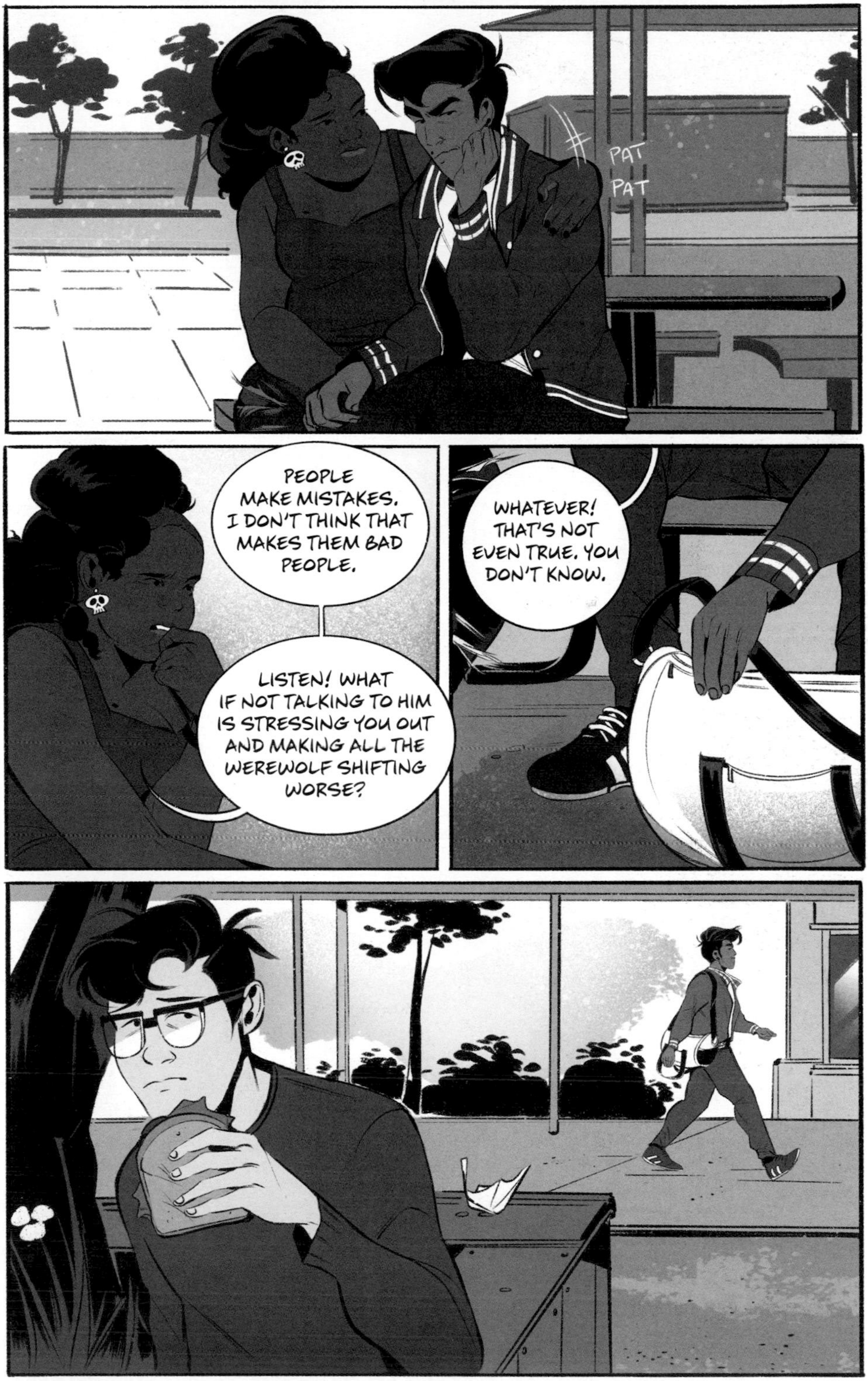
PAT
PAT
PEOPLE MAKE MISTAKES. I DON'T THINK THAT MAKES THEM BAD PEOPLE.
LISTEN! WHAT IF NOT TALKING TO HIM IS STRESSING YOU OUT AND MAKING ALL THE WEREWOLF SHIFTING WORSE?
WHATEVER! THAT'S NOT EVEN TRUE. YOU DON'T KNOW.

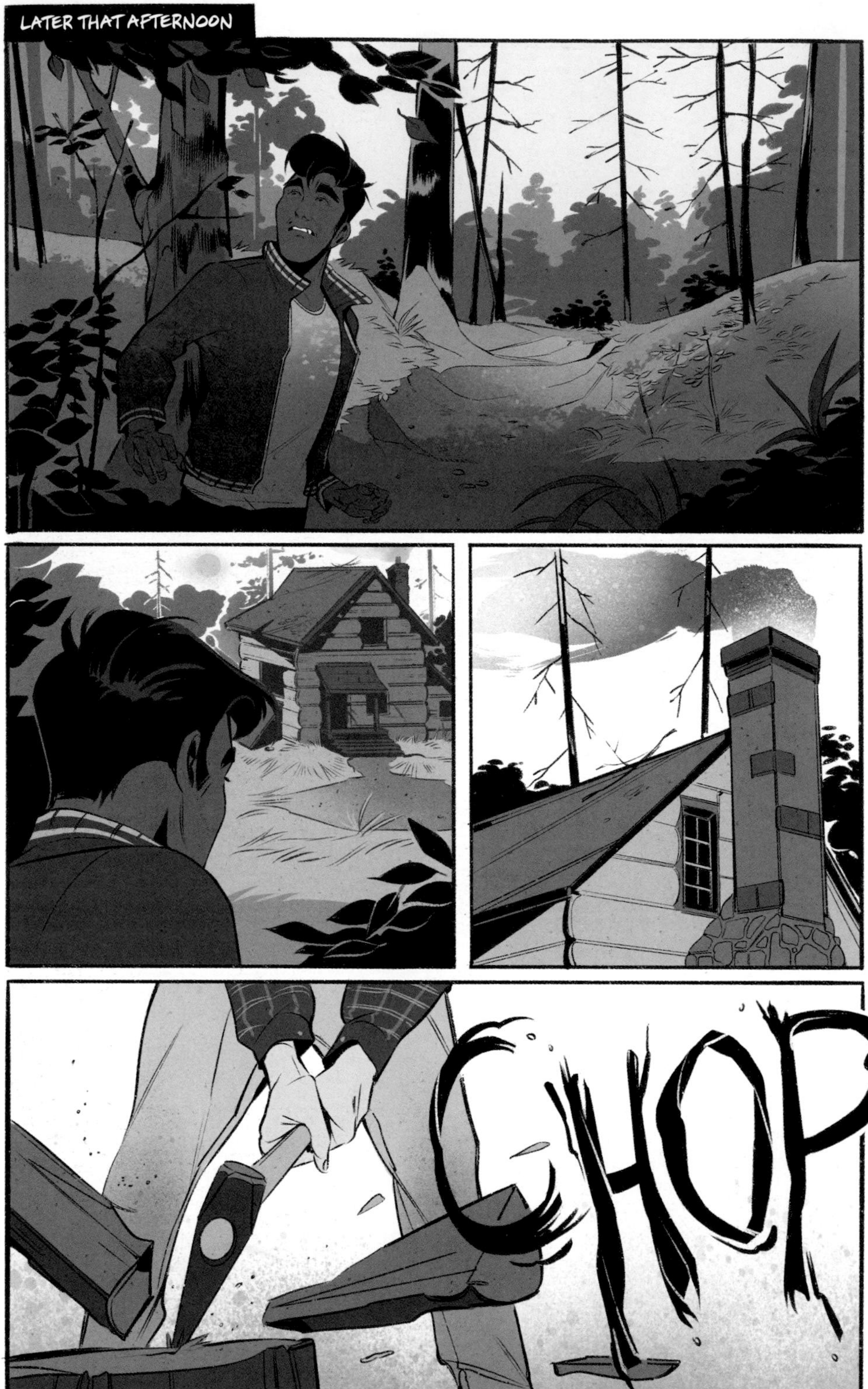
LATER THAT AFTERNOON
CHOP

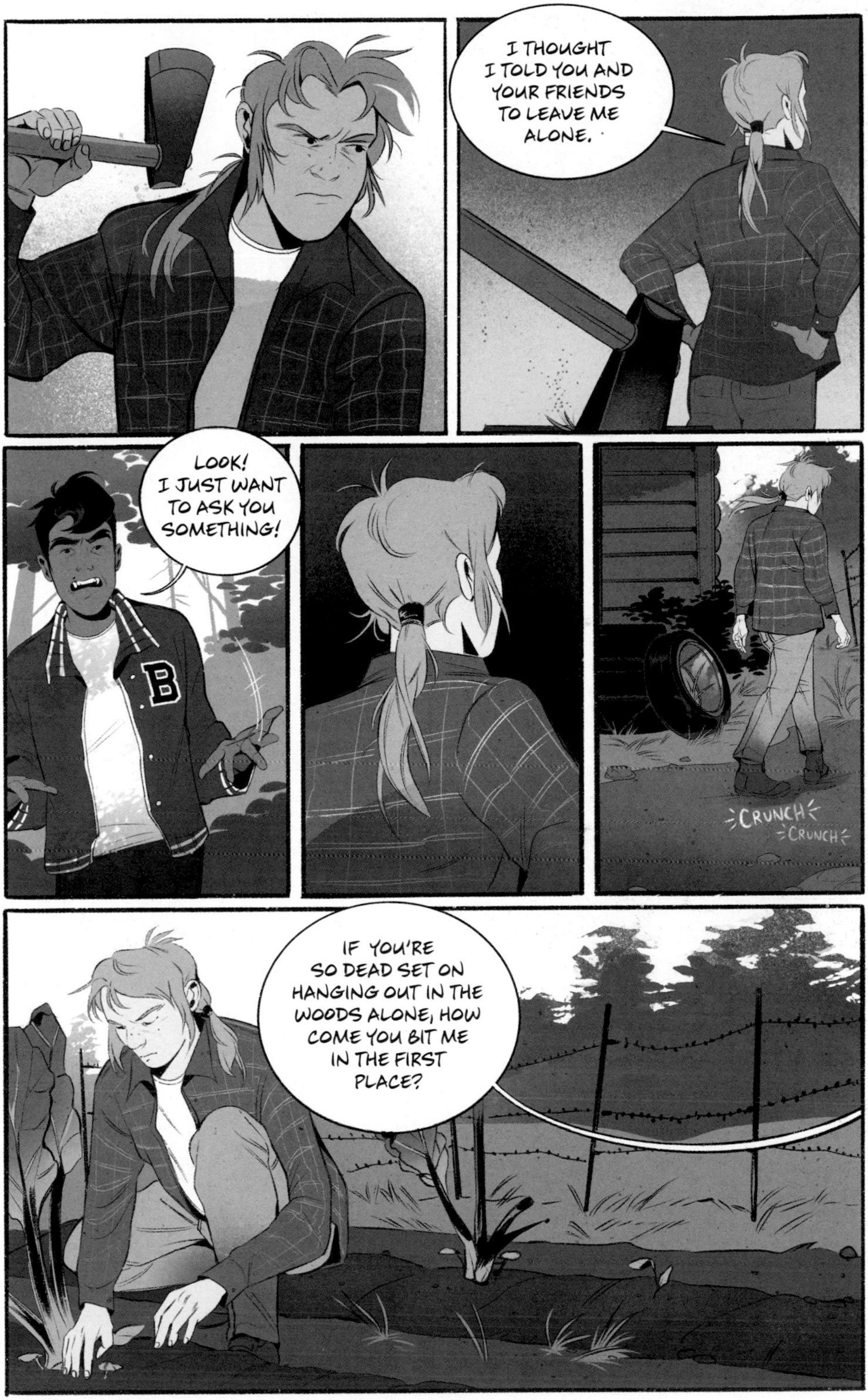
I THOUGHT I TOLD YOU AND YOUR FRIENDS TO LEAVE ME ALONE.
LOOK! I JUST WANT TO ASK YOU SOMETHING!
CRUNCH
CRUNCH
IF YOU'RE SO DEAD SET ON HANGING OUT IN THE WOODS ALONE, HOW COME YOU BIT ME IN THE FIRST PLACE?

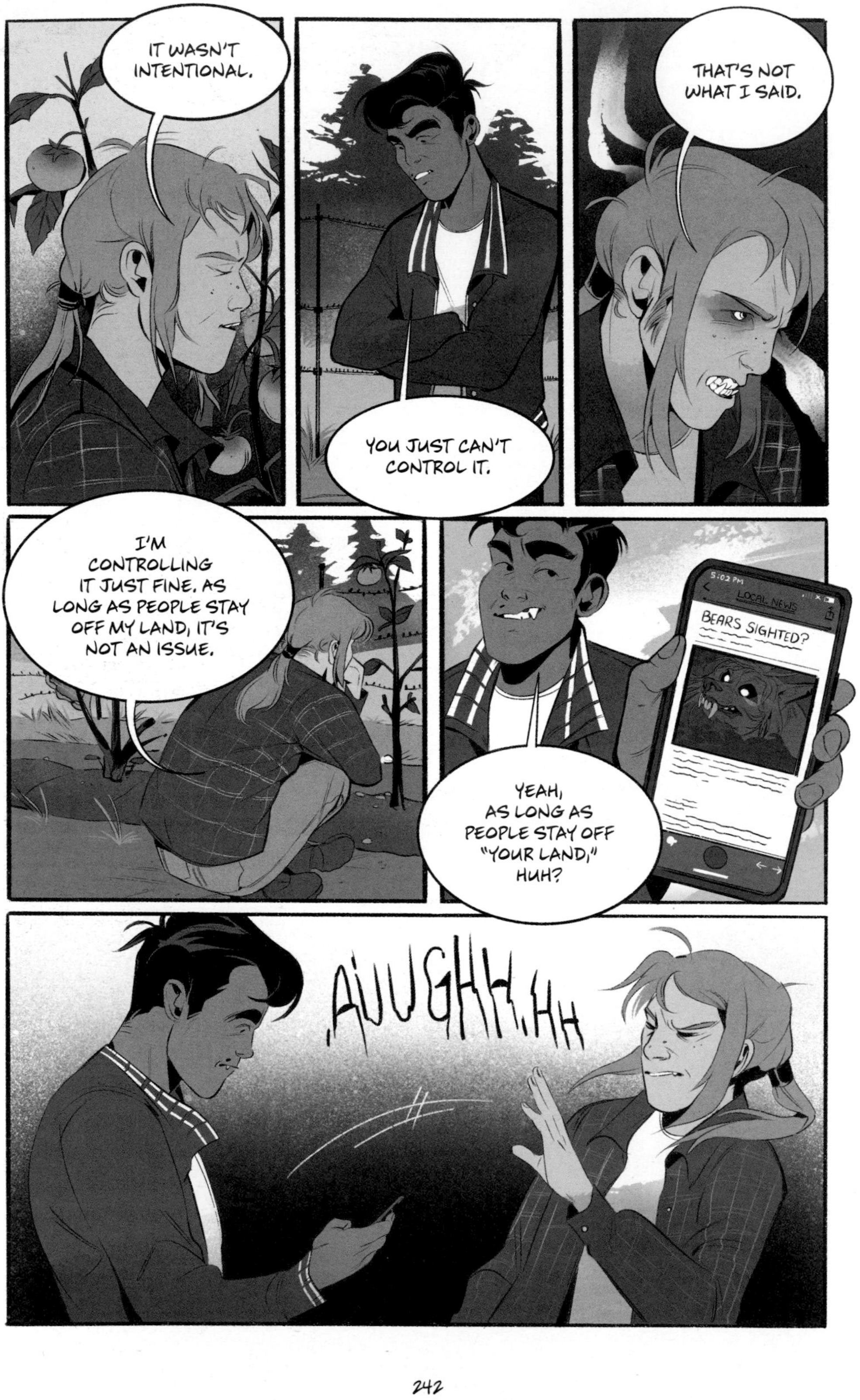
IT WASN'T INTENTIONAL.
YOU JUST CAN'T CONTROL IT.
THAT'S NOT WHAT I SAID.
I'M CONTROLLING IT JUST FINE. AS LONG AS PEOPLE STAY OFF MY LAND, IT'S NOT AN ISSUE.
5:02 PM
LOCAL NEWS
BEARS SIGHTED?
YEAH, AS LONG AS PEOPLE STAY OFF "YOUR LAND," HUH?
AUUGHHHH

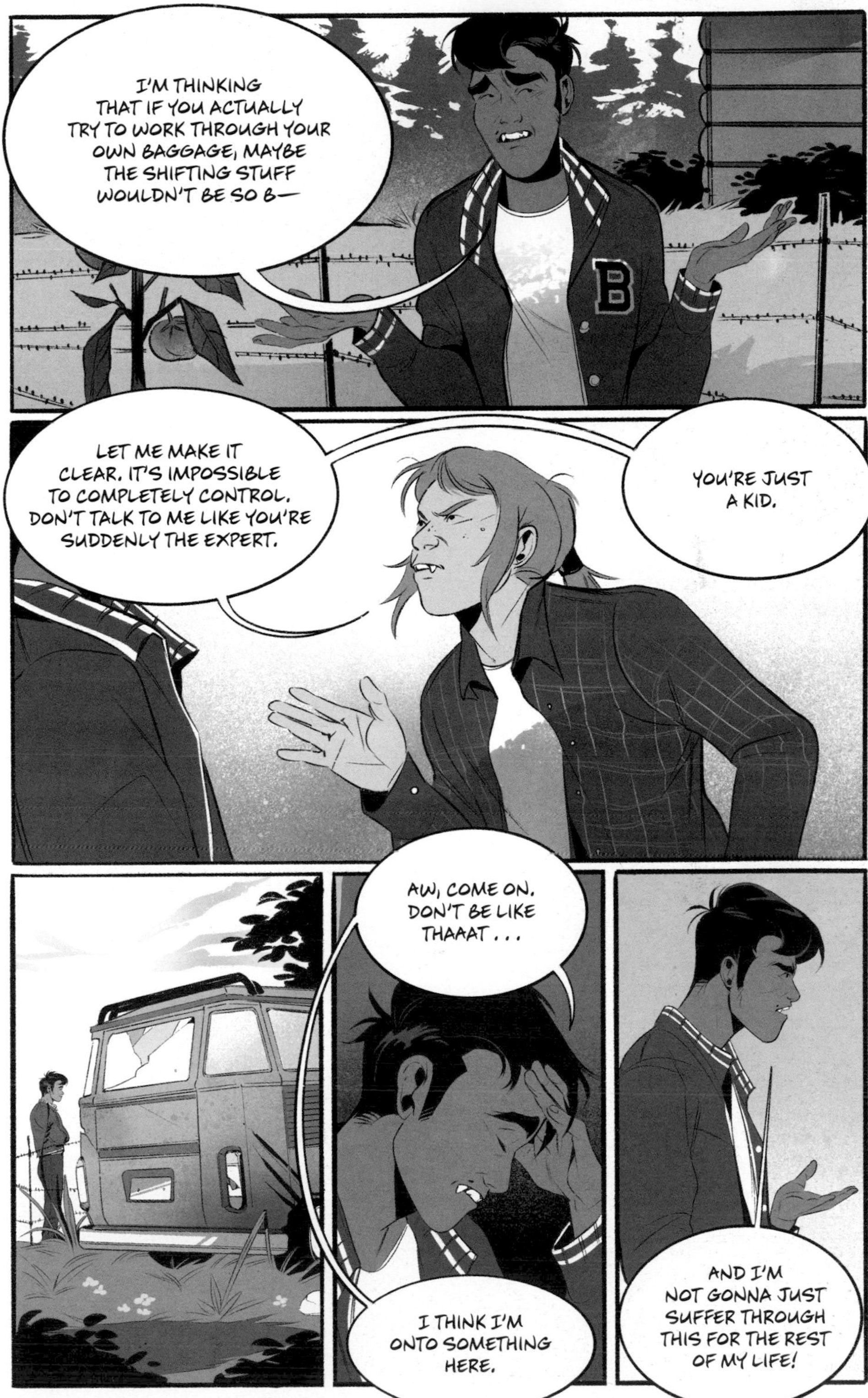
I'M THINKING THAT IF YOU ACTUALLY TRY TO WORK THROUGH YOUR OWN BAGGAGE, MAYBE THE SHIFTING STUFF WOULDN'T BE SO B—
LET ME MAKE IT CLEAR. IT'S IMPOSSIBLE TO COMPLETELY CONTROL. DON'T TALK TO ME LIKE YOU'RE SUDDENLY THE EXPERT.
YOU'RE JUST A KID.
AW, COME ON. DON'T BE LIKE THAAAT . . .
I THINK I'M ONTO SOMETHING HERE.
AND I'M NOT GONNA JUST SUFFER THROUGH THIS FOR THE REST OF MY LIFE!

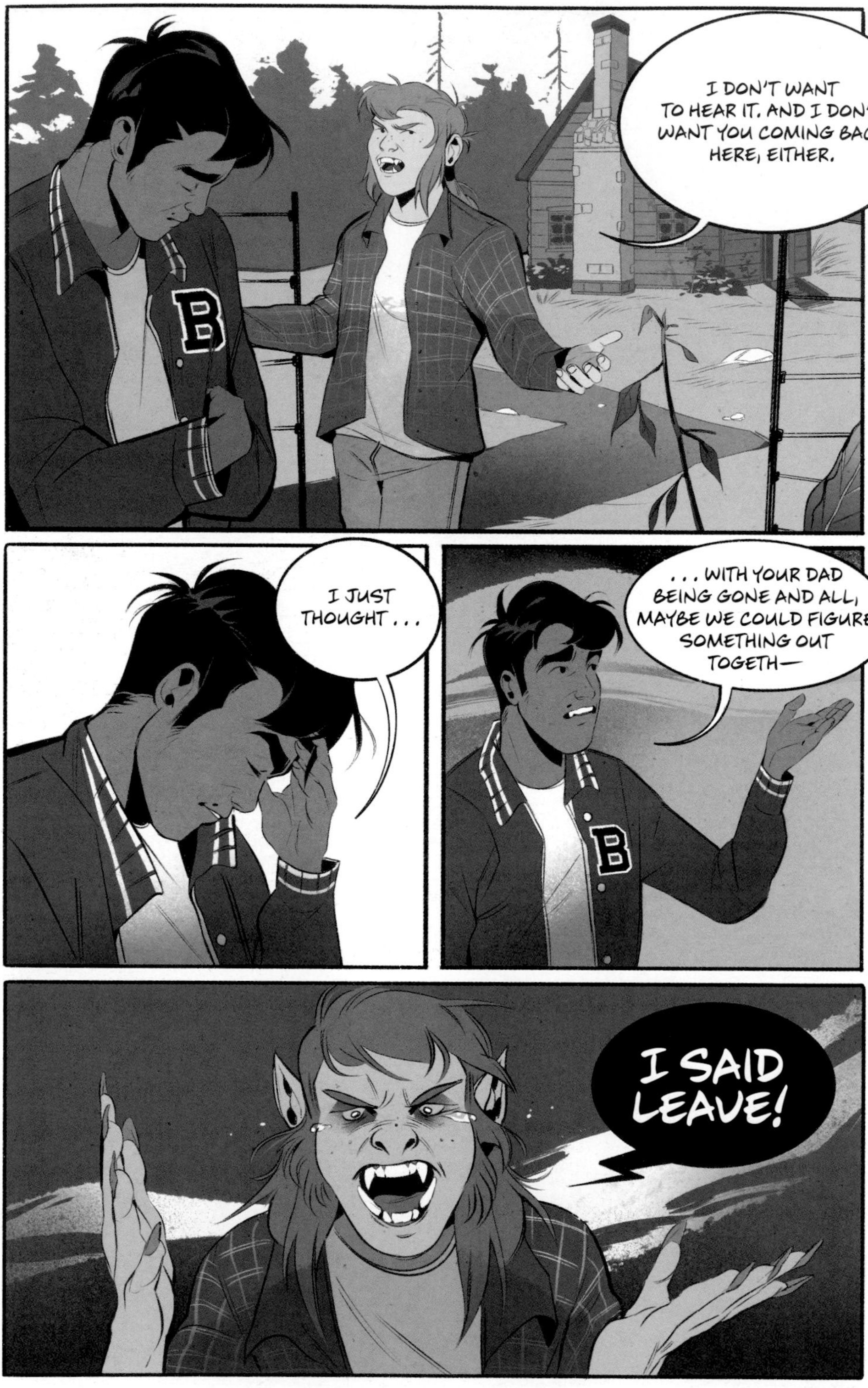
I DON'T WANT TO HEAR IT. AND I DON'T WANT YOU COMING BACK HERE, EITHER.
I JUST THOUGHT . . .
. . . WITH YOUR DAD BEING GONE AND ALL, MAYBE WE COULD FIGURE SOMETHING OUT TOGETH—
I SAID LEAVE!

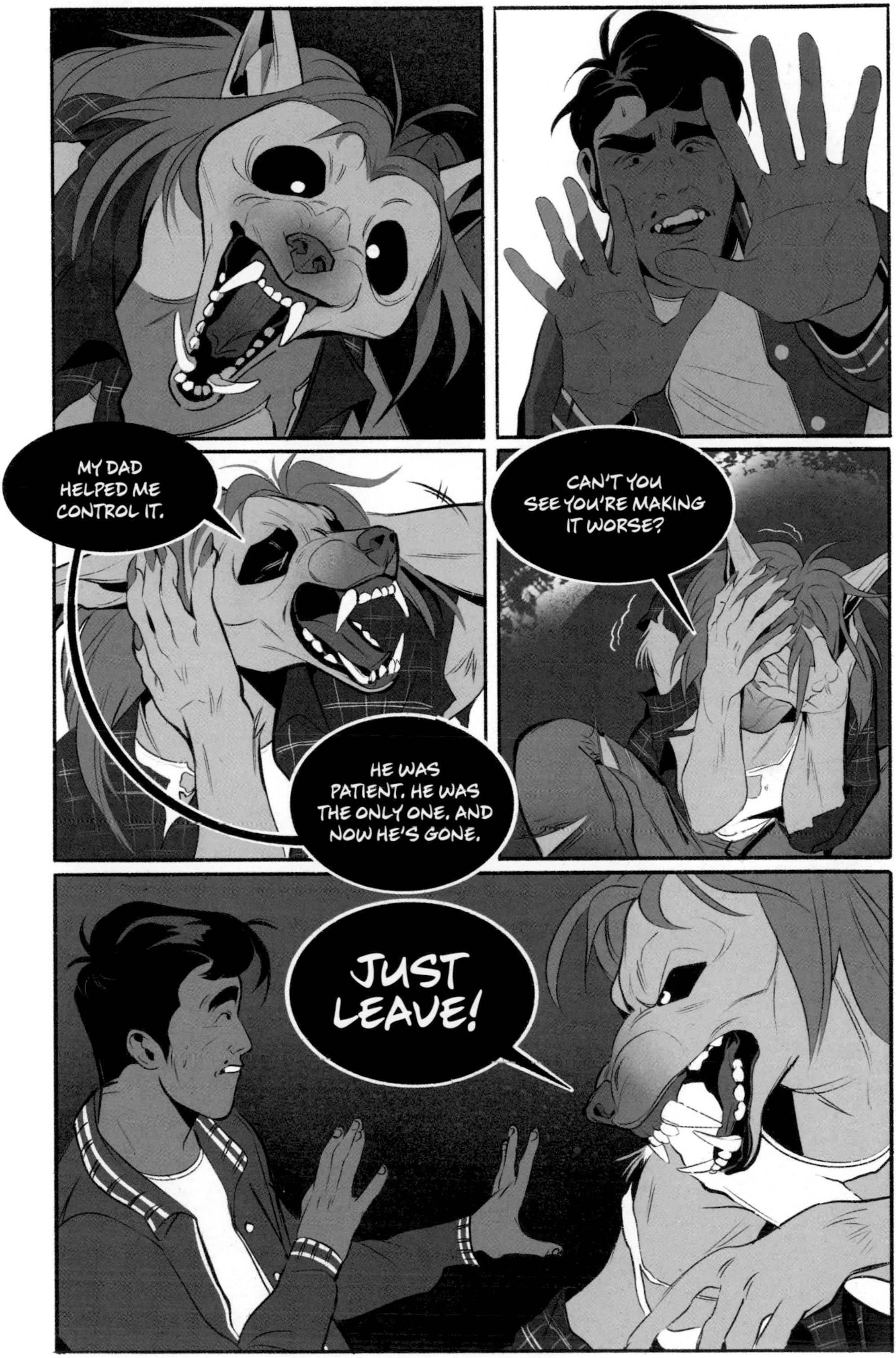
MY DAD HELPED ME CONTROL IT.
HE WAS PATIENT. HE WAS THE ONLY ONE. AND NOW HE'S GONE.
CAN'T YOU SEE YOU'RE MAKING IT WORSE?
JUST LEAVE!

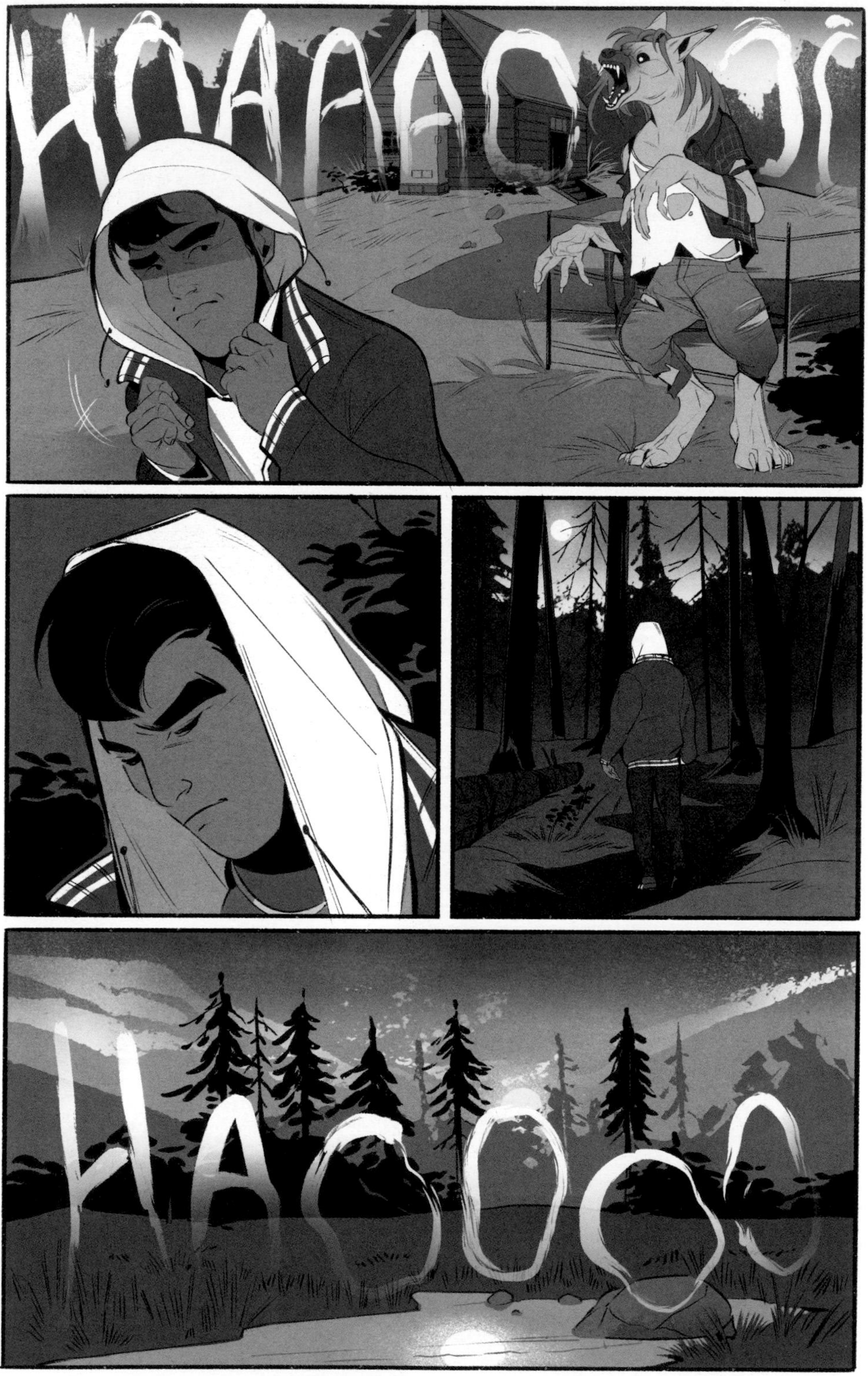
HOAAAOOO
HAOOOO

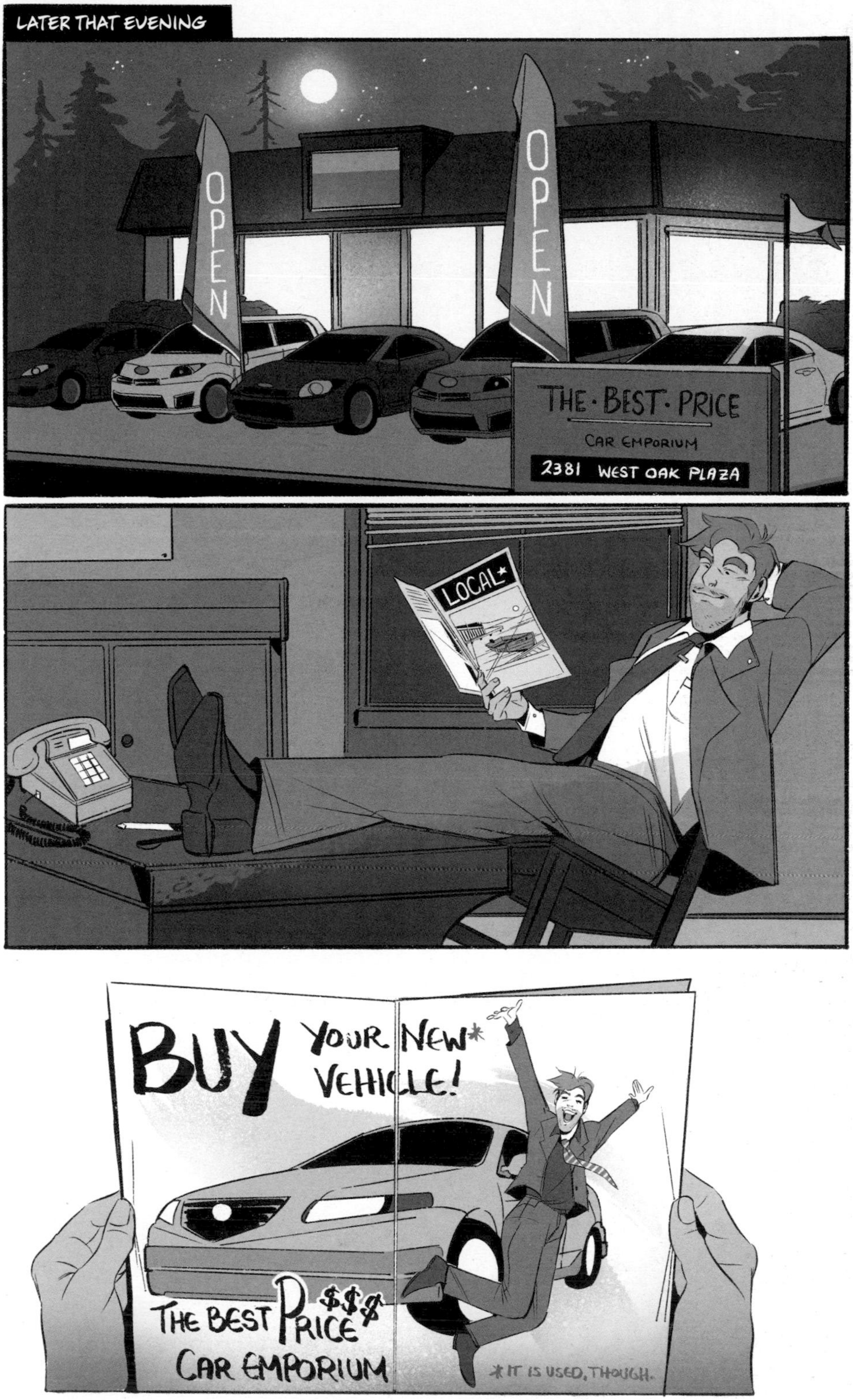
LATER THAT EVENING
OPEN
OPEN
THE · BEST · PRICE
CAR EMPORIUM
2381 WEST OAK PLAZA
LOCAL*
BUY YOUR NEW* VEHICLE!
THE BEST PRICE $$$
CAR EMPORIUM
*IT IS USED, THOUGH.

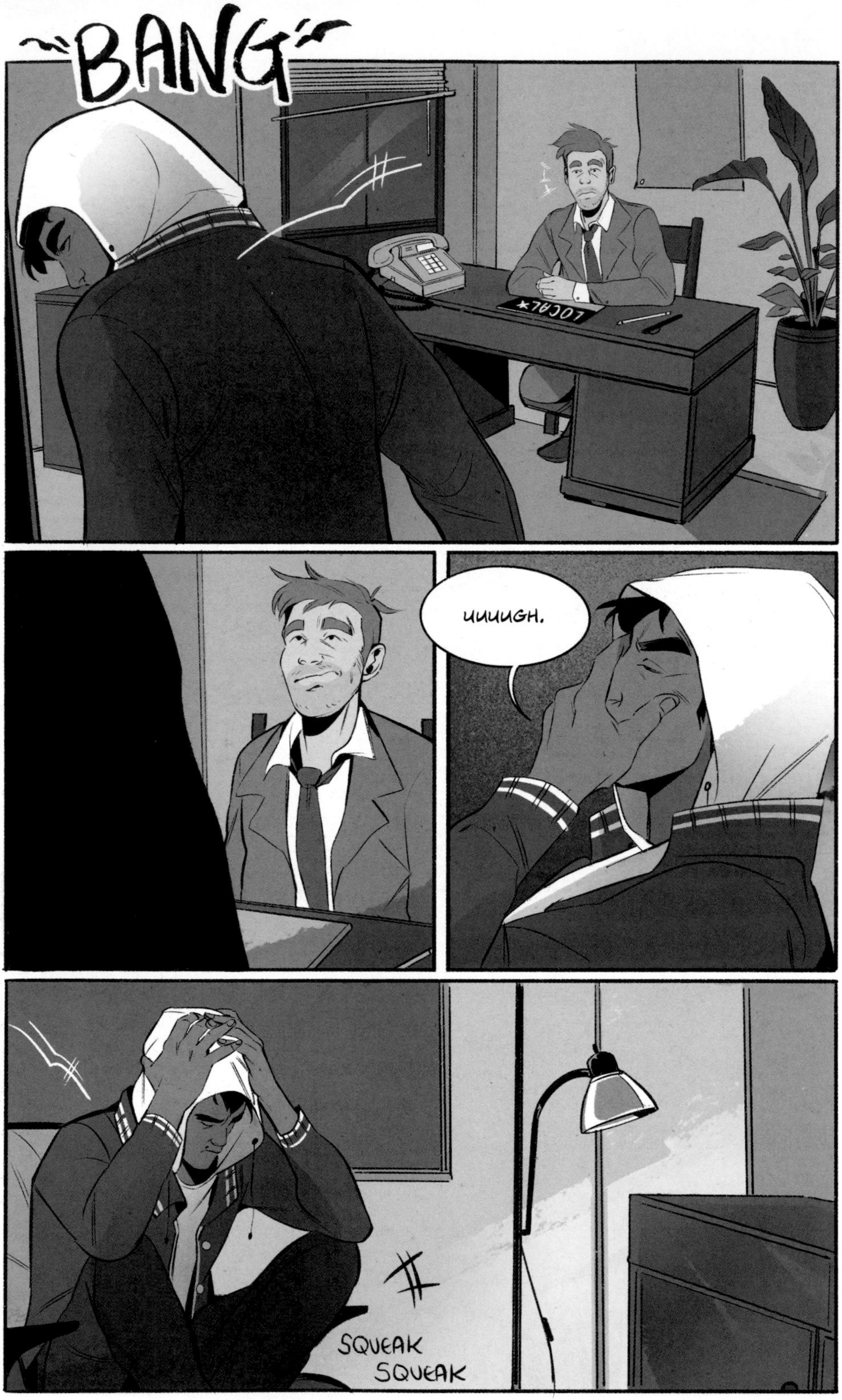
BANG
LOCAL
UUUUGH.
SQUEAK
SQUEAK

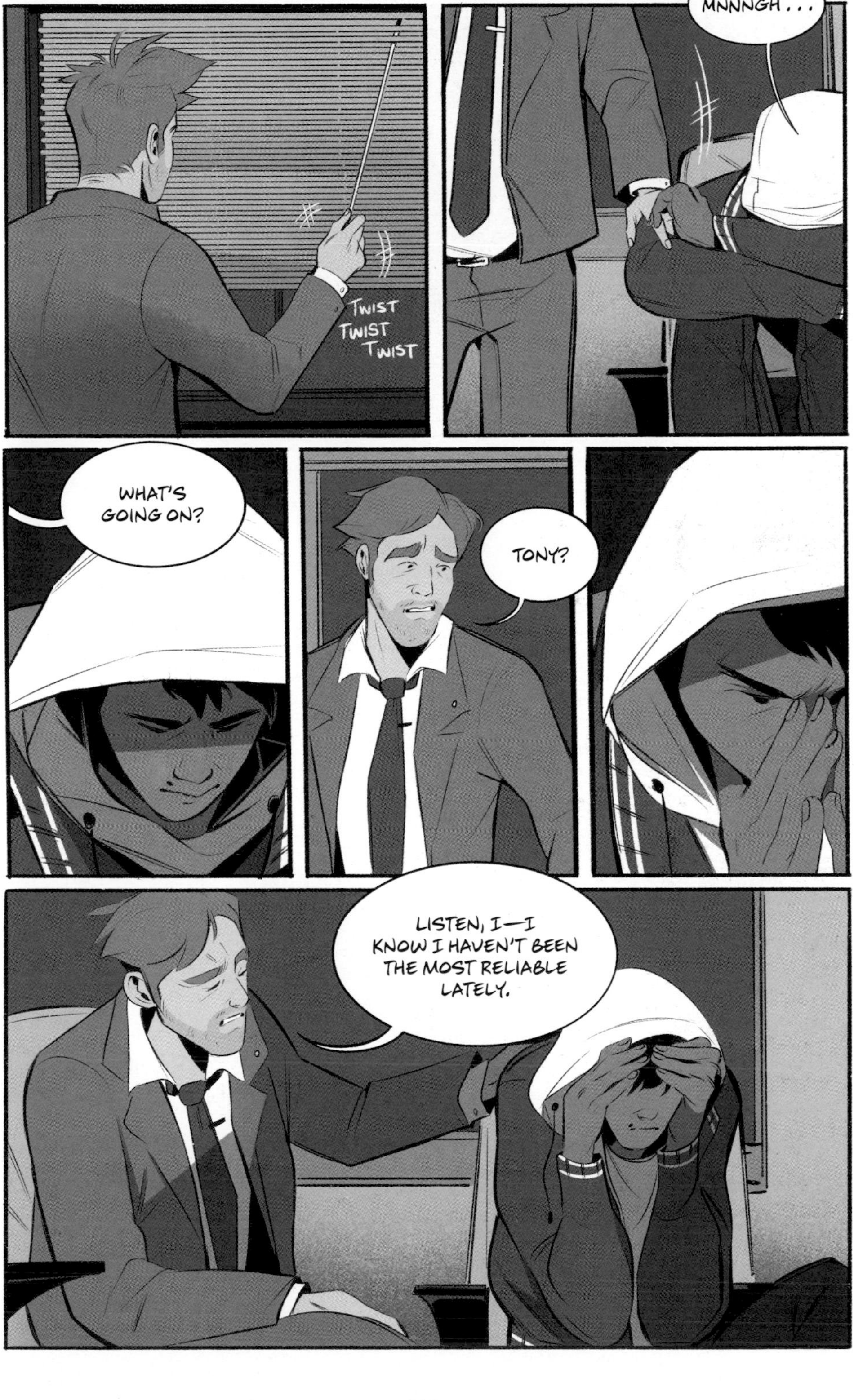
TWIST
TWIST
TWIST
MNNNGH . . .
WHAT'S GOING ON?
TONY?
LISTEN, I—I KNOW I HAVEN'T BEEN THE MOST RELIABLE LATELY.

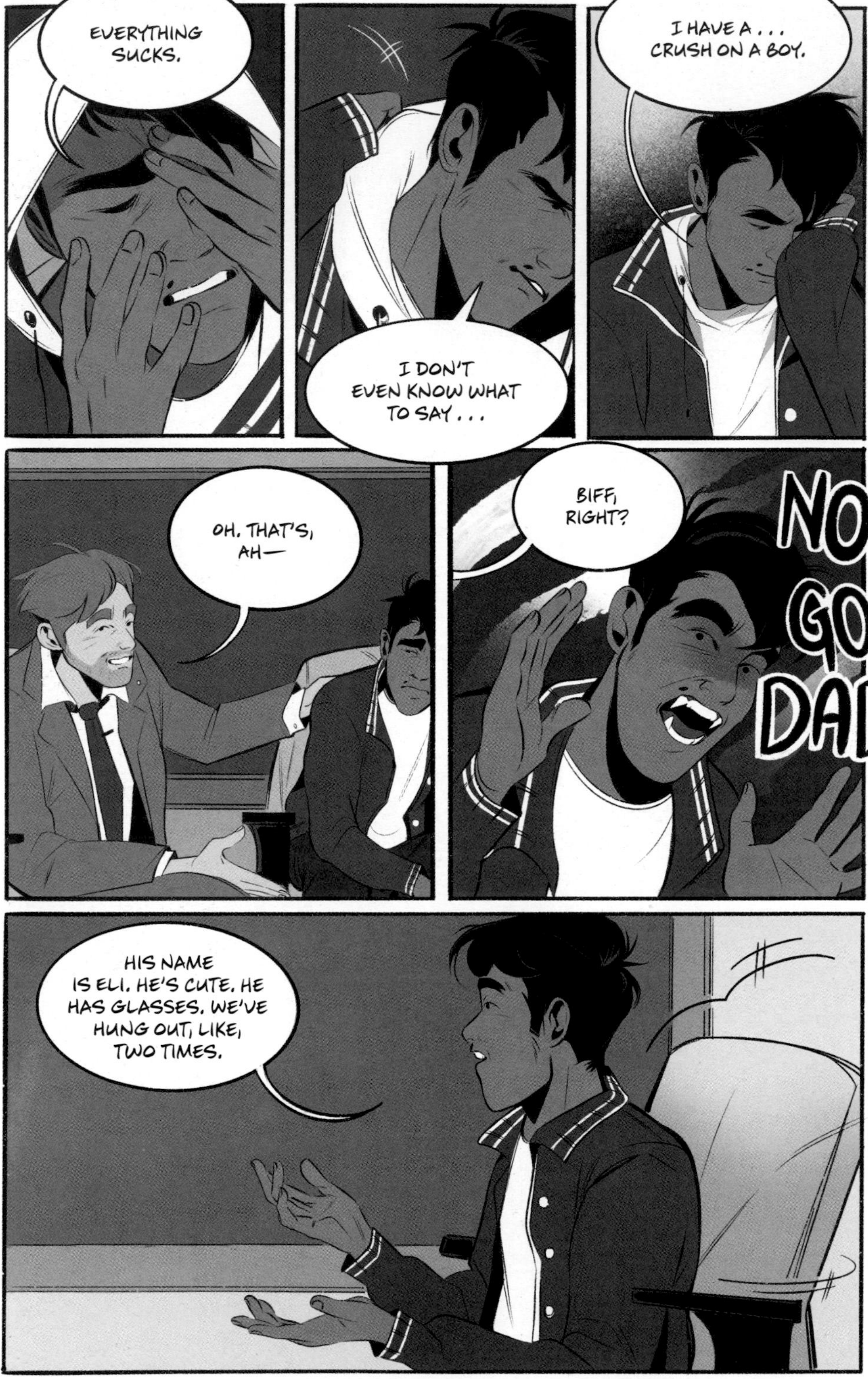
EVERYTHING SUCKS.
I DON'T EVEN KNOW WHAT TO SAY . . .
I HAVE A . . . CRUSH ON A BOY.
OH. THAT'S, AH—
BIFF, RIGHT?
NO, GOD. DAD.
HIS NAME IS ELI. HE'S CUTE. HE HAS GLASSES. WE'VE HUNG OUT, LIKE, TWO TIMES.

WELL, WHAT'S WRONG WITH THAT?

NOTHING.

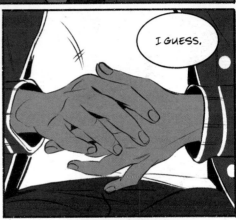

I GUESS.

IT'S JUST . . . DIFFERENT. IT'S WEIRD! IN THE PAST, I HAVEN'T REALLY HAD THESE KINDS OF FEELINGS BEFORE.

NOT FOR A GUY.

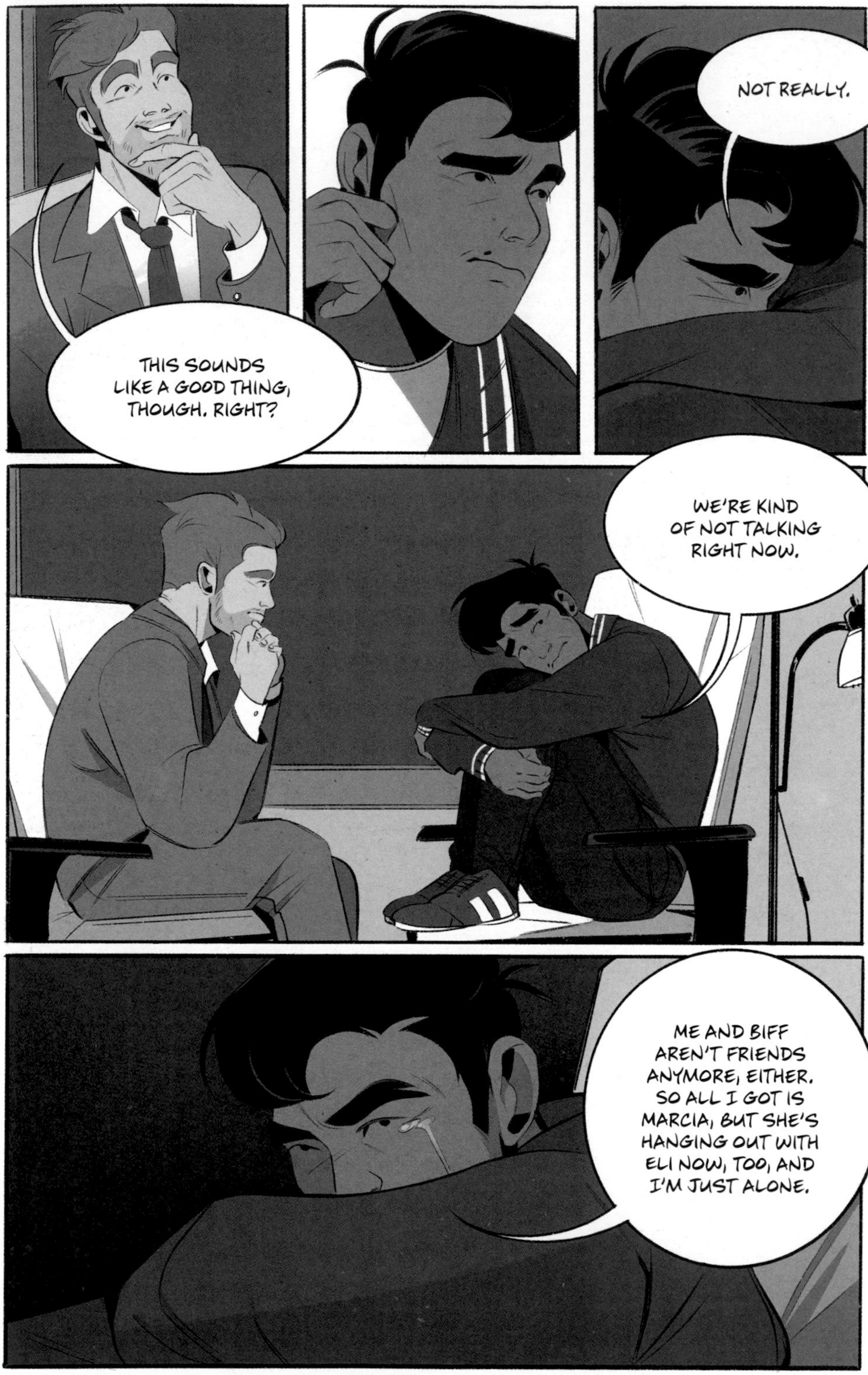
THIS SOUNDS LIKE A GOOD THING, THOUGH. RIGHT?
NOT REALLY.
WE'RE KIND OF NOT TALKING RIGHT NOW.
ME AND BIFF AREN'T FRIENDS ANYMORE, EITHER. SO ALL I GOT IS MARCIA, BUT SHE'S HANGING OUT WITH ELI NOW, TOO, AND I'M JUST ALONE.

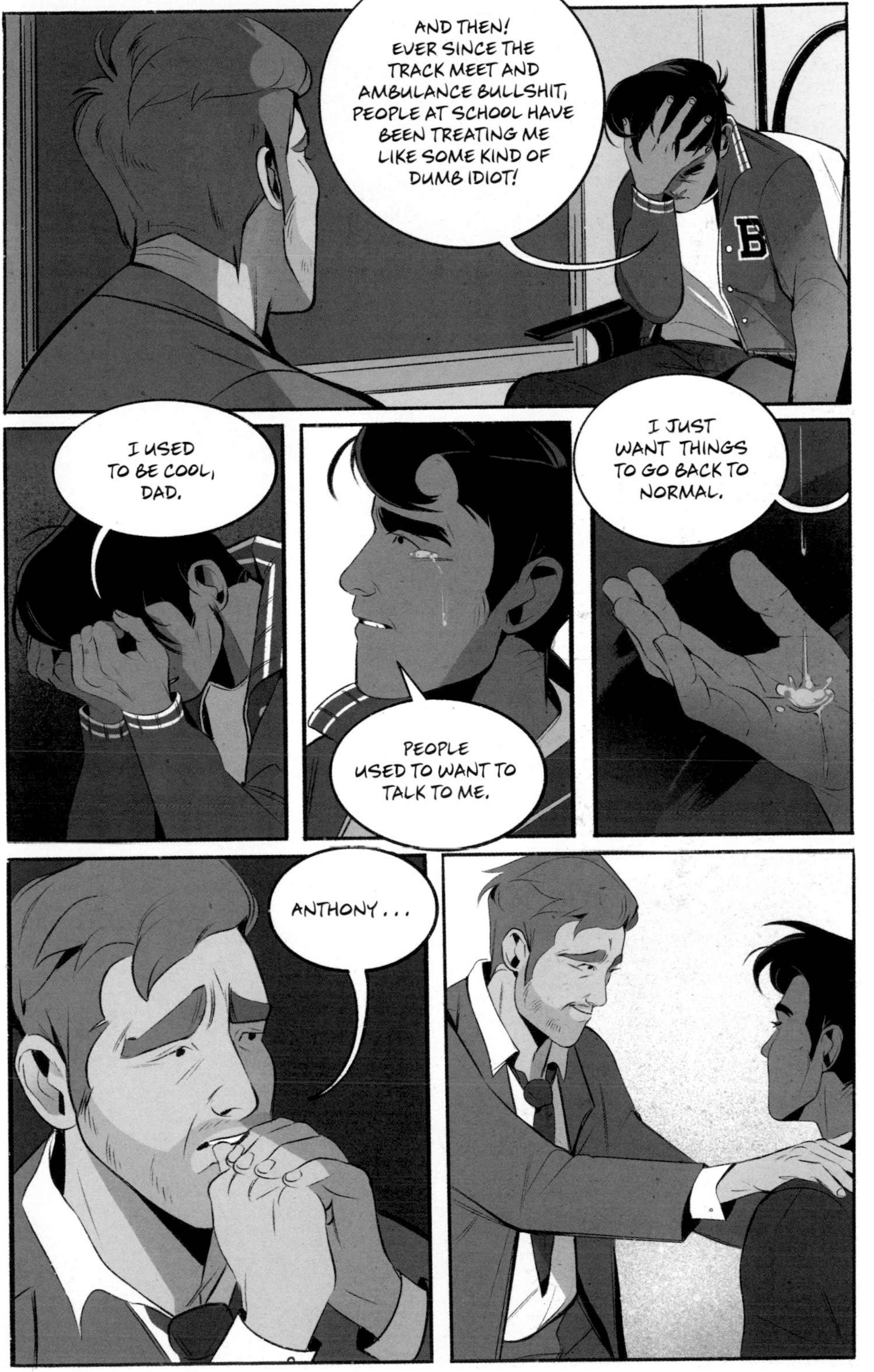
AND THEN! EVER SINCE THE TRACK MEET AND AMBULANCE BULLSHIT, PEOPLE AT SCHOOL HAVE BEEN TREATING ME LIKE SOME KIND OF DUMB IDIOT!
I USED TO BE COOL, DAD.
PEOPLE USED TO WANT TO TALK TO ME.
I JUST WANT THINGS TO GO BACK TO NORMAL.
ANTHONY . . .

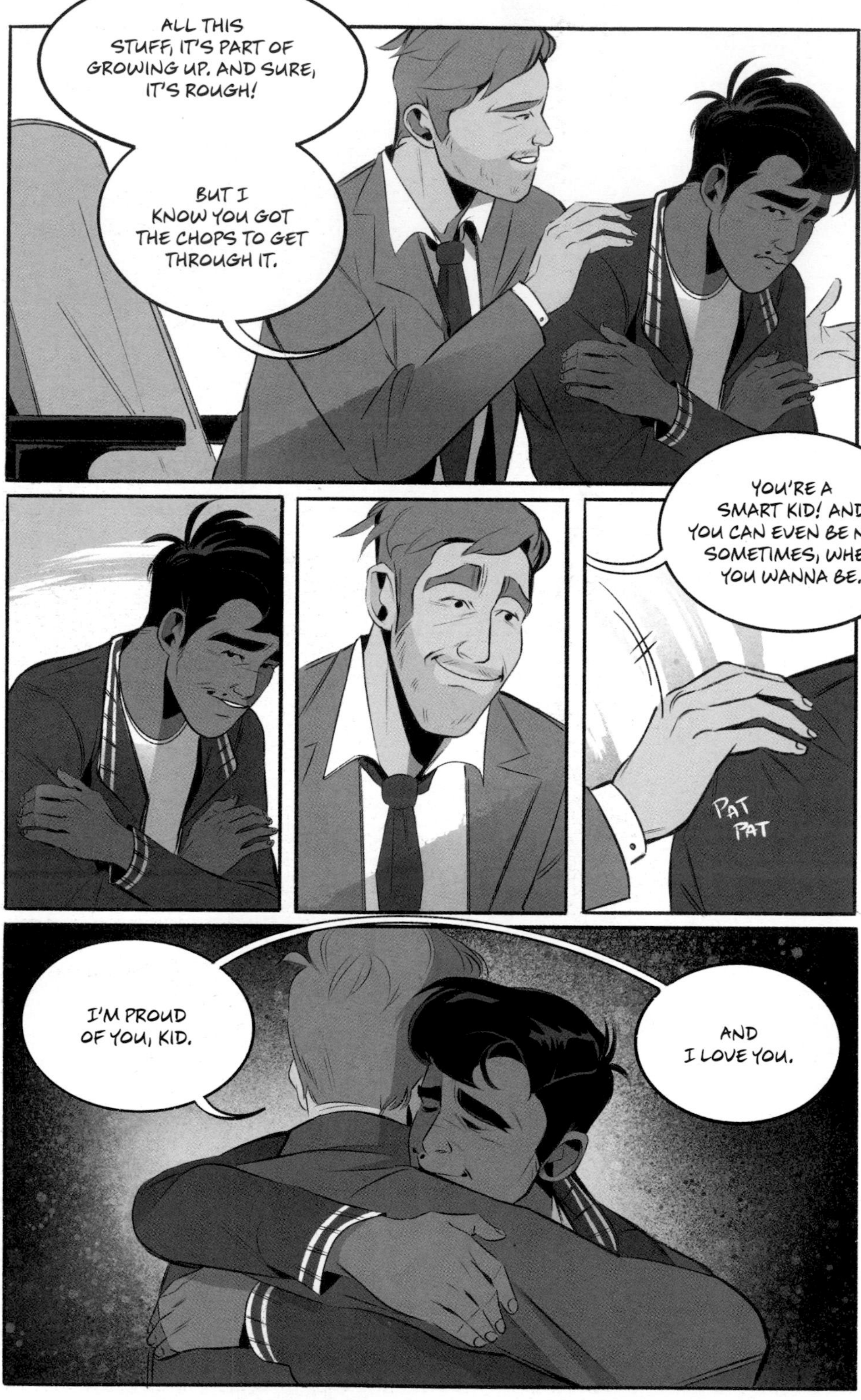
ALL THIS STUFF, IT'S PART OF GROWING UP. AND SURE, IT'S ROUGH!
BUT I KNOW YOU GOT THE CHOPS TO GET THROUGH IT.
YOU'RE A SMART KID! AND YOU CAN EVEN BE NICE SOMETIMES, WHEN YOU WANNA BE.
PAT PAT
I'M PROUD OF YOU, KID.
AND I LOVE YOU.

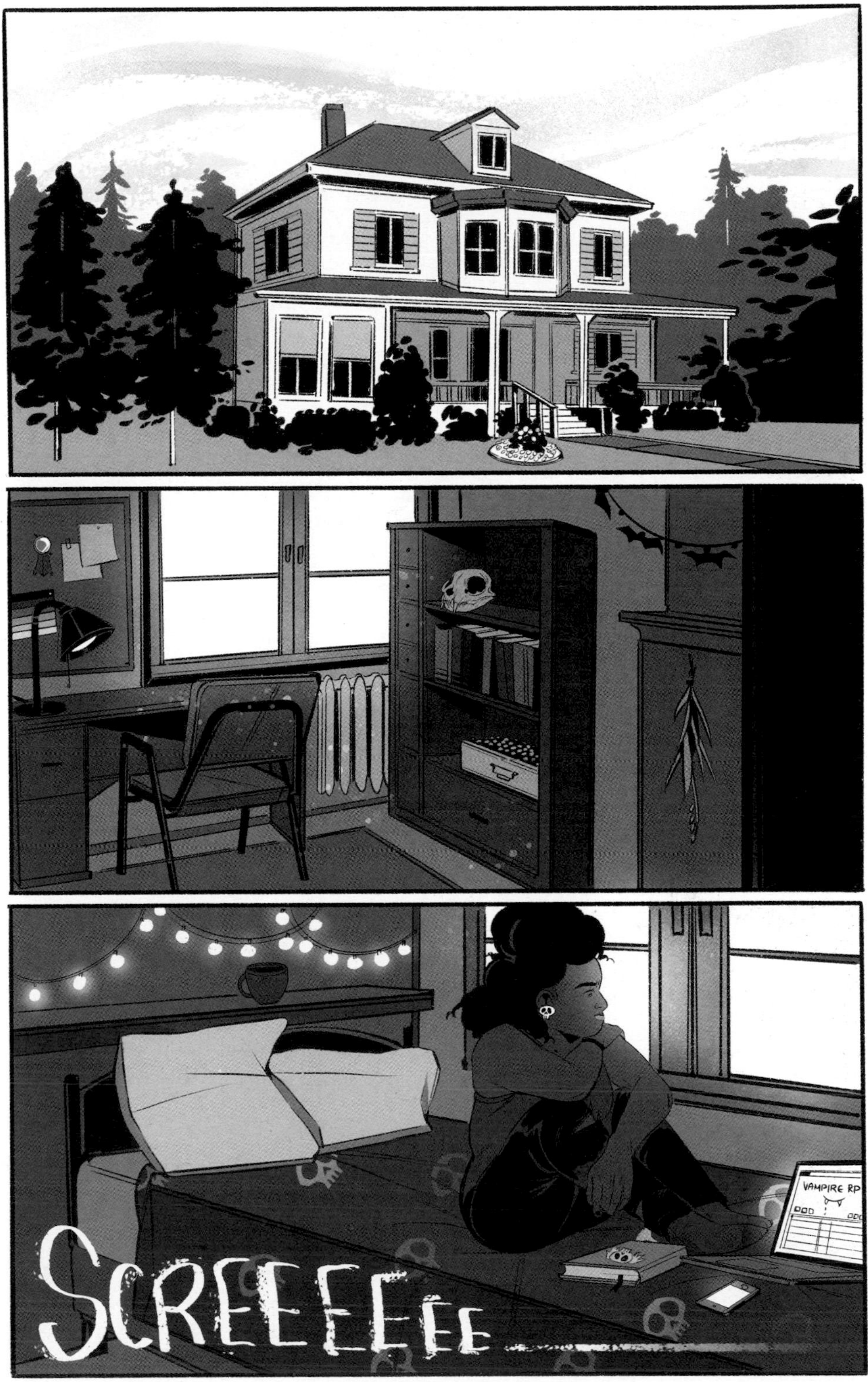
VAMPIRE RP
SCREEEEEE

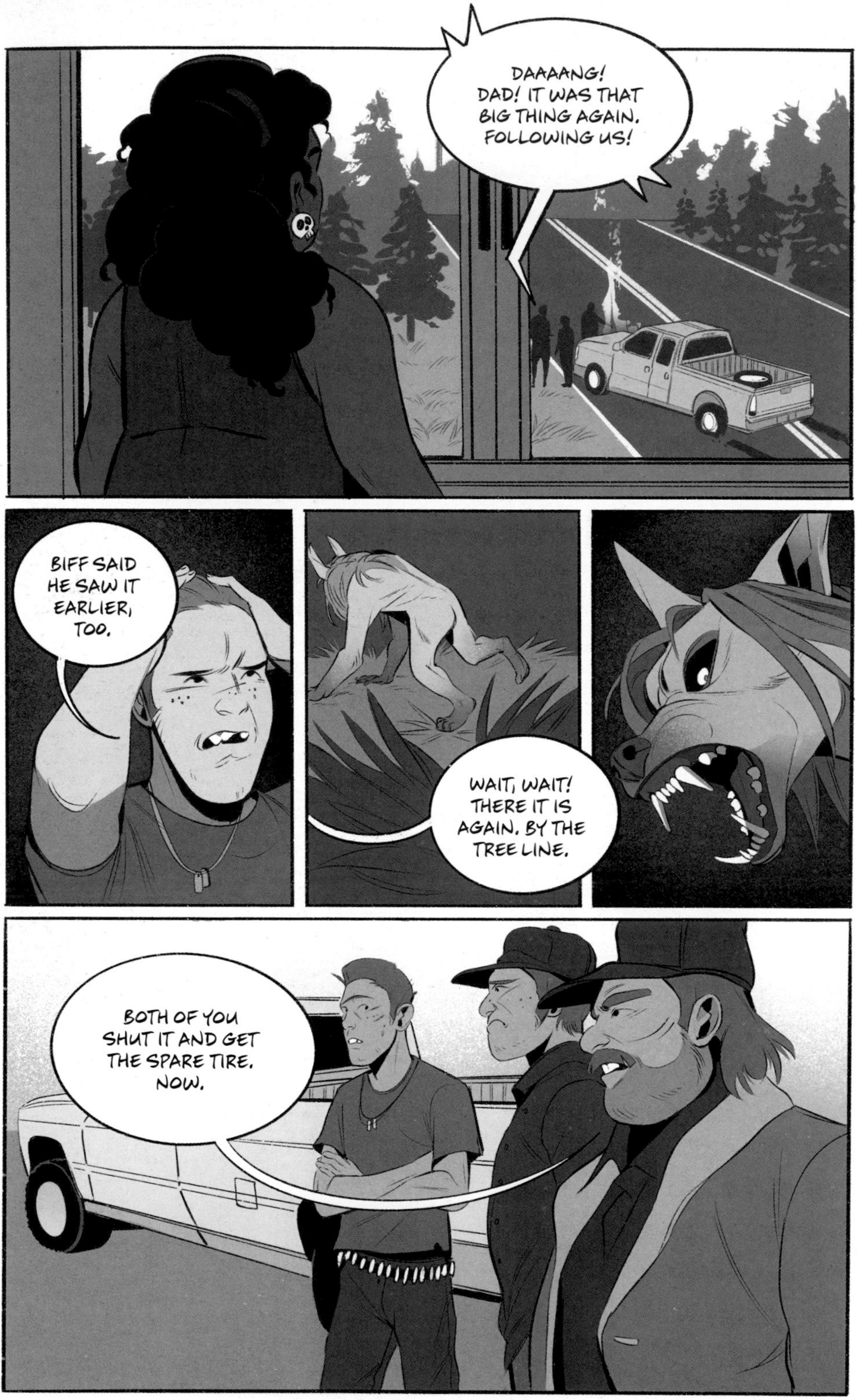
DAAAANG! DAD! IT WAS THAT BIG THING AGAIN. FOLLOWING US!
BIFF SAID HE SAW IT EARLIER, TOO.
WAIT, WAIT! THERE IT IS AGAIN. BY THE TREE LINE.
BOTH OF YOU SHUT IT AND GET THE SPARE TIRE. NOW.

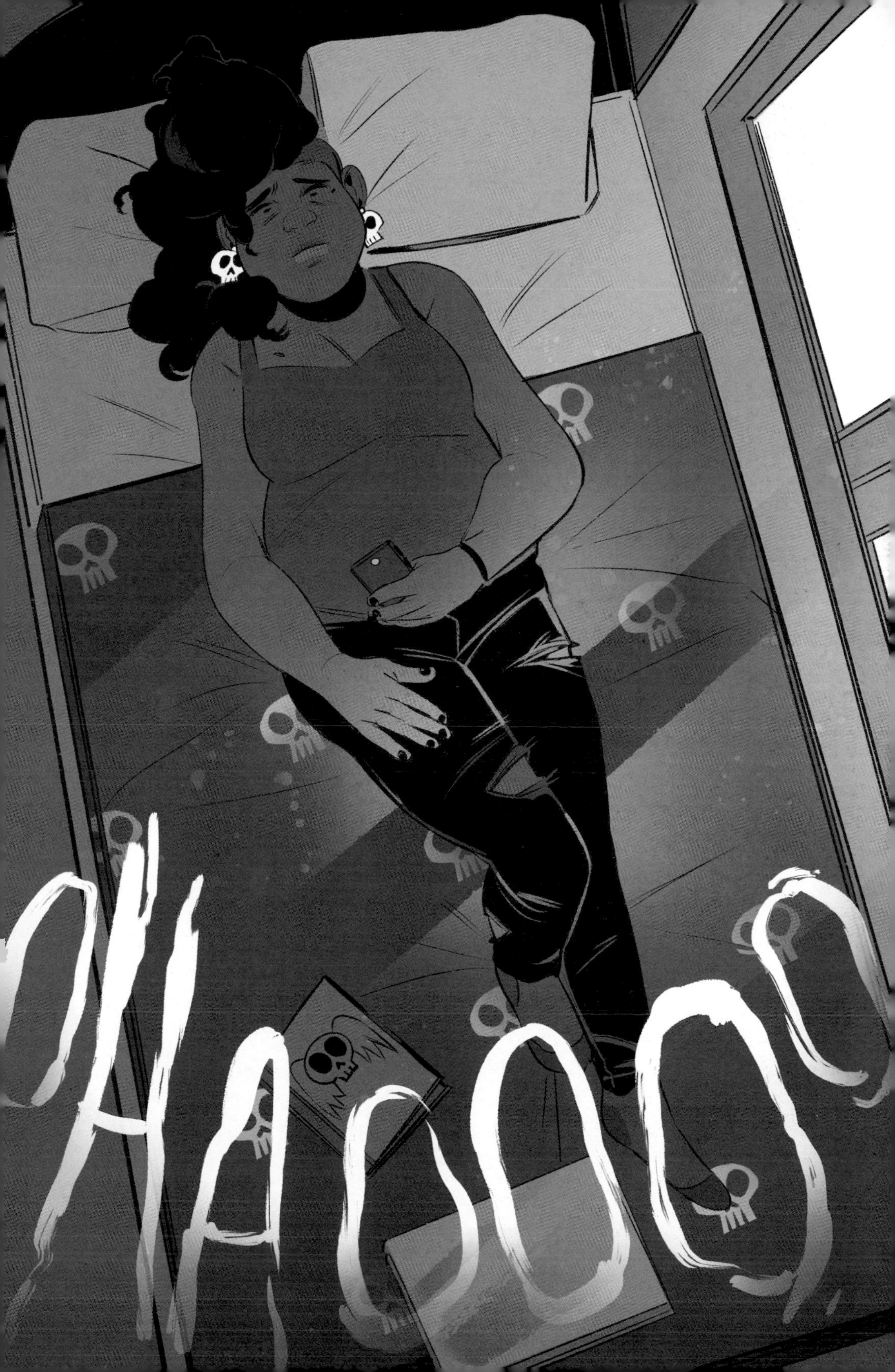
OHAOOOO

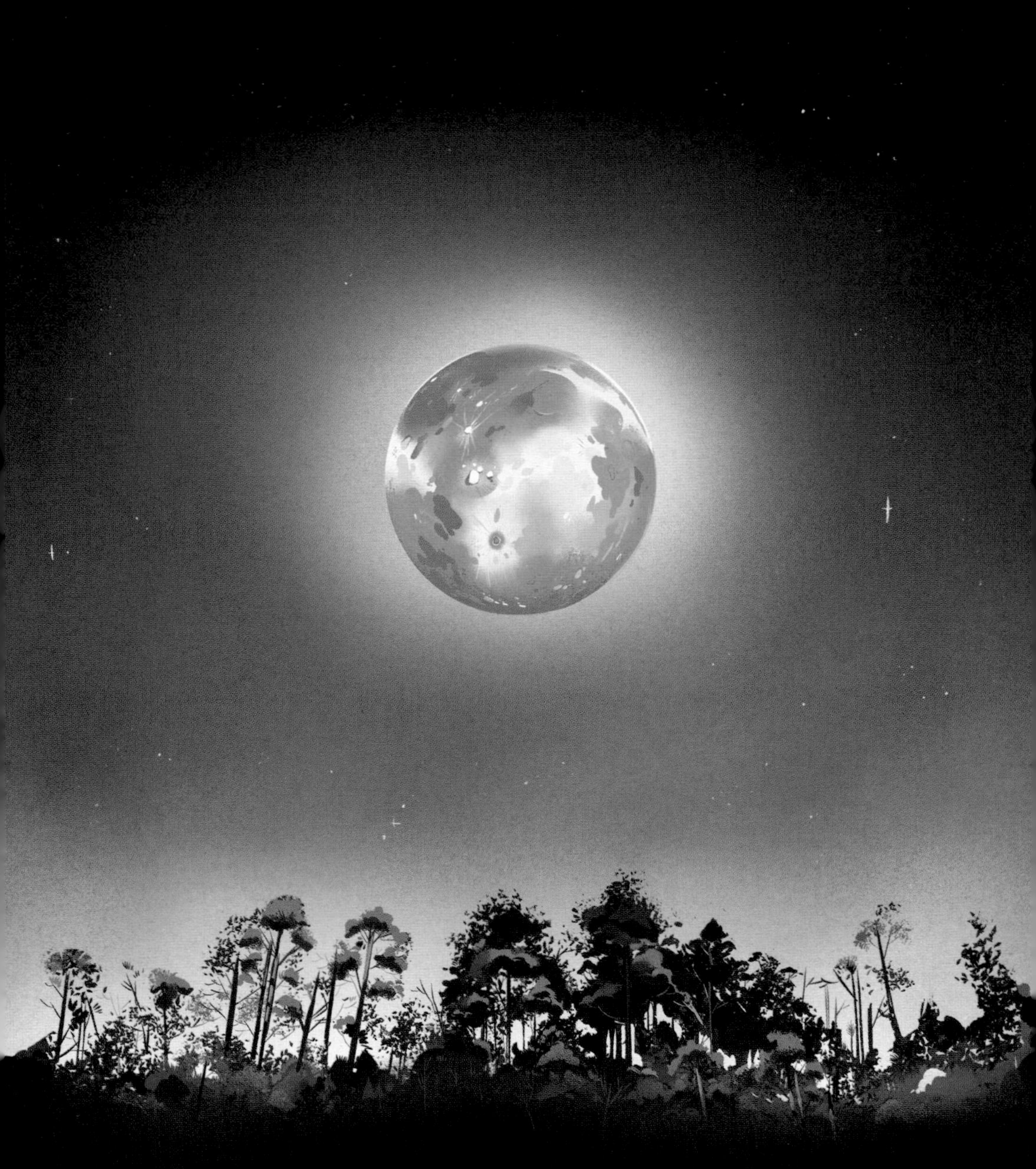

CHAPTER NINE
REUNION

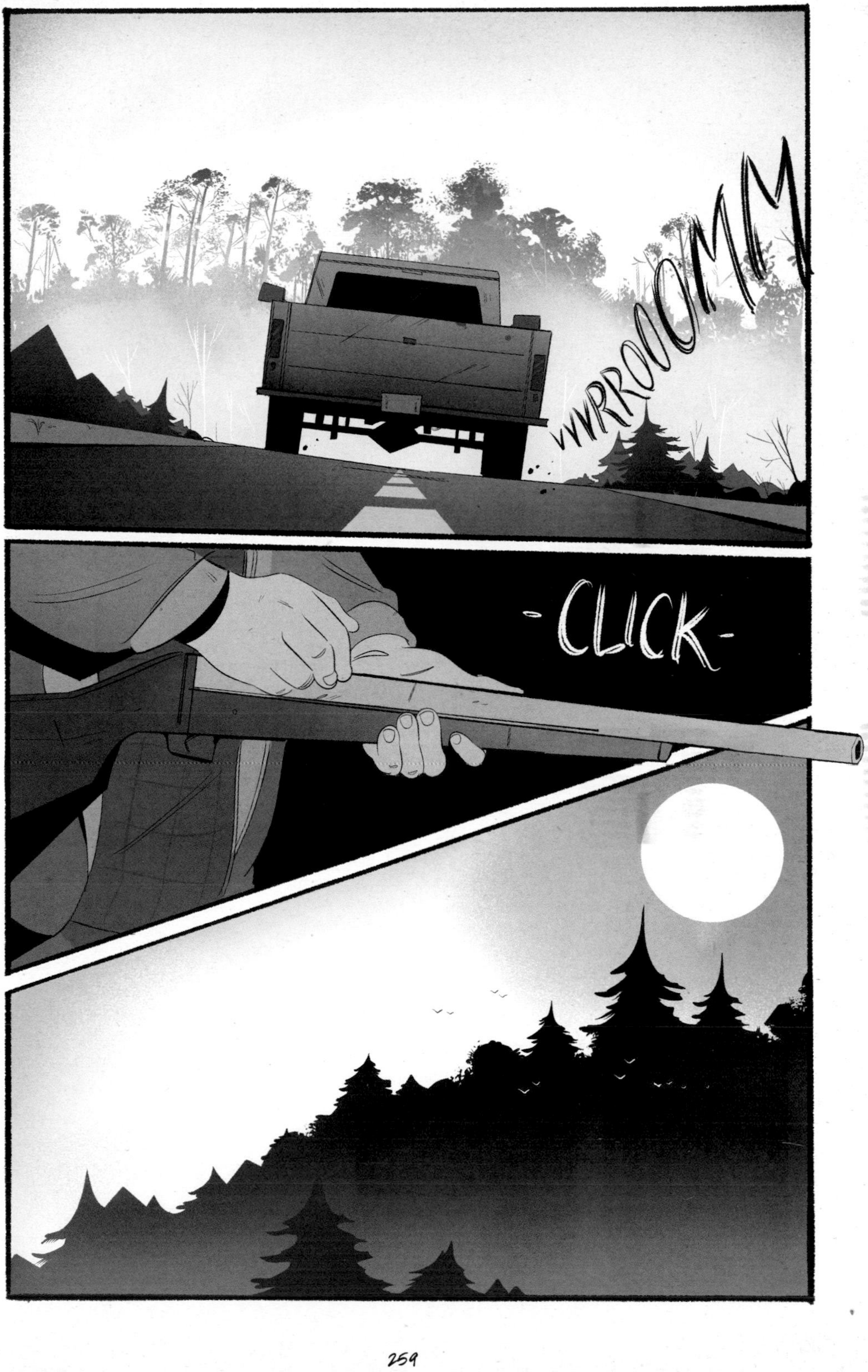
VVVRROOOOMMM
-CLICK-

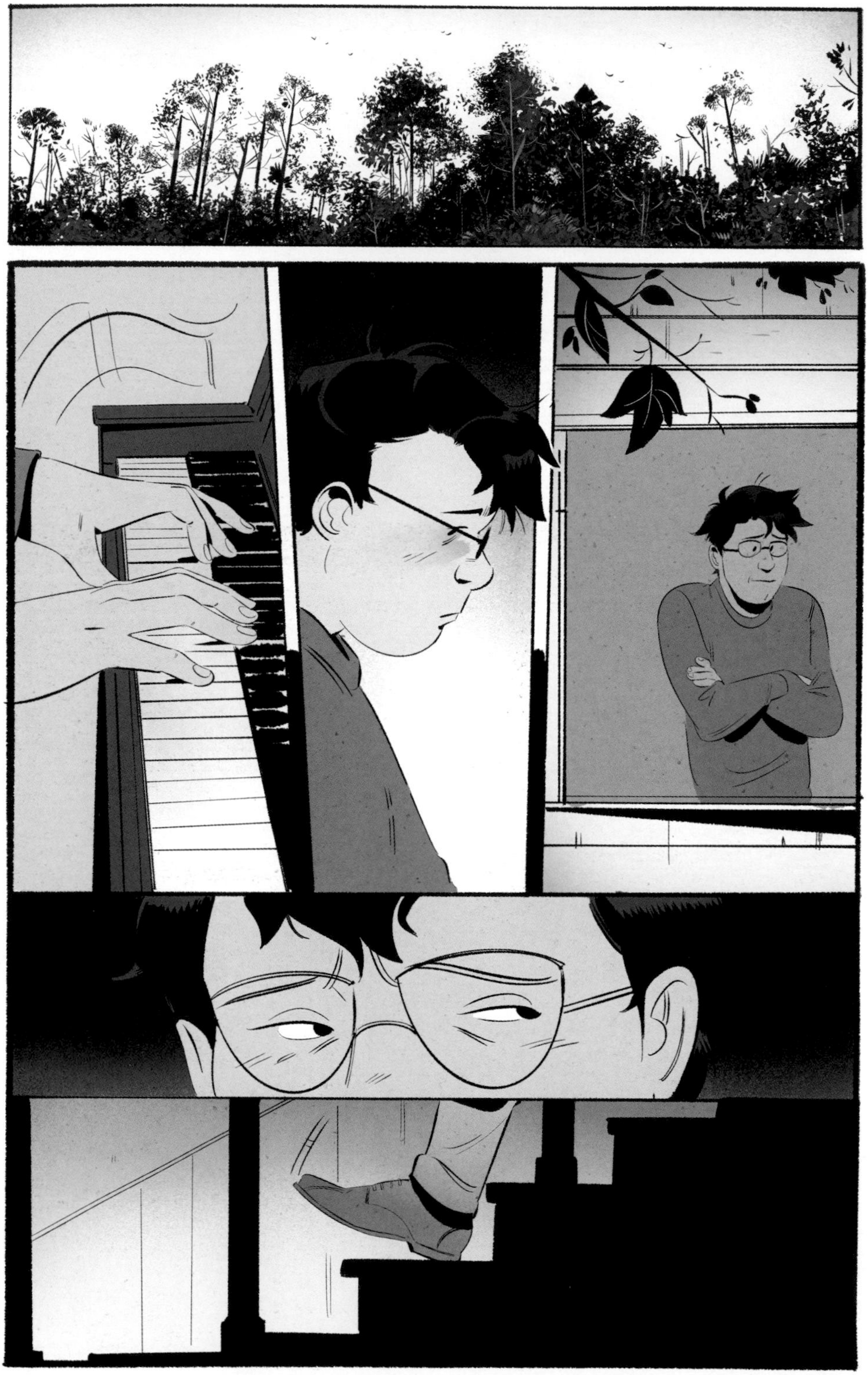

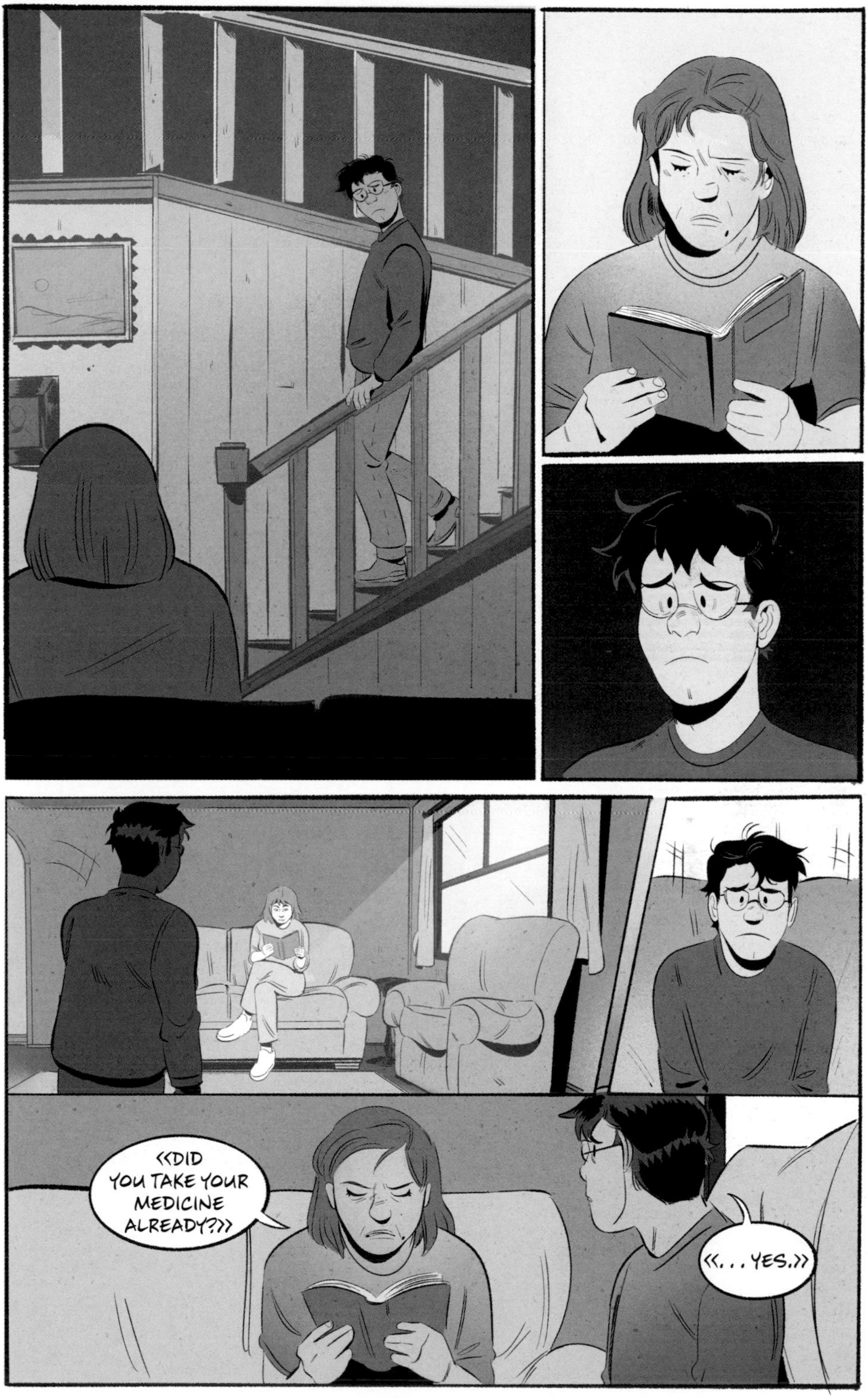

<<DID YOU TAKE YOUR MEDICINE ALREADY?>>
<<. . . YES.>>

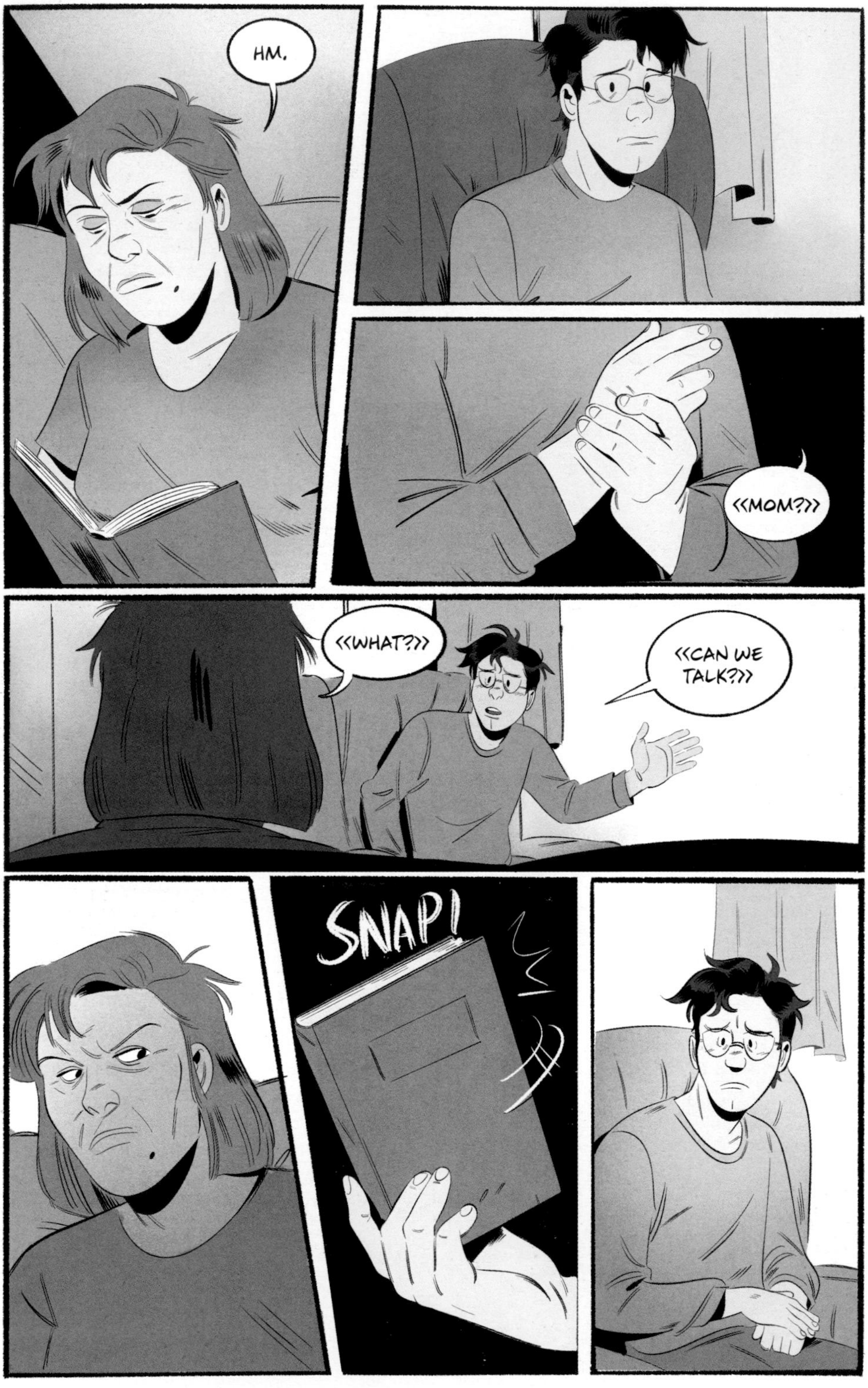
HM.
<<MOM?>>
<<WHAT?>>
<<CAN WE TALK?>>
SNAP!

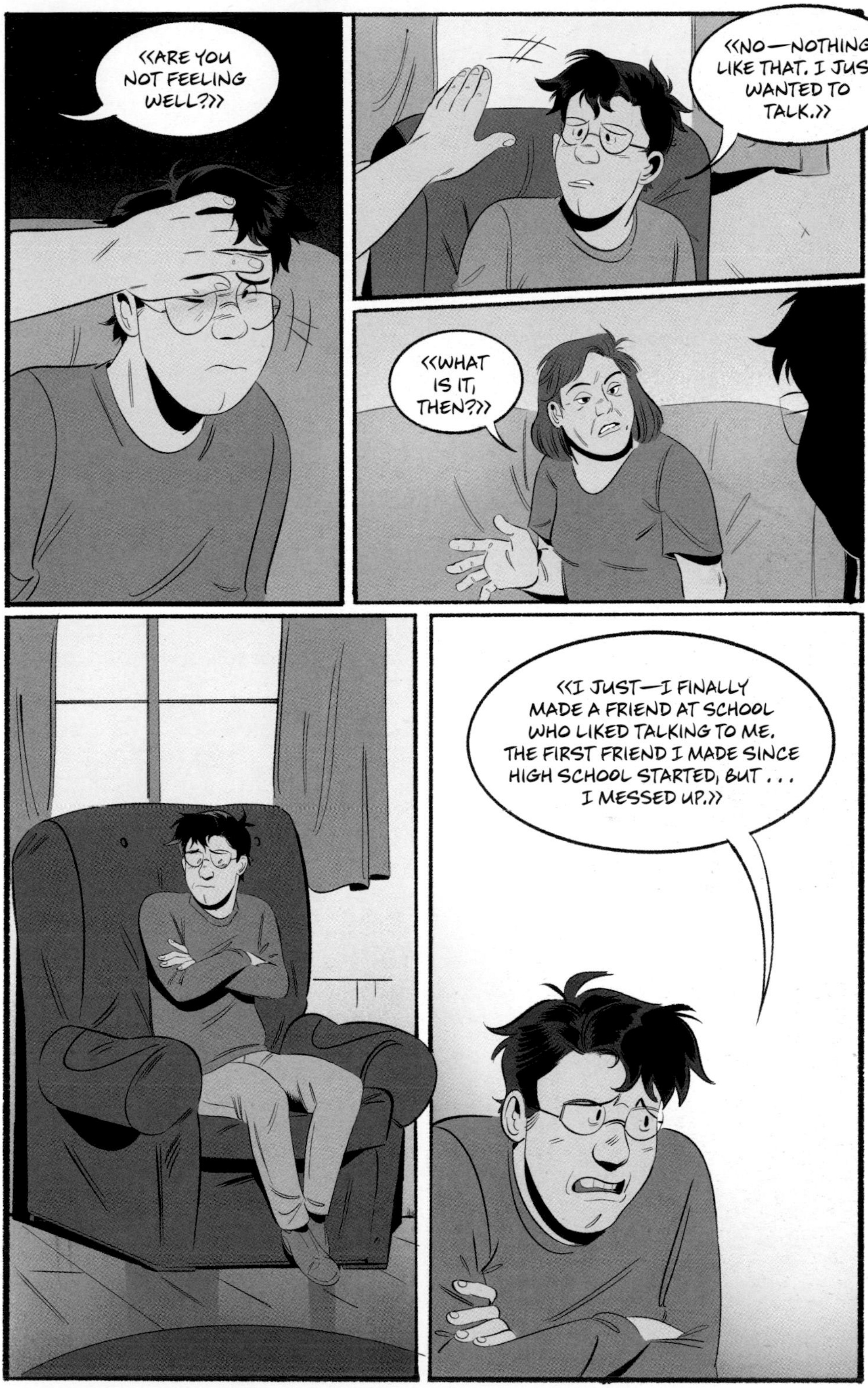

<<ARE YOU NOT FEELING WELL?>>
<<NO—NOTHING LIKE THAT. I JUST WANTED TO TALK.>>
<<WHAT IS IT, THEN?>>
<<I JUST—I FINALLY MADE A FRIEND AT SCHOOL WHO LIKED TALKING TO ME. THE FIRST FRIEND I MADE SINCE HIGH SCHOOL STARTED, BUT . . . I MESSED UP.>>

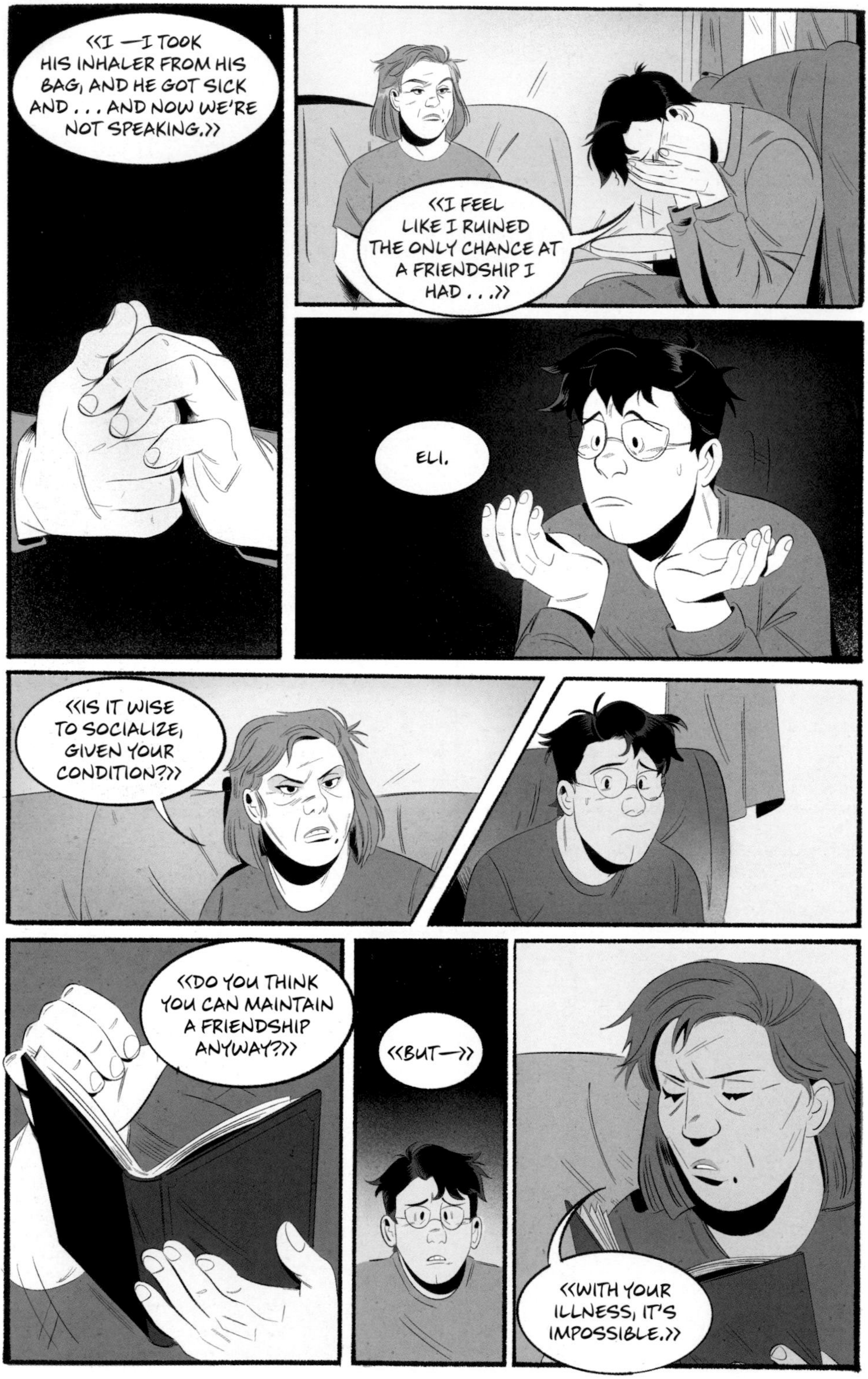
<<I —I TOOK HIS INHALER FROM HIS BAG, AND HE GOT SICK AND . . . AND NOW WE'RE NOT SPEAKING.>>
<<I FEEL LIKE I RUINED THE ONLY CHANCE AT A FRIENDSHIP I HAD . . .>>
ELI.
<<IS IT WISE TO SOCIALIZE, GIVEN YOUR CONDITION?>>
<<DO YOU THINK YOU CAN MAINTAIN A FRIENDSHIP ANYWAY?>>
<<BUT—>>
<<WITH YOUR ILLNESS, IT'S IMPOSSIBLE.>>

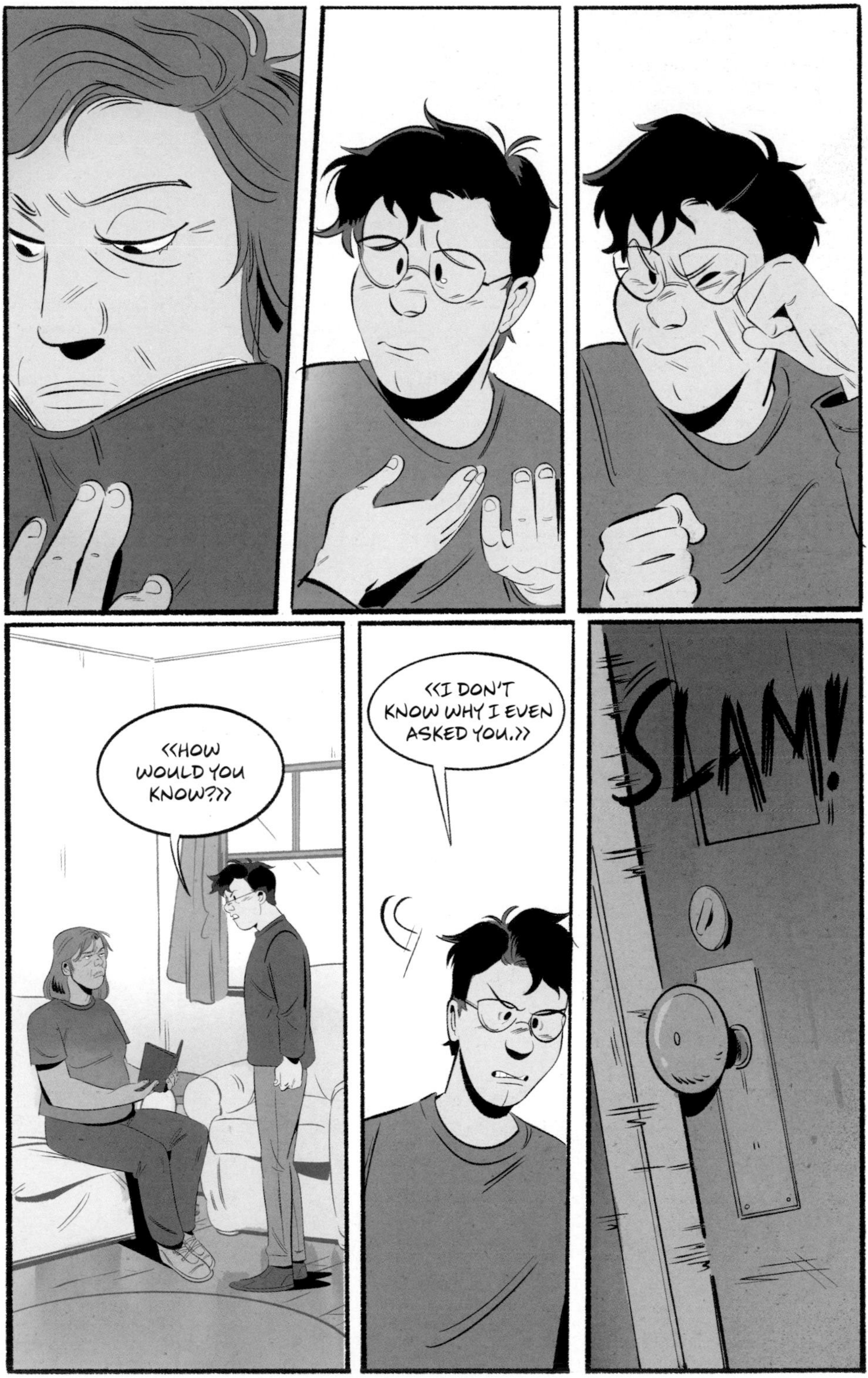

<<HOW WOULD YOU KNOW?>>
<<I DON'T KNOW WHY I EVEN ASKED YOU.>>
SLAM!

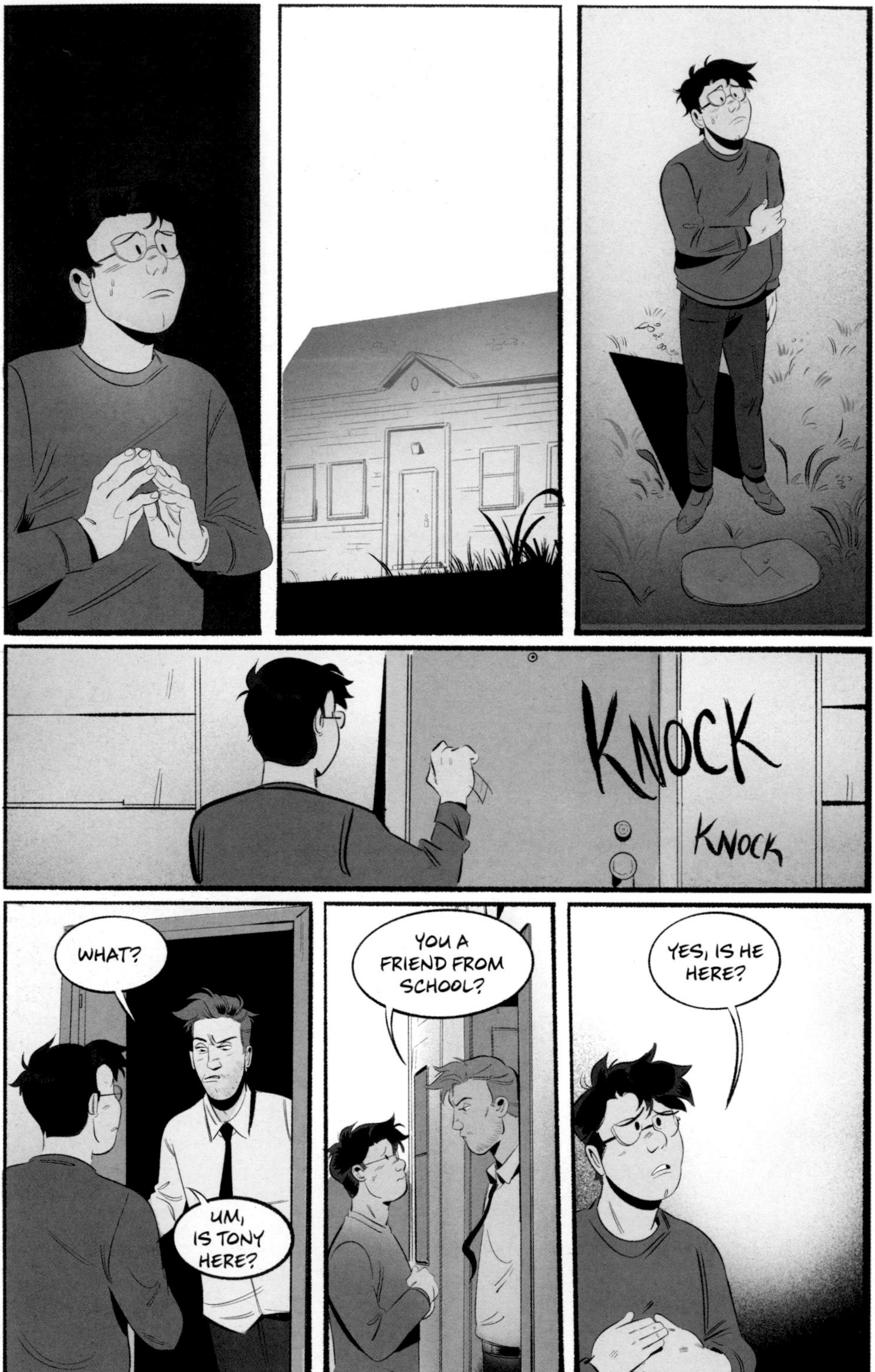
KNOCK
KNOCK
WHAT?
UM, IS TONY HERE?
YOU A FRIEND FROM SCHOOL?
YES, IS HE HERE?

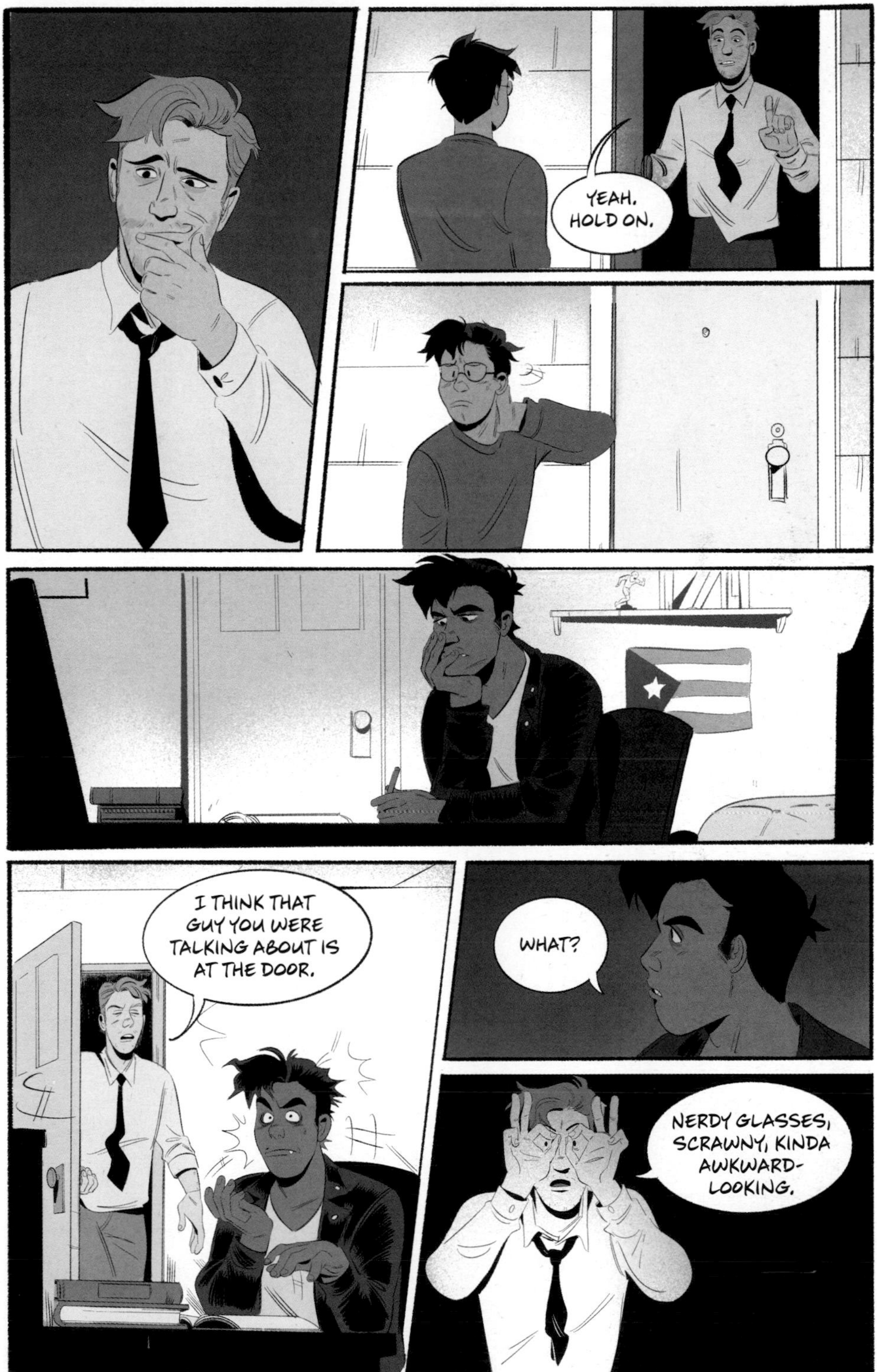
YEAH. HOLD ON.
I THINK THAT GUY YOU WERE TALKING ABOUT IS AT THE DOOR.
WHAT?
NERDY GLASSES, SCRAWNY, KINDA AWKWARD-LOOKING.

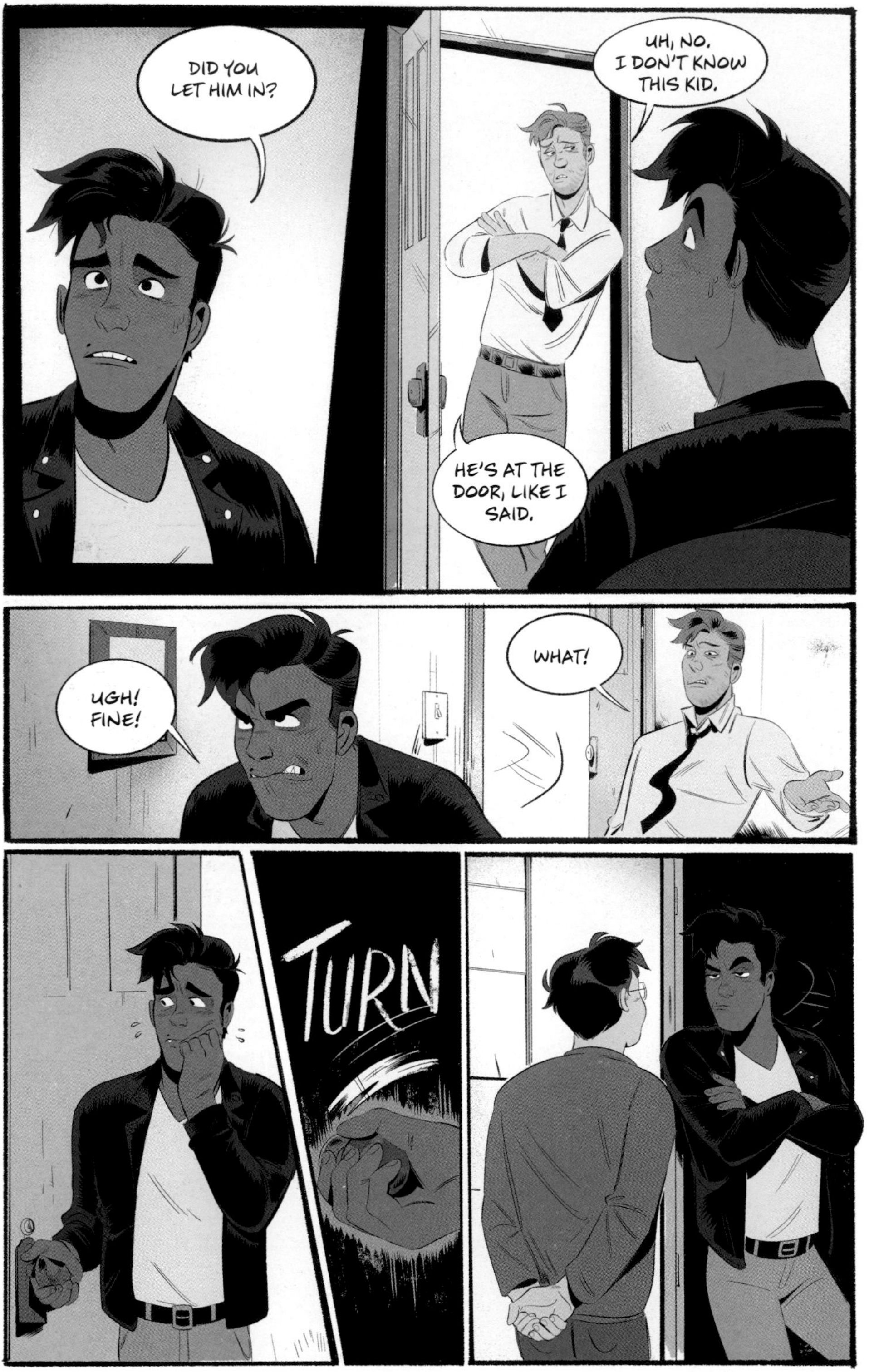
DID YOU LET HIM IN?
UH, NO. I DON'T KNOW THIS KID.
HE'S AT THE DOOR, LIKE I SAID.
UGH! FINE!
WHAT!
TURN

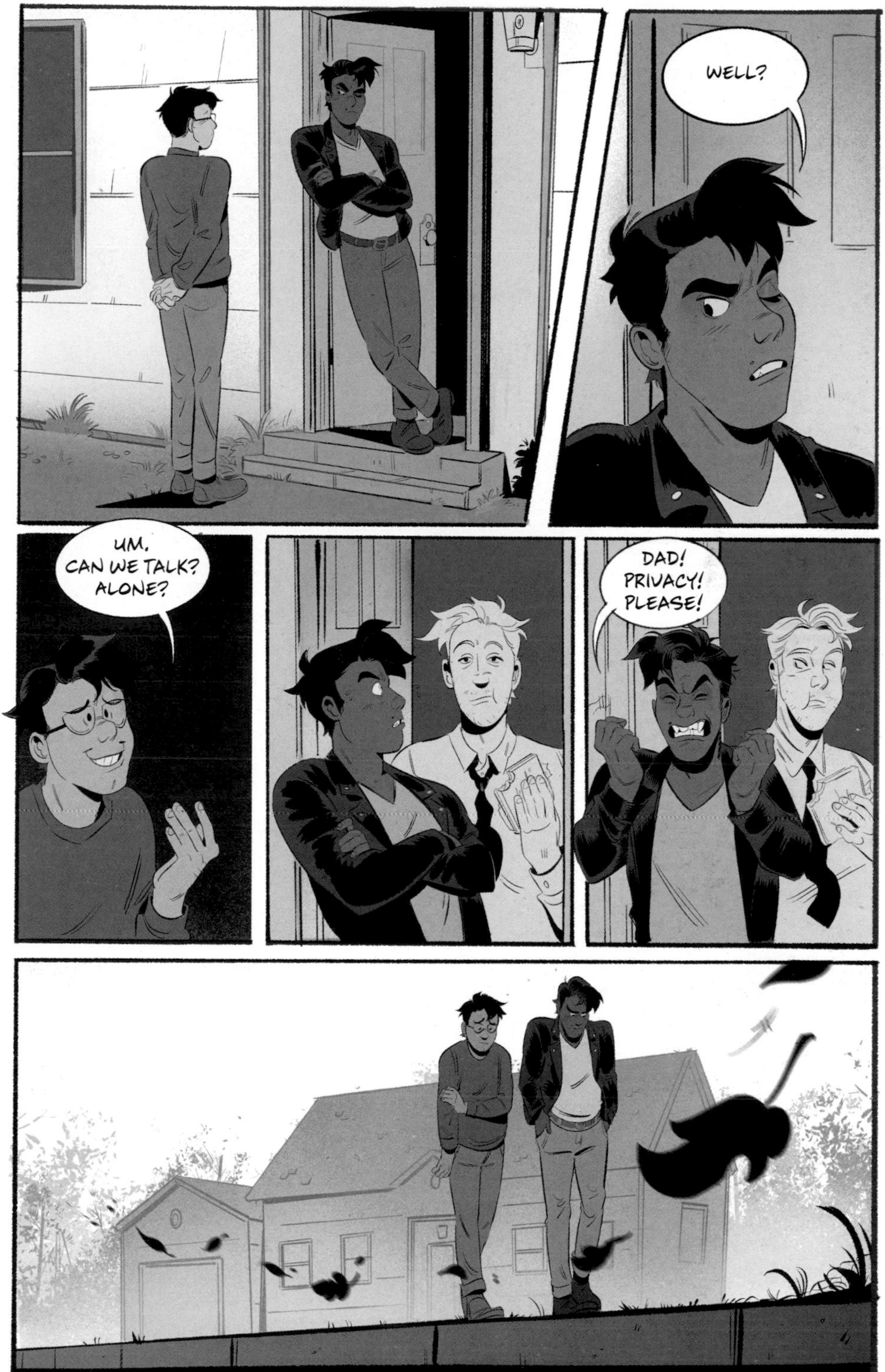
WELL?
UM. CAN WE TALK? ALONE?
DAD! PRIVACY! PLEASE!

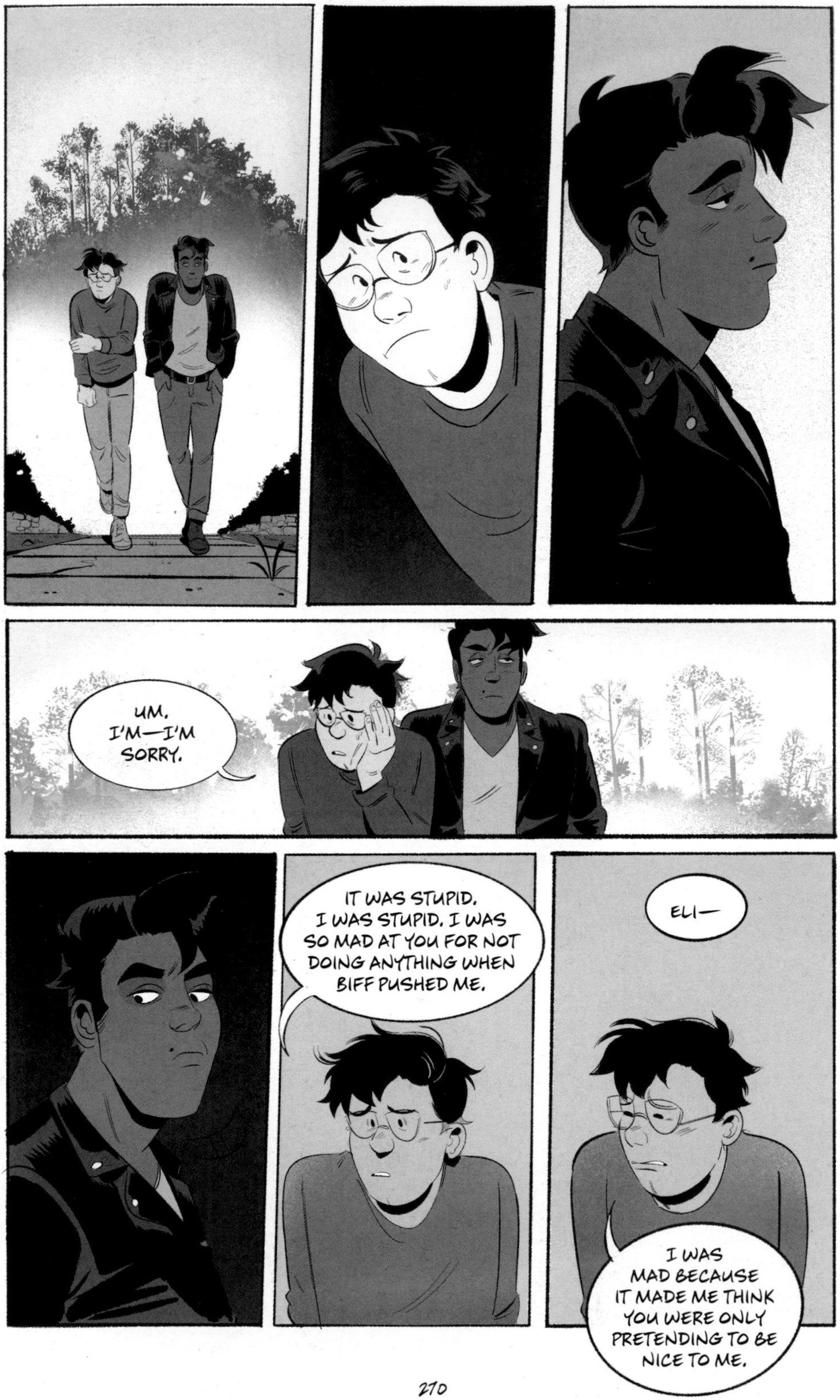
UM. I'M—I'M SORRY.
IT WAS STUPID. I WAS STUPID. I WAS SO MAD AT YOU FOR NOT DOING ANYTHING WHEN BIFF PUSHED ME.
ELI—
I WAS MAD BECAUSE IT MADE ME THINK YOU WERE ONLY PRETENDING TO BE NICE TO ME.

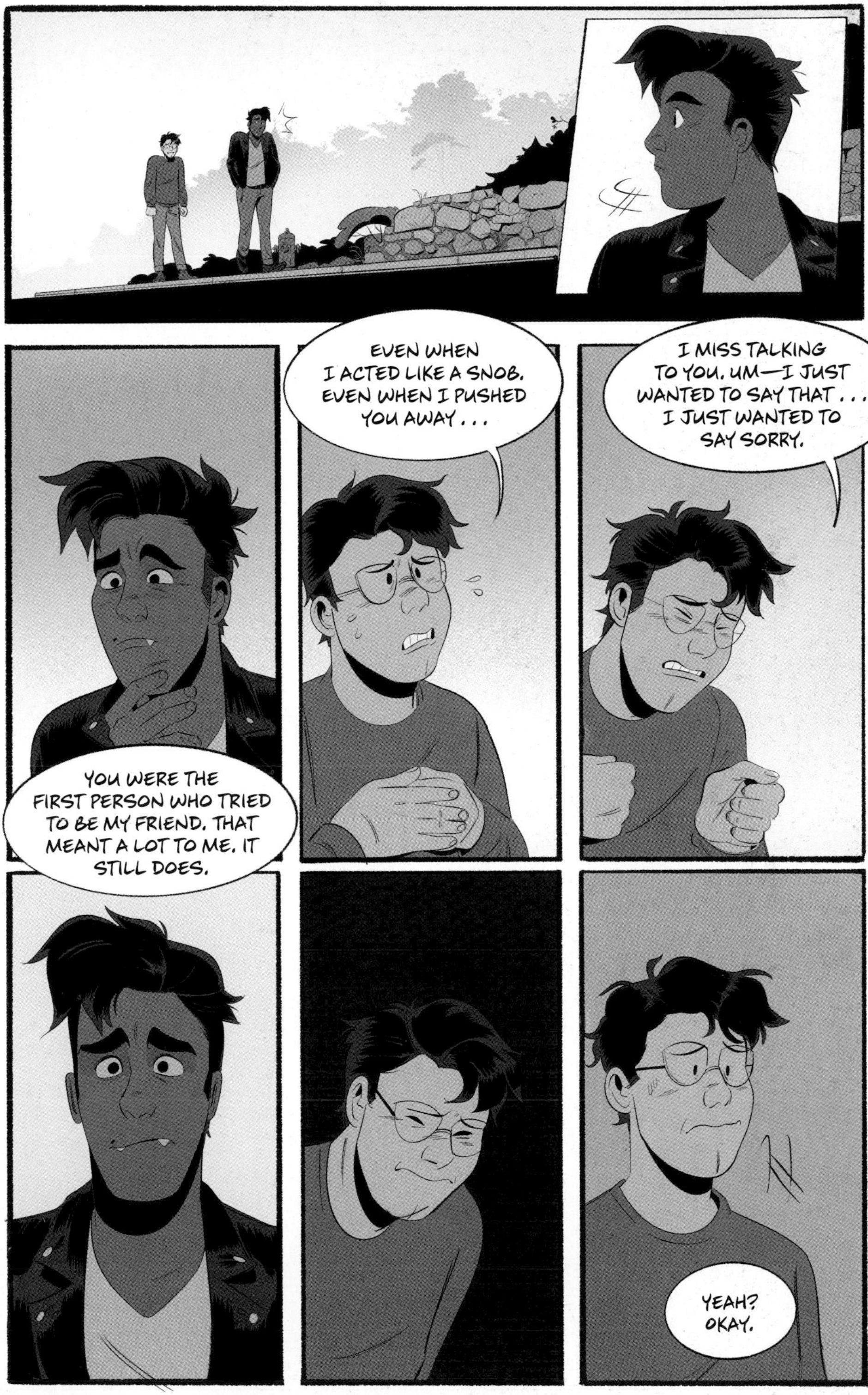

YOU WERE THE FIRST PERSON WHO TRIED TO BE MY FRIEND. THAT MEANT A LOT TO ME. IT STILL DOES.
EVEN WHEN I ACTED LIKE A SNOB. EVEN WHEN I PUSHED YOU AWAY . . .
I MISS TALKING TO YOU. UM—I JUST WANTED TO SAY THAT . . . I JUST WANTED TO SAY SORRY.
YEAH? OKAY.

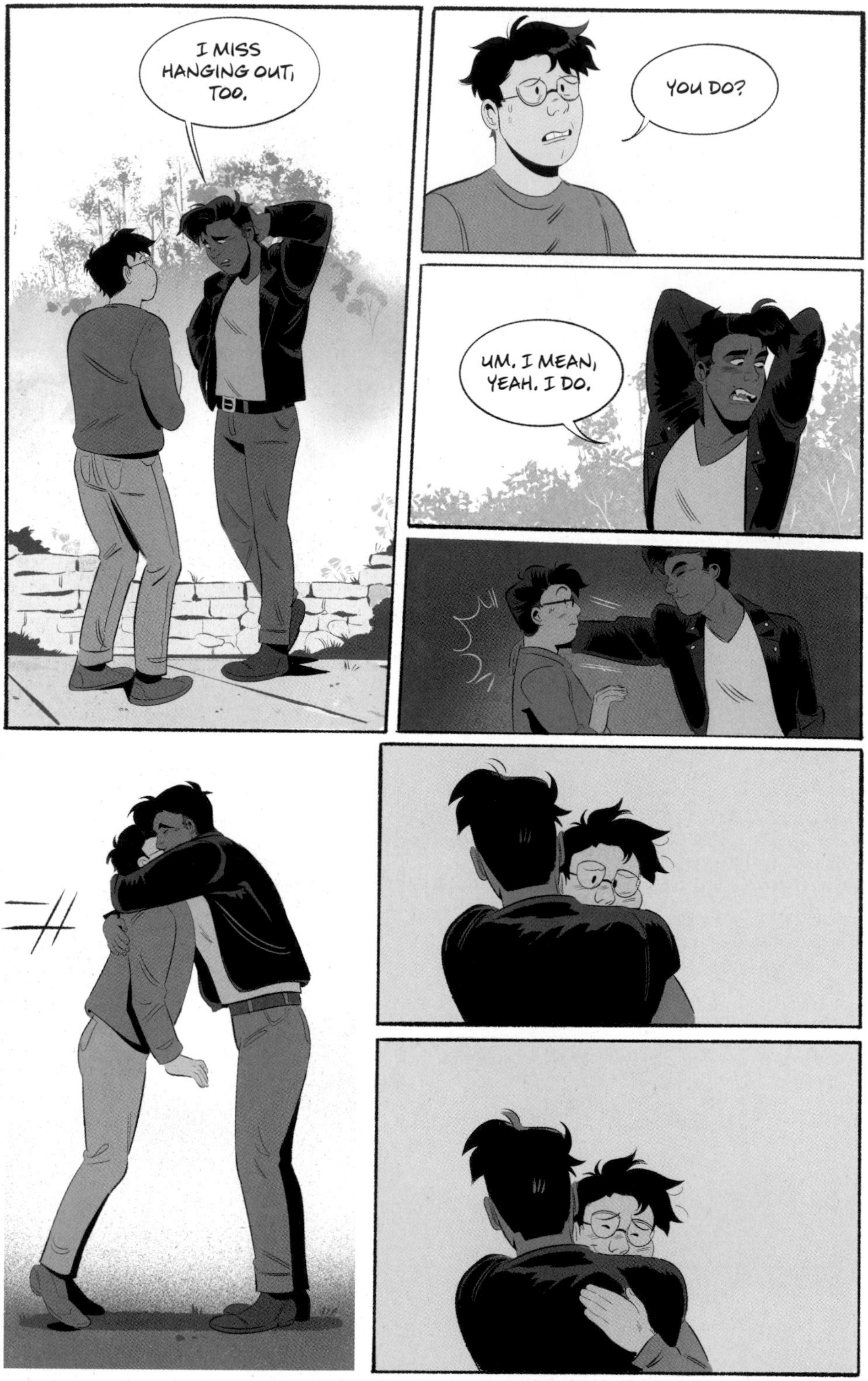
I MISS HANGING OUT, TOO.
YOU DO?
UM. I MEAN, YEAH. I DO.

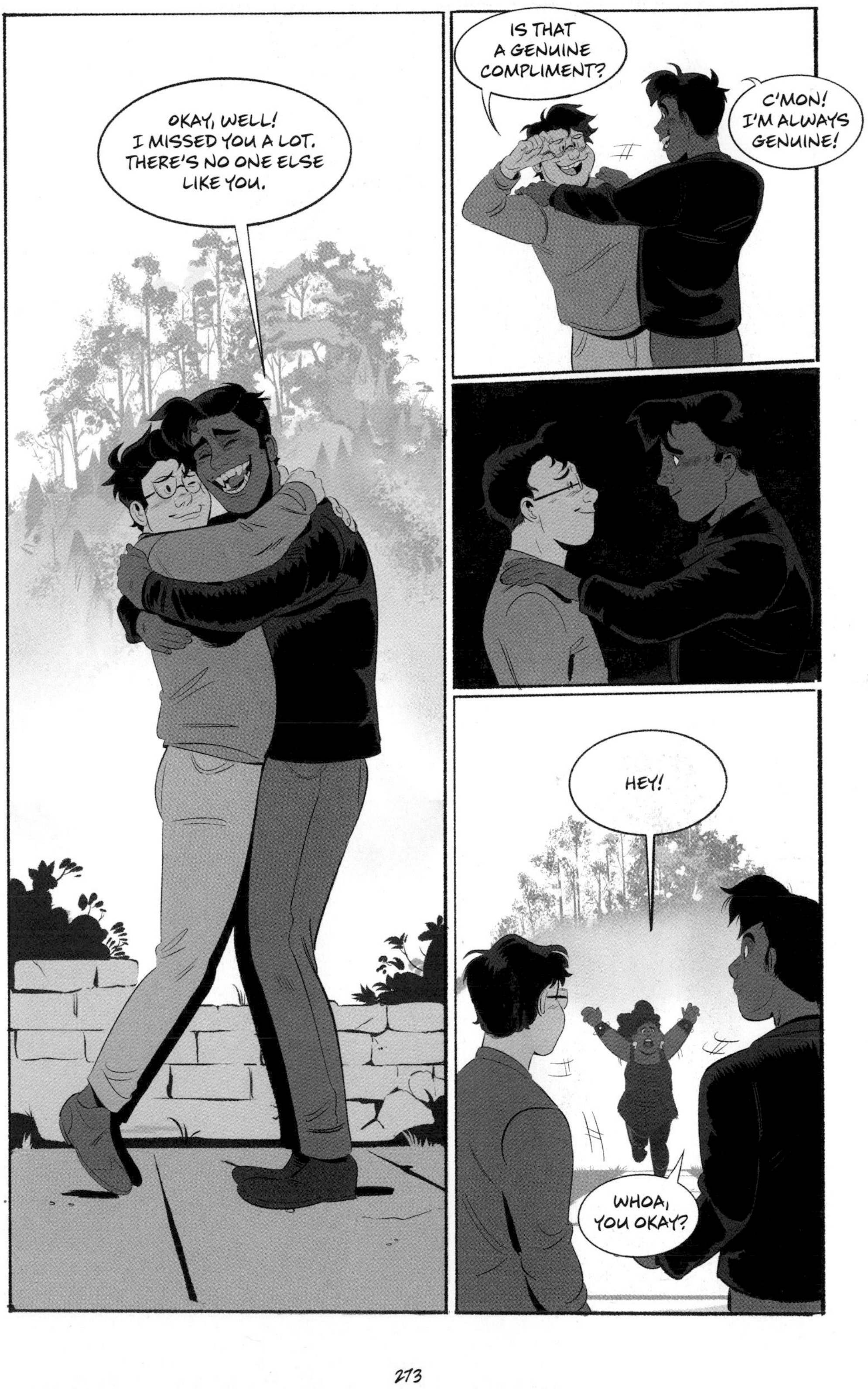
OKAY, WELL! I MISSED YOU A LOT. THERE'S NO ONE ELSE LIKE YOU.
IS THAT A GENUINE COMPLIMENT?
C'MON! I'M ALWAYS GENUINE!
HEY!
WHOA, YOU OKAY?

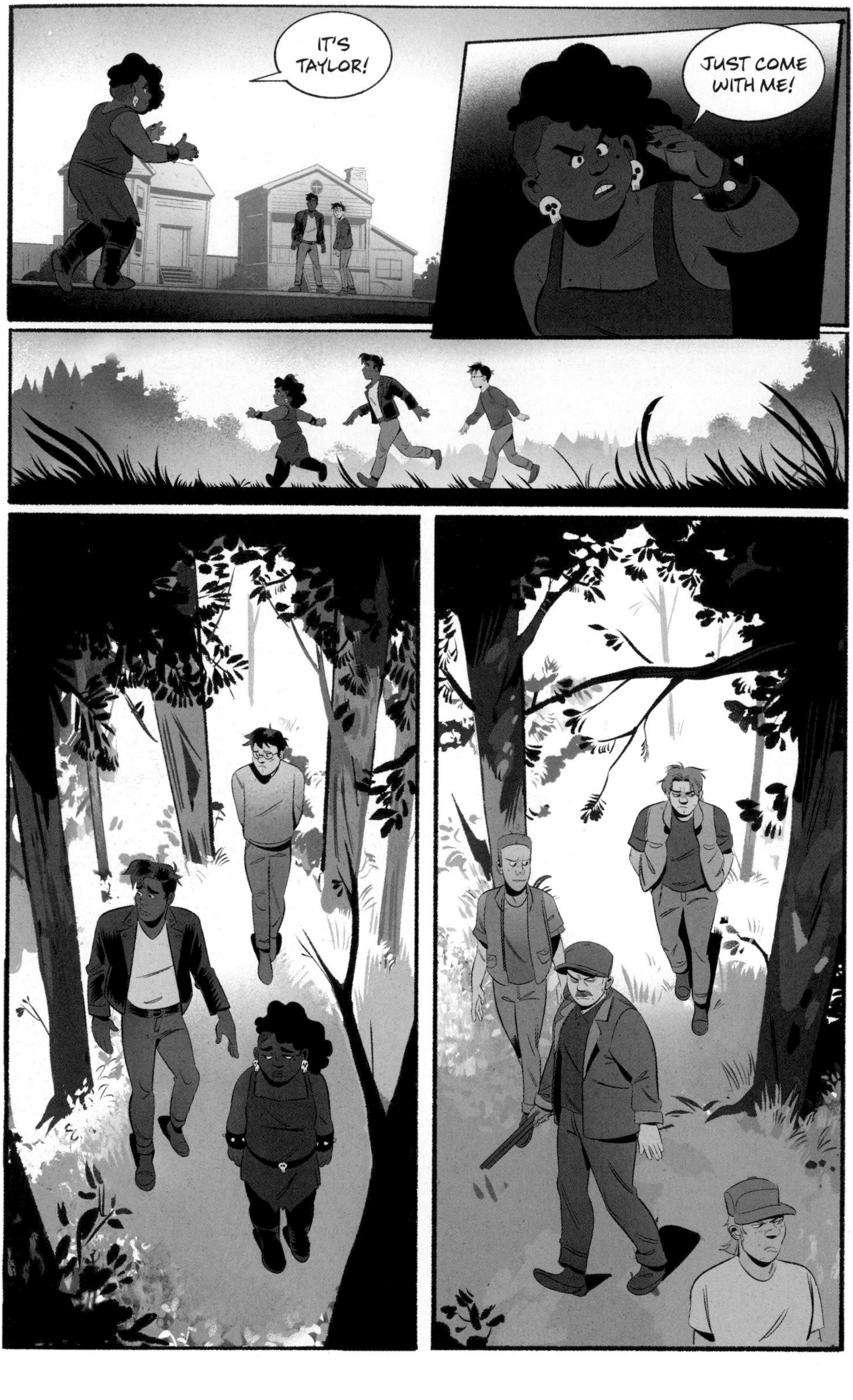
IT'S TAYLOR!
JUST COME WITH ME!

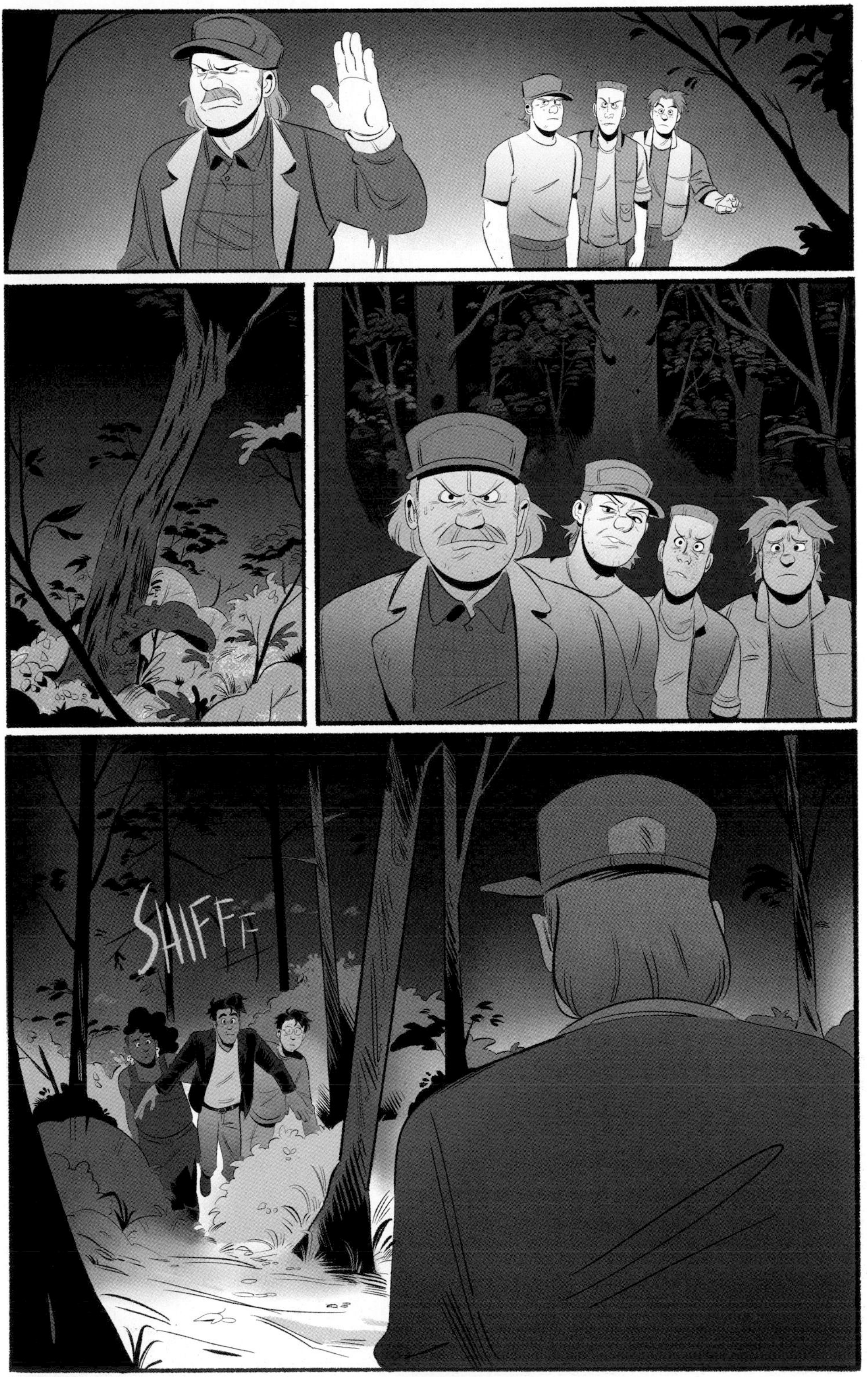
SHIFFF

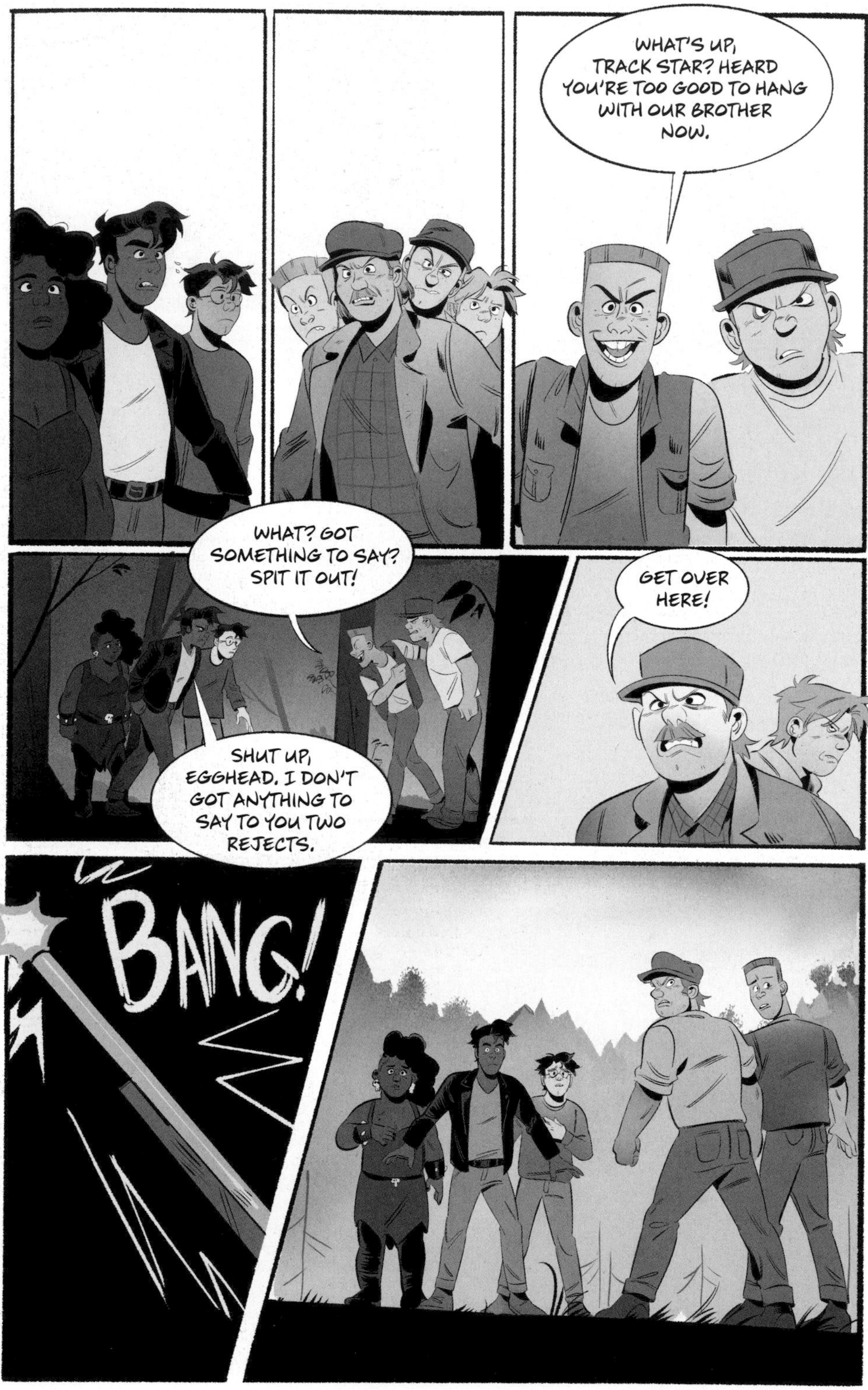

WHAT'S UP, TRACK STAR? HEARD YOU'RE TOO GOOD TO HANG WITH OUR BROTHER NOW.
WHAT? GOT SOMETHING TO SAY? SPIT IT OUT!
SHUT UP, EGGHEAD. I DON'T GOT ANYTHING TO SAY TO YOU TWO REJECTS.
GET OVER HERE!
BANG!

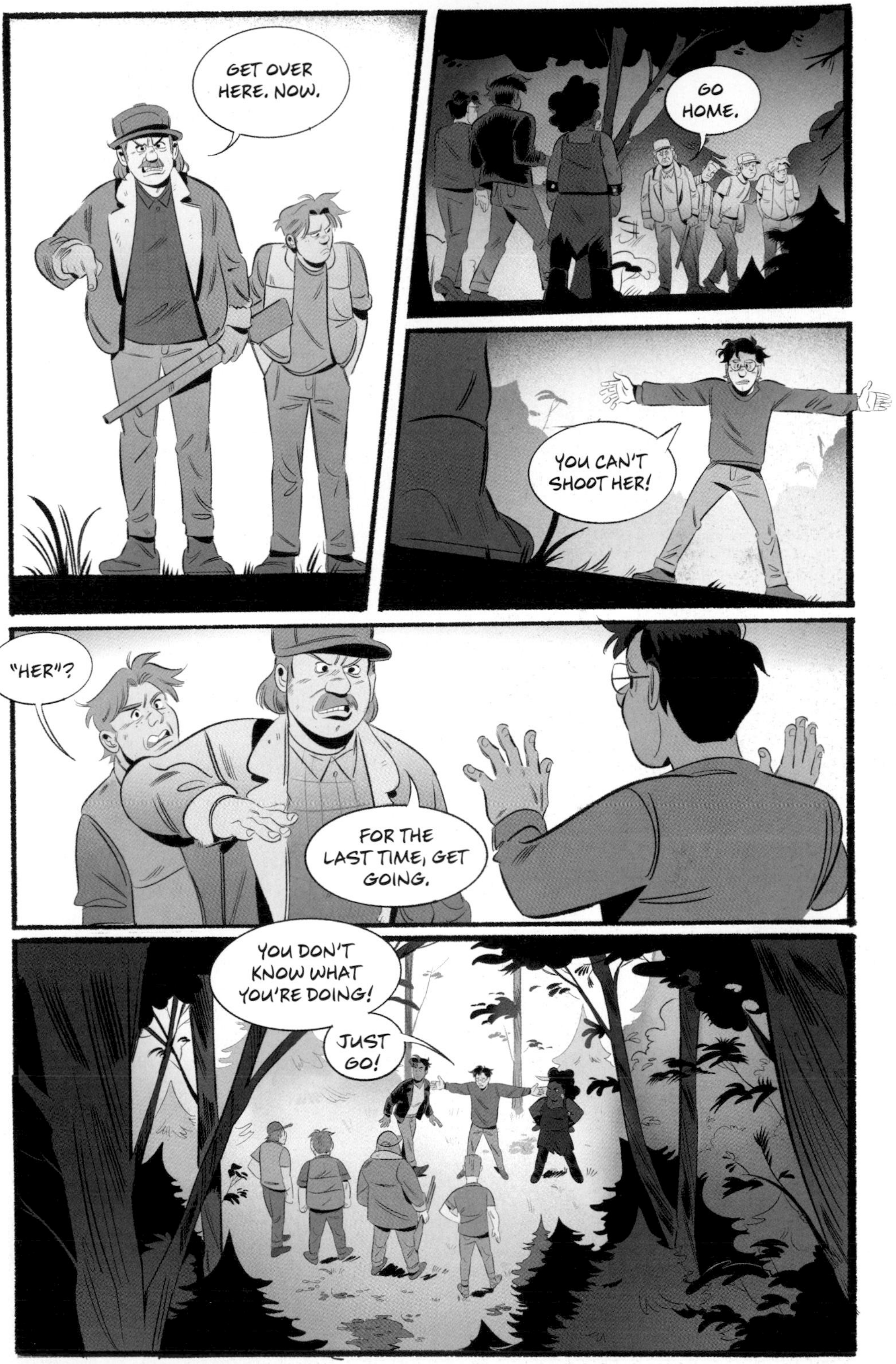
GET OVER HERE. NOW.
GO HOME.
YOU CAN'T SHOOT HER!
"HER"?
FOR THE LAST TIME, GET GOING.
YOU DON'T KNOW WHAT YOU'RE DOING!
JUST GO!

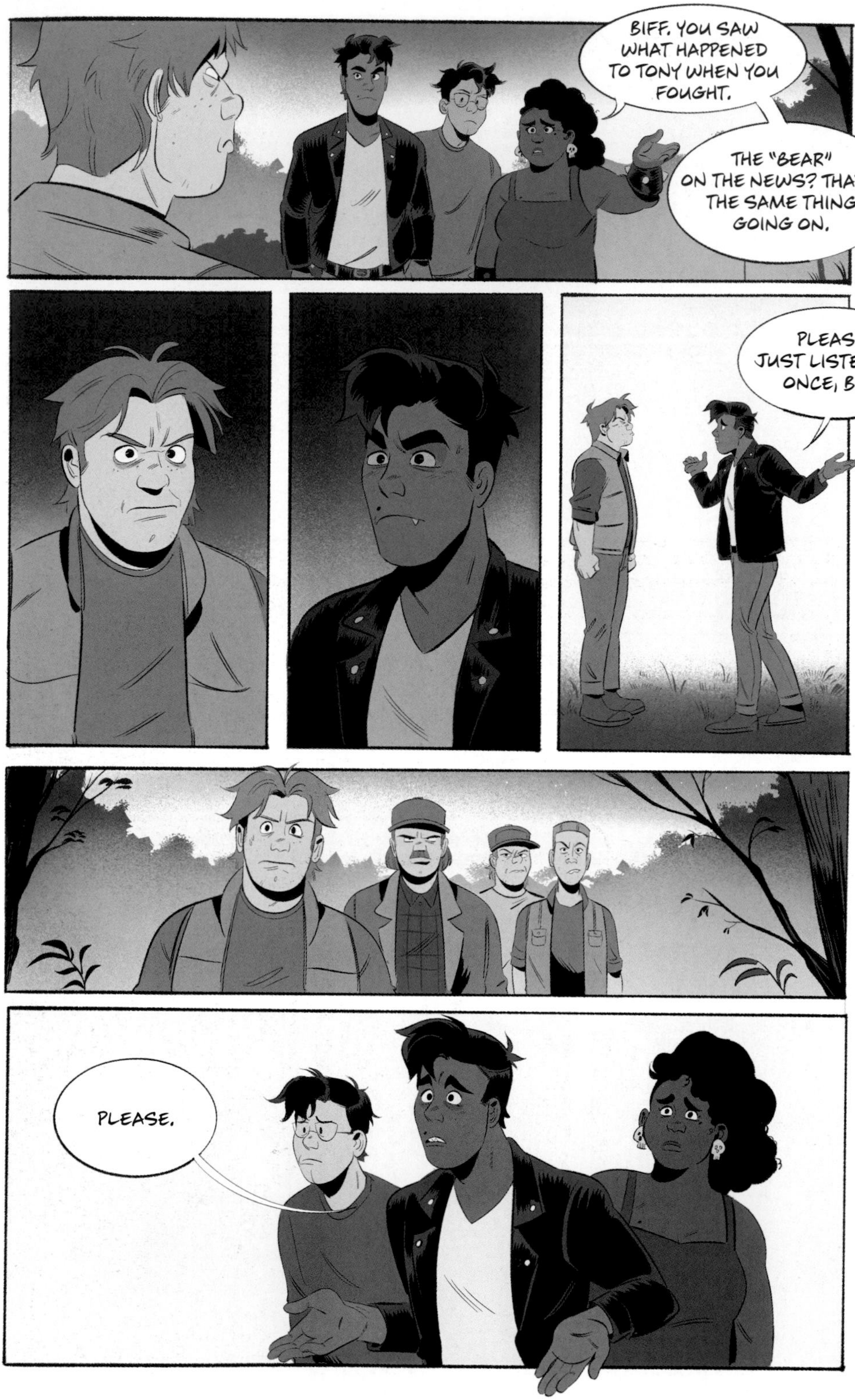
BIFF. YOU SAW WHAT HAPPENED TO TONY WHEN YOU FOUGHT.
THE "BEAR" ON THE NEWS? THAT'S THE SAME THING GOING ON.
PLEASE. JUST LISTEN FOR ONCE, BIFF.
PLEASE.

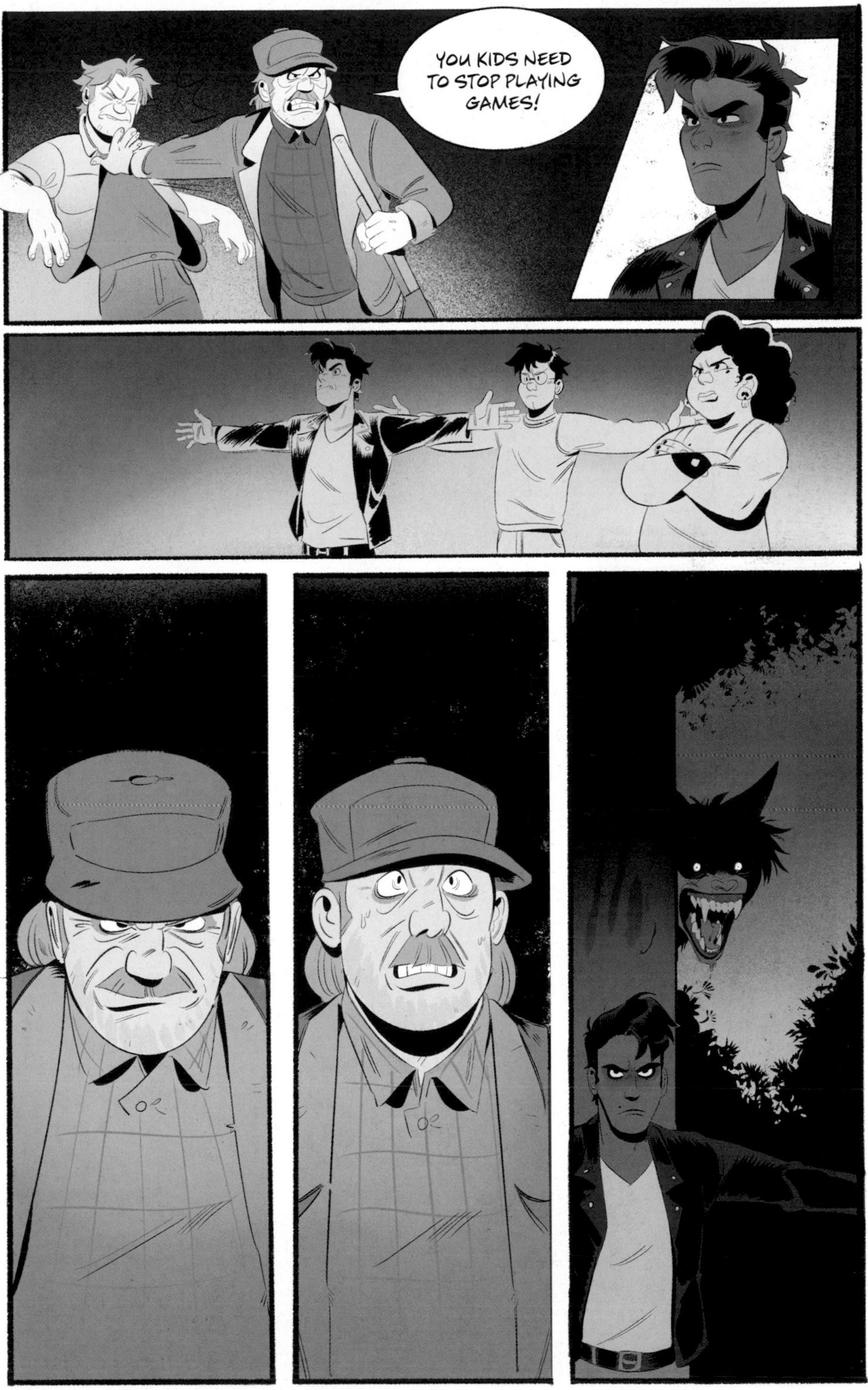
YOU KIDS NEED TO STOP PLAYING GAMES!

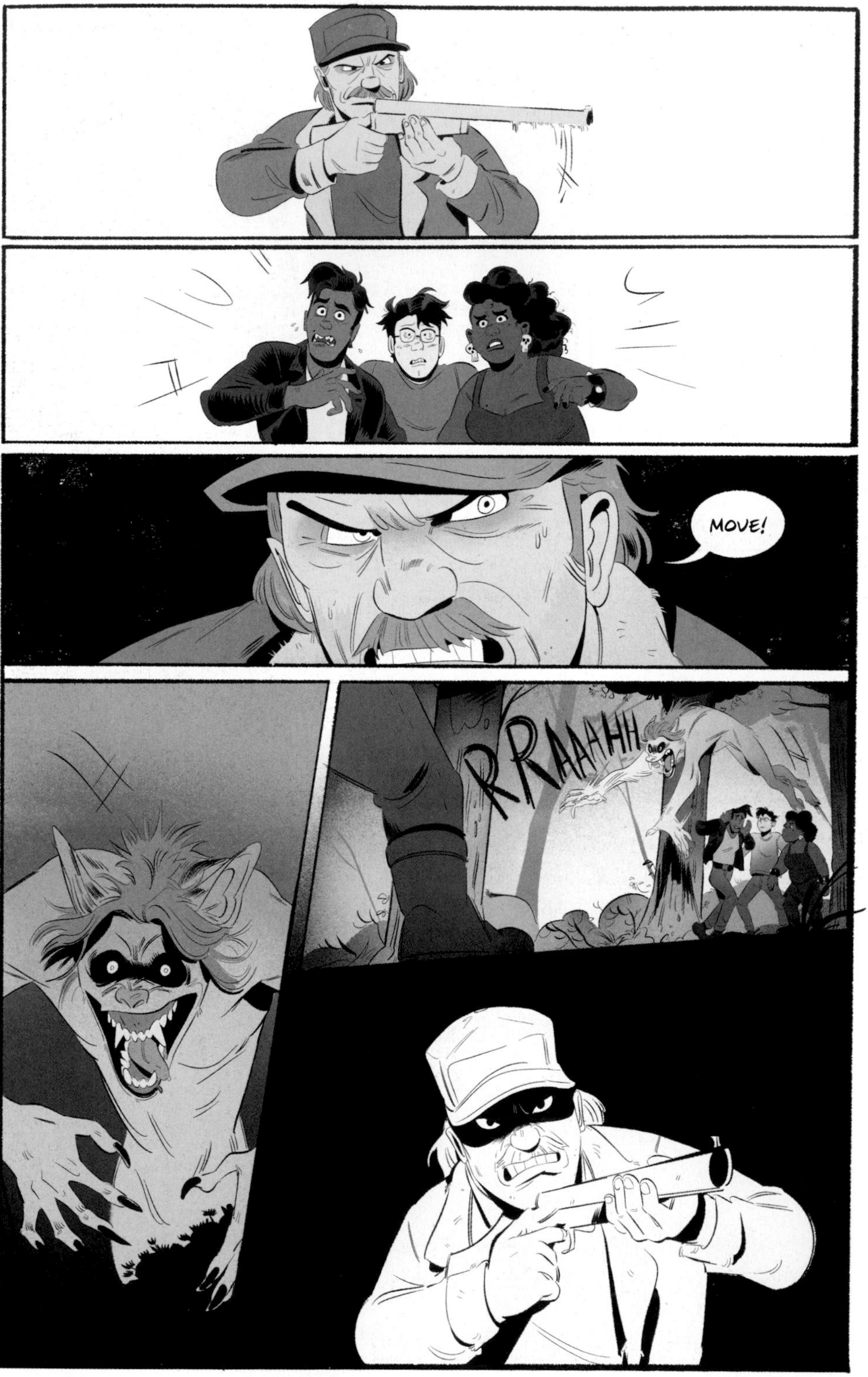
MOVE!
RRAAAHH

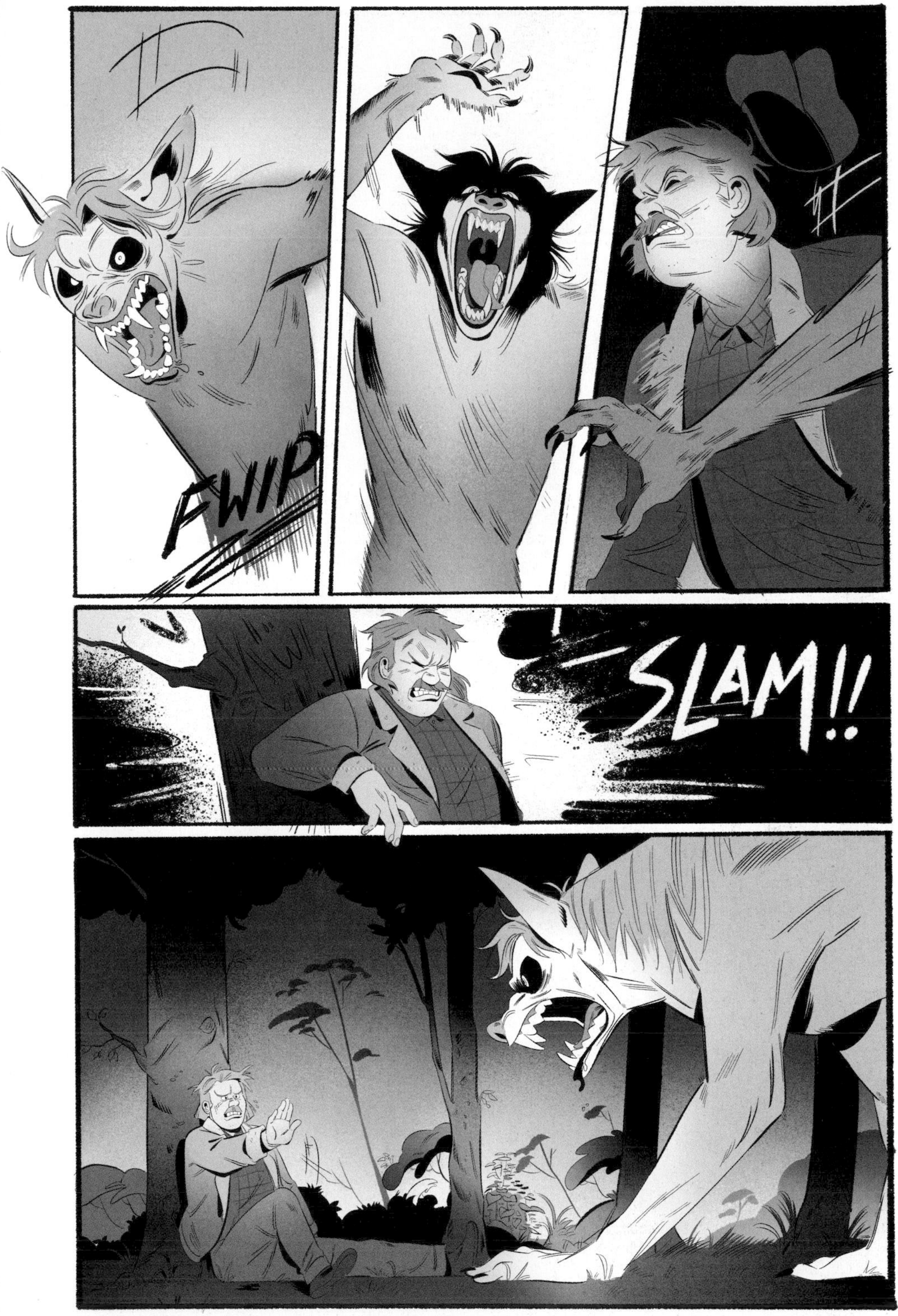
FWIP
SLAM!!

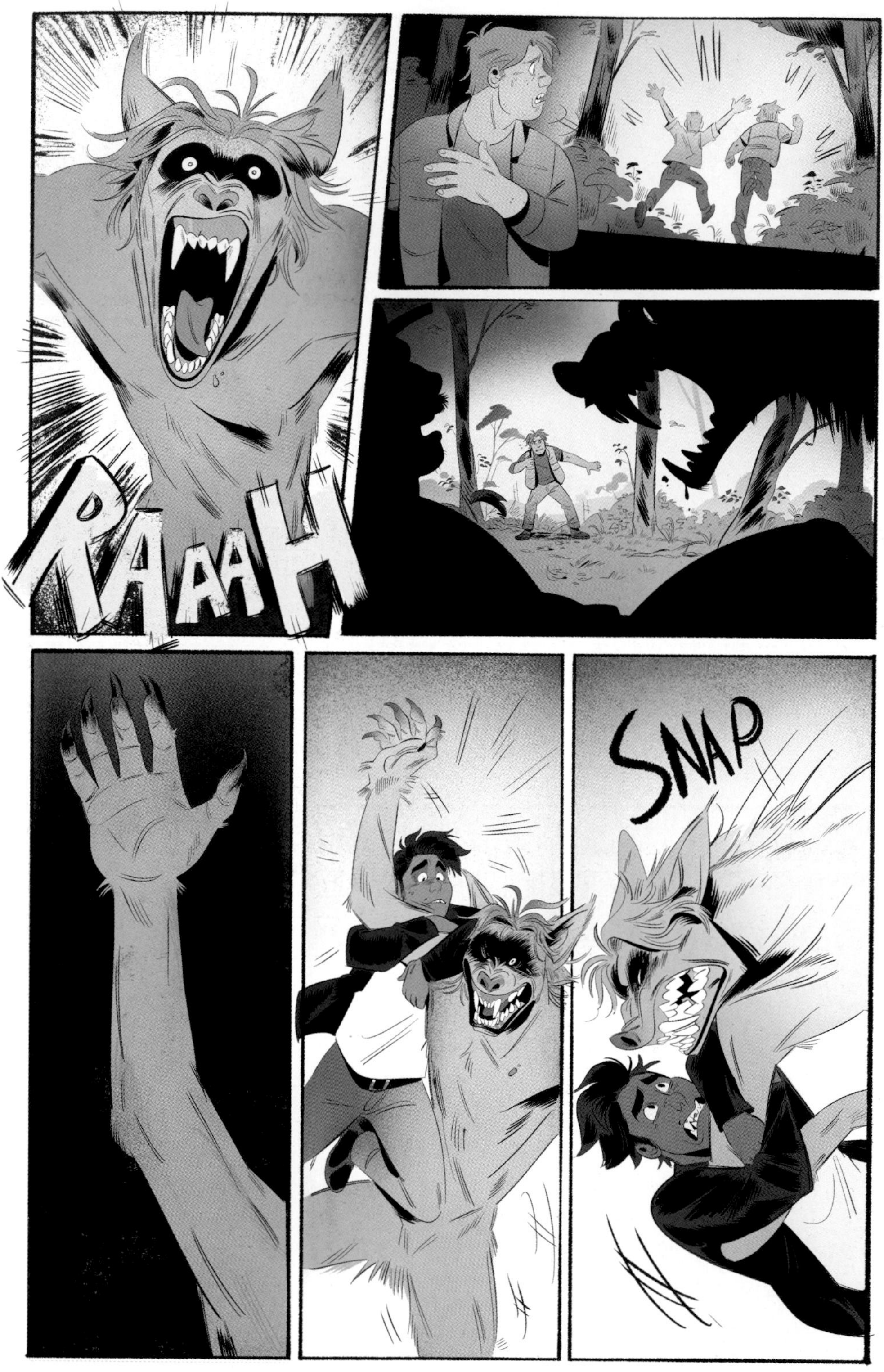
RAAAH
SNAP

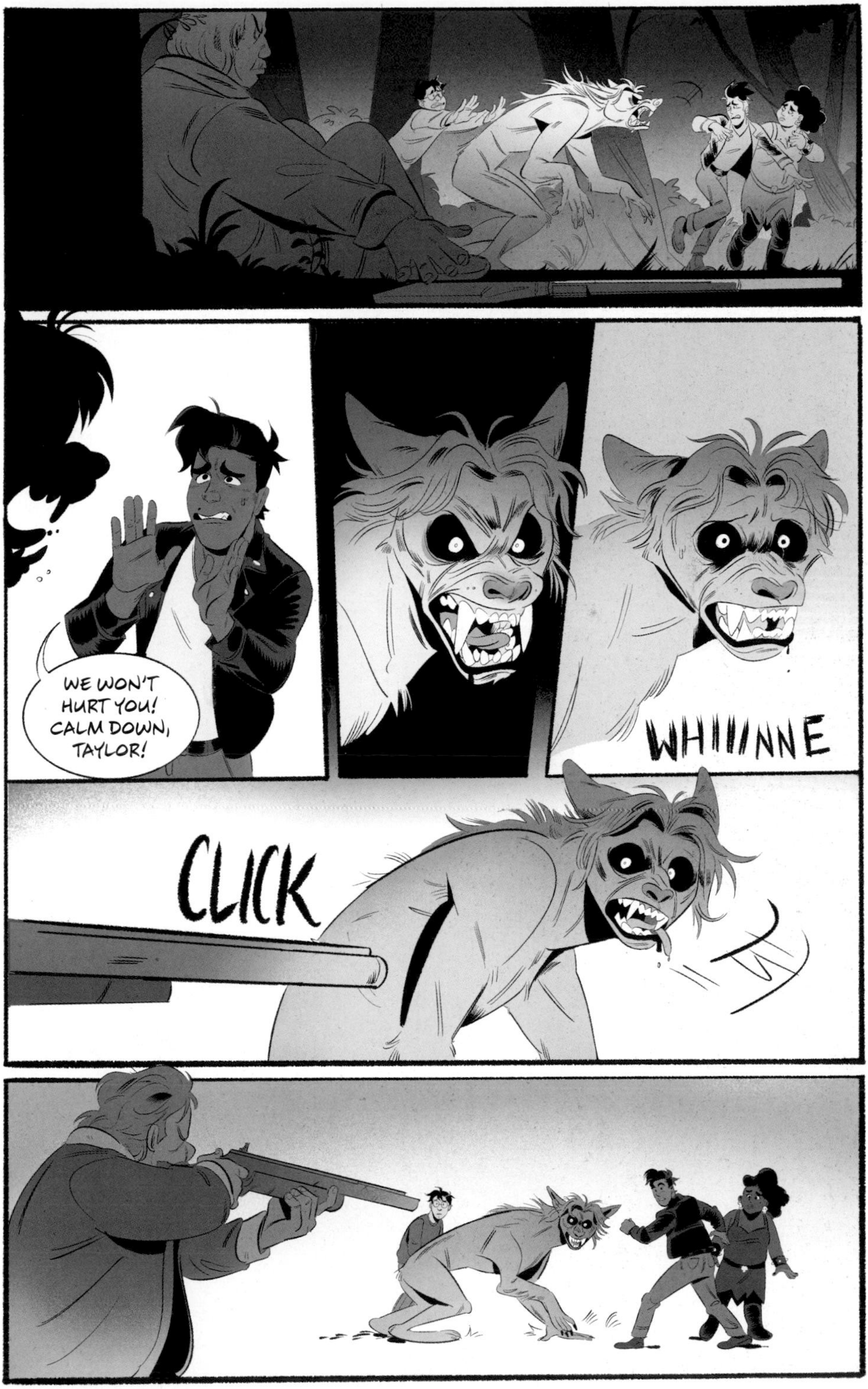
WE WON'T HURT YOU! CALM DOWN, TAYLOR!
WHIIINNE
CLICK

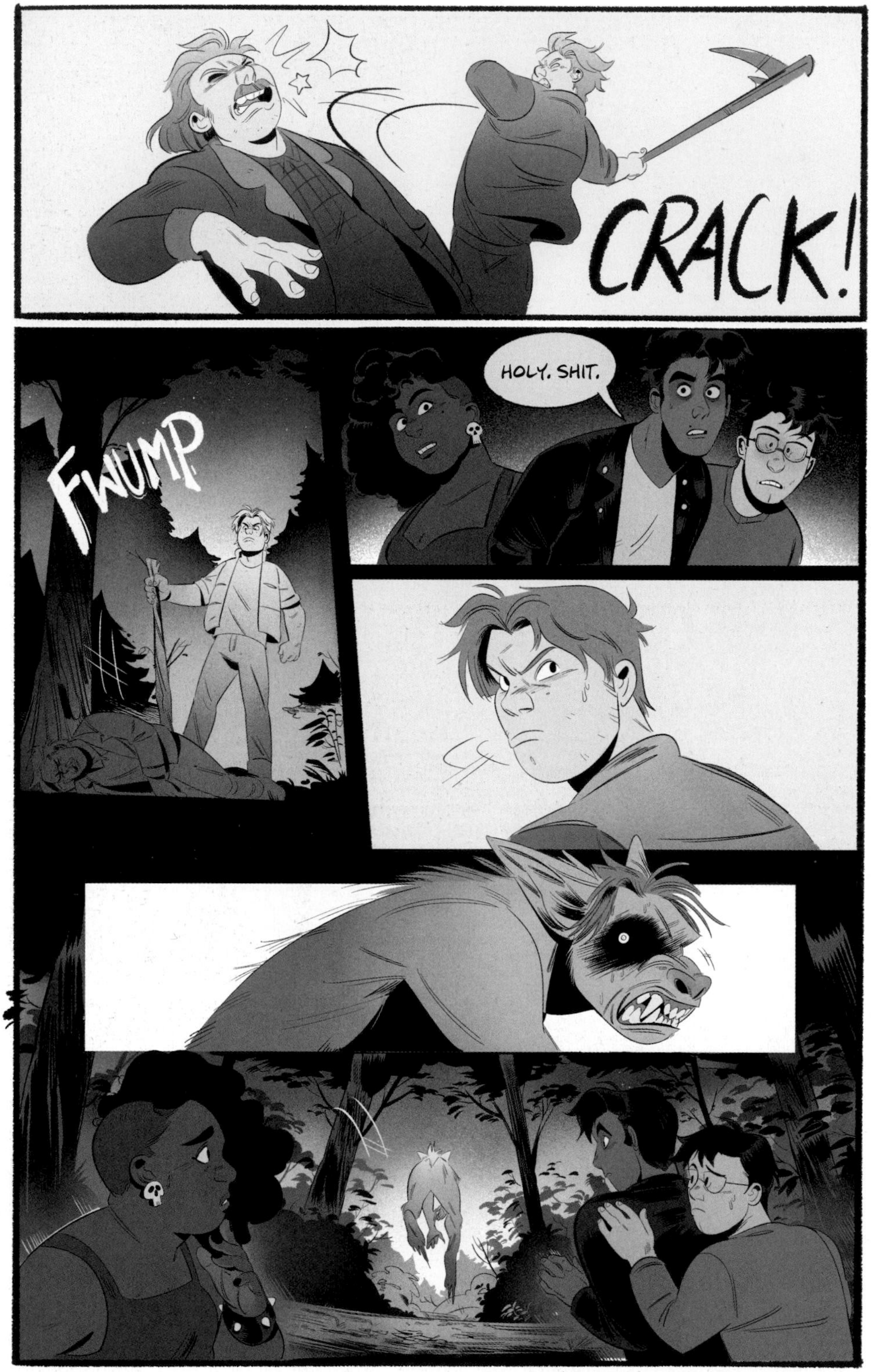
CRACK!
FWUMP
HOLY. SHIT.

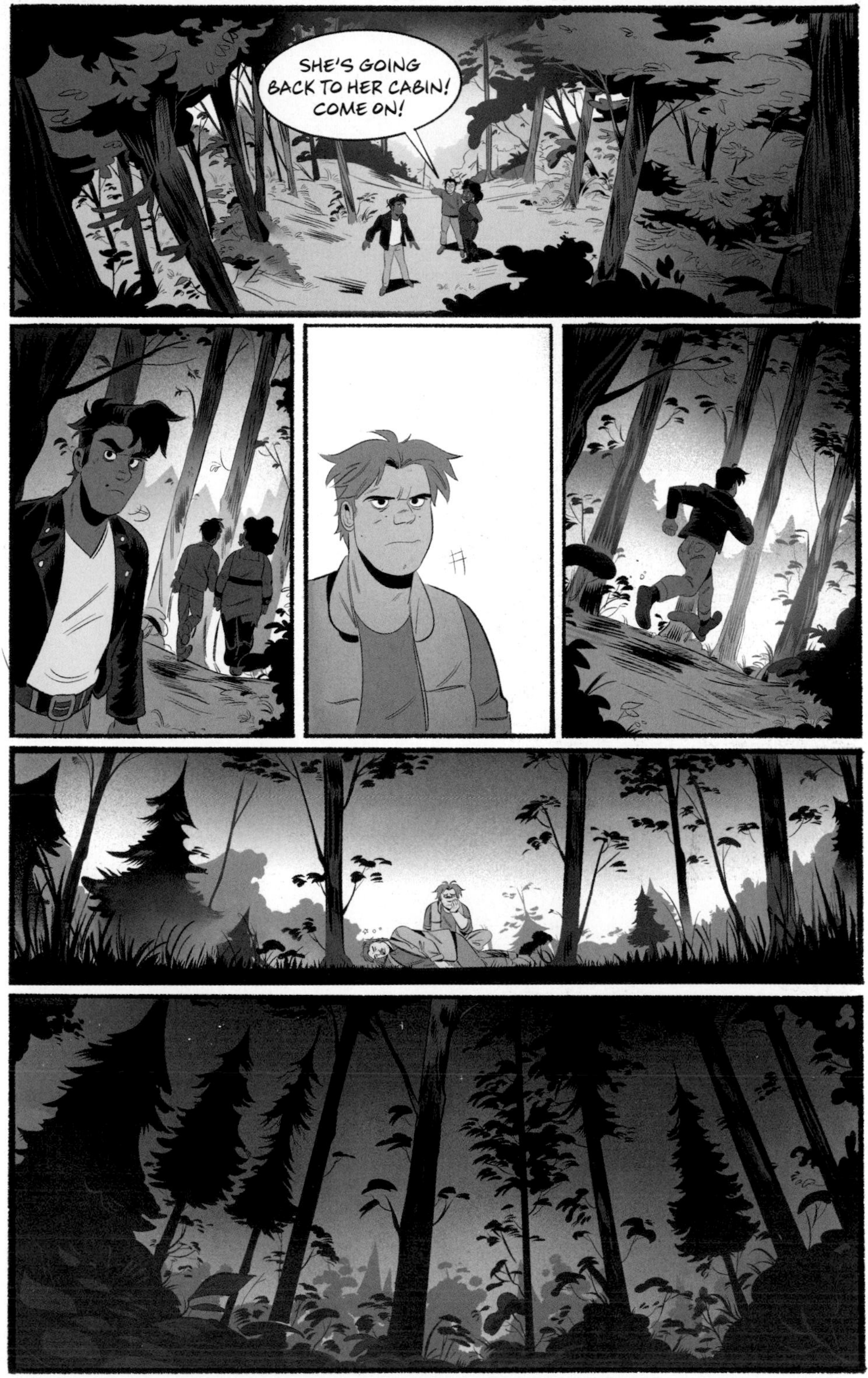
SHE'S GOING
BACK TO HER CABIN!
COME ON!

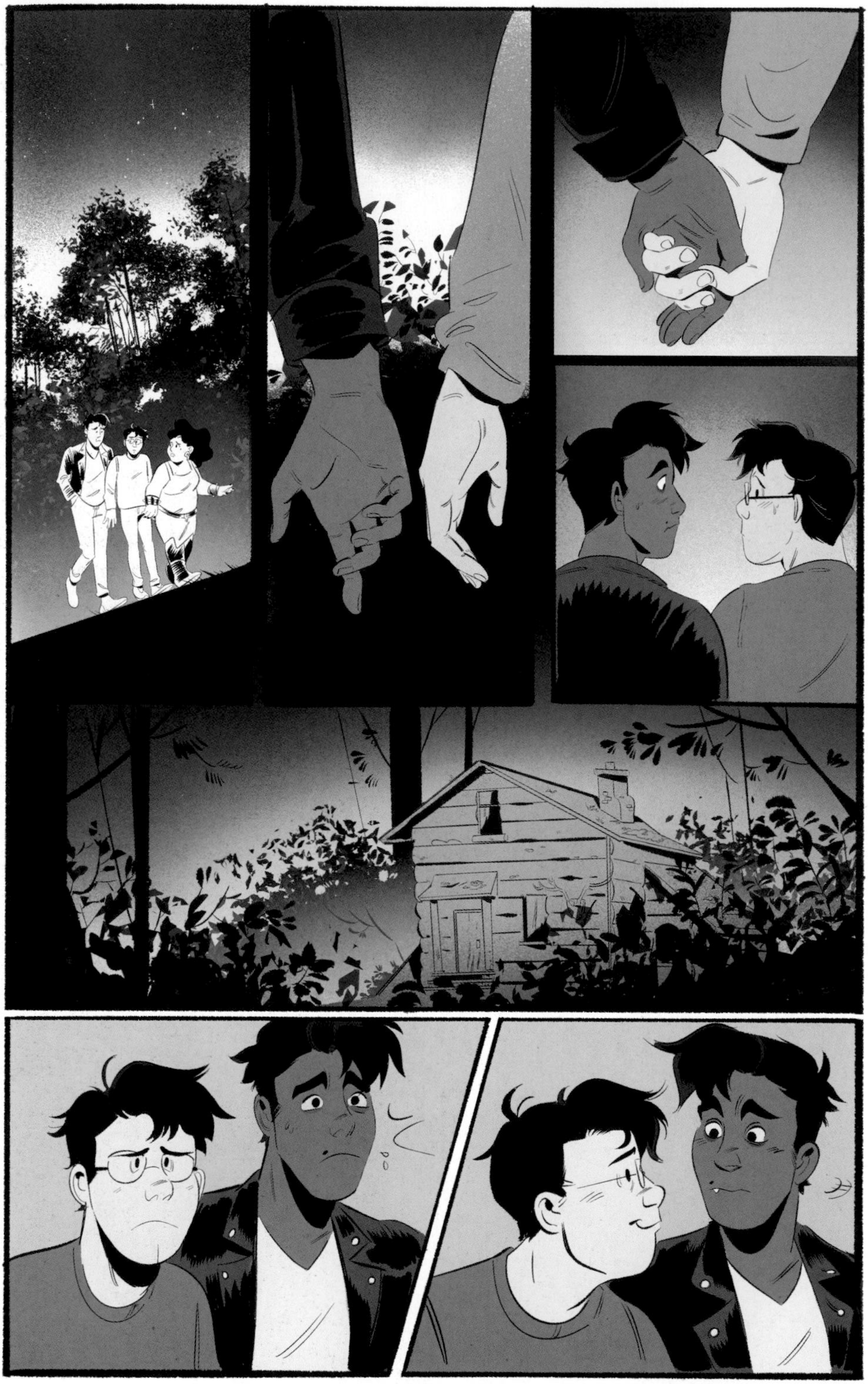

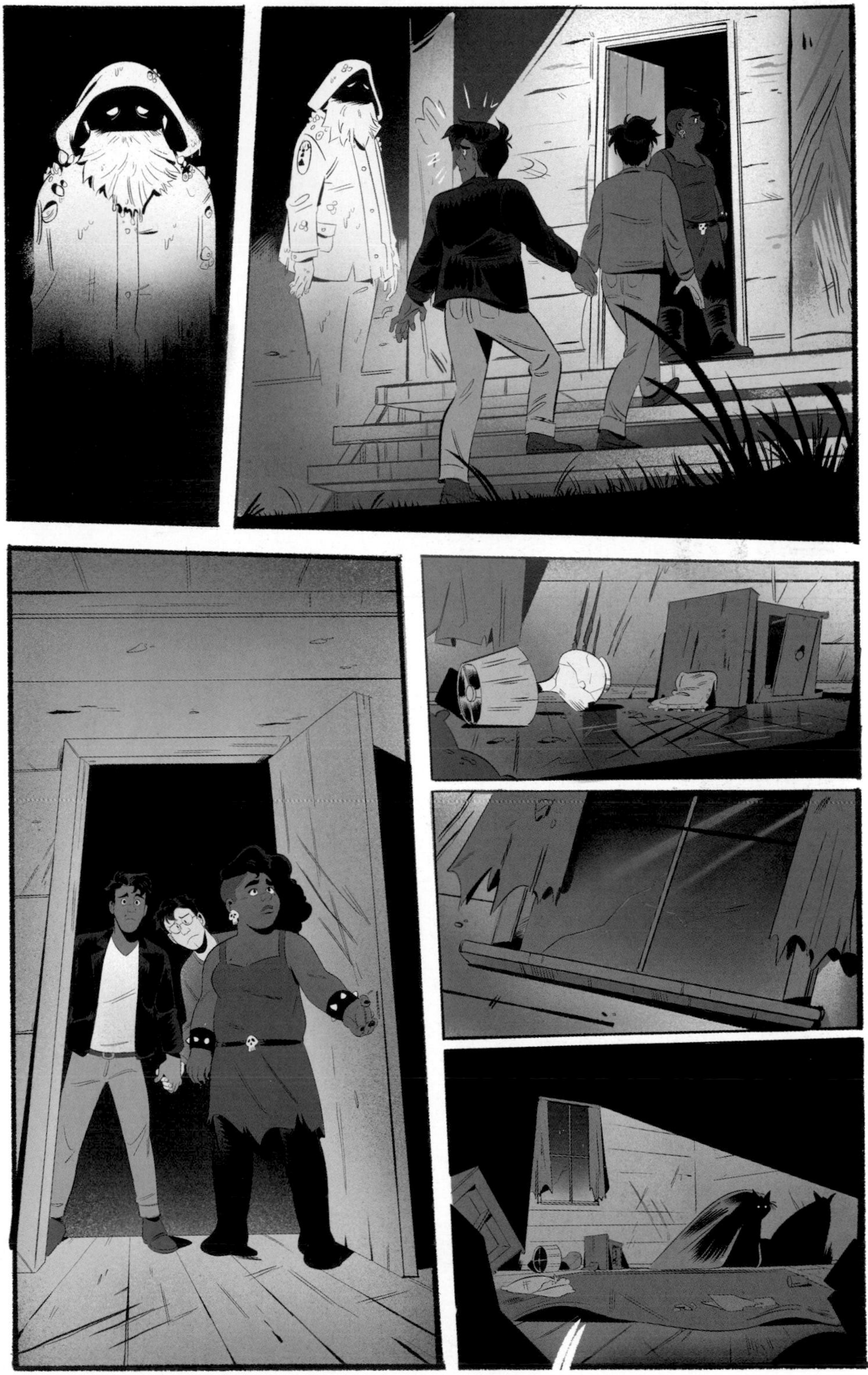

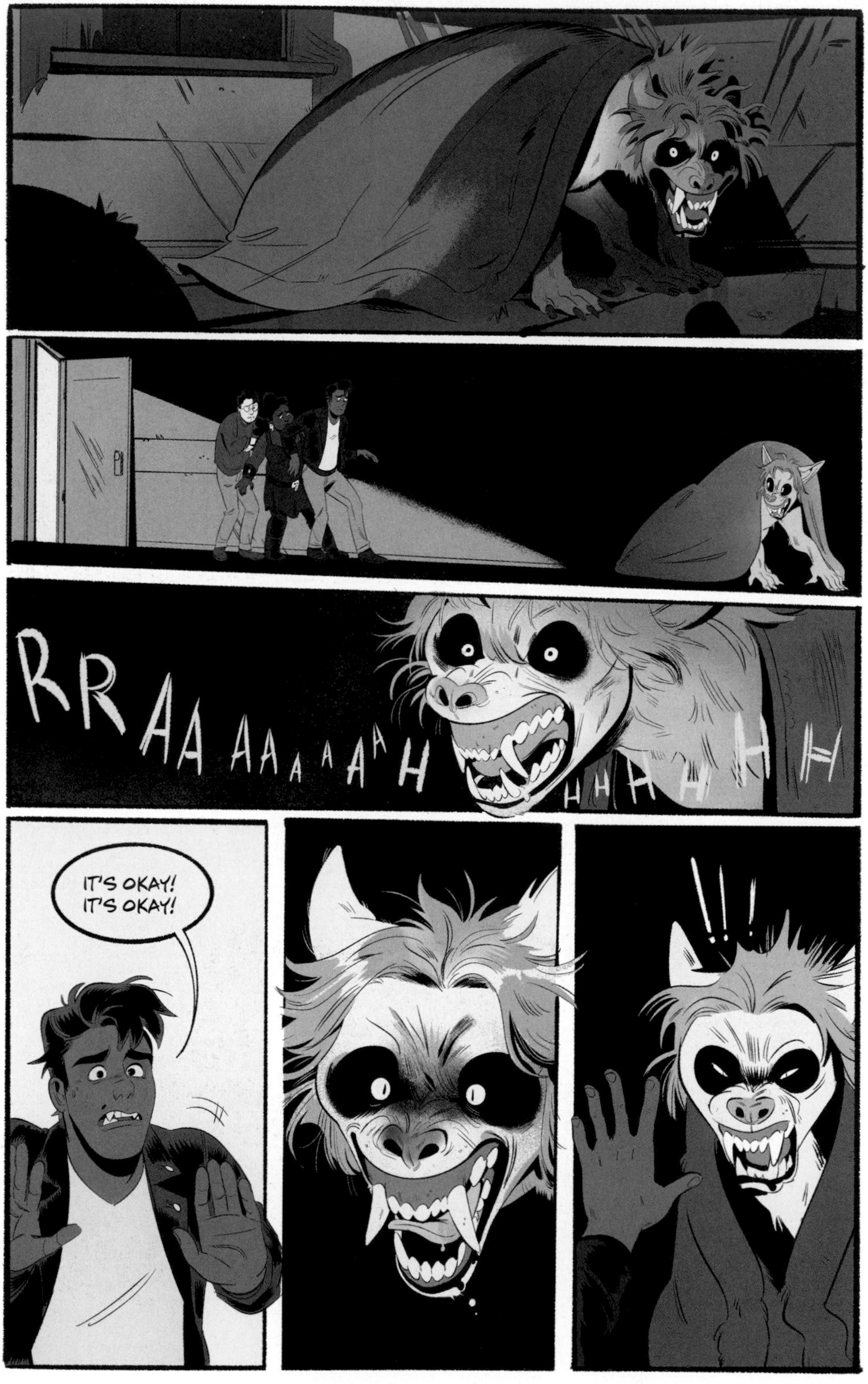
RRAAAAAAAAHHHHHHHH
IT'S OKAY! IT'S OKAY!
!!!

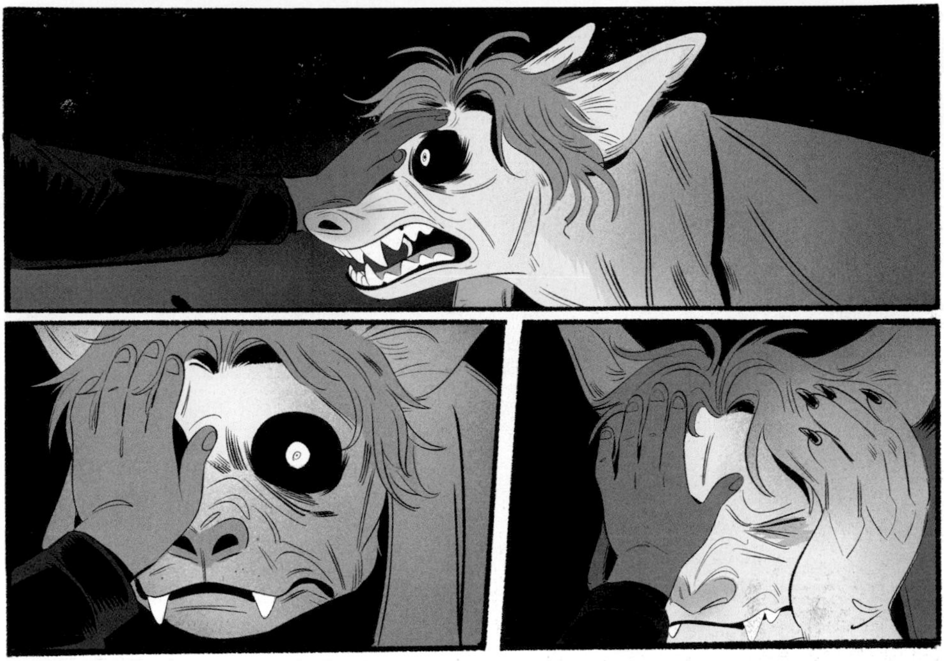

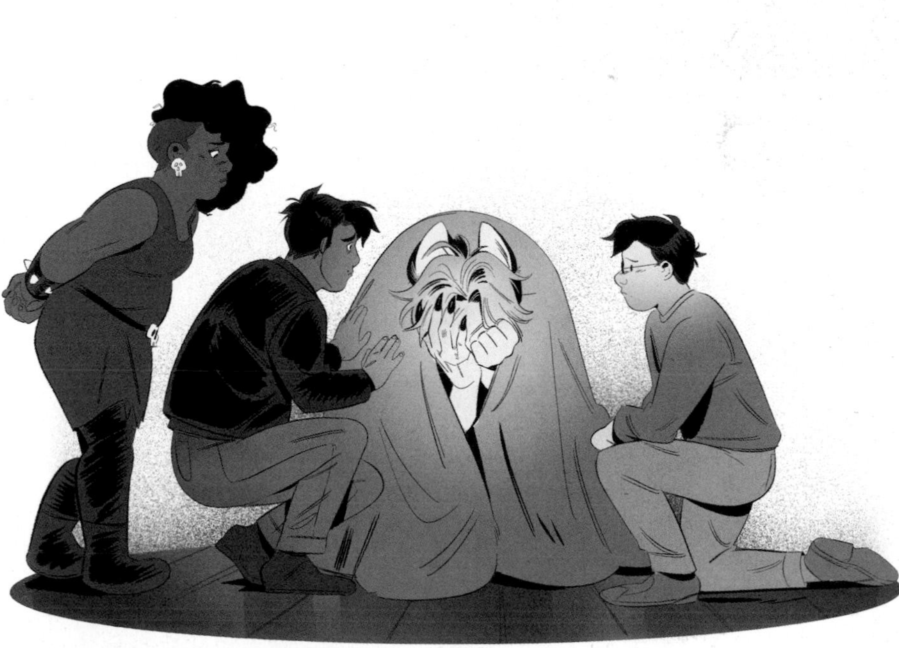

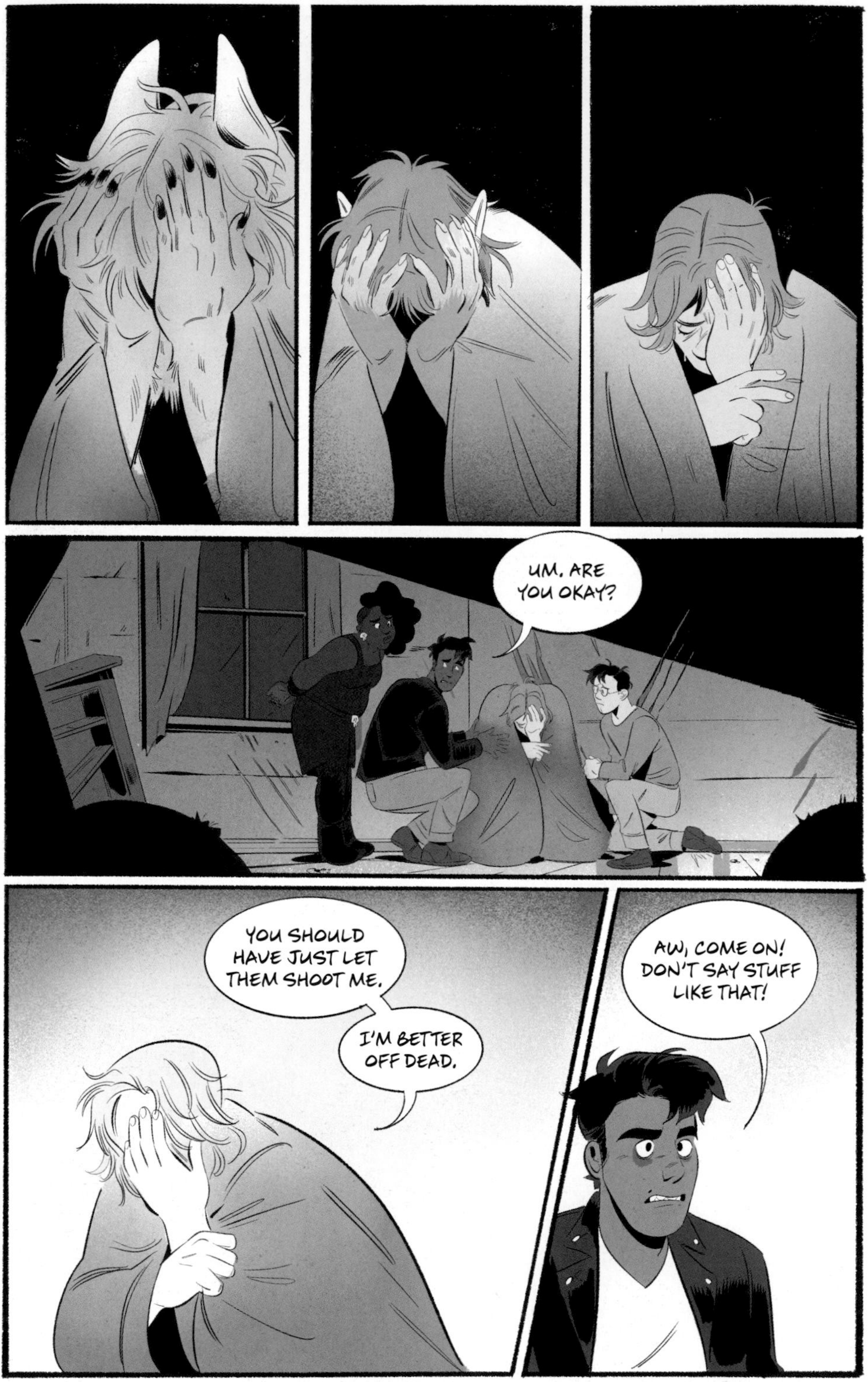
UM, ARE YOU OKAY?
YOU SHOULD HAVE JUST LET THEM SHOOT ME.
I'M BETTER OFF DEAD.
AW, COME ON! DON'T SAY STUFF LIKE THAT!

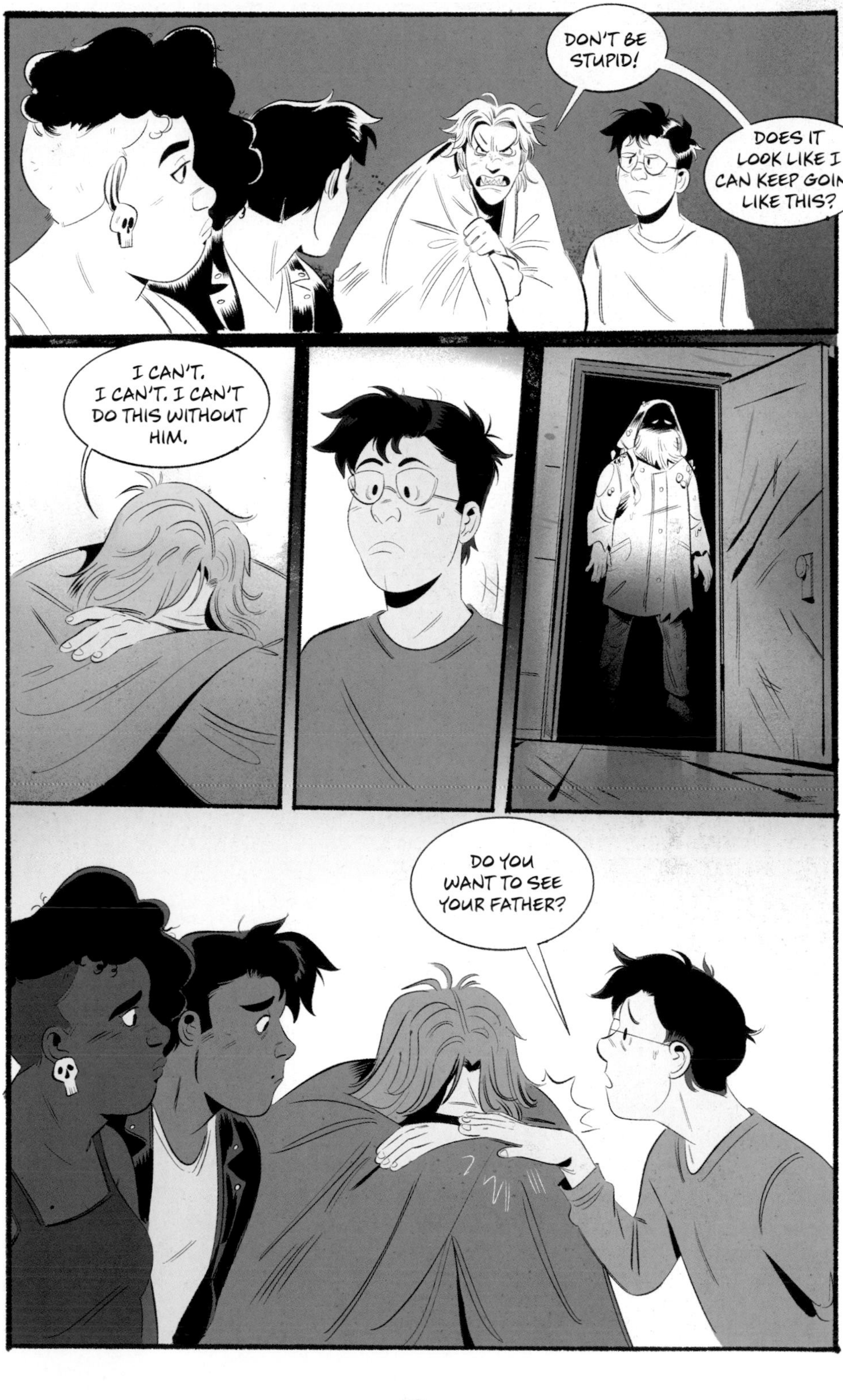
DON'T BE STUPID!
DOES IT LOOK LIKE I CAN KEEP GOING LIKE THIS?
I CAN'T. I CAN'T. I CAN'T DO THIS WITHOUT HIM.
DO YOU WANT TO SEE YOUR FATHER?

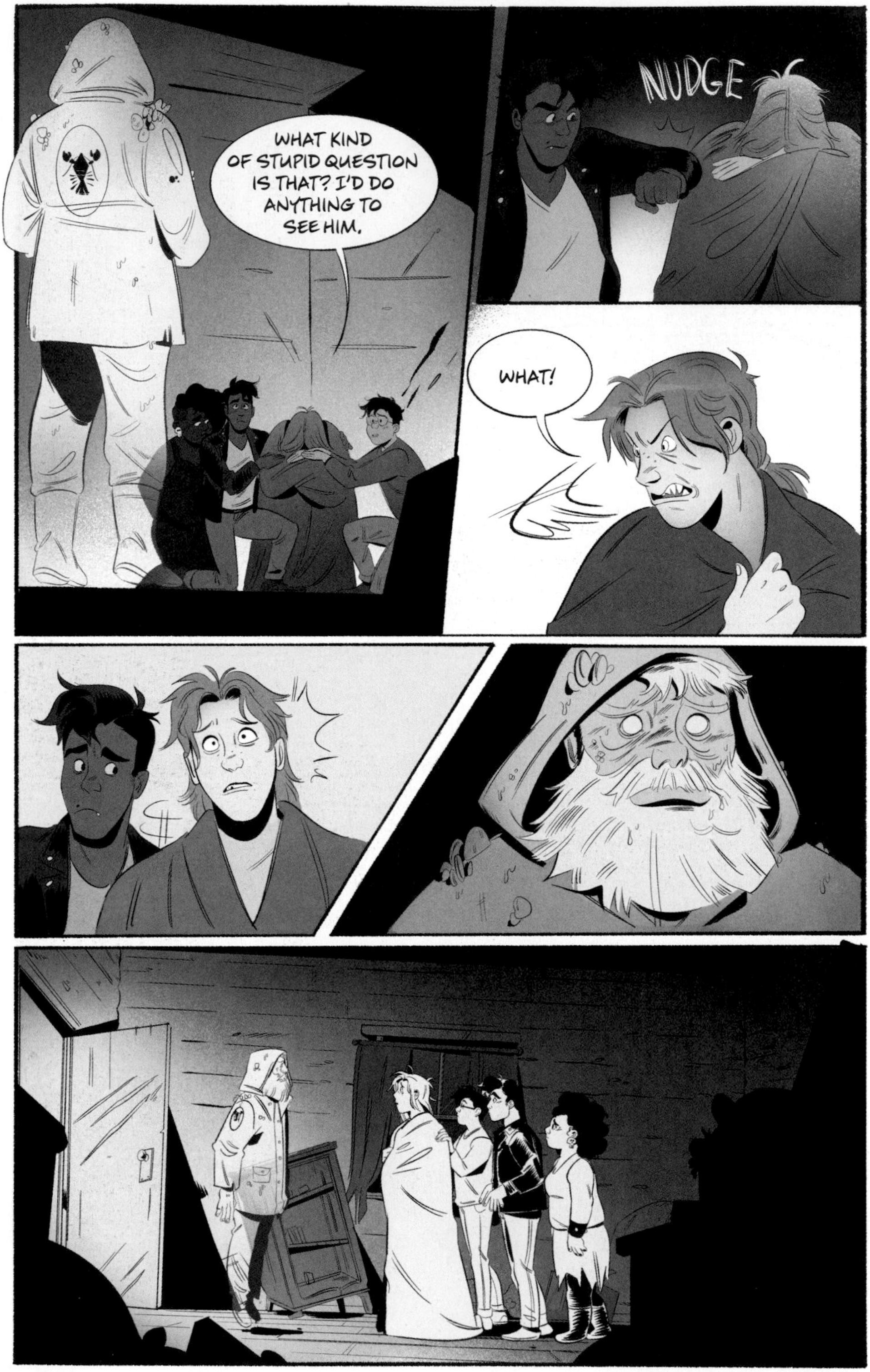
WHAT KIND OF STUPID QUESTION IS THAT? I'D DO ANYTHING TO SEE HIM.
NUDGE
WHAT!

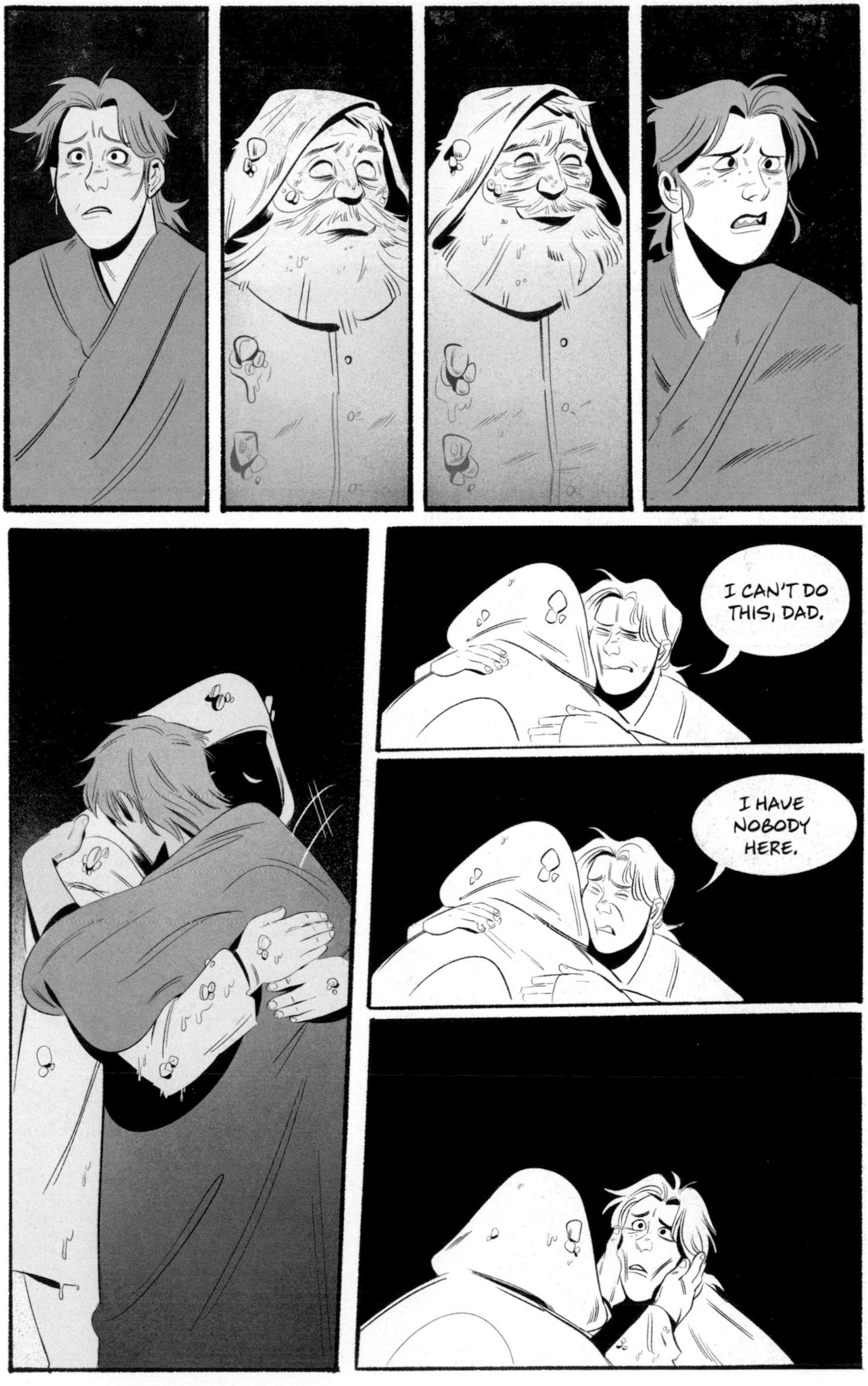
I CAN'T DO THIS, DAD.
I HAVE NOBODY HERE.

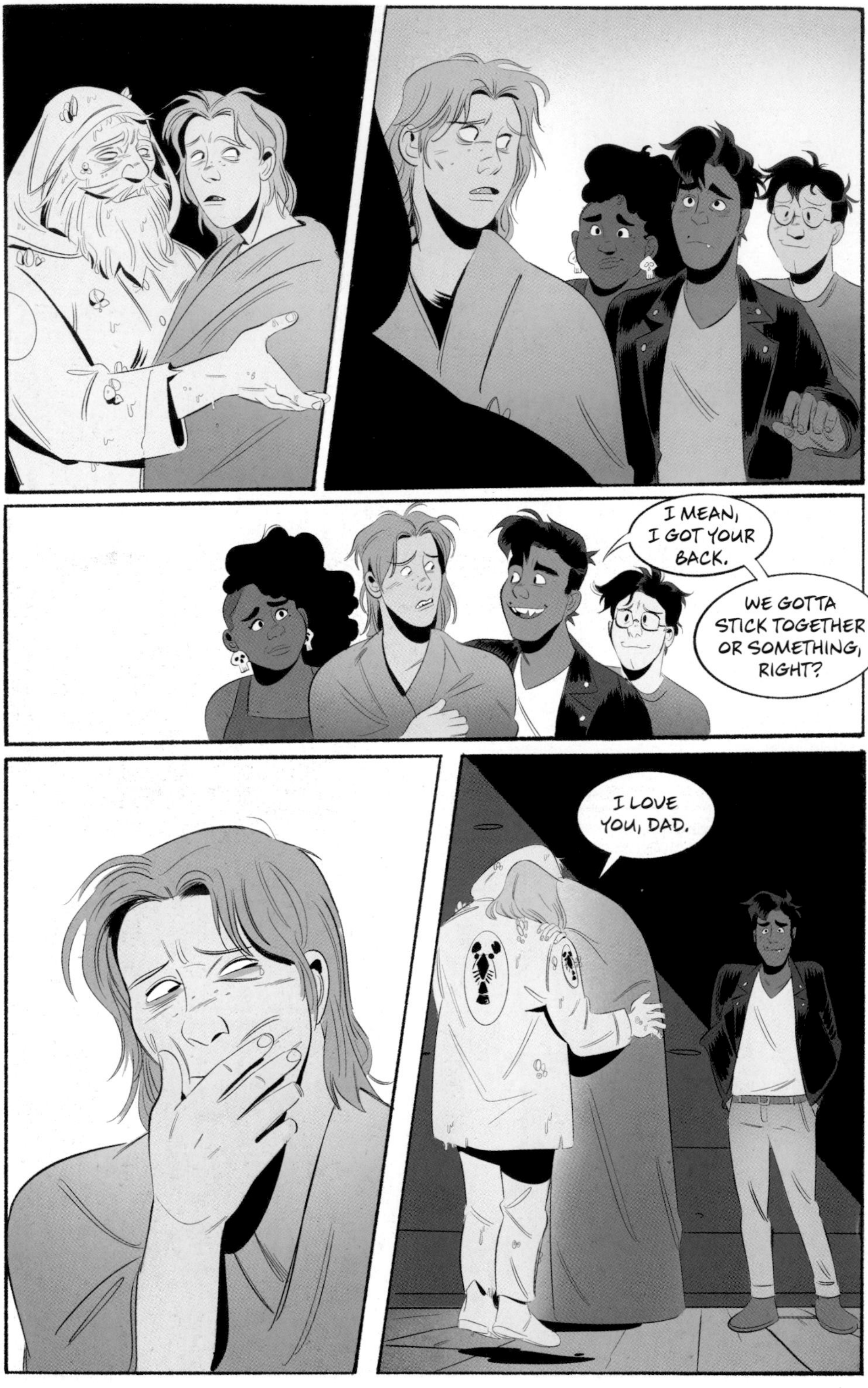
I MEAN, I GOT YOUR BACK.
WE GOTTA STICK TOGETHER OR SOMETHING, RIGHT?
I LOVE YOU, DAD.

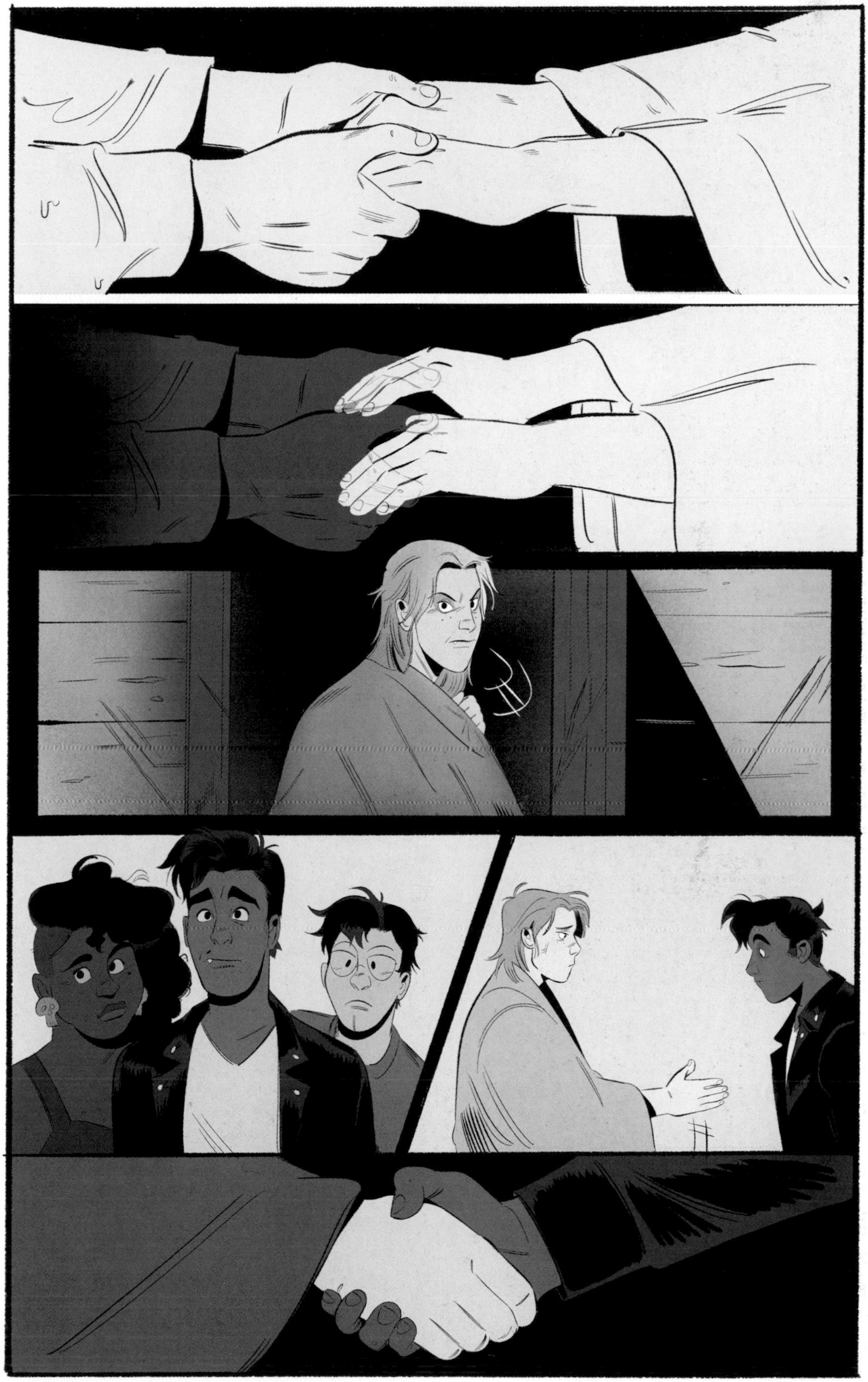

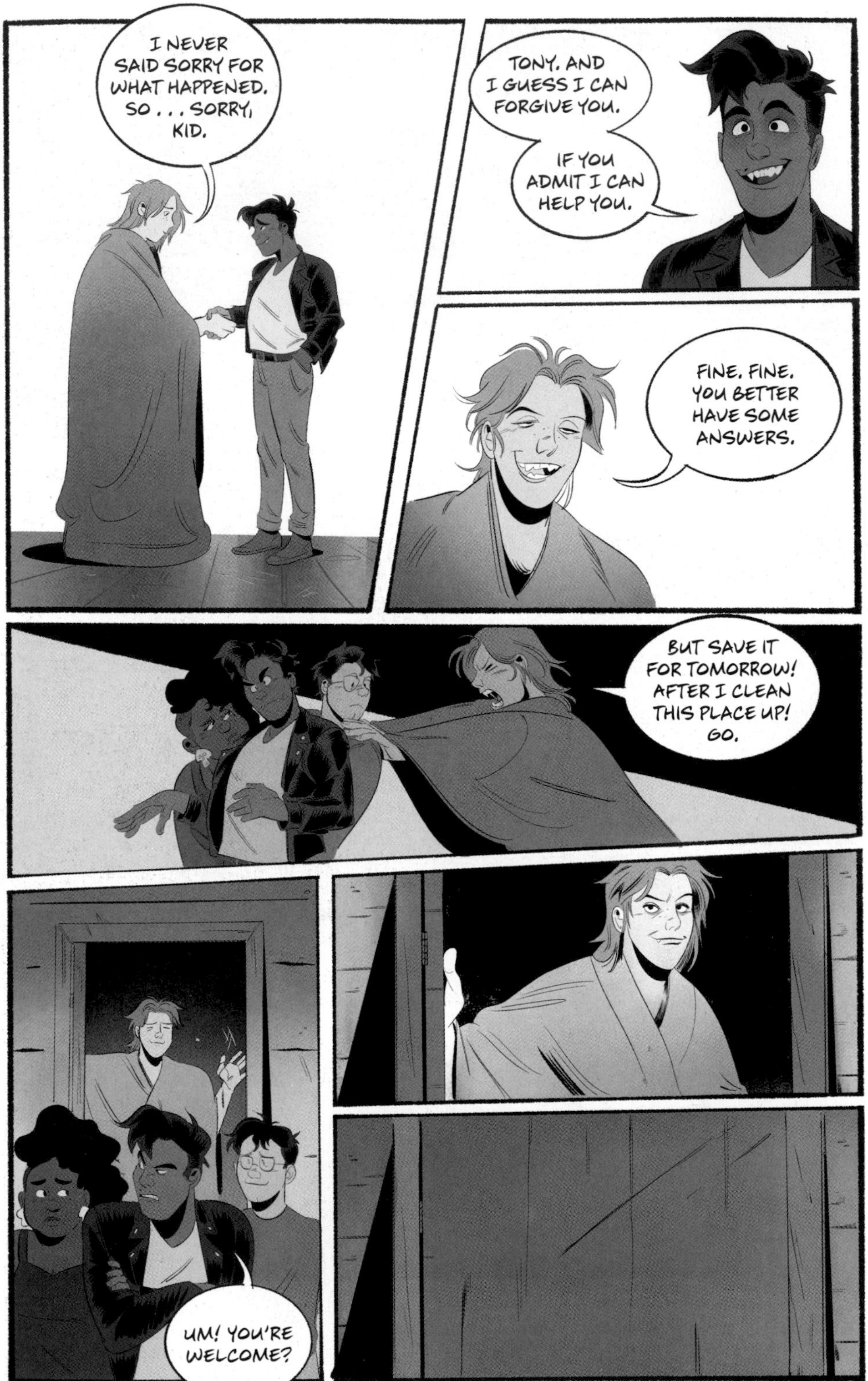
I NEVER SAID SORRY FOR WHAT HAPPENED. SO . . . SORRY, KID.
TONY. AND I GUESS I CAN FORGIVE YOU.
IF YOU ADMIT I CAN HELP YOU.
FINE. FINE. YOU BETTER HAVE SOME ANSWERS.
BUT SAVE IT FOR TOMORROW! AFTER I CLEAN THIS PLACE UP! GO.
UM! YOU'RE WELCOME?

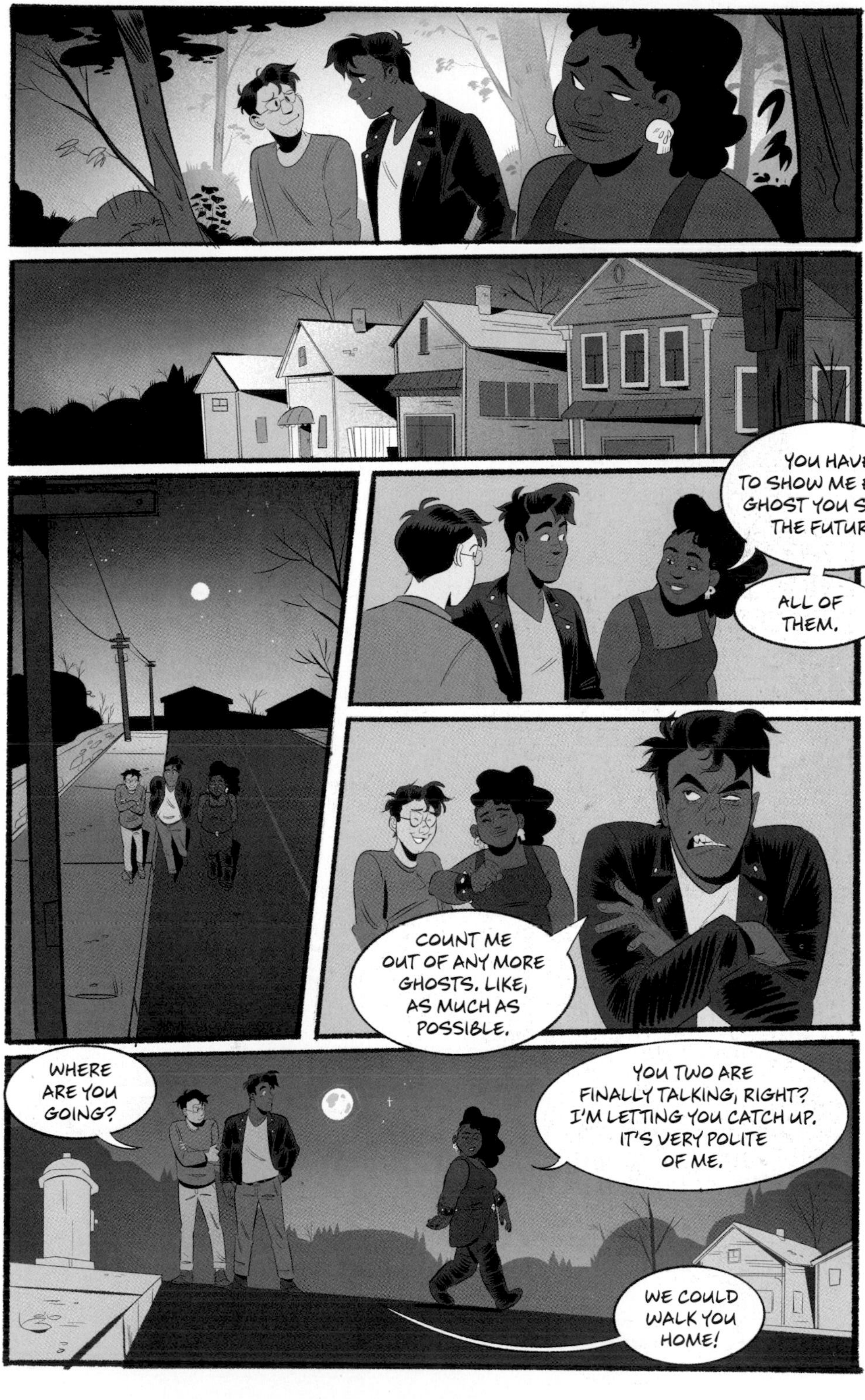
YOU HAVE TO SHOW ME EVERY GHOST YOU SEE IN THE FUTURE.
ALL OF THEM.
COUNT ME OUT OF ANY MORE GHOSTS. LIKE, AS MUCH AS POSSIBLE.
WHERE ARE YOU GOING?
YOU TWO ARE FINALLY TALKING, RIGHT? I'M LETTING YOU CATCH UP. IT'S VERY POLITE OF ME.
WE COULD WALK YOU HOME!

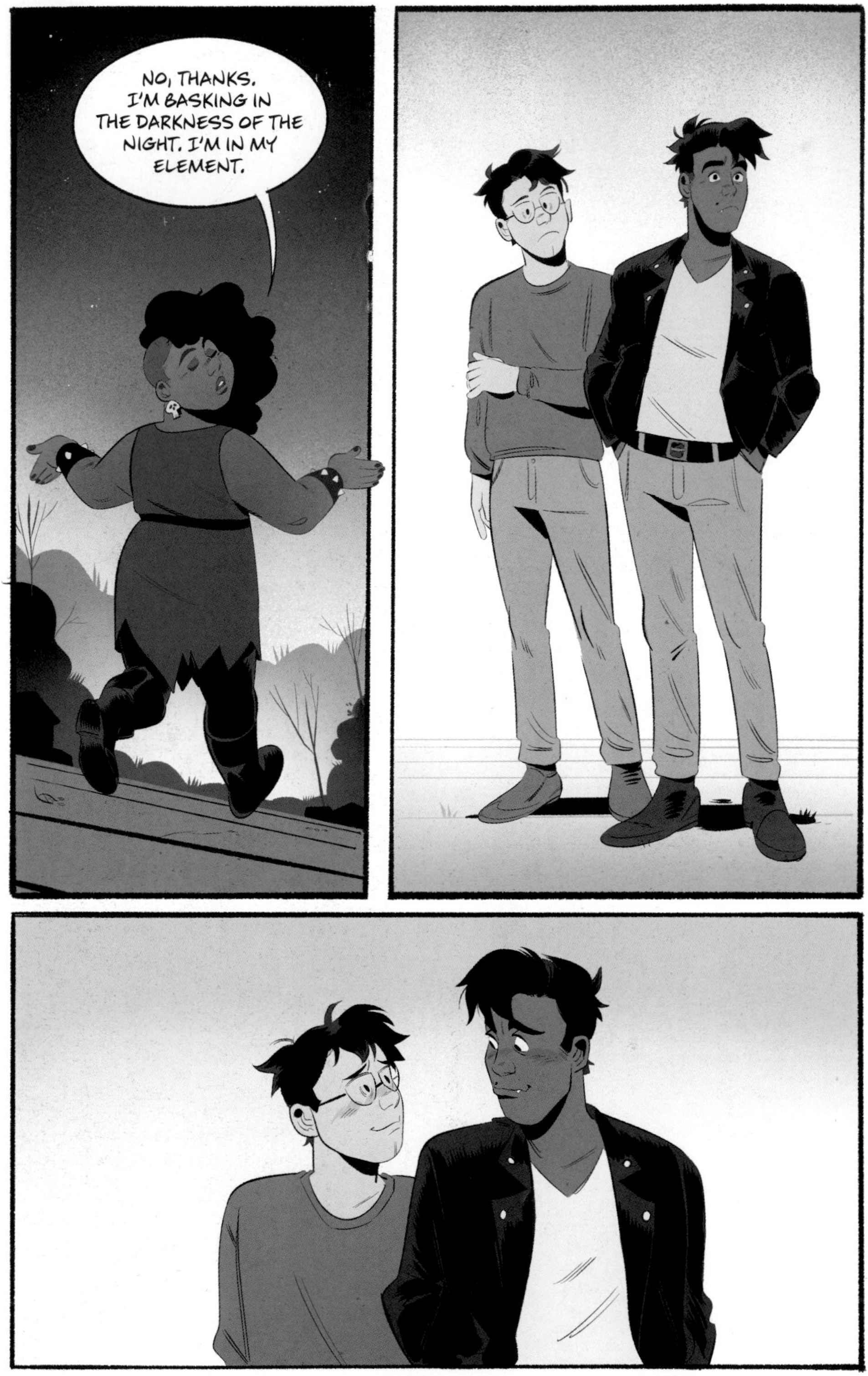
NO, THANKS. I'M BASKING IN THE DARKNESS OF THE NIGHT. I'M IN MY ELEMENT.

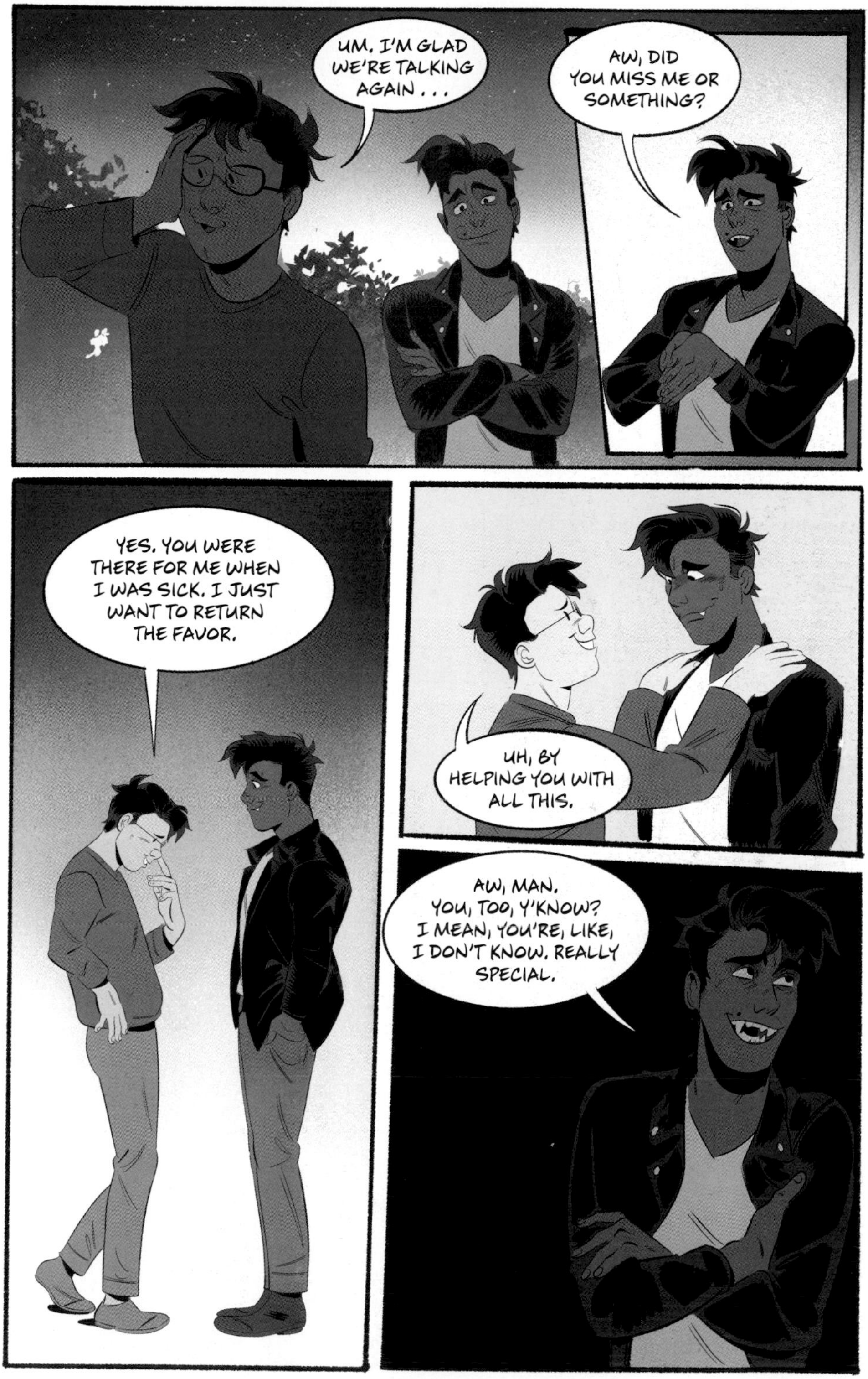
UM. I'M GLAD WE'RE TALKING AGAIN . . .
AW, DID YOU MISS ME OR SOMETHING?
YES. YOU WERE THERE FOR ME WHEN I WAS SICK. I JUST WANT TO RETURN THE FAVOR.
UH, BY HELPING YOU WITH ALL THIS.
AW, MAN. YOU, TOO, Y'KNOW? I MEAN, YOU'RE, LIKE, I DON'T KNOW. REALLY SPECIAL.

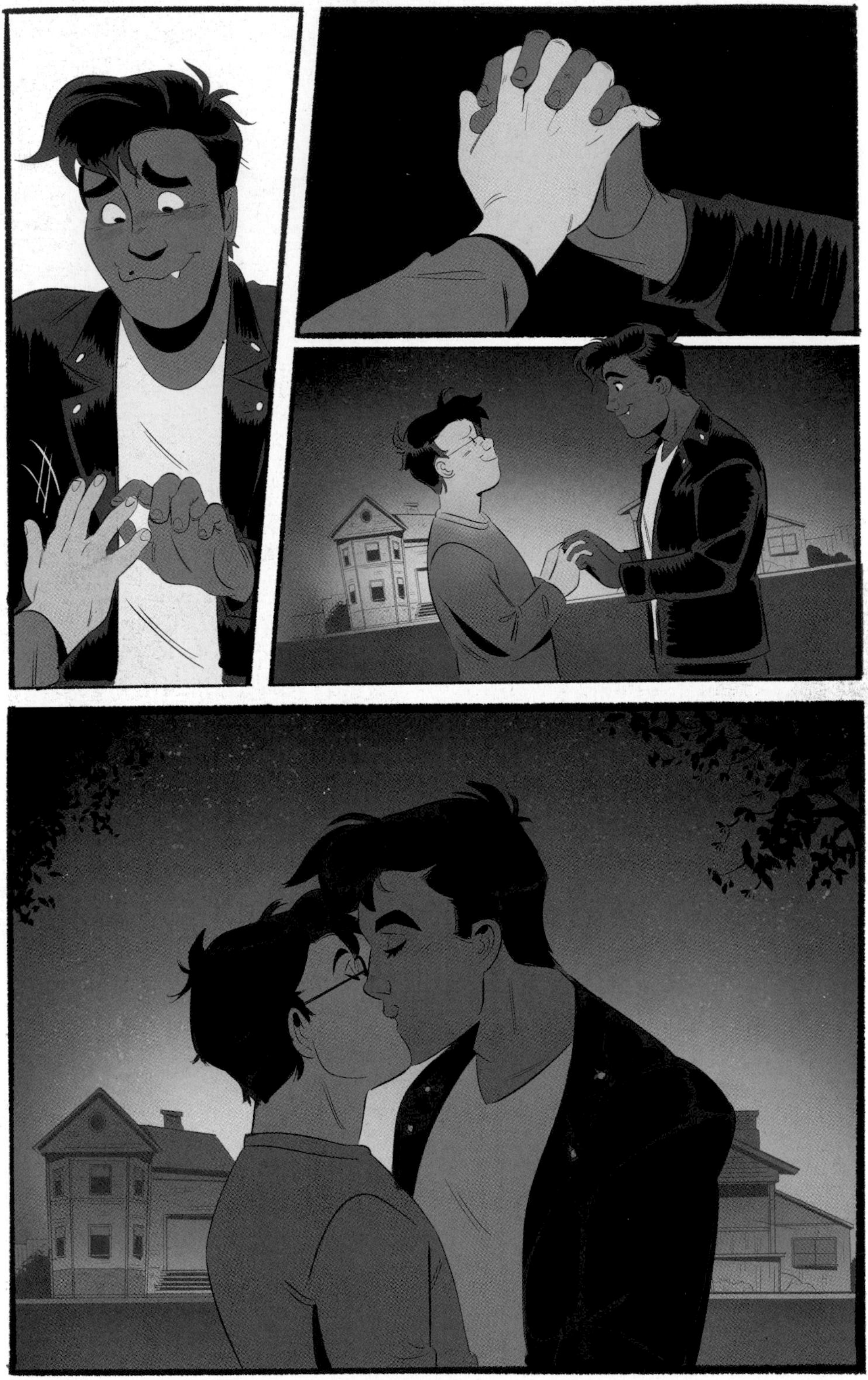

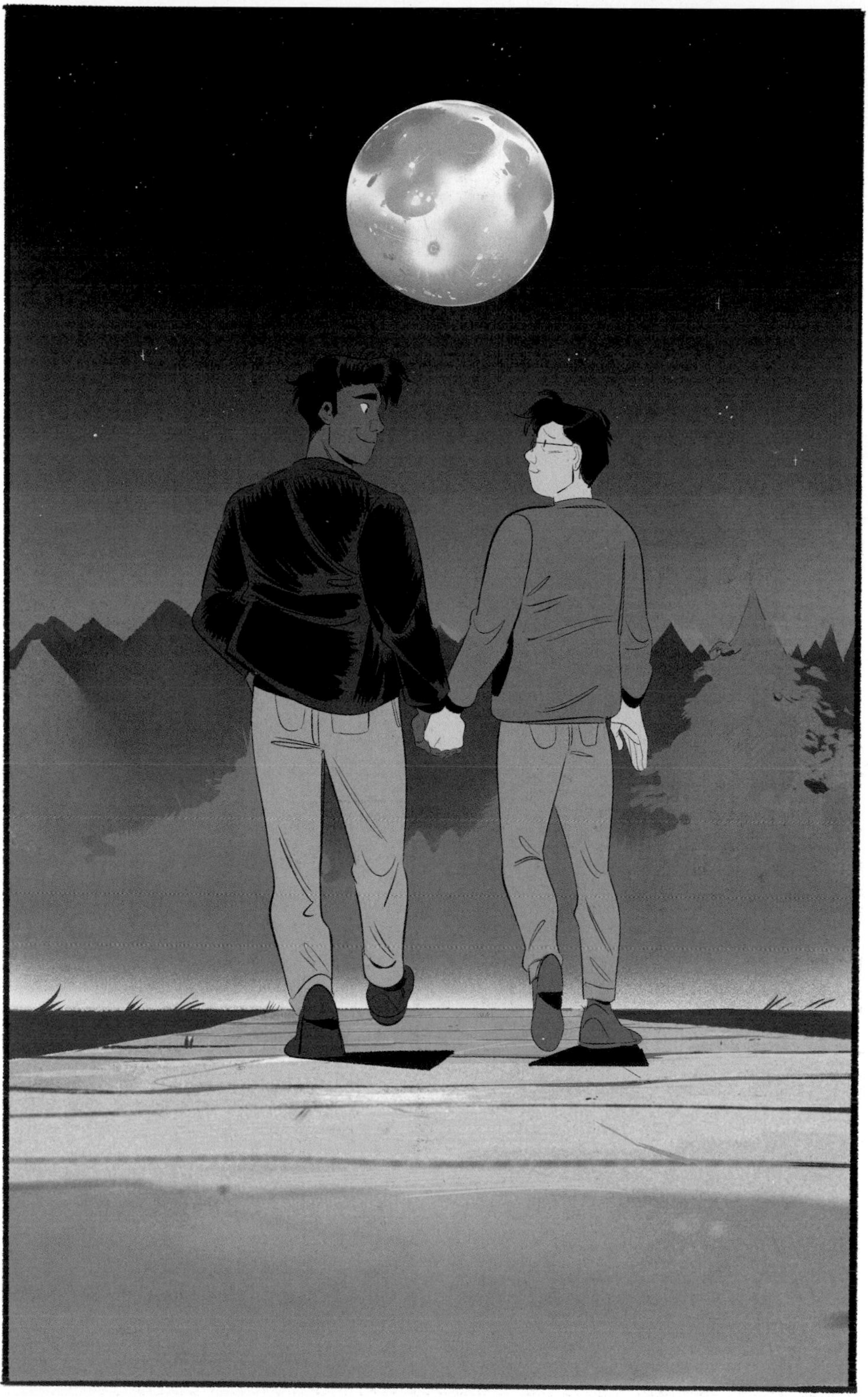

Jeannette Arroyo was born and raised in New Mexico but recently relocated to the rainier Seattle area. In addition to her first graphic novel, *Blackwater*, she has also done free-lance in animation and children's book illustration. A huge fan of the horror genre, Jeannette likes to mix in some lighthearted spooky elements in her work.

Ren Graham is a fiction writer and illustrator currently residing in the rainy Pacific Northwest. They have a BA in art history and a graduate studies certificate in science illustration, so biology, world mythology, and natural elements tend to influence and reappear in their work. Ren is interested in spooky stories, chilly hikes in the woods, and the ways in which art and science intersect.